RIENZI

THE LAST OF THE ROMAN TRIBUNES

The fierce Rienzi led on each assault.

RIENZI

THE LAST OF THE ROMAN TRIBUNES

By

EDWARD BULWER LYTTON

Illustrated by

L. W. ZEIGLER

Fredonia Books
Amsterdam, The Netherlands

Rienzi:
The Last of the Roman Tribunes

by
Edward Bulwer Lytton

ISBN: 1-4101-0102-9

Reprinted from the 1905 edition

Fredonia Books
Amsterdam, The Netherlands
http://www.fredoniabooks.com

In order to make original editions of historical works available to scholars at an economical price, this facsimile of the original edition of 1905 is reproduced from the best available copy and has been digitally enhanced to improve legibility, but the text remains unaltered to retain historical authenticity.

PREFACE

TO THE FIRST EDITION OF RIENZI

I began this tale two years ago at Rome. On removing to Naples, I threw it aside for "The Last Days of Pompeii," which required more than "Rienzi" the advantage of residence within reach of the scenes described. The fate of the Roman Tribune continued, however, to haunt and impress me, and some time after "Pompeii" was published, I renewed my earlier undertaking. I regarded the completion of these volumes, indeed, as a kind of duty;—for having had occasion to read the original authorities from which modern historians have drawn their accounts of the life of Rienzi, I was led to believe that a very remarkable man had been superficially judged, and a very important period crudely examined.* And this belief was sufficiently strong to induce me at first to meditate a more serious work upon the life and times of Rienzi.† Various reasons concurred against this project—and I renounced the biography to commence the fiction. I have still, however, adhered, with a greater fidelity than is customary in Romance, to all the leading events of the public life of the Roman Tribune; and the Reader will perhaps find in these pages a more full and detailed account of the rise and fall of Rienzi, than in any English work of which I am aware. I have, it is true, taken a view of his character different in some respects from that of Gib-

* See Appendix, Nos. I. and II.

† I have adopted the termination of *Rienzi* instead of *Rienzo*, as being more familiar to the general reader.—But the latter is perhaps the more accurate reading, since the name was a popular corruption from Lorenzo.

bon or Sismondi. But it is a view, in all its main features, which I believe (and I think I could prove) myself to be warranted in taking, not less by the facts of History than the laws of Fiction. In the meanwhile, as I have given the facts from which I have drawn my interpretation of the principal agent, the reader has sufficient data for his own judgment. In the picture of the Roman Populace, as in that of the Roman Nobles of the fourteenth century, I follow literally the descriptions left to us;—they are not flattering, but they are faithful, likenesses.

Preserving generally the real chronology of Rienzi's life, the plot of this work extends over a space of some years, and embraces the variety of characters necessary to a true delineation of events. The story, therefore, cannot have precisely that order of interest found in fictions strictly and genuinely *dramatic*, in which (to my judgment at least) the time ought to be as limited as possible, and the characters as few; —no new character of importance to the catastrophe being admissible towards the end of the work. If I may use the word Epic in its most modest and unassuming acceptation, this Fiction, in short, though indulging in dramatic situations, belongs, as a whole, rather to the Epic than the Dramatic school.

I cannot conclude without rendering the tribute of my praise and homage to the versatile and gifted Author of the beautiful Tragedy of Rienzi. Considering that our hero be the same—considering that we had the same materials from which to choose our several stories—I trust I shall be found to have little, if at all, trespassed upon ground previously occupied. With the single exception of a love-intrigue between a relative of Rienzi and one of the antagonist party, which makes the plot of Miss Mitford's Tragedy, and is little more than an episode in my Romance, having slight effect on the conduct and none on the fate of the hero, I am not aware of any resemblance between the two works; and even *this* coincidence I could easily have removed, had I deemed it the least advisable:—but it would be almost discreditable if I had *nothing* that resembled a performance possessing so much it were an honour to imitate.

In fact, the prodigal materials of the story—the rich and exuberant complexities of Rienzi's character—joined to the advantage possessed by the Novelist of embracing all that the Dramatist must reject *—are sufficient to prevent Dramatist and Novelist from interfering with each other.

LONDON, *December* 1, 1835.

* Thus the slender space permitted to the Dramatist does not *allow* Miss Mitford to be very faithful to facts; to distinguish between Rienzi's earlier and his later period of power; or to detail the true, but somewhat intricate causes of his rise, his splendour, and his fall.

PREFACE

TO THE EDITION OF 1848

From the time of its first appearance, "RIENZI" has had the good fortune to rank high amongst my most popular works—though its interest is rather drawn from a faithful narration of historical facts, than from the inventions of fancy. And the success of this experiment confirms me in my belief, that the true mode of employing history in the service of romance, is to study diligently the materials *as* history; conform to such views of the facts as the Author would adopt, if he related them in the dry character of historian; and obtain that warmer interest which fiction bestows, by tracing the causes of the facts in the characters and emotions of the personages of the time. The events of his work are thus already shaped to his hand—the characters already created—what remains for him, is the inner, not outer, history of man—the chronicle of the human heart; and it is by this that he introduces a new harmony between character and event, and adds the completer solution of what is actual and true, by those speculations of what is natural and probable, which are out of the province of history, but belong especially to the philosophy of romance. And—if it be permitted the tale-teller to come reverently for instruction in his art to the mightiest teacher of all, who, whether in the page or on the scene, would give to airy fancies the breath and the form of life,—such, we may observe, is the lesson the humblest craftsman in historical romance may glean from the Historical Plays of Shakespeare. Necessarily, Shakespeare consulted history according to the imperfect lights, and from the popular authorities of his age; and I do not say, therefore, that as an historian we can rely upon Shakespeare as correct. But to that in which he believed he rigidly adhered; nor did he seek, as lesser artists (such as Victor Hugo and his disciples) seek now, to turn perforce the Historical into the Poetical, but leaving history as he found it, to call forth from its arid prose the flower of the latent poem. Nay, even in the more imaginative plays which he has founded upon novels and legends popular in his time, it is curious and instructive to see how little he has altered the original ground-work—taking for granted the main materials of the story, and reserving all his matchless resources of wisdom and invention, to illustrate from mental analysis, the creations whose outline he was content to borrow. He receives, as a literal fact not to be altered, the somewhat incredible assertion of the novelist, that the pure and delicate and high-born Venetian loves the swarthy Moor—and that Romeo fresh from his "woes for Rosaline," becomes suddenly enamoured of Juliet: he found the Improbable, and employed his art to make it truthful.

That "RIENZI" should have attracted peculiar attention in Italy, is of course to be attributed to the choice of the subject rather than to the skill of the Author. It has been translated into the Italian language by eminent writers; and the authorities for the new view of Rienzi's times and character which the Author deemed himself warranted to take, have been compared with his text by careful critics and illustrious scholars, in those states in which the work has been permitted to circulate.* I may say, I trust without unworthy pride, that the result has confirmed the accuracy of delineations which English readers, relying only on the brilliant but disparaging account in Gibbon, deemed too favourable; and has tended to restore the great Tribune to his long forgotten claims

* In the Papal States, I believe, it was, neither prudently nor effectually proscribed.

to the love and reverence of the Italian land. Nor, if I may trust to the assurances that have reached me from many now engaged in the aim of political regeneration, has the effect of that revival of the honours due to a national hero, leading to the ennobling study of great examples, been wholly without its influence upon the rising generation of Italian youth, and thereby upon those stirring events which have recently drawn the eyes of Europe to the men and the lands beyond the Alps.

In preparing for the Press this edition of a work illustrative of the exertions of a Roman, in advance of his time, for the political freedom of his country, and of those struggles between contending principles, of which Italy was the most stirring field in the Middle Ages, it is not out of place or season to add a few sober words, whether as a student of the Italian past, or as an observer, with some experience of the social elements of Italy as it now exists, upon the state of affairs in that country.

It is nothing new to see the Papal Church in the capacity of a popular reformer, and in contra-position to the despotic potentates of the several states, as well as to the German Emperor, who nominally inherits the sceptre of the Cæsars. Such was its common character under its more illustrious Pontiffs; and the old Republics of Italy grew up under the shadow of the Papal throne, harbouring ever two factions—the one for the Emperor, the one for the Pope—the latter the more naturally allied to Italian independence. On the modern stage, we almost see the repetition of many an ancient drama. But the past should teach us to doubt the continuous and stedfast progress of any single line of policy under a principality so constituted as that of the Papal Church—a principality in which no race can be perpetuated, in which no objects can be permanent; in which the successor is chosen by a select ecclesiastical synod, under a variety of foreign as well as of national influences: in which the chief usually ascends the throne at an age that ill adapts his mind to the idea of human progress, and the active direction of mundane affairs;—a principality in which the peculiar sanctity that wraps the person of the Sovereign exonerates him from the healthful liabilities of a power purely temporal, and directly accountable to Man. A reforming Pope is a lucky accident, and dull indeed must be the brain which believes in the possibility of a long succession of reforming Popes, or which can regard as other than precarious and unstable the discordant combination of a constitutional government with an infallible head.

It is as true as it is trite that political freedom is not the growth of a day—it is not a flower without a stalk, and it must gradually develop itself amidst the unfolding leaves of kindred institutions.

In one respect, the Austrian domination, fairly considered, has been beneficial to the States over which it has been directly exercised, and may be even said to have unconsciously schooled them to the capacity for freedom. In those States the personal rights which depend on impartial and incorrupt administration of the law, are infinitely more secure than in most of the Courts of Italy. Bribery, which shamefully predominates in the judicature of certain Principalities, is as unknown in the juridical courts of Austrian Italy as in England. The Emperor himself is often involved in legal disputes with a subject, and justice is as free and as firm for the humblest suitor, as if his antagonist were his equal. Austria, indeed, but holds together the motley and inharmonious members of its vast domain on either side the Alps, by a general character of paternal mildness and forbearance in all that great circle of good government which lies without the one principle of constitutional liberty. It asks but of its subjects to submit to be well governed—without agitating the question " how and by what means that government is carried on." For every man except the politician, the innovator, Austria is no harsh stepmother. But it is obviously clear that the better in other respects the administration of a state, it does but foster the more the desire for that political security, which is only found in constitutional freedom: the reverence paid to personal rights but begets the passion for political; and under a mild despotism are already half matured the germs of a popular constitution. But it is still a grave question whether Italy is ripe for self-government—and whether, were it possible that the Austrian domination could be shaken off—the very passions so excited, the very bloodshed so poured forth, would not ultimately place the larger portion of Italy under auspices less favourable to the sure growth of freedom, than those which silently brighten under the sway of the German Cæsar.

The two kingdoms, at the opposite extremes of Italy, to which circumstance and nature seem to assign the main ascendancy, are Naples and Sardinia. Looking to the former, it is impossible to discover on the face of the earth a country more adapted for commercial prosperity. Nature formed it as the garden of Europe, and the mart of the Mediterranean. Its soil and climate could unite the products of the East with those of the Western hemisphere. The rich island of Sicily should be the great corn granary of the modern nations as it was of the ancient; the figs, the olives, the oranges of both the Sicilies, under skilful cultivation, should equal the produce of Spain and the Orient; and the harbours of the kingdom (the keys to three-quarters of the globe) should be crowded with the sails and busy with the life of commerce. But, in the character of its population, Naples has been invariably in the rear of Italian progress; it caught but partial inspiration from the free Republics, or even the wise Tyrannies, of the Middle Ages; the theatre of frequent revolutions without fruit; and all rational enthusiasm created by that insurrection, which has lately bestowed on Naples the boon of a representative system, cannot but be tempered by the conviction that of all the States in Italy, this is the one which least warrants the belief of permanence to political freedom, or of capacity to retain with vigour what may be seized by passion.*

Far otherwise is it with Sardinia. Many years since, the writer of these pages ventured to predict that the time must come when Sardinia would lead the van of Italian civilisation, and take proud place amongst the greater nations of Europe. In the great portion of this population there is visible the new blood of a young race; it is not, as with other Italian states, a worn-out stock; you do not see there a people fallen, proud of the past, and lazy amidst ruins, but a people rising, practical, industrious, active; there, in a word, is an eager youth to be formed to mature development, not a decrepit age to be restored to bloom and muscle. Progress is the great characteristic of the Sardinian state. Leave it for five years; visit it again, and you behold improvement. When you enter the kingdom and find, by the very skirts of its admirable roads, a raised footpath for the passengers and travellers from town to town, you become suddenly aware that you are in a land where close attention to the humbler classes is within the duties of a government. As you pass on from the more purely

* If the Electoral Chamber in the new Neapolitan Constitution give a fair share of members to the Island of Sicily, it will be rich in the inevitable elements of discord, and nothing save a wisdom and moderation, which cannot soberly be anticipated, can prevent the ultimate separation of the island from the dominion of Naples. Nature has set the ocean between the two countries—but differences in character, and degree and quality of civilisation—national jealousies, historical memories, have trebled the space of the seas that roll between them.—More easy to unite under one free Parliament, Spain with Flanders; or re-annex to England its old domains of Aquitaine and Normandy—than to unite in one Council Chamber *truly* popular, the passions, interests, and prejudices of Sicily and Naples.—Time will show. And now, in May, 1849—Time has already shown the impracticability of the first scheme proposed for cordial union between Naples and Sicily, and has rendered it utterly impossible, by mutual recollections of hatred, bequeathed by a civil war of singular barbarism, that Naples should permanently retain Sicily by any other hold than the brute force of conquest.

Italian part of the population,—from the Genoese country into that of Piedmont,—the difference between a new people and an old, on which I have dwelt, becomes visible in the improved cultivation of the soil, the better habitations of the labourer, the neater aspect of the towns, the greater activity in the thoroughfares. To the extraordinary virtues of the King, as King, justice is scarcely done, whether in England or abroad. Certainly, despite his recent concessions, Charles Albert is not and cannot be at heart, much of a constitutional reformer; and his strong religious tendencies, which, perhaps, unjustly, have procured him in philosophical quarters the character of a bigot, may link him more than his political, with the cause of the Father of his Church. But he is nobly and pre-eminently national, careful of the prosperity and jealous of the honour of his own state, while conscientiously desirous of the independence of Italy. His attention to business, is indefatigable. Nothing escapes his vigilance. Over all departments of the kingdom is the eye of a man ever anxious to improve. Already the silk manufacturers of Sardinia almost rival those of Lyons: in their own departments the tradesmen of Turin exhibit an artistic elegance and elaborate finish, scarcely exceeded in the wares of London and Paris. The King's internal regulations are admirable; his laws, administered with the most impartial justice—his forts and defences are in that order, without which, at least on the Continent, no land is safe—his army is the most perfect in Italy. His wise genius extends itself to the elegant as to the useful arts—an encouragement that shames England, and even France, is bestowed upon the School for Painters, which has become one of the ornaments of his illustrious reign. The character of the main part of the population, and the geographical position of his country, assist the monarch and must force on himself, or his successors, in the career of improvement so signally begun. In the character of the people, the vigour of the Northman ennobles the ardour and fancy of the West. In the position of the country, the public mind is brought into constant communication with the new ideas in the free lands of Europe. Civilisation sets in direct currents towards the streets and marts of Turin. Whatever the result of the present crisis in Italy, no power and no chance which statesmen can predict, can preclude Sardinia from ultimately heading all that is best in Italy. The King may improve his present position, or peculiar prejudices, inseparable perhaps from the heritage of absolute monarchy, and which the raw and rude councils of an Electoral Chamber, newly called into life, must often irritate and alarm, may check his own progress towards the master throne of the Ausonian land. But the people themselves, sooner or later will do the work of the King. And in now looking round Italy for a race worthy of Rienzi, and able to accomplish his proud dreams, I see but one for which the time is ripe or ripening, and I place the hopes of Italy in the men of Piedmont and Sardinia.

LONDON, *February* 14, 1848.

CONTENTS

BOOK I

The Time, the Place, and the Men

BOOK II

The Revolution

BOOK III

The Freedom Without Law

BOOK IV

The Triumph and the Pomp

BOOK V

The Crisis

BOOK VI

The Plague

BOOK VII

The Prison

BOOK VIII

The Grand Company

BOOK IX

The Return

BOOK X

The Lion of Basalt

APPENDIX I

APPENDIX II

LIST OF ILLUSTRATIONS

RIENZI

THE LAST OF THE TRIBUNES

BOOK I

THE TIME, THE PLACE, AND THE MEN

"Fuda sua gioventudine nutricato di latte di eloquenza; buono grammatico, megliore rettorico, autorista buono . . . Oh, come spesso diceva, 'Dove sono questi buoni Romani? Dove'è loro somma giustizia? Poterommi trovare in tempo che questi fioriscano?' Era bell'omo . . . Accadde che uno suo frate fu ucciso, e non ne fu fatta vendetta di sua morte; non lo poteò aiutare; pensa lungo mano vendicare 'l sangue di suo frate; pensa lunga mano dirizzare la cittate di Roma male guidata."—*Vita di Cola di Rienzi.* Ed. 1828. Forli.

"From his youth he was nourished with the milk of eloquence; a good grammarian, a better rhetorician, well versed in the writings of authors . . . Oh, how often would he say, 'Where are those good Romans? Where is their supreme justice? Shall I ever behold such times as those in which they flourished?' He was a handsome man . . . It happened that a brother of his was slain, and no retribution was made for his death: he could not help him; long did he ponder how to avenge his brother's blood; long did he ponder how to direct the misguided state of Rome."—*Life of Cola di Rienzi.*

CHAPTER I

THE BROTHERS

The celebrated name which forms the title to this work will sufficiently apprise the reader that it is in the earlier half of the fourteenth century that my story opens.

It was on a summer evening that two youths might be seen walking beside the banks of the Tiber, not far from that part of its winding course which sweeps by the base of Mount Aventine. The path they had selected was remote and tranquil. It was only at a distance that were seen the scattered and squalid houses that bordered the river, from amidst which rose, dark and frequent, the high roof and enormous towers which marked the fortified mansion of some Roman baron. On one side of the river, behind the cottages of the fishermen, soared Mount Janiculum, dark with massive foliage, from which gleamed at frequent intervals, the gray walls of many a castellated palace, and the spires and columns of a hundred churches; on the other side, the deserted Aventine rose abrupt and steep, covered with thick brushwood; while, on the height, from concealed but numerous convents, rolled, not unmusically, along the quiet landscape and the rippling waves, the sound of the holy bell.

Of the young men introduced in this scene, the elder, who might have somewhat passed his twentieth year, was of a tall and even commanding stature; and there was that in his presence remarkable and almost noble, despite the homeliness of his garb, which consisted of the long, loose gown and the plain tunic, both of dark-gray serge, which distinguished, at that time, the dress of the humbler scholars who frequented the monastery for such rude knowledge as then yielded a scanty return for intense toil. His countenance was handsome, and would have been rather gay than thoughtful in its expression, but for that vague and abstracted dreaminess of eye which so usually denotes a propensity to reverie and contemplation, and betrays that the past or the future is more congenial to the mind than the enjoyment and action of the present hour.

The younger, who was yet a boy, had nothing striking in his appearance or countenance, unless an expression of great sweetness and gentleness could be so called; and there was something almost feminine in the tender deference with which he appeared to listen to his companion. His dress was that usually worn by the humbler classes, though somewhat neater, perhaps, and newer; and the fond vanity of a mother might be detected in the care with which the long and silky ringlets had been smoothed and parted as they escaped from his cap and flowed midway down his shoulders.

As they thus sauntered on, beside the whispering reeds of the river, each with his arm round the form of his comrade, there was a grace in the bearing, in the youth, and in the evident affection of the brothers —for such their connection—which elevated the lowliness of their apparent condition.

"Dear brother," said the elder, "I cannot express to thee how I enjoy these evening hours. To you alone I feel as if I were not a mere visionary and idler when I talk of the uncertain future, and build up my palaces of the air. Our parents listen to me as if I were uttering fine things out of a book; and my dear mother, Heaven bless her! wipes her eyes, and says, 'Hark, what a scholar he is!' As for the monks, if I ever dare look from my Livy, and cry, 'Thus should Rome be again!' they stare, and gape, and frown, as though I had broached an heresy. But you, sweet brother, though you share not my studies, sympathise so kindly with all their results—you seem so to approve my wild schemes, and to encourage my ambitious hopes—that sometimes I forget our birth, our fortunes, and think and dare as if no blood save that of the Teuton Emperor flowed through our veins."

"Methinks, dear Cola," said the younger brother, "that Nature played us an unfair trick—to you she transmitted the royal soul, derived from our father's parentage; and to me only the quiet and lowly spirit of my mother's humble lineage."

"Nay," answered Cola, quickly, "you would then have the brighter share,—for I should have but the Barbarian origin, and you the Roman. Time was, when to be a simple Roman was to be nobler than a northern king.—Well, well, we may live to see great changes!"

"I shall live to see thee a great man, and that will content me," said the younger, smiling affectionately: "a great scholar all confess you to be already: our mother predicts your fortunes every time she hears of your welcome visits to the Colonna."

"The Colonna!" said Cola, with a bitter smile; "the Colonna—the pedants!—They affect, dull souls, the knowledge of the past, play the patron, and misquote Latin over their cups! They are pleased to welcome me at their board, because the Roman doctors call me learned, and because Nature gave me a wild wit, which to them is pleasanter than the stale jests of a hired buffoon. Yes, they would advance my fortunes—but how? by some place in the public offices, which would fill a dishonoured coffer, by wringing, yet more sternly, the hard earned coins from our famishing citizens! If there be a vile thing in the world, it is a plebeian, advanced by patricians, not for the purpose of righting his own order, but for playing the pander to the worst interests of theirs. He who is of the people but makes himself a traitor to his birth, if he furnishes the excuse for these tyrant hypocrites to lift up their hands and cry—'See what liberty exists in Rome, when *we*, the patricians, thus elevate a plebeian!' Did they ever elevate a plebeian if he sympathised with plebeians? No, brother; should I be lifted above our condition, I will be raised by the arms of my countrymen, and not upon their necks."

"All I hope, is, Cola, that you will not, in your zeal for your fellow-citizens, forget how dear you are to us. No greatness could ever reconcile me to the thought that it brought you danger."

"And *I* could laugh at all danger, if it led to greatness! But greatness—greatness! Vain dream! Let us keep it for our *night* sleep. Enough of *my* plans; now, dearest brother, of yours."

And, with the sanguine and cheerful elasticity which belonged to him, the young Cola, dismissing all wilder thoughts, bent his mind to listen, and to enter into, the humbler projects of his brother. The new boat and the holiday dress, and the cot removed to a quarter more secure from the oppression of the barons, and such distant pictures of love as a dark eye and a merry lip conjure up to the vague sentiments of a boy;—to schemes and aspirations of which such objects made the limit, did the scholar listen, with a relaxed brow and a tender smile; and often, in later life, did that conversation occur to him, when he shrank from asking his own heart which ambition was the wiser.

"And then," continued the younger brother, "by degrees I might save enough to purchase such a vessel as that which we now see, laden, doubtless, with corn and merchandise, bringing—oh, such a good return—that I could fill your room with books, and never hear you complain that you were not rich enough to purchase some crumbling old monkish manuscript. Ah, that would make me so happy!" Cola smiled as he pressed his brother closer to his breast.

"Dear boy," said he, "may it rather be mine to provide for your wishes! Yet methinks the masters of yon vessel have no enviable possession; see how anxiously the men look round, and behind, and before: peaceful traders though they be, they fear, it seems, even in this city (once the emporium of the civilised world), some pirate in pursuit; and ere the voyage be over, they may find that pirate in a Roman noble. Alas, to what are we reduced!"

The vessel thus referred to was speeding rapidly down the river, and some three or four armed men on deck were indeed intently surveying the quiet banks on either side, as if anticipating a foe. The bark soon, however, glided out of sight, and the brothers fell back upon those themes which require only the future for a text to become attractive to the young.

At length, as the evening darkened, they remembered that it was past the usual hour in which they returned home, and they began to retrace their steps.

"Stay," said Cola, abruptly, "how talk has beguiled me! Father Uberto promised me a rare manuscript, which the good friar confesses hath puzzled the whole convent. I was to seek his cell for it this evening. Tarry here a few minutes, it is but half-way up the Aventine. I shall soon return."

"Can I not accompany you?"

"Nay," returned Cola, with considerate kindness, "you have borne toil all the day, and must be wearied; my labours, of the body, at least, have been light enough. You are delicate, too, and seem fatigued already; the rest will refresh you. I shall not be long."

The boy acquiesced, though he rather wished to accompany his brother; but he was of a meek and yielding temper, and seldom resisted the lightest command of those he loved. He sat him down on a little bank by the river-side, and the firm step and towering form of his brother were soon hid from his gaze by the thick and melancholy foliage.

At first he sat very quietly, enjoying the cool air, and thinking over all the stories of ancient Rome that his brother had told him in their walk. At length he recollected that his little sister, Irene, had begged him to bring her home some flowers; and, gathering such as he could find at hand (and many a flower grew, wild and clustering, over that desolate spot), he again seated himself, and began weaving them into one of those garlands for which the southern peasantry still retain their ancient affection, and something of their classic skill.

While the boy was thus engaged, the tramp of horses and the loud shouting of men were heard at a distance. They came near, and nearer.

"Some baron's procession, perhaps, returning from a feast," thought the boy. "It will be a pretty sight—their white plumes and scarlet mantles! I love to see such sights, but I will just move out of their way."

So, still mechanically platting his garland, but with eyes turned towards the quarter of the expected procession, the young Roman moved yet nearer towards the river.

Presently the train came in view,—a gallant company, in truth; horsemen in front, riding two abreast, where the path permitted, their steeds caparisoned superbly, their plumes waving gaily, and the gleam of their corselets glittering through the shades of the dusky twilight. A large and miscellaneous crowd, all armed, some with pikes and mail, others with less warlike or worse fashioned weapons, followed the cavaliers; and high above plume and pike floated the blood-red banner of the Orsini, with the motto and device (in which was ostentatiously displayed the Guelfic badge of the keys of St. Peter) wrought in burnished gold. A momentary fear crossed the boy's mind, for at that time, and in that city, a nobleman begirt with his swordsmen was more dreaded than a wild beast by the plebeians; but it was already too late to fly—the train were upon him.

"Ho, boy!" cried the leader of the horsemen, Martino di Porto, one of the great House of the Orsini; "hast thou seen a boat pass up the river?—But thou must have seen it—how long since?"

"I saw a large boat about half an hour ago," answered the boy, terrified by the rough voice and imperious bearing of the cavalier.

"Sailing right a-head, with a green flag at the stern?"

"The same, noble sir."

"On, then! we will stop her course ere the moon rise," said the baron. "On!—let the boy go with us, lest he prove traitor, and alarm the Colonna."

"An Orsini, an Orsini!" shouted the multitude; "on, on!" and, despite the prayers and remonstrances of the boy, he was placed in the thickest of the crowd, and borne, or rather dragged along with the rest—frightened, breathless, almost weeping, with his poor little garland still hanging on his arm, while a sling was thrust into his unwilling hand. Still he felt, through all his alarm, a kind of childish curiosity to see the result of the pursuit.

By the loud and eager conversation of those about him, he learned that the vessel he had seen contained a supply of corn destined to a fortress up the river held by the Colonna, then at deadly feud with the Orsini; and it was the object of the expedition in which the boy had been thus lucklessly entrained to intercept the provision, and divert it to the garrison of Martino di Porto. This news somewhat increased his consternation, for the boy belonged to a family that claimed the patronage of the Colonna.

Anxiously and tearfully he looked with every moment up the steep ascent of the Aventine; but his guardian, his protector, still delayed his appearance.

They had now proceeded some way, when a winding in the road brought suddenly before them the object of their pursuit, as, seen by the light of the earliest stars, it scudded rapidly down the stream.

"Now, the Saints be blest!" quoth the chief; "she is ours!"

"Hold!" said a captain (a German) riding next to Martino, in a half whisper; "I hear sounds which I like not, by yonder trees—hark! the neigh of a horse! —by my faith, too, there is the gleam of a corselet."

"Push on, my masters," cried Martino; "the heron shall not balk the eagle—push on!"

With renewed shouts, those on foot pushed forward, till, as they had nearly gained the copse referred to by the German, a small compact body of horsemen, armed cap-à-pié, dashed from amidst the trees, and, with spears in their rests, charged into the ranks of the pursuers.

"A Colonna! a Colonna!" "An Orsini! an Orsini!" were shouts loudly and fiercely interchanged. Martino di Porto, a man of great bulk and ferocity, and his cavaliers, who were chiefly German Mercenaries, met the encounter unshaken. " Beware the bear's hug," cried the Orsini, as down went his antagonist, rider and steed, before his lance.

The contest was short and fierce; the complete armour of the horsemen protected them on either side from wounds,—not so unscathed fared the half-armed foot-followers of the Orsini, as they pressed, each pushed on by the other, against the Colonna. After a shower of stones and darts, which fell but as hailstones against the thick mail of the horsemen, they closed in, and, by their number, obstructed the movements of the steeds, while the spear, sword, and battle-axe of their opponents made ruthless havoc amongst their undisciplined ranks. And Martino, who cared little how many of his mere mob were butchered, seeing that his foes were for the moment embarrassed by the wild rush and gathering circle of his foot train (for the place of conflict, though wider than the previous road, was confined and narrow), made a sign to some of his horsemen, and was about to ride forward towards the boat, now nearly out of sight, when a bugle at some distance was answered by one of his enemy at hand; and the shout of " Colonna to the rescue!" was echoed afar off. A few moments brought in view a numerous train of horse at full speed, with the banners of the Colonna waving gallantly in the front.

" A plague on the wizards! who would have imagined they had divined us so craftily!" muttered Martino; " we must not abide these odds;" and the hand he had first raised for advance, now gave the signal of retreat.

Serried breast to breast and in complete order, the

horsemen of Martino turned to fly; the foot rabble who had come for spoil remained but for slaughter. They endeavoured to imitate their leaders; but how could they all elude the rushing chargers and sharp lances of their antagonists, whose blood was heated by the affray, and who regarded the lives at their mercy as a boy regards the wasp's nest he destroys. The crowd dispersing in all directions,—some, indeed, escaped up the hills, where the footing was impracticable to the horses; some plunged into the river and swam across to the opposite bank,—those less cool or experienced, who fled right onwards, served, by clogging the way of their enemy, to facilitate the flight of their leaders, but fell themselves, corpse upon corpse, butchered in the unrelenting and unresisted pursuit.

"No quarter to the ruffians—every Orsini slain is a robber the less—strike for God, the Emperor, and the Colonna!" such were the shouts which rung the knell of the dismayed and falling fugitives. Among those who fled onward, in the very path most accessible to the cavalry, was the young brother of Cola, so innocently mixed with the affray. Fast he fled, dizzy with terror—poor boy, scarce before ever parted from his parents' or his brother's side!—the trees glided past him—the banks receded:—on he sped, and fast behind came the tramp of the hoofs—the shouts—the curses—the fierce laughter of the foe, as they bounded over the dead and the dying in their path. He was now at the spot in which his brother had left him; hastily he glanced behind, and saw the couched lance and horrent crest of the horseman close at his rear; despairingly he looked up, and, behold! his brother bursting through the tangled brakes that clothed the mountain, and bounding to his succor.

"Save me! save me, brother!" he shrieked aloud, and the shriek reached Cola's ear;—the snort of the fiery charger breathed hot upon him;—a moment more, and with one wild shrill cry of "Mercy, mercy," he fell to the ground—a corpse: the lance of the pursuer passing through and through him, from back to breast, and nailing him on the very sod where he had sate, full of young life and careless hope, not an hour ago.

The horseman plucked forth his spear, and passed on in pursuit of new victims; his comrades following. Cola had descended,—was on the spot,—kneeling by his murdered brother. Presently, to the sound of horn and trumpet, came by a nobler company than most of those hitherto engaged; who had been, indeed, but the advanced-guard of the Colonna. At their head rode a man in years, whose long white hair escaped from his plumed cap and mingled with his venerable beard. "How is this?" said the chief, reining in his steed, "young Rienzi!"

The youth looked up, as he heard that voice, and then flung himself before the steed of the old noble, and, clasping his hands, cried out in a scarce articulate tone: "It is my brother, noble Stephen,—a boy, a mere child!—the best—the mildest! See how his blood dabbles the grass;—back, back—your horse's hoofs are in the stream! Justice, my Lord, justice!—you are a great man."

"Who slew him? an Orsini, doubtless; you shall have justice."

"Thanks, thanks," murmured Rienzi, as he tottered once more to his brother's side, turned the boy's face from the grass, and strove wildly to feel the pulse of his heart; he drew back his hand hastily, for it was crimsoned with blood, and lifting that hand on high, shrieked out again, "Justice! justice!"

The group round the old Stephen Colonna, hardened as they were in such scenes, were affected by the sight. A handsome boy, whose tears ran fast down his cheeks, and who rode his palfrey close by the side of the Colonna, drew forth his sword. "My Lord," said he, half sobbing, "an Orsini only could have butchered a harmless lad like this; let us lose not a moment,—let us on after the ruffians."

"No, Adrian, no!" cried Stephen, laying his hand on the boy's shoulder; "your zeal is to be lauded, but we must beware an ambush. Our men have ventured too far—what ho, there!—sound a return."

The bugles, in a few minutes, brought back the pursuers,—among them, the horseman whose spear had been so fatally misused. He was the leader of those engaged in the conflict with Martino di Porto; and the gold wrought into his armour, with the gorgeous trappings of his charger, betokened his rank.

"Thanks, my son, thanks," said the old Colonna to this cavalier, "you have done well and bravely. But tell me, knowest thou, for thou hast an eagle eye, which of the Orsini slew this poor boy?—a foul deed; his family, too, our clients!"

"Who? yon lad?" replied the horseman, lifting the helmet from his head, and wiping his heated brow; "say you so! how came he, then, with Martino's rascals? I fear me the mistake hath cost him dear. I could but suppose him of the Orsini rabble, and so—and so——"

"*You* slew him!" cried Rienzi, in a voice of thunder, starting from the ground. "Justice! then, my

Lord Stephen, justice! you promised me justice, and I will have it!"

"My poor youth," said the old man, compassionately, "you should have had justice against the Orsini; but see you not this has been an error? I do not wonder you are too grieved to listen to reason now. We must make this up to you."

"And let this pay for masses for the boy's soul: I grieve me much for the accident," said the younger Colonna, flinging down a purse of gold. "Ay, see us at the palace next week, young Cola—next week. My father, we had best return towards the boat; its safeguard may require us yet."

"Right, Gianni; stay, some two of you, and see to the poor lad's corpse;—a grievous accident! how could it chance?"

The company passed back the way they came, two of the common soldiers alone remaining, except the boy Adrian, who lingered behind a few moments, striving to console Rienzi, who, as one bereft of sense, remained motionless, gazing on the proud array as it swept along, and muttering to himself, "Justice, justice! I will have it yet."

The loud voice of the elder Colonna summoned Adrian, reluctantly and weeping, away. "Let me be your brother," said the gallant boy, affectionately pressing the scholar's hand to his heart; "I want a brother like you."

Rienzi made no reply; he did not heed or hear him—dark and stern thoughts, thoughts in which were the germ of a mighty revolution, were at his heart. He woke from them with a start, as the soldiers were now arranging their bucklers so as to make a kind of bier for the corpse, and then burst into tears as he fiercely motioned them away, and clasped the clay to his breast till he was literally soaked with the oozing blood.

The poor child's garland had not dropped from his arm even when he fell, and, entangled by his dress, it still clung around him. It was a sight that recalled to Cola all the gentleness, the kind heart, and winning graces of his only brother—his only friend! It was a sight that seemed to make yet more inhuman the untimely and unmerited fate of that innocent boy. "My brother! my brother!" groaned the survivor; "how shall I meet our mother?—how shall I meet even night and solitude again?—so young, so harmless! See ye, sirs, he was but too gentle. And they will not give us justice, because his murderer was a noble and a Colonna. And this gold, too—gold for a brother's blood! Will they not"—and the young man's eyes glared like fire—"will they not give us justice? Time shall show!" So saying, he bent his head over the corpse; his lips muttered, as with some prayer or invocation; and then rising, his face was as pale as the dead beside him,—but it was no longer pale with *grief!*

From that bloody clay, and that inward prayer, Cola di Rienzi rose a new being. With his young brother died his own youth. But for that event, the future liberator of Rome might have been but a dreamer, a scholar, a poet; the peaceful rival of Petrarch; a man of thoughts, not deeds. But from that time, all his faculties, energies, fancies, genius, became concentrated into a single point; and patriotism, before a vision, leapt into the life and vigour of a passion, lastingly kindled, stubbornly hardened, and awfully consecrated,—by revenge!

CHAPTER II

AN HISTORICAL SURVEY—NOT TO BE PASSED OVER, EXCEPT BY THOSE WHO DISLIKE TO UNDERSTAND WHAT THEY READ

Years had passed away, and the death of the Roman boy, amidst more noble and less excusable slaughter, was soon forgotten,—forgotten almost by the parents of the slain, in the growing fame and fortunes of their eldest son,—forgotten and forgiven never by that son himself. But, between that prologue of blood, and the political drama which ensues,—between the fading interest, as it were, of a dream, and the more busy, actual, and continuous excitements of sterner life,—this may be the most fitting time to place before the reader a short and rapid outline of the state and circumstances of that city in which the principal scenes of this story are laid;—an outline necessary, perhaps, to many, for a full comprehension of the motives of the actors, and the vicissitudes of the plot.

Despite the miscellaneous and mongrel tribes that had forced their settlements in the City of the Cæsars, the Roman population retained an inordinate notion of their own supremacy over the rest of the world; and, degenerated from the iron virtues of the Republic, possessed all the insolent and unruly turbulence which characterised the *Plebs* of the ancient Forum. Amongst a ferocious, yet not a brave populace, the nobles supported themselves less as sagacious tyrants than as relentless banditti. The popes had struggled in vain against these stubborn and stern patricians. Their state derided, their command defied, their persons publicly outraged, the pontiff-sovereigns of the rest of Europe resided, at the Vatican, as prisoners under terror of execution. When, thirty-eight years before the date of the events we are about to witness, a Frenchman under the name of Clement V., had ascended the chair of St. Peter, the new pope, with more prudence than valour, had deserted Rome for the tranquil retreat of Avignon; and the luxurious town of a foreign province became the court of the Roman pontiff, and the throne of the Christian Church.

Thus deprived of even the nominal check of the papal presence, the power of the nobles might be said to have no limits, save their own caprice, or their mutual jealousies and feuds. Though arrogating through fabulous genealogies their descent from the ancient Romans, they were, in reality, for the most part, the sons of the bolder barbarians of the North; and, contaminated by the craft of Italy, rather than imbued with its national affections, they retained the disdain of their foreign ancestors for a conquered soil and a degenerate people. While the rest of Italy, especially in Florence, in Venice, and in Milan, was fast and far advancing beyond the other states of Europe in civilisation and in art, the Romans appeared rather to recede than to improve;—unblest by laws, unvisited by art, strangers at once to the chivalry of a warlike, and the graces of a peaceful people. But they still possessed the sense and desire of liberty, and, by ferocious paroxysms and desperate struggles, sought to vindicate for their city the title it still assumed of "the Metropolis of the World." For the last two centuries they had known various revolutions,—brief, often bloody, and always unsuccessful. Still, there was the empty pageant of a popular form of government. The thirteen quarters of the city named each a chief; and the assembly of these magistrates, called Caporioni, by theory possessed an authority they had neither the power nor the courage to exert. Still there was the proud name of Senator; but, at the present time, the office was confined to one or to two persons, sometimes elected by the pope, sometimes by the nobles. The authority attached to the name seems to have had no definite limit; it was that of a stern dictator, or an indolent puppet, according as he who held it had the power to enforce the dignity he assumed. It was never conceded but to nobles, and it was by the nobles that all the outrages were committed. Private enmity alone was gratified whenever public justice was invoked: and the vindication of order was but the execution of revenge.

Holding their palaces as the castles and fortresses of princes, each asserting his own independency of all authority and law, and planting fortifications, and claiming principalities in the patrimonial territories of the Church, the barons of Rome made their state still more secure, and still more odious, by the maintenance of troops of foreign (chiefly of German) mercenaries, at once braver in disposition, more disciplined in service, and more skilful in arms, than even the freest Italians of that time. Thus they united the judicial and the military force, not for the protection, but for the ruin of Rome. Of these barons, the most powerful were the Orsini and Colonna; their feuds were hereditary and incessant, and every day witnessed the fruits of their lawless warfare, in bloodshed, in rape, and in conflagration. The flattery or the friendship of Petrarch, too credulously believed by modern historians, has invested the

Colonna, especially of the date now entered upon, with an elegance and a dignity not their own. Outrage, fraud, and assassination, a sordid avarice in securing lucrative offices to themselves, an insolent oppression of their citizens, and the most dastardly cringing to power superior to their own (with but few exceptions), mark the character of the first family of Rome. But, wealthier than the rest of the barons, they were, therefore, more luxurious, and, perhaps, more intellectual; and their pride was flattered in being patrons of those arts of which they could never have become the professors. From these multiplied oppressors the Roman citizens turned with fond and impatient regret to their ignorant and dark notions of departed liberty and greatness. They confounded the times of the Empire with those of the Republic; and often looked to the Teutonic king, who obtained his election from beyond the Alps, but his *title* of emperor from the Romans, as the deserter of his legitimate trust and proper home; vainly imagining that, if both the Emperor and the Pontiff fixed their residence in Rome, Liberty and Law would again seek their natural shelter beneath the resuscitated majesty of the Roman people.

The absence of the pope and the papal court served greatly to impoverish the citizens; and they had suffered yet more visibly by the depredations of hordes of robbers, numerous and unsparing, who infested Romagna, obstructing all the public ways, and were, sometimes secretly, sometimes openly, protected by the barons, who often recruited their banditti garrisons by banditti soldiers.

But besides the lesser and ignobler robbers, there had risen in Italy a far more formidable description of freebooters. A German, who assumed the lofty title of the Duke Werner, had, a few years prior to the period we approach, enlisted and organised a considerable force, styled "The Great Company," with which he besieged cities and invaded states, without any object less shameless than that of pillage. His example was soon imitated: numerous "Companies," similarly constituted, devastated the distracted and divided land. They appeared, suddenly raised, as if by magic, before the walls of a city, and demanded immense sums as the purchase of peace. Neither tyrant nor commonwealth maintained a force sufficient to resist them; and if other northern mercenaries were engaged to oppose them, it was only to recruit the standards of the freebooters with deserters. Mercenary fought not mercenary—nor German, German: and greater pay, and more unbridled rapine, made the tents of the "Companies" far more attractive than the regulated stipends of a city, or the dull fortress and impoverished coffers of a chief. Werner, the most implacable and ferocious of all these adventurers, and who had so openly gloried in his enormities as to wear upon his breast a silver plate, engraved with the words, "Enemy to God, to Pity, and to Mercy," had not long since ravaged Romagna with fire and sword. But, whether induced by money, or unable to control the fierce spirits he had raised, he afterwards led the bulk of his company back to Germany. Small detachments, however, remained, scattered throughout the land, waiting only an able leader once more to re-unite them: amongst those who appeared most fitted for that destiny was Walter de Montreal, a Knight of St. John, and gentleman of Provence, whose valour and military genius had already, though yet young, raised his name into dreaded celebrity; and whose ambition, experience, and sagacity, relieved by certain chivalric and noble qualities, were suited to enterprises far greater and more important than the violent depredations of the atrocious Werner. From these scourges, no state had suffered more grievously than Rome. The patrimonial territories of the pope,—in part wrested from him by petty tyrants, in part laid waste by these foreign robbers,—yielded but a scanty supply to the necessities of Clement VI., the most accomplished gentleman and the most graceful voluptuary of his time; and the good father had devised a plan, whereby to enrich at once the Romans and their pontiff.

Nearly fifty years before the time we enter upon, in order both to replenish the papal coffers and pacify the starving Romans, Boniface VIII. had instituted the Festival of the Jubilee, or Holy Year; in fact a revival of a Pagan ceremonial. A plenary indulgence was promised to every Catholic, who, in that year, and in the first year of every succeeding century, should visit the churches of St. Peter and St. Paul. An immense concourse of pilgrims, from every part of Christendom, had attested the wisdom of the invention: "and two priests stood night and day, with rakes in their hands, to collect without counting the heaps of gold and silver that were poured on the altar of St. Paul."

It is not to be wondered at that this most lucrative festival should, ere the next century was half expired, appear to a discreet pontiff to be too long postponed. And both pope and city agreed in thinking it might well bear a less distant renewal. Accordingly, Clement VI. had proclaimed, under the name of the *Mosaic* Jubilee, a second Holy Year for 1350—viz., three years distant from that date at which, in the next chapter, my narrative will commence. This circumstance had a great effect in whetting the popular indignation against the barons, and preparing the events I shall relate; for the roads were, as I before said, infested by the banditti, the creatures and allies of the barons. And if the roads were not cleared, the pilgrims might not attend. It was the object of the pope's vicar, Raimond, bishop of Orvietto (bad politician and good canonist), to seek, by every means, to remove all impediment between the offerings of devotion and the treasury of St. Peter.

Such, in brief, was the state of Rome at the period we are about to examine. Her ancient mantle of renown still, in the eyes of Italy and of Europe, cloaked her ruins. In name, at first she was still the queen of the earth; and from her hands came the crown of the emperor of the north, and the keys of the father of the church. Her situation was precisely that which presented a vast and glittering triumph to bold ambition,—an inspiring, if mournful, spectacle to determined patriotism,—and a fitting stage for that more august tragedy which seeks its incidents, selects its actors, and shapes its moral, amidst the vicissitudes and crimes of nations.

CHAPTER III

THE BRAWL

On an evening in April, 1347, and in one of those wide spaces in which Modern and Ancient Rome seemed blent together—equally desolate and equally in ruins—a miscellaneous and indignant populace were assembled. That morning the house of a Roman jeweller had been forcibly entered and pillaged by the soldiers of Martino di Porto, with a daring effrontery which surpassed even the ordinary licence of the barons. The sympathy and sensation throughout the city were deep and ominous.

"Never will I submit to this tyranny!"

"Nor I!"

"Nor I!"

"Nor, by the bones of St. Peter, will I!"

"And what, my friends, is this tyranny to which you will not submit?" said a young nobleman, addressing himself to the crowd of citizens who, heated, angry, half-armed, and with the vehement gestures of Italian passion, were now sweeping down the long and narrow street that led to the gloomy quarter occupied by the Orsini.

"Ah, my lord!" cried two or three of the citizens in a breath, "you will right us—you will see justice done to us—you are a Colonna."

"Ha, ha, ha!" laughed scornfully one man of gigantic frame, and wielding on high a huge hammer, indicative of his trade. "Justice and Colonna! body of God! those names are not often found together."

"Down with him! down with him! he is an Orsinist,—down with him!" cried at least ten of the throng: but no hand was raised against the giant.

"He speaks the truth," said a second voice, firmly.

"Ay, that doth he," said a third, knitting his brows, and unsheathing his knife, "and we will abide by it. The Orsini are tyrants—and the Colonnas are, at the best. as bad."

"Thou liest in thy teeth, ruffian!" cried the young noble, advancing into the press and confronting the last asperser of the Colonna.

Before the flashing eye and menacing gesture of the cavalier, the worthy brawler retreated some steps, so as to leave an open space between the towering form of the smith, and the small, slender, but vigorous frame of the young noble.

Taught from their birth to despise the courage of the plebeians, even while careless of much reputation as to their own, the patricians of Rome were not unaccustomed to the rude fellowship of these brawls; nor was it unoften that the mere presence of a noble sufficed to scatter whole crowds, that had the moment before been breathing vengeance against his order and his house.

Waving his hand, therefore, to the smith, and utterly unheeding either his brandished weapon or his vast stature, the young Adrian di Castello, a distant kinsman of the Colonna, haughtily bade him give way.

"To your homes, friends! and know," he added, with some dignity, "that ye wrong us much, if ye imagine we share the evil-doings of the Orsini, or are pandering solely to our own passions in the feud between their house and ours. May the Holy Mother so judge me," continued he, devoutly lifting up his eyes, "as I now with truth declare, that it is for your wrongs, and for the wrongs of Rome, that I have drawn this sword against the Orsini."

"So say all the tyrants," rejoined the smith, hardily, as he leant his hammer against a fragment of stone—some remnant of ancient Rome—"they never fight against each other, but it is for our good. One Colonna cuts me the throat of Orsini's baker—it is for our good! another Colonna seizes on the daughter of Orsini's tailor—it is for our good! *our* good—yes, for the good of the people!—the good of the bakers and tailors, eh?"

"Fellow," said the young nobleman, gravely, "if a Colonna did thus, he did wrong; but the holiest cause may have bad supporters."

"Yes, the holy Church itself is propped on very indifferent columns," answered the smith, in a rude witticism on the affection of the pope for the Colonna.

"He blasphemes! the smith blasphemes!" cried the partisans of that powerful house. "A Colonna, a Colonna!"

"An Orsini, an Orsini!" was no less promptly the counter cry.

"THE PEOPLE!" shouted the smith, waving his formidable weapon far above the heads of the group.

In an instant the whole throng, who had at first united against the aggression of one man, were divided by the hereditary wrath of faction. At the cry of Orsini, several new partisans hurried to the spot; the friends of the Colonna drew themselves on one side—the defenders of the Orsini on the other—and the few who agreed with the smith that both factions were equally odious, and the people was the sole legitimate cry in a popular commotion, would have withdrawn themselves from the approaching *mêlée*, if the smith himself, who was looked upon by them as an authority of great influence, had not—whether from resentment at the haughty bearing of the young Colonna, or from that appetite of contest not uncommon in men of a bulk and force which assure them in all personal affrays the lofty pleasure of superiority—if, I say, the smith himself had not, after a pause of indecision, retired among the Orsini, and entrained, by his example, the alliance of his friends with the favourers of that faction.

In popular commotions, each man is whirled along with the herd, often half against his own approbation or assent. The few words of peace by which Adrian di Castello commenced an address to his friends were drowned amidst their shouts. Proud to find in their ranks one of the most beloved, and one of the noblest of that name, the partisans of the Colonna placed him in their front, and charged impetuously on their foes. Adrian, however, who had acquired from circumstances something of that chivalrous code which he certainly could not have owed to his Roman birth, disdained at first to assault men among whom he recognised no equal, either in rank or the practice of arms. He contented himself with putting aside the few strokes that were aimed at him in the gathering confusion of the conflict—few; for those who recognised him, even amidst the bitterest partisans of the Orsini, were not willing to expose themselves to the danger and odium of spilling the blood of a man, who, in addition to his great birth and the terrible power of his connexions, was possessed of a personal popularity, which he owed rather to a comparison with the vices of his relatives than to any remarkable virtues hitherto displayed by himself. The smith alone, who had as yet taken no active part in the fray, seemed to gather himself up in determined opposition as the cavalier now advanced within a few steps of him.

"Did we not tell thee," quoth the giant, frowning, "that the Colonna were, not less than the Orsini, the foes of the people? Look at thy followers and clients: are they not cutting the throats of humble men by way of vengeance for the crime of a great one? But that is the way one patrician always scourges the insolence of another. He lays the rod on the backs of the people, and then cries, 'See how just I am!'"

"I do not answer thee now," answered Adrian; "but if thou regretest with me this waste of blood, join with me in attempting to prevent it."

"I—not I! let the blood of the slaves flow to-day: the time is fast coming when it shall be washed away by the blood of the lords."

"Away, ruffian!" said Adrian, seeking no further parley, and touching the smith with the flat side of his sword. In an instant the hammer of the smith swung in the air, and, but for the active spring of the young noble, would infallibly have crushed him to the earth. Ere the smith could gain time for a second blow, Adrian's sword passed twice through his right arm, and the weapon fell heavily to the ground.

"Slay him, slay him!" cried several of the clients of the Colonna, now pressing, dastard-like, round the disarmed and disabled smith.

"Ay, slay him!" said, in tolerable Italian, but with a barbarous accent, one man, half-clad in armour, who had but just joined the group, and who was one of those wild German bandits whom the Colonna held in their pay; "he belongs to a horrible gang of miscreants sworn against all order and peace. He is one of Rienzi's followers, and, bless the Three Kings! raves about the People."

"Thou sayest right, barbarian," said the sturdy smith, in a loud voice, and tearing aside the vest from his breast with his left hand; "come all—Colonna and Orsini—dig to this heart with your sharp blades, and when you have reached the centre, you will find there the object of your common hatred—'Rienzi and the People!'"

As he uttered these words, in language that would have seemed above his station (if a certain glow and exaggeration of phrase and sentiment were not common, when excited, to all the Romans), the loudness of his voice rose above the noise immediately round him, and stilled, for an instant, the general din; and when, at last, the words, "Rienzi and the People," rang forth, they penetrated midway through the increasing crowd, and were answered as by an echo, with a hundred voices—"Rienzi and the People!"

But whatever impression the words of the mechanic made on others, it was equally visible in the young Colonna. At the name of Rienzi the glow of excitement vanished from his cheek; he started back, muttered to himself, and for a moment seemed, even in the midst of that stirring commotion, to be lost in a moody and distant reverie. He recovered, as the shout died away; and saying to the smith, in a low tone, "Friend, I am sorry for thy wound; but seek me on the morrow, and thou shalt find thou hast wronged me;" he beckoned to the German to follow him, and threaded his way through the crowd, which generally gave back as he advanced. For the bitterest hatred to the order of the nobles was at that time in Rome mingled with a servile respect for their persons, and a mysterious awe of their uncontrollable power.

As Adrian passed through that part of the crowd in which the fray had not yet commenced, the murmurs that followed him were not those which many of his race could have heard.

"A Colonna," said one.

"Yet no ravisher," said another, laughing wildly.

"Nor murtherer," muttered a third, pressing his hand to his breast. "'Tis not against *him* that my father's blood cries aloud."

"Bless him," said a fourth, "for as yet no man curses him!"

"Ah, God help us!" said an old man, with a long gray beard, leaning on his staff: "the serpent's young yet; the fangs will show by and by."

"For shame, father! he is a comely youth, and not proud in the least. What a smile he hath!" quoth a fair matron, who kept on the outskirt of the *mêlée*.

"Farewell to a man's honour when a noble smiles on his wife!" was the answer.

"Nay," said Luigi, a jolly butcher, with a roguish eye, "what a man can win fairly from maid or wife, that let him do, whether plebeian or noble—that's my morality; but when an ugly old patrician finds fair words will not win fair looks, and carries me off a dame on the back of a German boar, with a stab in the side for comfort to the spouse,—then I say, he is a wicked man, and an adulterer."

While such were the comments and the murmurs that followed the noble, very different were the looks and words that attended the German soldier.

Equally, nay, with even greater promptitude, did the crowd make way at his armed and heavy tread; but not with looks of reverence:—the eye glared as he approached; but the cheek grew pale—the head bowed—the lip quivered; each man felt a shudder of hate and fear, as recognising a dread and mortal foe. And well and wrathfully did the fierce mercenary note the signs of the general aversion. He pushed on rudely—half-smiling in contempt, half-frowning in revenge, as he looked from side to side; and his long, matted, light hair, tawny-coloured moustache, and brawny front, contrasted strongly with the dark eyes, raven locks, and slender frames of the Italians.

"May Lucifer double damn those German cut-throats!" muttered, between his grinded teeth, one of the citizens.

"Amen!" answered, heartily, another.

"Hush!" said a third, timorously looking round; "if one of them hear thee, thou art a lost man."

"Oh, Rome! Rome! to what art thou fallen!" said bitterly one citizen, clothed in black, and of a higher seeming than the rest; "when thou shudderest in thy streets at the tread of a hired barbarian!"

"Hark to one of our learned men, and rich citizens!" said the butcher, reverently.

"'Tis a friend of Rienzi's," quoth another of the group, lifting his cap.

With downcast eyes, and a face in which grief, shame, and wrath were visibly expressed, Pandulfo di Guido, a citizen of birth and repute, swept slowly through the crowd, and disappeared.

Meanwhile, Adrian, having gained a street which, though in the neighbourhood of the crowd, was empty and desolate, turned to his fierce comrade. "Rodolf!" said he, "mark!—no violence to the citizens. Return to the crowd, collect the friends of our house, withdraw them from the scene; let not the Colonna be blamed for this day's violence; and assure our followers, in my name, that I swear, by the knighthood I received at the Emperor's hands, that by my sword shall Martino di Porto be punished for his outrage. Fain would I, in person, allay the tumult, but my presence only seems to sanction it. Go—thou hast weight with them all."

"Ay, signor, the weight of blows!" answered the grim soldier. "But the command is hard; I would fain let their puddle-blood flow an hour or two longer. Yet, pardon me; in obeying thy orders, do I obey those of my master, thy kinsman? It is old Stephen Colonna,—who seldom spares blood or treasure, God bless him—(save his own!)—whose money I hold, and to whose hests I am sworn."

"Diavolo!" muttered the cavalier, and the angry spot was on his cheek; but, with the habitual self-control of the Italian nobles, he smothered his rising choler, and said aloud, with calmness, but dignity,—

"Do as I bid thee; check this tumult,—make *us* the forbearing party. Let all be still within one hour hence, and call on me to-morrow for thy reward; be this purse an earnest of my future thanks. As for my kinsman, whom I command thee to name more reverently, 'tis in his name I speak. Hark! the din increases—the contest swells—go—lose not another moment."

Somewhat awed by the quiet firmness of the patrician, Rodolf nodded, without answer, slid the money into his bosom, and stalked away into the thickest of the throng. But, even ere he arrived, a sudden reaction had taken place.

The young cavalier, left alone in that spot, followed with his eyes the receding form of the mercenary, as the sun, now setting, shone slant upon his glittering casque, and said bitterly to himself—"Unfortunate city, fountain of all mighty memories—fallen queen of a thousand nations—how art thou decrowned and spoiled by thy recreant and apostate children! Thy nobles divided against themselves—thy people cursing thy nobles—thy priests, who should sow peace, planting discord—the father of thy church deserting thy stately walls, his home a refuge, his mitre a fief, his court a Gallic village—and we! we, of the haughtiest blood of Rome—we, the sons of Cæsars, and of the lineage of demigods, guarding an insolent and abhorred state by the swords of hirelings, who mock our cowardice while they receive our pay,—who keep our citizens slaves, and lord it over their very masters in return! Oh, that we, the hereditary chiefs of Rome, could but feel—oh, that we could but find, our only legitimate safeguard in the grateful hearts of our countrymen!"

So deeply did the young Adrian feel the galling truth of all he uttered, that the indignant tears rolled down his cheeks as he spoke. He felt no shame as he dashed them away; for that weakness which weeps for a fallen race, is the tenderness not of women but of angels.

As he turned slowly to quit the spot, his steps were suddenly arrested by a loud shout: "Rienzi! Rienzi!" smote the air. From the walls of the Capitol to the bed of the glittering Tiber, that name echoed far and wide; and, as the shout died away, it was swallowed up in a silence so profound, so universal, so breathless, that you might have imagined that death itself had fallen over the city. And now, at the extreme end of the crowd, and elevated above their level, on vast fragments of stone which had been dragged from the ruins of Rome in one of the late frequent tumults between contending factions, to serve as a barricade for citizens against citizens,—on these silent memorials of the past grandeur, the present misery, of Rome, stood that extraordinary man, who, above all his race, was the most penetrated with the glories of the one time, with the degradation of the other.

From the distance at which he stood from the scene, Adrian could only distinguish the dark outline of Rienzi's form; he could only hear the faint sound of his mighty voice; he could only perceive, in the subdued yet waving sea of human beings that spread around, their heads bared in the last rays of the sun, the unutterable effect which an eloquence, described by contemporaries almost as miraculous,—but in reality less so from the genius of the man than the sympathy of the audience,—created in all, who drank into their hearts and souls the stream of its burning thoughts.

It was but for a short time that that form was visible to the earnest eye, that that voice at intervals reached the straining ear, of Adrian di Castello; but that time sufficed to produce all the effect which Adrian himself had desired.

Another shout, more earnest, more prolonged than the first—a shout, in which spoke the release of swelling thoughts, of intense excitement—betokened the close of the harangue; and then you might see, after a minute's pause, the crowd breaking in all directions, and pouring down the avenues in various knots and groups, each testifying the strong and lasting impression made upon the multitude by that address. Every cheek was flushed—every tongue spoke: the animation of the orator had passed, like a living spirit, into the breasts of the audience. He had thundered against the disorders of the patricians, yet, by a word, he had disarmed the anger of the plebeians—he had preached freedom, yet he had opposed licence. He had calmed the present, by a promise of the future. He had chid their quarrels, yet had supported their cause. He had mastered the revenge of to-day, by a solemn assurance that there should come justice for the morrow. So great may be the power, so mighty the eloquence, so formidable the genius, of one man,—without arms, without rank, without sword or ermine, who addresses himself to a people that is oppressed.

CHAPTER IV

AN ADVENTURE

Avoiding the broken streams of the dispersed crowd, Adrian Colonna strode rapidly down one of the narrow streets leading to his palace, which was situated at no inconsiderable distance from the place in which the late contest had occurred. The education of his life made him feel a profound interest, not only in the divisions and disputes of his country, but also in the scene he had just witnessed, and the authority exercised by Rienzi.

An orphan of a younger, but opulent branch of the Colonna, Adrian had been brought up under the care and guardianship of his kinsman, that astute, yet valiant Stephen Colonna, who, of all the nobles of Rome, was the most powerful, alike from the favour of the pope, and the number of armed hirelings whom his wealth enabled him to maintain. Adrian had early manifested what in that age was considered an extraordinary disposition towards intellectual pursuits, and had acquired much of the little that was then known of the ancient language and the ancient history of his country.

Though Adrian was but a boy at the time in which, first presented to the reader, he witnessed the emotions of Rienzi at the death of his brother. his kind heart had been penetrated with sympathy for Cola's affliction, and shame for the apathy of his kinsmen at the result of their own feuds. He had earnestly sought the friendship of Rienzi, and, despite his years, had become aware of the power and energy of his character. But though Rienzi, after a short time, had appeared to think no more of his brother's death—though he again entered the halls of the Colonna, and shared their disdainful hospitalities, he maintained a certain distance and reserve of manner, which even Adrian could only partially overcome. He rejected every offer of service, favour, or promotion; and any unwonted proof of kindness from Adrian seemed, instead of making him more familiar, to offend him into colder distance. The easy humour and conversational vivacity which had first rendered him a welcome guest with those who passed their lives between fighting and feasting, had changed into a vein ironical, cynical, and severe. But the dull barons were equally amused at his wit, and Adrian was almost the only one who detected the serpent couched beneath the smile.

Often Rienzi sat at the feast, silent, but observant, as if watching every look, weighing every word, taking gauge and measurement of the intellect, policy, temperament, of every guest; and when he had seemed to satisfy himself, his spirits would rise, his words flow, and while his dazzling but bitter wit lit up the revel, none saw that the unmirthful flash was the token of the coming storm. But all the while, he neglected no occasion to mix with the humbler citizens, to stir up their minds, to inflame their imaginations, to kindle their emulation, with pictures of the present and with legends of the past. He grew in popularity and repute, and was yet more in power with the herd, because in favour with the nobles. Perhaps it was for that reason that he had continued the guest of the Colonna.

When, six years before the present date, the Capitol of the Cæsars witnessed the triumph of Petrarch, the scholastic fame of the young Rienzi had attracted the friendship of the poet,—a friendship that continued, with slight interruption, to the last, through careers so widely different; and afterwards, one among the Roman deputies to Avignon, he had been conjoined with Petrarch * to supplicate Clement VI. to remove the Holy See from Avignon to Rome. It was in this mission that, for the first time, he evinced his extraordinary powers of eloquence and persuasion. The pontiff, indeed, more desirous of ease than glory, was not convinced by the arguments, but he was enchanted with the pleader; and Rienzi returned to Rome, loaded with honours, and clothed with the dignity of high and responsible office. No longer the inactive scholar, the gay companion, he rose at once to pre-eminence above all his fellow-citizens. Never before had authority been borne with so austere an integrity, so uncorrupt a zeal. He had sought to impregnate his colleagues with the same loftiness of principle—he had failed. Now secure in his footing, he had begun openly to appeal to the people; and already a new spirit seemed to animate the populace of Rome.

While these were the fortunes of Rienzi, Adrian had been long separated from him, and absent from Rome.

* According to the modern historians; but it seems more probable that Rienzi's mission to Avignon was posterior to that of Petrarch. However this be, it was at Avignon that Petrarch and Rienzi became most intimate, as Petrarch himself observes in one of his letters.

The Colonna were staunch supporters of the imperial party and Adrian di Castello had received and obeyed an invitation to the Emperor's Court. Under that monarch he had initiated himself in arms, and, among the knights of Germany, he had learned to temper the natural Italian shrewdness with the chivalry of northern valour.

In leaving Bavaria, he had sojourned a short time in the solitude of one of his estates by the fairest lake of northern Italy; and thence, with a mind improved alike by action and study, had visited many of the free Italian states, imbibed sentiments less prejudiced than those of his order, and acquired an early reputation for himself while inly marking the characters and deeds of others. In him, the best qualities of the Italian noble were united. Passionately addicted to the cultivation of letters, subtle and profound in policy, gentle and bland of manner, dignifying a love of pleasure with a certain elevation of taste, he yet possessed a gallantry of conduct, and purity of honour, and an aversion from cruelty, which were then very rarely found in the Italian temperament, and which even the Chivalry of the North, while maintaining among themselves, usually abandoned the moment they came into contact with the systematic craft and disdain of honesty, which made the character of the ferocious, yet wily, South. With these qualities, he combined, indeed, the softer passions of his countrymen,—he adored Beauty, and he made a deity of Love.

He had but a few weeks returned to his native city, whither his reputation had already preceded him, and where his early affection for letters and gentleness of bearing were still remembered. He returned to find the position of Rienzi far more altered than his own.

Adrian had not yet sought the scholar. He wished first to judge with his own eyes, and at a distance, of the motives and object of his conduct; for partly he caught the suspicions which his own order entertained of Rienzi, and partly he shared in the trustful enthusiasm of the people.

"Certainly," said he now to himself, as he walked musingly onward, "certainly, no man has it more in his power to reform our diseased state, to heal our divisions, to awaken our citizens to the recollections of ancestral virtue. But that very power, how dangerous is it! Have I not seen, in the free states of Italy, men, called into authority for the sake of preserving the people, honest themselves at first, and then, drunk with the sudden rank, betraying the very cause which had exalted them? True, those men were chiefs and nobles; but are plebeians less human? Howbeit I have heard and seen enough from afar,—I will now approach, and examine the man himself."

While thus soliloquising, Adrian but little noted the various passengers, who, more and more rarely as the evening waned, hastened homeward. Among these were two females, who now alone shared with Adrian the long and gloomy street into which he had entered. The moon was already bright in the heavens, and, as the women passed the cavalier with a light and quick step, the younger one turned back and regarded him by the clear light with an eager, yet timid glance.

"Why dost thou tremble, my pretty one?" said her companion, who might have told some five-and-forty years, and whose garb and voice bespoke her of inferior rank to the younger female. "The streets seem quiet enough now, and, the Virgin be praised! we are not so far from home either."

"Oh! Benedetta, it is *he!* it is the young signor—it is Adrian!"

"That is fortunate," said the nurse, for such was her condition, "since they say he is as bold as a Northman: and as the Palazzo Colonna is not very far from hence, we shall be within reach of his aid should we want it: that is to say, sweet one, if you will walk a little slower than you have yet done."

The young lady slackened her pace, and sighed.

"He is certainly very handsome," quoth the nurse: "but thou must not think more of him; he is too far above thee for marriage, and for aught else, thou art too honest, and thy brother too proud——"

"And thou, Benedetta, art too quick with thy tongue. How canst thou talk thus, when thou knowest he hath never, since, at least, I was a mere child, even addressed me: nay, he scarce knows of my very existence. He, the Lord Adrian di Castello, dream of the poor Irene! the mere thought is madness!"

"Then why," said the nurse, briskly, "dost thou dream of *him?*"

Her companion sighed again more deeply than at first.

"Holy St. Catherine!" continued Benedetta, "if there were but one man in the world, I would die single ere I would think of him, until, at least, he had kissed my hand twice, and left it my own fault if it were not my lips instead."

The young lady still replied not.

"But how didst thou contrive to love him?" asked the nurse. "Thou canst not have seen him very often: it is but some four or five weeks since his return to Rome."

"Oh, how dull art thou?" answered the fair Irene.

"Have I not told thee, again and again, that I loved him six years ago?"

"When thou hadst told but thy tenth year, and a doll would have been thy most suitable lover! As I am a Christian, Signora, thou hast made good use of thy time."

"And during his absence," continued the girl, fondly, yet sadly, "did I not hear him spoken of, and was not the mere sound of his name like a love-gift that bade me remember? And when they praised him, have I not rejoiced? and when they blamed him, have I not resented? And when they said that his lance was victorious in the tourney, did I not weep with pride? and when they whispered that his vows were welcome in the bower, wept I not as fervently with grief? Have not the six years of his absence been a dream, and was not his return a waking into light—a morning of glory and the sun? And I see him now in the church when he wots not of me; and on his happy steed as he passes by my lattice: and is not that enough of happiness for love?"

"But if he loves not *thee?*"

"Fool! I ask not that; nay, I know not if I wish it. Perhaps I would rather dream of him, such as I would have him, than know him for what he is. He might be unkind, or ungenerous, or love me but little; rather would I not be loved at all, than loved coldly, and eat away my heart by comparing it with his. I can love him now as something abstract, unreal, and divine: but what would be my shame, my grief, if I were to find him less than I have imagined! Then, indeed, my life would have been wasted; then, indeed, the beauty of the earth would be gone!"

The good nurse was not very capable of sympathising with sentiments like these. Even had their characters been more alike, their disparity of age would have rendered such sympathy impossible. What but youth can echo back the soul of youth—all the music of its wild vanities and romantic follies? The good nurse did not sympathise with the sentiments of her young lady, but she sympathised with the deep earnestness with which they were expressed. She thought it wondrous silly, but wondrous moving; she wiped her eyes with the corner of her veil, and hoped in her secret heart that her young charge would soon get a real husband to put such unsubstantial fantasies out of her head. There was a short pause in their conversation, when, just where two streets crossed one another, there was heard a loud noise of laughing voices and trampling feet. Torches were seen on high affronting the pale light of the moon; and, at a very short distance from the two females, in the cross street, advanced a company of seven or eight men, bearing, as seen by the red light of the torches, the formidable badge of the Orsini.

Amidst the other disorders of the time, it was no unfrequent custom for the younger or more dissolute of the nobles, in small and armed companies, to parade the streets at night, seeking occasion for a licentious gallantry among the cowering citizens, or a skirmish at arms with some rival stragglers of their own order. Such a band had Irene and her companion now chanced to encounter.

"Holy Mother!" cried Benedetta, turning pale, and half running, "what curse has befallen us? How could we have been so foolish as to tarry so late at the Lady Nina's! Run, Signora,—run, or we shall fall into their hands!"

But the advice of Benedetta came too late,—the fluttering garments of the women had been already descried: in a moment more they were sourounded by the marauders. A rude hand tore aside Benedetta's veil, and at sight of features, which, if time had not spared, it could never very materially injure, the rough aggressor cast the poor nurse against the wall with a curse, which was echoed by a loud laugh from his comrades.

"Thou hast a fine fortune in faces, Giuseppe!"

"Yes; it was but the other day that he seized on a girl of sixty."

"And then, by way of improving her beauty, cut her across the face with his dagger, because she was not sixteen!"

"Hush, fellows! whom have we here?" said the chief of the party, a man richly dressed, and who, though bordering upon middle age, had only the more accustomed himself to the excesses of youth; as he spoke, he snatched the trembling Irene from the grasp of his followers. "Ho, there! the torches! *Oh che bella faccia!* what blushes—what eyes!—nay, look not down, pretty one; thou needst not be ashamed to win the love of an Orsini—yes; know the triumph thou hast achieved—it is Martino di Porto who bids thee smile upon him!"

"For the blest Mother's sake release me! Nay, sir, this must not be—I am not unfriended—this insult shall not pass!"

"Hark to her silver chiding; it is better than my best hound's bay! This adventure is worth a month's watching. What! will you not come?—restive—shrieks too!—Francesco Pietro, ye are the gentlest of the band. Wrap her veil around her,—muffle this music;—so! bear her before me to the palace, and to-morrow, sweet one, thou shalt go home with a basket of florins which thou mayest say thou hast bought at market."

But Irene's shrieks, Irene's struggles, had already brought succour to her side, and, as Adrian approached the spot, the nurse flung herself on her knees before him.

"Oh, sweet signor, for Christ's grace save us! deliver my young mistress—her friends love you well! We are all for the Colonna, my lord; yes, indeed, all for the Colonna! Save the kin of your own clients, gracious signor!"

"It is enough that she is a woman," answered Adrian, adding, between his teeth, "and that an Orsini is her assailant." He strode haughtily into the thickest of the group; the servitors laid hands on their swords, but gave way before him as they recognised his person; he reached the two men who had already seized Irene; in one moment he struck the foremost to the ground, in another he had passed his left arm round the light and slender form of the maiden, and stood confronting the Orsini with his drawn blade, which, however, he pointed to the ground.

"For shame, my lord—for shame!" said he, indignantly. "Will you force Rome to rise, to a man, against our order? Vex not too far the lion, chained though he be; war against *us* if ye will! draw your blades upon *men*, though they be of your own race, and speak your own tongue: but if ye would sleep at nights, and not dread the avenger's gripe,—if ye would walk the market-place secure,—wrong not a Roman woman! Yes, the very walls around us preach to you the punishment of such a deed: for that offence fell the Tarquins,—for that offence were swept away the

Decemvirs,—for that offence, if ye rush upon it, the blood of your whole house may flow like water. Cease then, my lord, from this mad attempt, so unworthy your great name; cease, and thank even a Colonna that he has come between you and a moment's frenzy!"

So noble, so lofty, were the air and gesture of Adrian, as he thus spoke, that even the rude servitors felt a thrill of approbation and remorse—not so Martino di Porto. He had been struck with the beauty of the prey thus suddenly snatched from him; he had been accustomed to long outrage and to long impunity; the very sight, the very voice of a Colonna, was a blight to his eye, and a discord to his ear: what, then, when a Colonna interfered with his lusts and rebuked his vices?

"Pedant!" he cried, with quivering lips, "prate not to me of thy vain legends and gossip's tales! think not to snatch from me my possession in another, when thine own life is in my hands. Unhand the maiden! throw down thy sword! return home without further parley, or, by my faith, and the blades of my followers—(look at them well)—thou diest!"

"Signor," said Adrian, calmly, yet while he spoke he retreated gradually with his fair burthen towards the neighbouring wall, so as at least to leave only his front exposed to those fearful odds: "Thou wilt not so misuse the present chances, and wrong thyself in men's mouths, as to attack with eight swords even thy hereditary foe, thus cumbered, too, as he is. But—nay hold!—if thou art so proposed, bethink thee well, one cry of my voice would soon turn the odds against thee. Thou art now in the quarter of my tribe; thou art surrounded by the habitations of the Colonna: yon palace swarms with men who sleep not, save with harness on their backs; men whom my voice can reach

"For shame, my lord, for shame."

even now, but from whom, if they once taste of blood, it could not save thee!"

"He speaks true, noble Lord," said one of the band: "we have wandered too far out of our beat; we are in their very den; the palace of old Stephen Colonna is within call: and, to my knowledge," added he, in a whisper, "eighteen fresh men-of-arms—ay, and Northmen too—marched through its gates this day."

"Were there eight hundred men at arm's length," answered Martino, furiously, "I would not be thus bearded amidst mine own train! Away with yon woman! To the attack! to the attack!"

Thus saying, he made a desperate lunge at Adrian, who, having kept his eye cautiously on the movements of his enemy, was not unprepared for the assault. As he put aside the blade with his own, he shouted with a loud voice—"Colonna! to the rescue, Colonna!"

Nor had it been without an ulterior object that the acute and self-controlling mind of Adrian had hitherto sought to prolong the parley. Even as he first addressed Orsini, he had perceived, by the moonlight, the glitter of armour upon two men advancing from the far end of the street, and judged at once, by the neighbourhood, that they must be among the mercenaries of the Colonna.

Gently he suffered the form of Irene, which now, for she had swooned with the terror, pressed too heavily upon him, to slide from his left arm, and standing over her form while sheltered from behind by the wall which he had so warily gained, he contented himself with parrying the blows hastily aimed at him, without attempting to retaliate. Few of the Romans, however accustomed to such desultory warfare, were then well and dexterously practised in the use of arms;

and the science Adrian had acquired in the schools of the martial north, befriended him now, even against such odds. It is true, indeed, that the followers of Orsini did not share the fury of their lord; partly afraid of the consequences to themselves should the blood of so high-born a signor be spilt by their hands, partly embarrassed with the apprehension that they should see themselves suddenly beset with the ruthless hirelings so close within hearing, they struck but aimless and random blows, looking every moment behind and aside, and rather prepared for flight than slaughter. Echoing the cry of "Colonna," poor Benedetta fled at the first clash of swords. She ran down the dreary street still shrieking that cry, and passed the very portals of Stephen's palace (where some grim forms yet loitered) without arresting her steps there, so great were her confusion and terror.

Meanwhile, the two armed men, whom Adrian had descried, proceeded leisurely up the street. The one was of a rude and common mould, his arms and his complexion testified his calling and race; and by the great respect he paid to his companion, it was evident that that companion was no native of Italy. For the brigands of the north, while they served the vices of the southern, scarce affected to disguise their contempt for his cowardice.

The companion of the brigand was a man of a martial, yet easy air. He wore no helmet, but a cap of crimson velvet, set off with a white plume; on his mantle, or surcoat, which was of scarlet, was wrought a broad white cross, both at back and breast; and so brilliant was the polish of his corselet, that, as from time to time the mantle waved aside and exposed it to the moonbeams, it glittered like light itself.

"Nay, Rodolf," said he, "if thou hast so good a lot of it here with that hoary schemer, Heaven forbid that I should wish to draw thee back again to our merry band. But tell me—this Rienzi—thinkest thou he has any solid and formidable power?"

"Pshaw! noble chieftain, not a whit of it. He pleases the mob; but as for the nobles, they laugh at him; and, as for the soldiers, he has no money!"

"He pleases the mob, then!"

"Ay, that doth he; and when he speaks aloud to them, all the roar of Rome is hushed."

"Humph!—when nobles are hated, and soldiers are bought, a mob may, in any hour, become the master. An honest people and a weak mob,—a corrupt people and a strong mob," said the other, rather to himself than to his comrade, and scarce, perhaps, conscious of the eternal truth of his aphorism. "He is no mere brawler, this Rienzi, I suspect—I must see to it. Hark! what noise is that? By the Holy Sepulchre, it is the ring of our own metal!"

"And that cry—'a Colonna!'" exclaimed Rodolf. "Pardon me, master,—I must away to the rescue!"

"Ay, it is the duty of thy hire;—run; yet stay, I will accompany thee, gratis for once, and from pure passion for mischief. By this hand, there is no music like clashing steel!"

Still Adrian continued gallantly and unwounded to defend himself, though his arm now grew tired, his breath well-nigh spent, and his eyes began to wink and reel beneath the glare of the tossing torches. Orsini himself, exhausted by his fury, had paused for an instant, fronting his foe with a heaving breast and savage looks, when, suddenly, his followers exclaimed, "Fly! fly!—the bandits approach—we are surrounded!" and two of the servitors, without further parley, took fairly to their heels. The other five remained irresolute, and waiting but the command of their master, when he of the white plume, whom I have just described, thrust himself into the *mêlée.*

"What! gentles," said he, "have ye finished already? Nay, let us not mar the sport; begin again, I beseech you. What are the odds? Ho! six to one! —nay, no wonder that ye have waited for fairer play. See, we too will take the weaker side. Now then, let us begin again."

"Insolent!" cried the Orsini. "Knowest thou him whom thou addressest thus arrogantly?—I am Martino di Porto. Who art thou?"

"Walter de Montreal, gentleman of Provence, and Knight of St. John!" answered the other, carelessly.

At that redoubted name—the name of one of the boldest warriors, and of the most accomplished freebooter of his time—even Martino's cheek grew pale, and his followers uttered a cry of terror.

"And this, my comrade," continued the Knight, "for we may as well complete the introduction, is probably better known to you than I am, gentles of Rome; and you doubtless recognise in him Rodolf of Saxony, a brave man and a true, where he is properly paid for his services."

"Signor," said Adrian to his enemy, who, aghast and dumb, remained staring vacantly at the two newcomers, "you are now in my power. See our own people, too, are approaching."

And, indeed, from the palace of Stephen Colonna, torches began to blaze, and armed men were seen rapidly advancing to the spot.

"Go home in peace, and if, to-morrow, or any day

more suitable to thee, thou wilt meet me alone, and lance to lance, as is the wont of the knights of the empire; or with band to band, and man for man, as is rather the Roman custom; I will not fail thee—there is my gage."

"Nobly spoken," said Montreal; "and, if ye choose the latter, by your leave, I will be one of the party."

Martino answered not; he took up the glove, thrust it in his bosom, and strode hastily away; only, when he had got some paces down the street, he turned back, and, shaking his clenched hand at Adrian, exclaimed, in a voice trembling with impotent rage—"Faithful to death!"

The words made one of the mottoes of the Orsini; and, whatever its earlier signification, had long passed into a current proverb, to signify their hatred to the Colonna.

Adrian, now engaged in raising, and attempting to revive Irene, who was still insensible, disdainfully left it to Montreal to reply.

"I doubt not, Signor," said the latter, coolly, "that thou wilt be faithful to Death: for Death, God wot, is the only contract which men, however ingenious, are unable to break or evade."

"Pardon me, gentle Knight," said Adrian, looking up from his charge, "if I do not yet give myself wholly to gratitude. I have learned enough of knighthood to feel thou wilt acknowledge that my first duty is here—"

"Oh, a lady, then, was the cause of the quarrel! I need not ask who was in the right, when a man brings to the rivalry such odds as yon caitiff."

"Thou mistakest a little, Sir Knight,—it is but a lamb I have rescued from the wolf."

"For thy own table! Be it so!" returned the Knight, gaily.

Adrian smiled gravely, and shook his head in denial. In truth, he was somewhat embarrassed by his situation. Though habitually gallant, he was not willing to expose to misconstruction the disinterestedness of his late conduct, and (for it was his policy to conciliate popularity) to sully the credit which his bravery would give him among the citizens, by conveying Irene (whose beauty, too, as yet he had scarcely noted) to his own dwelling; and yet, in her present situation, there was no alternative. She evinced no sign of life. He knew not her home, nor parentage. Benedetta had vanished. He could not leave her in the streets; he could not resign her to the care of another; and, as she lay now upon his breast, he felt her already endeared to him, by that sense of protection which is so grateful to the human heart. He briefly, therefore, explained to those now gathered round him, his present situation, and the cause of the past conflict; and bade the torch-bearers precede him to his home.

"You, Sir Knight," added he, turning to Montreal, "if not already more pleasantly lodged, will, I trust, deign to be my guest?"

"Thanks, Signor," answered Montreal, maliciously, "but I, also, perhaps, have my own affairs to watch over. Adieu! I shall seek you at the earliest occasion. Fair night, and gentle dreams!

'Robers Bertrams qui estoit tors
Maïs à ceval estoit mult fors
Cil avoit o lui grans effors
Multi ot 'homes per lui mors.'" *

* "An ill-favoured man, but a stout horseman, was Robert Bertram. Great deeds were his, and many a man died by his hand."

And, muttering this rugged chant from the old "Roman de Rou," the Provençal, followed by Rodolf, pursued his way.

The vast extent of Rome, and the thinness of its population, left many of the streets utterly deserted. The principal nobles were thus enabled to possess themselves of a wide range of buildings, which they fortified, partly against each other, partly against the people; their numerous relatives and clients lived around them, forming, as it were, petty courts and cities in themselves.

Almost opposite to the principal palace of the Colonna (occupied by his powerful kinsman, Stephen) was the mansion of Adrian. Heavily swung back the massive gates at his approach; he ascended the broad staircase, and bore his charge into an apartment which his tastes had decorated in a fashion not as yet common in that age. Ancient statues and busts were arranged around; the pictured arras of Lombardy decorated the walls, and covered the massive seats.

"What ho! Lights here, and wine!" cried the Seneschal.

"Leave us alone," said Adrian, gazing passionately on the pale cheek of Irene, as he now, by the clear light, beheld all its beauty; and a sweet yet burning hope crept into his heart.

CHAPTER V

THE DESCRIPTION OF A CONSPIRATOR, AND THE DAWN OF THE CONSPIRACY

Alone, by a table covered with various papers, sat a man in the prime of life. The chamber was low and long; many antique and disfigured bas-reliefs and torsos were placed around the wall, interspersed, here and there, with the short sword and close casque, time-worn relics of the prowess of ancient Rome. Right above the table at which he sate, the moonlight streamed through a high and narrow casement, deep sunk in the massy wall. In a niche to the right of this window, guarded by a sliding door, which was now partially drawn aside—but which, by its solid substance, and the sheet of iron with which it was plated, testified how valuable, in the eyes of the owner, was the treasure it protected—were ranged some thirty or forty volumes, then deemed no inconsiderable library; and being, for the most part, the laborious copies in manuscript by the hand of the owner, from immortal originals.

Leaning his cheek on his hand, his brow somewhat knit, his lip slightly compressed, that personage indulged in meditations far other than the indolent dreams of scholars. As the high and still moonlight shone upon his countenance, it gave an additional and solemn dignity to features which were naturally of a grave and majestic cast. Thick and auburn hair, the colour of which, not common to the Romans, was ascribed to his descent from the Teuton emperor, clustered in large curls above a high and expansive forehead; and even the present thoughtful compression of the brow could not mar the aspect of latent power, which is derived from that great breadth between the eyes, in which the Grecian sculptors of old so admirably conveyed the expression of authority, and the silent energy of command. But his features were not cast in the Grecian, still less in the Teuton mould. The iron jaw, the aquiline nose, the somewhat sunken cheek, strikingly recalled the character of the hard Roman race, and might not inaptly have suggested to a painter a model for the younger Brutus.

The marked outline of the face, and the short, firm upper lip, were not concealed by the beard and mustachios usually then worn; and, in the faded portrait of the person now described, still extant at Rome, may be traced a certain resemblance to the popular pictures of Napoleon; not indeed in the features, which are more stern and prominent in the portrait of the Roman, but in that peculiar expression of concentrated and tranquil power which so nearly realises the ideal of intellectual majesty. Though still young, the personal advantages most peculiar to youth,—the bloom and glow, the rounded cheek in which care has not yet ploughed its lines, the full unsunken eye, and the slender delicacy of frame,—these were not the characteristics of that solitary student. And, though considered by his contemporaries as eminently handsome, the judgment was probably formed less from the more vulgar claims to such distinction, than from the height of the stature, an advantage at that time more esteemed than at present, and that nobler order of beauty which cultivated genius and commanding character usually stamp upon even homely features;—the more rare in an age so rugged.

The character of Rienzi (for the youth presented to the reader in the first chapter of this history is now again before him in maturer years) had acquired greater hardness and energy with each stepping-stone to power. There was a circumstance attendant on his birth which had, probably, exercised great and early influence on his ambition. Though his parents were in humble circumstances, and of lowly calling, his father was the natural son of the Emperor, Henry VII.; * and it was the pride of the parents that probably gave to Rienzi the unwonted advantages of education. This pride transmitted to himself,—his descent from royalty dinned into his ear, infused into his thoughts, from his cradle,—made him, even in his earliest youth, deem himself the equal of the Roman signors, and half unconsciously aspire to be their superior. But, as the literature of Rome was unfolded to his eager eye and ambitious heart, he became imbued with that pride of country which is nobler than the pride of birth; and, save when stung by allusions to his origin, he unaffectedly valued himself more on being a Roman plebeian than the descendant of a Teuton king. His brother's death, and the vicissitudes he himself had already undergone, deepened the earnest and solemn qualities of his character; and, at length, all the faculties of a very uncommon intellect were concentrated into one object—

* De Sade supposes that the *mother* of Rienzi was the daughter of an illegitimate son of Henry VII., supporting his opinion from a MS. in the Vatican. But, according to the contemporaneous biographer, Rienzi, in addressing Charles, king of Bohemia, claims the relationship from his father. "Di vostro legnaggio sono—figlio di bastardo d'Enrico imperatore," &c. A more recent writer, il Padre Gabrini, cites an inscription in support of this descent: "Nicolaus Tribunus . . . *Laurentii Teutoniei* Filius." &c.

which borrowed from a mind strongly and mystically religious, as well as patriotic, a sacred aspect, and grew at once a duty and a passion.

"Yes," said Rienzi, breaking suddenly from his reverie, "yes, the day is at hand when Rome shall rise again from her ashes; Justice shall dethrone Oppression; men shall walk safe in their ancient Forum. We will rouse from his forgotten tomb the indomitable soul of Cato! There shall be a *people* once more in Rome! And I—I shall be the instrument of that triumph—the restorer of my race! mine shall be the first voice to swell the battle-cry of freedom—mine the first hand to rear her banner—yes, from the height of my own soul as from a mountain, I see already rising the liberties and the grandeur of the New Rome; and on the corner-stone of the mighty fabric posterity shall read my name."

Uttering these lofty boasts, the whole person of the speaker seemed instinct with his ambition. He strode the gloomy chamber with light and rapid steps, as if on air; his breast heaved, his eyes glowed. He felt that love itself can scarcely bestow a rapture equal to that which is felt, in his first virgin enthusiasm, by a patriot who knows himself *sincere!*

There was a slight knock at the door, and a servitor, in the rich liveries worn by the Pope's officials,* presented himself.

"Signor," said he, "my Lord, the Bishop of Orvieto, is without."

"Ha! that is fortunate. Lights there!—My Lord, this is an honour which I can estimate better than express."

* Not the present hideous habiliments which are said to have been the invention of Michael Angelo.

"Tut, tut! my good friend," said the Bishop, entering, and seating himself familiarly, "no ceremonies between the servants of the Church; and never, I ween well, had she greater need of true friends than now. These unholy tumults, these licentious contentions, in the very shrines and city of St. Peter, are sufficient to scandalise all Christendom."

"And so will it be," said Rienzi, "until his Holiness himself shall be graciously persuaded to fix his residence in the seat of his predecessors, and curb with a strong arm the excesses of the nobles."

"Alas, man!" said the Bishop, "thou knowest that these words are but as wind; for were the Pope to fulfil thy wishes, and remove from Avignon to Rome, by the blood of St. Peter! he would not curb the nobles, but the nobles would curb him. Thou knowest well that until his blessed predecessor, of pious memory, conceived the wise design of escaping to Avignon, the Father of the Christian world was but like many other fathers in their old age, controlled and guarded by his rebellious children. Recollectest thou not how the noble Boniface himself, a man of great heart, and nerves of iron, was kept in thraldom by the ancestors of the Orsini—his entrances and exits made but at their will—so that, like a caged eagle, he beat himself against his bars and died? Verily, thou talkest of the memories of Rome—these are not the memories that are very attractive to popes."

"Well," said Rienzi, laughing gently, and drawing his seat nearer to the Bishop's, "my Lord has certainly the best of the argument at present; and I must own, that strong, licentious, and unhallowed as the order of nobility was then, it is yet more so now."

"Even I," rejoined Raimond, colouring as he spoke,

"though Vicar of the Pope, and representative of his spiritual authority, was, but three days ago, subjected to a coarse affront from that very Stephen Colonna, who has ever received such favour and tenderness from the Holy See. His servitors jostled mine in the open streets, and I myself—I, the delegate of the sire of kings—was forced to draw aside to the wall, and wait until the hoary insolent swept by. Nor were blaspheming words wanting to complete the insult. 'Pardon, Lord Bishop,' said he, as he passed me; 'but this world, thou knowest, must necessarily take precedence of the other.'"

"Dared he so high?" said Rienzi, shading his face with his hand, as a very peculiar smile—scarcely itself joyous, though it made others gay, and which completely changed the character of his face, naturally grave even to sternness—played round his lips. "Then it is time for thee, holy father, as for us, to——"

"To what?" interrupted the Bishop, quickly. "Can we effect aught! Dismiss thy enthusiastic dreamings—descend to the real earth—look soberly round us. Against men so powerful, what *can* we do?"

"My Lord," answered Rienzi, gravely, "it is the misfortune of signors of your rank never to know the people, or the accurate signs of the time. As those who pass over the heights of mountains see the clouds sweep below, veiling the plains and valleys from their gaze, while they, only a little above the level, survey the movements and the homes of men; even so from your lofty eminence ye behold but the indistinct and sullen vapours—while from my humbler station I see the preparations of the shepherds, to shelter themselves and herds from the storm which those clouds betoken. Despair not, my Lord; endurance goes but to a certain limit—to that limit it is already stretched; Rome waits but the occasion (it will soon come, but not suddenly) to rise simultaneously against her oppressors."

The great secret of eloquence is to be in earnest—the great secret of Rienzi's eloquence was in the mightiness of his enthusiasm. He never spoke as one who doubted of success. Perhaps, like most men who undertake high and great actions, he himself was never thoroughly aware of the obstacles in his way. He saw the end, bright and clear, and overleaped, in the vision of his soul, the crosses and the length of the path; thus the deep convictions of his own mind stamped themselves irresistibly upon others. He seemed less to promise than to prophesy.

The Bishop of Orvietto, not over-wise, yet a man of cool temperament and much worldly experience, was forcibly impressed by the energy of his companion; perhaps, indeed, the more so, inasmuch as his own pride and his own passions were also enlisted against the arrogance and licence of the nobles. He paused ere he replied to Rienzi.

"But is it," he asked, at length, "only the plebeians who will rise? Thou knowest how they are caitiff and uncertain."

"My Lord," answered Rienzi, "judge, by one fact, how strongly I am surrounded by friends of no common class: thou knowest how loudly I speak against the nobles—I cite them by their name—I beard the Savelli, the Orsini, the Colonna, in their very hearing. Thinkest thou that they forgive me? thinkest thou that, were only the plebeians my safeguard and my favourers, they would not seize me by open force,—that I had not long ere this found a gag in their dungeons, or been swallowed up in the eternal dumbness of the grave? Observe," continued he, as, reading the Vicar's countenance, he perceived the impression he had made—"observe, that, throughout the whole world, a great revolution has begun. The barbaric darkness of centuries has been broken; the KNOWLEDGE which made men as demigods in the past time has been called from her urn; a Power, subtler than brute force, and mightier than armed men, is at work; we have begun once more to do homage to the Royalty of Mind. Yes, that same Power which, a few years ago, crowned Petrarch in the Capitol, when it witnessed, after the silence of twelve centuries, the glories of a TRIUMPH,—which heaped upon a man of obscure birth, and unknown in arms, the same honours given of old to emperors and the vanquishers of kings,—which united in one act of homage even the rival houses of Colonna and Orsini,—which made the haughtiest patricians emulous to bear the train, to touch but the purple robe of the son of the Florentine plebeian,—which still draws the eyes of Europe to the lowly cottage of Vaucluse,—which gives to the humble student the all-acknowledged licence to admonish tyrants, and approach, with haughty prayers, even the Father of the Church;—yes, that same Power, which, working silently throughout Italy, murmurs under the solid base of the Venetian oligarchy; * which, beyond the Alps, has wakened into visible and sudden life in Spain, in Germany, in Flanders; and which, even in

* It was about eight years afterwards that the long-smothered hate of the Venetian people to that wisest and most vigilant of all oligarchies, the Sparta of Italy, broke out in the conspiracy under Marino Faliero.

that barbarous Isle, conquered by the Norman sword, ruled by the bravest of living kings,* has roused a spirit Norman cannot break—kings to rule over must rule by—yes, that same Power is everywhere abroad: it speaks, it conquers in the voice even of him who is before you; it unites in his cause all on whom but one glimmering of light has burst, all in whom one generous desire can be kindled! Know, Lord Vicar, that there is not a man in Rome, save our oppressors themselves—not a man who has learned one syllable of our ancient tongue—whose heart and sword are not with me. The peaceful cultivators of letters—the proud nobles of the second order—the rising race, wiser than their slothful sires; above all, my Lord, the humbler ministers of religion, priests and monks, whom luxury hath not blinded, pomp hath not deafened, to the monstrous outrage to Christianity daily and nightly perpetrated in the Christian Capital; these, —all these,—are linked with the merchant and the artisan in one indissoluble bond, waiting but the signal to fall or to conquer, to live freemen, or to die martyrs, with Rienzi and their country!"

"Sayest thou so in truth?" said the Bishop, startled, and half rising. "Prove but thy words, and thou shalt not find the ministers of God are less eager than their lay brethren for the happiness of men."

"What I say," rejoined Rienzi, in a cooler tone, "that can I show! but I may only prove it to those who will be with us."

* Edward III., in whose reign opinions far more popular than those of the following century began to work. The Civil Wars threw back the action into the blood. It was indeed an age throughout the world which put forth abundant blossoms, but crude and unripened fruit;—a singular leap, followed by as singular a pause.

"Fear me not," answered Raimond: "I know well the secret mind of his Holiness, whose delegate and representative I am; and could he see but the legitimate and natural limit set to the power of the patricians, who, in their arrogance, have set at nought the authority of the Church itself, be sure that he would smile on the hand that drew the line. Nay, so certain of this am I, that if ye succeed, I, his responsible but unworthy vicar, will myself sanction the success. But beware of crude attempts; the Church must not be weakened by linking itself to failure."

"Right, my Lord," answered Rienzi; "and in this, the policy of religion is that of freedom. Judge of my prudence by my long delay. He who can see all around him impatient—himself not less so—and yet suppress the signal, and bide the hour, is not likely to lose his cause by rashness."

"More, then, of this anon," said the Bishop, resettling himself in his seat. "As thy plans mature, fear not to communicate with me. Believe that Rome has no firmer friend than he who, ordained to preserve order, finds himself impotent against aggression. Meanwhile, to the object of my present visit, which links itself, in some measure, perhaps, with the topics on which we have conversed . . . . Thou knowest that when his Holiness intrusted thee with thy present office, he bade thee also announce his beneficent intention of granting a general Jubilee at Rome for the year 1350—a most admirable design for two reasons, sufficiently apparent to thyself: first, that every Christian soul that may undertake the pilgrimage to Rome on that occasion, may thus obtain a general remission of sins; and secondly, because, to speak carnally, the concourse of pilgrims so assembled, usually, by the donations and offerings their piety suggests, very materially add to the revenues of the Holy See: at this time, by the way, in no very flourishing condition. This thou knowest, dear Rienzi."

Rienzi bowed his head in assent, and the prelate continued—

"Well, it is with the greatest grief that his Holiness perceives that his pious intentions are likely to be frustrated: for so fierce and numerous are now the brigands in the public approaches to Rome, that, verily, the boldest pilgrim may tremble a little to undertake the journey; and those who do so venture will, probably, be composed of the poorest of the Christian community,—men who, bringing with them neither gold, nor silver, nor precious offerings, will have little to fear from the rapacity of the brigands. Hence arise two consequences: on the one hand, the rich—whom, Heaven knows, and the Gospel has, indeed, expressly declared, have the most need of a remission of sins—will be deprived of this glorious occasion for absolution; and, on the other hand, the coffers of the Church will be impiously defrauded of that wealth which it would otherwise doubtless obtain from the zeal of her children."

"Nothing can be more logically manifest, my Lord," said Rienzi.

The Vicar continued—"Now, in letters received five days since from his Holiness, he bade me expose these fearful consequences to Christianity to the various patricians who are legitimately fiefs of the Church, and command their resolute combination against the marauders of the road. With these have I conferred, and vainly."

"For by the aid, and from the troops, of those very

brigands, these patricians have fortified their palaces against each other," added Rienzi.

"Exactly for that reason," rejoined the Bishop. "Nay, Stephen Colonna himself had the audacity to confess it. Utterly unmoved by the loss to so many precious souls, and, I may add, to the papal treasury, which ought to be little less dear to right-discerning men, they refuse to advance a step against the bandits. Now, then, hearken the second mandate of his Holiness:—'Failing the nobles,' saith he, in his prophetic sagacity, 'confer with Cola di Rienzi. He is a bold man, and a pious, and, thou tellest me, of great weight with the people; and say to him, that if his wit can devise the method for extirpating these sons of Belial, and rendering a safe passage along the public ways, largely, indeed, will he merit at our hands,—lasting will be the gratitude we shall owe to him; and whatever succour thou, and the servants of our See, can render to him, let it not be stinted.'"

"Said his Holiness thus!" exclaimed Rienzi. "I ask no more—the gratitude is mine that he hath thought thus of his servant, and intrusted me with this charge; at once I accept it—at once I pledge myself to success. Let us, my Lord, let us, then, clearly understand the limits ordained to my discretion. To curb the brigands without the walls, I must have authority over those within. If I undertake, at peril of my life, to clear all the avenues to Rome of the robbers who now infest it, shall I have full licence for conduct bold, peremptory, and severe?"

"Such conduct the very nature of the charge demands," replied Raimond.

"Ay—even though it be exercised against the arch offenders—against the supporters of the brigands—against the haughtiest of the nobles themselves?"

The Bishop paused, and looked hard in the face of the speaker. "I repeat," said he, at length, sinking his voice, and with a significant tone, "in these bold attempts, success is the sole sanction. *Succeed*, and we will excuse thee all—even to the——"

"Death of a Colonna or an Orsini, should justice demand it; and provided it be according to the law, and only incurred by the violation of the law!" added Rienzi, firmly.

The Bishop did not reply in words, but a slight motion of his head was sufficient answer to Rienzi.

"My Lord," said he, "from this time, then, all is well; I date the revolution—the restoration of order, of the state—from this hour, this very conference. Till now, knowing that justice must never wink upon great offenders, I had hesitated, through fear lest thou and his Holiness might deem it severity, and blame him who replaces the law, because he smites the violators of law. Now I judge ye more rightly. Your hand, my Lord."

The Bishop extended his hand; Rienzi grasped it firmly, and then raised it respectfully to his lips. Both felt that the compact was sealed.

This conference, so long in recital, was short in the reality; but its object was already finished, and the Bishop rose to depart. The outer portal of the house was opened, the numerous servitors of the Bishop held on high their torches, and he had just turned from Rienzi, who had attended him to the gate, when a female passed hastily through the Prelate's train, and starting as she beheld Rienzi, flung herself at his feet.

"Oh, hasten, Sir! hasten, for the love of God, hasten! or the young Signora is lost for ever!"

"The Signora!—Heaven and earth, Benedetta, of whom do you speak?—of my sister—of Irene? is she not within?"

"Oh, Sir—the Orsini—the Orsini!"

"What of them?—speak, woman!"

Here, breathlessly, and with many a break, Benedetta recounted to Rienzi, in whom the reader has already recognised the brother of Irene, so far of the adventure with Martino di Porto as she had witnessed: of the termination and result of the contest she knew nought.

Rienzi listened in silence; but the deadly paleness of his countenance, and the writhing of the nether lip, testified the emotions to which he gave no audible vent.

"You hear, my Lord Bishop—you hear," said he, when Benedetta had concluded; and turning to the Bishop, whose departure the narrative had delayed—"you hear to what outrage the citizens of Rome are subjected. My hat and sword! instantly! My Lord, forgive my abruptness."

"Whither art thou bent, then?" asked Raimond.

"Whither—whither!—Ay, I forgot, my Lord, you have no sister. Perhaps, too, you had no brother?—No, no; one victim at least I will live to save. Whither, you ask me?—to the palace of Martino di Porto."

"To an Orsini *alone*, and for justice?"

"Alone, and for *justice!*—No!" shouted Rienzi, in a loud voice, as he seized his sword, now brought to him by one of his servants, and rushed from the house; "but one man is sufficient for *revenge!*"

The Bishop paused for a moment's deliberation. "He must not be lost," muttered he, "as he well may be, if exposed thus solitary to the wolf's rage. What, ho!" he cried aloud; "advance the torches!—quick, quick! We ourself—we, the Vicar of the Pope—will see to this. Calm yourselves, good people; your young Signora shall be restored. On! to the palace of Martino di Porto!"

CHAPTER VI

IRENE IN THE PALACE OF ADRIAN DI CASTELLO

As the Cyprian gazed on the image in which he had embodied a youth of dreams, what time the living hues flushed slowly beneath the marble,—so gazed the young and passionate Adrian upon the form reclined before him, re-awakening gradually to life. And, if the beauty of that face were not of the loftiest or the most dazzling order, if its soft and quiet character might be outshone by many, of loveliness less really perfect, yet never was there a countenance that, to some eyes, would have seemed more charming, and never one in which more eloquently was wrought that ineffable and virgin expression which Italian art seeks for in its models,—in which modesty is the outward, and tenderness the latent, expression; the bloom of youth, both of form and heart, ere the first frail and delicate freshness of either is brushed away: and when even love itself, the only unquiet visitant that should be known at such an age, is but a sentiment, and not a passion!

"Benedetta!" murmured Irene, at length opening

her eyes, unconsciously, upon him who knelt beside her,—eyes of that uncertain, that most liquid hue, on which you might gaze for years and never learn the secret of the colour, so changed it with the dilating pupil,—darkening in the shade, and brightening into azure in the light:

"Benedetta," said Irene, "where art thou? Oh, Benedetta! I have had such a dream."

"And *I*, too, such a vision!" thought Adrian.

"Where am I?" cried Irene, rising from the couch. "This room—these hangings—Holy Virgin! do I dream still!—and you! Heavens!—it is the Lord Adrian di Castello!"

"Is that a name thou hast been taught to fear?" said Adrian; "if so, I will forswear it."

If Irene now blushed deeply, it was not in that wild delight with which her romantic heart might have foretold that she would listen to the first words of homage from Adrian di Castello. Bewildered and confused,—terrified at the strangeness of the place, and shrinking even from the thought of finding herself alone with one who for years had been present to her fancies,—alarm and distress were the emotions she felt the most, and which most were impressed upon her speaking countenance; and as Adrian now drew nearer to her, despite the gentleness of his voice and the respect of his looks, her fears, not the less strong that they were vague, increased upon her: she retreated to the further end of the room, looked wildly round her, and then, covering her face with her hands, burst into a paroxysm of tears.

Moved himself by these tears, and divining her thoughts, Adrian forgot for a moment all the more daring wishes he had formed.

"Fear not, sweet lady," said he earnestly: "recollect thyself, I beseech thee; no peril, no evil can reach thee here; it was this hand that saved thee from the outrage of the Orsini—this roof is but the shelter of a friend! Tell me, then, fair wonder, thy name and residence, and I will summon my servitors, and guard thee to thy home at once."

Perhaps the relief of tears, even more than Adrian's words, restored Irene to herself, and enabled her to comprehend her novel situation; and as her senses, thus cleared, told her what she owed to him whom her dreams had so long imaged as the ideal of all excellence, she recovered her self-possession, and uttered her thanks with a grace not the less winning, if it still partook of embarrassment.

"Thank me not," answered Adrian, passionately. "I have touched thy hand—I am repaid. Repaid! nay, all gratitude—all homage is for me to render!"

Blushing again, but with far different emotions than before, Irene, after a momentary pause, replied, "Yet, my Lord, I must consider it a debt the more weighty that you speak of it so lightly. And now, complete the obligation. I do not see my companion—suffer her to accompany me home; it is but a short way hence."

"Blessed, then, is the air that I have breathed so unconsciously!" said Adrian. "But thy companion, dear lady, is not here. She fled, I imagine, in the confusion of the conflict; and not knowing thy name, nor being able, in thy then state, to learn it from thy lips, it was my happy necessity to convey thee hither;—but I will be thy companion. Nay, why that timid glance? my people, also, shall attend us."

"My thanks, noble Lord, are of little worth; my brother, who is not unknown to thee, will thank thee more fittingly. May I depart?" and Irene, as she spoke, was already at the door.

"Art thou so eager to leave me?" answered Adrian, sadly. "Alas! when thou hast departed from my eyes, it will seem as if the moon had left the night!—but it is happiness to obey thy wishes, even though they tear thee from me."

A slight smile parted Irene's lips, and Adrian's heart beat audibly to himself, as he drew from that smile, and those downcast eyes, no unfavourable omen.

Reluctantly and slowly he turned towards the door, and summoned his attendants. "But," said he, as they stood on the lofty staircase, "thou sayest, sweet lady, that thy brother's name is not unknown to me. Heaven grant that he be, indeed, a friend of the Colonna!"

"His boast," answered Irene, evasively; "the boast of Cola di Rienzi is, to be a friend to the friends of Rome."

"Holy Virgin of Ara Cœli!—is thy brother that extraordinary man?" exclaimed Adrian, as he foresaw, at the mention of that name, a barrier to his sudden passion. "Alas! in a Colonna, in a noble, he will see no merit; even though thy fortunate deliverer, sweet maiden, sought to be his early friend!"

"Thou wrongest him much, my Lord," returned Irene, warmly; "he is a man above all others to sympathise with thy generous valour, even had it been exerted in defence of the humblest woman in Rome,—how much more, then, when in protection of his sister!"

"The times are, indeed, diseased," answered Adrian, thoughtfully, as they now found themselves in the open street, "when men who alike mourn for the woes of their country are yet suspicious of each other: when to be a patrician is to be regarded as an enemy to the people; when to be termed the friend of the people is to be considered a foe to the patricians: but come what may, oh! let me hope, dear lady, that no doubts, no divisions, shall banish from *thy* breast one gentle memory of me!"

"Ah! little, little do you know me!" began Irene, and stopped suddenly short.

"Speak! speak again!—of what music has this envious silence deprived my soul! Thou wilt not, then, forget me? And," continued Adrian, "we shall meet again? It is to Rienzi's house we are bound now; to-morrow I shall visit my old companion,—to-morrow I shall see thee. Will it not be so?"

In Irene's silence was her answer.

"And as thou hast told me thy brother's name, make it sweet to my ear, and add to it thine own."

"They call me Irene."

"Irene, Irene!—let me repeat it. It is a soft name, and dwells upon the lips as if loath to leave them—a fitting name for one like thee."

Thus making his welcome court to Irene, in that flowered and glowing language which, if more peculiar to that age and to the gallantry of the south, is also the language in which the poetry of youthful passion would, in all times and lands, utter its rich extravagance, could heart speak to heart, Adrian conveyed homeward his beautiful charge, taking, however, the most circuitous and lengthened route; an artifice which Irene either perceived not, or silently forgave. They were now within sight of the street in which Rienzi dwelt, when a party of men, bearing torches, came unexpectedly upon them. It was the train of the Bishop of Orvietto, returning from the palace of Martino di Porto, and in their way (accompanied by Rienzi) to that of Adrian. They had learned at the former, without an interview with the Orsini, from the retainers in the court below, the fortune of the conflict, and the name of Irene's champion; and, despite Adrian's general reputation for gallantry, Rienzi knew enough of his character, and the nobleness of his temper, to feel assured that Irene was safe in his protection. Alas! in that very safety to the person is often the most danger to the heart. Woman never so dangerously loves, as when he who loves her, for her sake, subdues himself.

Clasped to her brother's breast, Irene bade him thank her deliverer; and Rienzi, with that fascinating frankness which sits so well on those usually reserved, and which all who would rule the hearts of their fellow-men must at times command, advanced to the young Colonna, and poured forth his gratitude and praise.

"We have been severed too long,—we must know each other again," replied Adrian. "I shall seek thee, ere long, be assured."

Turning to take his leave of Irene, he conveyed her hand to his lips, and pressing it, as it dropped from his clasp, was he deceived in thinking that those delicate fingers lightly, involuntarily, returned the pressure?

CHAPTER VII

UPON LOVE AND LOVERS

If, in adopting the legendary love-tale of Romeo and Juliet, Shakespeare had changed the scene in which it is cast for a more northern clime, we may doubt whether the art of Shakespeare himself could have reconciled us at once to the suddenness and the strength of Juliet's passion. And even as it is, perhaps there are few of our rational and sober-minded islanders who would not honestly confess, it fairly questioned, that they deem the romance and fervour of those ill-starred lovers of Verona exaggerated and over-drawn. Yet in Italy, the picture of that affection born of a night—but "strong as death"—is one to which the veriest commonplaces of life would afford parallels without number. As in different ages, so in different climes, love varies wonderfully in the shapes it takes. And even at this day, beneath Italian skies, many a simple girl would feel as Juliet, and many a homely gallant would rival the extravagance of Romeo. Long suits in that sunny land, wherein, as whereof, I now write, are unknown. In no other land, perhaps, is there found so commonly the love at first sight, which in France is a jest, and in England a doubt; in no other land, too, is love, though so suddenly conceived, more faithfully preserved. That which is ripened in fancy comes at once to passion, yet is embalmed through all time by sentiment. And this must be my and their excuse, if the love of Adrian seem too prematurely formed, and that of Irene too romantically conceived;—it is the excuse which they take from the air and sun, from the customs of their ancestors, from the soft contagion of example. But while they yielded to the dictates of their hearts, it was with a certain though secret sadness—a presentiment that had, perhaps, its charm, though it was of cross and evil. Born of so proud a race, Adrian could scarcely dream of marriage with the sister of a plebeian; and Irene, unconscious of the future glory of her brother, could hardly have cherished any hope, save that of being loved. Yet these adverse circumstances, which, in the harder, the more prudent, the more self-denying, perhaps the more virtuous minds, that are formed beneath the northern skies, would have been an inducement to wrestle against love so placed, only contributed to feed and to strengthen *theirs* by an opposition which has ever its attraction for romance. They found frequent, though short, opportunities of meeting—not quite alone, but only in the conniving presence of Benedetta: sometimes in the public gardens, sometimes amidst the vast and deserted ruins by which the house of Rienzi was surrounded. They surrendered themselves, without much question of the future, to the excitement—the elysium—of the hour: they lived but from day to day; *their* future was the next time they should meet; beyond that epoch, the very mists of their youthful love closed in obscurity and shadow which they sought not to penetrate: and as yet they had not arrived at that period of affection when there was danger of their fall,—their love had not passed the golden portal where Heaven ceases and Earth begins. Everything for them was the poetry, the vagueness, the refinement,—not the power, the concentration, the mortality,—of desire. The look—the whisper—the brief pressure of the hand,—at most, the first kisses of love, rare and few,—these marked the human limits of that sentiment which filled them with a new life, which elevated them as with a new soul.

The roving tendencies of Adrian were at once fixed and centered; the dreams of his tender mistress had awakened to a life dreaming still, but " rounded with a *truth.*" All that earnestness, and energy, and fervour of emotion, which, in her brother, broke forth in the schemes of patriotism and the aspirations of power, were, in Irene, softened down into one object of existence, one concentration of soul,—and that was love. Yet, in this range of thought and action, so apparently limited, there was, in reality, no less boundless a sphere than in the wide space of her brother's many-pathed ambition. Not the less had she the power and scope for all the loftiest capacities granted to our clay. Equal was her enthusiasm for her idol; equal, had she been equally tried, would have been her generosity, her devotion:—greater, be sure, her courage; more inalienable her worship; more unsullied by selfish purposes and sordid views. Time, change, misfortune, ingratitude, would have left *her* the same! What state could fall, what liberty decay, if the zeal of man's noisy patriotism were as pure as the silent loyalty of a woman's love?

In them everything *was young!*—the heart unchilled, unblighted,—that fulness and luxuriance of life's life which has in it something of divine. At that age, when it seems as if we could never die, how deathless, how flushed and mighty as with the youngness of a god, is all that our hearts create! Our own youth is like that of the earth itself, when it peopled the woods and waters with divinities: when life ran riot, and yet only gave birth to beauty;—all its shapes, of poetry,—all its airs, the melodies of Arcady and Olympus! The Golden Age never leaves the world: it exists still, and shall exist, till love, health, poetry, are no more; but only for the young!

If I now dwell, though but for a moment, on this interlude in a drama calling forth more masculine passions than that of love, it is because I foresee that the occasion will but rarely recur. If I linger on the description of Irene and her hidden affection, rather than wait for circumstances to portray them better than the author's words can, it is because I foresee that that loving and lovely image must continue to the last rather a shadow than a portrait,—thrown in the background, as is the real destiny of such natures, by bolder figures and more gorgeous colours; a something whose presence is rather felt than seen, and whose very harmony with the whole consists in its retiring and subdued repose.

CHAPTER VIII

THE ENTHUSIASTIC MAN JUDGED BY THE DISCREET MAN

"Thou wrongest me," said Rienzi, warmly, to Adrian, as they sat alone, towards the close of a long conference; "I do not play the part of a mere demagogue; I wish not to stir the great deeps in order that my lees of fortune may rise to the surface. So long have I brooded over the past, that it seems to me as if I had become a part of it—as if I had no separate existence. I have coined my whole soul into one master passion,—and its end is the restoration of Rome."

"But by what means?"

"My Lord! my Lord! there is but one way to restore the greatness of a people—it is an appeal to the people themselves. It is not in the power of princes and barons to make a state permanently glorious; they raise themselves, but they raise not the people with them. All great regenerations are the universal movement of the mass."

"Nay," answered Adrian, "then have we read history differently. To me, all great regenerations seem to have been the work of the few, and tacitly accepted by the multitude. But let us not dispute after the manner of the schools. Thou sayest loudly that a vast crisis is at hand; that the Good Estate (*buono stato*) shall be established. How? where are your arms?—your soldiers? Are the nobles less strong than heretofore? is the mob more bold, more constant? Heaven knows that I speak not with the prejudices of my order—I weep for the debasement of my country! I am a Roman, and in that name I forget that I am a noble. But I tremble at the storm you would raise so hazardously. If your insurrection succeed, it will be violent: it will be purchased by blood—by the blood of all the loftiest names of Rome. You will aim at a second expulsion of the Tarquins; but it will be more like a second proscription of Sylla. Massacres and disorders never pave the way to peace. If, on the other hand, you fail, the chains of Rome are riveted for ever: an ineffectual struggle to escape is but an excuse for additional tortures to the slave."

"And what, then, would the Lord Adrian have us

do?" said Rienzi, with that peculiar and sarcastic smile which has before been noted. "Shall we wait till the Colonna and Orsini quarrel no more? shall we ask the Colonna for liberty, and the Orsini for justice? My Lord, we cannot appeal to the nobles against the nobles. We must not ask them to moderate their power; we must restore to ourselves that power. There may be danger in the attempt—but we attempt it amongst the monuments of the Forum: and if we fall—we shall perish worthy of our sires! Ye have high descent, and sounding titles, and wide lands, and you talk of *your* ancestral honours! We, too,—we plebeians of Rome,—we have *ours!* Our fathers were freemen! where is our heritage? not sold—not given away: but stolen from us, now by fraud, now by force—filched from us in our sleep; or wrung from us with fierce hands, amidst our cries and struggles. My Lord, we but ask that lawful heritage to be restored to us: to us—nay, to you it is the same; your liberty, alike, is gone. Can you dwell in your father's house, without towers, and fortresses, and the bought swords of bravos? can you walk in the streets at dark without arms and followers? True, *you*, a noble, may retaliate; though *we* dare not. You, in your turn, may terrify and outrage others; but does licence compensate for liberty? They have given you pomp and power—but the safety of equal laws were a better gift. Oh, were I you—were I Stephen Colonna himself, I should pant, ay, thirstily as I do now, for that free air which comes not through bars and bulwarks against my fellow-citizens, but in the open space of Heaven—safe, because protected by the silent Providence of Law, and not by the lean fears and hollow-eyed suspicions which are the comrades of a hated power. The tyrant thinks he is free, because he commands slaves: the meanest peasant in a free state is more free than he is. Oh, my Lord, that you—the brave, the generous, the enlightened—you, almost alone amidst your order, in the knowledge that we *had* a country—oh, would that you who can sympathise with our sufferings, would strike with us for their redress!"

"Thou wilt war against Stephen Colonna, my kinsman; and though I have seen him but little, nor, truth to say, esteem him much, yet he is the boast of our house,—how can I join thee?"

"His life will be safe, his possessions safe, his rank safe. What do we war against? His power to do wrong to others?"

"Should he discover that thou hast force beyond words, he would be less merciful to *thee*."

"And has he not discovered that? Do not the shouts of the people tell him that I am a man whom he should fear? Does he—the cautious, the wily, the profound—does he build fortresses, and erect towers, and not see from his battlements the mighty fabric that I, too, have erected?"

"You! where, Rienzi?"

"In the hearts of Rome! Does he not see?" continued Rienzi. "No, no; he—all, all his tribe are blind. Is it not so?"

"Of a certainty, my kinsman has no belief in your power, else he would have crushed you long ere this. Nay, it was but three days ago that he said, gravely, he would rather *you* addressed the populace than the best priest in Christendom; for that other orators inflamed the crowd, and no man so stilled and dispersed them as you did."

"And I called *him* profound! Does not Heaven

hush the air most when most it prepares the storm? Ay, my Lord, I understand. Stephen Colonna despises me. I have been "—(here, as he continued, a deep blush mantled over his cheek)—" you remember it—at his palace in my younger days, and pleased him with witty tales and light apophthegms. Nay—ha! ha!—he would call me, I think, sometimes, in gay compliment, his jester—his buffoon! I have brooked his insult; I have even bowed to his applause. I would undergo the same penance, stoop to the same shame, for the same motive, and in the same cause. What did I desire to effect? Can you tell me? No! I will whisper it, then, to you: it was—the contempt of Stephen Colonna. Under that contempt I was protected, till protection became no longer necessary. I desired not to be thought formidable by the patricians, in order that, quietly and unsuspected, I might make my way amongst the people. I have done so; I now throw aside the mask. Face to face with Stephen Colonna, I could tell him, this very hour, that I brave his anger; that I laugh at his dungeons and armed men. But if he think me the same Rienzi as of old, let him; I can wait my hour."

"Yet," said Adrian, waiving an answer to the haughty language of his companion, "tell me, what dost thou ask for the people, in order to avoid an appeal to their passions?—ignorant and capricious as they are, thou canst not appeal to their reason."

"I ask full justice and safety for all men. I will be contented with no less a compromise. I ask the nobles to dismantle their fortresses; to disband their armed retainers; to acknowledge no impunity for crime in high lineage; to claim no protection save in the courts of the common law."

"Vain desire!" said Adrian. "Ask what may yet be granted."

"Ha—ha! ha!" replied Rienzi, laughing bitterly, "did I not tell you it was a vain dream to ask for law and justice at the hands of the great? Can you blame me, then, that I ask it elsewhere?" Then, suddenly changing his tone and manner, he added with great solemnity—"Waking life hath false and vain dreams; but sleep is sometimes a mighty prophet. By sleep it is that Heaven mysteriously communes with its creatures, and guides and sustains its earthly agents in the path to which its providence leads them on."

Adrian made no reply. This was not the first time he had noted that Rienzi's strong intellect was strangely conjoined with a deep and mystical superstition. And this yet more inclined the young noble, who, though sufficiently devout, yielded but little to the wilder credulities of the time, to doubt the success of the schemer's projects. In this he erred greatly, though his error was that of the worldly wise. For nothing ever so inspires human daring, as the fond belief that it is the agent of a Diviner Wisdom. Revenge and patriotism, united in one man of genius and ambition—such are the Archimedian levers that find, in FANATICISM, the spot *out* of the world by which to move the world. The prudent man may direct a state; but it is the enthusiast who regenerates it,—or ruins.

CHAPTER IX

"WHEN THE PEOPLE SAW THIS PICTURE EVERY ONE MARVELLED"

Before the market-place, and at the foot of the Capitol, an immense crowd was assembled. Each man sought to push before his neighbour; each struggled to gain access to one particular spot, round which the crowd was wedged thick and dense.

"Corpo di Dio!" said a man of huge stature, pressing onward, like some bulky ship, casting the noisy waves right and left from its prow, "this is hot work; but for what, in the Holy Mother's name, do ye crowd so? See you not, Sir Ribald, that my right arm is disabled, swathed, and bandaged, so that I cannot help myself better than a baby? and yet, you push against me as if I were an old wall!"

"Ah, Cecco del Vecchio!—what, man! we must make way for you—you are too small and tender to bustle through a crowd! Come, I will protect you!" said a dwarf of some four feet high, glancing up at the giant.

"Faith," said the grim smith, looking round on the mob, who laughed loud at the dwarf's proffer, "we all do want protection, big and small. What do you laugh for, ye apes?—ay, you don't understand parables."

"And yet it is a parable we are come to gaze upon," said one of the mob, with a slight sneer.

"Pleasant day to you, Signor Baroncelli," answered Cecco del Vecchio; "you are a good man, and love the people; it makes one's heart smile to see you. What's all this pother for?"

"Why the Pope's Notary hath set up a great picture in the market-place, and the gapers say it relates to Rome; so they are melting their brains out, this hot day, to guess at the riddle."

"Ho! ho!" said the smith, pushing on so vigorously that he left the speaker suddenly in the rear; "if Cola di Rienzi hath aught in the matter, I would break through stone rocks to get to it."

"Much good will a dead daub do us," said Baroncelli, sourly, and turning to his neighbours; but no man listened to him, and he, a would-be demagogue, gnawed his lip in envy.

Amidst half-awed groans and curses from the men whom he jostled aside, and open objurgations and shrill cries from the women, to whose robes and head-gear he showed as little respect, the sturdy smith won his way to a space fenced round by chains, in the centre of which was placed a huge picture.

"How came it hither?" cried one; "I was first at the market."

"We found it here at daybreak," said a vendor of fruit: "no one was by."

"But why do you fancy Rienzi had a hand in it?"

"Why, who else could?" answered twenty voices.

"True! Who else?" echoed the gaunt smith. "I dare be sworn the good man spent the whole night in painting it himself. Blood of St. Peter! but it is mighty fine! What is it about?"

"That's the riddle," said a meditative fish-woman; "if I could make it out I should die happy."

"It is something about liberty and taxes, no doubt," said Luigi, the butcher, leaning over the chains. "Ah, if Rienzi were minded, every poor man would have his bit of meat in his pot."

"And as much bread as he could eat," added a pale baker.

"Chut! bread and meat—everybody has that now!—but what wine the poor folks drink! One has no encouragement to take pains with one's vineyard," said a vine-dresser.

"Ho, hollo!—long life to Pandulfo di Guido! make way for master Pandulfo; he is a learned man; he is a friend of the great Notary's: he will tell us all about the picture; make way, there—make way!"

Slowly and modestly, Pandulfo di Guido, a quiet, wealthy, and honest man of letters, whom nought save the violence of the times could have roused from his tranquil home, or his studious closet, passed to the chains. He looked long and hard at the picture, which was bright with new, and yet moist colours, and exhibited somewhat of the reviving art, which, though hard and harsh in its features, was about that time visible, and, carried to a far higher degree, we yet gaze upon in the paintings of Perugino, who flourished during the succeeding generation. The people pressed round the learned man, with open mouths; now turning their eyes to the picture, now to Pandulfo.

"Know you not," at length said Pandulfo, "the easy and palpable meaning of this design? Behold how the painter has presented to you a vast and stormy sea—mark how its waves—"

"Speak louder—louder!" shouted the impatient crowd.

"Hush!" cried those in the immediate vicinity of Pandulfo, "the worthy Signor is perfectly audible!"

Meanwhile, some of the more witty, pushing

towards a stall in the market-place, bore from it a rough table, from which they besought Pandulfo to address the people. The pale citizen, with some pain and shame, for he was no practised spokesman, was obliged to assent; but when he cast his eyes over the vast and breathless crowd, his own deep sympathy with their cause inspired and emboldened him. A light broke from his eyes; his voice swelled into power; and his head, usually buried in his breast, became erect and commanding in its air.

"You see before you in the picture" (he began again) "a mighty and tempestuous sea: upon its waves you behold five ships; four of them are already wrecks,—their masts are broken, the waves are dashing through the rent planks, they are past all aid and hope: on each of these ships lies the corpse of a woman. See you not, in the wan face and livid limbs, how faithfully the limner hath painted the hues and loathsomeness of death? Below each of these ships is a word that applies the metaphor to truth. Yonder, you see the name of Carthage; the other three are Troy, Jerusalem, and Babylon. To these four is one common inscription. 'To exhaustion were we brought by injustice!' Turn now your eyes to the middle of the sea,—there you behold the fifth ship, tossed amidst the waves, her mast broken, her rudder gone, her sails shivered, but not yet a wreck like the rest, though she soon may be. On her deck kneels a female, clothed in mourning; mark the woe upon her countenance,—how cunningly the artist has conveyed its depth and desolation; she stretches out her arms in prayer, she implores your and Heaven's assistance. Mark now the superscription—'This is Rome!'—Yes, it is your country that addresses you in this emblem!"

The crowd waved to and fro, and a deep murmur crept gathering over the silence which they had hitherto kept.

" Now," continued Pandulfo, " turn your gaze to the right of the picture, and you will behold the cause of the tempest,—you will see why the fifth vessel is thus perilled, and her sisters are thus wrecked. Mark, four different kinds of animals, who, from their horrid jaws, send forth the winds and storms which torture and rack the sea. The first are the lions, the wolves, the bears. These, the inscription tells you, are the lawless and savage signors of the state. The next are the dogs and swine,—these are the evil counsellors and parasites. Thirdly, you behold the dragons and the foxes,—and these are false judges and notaries, and they who sell justice. Fourthly, in the hares, the goats, the apes, that assist in creating the storm, you perceive, by the inscription, the emblems of the popular thieves and homicides, ravishers and spoliators. Are ye bewildered still, O Romans! or have ye mastered the riddle of the picture? "

Far in their massive palaces the Savelli and Orsini heard the echo of the shouts that answered the question of Pandulfo.

" Are ye, then, without hope! " resumed the scholar, as the shout ceased, and hushing, with the first sound of his voice, the ejaculations and speeches which each man had turned to utter to his neighbour. " Are ye without hope? Doth the picture, which shows your tribulation, promise you no redemption? Behold, above that angry sea, the heavens open, and the majesty of God descends gloriously, as to judgment; and, from the rays that surround the spirit of God extend two flaming swords, and on those swords stand, in wrath, but in deliverance, the two patron saints—the two mighty guardians of your city! People of Rome, farewell! the parable is finished." *

CHAPTER X

A ROUGH SPIRIT RAISED, WHICH MAY HEREAFTER REND THE WIZARD

While thus animated was the scene around the Capitol, *within* one of the apartments of the palace sat the agent and prime cause of that excitement. In the company of his quiet scribes, Rienzi appeared absorbed in the patient details of his avocation. While the murmur and the hum, the shout and the tramp, of multitudes, rolled to his chamber, he seemed not to heed them, nor to rouse himself a moment from his task. With the unbroken regularity of an automaton, he continued to enter in his large book, and with the clear and beautiful characters of the period, those damning figures which taught him, better than declamations, the frauds practised on the people, and armed him with that weapon of plain fact which it is so difficult for abuse to parry.

"Page 2, Vol. B.," said he, in the tranquil voice of business, to the clerks; "see there, the profits of the salt duty; department No. 3—very well. Page 9, Vol.

* M. Sismondi attributes to Rienzi a fine oration at the showing of the picture, in which he thundered against the vices of the patricians. The contemporary biographer of Rienzi says nothing of this harangue. But, apparently (since history has its liberties as well as fiction), M. Sismondi has thought it convenient to confound two occasions very distinct in themselves.

D.—what is the account rendered by Vescobaldi, the collector? What! twelve thousand florins?—no more?—unconscionable rascal!" (Here was a loud shout without of "Pandulfo!—long live Pandulfo!") "Pastrucci, my friend, your head wanders; you are listening to the noise without—please to amuse yourself with the calculation I entrusted to you. Santi, what is the entry given in by Antonio Tralli?"

A slight tap was heard at the door, and Pandulfo entered.

The clerks continued their labour, though they looked up hastily at the pale and respectable visitor, whose name, to their great astonishment, had thus become a popular cry.

"Ah, my friend," said Rienzi, calmly enough in voice, but his hands trembled with ill-suppressed emotion, "you would speak to me alone, eh? well, well,—this way." Thus saying, he led the citizen into a small cabinet in the rear of the room of office, carefully shut the door, and then giving himself up to the natural impatience of his character, seized Pandulfo by the hand: "Speak!" cried he: "do they take the interpretation?—have you made it plain and palpable enough?—has it sunk deep into their souls?"

"Oh, by St. Peter! yes!" returned the citizen, whose spirits were elevated by his recent discovery that he, too, was an orator—a luxurious pleasure for a timid man. "They swallowed every word of the interpretation; they are moved to the marrow—you might lead them this very hour to battle, and find them heroes. As for the sturdy smith—"

"What! Cecco del Vecchio?" interrupted Rienzi; "ah, his heart is wrought in bronze—what did he?"

"Why, he caught me by the hem of my robe as I

descended my rostrum (oh! would you could have seen me!—*per fede* I had caught your mantle!—I was a second *you!*) and said, weeping like a child, 'Ah, Signor, I am but a poor man, and of little worth; but if every drop of blood in this body were a life, I would give it for my country!'"

"Brave soul," said Rienzi, with emotion; "would Rome had but fifty such! No man hath done us more good among his own class than Cecco del Vecchio."

"They feel a protection in his very size," said Pandulfo. "It is something to hear such big words from such a big fellow."

"Were there *any* voices lifted in disapprobation of the picture and its sentiment?"

"None."

"The time is nearly ripe, then—a few suns more, and the fruit must be gathered. The Aventine,—the Lateran,—and then *the solitary trumpet!*" Thus saying, Rienzi, with folded arms and downcast eyes, seemed sunk into a reverie.

"By the way," said Pandulfo, "I had almost forgot to tell thee, that the crowd would have poured themselves hither, so impatient were they to see thee; but I bade Cecco del Vecchio mount the rostrum, and tell them, in his blunt way, that it would be unseemly at the present time, when thou wert engaged in the Capitol on civil and holy affairs, to rush in so great a body into thy presence. Did I not right?"

"Most right, my Pandulfo."

"But Cecco del Vecchio says he must come and kiss thy hand: and thou mayest expect him here the moment he can escape unobserved from the crowd."

"He is welcome!" said Rienzi, half mechanically, for he was still absorbed in thought.

"And lo! here he is,"—as one of the scribes announced the visit of the smith.

"Let him be admitted!" said Rienzi, seating himself composedly.

When the huge smith found himself in the presence of Rienzi, it amused Pandulfo to perceive the wonderful influences of mind over matter. That fierce and sturdy giant, who, in all popular commotions, towered above his tribe, with thews of stone, and nerves of iron, the rallying point and bulwark of the rest,—stood now colouring and trembling before the intellect, which (so had the eloquent spirit of Rienzi waked and fanned the spark which, till then, had lain dormant in that rough bosom) might almost be said to have created his own. And he, indeed, who first arouses in the bondsman the sense and soul of freedom, comes as near as is permitted to man, nearer than the philosopher, nearer even than the poet, to the great creative attribute of God!—But, if the breast be uneducated, the gift may curse the giver; and he who passes at once from the slave to the freeman may pass as rapidly from the freeman to the ruffian.

"Approach, my friend," said Rienzi, after a moment's pause; "I know all that thou hast done, and wouldst do, for Rome! Thou are worthy of her best days, and thou art born to share in their return."

The smith dropped at the feet of Rienzi, who held out his hand to raise him, which Cecco del Vecchio seized, and reverently kissed.

"This kiss doth not betray," said Rienzi, smiling; "but rise, my friend,—this posture is only due to God and his saints!"

"He is a saint who helps us at need!" said the smith, bluntly, "and that no man has done as thou hast. But when," he added, sinking his voice, and fixing his eyes hard on Rienzi, as one may do who waits a signal to strike a blow, "when—when shall we make the great effort?"

"Thou hast spoken to all the brave men in thy neighbourhood,—are they well prepared?"

"To live or die, as Rienzi bids them!"

"I must have the list—the number—names—houses and callings, this night."

"Thou shalt."

"Each man must sign his name or mark with his own hand."

"It shall be done."

"Then, harkye! attend Pandulfo di Guido at his house this evening, at sunset. He shall instruct thee where to meet this night some brave hearts;—thou art worthy to be ranked amongst them. Thou wilt not fail!"

"By the Holy Stairs! I will count every minute till then," said the smith, his swarthy face lighted with pride at the confidence shown him.

"Meanwhile, watch all your neighbours; let no man flag or grow faint-hearted,—none of thy friends must be branded as a traitor!"

"I will cut his throat, were he my own mother's son, if I find one pledged man flinch!" said the fierce smith.

"Ha, ha!" rejoined Rienzi, with that strange laugh which belonged to him; "a miracle! a miracle! The Picture speaks now!"

It was already nearly dusk when Rienzi left the Capitol. The broad space before its walls was empty and deserted, and wrapping his mantle closely round him, he walked musingly on.

"I have almost climbed the height," thought he, "and now the precipice yawns before me. If I fail, what a fall! The last hope of my country falls with me. Never will a noble rise against the nobles. Never will another plebeian have the opportunities and the power that I have! Rome is bound up with me—with a single life. The liberties of all time are fixed to a reed that a wind may uproot. But oh, Providence! hast thou not reserved and marked me for great deeds? How, step by step, have I been led on to this solemn enterprise! How has each hour prepared its successor! And yet what danger! *if* the inconstant people, made cowardly by long thraldom, do but waver in the crisis, I am swept away!"

As he spoke, he raised his eyes, and lo, before him, the first star of twilight shone calmly down upon the crumbling remnants of the Tarpeian Rock. It was no favouring omen, and Rienzi's heart beat quicker as that dark and ruined mass frowned thus suddenly on his gaze.

"Dread monument," thought he, "of what dark catastrophes, to what unknown schemes, hast thou been the witness! To how many enterprises, on which history is dumb, hast thou set the seal! How know we whether they were criminal or just? How know we whether he, thus doomed as a traitor, would not, if successful, have been immortalised as a deliverer? If I fall, who will write my chronicle? One of the people? alas! blinded and ignorant, they furnish forth no minds that can appeal to posterity. One of the patricians? in what colours then shall I be painted! No tomb will rise for me amidst the wrecks; no hand scatter flowers upon my grave!"

Thus meditating on the verge of that mighty enterprise to which he had devoted himself, Rienzi pursued his way. He gained the Tiber, and paused for a few moments beside its legendary stream, over which the purple and star-lit heaven shone deeply down. He crossed the bridge which leads to the quarter of the Trastevere, whose haughty inhabitants yet boast themselves the sole true descendants of the ancient Romans. Here his step grew quicker and more light; brighter, if less solemn, thoughts crowded upon his breast; and ambition, lulled for a moment, left his strained and over-laboured mind to the reign of a softer passion.

CHAPTER XI

NINA DI RASELLI

"I tell you, Lucia, I do not love those stuffs; they do not become me. Saw you ever so poor a dye?—this purple, indeed! that crimson! Why did you let the man leave them? Let him take them elsewhere to-morrow. They may suit the signoras on the other side the Tiber, who imagine everything Venetian must be perfect; but I, Lucia, *I* see with my own eyes, and judge from my own mind."

"Ah, dear lady," said the serving-maid, "if you were, as you doubtless will be, some time or other, a grand signora, how worthily you would wear the honours! Santa Cecilia! no other dame in Rome would be looked at while the Lady Nina were by!"

"Would we not teach them what pomp was?" answered Nina. "Oh! what festivals would we hold! Saw you not from the gallery the revels given last week by the Lady Giulia Savelli?"

"Ay, Signora; and when you walked up the hall in your silver and pearl tissue, there ran such a murmur through the gallery; every one cried, 'The Savelli have entertained an angel!'"

"Pish! Lucia; no flattery, girl."

"It is naked truth, lady. But that *was* a revel, was it not? There was grandeur!—fifty servitors in scarlet and gold! and the music playing all the while. The minstrels were sent for from Bergamo. Did not that festival please you? Ah, I warrant many were the fine speeches made to you that day!"

"Heigho!—no, there was one voice wanting, and all the music was marred. But, girl, were *I* the Lady Giulia, I would not have been contented with so poor a revel."

"How, poor! Why all the nobles say it outdid the proudest marriage feast of the Colonna. Nay, a Neapolitan who sat next me, and who had served under the young Queen Joanna, at her marriage, says, that even Naples was outshone."

"That may be. I know nought of Naples; but I know what *my* court should have been, were I what—what I am not, and may never be! The banquet vessels should have been of gold; the cups jewelled to the brim; not an inch of the rude pavement should have been visible; all should have glowed with cloth of gold. The fountain in the court should have showered up the perfumes of the East; my pages should not have been rough youths, blushing at their own uncouthness, but fair boys, who had not told their twelfth year, culled from the daintiest palaces of Rome; and, as for the music, oh Lucia!—each musician should have worn a chaplet, and deserved it; and he who played best should have had a reward, to inspire all the rest—

a rose from me. Saw you, too, the Lady Giulia's robe? What colours! they might have put out the sun at noonday!—yellow, and blue, and orange, and scarlet! Oh, sweet Saints!—but my eyes ached all the next day!"

"Doubtless, the Lady Giulia lacks your skill in the mixture of colours," said the complaisant waiting-woman.

"And then, too, what a mien!—no royalty in it! She moved along the hall, so that her train well-nigh tripped her every moment; and then she said, with a foolish laugh, 'These holyday robes are but troublesome luxuries.' Troth, for the great there should be no holyday robes; 'tis for myself, not for others, that I would attire! Every day should have its new robe, more gorgeous than the last;—every day should be a holyday!"

"Methought," said Lucia, "that the Lord Giovanni Orsini seemed very devoted to my Lady."

"He! the bear!"

"Bear, he may be! but he has a costly skin. His riches are untold."

"And the fool knows not how to spend them."

"Was not that the young Lord Adrian who spoke to you just by the columns, where the music played?"

"It might be,—I forget."

"Yet, I hear that few ladies forget when Lord Adrian di Castello woos them."

"There was but one man whose company seemed to me worth the recollection," answered Nina, unheeding the insinuation of the artful handmaid.

"And who was he?" asked Lucia.

"The old scholar from Avignon!"

"What! he with the gray beard? Oh, Signora!"

"Yes," said Nina, with a grave and sad voice; "when he spoke, the whole scene vanished from my eyes,—for he spoke to me of HIM!"

As she said this the Signora sighed deeply, and the tears gathered to her eyes.

The waiting-woman raised her lips in disdain, and her looks in wonder; but she did not dare to venture a reply.

"Open the lattice," said Nina, after a pause, "and give me yon paper. Not that, girl—but the verses sent me yesterday. What! art thou Italian, and dost thou not know, by instinct, that I spoke of the rhyme of Petrarch?"

Seated by the open casement, through which the moonlight stole soft and sheen, with one lamp beside her, from which she seemed to shade her eyes, though in reality she sought to hide her countenance from Lucia, the young Signora appeared absorbed in one of those tender sonnets which then turned the brains and inflamed the hearts of Italy.*

Born of an impoverished house, which, though boasting its descent from a consular race of Rome, scarcely at that day maintained a rank amongst the inferior order of nobility, Nina di Raselli was the spoiled child—the idol and the tyrant—of her parents. The energetic and self-willed character of her mind made her rule where she should have obeyed; and as in all ages dispositions can conquer custom, she had, though in a clime and land where the young and

* Although it is true that the love sonnets of Petrarch were not then, as now, the most esteemed of his works, yet it has been a great, though a common error, to represent them as little known and coldly admired. Their effect was, in reality, prodigious and universal. Every ballad-singer sung them in the streets (says Filippo Villani), "Gravissimi nesciebant abstinere"—"Even the gravest could not abstain from them."

unmarried of her sex are usually chained and fettered, assumed, and by assuming won, the prerogative of independence. She possessed, it is true, more learning and more genius than generally fell to the share of women in that day; and enough of both to be deemed a miracle by her parents;—she had, also, what they valued more, a surpassing beauty; and, what they feared more, an indomitable haughtiness;—a haughtiness mixed with a thousand soft and endearing qualities where she loved; and which, indeed, where she loved, seemed to vanish. At once vain yet high-minded, resolute yet impassioned, there was a gorgeous magnificence in her very vanity and splendour, —an ideality in her waywardness: her defects made a part of her brilliancy; without them she would have seemed less woman; and, knowing her, you would have compared all women by her standard. Softer qualities beside her seemed not more charming, but more insipid. She had no vulgar ambition, for she had obstinately refused many alliances which the daughter of Raselli could scarcely have hoped to form. The untutored minds and savage power of the Roman nobles seemed to her imagination, which was full of the *poetry* of rank, its luxury and its graces, as something barbarous and revolting, at once to be dreaded and despised. She had, therefore, passed her twentieth year unmarried, but not without love. The faults, themselves, of her character, elevated that ideal of love which she had formed. She required some being round whom all her vainer qualities could rally; she felt that where she loved she must adore; she demanded no common idol before which to humble so strong and imperious a mind. Unlike women of a gentler mould, who desire, for a short period, to exercise the caprices of sweet empire,—when she loved she must cease to command; and pride, at once, be humbled to devotion. So rare were the qualities that could attract her; so imperiously did her haughtiness require that those qualities should be above her own, yet of the same order; that her love elevated its object like a god. Accustomed to despise, she felt all the luxury it is to venerate! And if it were her lot to be united with one thus loved, her nature was that which might become elevated by the nature that it gazed on. For her beauty—Reader, shouldst thou ever go to Rome, thou wilt see in the Capitol the picture of the Cumæan Sibyl, which, often copied, no copy can even faintly represent. I beseech thee, mistake not this sibyl for another, for the Roman galleries abound in sibyls.* The sibyl I speak of is dark, and the face has an Eastern cast; the robe and turban, gorgeous though they be, grow dim before the rich, but transparent roses of the cheek; the hair would be black, save for that golden glow which mellows it to a hue and lustre never seen but in the south, and even in the south most rare; the features, not Grecian, are yet faultless; the mouth, the brow, the ripe and exquisite contour, all are human and voluptuous; the expression, the aspect, is something more; the form is, perhaps, too full for the perfection of loveliness, for the proportions of sculpture, for the delicacy of Athenian models; but the luxuriant fault has a majesty. Gaze long upon that picture: it charms, yet commands, the eye. While you gaze, you call back five centuries. You see before you the breathing image of Nina di Raselli!

* The sibyl referred to is the well-known one by Domenichino. As a mere work of art, that by Guercino, called the Persian sibyl, in the same collection, is perhaps superior: but in beauty, in character there is no comparison.

But it was not those ingenious and elaborate conceits in which Petrarch, great Poet though he be, has so often mistaken pedantry for passion, that absorbed at that moment the attention of the beautiful Nina. Her eyes rested not on the page, but on the garden that stretched below the casement. Over the old fruit-trees and hanging vines fell the moonshine; and in the centre of the green, but half-neglected sward, the waters of a small and circular fountain, whose perfect proportions spoke of days long past, played and sparkled in the starlight. The scene was still and beautiful; but neither of its stillness nor its beauty thought Nina: towards one, the gloomiest and most rugged, spot in the whole garden, turned her gaze; there, the trees stood densely massed together, and shut from view the low but heavy wall which encircled the mansion of Raselli. The boughs on those trees stirred gently, but Nina saw them wave; and now from the copse emerged, slowly and cautiously, a solitary figure, whose shadow threw itself, long and dark, over the sward. It approached the window, and a low voice breathed Nina's name.

"Quick, Lucia!" cried she, breathlessly, turning to her handmaid: "quick! the rope-ladder! it is he! he is come! How slow you are! haste, girl,—he may be discovered! There,—O joy,—O joy!—My lover! my hero! my Rienzi!"

"It is you!" said Rienzi, as, now entering the chamber, he wound his arms around her half-averted form, "and what is night to others is day to me!"

The first sweet moments of welcome were over; and Rienzi was seated at the feet of his mistress: his head rested on her knees—his face looking up to hers—their hands clasped each in each.

"And for me thou bravest these dangers!" said the lover; "the shame of discovery, the wrath of thy parents!"

"But what are my perils to thine? Oh, Heaven! if my father found thee here thou wouldst die!"

"He would think it then so great a humiliation, that thou, beautiful Nina, who mightst match with the haughtiest names of Rome, shouldst waste thy love on a plebeian—even though the grandson of an emperor!"

The proud heart of Nina could sympathise well with the wounded pride of her lover: she detected the soreness which lurked beneath his answer, carelessly as it was uttered.

"Hast thou not told me," she said, "of that great Marius, who was no noble, but from whom the loftiest Colonna would rejoice to claim his descent? and do I not know in thee one who shall yet eclipse the power of Marius, unsullied by his vices?"

"Delicious flattery! sweet prophet!" said Rienzi, with a melancholy smile; "never were thy supporting promises of the future more welcome to me than now; for to thee I will say what I would utter to none else—my soul half sinks beneath the mighty burthen I have heaped upon it. I want new courage as the dread hour approaches; and from thy words and looks I drink it."

"Oh!" answered Nina, blushing as she spoke, "glorious is indeed the lot which I have bought by my love for thee: glorious to share thy schemes, to cheer thee in doubt, to whisper hope to thee in danger."

"And give grace to me in triumph!" added Rienzi, passionately. "Ah! should the future ever place upon these brows the laurel-wreath due to one who has saved his country, what joy, what recompence, to lay it at thy feet! Perhaps, in those long and solitary hours of languor and exhaustion which fill up the interstices of time,—the dull space for sober thought between the epochs of exciting action,—perhaps I should have failed and flagged, and renounced even my dreams for Rome, had they not been linked also with my dreams for thee!—had I not pictured to myself the hour when my fate should elevate me beyond my birth; when thy sire would deem it no disgrace to give thee to my arms; when thou, too, shouldst stand amidst the dames of Rome, more honoured, as more beautiful, than all; and when I should see that pomp, which my own soul disdains,* made dear and grateful to me because associated with thee! Yes, it is these thoughts that have inspired me, when sterner ones have shrunk back appalled from the spectres that surround their goal. And oh! my Nina, sacred, strong, enduring must be, indeed, the love which lives in the same pure and elevated air as that which sustains my hopes of liberty and fame!"

This was the language which, more even than the vows of fidelity and the dear adulation which springs from the heart's exuberance, had bound the proud and vain soul of Nina to the chains that it so willingly wore. Perhaps, indeed, in the absence of Rienzi, her weaker nature pictured to herself the triumph of humbling the high-born signoras, and eclipsing the barbarous magnificence of the chiefs of Rome; but in his presence, and listening to his more elevated and

* "Quem semper abhorrui sicut cenum" is the expression used by Rienzi, in his letter to his friend at Avignon, and which was probably sincere. Men rarely act according to the bias of their own tastes.

generous ambition, as yet all unsullied by one private feeling save the hope of her, her higher sympathies were enlisted with his schemes, her mind aspired to raise itself to the height of his, and she thought less of her own rise than of his glory. It was sweet to her pride to be the sole confidante of his most secret thoughts, as of his most hardy undertakings; to see bared before her that intricate and plotting spirit; to be admitted even to the knowledge of its doubts and weakness, as of its heroism and power.

Nothing could be more contrasted than the loves of Rienzi and Nina, and those of Adrian and Irene: in the latter all were the dreams, the phantasies, the extravagance, of youth; they never talked of the future; they mingled no other aspirations with those of love. Ambition, glory, the world's high objects, were nothing to them when together; their love had swallowed up the world, and left nothing visible beneath the sun, save itself. But the passion of Nina and *her* lover was that of more complicated natures and more mature years: it was made up of a thousand feelings, each naturally severed from each, but compelled into one focus by the mighty concentration of love; their talk was of the world; it was from the world that they drew the aliment which sustained it; it was of the future they spoke and thought; of its dreams and imagined glories they made themselves a home and altar; their love had in it more of the Intellectual than that of Adrian and Irene; it was more fitted for this hard earth; it had in it, also, more of the leaven of the later and iron days, and less of poetry and the first golden age.

"And must thou leave me now?" said Nina, her cheek no more averted from his lips, nor her form from his parting embrace. "The moon is high yet; it is but a little hour thou hast given me."

"An hour! Alas!" said Rienzi, "it is near upon midnight—our friends await me."

"Go, then, my soul's best half! go; Nina shall not detain thee one moment from those higher objects which make thee so dear to Nina. When—when shall we meet again!"

"Not," said Rienzi, proudly, and with all his soul upon his brow, "not thus, by stealth! no! nor as I thus have met thee, the obscure and contemned bondsman! When next thou seest me, it shall be at the head of the sons of Rome! her champion! her restorer! or——" said he, sinking his voice—

"There is no *or!*" interrupted Nina, weaving her arms round him, and catching his enthusiasm; "thou hast uttered thine own destiny!"

"One kiss more!—farewell!—the tenth day from the morrow shines upon the restoration of Rome!"

CHAPTER XII

THE STRANGE ADVENTURES THAT BEFEL WALTER DE MONTREAL

It was upon that same evening, and while the earlier stars yet shone over the city, that Walter de Montreal, returning, alone, to the convent then associated with the church of Santa Maria del Priorta (both of which belonged to the Knights of the Hospital, and in the first of which Montreal had taken his lodgment), paused amidst the ruins and desolation which lay around his path. Though little skilled in the classic memories and associations of the spot, he could not but be impressed with the surrounding witnesses of departed empire; the vast skeleton, as it were, of the dead giantess.

"Now," thought he, as he gazed around upon the roofless columns and shattered walls, everywhere visible, over which the starlight shone, ghastly and transparent, backed by the frowning and embattled fortresses of the Frangipani, half hid by the dark foliage that sprung up amidst the very fanes and palaces of old—Nature exulting over the frailer Art; "now," thought he, "bookmen would be inspired, by this scene, with fantastic and dreaming visions of the past. But to me these monuments of high ambition and royal splendour create only images of the future. Rome may yet be, with her seven-hilled diadem, as Rome has been before, the prize of the strongest hand and the boldest warrior,—revived, not by her own degenerate sons, but the infused blood of a new race. William the Bastard could scarce have found the hardy Englishers so easy a conquest as Walter the Well-born may find these eunuch Romans. And which conquest were the more glorious,—the barbarous Isle, or the Metropolis of the World? Short step from the general to the podesta—shorter step from the podesta to the king!"

While thus revolving his wild, yet not altogether chimerical ambition, a quick light step was heard amidst the long herbage, and, looking up, Montreal perceived the figure of a tall female descending from that part of the hill then covered by many convents, towards the base of the Aventine. She supported her steps with a long staff, and moved with such elasticity and erectness, that now, as her face became visible by the starlight, it was surprising to perceive that it was the face of one advanced in years,—a harsh, proud countenance, withered, and deeply wrinkled, but not without a certain regularity of outline.

"Merciful Virgin!" cried Montreal, starting back as that face gleamed upon him: "is it possible? It is she!—it is——"

He sprung forward, and stood right before the old woman, who seemed equally surprised, though more dismayed at the sight of Montreal.

"I have sought thee for years," said the Knight, first breaking the silence; "years, long years,—thy conscience can tell thee why."

"*Mine*, man of blood!" cried the female, trembling with rage or fear; "darest *thou* talk of conscience? *Thou*, the dishonourer—the robber—the professed homicide! *Thou*, disgrace to knighthood and to birth! *Thou*, with the cross of chastity and of peace upon thy breast! *Thou* talk of conscience, hypocrite!—thou?"

"Lady—lady!" said Montreal, deprecatingly, and almost quailing beneath the fiery passion of that feeble woman, "I have sinned against thee and thine. But remember all my excuses!—early love—fatal obstacles—rash vow—irresistible temptation! Perhaps," he added, in a more haughty tone, "perhaps, yet I may have the power to atone my error, and wring, with mailed hand, from the successor of St. Peter, who hath power to loose as to bind——"

"Perjured and abandoned!" interrupted the female; "dost thou dream that violence can purchase absolution, or that thou canst ever atone the past? a noble name disgraced, a father's broken heart and dying curse! Yes, that curse, I hear it now! it rings upon me thrillingly, as when I watched the expiring clay!

it cleaves to thee—it pursues thee—it shall pierce thee through thy corselet—it shall smite thee in the meridian of thy power! Genius wasted—ambition blasted—penitence deferred—a life of brawls, and a death of shame—thy destruction the offspring of thy crime!—To this, to this, an old man's curse hath doomed thee!—AND THOU ART DOOMED!"

These words were rather shrieked than spoken: and the flashing eye, the lifted hand, the dilated form of the speaker—the hour—the solitude of the ruins around—all conspired to give to the fearful execration the character of prophecy. The warrior, against whose undaunted breast a hundred spears had shivered in vain, fell appalled and humbled to the ground. He seized the hem of his fierce denouncer's robe, and cried, in a choked and hollow voice, "Spare me! spare me!"

"Spare thee!" said the unrelenting crone; "hast *thou* ever spared man in thy hatred, or woman in thy lust? Ah, grovel in the dust!—crouch—crouch!—wild beast as thou art; whose sleek skin and beautiful hues have taught the unwary to be blind to the talons that rend, and the grinders that devour;—crouch, that the foot of the old and impotent may spurn thee!"

"Hag!" cried Montreal, in the reaction of sudden fury and maddened pride, springing up to the full height of his stature. "Hag! thou hast passed the limits to which, remembering who thou art, my forbearance gave the licence. I had well-nigh forgot that thou hadst assumed my part—*I* am the Accuser! Woman!—the boy!—shrink not! equivocate not! lie not!—thou wert the thief!"

"I was. Thou taughtest me the lesson how to steal a——"

"Render—restore him!" interrupted Montreal, stamping on the ground with such force that the splinters of the marble fragments on which he stood shivered under his armed heel.

The woman little heeded a violence at which the fiercest warrior of Italy might have trembled; but she did not make an immediate answer. The character of her countenance altered from passion into an expression of grave, intent, and melancholy thought. At length she replied to Montreal; whose hand had wandered to his dagger-hilt, with the instinct of long habit, whenever enraged or thwarted, rather than from any design of blood; which, stern and vindictive as he was, he would have been incapable of forming against any woman,—much less against the one then before him.

"Walter de Montreal," said she, in a voice so calm that it almost sounded like that of compassion, "the boy, I think, has never known brother or sister: the only child of a once haughty and lordly race, on both sides, though now on both dishonoured—nay, why so impatient? thou wilt soon learn the worst—the boy is dead!"

"Dead!" repeated Montreal, recoiling and growing pale; "dead!—no, no—say not that! He has a mother,—you know he has!—a fond, meekhearted, anxious, hoping mother!—no!—no, he is not dead!"

"Thou canst feel then, for a mother?" said the old woman, seemingly touched by the tone of the Provençal. "Yet, bethink thee; is it not better that the grave should save him from a life of riot, of bloodshed, and of crime? Better to sleep with God than to wake with the fiends!"

"Dead?" echoed Montreal; "dead!—the pretty

one! so young!—those eyes—the mother's eyes—closed so soon?"

"Hast thou aught else to say? Thy sight scares my very womanhood from my soul!—let me be gone."

"Dead!—may I believe thee? or dost thou mock me? Thou has uttered *thy* curse, hearken to *my* warning:—If thou hast lied in this, thy last hour shall dismay thee, and thy death-bed shall be the death-bed of despair!"

"Thy lips," replied the female, with a scornful smile, "are better adapted for lewd vows to unhappy maidens, than for the denunciations which sound solemn only when coming from the good. Farewell!"

"Stay! inexorable woman! stay!—where sleeps he? Masses shall be sung! priests shall pray!—the sins of the father shall not be visited on that young head!"

"At Florence!" returned the woman, hastily. "But no stone records the departed one!—The dead boy had no name!"

Waiting for no further questionings, the woman now passed on,—pursued her way;—and the long herbage, and the winding descent, soon snatched her ill-omened apparition from the desolate landscape.

Montreal, thus alone, sunk with a deep and heavy sigh upon the ground, covered his face with his hands, and burst into an agony of grief; his chest heaved, his whole frame trembled, and he wept and sobbed aloud, with all the fearful vehemence of a man whose passions are strong and fierce, but to whom the violence of grief alone is novel and unfamiliar.

He remained thus, prostrate and unmanned, for a considerable time, growing slowly and gradually more calm as tears relieved his emotion; and, at length, rather indulging a gloomy reverie than a passionate grief. The moon was high and the hour late when he arose, and then few traces of the past excitement remained upon his countenance; for Walter de Montreal was not of that mould in which woe can force a settlement, or to which any affliction can bring the continued and habitual melancholy that darkens those who feel more enduringly, though with emotions less stormy. His were the elements of the true Franc character, though carried to excess: his sternest and his deepest qualities were mingled with fickleness and caprice; his profound sagacity often frustrated by a whim; his towering ambition deserted for some frivolous temptation; and his elastic, sanguine, and high-spirited nature, faithful only to the desire of military glory, to the poetry of a daring and stormy life, and to the susceptibilities of that tender passion without whose colourings no portrait of chivalry is complete, and in which he was capable of a sentiment, a tenderness, and a loyal devotion, which could hardly have been supposed compatible with his reckless levity and his undisciplined career.

"Well," said he, as he rose slowly, folded his mantle round him, and resumed his way, "it was not for *myself* I grieved thus. But the pang is past, and the worst is known. Now, then, back to those things that never die—restless projects and daring schemes. That hag's curse keeps my blood cold still, and this solitude has something in it weird and awful. Ha!—what sudden light is that?"

The light which caught Montreal's eye broke forth almost like a star, scarcely larger, indeed, but more red and intense in its ray. Of itself it was nothing uncommon, and might have shone either from convent or cottage. But it streamed from a part of the Aventine which contained no habitations of the living, but only the empty ruins and shattered porticoes, of which even the names and memories of the ancient inhabitants were dead. Aware of this, Montreal felt a slight awe (as the beam threw its steady light over the dreary landscape); for he was not without the knightly superstitions of the age, and it was now the witching hour consecrated to ghost and spirit. But fear, whether of this world or the next, could not long daunt the mind of the hardy freebooter; and, after a short hesitation, he resolved to make a digression from his way, and ascertain the cause of the phenomenon. Unconsciously, the martial tread of the barbarian passed over the site of the famed, or infamous temple of Isis, which had once witnessed those wildest orgies commemorated by Juvenal; and came at last to a thick and dark copse, from an opening in the centre of which gleamed the mysterious light. Penetrating the gloomy foliage, the Knight now found himself before a large ruin, gray and roofless, from within which came, indistinct and muffled, the sound of voices. Through a rent in the wall, forming a kind of casement, and about ten feet from the ground, the light now broke over the matted and rank soil, embedded, as it were, in vast masses of shade, and streaming through a mouldering portico hard at hand. The Provençal stood, though he knew it not, on the very place once consecrated by the Temple: the Portico and the Library of Liberty (the first public library instituted in Rome). The wall of the ruin was covered with innumerable creepers and wild brushwood, and it required but little agility on the part of Montreal, by the help of these, to raise himself to the height of the aperture, and, concealed by the luxuriant foliage, to gaze within. He saw a table, lighted with tapers, in the centre of which was a crucifix; a dagger, unsheathed; an open scroll, which the event proved to be of sacred character; and a brazen bowl. About a hundred men, in cloaks, and with black vizards, stood motionless around; and one, taller than the rest, without disguise or mask—whose pale brow and stern features seemed by that light yet paler and yet more stern—appeared to be concluding some address to his companions.

"Yes," said he, "in the church of the Lateran I will make the last appeal to the people. Supported by the Vicar of the Pope, myself an officer of the Pontiff, it will be seen that Religion and Liberty—the heroes and the martyrs—are united in one cause. After that time, words are idle; action must begin. By this crucifix I pledge my faith, on this blade I devote my life, to the regeneration of Rome! And you (then no need for mask or mantle!), when the solitary trump is heard, when the solitary horseman is seen,—*you*, swear to rally round the standard of the Republic, and resist—with heart and hand, with life and soul, in defiance of death, and in hope of redemption—the arms of the oppressor!"

"We swear—we swear!" exclaimed every voice: and, crowding toward cross and weapon, the tapers were obscured by the intervening throng, and Montreal could not perceive the ceremony, nor hear the muttered formula of the oath: but he could guess that the rite then common to conspiracies—and which required each conspirator to shed some drops of his own blood, in token that life itself was devoted to the enterprise—had not been omitted, when, the group again receding, the same figure as before had addressed the meeting, holding on high the bowl with both hands,—while from the left arm, which was bared, the blood weltered slowly, and trickled, drop by drop, upon the ground,—said, in a solemn voice and with upturned eyes:

"Amidst the ruins of thy temple, O Liberty! we, Romans, dedicate to thee this libation! We, befriended and inspired by no unreal and fabled idols, but by the Lord of Hosts, and Him who, descending to earth, appealed not to emperors and to princes, but to the fisherman and the peasant,—giving to the lowly and the poor the mission of Revelation." Then, turning suddenly to his companions, as his features, singularly varying in their character and expression, brightened, from solemn awe, into a martial and kindling enthusiasm, he cried aloud, "Death to the Tyranny! Life to the Republic!" The effect of the transition was startling. Each man, as by an involuntary and irresistible impulse, laid his hand upon his sword, as he echoed the sentiment; some, indeed, drew forth their blades, as if for instant action.

"I have seen enow: they will break up anon," said Montreal to himself: "and I would rather face an army of thousands, than even half-a-dozen enthusiasts, so inflamed,—and I thus detected." And, with this thought, he dropped on the ground, and glided away, as, once again, through the still midnight air, broke upon his ear the muffled shout—"DEATH TO THE TYRANNY!—LIFE TO THE REPUBLIC!"

BOOK II

THE REVOLUTION

"Ogni Lascivia, ogni male, nulla giustizia, nullo freno. Non c'era piu remedia, ogni persona periva. Allora Cola di Rienzi," &c.—*Vita di Cola di Rienzi,* lib. i. chap. 2.

"Every kind of lewdness, every form of evil; no justice, no restraint. Remedy there was none; perdition fell on all. Then Cola di Rienzi," &c.—*Life of Cola di Rienzi.*

CHAPTER I

THE KNIGHT OF PROVENCE, AND HIS PROPOSAL

It was nearly noon as Adrian entered the gates of the palace of Stephen Colonna. The palaces of the nobles were not then as we see them now, receptacles for the immortal canvas of Italian, and the imperishable sculpture of Grecian Art; but still to this day are retained the massive walls, and barred windows, and spacious courts, which at that time protected their rude retainers. High above the gates rose a lofty and solid tower, whose height commanded a wide view of the mutilated remains of Rome: the gate itself was adorned and strengthened on either side by columns of granite, whose Doric capitals betrayed the sacrilege that had torn them from one of the many temples that had formerly crowded the sacred Forum. From the same spoils came, too, the vast fragments of travertine which made the walls of the outer court. So common at that day were these barbarous appropriations of the most precious monuments of art, that the columns and domes of earlier Rome were regarded by all classes but as quarries, from which every man was free to gather the materials, whether for his castle or his cottage,—a wantonness of outrage far greater than the Goths', to whom a later age would fain have attributed all the disgrace, and which, more perhaps than even heavier offences, excited the classical indignation of Petrarch, and made him sympathise with Rienzi in his hopes of Rome. Still may you see the churches of that or even earlier dates, of the most shapeless architecture, built on the sites, and from the marbles, consecrating (rather than consecrated by) the names of Venus, of Jupiter, of Minerva. The palace of the Prince of the Orsini, duke of Gravina, is yet reared above the graceful arches (still visible) of the theatre of Marcellus; then a fortress of the Savelli.

As Adrian passed the court, a heavy waggon blocked up the way, laden with huge marbles, dug from the unexhausted mine of the Golden House of Nero: they were intended for an additional tower. by which Stephen Colonna proposed yet more to strengthen the tasteless and barbarous edifice in which the old noble maintained the dignity of outraging the law.

The friend of Petrarch and the pupil of Rienzi sighed deeply as he passed this vehicle of new spoliations, and as a pillar of fluted alabaster, rolling carelessly from the waggon, fell with a loud crash upon the pavement. At the foot of the stairs grouped some dozen of the bandits whom the old Colonna entertained: they were playing at dice upon an ancient tomb, the clear and deep inscription on which (so different from the slovenly character of the later empire) bespoke it a memorial of the most powerful age of Rome, and which, now empty even of ashes, and upset, served for a table to these foreign savages, and was strewn, even at that early hour, with fragments of meat and flasks of wine. They scarcely stirred, they scarcely looked up, as the young noble passed them; and their fierce oaths and loud ejaculations, uttered in a northern *patois,* grated harsh upon his ear, as he mounted, with a slow step, the lofty and unclean stairs. He came into a vast ante-chamber, which was half-filled with the higher class of the patrician's retainers: some five or six pages, chosen from the inferior noblesse, congregated by a narrow and deep-sunk casement, were discussing the grave matters of gallantry and intrigue; three petty chieftains of the band below, with their corselets donned, and their swords and casques beside them, were sitting, stolid and silent, at a table, in the middle of the room, and might have been taken for automatons, save for the solemn regularity with which they ever and anon lifted to their moustachioed lips their several goblets, and then, with a complacent grunt, re-settled to their contemplations. Striking was the contrast which their northern phlegm presented to a crowd of Italian clients, and petitioners, and parasites, who walked restlessly to and fro, talking loudly to each other, with all the vehement gestures and varying physiognomy of southern vivacity. There was a general stir and sensation as Adrian broke upon this miscellaneous company. The bandit captains nodded their heads mechanically; the pages bowed, and admired the fashion of his plume and hose; the clients, and petitioners, and parasites, crowded round him, each with a separate request for interest with his potent kinsman. Great need had Adrian of his wonted urbanity and address, in extricating himself from their grasp; and painfully did he win, at last, the low and narrow door, at which stood a tall servitor, who admitted or rejected the applicants, according to his interest or caprice.

"Is the Baron alone?" asked Adrian.

"Why, no, my Lord: a foreign signor is with him—but to you he is of course visible."

"Well, you may admit me. I would inquire of his health."

The servitor opened the door—through whose aperture peered many a jealous and wistful eye—and consigned Adrian to the guidance of a page, who, older and of greater esteem than the loiterers in the anteroom, was the especial henchman of the Lord of the Castle. Passing another, but empty chamber, vast and dreary, Adrian found himself in a small cabinet, and in the presence of his kinsman.

Before a table, bearing the implements of writing, sate the old Colonna: a robe of rich furs and velvet hung loose upon his tall and stately frame: from a round skull-cap, of comforting warmth and crimson hue, a few gray locks descended, and mixed with a long and reverent beard. The countenance of the aged noble, who had long passed his eightieth year, still retained the traces of a comeliness for which in earlier manhood he was remarkable. His eyes, if deep-sunken, were still keen and lively, and sparkled with all the fire of youth; his mouth curved upward in a pleasant, though half-satiric, smile; and his appearance on the whole was prepossessing and commanding, indicating rather the high blood, the shrewd wit, and the gallant valour of the patrician, than his craft, hypocrisy, and habitual but disdainful spirit of oppression.

Stephen Colonna, without being absolutely a hero, was indeed far braver than most of the Romans, though he held fast to the Italian maxim—never to fight an enemy while it is possible to cheat him. Two faults, however, marred the effect of his sagacity: a supreme insolence of disposition, and a profound belief in the lights of his experience. He was incapable of analogy. What had never happened in his time, he was perfectly persuaded never could happen. Thus, though generally esteemed an able diplomatist, he had the cunning of the intriguant, and not the providence of a statesman. If, however, pride made him arrogant in prosperity, it supported him in misfortune. And in the earlier vicissitudes of a life which had partly been consumed in exile, he had developed many noble qualities of fortitude, endurance, and real greatness of soul; which showed that his failings were rather acquired by circumstance than derived from nature. His numerous and high-born race were proud of their chief; and with justice; for he was the ablest and most honoured, not only of the direct branch of the Colonna, but also, perhaps, of all the more powerful barons.

Seated at the same table with Stephen Colonna was a man of noble presence, of about three or four and thirty years of age, in whom Adrian instantly recognised Walter de Montreal. This celebrated knight was scarcely of the personal appearance which might have corresponded with the terror his name generally excited. His face was handsome, almost to the extreme of womanish delicacy. His fair hair waved long and freely over a white and unwrinkled forehead: the life of a camp and the suns of Italy had but little embrowned his clear and healthful complexion, which retained much of the bloom of youth. His features were aquiline and regular; his eyes, of a light hazel, were large, bright, and penetrating; and a short, but curled beard and moustachio, trimmed with soldier-like precision, and very little darker than the hair, gave indeed a martial expression to his comely countenance, but rather the expression which might have suited the hero of courts and tournaments, than the chief of a brigand's camp. The aspect, manner, and bearing, of the Provençal were those which captivate rather than awe,—blending, as they did, a certain military frankness with the easy and graceful dignity of one conscious of gentle birth, and accustomed to mix, on equal terms, with the great and noble. His form happily contrasted and elevated the character of a countenance which required strength and stature to free its uncommon beauty from the charge of effeminacy, being of great height and remarkable muscular power, without the least approach to clumsy and unwieldy bulk: it erred, indeed, rather to the side of leanness than flesh,—at once robust and slender. But the chief personal distinction of this warrior, the most redoubted lance of Italy, was an air and carriage of chivalric and heroic grace, greatly set off at this time by his splendid dress, which was of brown velvet sown with pearls, over which hung the surcoat worn by the Knights of the Hospital, whereon was wrought, in white, the eight-pointed cross that made the badge of his order. The Knight's attitude was that of earnest conversation, bending slightly forward towards the Colonna, and resting both his hands—which (according to the usual distinction of the old Norman race,* from whom, though born in Provence, Montreal boasted his descent) were small and delicate, the fingers being covered with jewels, as was the fashion of the day—upon the golden hilt of an enormous sword, on the sheath of which was elaborately wrought the silver lilies that made the device of the Provençal Brotherhood of Jerusalem.

"Good morrow, fair kinsman!" said Stephen. "Seat thyself, I pray; and know in this knightly visitor the celebrated Sieur de Montreal."

"Ah, my Lord," said Montreal, smiling, as he saluted Adrian; "and how is my lady at home?"

"You mistake, Sir Knight," quoth Stephen: "my young kinsman is not yet married: 'faith, as Pope Boniface remarked, when he lay stretched on a sick bed, and his confessor talked to him about Abraham's bosom, 'that is a pleasure the greater for being deferred.'"

"The Signor will pardon my mistake," returned Montreal.

"But not," said Adrian, "the neglect of Sir Walter in not ascertaining the fact in person. My thanks to him, noble kinsman, are greater than you weet of; and he promised to visit me, that he might receive them at leisure."

"I assure you, Signor," answered Montreal, "that I have not forgotten the invitation; but so weighty hitherto have been my affairs at Rome, that I have

* Small hands and feet, however disproportioned to the rest of the person, were at that time deemed no less a distinction of the well-born, than they have been in a more refined age. Many readers will remember the pain occasioned to Petrarch by his tight shoes. The supposed beauty of this peculiarity is more derived from the feudal than the classic time.

been obliged to parley with my impatience to better our acquaintance."

"Oh, ye knew each other before?" said Stephen. "And how?"

"My Lord, there is a damsel in the case!" replied Montreal. "Excuse my silence."

"Ah, Adrian, Adrian! when will you learn my continence!" said Stephen, solemnly stroking his gray beard. "What an example I set you! But a truce to this light conversation,—let us resume our theme. You must know, Adrian, that it is to the brave band of my guest I am indebted for those valiant gentlemen below, who keep Rome so quiet, though my poor habitation so noisy. He has called to proffer more assistance, if need be; and to advise me on the affairs of Northern Italy. Continue, I pray thee, Sir Knight; I have no disguises from my kinsman."

"Thou seest," said Montreal, fixing his penetrating eyes on Adrian, "thou seest, doubtless, my Lord, that Italy at this moment presents to us a remarkable spectacle. It is a contest between two opposing powers, which shall destroy the other. The one power is that of the unruly and turbulent people—a power which they call 'Liberty'; the other power is that of the chiefs and princes—a power which they more appropriately call 'Order.' Between these parties the cities of Italy are divided. In Florence, in Genoa, in Pisa, for instance, is established a Free State—a Republic, God wot! and a more riotous, unhappy state of government, cannot well be imagined."

"That is perfectly true," quoth Stephen; "they banished my own first cousin from Genoa."

"A perpetual strife, in short," continued Montreal,

"between the great families; an alternation of prosecutions, and confiscations, and banishments: to-day, the Guelfs proscribe the Ghibellines—to-morrow, the Ghibellines drive out the Guelfs. This may be liberty, but it is the liberty of the strong against the weak. In the other cities, as Milan, as Verona, as Bologna, the people are under the rule of one man,—who calls himself a prince, and whom his enemies call a tyrant. Having more force than any other citizen, he preserves a firm government; having more constant demand on his intellect and energies than the other citizens, he also preserves a wise one. These two orders of government are enlisted against each other: whenever the people in the one rebel against their prince, the people of the other—that is the Free States—send arms and money to their assistance."

"You hear, Adrian, how wicked those last are," quoth Stephen.

"Now it seems to me," continued Montreal, "that this contest must end some time or other. All Italy must become republican or monarchical. It is easy to predict which will be the result."

"Yes, Liberty must conquer in the end!" said Adrian, warmly.

"Pardon me, young Lord; my opinion is entirely the reverse. You perceive that these republics are commercial,—are traders; they esteem wealth, they despise valour, they cultivate all trades save that of the armourer. Accordingly, how do they maintain themselves in war? By their own citizens? Not a whit of it! Either they send to some foreign chief, and promise, if he grant them his protection, the principality of the city for five or ten years in return; or else they borrow from some hardy adventurer, like myself, as many troops as they can afford to pay for. Is it not so, Lord Adrian?"

Adrian nodded his reluctant assent.

"Well, then, it is the fault of the foreign chief if he do not make his power permanent; as has been already done in States once free by the Visconti and the Scala: or else it is the fault of the captain of the mercenaries if he do not convert his brigands into senators, and himself into a king. These are events so natural, that one day or other they will occur throughout all Italy. And all Italy will then become monarchical. Now it seems to me the interest of all the powerful families—your own, at Rome, as that of the Visconti at Milan—to expedite this epoch, and to check, while you yet may with ease, that rebellious contagion amongst the people which is now rapidly spreading, and which ends in the fever of licence to them, but in the corruption of death to you. In these free States, the nobles are the first to suffer: first your privileges, then your property, are swept away. Nay, in Florence, as ye well know, my Lords, no noble is even capable of holding the meanest office in the State!"

"Villains!" said Colonna, "they violate the first law of nature!"

"At this moment," resumed Montreal, who, engrossed with his subject, little heeded the interruptions he received from the holy indignation of the Baron: "at this moment, there are many—the wisest, perhaps, in the free States—who desire to renew the old Lombard leagues, in defence of their common freedom everywhere, and against whosoever shall aspire to be prince. Fortunately, the deadly jealousies between these merchant States—the base plebeian jealousies—

more of trade than of glory—interpose at present an irresistible obstacle to this design; and Florence, the most stirring and the most esteemed of all, is happily so reduced by reverses of commerce as to be utterly unable to follow out so great an undertaking. Now, then, is the time for us, my Lords; while these obstacles are so great for our foes, now is the time for us to form and cement a counter-league between all the princes of Italy. To you, noble Stephen, I have come, as your rank demands,—alone of all the barons of Rome,—to propose to you this honourable union. Observe what advantages it proffers to your house. The popes have abandoned Rome for ever; there is no counterpoise to your ambition,—there need be none to your power. You see before you the examples of Visconti and Taddeo di Pepoli. You may found in Rome, the first city of Italy, a supreme and uncontrolled principality, subjugate utterly your weaker rivals,—the Savelli, the Malatesta, the Orsini, —and leave to your sons' sons an hereditary kingdom that may aspire once more, perhaps, to the empire of the world."

Stephen shaded his face with his hand as he answered: "But this, noble Montreal, requires means: —money and men."

"Of the last, you can command from me enow—my small company, the best disciplined, can (whenever I please) swell to the most numerous in Italy: in the first, noble Baron, the rich house of Colonna cannot fail; and even a mortgage on its vast estates may be well repaid when you have possessed yourselves of the whole revenues of Rome. You see," continued Montreal, turning to Adrian, in whose youth he expected a more warm ally than in his hoary kinsman: "you see at a glance how feasible is this project, and what a mighty field it opens to your House."

"Sir Walter de Montreal," said Adrian, rising from his seat, and giving vent to the indignation he had with difficulty suppressed, "I grieve much that, beneath the roof of the first citizen of Rome, a stranger should attempt thus calmly, and without interruption, to excite the ambition of emulating the execrated celebrity of a Visconti or a Pepoli. Speak, my Lord! (turning to Stephen)—speak, noble kinsman! and tell this Knight of Provence, that if by a Colonna the ancient grandeur of Rome cannot be restored, it shall not be, at least, by a Colonna that her last wrecks of liberty shall be swept away."

"How now, Adrian!—how now, sweet kinsman!" said Stephen, thus suddenly appealed to, "calm thyself, I pr'ythee. Noble Sir Walter, he is young—young and hasty—he means not to offend thee."

"Of that I am persuaded," returned Montreal, coldly, but with great and courteous command of temper. "He speaks from the impulse of the moment,—a praiseworthy fault in youth. It was mine at his age, and many a time have I nearly lost my life for the rashness. Nay, Signor, nay!—touch not your sword so meaningly, as if you fancied I intimated a threat; far from me such presumption. I have learned sufficient caution, believe me, in the wars, not wantonly to draw against me a blade which I have seen wielded against such odds."

Touched, despite himself, by the courtesy of the Knight, and the allusion to a scene in which, perhaps, his life had been preserved by Montreal, Adrian extended his hand to the latter.

"I was to blame for my haste," said he, frankly;

"but know, by my very heat," he added more gravely, "that your project will find no friends among the Colonna. Nay, in the presence of my noble kinsman, I dare to tell you, that could even his high sanction lend itself to such a scheme, the best hearts of his house would desert him; and I myself, his kinsman, would man yonder castle against so unnatural an ambition!"

A slight and scarce perceptible cloud passed over Montreal's countenance at these words; and he bit his lip ere he replied:

"Yet if the Orsini be less scrupulous, their first exertion of power would be heard in the crashing house of the Colonna."

"Know you," returned Adrian, "that one of our mottoes is this haughty address to the Romans,—'If we fall, ye fall also'? And better that fate, than a rise upon the wrecks of our native city."

"Well, well, well!" said Montreal, re-seating himself, "I see that I must leave Rome to herself,—the League must thrive without her aid. I did but jest, touching the Orsini, for they have not the power that would make their efforts safe. Let us sweep, then, our past conference from our recollection. It is the nineteenth, I think, Lord Colonna, on which you propose to repair to Corneto, with your friends and retainers, and on which you have invited my attendance?"

"It is on that day, Sir Knight," replied the Baron, evidently much relieved by the turn the conversation had assumed. "The fact is, that we have been so charged with indifference to the interests of the good people, that I strain a point in this expedition to contradict the assertion; and we propose, therefore, to escort and protect, against the robbers of the road, a convoy of corn to Corneto. In truth, I may add another reason, besides fear of the robbers, that makes me desire as numerous a train as possible. I wish to show my enemies, and the people generally, the solid and growing power of my house; the display of such an armed band as I hope to levy, will be a magnificent occasion to strike awe into the riotous and refractory. Adrian, you will collect your servitors, I trust, on that day; we would not be without you."

"And as we ride along, fair Signor," said Montreal, inclining to Adrian, "we will find at least one subject on which we can agree: all brave men and true knights have one common topic,—and its name is Woman. You must make me acquainted with the names of the fairest dames of Rome; and we will discuss old adventures in the Parliament of Love, and hope for new. By the way, I suppose, Lord Adrian, you, with the rest of your countrymen, are Petrarch-stricken?"

"Do you not share our enthusiasm? slur not so your gallantry, I pray you."

"Come, we must not again disagree; but, by my halidame, I think one troubadour roundel worth all that Petrarch ever wrote. He has but borrowed from our knightly poesy to disguise it, like a carpet coxcomb."

"Well," said Adrian, gaily, "for every line of the troubadours that you quote, I will cite you another. I will forgive you for injustice to Petrarch, if you are just to the troubadours."

"Just!" cried Montreal, with real enthusiasm: "I am of the land, nay, the very blood of the troubadour! But we grow too light for your noble kinsman; and it is time for me to bid you, for the present, farewell. My Lord Colonna, peace be with you; farewell, Sir Adrian,—brother mine in knighthood,—remember your challenge."

And with an easy and careless grace the Knight of St. John took his leave. The old Baron, making a dumb sign of excuse to Adrian, followed Montreal into the adjoining room.

"Sir Knight!" said he, "Sir Knight!" as he closed the door upon Adrian, and then drew Montreal to the recess of the casement,—"a word in your ear. Think not I slight your offer, but these young men must be managed; the plot is great—noble—grateful to my heart; but it requires time and caution. I have many of my house, scrupulous as yon hot-skull, to win over; the way is pleasant, but must be sounded well and carefully; you understand?"

From under his bent brows, Montreal darted one keen glance at Stephen, and then answered:

"My friendship for you dictated my offer. The League may stand without the Colonna,—beware a time when the Colonna cannot stand without the League. My Lord, look well around you; there are more freemen—ay, bold and stirring ones, too—in Rome, than you imagine. Beware Rienzi! Adieu, we meet soon again."

Thus saying, Montreal departed, soliloquising as he passed with his careless step through the crowded ante-room:

"I shall fail here!—these caitiff nobles have neither the courage to be great, nor the wisdom to be honest. Let them fall!—I may find an adventurer from the people, an adventurer like myself, worth them all."

No sooner had Stephen returned to Adrian than he

flung his arms affectionately round his ward, who was preparing his pride for some sharp rebuke for his petulance.

"Nobly feigned,—admirable, admirable!" cried the Baron; "you have learned the true art of a statesman at the Emperor's court. I always thought you would—always said it. You saw the dilemma I was in, thus taken by surprise by that barbarian's mad scheme; afraid to refuse,—more afraid to accept. You extricated me with consummate address: that passion,—so natural to your age,—was a famous feint; drew off the attacks; gave me time to breathe; allowed me to play with the savage. But we must not offend him, you know: all my retainers would desert me, or sell me to the Orsini, or cut my throat, if he but held up his finger. Oh! it was admirably managed, Adrian—admirably!"

"Thank Heaven!" said Adrian, with some difficulty recovering the breath which his astonishment had taken away, "you do not think of embracing that black proposition?"

"Think of it! no, indeed!" said Stephen, throwing himself back on his chair. "Why, do you not know my age, boy? Hard on my ninetieth year, I should be a fool indeed to throw myself into such a whirl of turbulence and agitation. I want to keep what I have, not risk it by grasping more. Am I not the beloved of the pope? shall I hazard his excommunication? Am I not the most powerful of the nobles? should I be more if I were king? At my age, to talk to me of such stuff!—the man's an idiot. Besides," added the old man, sinking his voice, and looking fearfully round, "if I were a king, my sons might poison me for the succession. They are good lads, Adrian, very!

But such a temptation!—I would not throw it in their way; these gray hairs have experience! Tyrants don't die a natural death; no, no! Plague on the Knight, say I; he has already cast me into a cold sweat."

Adrian gazed on the working features of the old man, whose selfishness thus preserved him from crime. He listened to his concluding words—full of the dark truth of the times; and as the high and pure ambition of Rienzi flashed upon him in contrast, he felt that he could not blame its fervour or wonder at its excess.

"And then, too," resumed the Baron, speaking more deliberately as he recovered his self-possession, "this man, by way of a warning, shows me, at a glance, his whole ignorance of the state. What think you? he has mingled with the mob, and taken their rank breath for power; yes, he thinks words are soldiers, and bade me—me, Stephen Colonna—beware—of whom, think you? No, you will never guess!—of that speech-maker, Rienzi! my own old jesting guest! Ha! ha! ha!—the ignorance of these barbarians! ha! ha! ha!" and the old man laughed till the tears ran down his cheeks.

"Yet many of the nobles fear that same Rienzi," said Adrian, gravely.

"Ah! let them, let them!—they have not our experience—our knowledge of the world, Adrian. Tut, man,—when did declamation ever overthrow castles, and conquer soldiery? I like Rienzi to harangue the mob about old Rome, and such stuff; it gives them something to think of and prate about, and so all their fierceness evaporates in words; they might burn a house if they did not hear a speech. But, now I am on that score, I must own the pedant has grown impudent in his new office; here, here,—I received this paper ere I rose to-day. I hear a similar insolence has been shown to all the nobles. Read it, will you," and the Colonna put a scroll into his kinsman's hand.

"I have received the like," said Adrian, glancing at it. "It is a request of Rienzi's to attend at the Church of St. John of Lateran, to hear explained the inscription on a Table just discovered. It bears, he saith, the most intimate connexion with the welfare and state of Rome."

"Very entertaining, I dare to say, to professors and bookmen. Pardon me, kinsman; I forgot your taste for these things; and my son, Gianni, too, shares your fantasy. Well, well! it is innocent enough! Go—the man talks well."

"Will you not attend, too?"

"I—my dear boy—I!" said the old Colonna, opening his eyes in such astonishment that Adrian could not help laughing at the simplicity of his own question.

CHAPTER II

THE INTERVIEW, AND THE DOUBT

As Adrian turned from the palace of his guardian, and bent his way in the direction of the Forum, he came somewhat unexpectedly upon Raimond, Bishop of Orvietto, who, mounted upon a low palfrey, and accompanied by some three or four of his waiting-men, halted abruptly when he recognised the young noble.

"Ah, my son! it is seldom that I see thee: how fares it with thee?—well? So, so! I rejoice to hear it.

Alas! what a state of society is ours, when compared to the tranquil pleasures of Avignon! There, all men who, like us, are fond of the same pursuits, the same studies, *deliciæ musarum*, hum! hum! (the Bishop was proud of an occasional quotation, right or wrong), are brought easily and naturally together. But here we scarcely dare stir out of our houses, save upon great occasions. But, talking of great occasions, and the Muses, reminds me of our good Rienzi's invitation to the Lateran: of course you will attend; 'tis a mighty knotty piece of Latin he proposes to solve—so I hear, at least: very interesting to us, my son,—very!"

"It is to-morrow," answered Adrian. "Yes, assuredly; I will be there."

"And harkye, my son," said the Bishop, resting his hand affectionately on Adrian's shoulder, "I have reason to hope that he will remind our poor citizens of the Jubilee for the year Fifty, and stir them towards clearing the road of the brigands: a necessary injunction, and one to be heeded timeously; for who will come here for absolution when he stands a chance of rushing unannealed upon purgatory by the way? You have heard Rienzi,—ay? quite a Cicero—quite! Well, Heaven bless you, my son! you will not fail?"

"Nay, not I!"

"Yet, stay—a word with you: just suggest to all whom you may meet the advisability of a full meeting; it looks well for the city to show respect to letters."

"To say nothing of the Jubilee," added Adrian, smiling.

"Ah, to say nothing of the Jubilee—very good! Adieu for the present!" And the Bishop, resettling himself on his saddle, ambled solemnly on to visit his various friends, and press them to the meeting.

Meanwhile, Adrian continued his course till he had passed the Capitol, the Arch of Severus, the crumbling columns of the fane of Jupiter, and found himself amidst the long grass, the whispering reeds, and the neglected vines that wave over the now-vanished pomp of the Golden House of Nero. Seating himself on a fallen pillar—by that spot where the traveller descends to the (so-called) Baths of Livia—he looked impatiently to the sun, as if to blame it for the slowness of its march.

Not long, however, had he to wait before a light step was heard crushing the fragrant grass; and presently through the arching vines gleamed a face that might well have seemed the nymph, the goddess of the scene.

"My beautiful! my Irene!—how shall I thank thee!"

It was long before the delighted lover suffered himself to observe upon Irene's face a sadness that did not usually cloud it in his presence. Her voice, too, trembled; her words seemed constrained and cold.

"Have I offended thee?" he asked; "or what less misfortune hath occurred?"

Irene raised her eyes to her lover's, and said, looking at him earnestly, "Tell me, my Lord, in sober and simple truth, tell me, would it grieve thee much were this to be our last meeting?"

Paler than the marble at his feet grew the dark cheek of Adrian. It was some moments ere he could reply, and he did so then with a forced smile and a quivering lip.

"Jest not so, Irene! Last!—that is not a word for us!"

"But hear me, my Lord——"

"Why so cold?—call me Adrian!—friend!—lover! or be dumb!"

"Well, then, my soul's soul! my all of hope! my life's life!" exclaimed Irene, passionately, "hear me! I fear that we stand at this moment upon some gulf whose depth I see not, but which may divide us for ever! Thou knowest the real nature of my brother, and dost not misread him as many do. Long has he planned, and schemed, and communed with himself, and, feeling his way amidst the people, prepared the path to some great design. But now——(thou wilt not betray—thou wilt not injure him?—he is *thy* friend!)"

"And thy brother! I would give my life for his! Say on!"

"But now, then," resumed Irene, "the time for that enterprise, whatever it be, is coming fast. I know not of its exact nature, but I know that it is against the nobles—against thy order—against thy house itself! If it succeed—oh, Adrian! thou thyself mayst not be free from danger; and my name, at least, will be coupled with the name of thy foes. If it fail,—my brother, my bold brother, is swept away! He will fall a victim to revenge or justice, call it as you will. Your kinsman may be his judge—his executioner; and I—even if I should yet live to mourn over the boast and glory of my humble line—could I permit myself to love, to see, one in whose veins flowed the blood of his destroyer? Oh! I am wretched!—wretched! these thoughts make me well-nigh mad!" and wringing her hands bitterly Irene sobbed aloud.

Adrian himself was struck forcibly by the picture thus presented to him, although the alternative it embraced had often before forced itself dimly on his mind. It was true, however, that, not seeing the schemes of Rienzi backed by any physical power, and never yet having witnessed the mighty force of a moral revolution, he did not conceive that any rise to which he might instigate the people could be permanently successful: and, as for his punishment, in that city, where all justice was the slave of interest, Adrian knew himself powerful enough to obtain forgiveness even for the greatest of all crimes—armed insurrection against the nobles. As these thoughts recurred to him, he gained the courage to console and cheer Irene. But his efforts were only partially successful. Awakened by her fears to that consideration of the future which hitherto she had forgotten, Irene, for the first time, seemed deaf to the charmer's voice.

"Alas!" said she, sadly, "even at the best, what can this love, that we have so blindly encouraged—what can it end in? Thou must not wed with one like me! and I! how foolish I have been!"

"Recall thy senses then, Irene," said Adrian, proudly, partly perhaps in anger, partly in his experience of the sex. "Love another, and more wisely, if thou wilt; cancel thy vows with me, and continue to think it a crime to love, and a folly to be true!"

"Cruel!" said Irene, falteringly, and in her turn alarmed. "Dost thou speak in earnest?"

"Tell me, ere I answer you, tell me this: come death, come anguish, come a whole life of sorrow, as the end of this love, wouldst thou yet repent that thou hast loved? If so, thou knowest not the love that I feel for thee."

"Never! never can I repent!" said Irene, falling upon Adrian's neck; "forgive me!"

"But is there, in truth," said Adrian, a little while

after this lover-like quarrel and reconciliation, "is there, in truth, so marked a difference between thy brother's past and his present bearing? How knowest thou that the time for action is so near?"

"Because now he sits closeted whole nights with all ranks of men; he shuts up his books,—he reads no more,—but when alone, walks to and fro his chamber, muttering to himself. Sometimes he pauses before the calendar, which of late, he has fixed with his own hand against the wall, and passes his finger over the letters, till he comes to some chosen date, and then he plays with his sword and smiles. But two nights since, arms, too, in great number were brought to the house; and I heard the chief of the men who brought them, a grim giant, known well amongst the people, say, as he wiped his brow,—'these will see work soon!'"

"Arms! Are you sure of that?" said Adrian, anxiously. "Nay, then, there is more in these schemes than I imagined! But" (observing Irene's gaze bent fearfully on him as his voice changed, he added more gaily)—"but come what may—believe me,—my beautiful! my adored! that while I live, thy brother shall not suffer from the wrath he may provoke,—nor I, though he forget our ancient friendship, cease to love thee less."

"Signora! Signora! child! it is time! we must go!" said the shrill voice of Benedetta, now peering through the foliage. "The working men pass home this way; I see them approaching."

The lovers parted; for the first time the serpent had penetrated into their Eden,—they had conversed, they had thought, of other things than Love.

CHAPTER III

THE SITUATION OF A POPULAR PATRICIAN IN TIMES OF POPULAR DISCONTENT.—SCENE OF THE LATERAN

The situation of a Patrician who honestly loves the people is, in those evil times, when power oppresses and freedom struggles,—when the two divisions of men are wrestling against each other,—the most irksome and perplexing that destiny can possibly contrive. Shall he take part with the nobles?—he betrays his conscience! With the people?—he deserts his friends! But that consequence of the last alternative is not the sole—nor, perhaps to a strong mind, the most severe. All men are swayed and chained by public opinion—it is the public judge; but public opinion is not the same for all ranks. The public opinion that excites or deters the plebeian, is the opinion of the plebeians,—of those whom he sees, and meets, and knows; of those with whom he is brought in contact,—those with whom he has mixed from childhood,—those whose praises are daily heard,—whose censure frowns upon him with every hour.* So, also, the public opinion of the great is the opinion

*It is the same in still smaller divisions. The public opinion for lawyers is that of lawyers; of soldiers, that of the army; of scholars, it is that of men of literature and science. And to the susceptible amongst the latter, the hostile criticism of learning has been more stinging than the severest moral censures of the vulgar. Many a man has done a great act, or composed a great work, solely to please the two or three persons constantly present to him. Their voice was *his* public opinion. The public opinion that operated on Bishop, the murderer, was the opinion of the Burkers, his comrades. Did that condemn him? No! He knew no other public opinion till he came to be hanged, and caught the loathing eyes, and heard the hissing execrations of the crowd below his gibbet.

of *their* equals,—of those whom birth and accident cast for ever in their way. This distinction is full of important practical deductions; it is one which, more than most maxims, should never be forgotten by a politician who desires to be profound. It is, then, an ordeal terrible to pass—which few plebeians ever pass, which it is therefore unjust to expect patricians to cross unfalteringly—the ordeal of opposing the public opinion which exists for *them*. They cannot help doubting their own judgment,—they cannot help thinking the voice of wisdom or of virtue speaks in those sounds which have been deemed oracles from their cradle. In the tribunal of Sectarian Prejudice they imagine they recognise the court of the Universal Conscience. Another powerful antidote to the activity of a patrician so placed, is in the certainty that to the last the motives of such activity will be alike misconstrued by the aristocracy he deserts and the people he joins. It seems so unnatural in a man to fly in the face of his own order, that the world is willing to suppose any clue to the mystery save that of honest conviction or lofty patriotism. "Ambition!" says one. "Disappointment!" cries another. "Some private grudge!" hints a third. "Mob-courting vanity!" sneers a fourth. The people admire at first, but suspect afterwards. The moment he thwarts a popular wish, there is no redemption for him: he is accused of having acted the hypocrite,—of having worn the sheep's fleece: and now, say they,—"See! the wolf's teeth peep out!" Is he familiar with the people?—it is cajolery! Is he distant?—it is pride! What then, sustains a man in such a situation, following his own conscience, with his eyes opened to all the perils of the path? Away with the cant of public opinion,—

away with the poor delusion of posthumous justice; he will offend the first, he will never obtain the last. What sustains him? His OWN SOUL! A man thoroughly great has a certain contempt for his kind while he aids them: their weal or woe are all: their applause—their blame—are nothing to him. He walks forth from the circle of birth and habit; he is deaf to the little motives of little men. High, through the widest space his orbit may describe, he holds on his course to guide or to enlighten; but the noises below reach him not! Until the wheel is broken,—until the dark void swallow up the star—it makes melody, night and day, to its own ear; thirsting for no sound from the earth it illumines, anxious for no companionship in the path through which it rolls, conscious of its own glory, and contented, therefore, to be *alone!*

But minds of this order are rare. All ages cannot produce them. They are exceptions to the ordinary and human virtue, which is influenced and regulated by external circumstance. At a time when even to be merely susceptible to the voice of fame was a great pre-eminence in moral energies over the rest of mankind, it would be impossible that any one should ever have formed the conception of that more refined and metaphysical sentiment, that purer excitement to high deeds—that glory in one's own heart, which is so immeasurably above the desire of a renown that lackeys the heels of others. In fact, before we can dispense with the world, we must, by a long and severe novitiate—by the probation of much thought, and much sorrow—by deep and sad conviction of the vanity of all that the world can give us, have raised ourselves—not in the fervour of an hour, but habitually—*above* the world: an abstraction—an idealism—

which, in our wiser age, how few even of the wisest can attain! Yet, till we are thus fortunate, we know not the true divinity of contemplation, nor the all-sufficing mightiness of conscience: nor can we retreat with solemn footsteps into that Holy of Holies in our own souls, wherein we know, and feel, how much our nature is capable of the self-existence of a God!

But to return to the things and thoughts of earth. Those considerations, and those links of circumstance, which in a similar situation have changed so many honest and courageous minds, changed also the mind of Adrian. He felt in a false position. His reason and conscience shared in the schemes of Rienzi, and his natural hardihood and love of enterprise would have led him actively to share the danger of their execution. But this, all his associations, his friendships, his private and household ties, loudly forbade. Against his order, against his house, against the companions of his youth, how could he plot secretly, or act sternly? By the goal to which he was impelled by patriotism, stood hypocrisy and ingratitude. Who would believe him the honest champion of his country who was a traitor to his friends? Thus, indeed,

> "The native hue of resolution
> Was sicklied o'er with the pale cast of thought!"

And he who should have been by nature a leader of the time become only its spectator. Yet Adrian endeavoured to console himself for his present passiveness in a conviction of the policy of his conduct. He who takes no share in the commencement of civil revolutions, can often become, with the most effect, a mediator between the passions and the parties subsequently formed. Perhaps, under Adrian's circumstances, delay was really the part of a prudent statesman; the very position which cripples at the first, often gives authority before the end. Clear from the excesses, and saved from the jealousies, of rival factions, all men are willing to look with complaisance and respect to a new actor in a turbulent drama; his moderation may make him trusted by the people; his rank enable him to be a fitting mediator with the nobles; and thus the qualities that would have rendered him a martyr at one period of the Revolution, raise him perhaps into a saviour at another.

Silent, therefore, and passive, Adrian waited the progress of events. If the projects of Rienzi failed, he might, by that inactivity, the better preserve the people from new chains, and their champion from death. If those projects succeeded, he might equally save his house from the popular wrath—and, advocating liberty, check disorder. Such, at least, were his hopes; and thus did the Italian sagacity and caution of his character control and pacify the enthusiasm of youth and courage.

The sun shone, calm and cloudless, upon the vast concourse gathered before the broad space that surrounds the Church of St. John of Lateran. Partly by curiosity—partly by the desire of the Bishop of Orvieto—partly because it was an occasion in which they could display the pomp of their retinues—many of the principal Barons of Rome had gathered to this spot.

On one of the steps ascending to the church, with his mantle folded round him, stood Walter de Montreal, gazing on the various parties that, one after another, swept through the lane which the soldiers of the Church preserved unimpeded, in the middle of the crowd, for the access of the principal nobles. He watched with interest, though with his usual carelessness of air and roving glance, the different marks and looks of welcome given by the populace to the different personages of note. Banners and pennons preceded each Signor, and, as they waved aloft, the witticisms or nicknames—the brief words of praise or censure, that imply so much—which passed to and fro among that lively crowd, were treasured carefully in his recollection.

"Make way, there!—way for my Lord Martino Orsini—Baron di Porto!"

"Peace, minion!—draw back! way for the Signor Adrian Colonna, Baron di Castello, and Knight of the Empire."

And at those two rival shouts, you saw waving on high the golden bear of the Orsini, with the motto—"Beware my embrace!" and the solitary column on an azure ground, of the Colonna, with Adrian's especial device—"Sad, but strong." The train of Martino Orsini was much more numerous than that of Adrian, which last consisted but of ten servitors. But Adrian's men attracted far greater admiration amongst the crowd, and pleased more the experienced eye of the warlike Knight of St. John. Their arms were polished like mirrors, their height was to an inch the same; their march was regular and sedate; their mien erect; they looked neither to the right nor left; they betrayed that ineffable discipline—that harmony of order—which Adrian had learned to impart to his men during his own apprenticeship of arms. But the disorderly train of the Lord of Porto was composed of men of all heights. Their arms were ill-polished and ill-fashioned, and they pressed confusedly on each other; they laughed and spoke aloud; and in their mien and bearing expressed all the insolence of men who despised alike the master they served and the people they awed. The two bands coming unexpectedly on each other through this narrow defile, the jealousy of the two houses presently declared itself. Each pressed forward for the precedence; and, as the quiet regularity of Adrian's train, and even its compact paucity of numbers, enabled it to pass before the servitors of his rival, the populace set up a loud shout,—"A Colonna for ever!"—"Let the Bear dance after the Column!"

"On, ye knaves!" said Orsini aloud to his men. "How have ye suffered this affront?" And passing himself to the head of his men, he would have advanced through the midst of his rival's train, had not a tall guard, in the Pope's livery, placed his baton in the way.

"Pardon, my Lord! we have the Vicar's express commands to suffer no struggling of the different trains one with another."

"Knave! dost thou bandy words with me?" said the fierce Orsini; and with his sword he clove the baton in two.

"In the Vicar's name, I command you to fall back!" said the sturdy guard, now placing his huge bulk in the very front of the noble's path.

"It is Cecco de Vecchio!" cried those of the populace, who were near enough to perceive the interruption and its cause.

"Ay," said one, "the good Vicar has put many of the stoutest fellows in the Pope's livery, in order the better to keep peace. He could have chosen none better than Cecco."

"But he must not fall!" cried another, as Orsini, glaring on the smith, drew back his sword as if to plunge it through his bosom.

"Shame—shame! shall the Pope be thus insulted in his own city?" cried several voices. "Down with the sacrilegious—down!" And, as if by a preconcerted plan, a whole body of the mob broke at once through the lane, and swept like a torrent over Orsini and his jostled and ill-assorted train. Orsini himself was thrown on the ground with violence, and trampled upon by a hundred footsteps; his men, huddled and struggling as much against themselves as against the mob, were scattered and overset; and when, by a great effort of the guards, headed by the smith himself, order was again restored, and the line reformed, Orsini, well-nigh choked with his rage and humiliation, and greatly bruised by the rude assaults he had received, could scarcely stir from the ground. The officers of the Pope raised him, and, when he was on his legs, he looked wildly around for his sword, which, falling from his hand, had been kicked amongst the crowd, and seeing it not, he said, between his ground teeth, to Cecco del Vecchio—

"Fellow, thy neck shall answer this outrage, or may God desert me!" and passed along through the space; while a half-suppressed and exultant hoot from the bystanders followed his path.

"Way there!" cried the smith, "for the Lord Martino di Porto, and may all the people know that he has threatened to take my life for the discharge of my duty in obedience to the Pope's Vicar!"

"He dare not!" shouted out a thousand voices; "the people can protect their own!"

This scene had not been lost on the Provençal, who

well knew how to construe the wind by the direction of straws, and saw at once, by the boldness of the populace, that they themselves were conscious of a coming tempest. "*Par Dieu*," said he, as he saluted Adrian, who, gravely, and without looking behind, had now won the steps of the church, "yon tall fellow has a brave heart, and many friends, too. What think you," he added, in a low whisper, "is not this scene a proof that the nobles are less safe than they wot of?"

"The beast begins to kick against the spur, Sir Knight," answered Adrian, "a wise horseman should, in such a case, take care how he pull the rein too tight, lest the beast should rear, and he be overthrown—yet that is the policy thou wouldst recommend."

"You mistake," returned Montreal, "my wish was to give Rome one sovereign instead of many tyrants,—but hark! what means that bell?"

"The ceremony is about to begin," answered Adrian. "Shall we enter the church together?"

Seldom had a temple consecrated to God witnessed so singular a spectacle as that which now animated the solemn space of the Lateran.

In the centre of the church, seats were raised in an amphitheatre, at the far end of which was a scaffolding, a little higher than the rest; below this spot, but high enough to be in sight of all the concourse, was placed a vast table of iron, on which was graven an ancient inscription, and bearing in its centre a clear and prominent device, presently to be explained.

The seats were covered with cloth and rich tapestry. In the rear of the church was drawn a purple curtain. Around the amphitheatre were the officers of the Church, in the party-coloured liveries of the Pope. To the right of the scaffold sate Raimond, Bishop of

Orvietto, in his robes of state. On the benches round him you saw all the marked personages of Rome—the judges, the men of letters, the nobles, from the lofty rank of the Savelli to the inferior grade of a Raselli. The space beyond the amphitheatre was filled with the people, who now poured fast in, stream after stream: all the while rang, clear and loud, the great bell of the church.

At length, as Adrian and Montreal seated themselves at a little distance from Raimond, the bell suddenly ceased—the murmurs of the people were stilled—the purple curtain was withdrawn, and Rienzi came forth with slow and majestic steps. He came—but not in his usual sombre and plain attire. Over his broad breast he wore a vest of dazzling whiteness—a long robe, in the ample fashion of the toga, descended to his feet and swept the floor. On his head he wore a fold of white cloth, in the centre of which shone a golden crown. But the crown was divided, or cloven, as it were, by the mystic ornament of a silver sword, which, attracting the universal attention, testified at once that this strange garb was worn, not from the vanity of display, but for the sake of presenting to the concourse—in the person of the citizen—a type and emblem of that state of the city on which he was about to descant.

"Faith," whispered one of the old nobles to his neighbour, "the plebeian assumes it bravely."

"It will be rare sport," said a second. "I trust the good man will put some jests in his discourse."

"What showman's tricks are these?" said a third.

"He is certainly crazed!" said a fourth.

"How handsome he is!" said the women, mixed with the populace.

"This is a man who has learned the people by heart," observed Montreal to Adrian. "He knows he must speak to the eye, in order to win the mind: a knave,—a wise knave!"

And now Rienzi had ascended the scaffold; and as he looked long and steadfastly around the meeting, the high and thoughtful repose of his majestic countenance, its deep and solemn gravity, hushed all the murmurs, and made its effect equally felt by the sneering nobles as the impatient populace.

"Signors of Rome," said he, at length, "and ye, friends, and citizens, you have heard why we are met together this day; and you, my Lord Bishop of Orvietto,—and ye, fellow labourers with me in the field of letters,—ye, too, are aware that it is upon some matter relative to that ancient Rome, the rise and the decline of whose past power and glories we have spent our youth in endeavouring to comprehend. But this, believe me, is no vain enigma of erudition, useful but to the studious,—referring but to the dead. Let the Past perish!—let darkness shroud it!—let it sleep for ever over the crumbling temples and desolate tombs of its forgotten sons,—if it cannot afford us, from its disburied secrets, a guide for the Present and the Future. What, my Lords, ye have thought that it was for the sake of antiquity alone that we have wasted our nights and days in studying what antiquity can teach us! You are mistaken; it is nothing to know what we have been, unless it is with the desire of knowing that which we ought to be. Our ancestors are mere dust and ashes, save when they speak to our posterity; and then their voices resound, not from the earth below, but the heaven above. There is an eloquence in Memory, because it is the nurse of Hope. There is a sanctity in the Past, but only because of the chronicles it retains,—chronicles of the progress of mankind,—stepping-stones in civilisation, in liberty, and in knowledge. Our fathers forbid us to recede, —they teach us what is our rightful heritage,—they bid us reclaim, they bid us augment, that heritage,—preserve their virtues, and avoid their errors. These are the true uses of the Past. Like the sacred edifice in which we are,—it is a tomb upon which to rear a temple. I see that you marvel at this long beginning; ye look to each other—ye ask to what it tends. Behold this broad plate of iron; upon it is graven an inscription but lately disinterred from the heaps of stone and ruin, which—O shame to Rome!—were once the palaces of empire, and the arches of triumphant power. The device in the centre of the table, which you behold, conveys the act of the Roman Senators,—who are conferring upon Vespasian the imperial authority. It is this inscription which I have invited you to hear read! It specifies the very terms and limits of the authority thus conferred. To the Emperor was confided the power of making laws and alliances with whatsoever nation,—of increasing, or of diminishing the limits of towns and districts,—of—mark this, my Lords!—exalting men to the rank of dukes and kings,—ay, and of deposing and degrading them:—of making cities, and of unmaking: in short, of all the attributes of imperial power. Yes, to that Emperor was confided this vast authority; but, by whom? Heed—listen, I pray you —let not a word be lost;—by whom, I say? By the Roman Senate! What was the Roman Senate? The Representative of the Roman People!"

"I knew he would come to that!" said the smith.

who stood at the door with his fellows, but to whose ear, clear and distinct, rolled the silver voice of Rienzi.

"Brave fellow! and this, too, in the hearing of the Lords!"

"Ay, you see what the people were, and we should never have known this but for him."

"Peace, fellows!" said the officer to those of the crowd, from whom came these whispered sentences.

Rienzi continued.—"Yes, it is the people who intrusted this power—to the people, therefore, it belongs! Did the haughty Emperor arrogate the crown? Could he assume the authority of himself? Was it born with him? Did he derive it, my Lord Barons, from the possession of towered castles—of lofty lineage? No! all-powerful as he was, he had no right to one atom of that power, save from the voice and trust of the Roman people. Such, O my countrymen! such was even at that day, when Liberty was but the shadow of her former self,—such was the acknowledged prerogative of your fathers! All power was the gift of the people. What have ye to give now? Who, who, I say,—what single person, what petty chief, asks *you* for the authority he assumes? His senate is his sword; his chart of licence is written, not with ink, but blood. The people!—there is *no* people! Oh! would to God that we might disentomb the spirit of the Past as easily as her records!"

"If I were your kinsman," whispered Montreal to Adrian, "I would give this man short breathing-time between his peroration and confession."

"What is your Emperor?" continued Rienzi; "a stranger! What the great head of your Church?—an exile! Ye are without your lawful chiefs; and why? Because ye are *not* without your law-defying tyrants!

The licence of your nobles, their discords, their dissensions, have driven our Holy Father from the heritage of St. Peter;—they have bathed your streets in your own blood; they have wasted the wealth of your labours on private quarrels and the maintenance of hireling ruffians! Your forces are exhausted against yourselves. You have made a mockery of your country, once the mistress of the world. You have steeped her lips in gall—ye have set a crown of thorns upon her head! What, my Lords!" cried he, turning sharply round towards the Savelli and Orsini, who, endeavouring to shake off the thrill which the fiery eloquence of Rienzi had stricken to their hearts, now, by contemptuous gestures and scornful smiles, testified the displeasure they did not dare loudly to utter in the presence of the Vicar and the people.—"What! even while I speak—not the sanctity of this place restrains you! I am an humble man—a citizen of Rome;—but I have this distinction: I have raised against myself many foes and scoffers for that which I have done for Rome. I am hated, because I love my country; I am despised, because I would exalt her. I retaliate—I shall be avenged. Three traitors in your own palaces shall betray you: their names are—Luxury, Envy, and Dissension!"

"There he had them on the hip!"

"Ha, ha! by the Holy Cross, that was good!"

"I would go to the hangman for such another keen stroke as that!"

"It is a shame if *we* are cowards, when one man is thus brave," said the smith.

"This is the man we have always wanted!"

"Silence!" proclaimed the officer.

"O Romans!" resumed Rienzi, passionately—

"awake! I conjure you! Let this memorial of your former power—your ancient liberties—sink deep into your souls. In a propitious hour, if ye seize it,—in an evil one, if ye suffer the golden opportunity to escape,—has this record of the past been unfolded to your eyes. Recollect that the Jubilee approaches."

The Bishop of Orvietto smiled, and bowed approvingly; the people, the citizens, the inferior nobles, noted well those signs of encouragement; and, to their minds, the Pope himself, in the person of his Vicar, looked benignly on the daring of Rienzi.

"The jubilee approaches,—the eyes of all Christendom will be directed hither. Here, where, from all quarters of the globe, men come for peace, shall they find discord?—seeking absolution, shall they perceive but crime? In the centre of God's dominion, shall they weep at your weakness?—in the seat of the martyred saints, shall they shudder at your vices?—in the fountain and source of Christ's law, shall they find all law unknown? You were the glory of the world—will you be its by-word? You were its example—will you be its warning? Rise, while it is yet time!—clear your roads from the bandits that infest them!—your walls from the hirelings that they harbour! Banish these civil discords, or the men—how proud, how great, soever—who maintain them! Pluck the scales from the hand of Fraud!—the sword from the hand of Violence!—the balance and the sword are the ancient attributes of Justice!—restore them to *her* again! This be your high task,—these be your great ends! Deem any man who opposes them a traitor to his country. Gain a victory greater than those of the Cæsars—a victory over yourselves! Let the pilgrims of the world behold the resurrection of Rome!

Make one epoch of the Jubilee of Religion and the Restoration of Law! Lay the sacrifice of your vanquished passions—the first-fruits of your renovated liberties—upon the very altar that these walls contain! and never! oh, never! since the world began, shall men have made a more grateful offering to their God!"

So intense was the sensation these words created in the audience—so breathless and overpowered did they leave the souls which they took by storm—that Rienzi had descended the scaffold, and already disappeared behind the curtain from which he had emerged, ere the crowd were fully aware that he had ceased.

The singularity of this sudden apparition—robed in mysterious splendour, and vanishing the moment its errand was fulfilled—gave additional effect to the words it had uttered. The whole character of that bold address became invested with a something preternatural and inspired; to the minds of the vulgar, the mortal was converted into the oracle; and, marvelling at the unhesitating courage with which their idol had rebuked and conjured the haughty barons,—each of whom they regarded in the light of sanctioned executioners, whose anger could be made manifest at once by the gibbet or the axe,—the people could not but superstitiously imagine that nothing less than authority from above could have gifted their leader with such hardihood, and preserved him from the danger it incurred. In fact, it was in this very courage of Rienzi that his safety consisted; he was placed in those circumstances where audacity is prudence. Had he been less bold, the nobles would have been more severe; but so great a licence of speech in an officer of the Holy See, they naturally imagined, was not unauthorised by the assent of the Pope, as well as by the approbation of the people. Those who did not (like Stephen Colonna) despise words as wind, shrank back from the task of punishing one whose voice might be the mere echo of the wishes of the pontiff. The dissensions of the nobles among each other, were no less favourable to Rienzi. He attacked a body, the members of which had no union.

"It is not *my* duty to slay him!" said one.

"I am not the representative of the barons!" said another.

"If Stephen Colonna heeds him not, it would be absurd, as well as dangerous, in a meaner man to make himself the champion of the order!" said a third.

The Colonna smiled approval, when Rienzi denounced an Orsini—an Orsini laughed aloud, when the eloquence burst over a Colonna. The lesser nobles were well pleased to hear attacks upon both: while, on the other hand, the Bishop, by the long impunity of Rienzi, had taken courage to sanction the conduct of his fellow-officer. He affected, indeed, at times, to blame the excess of his fervour, but it was always accompanied by the praises of his honesty; and the approbation of the Pope's Vicar confirmed the impression of the nobles as to the approbation of the Pope. Thus, from the very rashness of his enthusiasm had grown his security and success.

Still, however, when the barons had a little recovered from the stupor into which Rienzi had cast them, they looked round to each other; and their looks confessed their sense of the insolence of the orator, and the affront offered to themselves.

"*Per fede!*" quoth Reginaldo di Orsini, "this is past bearing,—the plebeian has gone too far!"

"Look at the populace below! how they murmur and gape,—and how their eyes sparkle—and what looks they bend at us!" said Luca di Savelli to his mortal enemy, Castruccio Malatesta: the sense of a common danger united in one moment, but only *for* a moment, the enmity of years.

"Diavolo!" muttered Raselli (Nina's father) to a baron, equally poor, "but the clerk has truth in his lips. 'Tis a pity he is not noble."

"What a clever brain marred!" said a Florentine merchant. "That man might be something, if he were sufficiently rich."

Adrian and Montreal were silent: the first seemed lost in thought,—the last was watching the various effects produced upon the audience.

"Silence!" proclaimed the officers. "Silence, for my Lord Vicar."

At this announcement, every eye turned to Raimond, who, rising with much clerical importance, thus addressed the assembly:—

"Although, Barons and Citizens of Rome, my well-beloved flock, and children,—I, no more than yourselves, anticipated the exact nature of the address ye have just heard,—and, albeit, I cannot feel unalloyed contentment at the manner, nor, I may say, at the whole matter of that fervent exhortation—*yet*" (laying great emphasis on the last word), "I cannot suffer you to depart without adding to the prayers of our Holy Father's servant, those, also, of his Holiness's spiritual representative. It is true! the Jubilee approaches! The Jubilee approaches—and yet our roads, even to the gates of Rome, are infested with murderous and godless ruffians! What pilgrim can venture across the Apennines to worship at the altars of St. Peter? The Jubilee approaches: what scandal shall it be to Rome if these shrines be without pilgrims—if the timid recoil from, if the bold fall victims to, the dangers of the way! Wherefore, I pray you all, citizens and chiefs alike,—I pray you all to lay aside those unhappy dissensions which have so long consumed the strength of our sacred city; and, uniting with each other in the ties of amity and brotherhood, to form a blessed league against the marauders of the road. I see amongst you, my Lords, many of the boasts and pillars of the state; but, alas! I think with grief and dismay on the causeless and idle hatred that has grown up between you!—a scandal to our city, and reflecting, let me add, my Lords, no honour on your faith as Christians, nor on your dignity as defenders of the Church."

Amongst the inferior nobles—along the seats of the judges and the men of letters—through the vast concourse of the people—ran a loud murmur of approbation at these words. The greater barons looked proudly, but not contemptuously, at the countenance of the prelate, and preserved a strict and unrevealing silence.

"In this holy spot," continued the Bishop, "let me beseech you to bury those fruitless animosities which have already cost enough of blood and treasure; and let us quit these walls with one common determination to evince our courage and display our chivalry only against our universal foes;—those ruffians who lay waste our fields, and infest our public ways,—the foes alike of the people we should protect, and the God whom we should serve!"

The Bishop resumed his seat; the nobles looked at each other without reply; the people began to whisper loudly amongst themselves; when, after a short pause, Adrian di Castello rose.

"Pardon me, my Lords, and you, reverend Father, if I, inexperienced in years and of little mark or dignity amongst you, presume to be the first to embrace the proposal we have just heard. Willingly do I renounce all ancient cause of enmity with any of my compeers. Fortunately for me, my long absence from Rome has swept from my remembrance the feuds and rivalries familiar to my early youth; and in this noble conclave I see but one man" (glancing at Martino di Porto, who sat sullenly looking down) "against whom I have, at any time, deemed it a duty to draw my sword; the gage that I once cast to that noble is yet, I rejoice to think, unredeemed. I withdraw it. Henceforth my only foes shall be the foes of Rome!"

"Nobly spoken!" said the Bishop, aloud.

"And," continued Adrian, casting down his glove amongst the nobles, "I throw, my Lords, the gage, thus resumed, amongst you all, in challenge to a wider rivalry, and a more noble field. I invite any man to vie with me in the zeal that he shall show to restore tranquillity to our roads, and order to our state. It is a contest in which, if I be vanquished with reluctance, I will yield the prize without envy. In ten days from this time, reverend Father, I will raise forty horsemen-at-arms, ready to obey whatever orders shall be agreed upon for the security of the Roman state. And you, O Romans, dismiss, I pray you, from your minds, those eloquent invectives against your fellow-citizens which ye have lately heard. All of us, of what rank soever, may have shared in the excesses of these unhappy times; let us endeavour, not to avenge nor to imitate, but to reform and to unite. And may the people hereafter find, that the true boast of a patrician is, that his power the better enables him to serve his country."

"Brave words!" quoth the smith, sneeringly.

"If they were all like him!" said the smith's neighbour.

"He has helped the nobles out of a dilemma," said Pandulfo.

"He has shown gray wit under young hairs," said an aged Malatesta.

"You have turned the tide, but not stemmed it, noble Adrian," whispered the ever-boding Montreal, as, amidst the murmurs of the general approbation, the young Colonna resumed his seat.

"How mean you?" said Adrian.

"That your soft words, like all patrician conciliations, have come too late."

Not another noble stirred, though they felt, perhaps, disposed to join in the general feeling of amnesty, and appeared, by signs and whispers, to applaud the speech of Adrian. They were too habituated to the ungracefulness of an unlettered pride, to bow themselves to address conciliating language either to the people or their foes. And Raimond, glancing round, and not willing that their unseemly silence should be long remarked, rose at once, to give it the best construction in his power.

"My son, thou hast spoken as a patriot and a Christian; by the approving silence of your peers we all feel that they share your sentiments. Break we up the meeting—its end is obtained. The manner of our proceeding against the leagued robbers of the road requires maturer consideration elsewhere. This day shall be an epoch in our history."

"It shall," quoth Cecco del Vecchio, gruffly, between his teeth.

"Children, my blessing upon you all!" concluded the Vicar, spreading his arms.

And in a few minutes more the crowd poured from the church. The different servitors and flag-bearers ranged themselves on the steps without, each train anxious for their master's precedence; and the nobles, gravely collecting in small knots, in the which was no mixture of rival blood, followed the crowd down the aisles. Soon rose again the din, and the noise, and the wrangling, and the oaths, of the hostile bands, as, with pain and labour, the Vicar's officers marshalled them in "order most disorderly."

But so true were Montreal's words to Adrian, that the populace already half forgot the young noble's generous appeal, and were only bitterly commenting on the ungracious silence of his brother Lords. What, too, to them was this crusade against the robbers of the road? They blamed the good Bishop for not saying boldly to the nobles—"*Ye* are the first robbers we must march against!" The popular discontents had gone far beyond palliatives; they had arrived at that point when the people longed less for reform than change. There are times when a revolution cannot be warded off; it must come—come alike by resistance or by concession. Woe to that race in which a revolution produces no fruits!—in which the thunderbolt smites the high place, but does not purify the air! To suffer in vain is often the lot of the noblest individuals; but when a People suffer in vain, let them curse themselves!

CHAPTER IV

THE AMBITIOUS CITIZEN, AND THE AMBITIOUS SOLDIER

The Bishop of Orvietto lingered last, to confer with Rienzi, who awaited him in the recesses of the Lateran. Raimond had the penetration not to be seduced into believing that the late scene could effect any reformation amongst the nobles, heal their divisions, or lead them actively against the infestors of the Campagna. But, as he detailed to Rienzi all that had occurred subsequent to the departure of that hero of the scene, he concluded with saying:—

"You will perceive from this, one good result will be produced: the first armed dissension—the first fray among the nobles—will seem like a breach of promise; and, to the people and to the Pope, a reasonable excuse for despairing of all amendment amongst the Barons,—an excuse which will sanction the efforts of the first, and the approval of the last."

"For such a fray we shall not long wait," answered Rienzi.

"I believe the prophecy," answered Raimond, smiling; "at present all runs well. Go you with us homeward?"

"Nay, I think it better to tarry here till the crowd is entirely dispersed; for if they were to see me, in their present excitement, they might insist on some rash and hasty enterprise. Besides, my Lord," added Rienzi, "with an ignorant people, however honest and enthusiastic, this rule must be rigidly observed—stale not your presence by custom. Never may men like me, who have no external rank, appear amongst the crowd, save on those occasions when the mind is itself a rank."

"That is true, as you have no train," answered Raimond, thinking of his own well-liveried menials. "Adieu, then! we shall meet soon."

"Ay, at Philippi, my Lord. Reverend Father, your blessing!"

It was some time subsequent to this conference that Rienzi quitted the sacred edifice. As he stood on the steps of the church—now silent and deserted—the hour that precedes the brief twilight of the South lent its magic to the view. There he beheld the sweeping arches of the mighty Aqueduct extending far along the scene, and backed by the distant and purpled hills. Before—to the right—rose the gate which took its Roman name from the Cœlian Mount, at whose declivity it yet stands. Beyond—from the height of the steps—he saw the villages scattered through the gray Campagna, whitening in the sloped sun; and in the furthest distance the mountain shadows began to darken over the roofs of the ancient Tusculum, and the second Alban * city, which yet rises, in desolate neglect, above the vanished palaces of Pompey and Domitian.

The Roman stood absorbed and motionless for some moments, gazing on the scene, and inhaling the sweet balm of the mellow air. It was the soft spring-time—the season of flowers, and green leaves, and whispering winds—the pastoral May of Italia's poets: but hushed was the voice of song on the banks of the Tiber—the reeds gave music no more. From the sacred Mount

* The first Alba—the Alba Longa—whose origin Fable ascribes to Ascanius, was destroyed by Tullus Hostilius. The second Alba, or modern Albano, was erected on the plain below the ancient town, a little before the time of Nero.

in which Saturn held his home, the Dryad and the Nymph, and Italy's native Sylvan, were gone for ever. Rienzi's original nature—its enthusiasm—its veneration for the past—its love of the beautiful and the great—that very attachment to the graces and pomp which give so florid a character to the harsh realities of life, and which power afterwards too luxuriantly developed; the exuberance of thoughts and fancies, which poured itself from his lips in so brilliant and inexhaustible a flood—all bespoke those intellectual and imaginative biasses, which, in calmer times, might have raised him in literature to a more indisputable eminence than that to which action can ever lead; and something of such consciousness crossed his spirit at that moment.

"Happier had it been for me," thought he, "had I never looked out from my own heart upon the world. I had all within me that makes contentment of the present, because I had that which can make me forget the present. I had the power to re-people—to create: the legends and dreams of old—the divine faculty of verse, in which the beautiful superfluities of the heart can pour themselves—these were mine! Petrarch chose wisely for himself! To address the world, but from without the world; to persuade—to excite—to command,—for these are the aim and glory of ambition;—but to shun its tumult, and its toil! His the quiet cell which he fills with the shapes of beauty—the solitude, from which he can banish the evil times whereon we are fallen, but in which he can dream back the great hearts and the glorious epochs of the past. For me—to what cares I am wedded! to what labours I am bound! what instruments I must use! what disguises I must assume! to tricks and artifice

I must bow my pride! base are my enemies—uncertain my friends! and verily, in this struggle with blinded and mean men, the soul itself becomes warped and dwarfish. Patient and darkling, the Means creep through caves and the soiling mire, to gain at last the light which is the End."

In these reflections there was a truth, the whole gloom and sadness of which the Roman had not yet experienced. However august be the object we propose to ourselves, every less worthy path we take to insure it distorts the mental sight of our ambition; and the means, by degrees, abase the end to their own standard. This is the true misfortune of a man nobler than his age—that the instruments he must use soil himself: half he reforms his times; but half, too, the times will corrupt the reformer. His own craft undermines his safety;—the people, whom he himself accustoms to a false excitement, perpetually crave it; and when their ruler ceases to seduce their fancy, he falls their victim. The reform he makes by these means is hollow and momentary—it is swept away with himself: it was but the trick—the show—the wasted genius of a conjuror: the curtain falls—the magic is over—the cup and balls are kicked aside. Better one slow step in enlightenment,—which being made by the reason of a whole people, cannot recede,—than these sudden flashes in the depth of the general night, which the darkness, by contrast doubly dark, swallows up everlastingly again!

As, slowly and musingly, Rienzi turned to quit the church, he felt a light touch upon his shoulder.

"Fair evening to you, Sir Scholar," said a frank voice.

"To you, I return the courtesy," answered Rienzi,

gazing upon the person who thus suddenly accosted him, and in whose white cross and martial bearing the reader recognises the Knight of St. John.

" You know me not, I think? " said Montreal; " but that matters little, we may easily commence our acquaintance: for me, indeed, I am fortunate enough to have made myself already acquainted with you."

" Possibly we have met elsewhere, at the house of one of those nobles to whose rank you seem to belong? "

" Belong! no, not exactly! " returned Montreal, proudly. " High-born and great as your magnates deem themselves, I would not, while the mountains can yield one free spot for my footstep, change my place in the world's many grades for theirs. To the brave, there is but one sort of plebeian, and that is the coward. But you, sage Rienzi," continued the Knight, in a gayer tone, " I have seen in more stirring scenes than the hall of a Roman Baron."

Rienzi glanced keenly at Montreal, who met his eye with an open brow.

" Yes! " resumed the Knight—" but let us walk on; suffer me for a few moments to be your companion. Yes! I have listened to you—the other eve, when you addressed the populace, and to-day, when you rebuked the nobles; and at midnight, too, not long since, when (your ear, fair Sir!—lower, it is a secret!) —at midnight, too, when you administered the oath of brotherhood to the bold conspirators, on the ruined Aventine! "

As he concluded, the Knight drew himself aside to watch, upon Rienzi's countenance, the effect which his words might produce.

A slight tremor passed over the frame of the conspirator—for so, unless the conspiracy succeed, would Rienzi be termed, by others than Montreal: he turned abruptly round to confront the Knight, and placed his hand involuntarily on his sword, but presently relinquished the grasp.

"Ha!" said the Roman, slowly, "if this be true, fall Rome! There is treason even among the free!"

"No treason, brave Sir!" answered Montreal; "I possess thy secret—but none have betrayed it to me."

"And is it as friend or foe that thou hast learned it?"

"That as it may be," returned Montreal, carelessly. "Enough, at present, that I could send thee to the gibbet, if I said but a word,—to show my power to be thy foe: enough, that I have not done it, to prove my disposition to be thy friend."

"Thou mistakest, stranger! that man does not live who could shed my blood in the streets of Rome! The gibbet! Little dost thou know of the power which surrounds Rienzi."

These words were said with some scorn and bitterness; but, after a moment's pause, Rienzi resumed, more calmly:—

"By the cross on thy mantle, thou belongest to one of the proudest orders of knighthood: thou art a foreigner, and a cavalier. What generous sympathies can convert thee into a friend of the Roman people?"

"Cola di Rienzi," returned Montreal, "the sympathies that unite us are those which unite all men who, by their own efforts, rise above the herd. True, I was born noble—but powerless and poor: at my beck now move, from city to city, the armed instruments of authority: my breath is the law of thousands. This empire I have not inherited; I won it by a cool brain and a fearless arm. Know me for Walter de Montreal; is it not a name that speaks a spirit kindred to thine own? Is not ambition a common sentiment between us? I do not marshal soldiers for gain only, though men have termed me avaricious—nor butcher peasants for the love of blood, though men have called me cruel. Arms and wealth are the sinews of power; it is power that I desire;—thou, bold Rienzi, strugglest thou not for the same? Is it the rank breath of the garlic-chewing mob—is it the whispered envy of schoolmen—is it the hollow mouthing of boys who call thee patriot and freeman, words to trick the ear—that will content thee? These are but *thy* instruments to *power*. Have I spoken truly?"

Whatever distaste Rienzi might conceive at this speech he masked effectually. "Certes," said he, "it would be in vain, renowned Captain, to deny that I seek but that power of which thou speakest. But what union can there be between the ambition of a Roman citizen and the leader of paid armies that take their cause only according to their hire—to-day, fight for liberty in Florence—to-morrow, for tyranny in Bologna? Pardon my frankness; for in this age that is deemed no disgrace which I impute to thy armies. Valour and generalship are held to consecrate any cause they distinguish; and he who is the master of princes, may be well honoured by them as their equal."

"We are entering into a less deserted quarter of the town," said the Knight; "is there no secret place—no Aventine—in this direction, where we can confer?"

"Hush!" replied Rienzi, cautiously looking round.

"I thank thee, noble Montreal, for the hint; nor may it be well for us to be seen together. Wilt thou deign to follow me to my home, by the Palatine Bridge? * there we can converse undisturbed and secure."

"Be it so," said Montreal, falling back.

With a quick and hurried step, Rienzi passed through the town, in which, wherever he was discovered, the scattered citizens saluted him with marked respect; and, turning through a labyrinth of dark alleys, as if to shun the more public thoroughfares, arrived at length at a broad space near the river. The first stars of night shone down on the ancient temple of Fortuna Virilis, which the chances of Time had already converted into the Church of St. Mary of Egypt; and facing the twice-hallowed edifice stood the house of Rienzi.

"It is a fair omen to have my mansion facing the ancient Temple of Fortune," said Rienzi, smiling, as Montreal followed the Roman into the chamber I have already described.

"Yet Valour need never pray to Fortune," said the Knight; "the first commands the last."

Long was the conference between these two men, the most enterprising of their age. Meanwhile, let me make the reader somewhat better acquainted with the character and designs of Montreal, than the hurry of events has yet permitted him to become.

Walter de Montreal, generally known in the chronicles of Italy by the designation of Fra Moreale, had

* The picturesque ruins shown at this day as having once been the habitation of the celebrated Cola di Rienzi, were long asserted by the antiquarians to have belonged to another Cola or Nicola. I believe, however that the dispute has been lately decided: and, indeed, no one but an antiquary, and that a Roman one, could suppose that there were two Colas to whom the inscription on the house would apply.

passed into Italy—a bold adventurer, worthy to become a successor of those roving Normans (from one of the most eminent of whom, by the mother's side, he claimed descent) who had formerly played so strange a part in the chivalric errantry of Europe,—realising the fables of Amadis and Palmerin—(each knight, in himself a host), winning territories and oversetting thrones; acknowledging no laws save those of knighthood; never confounding themselves with the tribe amongst which they settled; incapable of becoming citizens, and scarcely contented with aspiring to be kings. At that time, Italy was the India of all those well-born and penniless adventurers who, like Montreal, had inflamed their imagination by the ballads and legends of the Roberts and the Godfreys of old; who had trained themselves from youth to manage the barb, and bear, through the heats of summer, the weight of arms; and who, passing into an effeminate and distracted land, had only to exhibit bravery in order to command wealth. It was considered no disgrace for some powerful chieftain to collect together a band of these hardy aliens,—to subsist amidst the mountains on booty and pillage,—to make war upon tyrant or republic, as interest suggested, and to sell, at enormous stipends, the immunities of peace. Sometimes they hired themselves to one state to protect it against the other; and the next year beheld them in the field against their former employers. These bands of Northern stipendiaries assumed, therefore, a civil, as well as a military, importance; they were as indispensable to the safety of one state as they were destructive to the security of all. But five years before the present date, the Florentine Republic had hired the services of a celebrated leader of these foreign soldiers,—Gualtier, Duke of Athens. By acclamation, the people themselves had elected that warrior to the state of prince, or tyrant, of their state; before the year was completed, they revolted against his cruelties, or rather against his exactions,—for, despite all the boasts of their historians, they felt an attack on their purses more deeply than an assault on their liberties,—they had chased him from their city, and once more proclaimed themselves a Republic. The bravest, and most favoured of the soldiers of the Duke of Athens had been Walter de Montreal; he had shared the rise and the downfall of his chief. Amongst popular commotions, the acute and observant mind of the Knight of St. John had learned no mean civil experience; he had learned to sound a people—to know how far they would endure—to construe the signs of revolution—to be a reader of the times. After the downfall of the Duke of Athens, as a Free Companion, in other words a Freebooter, Montreal had augmented under the fierce Werner his riches and his renown. At present without employment worthy his spirit of enterprise and intrigue, the disordered and chiefless state of Rome had attracted him thither. In the league he had proposed to Colonna—in the suggestions he had made to the vanity of that Signor—his own object was to render his services indispensable—to constitute himself the head of the soldiery whom his proposed designs would render necessary to the ambition of the Colonna, could it be excited—and, in the vastness of his hardy genius for enterprise, he probably foresaw that the command of such a force would be, in reality, the command of Rome; a counter-revolution might easily unseat the Colonna and elect himself to the principality. It had sometimes been the custom of Roman, as of other Italian, States, to prefer for a chief magistrate, under the title of *Podesta,* a foreigner to a native. And Montreal hoped that he might possibly become to Rome what the Duke of Athens had been to Florence—an ambition he knew well enough to be above the gentleman of Provence, but not above the leader of an army. But, as we have already seen, his sagacity perceived at once that he could not move the aged head of the patricians to those hardy and perilous measures which were necessary to the attainment of supreme power. Contented with his present station, and taught moderation by his age and his past reverses, Stephen Colonna was not the man to risk a scaffold from the hope to gain a throne. The contempt which the old patrician professed for the people, and their idol, also taught the deep-thinking Montreal that, if the Colonna possessed not the ambition, neither did he possess the policy, requisite for empire. The Knight found his caution against Rienzi in vain, and he turned to Rienzi himself. Little cared the Knight of St. John which party were uppermost—prince or people—so that his own objects were attained; in fact, he had studied the humours of a people, not in order to serve, but to rule them; and, believing all men actuated by a similar ambition, he imagined that, whether a demagogue or a patrician reigned, the people were equally to be victims, and that the cry of "Order" on the one hand, or of "Liberty" on the other, was but the mere pretext by which the energy of one man sought to justify his ambition over the herd. Deeming himself one of the most honourable spirits of his age, he believed in no honour which *he* was unable to feel; and, sceptic in virtue. was therefore credulous of vice.

But the boldness of his own nature inclined him, perhaps, rather to the adventurous Rienzi than to the self-complacent Colonna; and he considered that to the safety of the first he and his armed minions might be even more necessary than to that of the last. At present his main object was to learn from Rienzi the exact strength which he possessed, and how far he was prepared for any actual revolt.

The acute Roman took care, on the one hand, how he betrayed to the Knight more than he yet knew, or he disgusted him by apparent reserve on the other. Crafty as Montreal was, he possessed not that wonderful art of mastering others which was so pre-eminently the gift of the eloquent and profound Rienzi, and the difference between the grades of their intellect was visible in their present conference.

"I see," said Rienzi, "that amidst all the events which have lately smiled upon my ambition, none is so favourable as that which assures me of your countenance and friendship. In truth, I require some armed alliance. Would you believe it, our friends, so bold in private meetings, yet shrink from a public explosion. They fear not the patricians, but the soldiery of the patricians; for it is the remarkable feature in the Italian courage, that they have no terror for each other, but the casque and sword of a foreign hireling make them quail like deer."

"They will welcome gladly, then, the assurance that such hirelings shall be in their service—not against them; and as many as you desire for the revolution, so many shall you receive."

"But the pay and the conditions," said Rienzi, with his dry, sarcastic smile. "How shall we arrange the first. and what shall we hold to be the second?"

"That is an affair easily concluded," replied Montreal. "For me, to tell you frankly, the glory and excitement of so great a revulsion would alone suffice. I like to feel myself necessary to the completion of high events. For my men it is otherwise. Your first act will be to seize the revenues of the state. Well, whatever they amount to, the product of the first year, great or small, shall be divided amongst us. You the one half, I and my men the other half."

"It is much," said Rienzi, gravely, and as if in calculation,—"but Rome cannot purchase her liberties too dearly. So be it then decided."

"Amen!—and now, then, what is your force? for these eighty or a hundred signors of the Aventine,—worthy men, doubtless,—scarce suffice for a revolt!"

Gazing cautiously round the room, the Roman placed his hand on Montreal's arm—

"Between you and me, it requires time to cement it. We shall be unable to stir these five weeks. I have too rashly anticipated the period. The corn is indeed cut, but I must now, by private adjuration and address, bind up the scattered sheaves."

"Five weeks," repeated Montreal; "that is far longer than I anticipated."

"What I desire," continued Rienzi, fixing his searching eyes upon Montreal, "is, that, in the meanwhile, we should preserve a profound calm,—we should remove every suspicion. I shall bury myself in my studies, and convoke no more meetings."

"Well——"

"And for yourself, noble Knight, might I venture to dictate, I would pray you to mix with the nobles—to profess for me and for the people the profoundest contempt—and to contribute to rock them yet more in the cradle of their false security. Meanwhile, you could quietly withdraw as many of the armed mercenaries as you influence from Rome, and leave the nobles without their only defenders. Collecting these hardy warriors in the recesses of the mountains, a day's march from hence, we may be able to summon them at need, and they shall appear at our gates, and in the midst of our rising—hailed as deliverers by the nobles, but in reality allies with the people. In the confusion and despair of our enemies at discovering their mistake, they will fly from the city."

"And its revenues and its empire will become the appanage of the hardy soldier and the intriguing demagogue!" cried Montreal, with a laugh.

"Sir Knight, the division shall be equal."

"Agreed!"

"And now, noble Montreal, a flask of our best vintage!" said Rienzi, changing his tone.

"You know the Provençals," answered Montreal, gaily.

The wine was brought, the conversation became free and familiar, and Montreal, whose craft was acquired, and whose frankness was natural, unwittingly committed his secret projects and ambition more nakedly to Rienzi than he had designed to do. They parted apparently the best of friends.

"By the way," said Rienzi, as they drained the last goblet, "Stephen Colonna betakes him to Corneto, with a convoy of corn, on the 19th. Will it not be as well if you join him? You can take that opportunity to whisper discontent to the mercenaries that accompany him on his mission, and induce them to our plan."

"I thought of that before," returned Montreal; "it shall be done. For the present, farewell!"

"'His barb, and his sword,
And his lady, the peerless,
Are all that are prized
By Orlando the fearless.

"'Success to the Norman,
The darling of story;
His glory is pleasure—
His pleasure is glory.'"

Chanting this rude ditty as he resumed his mantle, the Knight waved his hand to Rienzi, and departed.

Rienzi watched the receding form of his guest with an expression of hate and fear upon his countenance. "Give that man the power," he muttered, "and he may be a second Totila.* Methinks I see, in his griping and ferocious nature,—through all the gloss of its gaiety and knightly grace,—the very personification of our old Gothic foes. I trust I have lulled him! Verily, two suns could no more blaze in one hemisphere, than Walter de Montreal and Cola di Rienzi live in the same city. The star-seers tell us that we feel a secret and uncontrollable antipathy to those whose astral influences destine them to work us evil; such antipathy do I feel for yon fair-faced homicide. Cross not my path, Montreal!—cross not my path!"

With this soliloquy Rienzi turned within, and, retiring to his apartment, was seen no more that night.

* Innocent VI., some years afterwards, proclaimed Montreal to be *worse* than Totila.

CHAPTER V

THE PROCESSION OF THE BARONS.—THE BEGINNING OF THE END

It was the morning of the 19th of May, the air was brisk and clear, and the sun, which had just risen, shone cheerily upon the glittering casques and spears of a gallant procession of armed horsemen, sweeping through the long and principal street of Rome. The neighing of the horses, the ringing of the hoofs, the dazzle of the armour, and the tossing to and fro of the standards, adorned with the proud insignia of the Colonna, presented one of the gay and brilliant spectacles peculiar to the middle ages.

At the head of the troop, on a stout palfrey, rode Stephen Colonna. At his right was the Knight of Provence, curbing, with an easy hand, a slight, but fiery steed of the Arab race: behind him followed two squires, the one leading his war-horse, the other bearing his lance and helmet. At the left of Stephen Colonna rode Adrian, grave and silent, and replying only by monosyllables to the gay bavardage of the Knight of Provence. A considerable number of the flower of the Roman nobles followed the old Baron; and the train was closed by a serried troop of foreign horsemen, completely armed.

There was no crowd in the street,—the citizens looked with seeming apathy at the procession from their half-closed shops.

"Have these Romans no passion for shows?" asked Montreal; "if they could be more easily amused they would be more easily governed."

"Oh, Rienzi, and such buffoons, amuse them. We do better,—we terrify!" replied Stephen.

"What sings the troubadour, Lord Adrian?" said Montreal.

"'Smiles, false smiles, should form the school
For those who rise, and those who rule:
The brave they trick, the fair subdue,
Kings deceive, and States undo.
Smiles, false smiles!

"'Frowns, true frowns, ourselves betray,
The brave arouse, the fair dismay,
Sting the pride, which blood must heal,
Mix the bowl, and point the steel.
Frowns, true frowns!'

"The lay is of France, Signor; yet methinks it brings its wisdom from Italy;—for the serpent smile is your countrymen's proper distinction, and the frown ill becomes them."

"Sir Knight," replied Adrian, sharply, and incensed at the taunt, "you foreigners have taught us how to frown:—a virtue sometimes."

"But not wisdom, unless the hand could maintain what the brow menaced," returned Montreal, with haughtiness; for he had much of the Franc vivacity which often overcame his prudence; and he had conceived a secret pique against Adrian since their interview at Stephen's palace.

"Sir Knight," answered Adrian, colouring, "our conversation may lead to warmer words than I would desire to have with one who has rendered me so gallant a service."

"Nay, then, let us go back to the troubadours," said Montreal, indifferently. "Forgive me if I do not think highly, in general, of Italian honour, or Italian valour; *your* valour I acknowledge, for I have witnessed it, and valour and honour go together,—let that suffice!"

As Adrian was about to answer, his eye fell suddenly on the burly form of Cecco del Vecchio, who was leaning his bare and brawny arms over his anvil, and gazing, with a smile, upon the group. There was something in that smile which turned the current of Adrian's thoughts, and which he could not contemplate without an unaccountable misgiving.

"A strong villain, that," said Montreal, also eyeing the smith. "I should like to enlist him. Fellow!" cried he, aloud, "you have an arm that were as fit to wield the sword as to fashion it. Desert your anvil, and follow the fortunes of Fra Moreale!"

The smith nodded his head. "Signor Cavalier," said he, gravely, "we poor men have no passion for war; we want not to kill others—we desire only ourselves to live,—if you will let us!"

"By the Holy Mother, a slavish answer! But you Romans——"

"*Are* slaves!" interrupted the smith, turning away to the interior of his forge.

"The dog is mutinous!" said the old Colonna. And as the band swept on, the rude foreigners, encouraged by their leaders, had each some taunt or jest, uttered in a barbarous attempt at the southern *patois*, for the lazy giant, as he again appeared in front of his forge, leaning on his anvil as before, and betraying no sign of attention to his insulters, save by a heightened glow of his swarthy visage;—and so the gallant procession passed through the streets, and quitted the Eternal City.

There was a long interval of deep silence—of general calm—throughout the whole of Rome: the shops were still but half-opened; no man betook himself to his business; it was like the commencement of some holiday, when indolence precedes enjoyment.

About noon, a few small knots of men might be seen scattered about the streets, whispering to each other, but soon dispersing; and every now and then, a single passenger, generally habited in the long robes used by the men of letters, or in the more sombre garb of monks, passed hurriedly up the street towards the Church of St. Mary of Egypt, once the Temple of Fortune. Then, again, all was solitary and deserted. Suddenly, there was heard *the sound of a single trumpet!* It swelled—it gathered on the ear. Cecco del Vecchio looked up from his anvil! *A solitary horseman* paced slowly by the forge, and wound a long loud blast of the trumpet suspended round his neck, as he passed through the middle of the street. Then might you see a crowd, suddenly, and as by magic, appear emerging from every corner; the street became thronged with multitudes; but it was only by the tramp of their feet, and an indistinct and low murmur, that they broke the silence. Again the horseman wound his trump, and when the note ceased, he cried aloud—"Friends and Romans! to-morrow, at dawn of day, let each man find himself unarmed before the Church of St. Angelo. Cola di Rienzi convenes the Romans to provide for the good state of Rome." A shout, that seemed to shake the bases of the seven hills, broke forth at the end of this brief exhortation; the horseman rode slowly on, and the crowd followed.—This was the commencement of the Revolution!

CHAPTER VI

THE CONSPIRATOR BECOMES THE MAGISTRATE

At midnight, when the rest of the city seemed hushed in rest, lights were streaming from the windows of the Church of St. Angelo. Breaking from its echoing aisles, the long and solemn notes of sacred music stole at frequent intervals upon the air. Rienzi was praying within the church; thirty masses consumed the hours from night till morn, and all the sanction of religion was invoked to consecrate the enterprise of liberty.* The sun had long risen, and the crowd had long been assembled before the church door, and in vast streams along every street that led to it,—when the bell of the church tolled out long and merrily; and as it ceased, the voices of the choristers within chanted the following hymn, in which were somewhat strikingly, though barbarously, blended, the spirit of the classic patriotism with the fervour of religious zeal:—

THE ROMAN HYMN OF LIBERTY

Let the mountains exult around! †
On her seven-hill'd throne renown'd,
Once more old Rome is crown'd!
Jubilate!

* In fact, I apprehend that if ever the life of Cola di Rienzi shall be written by a hand worthy of the task, *it will be shown that a strong religious feeling was blended with the political enthusiasm of the people,—the religious feeling of a premature and crude reformation, the legacy of Arnold of Brescia.* It was not, however, one excited against the priests, but favoured by them. The principal conventual orders declared for the Revolution.

† "Exultent in circuito Vestro Montes," &c.—Let the mountains exult around! So begins Rienzi's letter to the Senate and Roman people: preserved by Hocsemius.

Sing out, O Vale and Wave!
Look up from each laurell'd grave,
Bright dust of the deathless brave!
Jubilate!

Pale Vision, what art thou?—Lo,
From Time's dark deeps,
Like a wind, It sweeps,
Like a Wind, when the tempests blow;

A shadowy form—as a giant ghost—
It stands in the midst of the armed host!
The dead man's shroud on Its awful limbs;
And the gloom of Its presence the day-light dims:
And the trembling world looks on aghast—
All hail to the SOUL OF THE MIGHTY PAST!
Hail! all hail!

As we speak—as we hallow—It moves, It breathes;
From its clouded crest bud the laurel wreaths—
As a Sun that leaps up from the arms of Night,
The shadow takes shape, and the gloom takes light.
Hail! all hail!

THE SOUL OF THE PAST, again
To its ancient home,
In the hearts of Rome,
Hath come to resume its reign!

O Fame, with a prophet's voice,
Bid the ends of the earth rejoice!
Wherever the Proud are Strong,
And Right is oppress'd by Wrong;—
Wherever the day dim shines
Through the cell where the captive pines;—
Go forth, with a trumpet's sound!
And tell to the Nations round—
On the Hills which the Heroes trod—
In the shrines of the Saints of God—
In the Cæsars' hall, and the Martyrs' prison—
That the slumber is broke, and the Sleeper arisen!
That the reign of the Goth and the Vandal is o'er:
And earth feels the tread of THE ROMAN once more.

As the hymn ended, the gate of the church opened; the crowd gave way on either side, and, preceded by three of the young nobles of the inferior order, bearing standards of allegorical design, depicting the triumph of Liberty, Justice, and Concord, forth issued Rienzi, clad in complete armour, the helmet alone excepted. His face was pale with watching and intense excitement—but stern, grave, and solemnly composed; and its expression so repelled any vociferous and vulgar burst of feeling, that those who beheld it hushed the shout on their lips, and stilled, by a simultaneous cry of reproof, the gratulations of the crowd behind. Side by side with Rienzi moved Raimond, Bishop of Orvietto: and behind, marching two by two, followed a hundred men-at-arms. In complete silence the procession began its way, until, as it approached the Capitol, the awe of the crowd gradually vanished, and thousands upon thousands of voices rent the air with shouts of exultation and joy.

Arrived at the foot of the great staircase, which then made the principal ascent to the square of the Capitol, the procession halted; and as the crowd filled up that vast space in front—adorned and hallowed by many of the most majestic columns of the temples of old—Rienzi addressed the Populace, whom he had suddenly elevated into a People.

He depicted forcibly the servitude and misery of the citizens—the utter absence of all law—the want even of common security to life and property. He declared that, undaunted by the peril he incurred, he devoted his life to the regeneration of their common country; and he solemnly appealed to the people to assist the enterprise, and at once to sanction and consolidate the Revolution by an established code of law

Forth issued Rienzi, clad in complete armour.

and a Constitutional Assembly. He then ordered the chart and outline of the Constitution he proposed, to be read by the Herald to the multitude.

It created,—or rather revived, with new privileges and powers,—a Representative Assembly of Councillors. It proclaimed, as its first law, one that seems simple enough to our happier times, but never hitherto executed at Rome: Every wilful homicide, of whatever rank, was to be punished by death. It enacted, that no private noble or citizen should be suffered to maintain fortifications and garrisons in the city or the country; that the gates and bridges of the State should be under the control of whomsoever should be elected Chief Magistrate. It forbade all harbour of brigands, mercenaries, and robbers, on payment of a thousand marks of silver; and it made the Barons who possessed the neighbouring territories responsible for the safety of the roads, and the transport of merchandise. It took under the protection of the State the widow and the orphan. It appointed, in each of the quarters of the city, an armed militia, whom the tolling of the bell of the Capitol, at any hour, was to assemble to the protection of the State. It ordained, that in each harbour of the coast, a vessel should be stationed, for the safeguard of commerce. It decreed the sum of one hundred florins to the heirs of every man who died in the defence of Rome; and it devoted the public revenues to the service and protection of the State.

Such, moderate at once and effectual, was the outline of the New Constitution; and it may amuse the reader to consider how great must have been the previous disorders of the city, when the common and elementary provisions of civilisation and security made the character of the code proposed, and the limit of a popular revolution.

The most rapturous shouts followed this sketch of the New Constitution: and, amidst the clamour, up rose the huge form of Cecco del Vecchio. Despite his condition, he was a man of great importance at the present crisis: his zeal and his courage, and, perhaps, still more, his brute passion and stubborn prejudice, had made him popular. The lower order of mechanics looked to him as their head and representative; out, then, he spake loud and fearlessly,—speaking well, because his mind was full of what he had to say.

"Countrymen and Citizens!—This New Constitution meets with your approbation—so it ought. But what are good laws, if we do not have good men to execute them? Who can execute a law so well as the man who designs it? If you ask me to give you a notion how to make a good shield, and my notion pleases you, would you ask me, or another smith, to make it for you? If you ask another, he may make a good shield, but it would not be the same as that which I should have made, and the description of which contented you. Cola di Rienzi has proposed a Code of Law that shall be our shield. Who should see that the shield become what he proposes, but Cola di Rienzi? Romans! I suggest that Cola di Rienzi be intrusted by the people with the authority, by whatsoever name he pleases, of carrying the New Constitution into effect;—and whatever be the means, we, the People, will bear him harmless."

"Long life to Rienzi!—long live Cecco del Vecchio! He hath spoken well!—none but the Lawmaker shall be the Governor!"

Such were the acclamations which greeted the ambitious heart of the Scholar. The voice of the people invested him with the supreme power. He had created a Commonwealth—to become, if he desired it, a Despot!

CHAPTER VII

LOOKING AFTER THE HALTER WHEN THE MARE IS STOLEN

While such were the events at Rome, a servitor of Stephen Colonna was already on his way to Corneto. The astonishment with which the old Baron received the intelligence may be easily imagined. He lost not a moment in convening his troop; and, while in all the bustle of departure, the Knight of St. John abruptly entered his presence. His mien had lost its usual frank composure.

"How is this?" said he, hastily; "a revolt?—Rienzi sovereign of Rome?—can the news be believed?"

"It is too true!" said Colonna, with a bitter smile. "Where shall we hang him on our return?"

"Talk not so wildly, Sir Baron," replied Montreal, discourteously; "Rienzi is stronger than you think for. I know what men are, and you only know what noblemen are! Where is your kinsman, Adrian?"

"He is here, noble Montreal," said Stephen, shrugging his shoulders, with a half-disdainful smile at the rebuke, which he thought it more prudent not to resent; "he is here!—see him enter!"

"You have heard the news?" exclaimed Montreal.

"I have."

"And despise the revolution?"

"I fear it!"

"Then you have some sense in you. But this is none of my affair: I will not interrupt your consultations. Adieu for the present!" and, ere Stephen could prevent him, the Knight had quitted the chamber.

"What means this demagogue?" Montreal muttered to himself. "Would he trick me?—has he got rid of my presence in order to monopolise all the profit of the enterprise? I fear me so!—the cunning Roman! We northern warriors could never compete with the intellect of these Italians but for their cowardice. But what shall be done? I have already bid Rodolf communicate with the brigands, and they are on the eve of departure from their present lord. Well! let it be so! Better that I should first break the power of the Barons, and then make my own terms, sword in hand, with the plebeian. And if I fail in this,—sweet Adeline! I shall see thee again!—that is some comfort!—and Louis of Hungary will bid high for the arm and brain of Walter de Montreal. What, ho! Rodolf!" he exclaimed aloud, as the sturdy form of the trooper, half-armed and half-intoxicated, reeled along the court-yard. "Knave! art thou drunk at this hour?"

"Drunk or sober," answered Rodolf, bending low, "I am at thy bidding."

"Well said!—are thy friends ripe for the saddle?"

"Eighty of them already tired of idleness and the dull air of Rome, will fly wherever Sir Walter de Montreal wishes."

"Hasten, then,—bid them mount; we go not hence with the Colonna—we leave while they are yet talking!—Bid my squires attend me!"

And when Stephen Colonna was settling himself on

his palfrey, he heard, for the first time, that the Knight of Provence, Rodolf the trooper, and eighty of the stipendiaries, had already departed,—whither, none knew.

"To precede us to Rome! gallant barbarian!" said Colonna. "Sirs, on!"

CHAPTER VIII

THE ATTACK—THE RETREAT—THE ELECTION—AND THE ADHESION

Arriving at Rome, the company of the Colonna found the gates barred, and the walls manned. Stephen bade advance his trumpeters, with one of his captains, imperiously to demand admittance.

"We have orders," replied the chief of the town-guard, "to admit none who bear arms, flags, or trumpets. Let the Lords Colonna dismiss their train, and they are welcome."

"Whose are these insolent mandates?" asked the captain.

"Those of the Lord Bishop of Orvietto and Cola di Rienzi, joint protectors of the Buono Stato."*

The captain of the Colonna returned to his chief with these tidings. The rage of Stephen was indescribable. "Go back," he cried, as soon as he could summon voice, "and say, that, if the gates are not forthwith opened to me and mine, the blood of the plebeians be on their own head. As for Raimond, Vicars of the Pope have high spiritual authority, none temporal. Let him prescribe a fast, and he shall be

* Good Estate.

obeyed; but, for the rash Rienzi, say that Stephen Colonna will seek him in the Capitol to-morrow, for the purpose of throwing him out of the highest window."

These messages the envoy failed not to deliver.

The captain of the Romans was equally stern in his reply.

"Declare to your Lord," said he, "that Rome holds him and his as rebels and traitors; and that the moment you regain your troop, our archers receive our command to draw their bows—in the name of the Pope, the City, and the Liberator."

This threat was executed to the letter; and ere the old Baron had time to draw up his men in the best array, the gates were thrown open, and a well-armed, if undisciplined, multitude poured forth, with fierce shouts, clashing their arms, and advancing the azure banners of the Roman State. So desperate their charge, and so great their numbers, that the Barons, after a short and tumultuous conflict, were driven back, and chased by their pursuers for more than a mile from the walls of the city.

As soon as the Barons recovered their disorder and dismay, a hasty council was held, at which various and contradictory opinions were loudly urged. Some were for departing on the instant to Palestrina, which belonged to the Colonna, and possessed an almost inaccessible fortress. Others were for dispersing, and entering peaceably, and in detached parties, through the other gates. Stephen Colonna—himself incensed and disturbed from his usual self-command—was unable to preserve his authority; Luca di Savelli,* a timid,

* The more correct orthography were Luca di Savello, but the one in the text is preserved as more familiar to the English reader.

though treacherous and subtle man, already turned his horse's head, and summoned his men to follow him to his castle in Romagna, when the old Colonna bethought himself of a method by which to keep his band from a disunion that he had the sense to perceive would prove fatal to the common cause. He proposed that they should at once repair to Palestrina, and there fortify themselves; while one of the chiefs should be selected to enter Rome alone, and apparently submissive, to examine the strength of Rienzi; and with the discretionary power to resist if possible,—or to make the best terms he could for the admission of the rest.

"And who," asked Savelli, sneeringly, "will undertake this dangerous mission? Who, unarmed and alone, will expose himself to the rage of the fiercest populace of Italy, and the caprice of a demagogue in the first flush of his power?"

The Barons and the Captains looked at each other in silence. Savelli laughed.

Hitherto Adrian had taken no part in the conference, and but little in the previous contest. He now came to the support of his kinsman.

"Signors!" said he, "I will undertake this mission,—but on mine own account, independently of yours;—free to act as I may think best, for the dignity of a Roman noble, and the interests of a Roman citizen; free to raise my standard on mine own tower, or to yield fealty to the new estate."

"Well said!" cried the old Colonna, hastily. "Heaven forbid we should enter Rome as foes, if to enter it as friends be yet allowed us! What say ye, gentles?"

"A more worthy choice could not be selected," said

Savelli; "but I should scarce deem it possible that a Colonna could think there was an option between resistance and fealty to this upstart revolution."

"Of that, Signor, I will judge for myself; if you demand an agent for yourselves, choose another. I announce to ye frankly, that I have seen enough of other states to think the recent condition of Rome demanded some redress. Whether Rienzi and Raimond be worthy of the task they have assumed, I know not."

Savelli was silent. The old Colonna seized the word.

"To Palestrina, then!—are ye all agreed on this? At the worst, or at the best, we should not be divided! On this condition alone I hazard the safety of my kinsman!"

The Barons murmured a little among themselves;—the expediency of Stephen's proposition was evident, and they at length assented to it.

Adrian saw them depart, and then, attended only by his 'squire, slowly rode towards a more distant entrance into the city. On arriving at the gates, his name was demanded—he gave it freely.

"Enter, my Lord," said the warder, "our orders were to admit all that came unarmed and unattended. But to the Lord Adrian di Castello, alone, we had a special injunction to give the honours due to a citizen and a friend."

Adrian, a little touched by this implied recollection of friendship, now rode through a long line of armed citizens, who saluted him respectfully as he passed, and, as he returned the salutation with courtesy, a loud and approving shout followed his horse's steps.

So, save by one attendant, alone, and in peace, the

young patrician proceeded leisurely through the long streets, empty and deserted,—for nearly one half of the inhabitants were assembled at the walls, and nearly the other half were engaged in a more peaceful duty,—until, penetrating the interior, the wide and elevated space of the Capitol broke upon his sight. The sun was slowly setting over an immense multitude that overspread the spot, and high above a scaffold raised in the centre, shone, to the western ray, the great Gonfalon of Rome, studded with silver stars.

Adrian reined in his steed. "This," thought he, "is scarcely the hour thus publicly to confer with Rienzi; yet fain would I, mingled with the crowd, judge how far his power is supported, and in what manner it is borne." Musing a little, he withdrew into one of the obscurer streets, then wholly deserted, surrendered his horse to his 'squire, and, borrowing of the latter his morion and long mantle, passed to one of the more private entrances of the Capitol, and, enveloped in his cloak, stood—one of the crowd—intent upon all that followed.

"And what," he asked of a plainly dressed citizen, "is the cause of this assembly?"

"Heard you not the proclamation?" returned the other in some surprise. "Do you not know that the Council of the City and the Guilds of the Artizans have passed a vote to proffer to Rienzi the title of king of Rome?"

The Knight of the Emperor, to whom belonged that august dignity, drew back in dismay.

"And," resumed the citizen, "this assembly of all the lesser Barons, Councillors, and Artificers, is convened to hear the answer."

"Of course it will be assent?"

"I know not—there are strange rumours; hitherto the Liberator has concealed his sentiments."

At that instant a loud flourish of martial music announced the approach of Rienzi. The crowd tumultuously divided, and presently, from the Palace of the Capitol to the scaffold, passed Rienzi, still in complete armour, save the helmet, and with him, in all the pomp of his episcopal robes, Raimond of Orvietto.

As soon as Rienzi had ascended the platform, and was thus made visible to the whole concourse, no words can suffice to paint the enthusiasm of the scene—the shouts, the gestures, the tears, the sobs, the wild laughter, in which the sympathy of those lively and susceptible children of the South broke forth. The windows and balconies of the Palace were thronged with the wives and daughters of the lesser Barons and more opulent citizens; and Adrian, with a slight start, beheld amongst them,—pale—agitated—tearful,—the lovely face of his Irene—a face that even thus would have outshone all present, but for one by her side, whose beauty the emotion of the hour only served to embellish. The dark, large, and flashing eyes of Nina di Raselli, just bedewed, were fixed proudly on the hero of her choice: and pride, even more than joy, gave a richer carnation to her cheek, and the presence of a queen to her noble and rounded form. The setting sun poured its full glory over the spot; the bared heads—the animated faces of the crowd—the gray and vast mass of the Capitol; and, not far from the side of Rienzi, it brought into a strange and startling light the sculptured form of a colossal Lion of Basalt,*

* The existent Capitol is very different from the building at the time of Rienzi; and the reader must not suppose that the present staircase, designed by Michael Angelo, at the base of which are two marble lions, removed by Pius IV. from the

which gave its name to a staircase leading to the Capitol. It was an old Egyptian relic,—vast, worn, and grim; some symbol of a vanished creed, to whose face the sculptor had imparted something of the aspect of the human countenance. And this producing the effect probably sought, gave at all times a mystic, preternatural, and fearful expression to the stern features, and to that solemn and hushed repose, which is so peculiarly the secret of Egyptian sculpture. The awe which this colossal and frowning image was calculated to convey, was felt yet more deeply by the vulgar, because "the Staircase of the Lion" was the wonted place of the state executions, as of the state ceremonies. And seldom did the stoutest citizen forget to cross himself, or feel unchilled with a certain terror, whenever, passing by the place, he caught, suddenly fixed upon him, the stony gaze and ominous grin of that old monster from the cities of the Nile.

It was some minutes before the feelings of the assembly allowed Rienzi to be heard. But when, at length, the last shout closed with a simultaneous cry of "Long live Rienzi! Deliverer and King of Rome!" he raised his hand impatiently, and the curiosity of the crowd procured a sudden silence.

"Deliverer of Rome, my countrymen!" said he. "Yes! change not that title—I am too ambitious to be a King! Preserve your obedience to your Pontiff—your allegiance to your Emperor—but be faithful to your own liberties. Ye have a right to your ancient constitution; but that constitution needed not a king. Emulous of the name of Brutus, I am above the titles

Church of St. Stephen del Cacco, was the staircase of the Lion of Basalt, which bears so stern a connexion with the history of Rienzi. That mute witness of dark deeds is no more.

of a Tarquin! Romans, awake! awake! be inspired with a nobler love of liberty than that which, if it dethrones the tyrant of to-day, would madly risk the danger of tyranny for to-morrow! Rome wants still a liberator—never an usurper!—Take away yon bauble!"

There was a pause; the crowd were deeply affected —but they uttered no shouts; they looked anxiously for a reply from their councillors, or popular leaders.

"Signor," said Pandulfo di Guido, who was one of the Caporioni, "your answer is worthy of your fame. But, in order to enforce the law, Rome must endow you with a legal title—if not that of King, deign to accept that of Dictator or of Consul."

"Long live the Consul Rienzi!" cried several voices.

Rienzi waved his hand for silence.

"Pandulfo di Guido! and you, honoured Councillors of Rome! such title is at once too august for my merits, and too inapplicable to my functions. I am one of the people—the people are my charge; the nobles can protect themselves. Dictator and Consul are the appellations of patricians. No," he continued after a short pause, "if ye deem it necessary, for the preservation of order, that your fellow-citizen should be entrusted with a formal title and a recognised power, be it so: but let it be such as may attest the nature of our new institutions, the wisdom of the people, and the moderation of their leaders. Once, my countrymen, the people elected, for the protectors of their rights and the guardians of their freedom, certain officers responsible to the people,—chosen from the people,—provident *for* the people. Their power was great, but it was delegated: a dignity, but a trust. The name of these officers was that of Tribune. Such is the title that conceded, not by clamour alone, but in the full Parliament of the people, and accompanied *by*, such Parliament, ruling *with* such Parliament,—such is the title I will gratefully accept."*

The speech, the sentiments of Rienzi were rendered far more impressive by a manner of earnest and deep sincerity; and some of the Romans, despite their corruption, felt a momentary exultation in the forbearance of their chief. "Long live the Tribune of Rome!" was shouted, but less loud than the cry of "Live the King!" And the vulgar almost thought the revolution was incomplete, because the loftier title was not assumed. To a degenerate and embruted people, liberty seems too plain a thing, if unadorned by the pomp of the very despotism they would dethrone. Revenge is their desire, rather than Release; and the greater the new power they create, the greater seems their revenge against the old. Still all that was most respected, intelligent, and powerful amongst the assembly, were delighted at a temperance which they foresaw would free Rome from a thousand dangers, whether from the Emperor or the Pontiff. And their delight was yet increased, when Rienzi added, so soon as returning silence permitted—"And since we have been equal labourers in the same cause, whatever honours be awarded to me, should be extended also to the

* Gibbon and Sismondi alike, (neither of whom appears to have consulted with much attention the original documents preserved by Hocsemius,) say nothing of the Representative Parliament, which it was almost Rienzi's first public act to institute or model. Six days from the memorable 19th of May, he addressed the people of Viterbo in a letter yet extant. He summons them to elect and send two syndics, or ambassadors, to the general Parliament.

Vicar of the Pope, Raimond, Lord Bishop of Orvietto. Remember, that both Church and State are properly the rulers of the people, only because their benefactors.—Long live the first Vicar of a Pope that was ever also the Liberator of a State!"

Whether or not Rienzi was only actuated by patriotism in his moderation, certain it is, that his sagacity was at least equal to his virtue; and perhaps nothing could have cemented the revolution more strongly, than thus obtaining for a colleague the Vicar, and Representative of the Pontifical power: it borrowed, for the time, the sanction of the Pope himself—thus made to share the responsibility of the revolution, without monopolising the power of the State.

While the crowd hailed the proposition of Rienzi; while their shouts yet filled the air; while Raimond, somewhat taken by surprise, sought by signs and gestures to convey at once his gratitude and his humility, the Tribune-Elect, casting his eyes around, perceived many hitherto attracted by curiosity, and whom, from their rank and weight, it was desirable to secure in the first heat of the public enthusiasm. Accordingly, as soon as Raimond had uttered a short and pompous harangue,—in which his eager acceptance of the honour proposed him was ludicrously contrasted by his embarrassed desire not to involve himself or the Pope in any untoward consequences that might ensue,—Rienzi motioned to two heralds that stood behind upon the platform, and one of these advancing, proclaimed—"That as it was desirable that all hitherto neuter should now profess themselves friends or foes, so they were invited to take at once the oath of obedience to the laws, and subscription to the Buono Stato."

So great was the popular fervour, and so much had

it been refined and deepened in its tone by the addresses of Rienzi, that even the most indifferent had caught the contagion: and no man liked to be seen shrinking from the rest: so that the most neutral, knowing themselves the most marked, were the most entrapped into allegiance to the Buono Stato. The first who advanced to the platform and took the oath was the Signor di Raselli, the father of Nina.—Others of the lesser nobility followed his example.

The presence of the Pope's Vicar induced the aristocratic; the fear of the people urged the selfish; the encouragement of shouts and congratulations excited the vain. The space between Adrian and Rienzi was made clear. The young noble suddenly felt the eyes of the Tribune were upon him; he felt that those eyes recognised and called upon him—he coloured—he breathed short. The noble forbearance of Rienzi had touched him to the heart;—the applause—the pageant—the enthusiasm of the scene, intoxicated—confused him.—He lifted his eyes and saw before him the sister of the Tribune—the lady of his love! His indecision—his pause—continued, when Raimond, observing him, and obedient to a whisper from Rienzi, artfully cried aloud—"Room for the Lord Adrian di Castello! a Colonna! a Colonna!" Retreat was cut off. Mechanically, and as if in a dream, Adrian ascended to the platform: and to complete the triumph of the Tribune, the sun's last ray beheld the flower of the Colonna—the best and bravest of the Barons of Rome—confessing his authority, and subscribing to his laws.

BOOK III

THE FREEDOM WITHOUT LAW

" Ben furo avventurosi i cavalieri
Ch' erano a quella età, che nei valloni,
Nelle scure spelonche e boschi fieri,
Tane di serpi, d' orsi e di leoni,
Trovavan quel che nei palazzi altieri
Appena or trovar pon giudici buoni;
Donne che nella lor più fresca etade
Sien degne di aver titol di beltade."

ARIOSTO, *Orl. Fur.* can. xiii, 1

CHAPTER I

THE RETURN OF WALTER DE MONTREAL TO HIS FORTRESS

When Walter de Montreal and his mercenaries quitted Corneto, they made the best of their way to Rome; arriving there, long before the Barons, they met with a similar reception at the gates, but Montreal prudently forbore all attack and menace, and contented himself with sending his trusty Rodolf into the city to seek Rienzi, and to crave permission to enter with his troop. Rodolf returned in a shorter time than was anticipated. "Well," said Montreal impatiently, "you have the order I suppose. Shall we bid them open the gates?"

"Bid them open our graves," replied the Saxon, bluntly. "I trust my next heraldry will be to a more friendly court."

"How! what mean you?"

"Briefly this:—I found the new governor, or whatever his title, in the palace of the Capitol, surrounded by guards and councillors, and in a suit of the finest armour I ever saw out of Milan."

"Pest on his armour! give us his answer."

"'Tell Walter de Montreal,' said he, then, if you will have it, 'that Rome is no longer a den of thieves; tell him, that if he enters, he must abide a trial——'"

"A trial!" cried Montreal, grinding his teeth.

"'For participation in the evil doings of Werner and his freebooters.'"

"Ha!"

"'Tell him, moreover, that Rome declares war against all robbers, whether in tent or tower, and that we order him in forty-eight hours to quit the territories of the Church.'"

"He thinks, then, not only to deceive, but to menace me? Well, proceed."

"That was all his reply to you; to me, however, he vouchsafed a caution still more obliging. 'Hark ye, friend,' said he, 'for every German bandit found in Rome after to-morrow, our welcome will be cord and gibbet! Begone.'"

"Enough! enough!" cried Montreal, colouring with rage and shame. "Rodolf, you have a skilful eye in these matters, how many Northmen would it take to give that same gibbet to the upstart?"

Rodolf scratched his huge head, and seemed awhile lost in calculation; at length he said, "You, Captain, must be the best judge, when I tell you, that twenty thousand Romans are the least of his force; so I heard by the way; and this evening he is to accept the crown, and depose the Emperor."

"Ha, ha!" laughed Montreal, "is he so mad? then he will want not our aid to hang himself. My friends, let us wait the result. At present neither barons nor people seem likely to fill our coffers. Let us across the country to Terracina. Thank the saints," and Montreal (who was not without a strange kind of devotion,—indeed he deemed that virtue essential to chivalry) crossed himself piously, "the free companions are never long without quarters!"

"Hurrah for the Knight of St. John!" cried the mercenaries. "And hurrah for fair Provence and bold Germany!" added the Knight, as he waved his hand on high, struck spurs into his already wearied horse, and, breaking out into his favourite song,

> "His steed and his sword,
> And his lady the peerless," &c.,

Montreal, with his troop, struck gallantly across the Campagna.

The Knight of St. John soon, however, fell into an absorbed and moody reverie; and his followers imitating the silence of their chief, in a few minutes the clatter of their arms and the jingle of their spurs, alone disturbed the stillness of the wide and gloomy plains across which they made towards Terracina. Montreal was recalling with bitter resentment his conference with Rienzi; and, proud of his own sagacity and talent for scheming, he was humbled and vexed at the discovery that he had been duped by a wilier intriguer. His ambitious designs on Rome, too, were crossed, and even crushed for the moment, by the very means to which he had looked for their execution. He had seen enough of the barons to feel assured that while

Stephen Colonna lived, the head of the order, he was not likely to obtain that mastery in the state which, if leagued with a more ambitious or a less timid and less potent signor, might reward his aid in expelling Rienzi. Under all circumstances, he deemed it advisable to remain aloof. Should Rienzi grow strong, Montreal might make the advantageous terms he desired with the Barons; should Rienzi's power decay, his pride, necessarily humbled, might drive him to seek the assistance, and submit to the proposals, of Montreal. The ambition of the Provençal, though vast and daring, was not of a consistent and persevering nature. Action and enterprise were dearer to him, as yet, than the rewards which they proffered; and if baffled in one quarter, he turned himself, with the true spirit of the knight-errant, to any other field for his achievements. Louis, king of Hungary, stern, warlike, implacable, seeking vengeance for the murder of his brother, the ill-fated husband of Joanna, (the beautiful and guilty Queen of Naples—the Mary Stuart of Italy,) had already prepared himself to subject the garden of Campania to the Hungarian yoke. Already his bastard brother had entered Italy—already some of the Neapolitan states had declared in his favour—already promises had been held out by the northern monarch to the scattered Companies—and already those fierce mercenaries gathered menacingly round the frontiers of that Eden of Italy, attracted, as vultures to the carcass, by the preparation of war and the hope of plunder. Such was the field to which the bold mind of Montreal now turned its thoughts; and his soldiers had joyfully conjectured his design when they had heard him fix Terracina as their bourne. Provident of every resource, and refining his audacious and unprincipled valour by a sagacity which promised, when years had more matured and sobered his restless chivalry, to rank him among the most dangerous enemies Italy had ever known, on the first sign of Louis's warlike intentions, Montreal had seized and fortified a strong castle on that delicious coast beyond Terracina, by which lies the celebrated pass once held by Fabius against Hannibal, and which Nature has so favoured for war as for peace, that a handful of armed men might stop the march of an army. The possession of such a fortress on the very frontiers of Naples, gave Montreal an importance of which he trusted to avail himself with the Hungarian king: and now, thwarted in his more grand and aspiring projects upon Rome, his sanguine, active, and elastic spirit congratulated itself upon the resource it had secured.

The band halted at nightfall on this side the Pontine Marshes, seizing without scruple some huts and sheds, from which they ejected the miserable tenants, and slaughtering with no greater ceremony the swine, cattle, and poultry of a neighbouring farm. Shortly after sunrise they crossed those fatal swamps which had already been partially drained by Boniface VIII.; and Montreal, refreshed by sleep, reconciled to his late mortification by the advantages opened to him in the approaching war with Naples, and rejoicing as he approached a home which held one who alone divided his heart with ambition, had resumed all the gaiety which belonged to his Gallic birth and his reckless habits. And that deadly but consecrated road, where yet may be seen the labours of Augustus, in the canal which had witnessed the Voyage so humorously described by Horace, echoed with the loud laughter and frequent snatches of wild song by which the barbarian robbers enlivened their rapid march.

It was noon when the company entered upon that romantic pass I have before referred to—the ancient Lantulæ. High to the left rose steep and lofty rocks, then covered by the prodigal verdure, and the countless flowers, of the closing May; while to the right the sea, gentle as a lake, and blue as heaven, rippled musically at their feet. Montreal, who largely possessed the poetry of his land, which is so eminently allied with a love of nature, might at another time have enjoyed the beauty of the scene; but at that moment less external and more household images were busy within him.

Abruptly ascending where a winding path up the mountain offered a rough and painful road to their horses' feet, the band at length arrived before a strong fortress of gray stone, whose towers were concealed by the lofty foliage, until they emerged sullenly and suddenly from the laughing verdure. The sound of the bugle, the pennon of the knight, the rapid watchword, produced a loud shout of welcome from a score or two of grim soldiery on the walls; the portcullis was raised, and Montreal, throwing himself hastily from his panting steed, sprung across the threshold of a jutting porch, and traversed a huge hall, when a lady—young, fair, and richly dressed—met him with a step equally swift, and fell breathless and overjoyed into his arms.

"My Walter! my dear, dear Walter; welcome—ten thousand welcomes!"

"Adeline, my beautiful—my adored—I see thee again!"

Such were the greetings interchanged as Montreal

pressed his lady to his heart, kissing away her tears, and lifting her face to his, while he gazed on its delicate bloom with all the wistful anxiety of affection after absence.

"Fairest," said he, tenderly, "thou hast pined, thou hast lost roundness and colour since we parted. Come, come, thou art too gentle, or too foolish, for a soldier's love."

"Ah, Walter!" replied Adeline, clinging to him, "now thou art returned, and I shall be well. Thou wilt not leave me again a long, long time."

"Sweet one, no;" and flinging his arm round her waist, the lovers—for alas! they were not wedded!—retired to the more private chambers of the castle.

CHAPTER II

THE LIFE OF LOVE AND WAR—THE MESSENGER OF PEACE—THE JOUST

Girt with his soldiery, secure in his feudal hold, enchanted with the beauty of the earth, sky, and sea around, and passionately adoring his Adeline, Montreal for awhile forgot all his more stirring projects and his ruder occupations. His nature was capable of great tenderness, as of great ferocity; and his heart smote him when he looked at the fair cheek of his lady, and saw that even his presence did not suffice to bring back the smile and the fresh hues of old. Often he cursed that fatal oath of his knightly order which forbade him to wed, though with one more than his equal; and remorse embittered his happiest hours. That gentle lady in that robber hold, severed from all she had been taught most to prize—mother, friends, and fair fame—only loved her seducer the more intensely; only the more concentrated upon one object all the womanly and tender feelings denied every other and less sinful vent. But she felt her shame, though she sought to conceal it, and a yet more gnawing grief than even that of shame contributed to prey upon her spirits and undermine her health. Yet, withal, in Montreal's presence she was happy, even in regret; and in her declining health she had at least a consolation in the hope to die while his love was undiminished. Sometimes they made short excursions, for the disturbed state of the country forbade them to wander far from the castle, through the sunny woods, and along the glassy sea, which make the charm of that delicious scenery; and that mixture of the savage with the tender, the wild escort, the tent in some green glade in the woods at noon, the lute and voice of Adeline, with the fierce soldiers grouped and listening at the distance, might have well suited the verse of Ariosto, and harmonised singularly with that strange, disordered, yet chivalric time, in which the Classic South became the seat of the Northern Romance. Still, however, Montreal maintained his secret intercourse with the Hungarian king, and, plunged in new projects, willingly forsook for the present all his designs on Rome. Yet deemed he that his more august ambition was only delayed, and, bright in the more distant prospects of his adventurous career, rose the Capitol of Rome and shone the sceptre of the Cæsars.

One day, as Montreal, with a small troop in attendance, passed on horseback near the walls of Terracina, the gates were suddenly thrown open, and a numerous throng issued forth, preceded by a singular figure, whose steps they followed bareheaded and with loud blessings; a train of monks closed the procession, chanting a hymn, of which the concluding words were as follows:—

Beauteous on the mountains—lo,
  The feet of him glad tidings gladly bringing;
The flowers along his pathway grow,
  And voices, heard aloft, to angel harps are singing:
And strife and slaughter cease
Before thy blessed way, Young Messenger of Peace!
  O'er the mount, and through the moor,
  Glide thy holy steps secure.
  Day and night no fear thou knowest,
  Lonely—but with God thou goest.
  Where the heathen rage the fiercest,
  Through the armed throng thou piercest.
  For thy coat of mail, bedight
  In thy spotless robe of white.
  For the sinful sword—thy hand
  Bearing bright the silver wand:
  Through the camp and through the court,
  Through the bandit's gloomy fort,
  On the mission of the dove,
  Speeds the minister of love;
  By a word the wildest taming,
  And the world to Christ reclaiming:
  While, as once the waters trod
  By the footsteps of thy God,
  War, and wrath, and rapine cease,
Hush'd round thy charmed path, O Messenger of Peace!

The stranger to whom these honours were paid was a young, unbearded man, clothed in white wrought with silver; he was unarmed and barefooted: in his hand he held a tall silver wand. Montreal and his party halted in astonishment and wonder, and the knight, spurring his horse toward the crowd, confronted the stranger.

"How, friend," quoth the Provençal, "is thine a new order of pilgrims, or what especial holiness has won thee this homage?"

"Back, back," cried some of the bolder of the crowd, "let not the robber dare arrest the Messenger of Peace."

Montreal waved his hand disdainfully.

"I speak not to you, good sirs, and the worthy friars in your rear know full well that I never injured herald or palmer."

The monks, ceasing from their hymn, advanced hastily to the spot; and indeed the devotion of Montreal had ever induced him to purchase the goodwill of whatever monastery neighboured his wandering home.

"My son," said the eldest of the brethren, "this is a strange spectacle, and a sacred: and when thou learnest all, thou wilt rather give the messenger a passport of safety from the unthinking courage of thy friends than intercept his path of peace."

"Ye puzzle still more my simple brain," said Montreal, impatiently, "let the youth speak for himself; I perceive that on his mantle are the arms of Rome blended with other quarterings, which are a mystery to me,—though sufficiently versed in heraldic art as befits a noble and a knight."

"Signor," said the youth, gravely, "know in me the messenger of Cola di Rienzi, Tribune of Rome, charged with letters to many a baron and prince in the ways between Rome and Naples. The arms wrought upon my mantle are those of the Pontiff, the City, and the Tribune."

"Umph; thou must have bold nerves to traverse the Campagna with no other weapon than that stick of silver!"

"Thou art mistaken, Sir Knight," replied the youth, boldly, "and judgest of the present by the past; know that not a single robber now lurks within the Campagna, the arms of the Tribune have rendered every road around the city as secure as the broadest street of the city itself."

"Thou tellest me wonders."

"Through the forest—and in the fortress,—through the wildest solitudes,—through the most populous towns,—have my comrades borne this silver wand unmolested and unscathed; wherever we pass along, thousands hail us, and tears of joy bless the messengers of him who hath expelled the brigand from his hold, the tyrant from his castle, and ensured the gains of the merchant and the hut of the peasant."

"*Pardieu,*" said Montreal, with a stern smile, "I ought to be thankful for the preference shown to me; I have not yet received the commands, nor felt the vengeance, of the Tribune; yet, methinks, my humble castle lies just within the patrimony of St. Peter."

"Pardon me, Signor Cavalier," said the youth; "but do I address the renowned Knight of St. John, warrior of the Cross, yet leader of banditti?"

"Boy, you are bold; I am Walter de Montreal."

"I am bound, then, Sir Knight, to your castle."

"Take care how thou reach it before me, or thou standest a fair chance of a quick exit. How now, my friends!" seeing that the crowd at these words gathered closer round the messenger, "Think ye that I, who have my mate in kings, would find a victim in an unarmed boy? Fie! give way—give way. Young man, follow me homeward; you are safe in my castle as in your mother's arms." So saying, Montreal, with great dignity and deliberate gravity, rode slowly towards his castle, his soldiers, wondering, at a little distance, and the white-robed messenger following with the crowd, who refused to depart; so great was their enthusiasm, that they even ascended to the gates of the dreaded castle, and insisted on waiting without until the return of the youth assured them of his safety.

Montreal, who, however lawless elsewhere, strictly preserved the rights of the meanest boor in his immediate neighbourhood, and rather affected popularity with the poor, bade the crowd enter the court-yard, ordered his servitors to provide them with wine and refreshment, regaled the good monks in his great hall, and then led the way to a small room, where he received the messenger.

"This," said the youth, "will best explain my mission," as he placed a letter before Montreal.

The Knight cut the silk with his dagger, and read the epistle with great composure.

"Your Tribune," said he, when he had finished it, "has learned the laconic style of power very soon. He orders me to render this castle, and vacate the Papal territory within ten days. He is obliging; I must have breathing time to consider the proposal; be seated, I pray you, young sir. Forgive me, but I should have imagined that your lord had enough upon his hands with his Roman barons, to make him a little more indulgent to us foreign visitors. Stephen Colonna——"

"Is returned to Rome, and has taken the oath of allegiance; the Savelli, the Orsini, the Frangipani, have all subscribed their submission to the *Buono Stato.*"

"How!" cried Montreal, in great surprise.

"Not only have they returned, but they have submitted to the dispersion of all their mercenaries, and the dismantling of all their fortifications. The iron of the Orsini palace now barricades the Capitol, and the stonework of the Colonna and the Savelli has added new battlements to the gates of the Lateran and St. Laurence."

"Wonderful man!" said Montreal, with reluctant admiration. "By what means was this effected?"

"A stern command and a strong force to back it. At the first sound of the great bell, twenty thousand Romans rise in arms. What to such an army are the brigands of an Orsini or a Colonna?—Sir Knight, your valour and renown make even Rome admire you; and I, a Roman, bid you beware."

"Well, I thank thee—thy news, friend, robs me of breath. So the Barons submit, then?"

"Yes: on the first day, one of the Colonna, the Lord Adrian, took the oath; within a week, Stephen, assured of safe conduct, left Palestrina, the Savelli in his train; the Orsini followed—even Martino di Porto has silently succumbed."

"The Tribune—but is that his dignity—methought he was to be king——"

"He was offered, and he refused, the title. His present rank, which arrogates no patrician honours, went far to conciliate the nobles."

"A wise knave!—I beg pardon, a sagacious prince!—Well, then, the Tribune lords it mightily, I suppose, over the great Roman names?"

"Pardon me—he enforces impartial justice from peasant or patrician; but he preserves to the nobles all their just privileges and legal rank."

"Ha!—and the vain puppets, so they keep the

semblance, scarce miss the substance—I understand. But this shows genius—the Tribune is unwed, I think. Does he look among the Colonna for a wife?"

"Sir Knight, the Tribune is already married; within three days after his ascension to power, he won and bore home the daughter of the Baron di Raselli."

"Raselli! no great name; he might have done better."

"But it is said," resumed the youth, smiling, "that the Tribune will shortly be allied to the Colonna, through his fair sister the Signora Irene. The Baron di Castello woos her."

"What, Adrian Colonna! Enough! you have convinced me that a man who contents the people and awes or conciliates the nobles is born for empire. My answer to this letter I will send myself. For your news, Sir Messenger, accept this jewel," and the knight took from his finger a gem of some price. "Nay, shrink not, it was as freely given to me as it is now to thee."

The youth, who had been agreeably surprised, and impressed, by the manner of the renowned freebooter, and who was not a little astonished himself with the ease and familiarity with which he had been relating to Fra Moreale, in his own fortress, the news of Rome, bowed low as he accepted the gift.

The astute Provençal, who saw the evident impression he had made, perceived also that it might be of advantage in delaying the measures he might deem it expedient to adopt. "Assure the Tribune," said he, on dismissing the messenger, "shouldst thou return ere my letter arrive, that I admire his genius, hail his power, and will not fail to consider as favourably as I may of his demand."

"Better," said the messenger, warmly (he was of good blood, and gentle bearing),—"better ten tyrants for our enemy, than one Montreal."

"An enemy! believe me, sir, I seek no enmity with princes who know how to govern, or a people that has the wisdom at once to rule and to obey."

The whole of that day, however, Montreal remained thoughtful and uneasy; he despatched trusty messengers to the Governor of Aquila (who was then in correspondence with Louis of Hungary), to Naples, and to Rome:—the last charged with a letter to the Tribune, which, without absolutely compromising himself, affected submission, and demanded only a longer leisure for the preparations of departure. But, at the same time, fresh fortifications were added to the castle, ample provisions were laid in, and, night and day, spies and scouts were stationed along the pass, and in the town of Terracina. Montreal was precisely the chief who prepared most for war when most he pretended peace.

One morning, the fifth from the appearance of the Roman messenger, Montreal, after narrowly surveying his outworks and his stores, and feeling satisfied that he could hold out at least a month's siege, repaired, with a gayer countenance than he had lately worn, to the chamber of Adeline.

The lady was seated by the casement of the tower, from which might be seen the glorious landscape of woods, and vales, and orange groves—a strange garden for such a palace! As she leant her face upon her hand, with her profile slightly turned to Montreal, there was something ineffably graceful in the bend of her neck,—the small head so expressive of gentle blood,—with the locks parted in front in that simple fashion which modern times have so happily revived. But the expression of the half-averted face, the abstracted intentness of the gaze, and the profound stillness of the attitude, were so sad and mournful, that Montreal's purposed greeting of gallantry and gladness died upon his lips. He approached in silence, and laid his hand upon her shoulder.

Adeline turned, and taking the hand in hers, pressed it to her heart, and smiled away all her sadness. "Dearest," said Montreal, "couldst thou know how much any shadow of grief on thy bright face darkens my heart, thou wouldst never grieve. But no wonder that in these rude walls—no female of equal rank near thee, and such mirth as Montreal can summon to his halls, grating to thy ear—no wonder that thou repentest thee of thy choice."

"Ah, no—no, Walter, I never repent. I did but think of our child as you entered. Alas! he was our only child! How fair he was, Walter; how he resembled thee!"

"Nay, he had thine eyes and brow," replied the Knight, with a faltering voice, and turning away his head.

"Walter," resumed the lady, sighing, "do you remember?—this is his birthday. He is ten years old to-day. We have loved each other eleven years. and thou hast not tired yet of thy poor Adeline."

"As well might the saints weary of Paradise," replied Montreal, with an enamoured tenderness, which changed into softness the whole character of his heroic countenance.

"Could I think so, I should indeed be blest!" answered Adeline. "But a little while longer, and the few charms I yet possess must fade; and what other claim have I on thee?"

"All claim;—the memory of thy first blushes—thy first kiss—of thy devoted sacrifices—of thy patient wanderings—of thy uncomplaining love! Ah, Adeline, we are of Provence, not of Italy; and when did Knight of Provence avoid his foe, or forsake his love? But enough, dearest, of home and melancholy for to-day. I come to bid thee forth. I have sent on the servitors to pitch our tent beside the sea,—we will enjoy the orange blossoms while we may. Ere another week pass over us, we may have sterner pastime and closer confines."

"How, dearest Walter! thou dost not apprehend danger?"

"Thou speakest, lady-bird," said Montreal, laughing, "as if danger were novelty; methinks by this time, thou shouldst know it as the atmosphere we breathe."

"Ah, Walter, is this to last for ever? Thou art now rich and renowned; canst thou not abandon this career of strife?"

"Now, out on thee, Adeline. What are riches and renown but the means to power! And for strife, the shield of warriors was my cradle—pray the saints it be my bier! These wild and wizard extremes of life—from the bower to the tent—from the cavern to the palace—to-day a wandering exile, to-morrow the equal of kings—make the true element of the chivalry of my Norman sires. Normandy taught me war, and sweet Provence love. Kiss me, dear Adeline; and now let thy handmaids attire thee. Forget not thy lute, sweet one. We will rouse the echoes with the songs of Provence."

The ductile temper of Adeline yielded easily to the gaiety of her lord; and the party soon sallied from the castle towards the spot in which Montreal had designed their resting-place during the heats of day. But already prepared for all surprise, the castle was left strictly guarded, and besides the domestic servitors of the castle, a detachment of ten soldiers, completely armed, accompanied the lovers. Montreal himself wore his corselet, and his 'squires followed with his helmet and lance. Beyond the narrow defile at the base of the castle, the road at that day opened into a broad patch of verdure, circled on all sides, save that open to the sea, by wood, interspersed with myrtle and orange, and a wilderness of odorous shrubs. In this space, and sheltered by the broad-spreading and classic *fagus* (so improperly translated into the English *beech*), a gay pavilion was prepared, which commanded the view of the sparkling sea;—shaded from the sun, but open to the gentle breeze. This was poor Adeline's favourite recreation, if recreation it might be called. She rejoiced to escape from the gloomy walls of her castellated prison, and to enjoy the sunshine and the sweets of that voluptuous climate without the fatigue which of late all exercise occasioned her. It was a gallantry on the part of Montreal, who foresaw how short an interval might elapse before the troops of Rienzi besieged his walls; and who was himself no less at home in the bower than in the field.

As they reclined within the pavilion—the lover and his lady,—of the attendants without, some lounged idly on the beach; some prepared the awning of a pleasure-boat against the decline of the sun; some, in a ruder tent, out of sight in the wood, arranged the mid-day repast; while the strings of the lute, touched by Montreal himself with a careless skill, gave their music to the dreamy stillness of the noon.

While thus employed, one of Montreal's scouts arrived breathless and heated at the tent.

"Captain," said he, "a company of thirty lances completely armed, with a long retinue of 'squires and pages, have just quitted Terracina. Their banners bear the two-fold insignia of Rome and the Colonna."

"Ho!" said Montreal, gaily, "such a troop is a welcome addition to our company; send our 'squire hither."

The 'squire appeared.

"Hie thee on thy steed towards the procession thou wilt meet with in the pass, (nay, sweet lady mine, no forbiddal!) seek the chief, and say that the good Knight Walter de Montreal sends him greeting, and prays him, in passing our proper territory, to rest awhile with us a welcome guest; and—stay,—add, that if to while an hour or so in gentle pastime be acceptable to him, Walter de Montreal would rejoice to break a lance with him, or any knight in his train, in honour of our respective ladies. Hie thee quick!"

"Walter, Walter," began Adeline, who had that keen and delicate sensitiveness to her situation, which her reckless lord often wantonly forgot; "Walter, dear Walter, canst thou think it honour to——"

"Hush thee, sweet *Fleur de lis!* Thou hast not seen pastime this many a day; I long to convince thee that thou art still the fairest lady in Italy—ay, and of Christendom. But these Italians are craven knights, and thou needst not fear that my proffer will be accepted. But in truth, lady mine, I rejoice for graver objects, that chance throws a Roman noble, perhaps a Colonna, in my way;—women understand not these matters; and aught concerning Rome touches us home at this moment."

With that the Knight frowned, as was his wont in thought, and Adeline ventured to say no more, but retired to the interior division of the pavilion.

Meanwhile the 'squire approached the procession that had now reached the middle of the pass. And a stately and gallant company it was:—if the complete harness of the soldiery seemed to attest a warlike purpose, it was contradicted on the other hand by a numerous train of unarmed 'squires and pages gorgeously attired, while the splendid blazon of two heralds preceding the standard-bearers, proclaimed their object as peaceful, and their path as sacred. It required but a glance at the company to tell the leader. Arrayed in a breastplate of steel, wrought profusely with gold arabesques, over which was a mantle of dark-green velvet, bordered with pearls, while above his long dark locks waved a black ostrich plume in a high Macedonian cap, such as, I believe, is now worn by the Grand Master of the order of St. Constantine, rode in the front of the party, a young cavalier, distinguished from his immediate comrades, partly by his graceful presence and partly by his splendid dress.

The 'squire approached respectfully, and dismounting, delivered himself of his charge.

The young cavalier smiled, as he answered, "Bear back to Sir Walter de Montreal the greeting of Adrian Colonna, Baron di Castello, and say, the solemn object of my present journey will scarce permit me to encounter the formidable lance of so celebrated a knight; and I regret this the more, inasmuch as I may not yield to any dame the palm of my liege lady's beauty. I must live in hope of a happier occasion. For the rest, I will cheerfully abide for some few hours the guest of so courteous a host."

The 'squire bowed low. "My master," said he, hesitatingly, "will grieve much to miss so noble an opponent. But my message refers to all this knightly and gallant train; and if the Lord Adrian di Castello deems himself forbidden the joust by the object of his present journey, surely one of his comrades will be his proxy with my master."

Out and quickly spoke a young noble by the side of Adrian, Riccardo Annibaldi, who afterwards did good service both to the Tribune and to Rome, and whose valour brought him, in later life, to an untimely end.

"By the Lord Adrian's permission," cried he, "I will break a lance with——"

"Hush! Annibaldi," interrupted Adrian. "And you, Sir 'Squire, know, that Adrian di Castello permits no proxy in arms. Avise the Knight of St. John that we accept his hospitality, and if, after some converse on graver matters, he should still desire so light an entertainment, I will forget that I am the ambassador to Naples, and remember only that I am a Knight of the Empire. You have your answer."

The 'squire with much ceremony made his obeisance, remounted his steed, and returned in a half-gallop to his master.

"Forgive me, dear Annibaldi," said Adrian, "that I balked your valour; and believe me that I never more longed to break a lance against any man than I do against this boasting Frenchman. But bethink you, that though to us, brought up in the dainty laws of chivalry, Walter de Montreal is the famous Knight of Provence, to the Tribune of Rome, whose grave mission we now fulfil, he is but the mercenary captain of a Free Company. Grievously in his eyes should we sully our dignity by so wanton and irrelevant a holiday conflict with a declared and professional brigand."

"For all that," said Annibaldi, "the brigand ought not to boast that a Roman knight shunned a Provençal lance."

"Cease, I pray thee!" said Adrian, impatiently. In fact, the young Colonna, already chafed bitterly against his discreet and dignified rejection of Montreal's proffer, and recollecting with much pique the disparaging manner in which the Provençal had spoken of the Roman chivalry, as well as a certain tone of superiority, which in all warlike matters Montreal had assumed over him,—he now felt his cheek burn, and his lip quiver. Highly skilled in the martial accomplishments of his time, he had a natural and excusable desire to prove that he was at least no unworthy antagonist even of the best lance in Italy: and, added to this, the gallantry of the age made him feel it a sort of treason to his mistress to forego any means of asserting her perfections.

It was, therefore, with considerable irritation that Adrian, as the pavilion of Montreal became visible, perceived the 'squire returning to him. And the reader will judge how much this was increased when the latter, once more dismounting, accosted him thus:

"My master, the Knight of St. John, on hearing the courteous answer of the Lord Adrian di Castello, bids me say, that lest the graver converse the Lord Adrian refers to should mar gentle and friendly sport, he ventures respectfully to suggest, that the tilt should preface the converse. The sod before the tent is so soft and smooth, that even a fall could be attended with *no danger* to knight or steed."

"By our Lady!" cried Adrian and Annibaldi in a breath, "but thy last words are discourteous; and" (proceeded Adrian, recovering himself) "since thy master will have it so, let him look to his horse's girths. I will not gainsay his fancy."

Montreal, who had thus insisted upon the exhibition, partly, it may be, from the gay and ruffling bravado, common still amongst his brave countrymen; partly because he was curious of exhibiting before those who might soon be his open foes his singular and unrivalled address in arms, was yet more moved to it on learning the name of the leader of the Roman Company; for his vain and haughty spirit, however it had disguised resentment at the time, had by no means forgiven certain warm expressions of Adrian in the palace of Stephen Colonna, and in the unfortunate journey to Corneto. While Adrian, halting at the entrance of the defile, aided by his 'squires, indignantly, but carefully, indued the rest of his armour, and saw, himself, to the girths, stirrup-leathers, and various buckles in the caparison of his noble charger, Montreal in great glee kissed his lady, who, though too soft to be angry, was deeply vexed, (and yet her vexation half forgotten in fear for his safety,) snatched up her scarf of blue, which he threw over his breastplate, and completed his array with the indifference of a man certain of victory. He was destined, however, to one disadvantage, and that the greatest; his armour and lance had been brought from the castle—not his war-horse. His palfrey was too slight to bear the great weight of his armour, nor amongst his troop was there one horse that for power and bone could match with Adrian's. He chose, however, the strongest that was at hand, and a loud shout from his wild followers testified their admiration when he sprung unaided from the ground into the saddle—a rare and difficult feat of agility in a man completely arrayed in the ponderous armour which issued at that day from the forges of Milan, and was worn far more weighty in Italy than any other part of Europe. While both companies grouped slowly, and mingled in a kind of circle round the green turf, and the Roman heralds, with bustling importance, attempted to marshal the spectators into order, Montreal rode his charger round the sward, forcing it into various caracoles, and exhibiting, with the vanity that belonged to him, his exquisite and practised horsemanship.

At length, Adrian, his visor down, rode slowly into the green space, amidst the cheers of his party. The two Knights, at either end, gravely fronted each other; they made the courtesies with their lances, which, in friendly and sportive encounters, were customary; and, as they thus paused for the signal of encounter, the Italians trembled for the honour of their chief: Montreal's stately height and girth of chest forming a strong contrast, even in armour, to the form of his opponent, which was rather under the middle standard, and though firmly knit, slightly and slenderly built. But to that perfection was skill in arms brought in those times, that great strength and size were far from being either the absolute requisites, or even the usual attributes, of the more celebrated knights; in fact, so much was effected by the power and the management of the steed, that a light weight in the rider was often rather to his advantage than his prejudice: and, even at a later period, the most accomplished victors in the tourney, the French Bayard and the English Sydney, were far from remarkable either for bulk or stature.

Whatever the superiority of Montreal in physical power, was, in much, counterbalanced by the inferiority of his horse, which, though a thick-built and strong Calabrian, had neither the blood, bone, nor practised discipline of the northern charger of the Roman. The shining coat of the latter, coal black, was set off by a scarlet cloth wrought in gold; the neck and shoulders were clad in scales of mail; and from the forehead projected a long point, like the horn of an unicorn, while on its crest waved a tall plume of scarlet and white feathers. As the mission of Adrian to Naples was that of pomp and ceremony to a court of great splendour, so his array and retinue were befitting the occasion and the passion for show that belonged to the time: and the very bridle of his horse, which was three inches broad, was decorated with gold, and even jewels. The Knight himself was clad in mail, which had tested the finest art of the celebrated Ludovico of Milan; and, altogether, his appearance was unusually gallant and splendid, and seemed still more so beside the plain but brightly polished and artfully flexile armour of Montreal, (adorned only with his lady's scarf,) and the common and rude mail of his charger. This contrast, however, was not welcome to the Provençal, whose vanity was especially indulged in warlike equipments; and who, had he foreseen the "pastime" that awaited him, would have outshone even the Colonna.

The trumpeters of either party gave a short blast—the Knights remained erect as statues of iron; a second, and each slightly bent over his saddle-bow;

a third, and with spears couched, and slackened reins, and at full speed, on they rushed, and fiercely they met midway. With the reckless arrogance which belonged to him, Montreal had imagined, that at the first touch of his lance Adrian would have been unhorsed; but to his great surprise the young Roman remained firm, and amidst the shouts of his party, passed on to the other end of the lists. Montreal himself was rudely shaken, but lost neither seat nor stirrup.

"This can be no carpet knight," muttered Montreal between his teeth, as, this time, he summoned all his skill for a second encounter; while Adrian, aware of the great superiority of his charger, resolved to bring it to bear against his opponent. Accordingly, when the Knights again rushed forward, Adrian, covering himself well with his buckler, directed his care less against the combatant, whom he felt no lance wielded by mortal hand was likely to dislodge, than against the less noble animal he bestrode. The shock of Montreal's charge was like an avalanche—his lance shivered into a thousand pieces. Adrian lost both stirrups, and but for the strong iron bows which guarded the saddle in front and rear, would have been fairly unhorsed; as it was, he was almost doubled back by the encounter, and his ears rung and his eyes reeled, so that for a moment or two he almost lost all consciousness. But his steed had well repaid its nurture and discipline. Just as the combatants closed, the animal, rearing on high, pressed forward with its mighty crest against its opponent with a force so irresistible as to drive back Montreal's horse several paces: while Adrian's lance, poised with exquisite skill, striking against the Provençal's helmet, somewhat rudely diverted the Knight's attention for the moment from his rein. Montreal, drawing the curb too tightly in the suddenness of his recovery, the horse reared on end; and, receiving at that instant, full upon his breastplate, the sharp horn and mailed crest of Adrian's charger—fell back over its rider upon the sward. Montreal disencumbered himself in great rage and shame, as a faint cry from his pavilion reached his ear, and redoubled his mortification. He rose with a lightness which astonished the beholders; for so heavy was the armour worn at that day, that few knights once stretched upon the ground could rise without assistance; and drawing his sword, cried out fiercely—"On foot, on foot!—the fall was not mine, but this accursed beast's, that I must needs for my sins raise to the rank of a charger. Come on——"

"Nay, Sir Knight," said Adrian, drawing off his gauntlets and unbuckling his helmet, which he threw on the ground. "I come to thee a guest and a friend; but to fight on foot is the encounter of mortal foes. Did I accept thy offer, my defeat would but stain thy knighthood."

Montreal, whose passion had beguiled him for the moment, sullenly acquiesced in this reasoning. Adrian hastened to soothe his antagonist. "For the rest," said he, "I cannot pretend to the prize. Your lance lost me my stirrups—mine left you unshaken. You say right! the defeat, if any, was that of your steed."

"We may meet again when I am more equally horsed," said Montreal, still chafing.

"Now, our Lady forbid!" exclaimed Adrian, with so devout an earnestness that the bystanders could not refrain from laughing; and even Montreal grimly and half-reluctantly joined in the merriment. The courtesy of his foe, however, conciliated and touched the more frank and soldierly qualities of his nature, and composing himself, he replied:—

"Signor di Castello, I rest your debtor for a courtesy that I have but little imitated. Howbeit, if thou wouldst bind me to thee for ever, thou wilt suffer me to send for my own charger, and afford me a chance to retrieve mine honour. With that steed, or with one equal to thine, which seems to me of the English breed, I will gage all I possess, lands, castle, and gold, sword and spurs, to maintain this pass, one by one, against all thy train."

Fortunately, perhaps, for Adrian, ere he could reply, Riccardo Annibaldi cried, with great warmth, "Sir Knight, I have with me two steeds well practised in the tourney; take thy choice, and accept in me a champion of the Roman against the French chivalry; —there is my gage."

"Signor," replied Montreal, with ill-suppressed delight, "thy proffer shows so gallant and free a spirit, that it were foul sin in me to balk it. I accept thy gage, and whichever of thy steeds thou rejectest, in God's name bring it hither, and let us waste no words before action."

Adrian, who felt that hitherto the Romans had been more favoured by fortune than merit, vainly endeavoured to prevent this second hazard. But Annibaldi was greatly chafed, and his high rank rendered it impolitic in Adrian to offend him by peremptory prohibition; the Colonna reluctantly, therefore, yielded his assent to the engagement. Annibaldi's steeds were led to the spot, the one a noble roan, the other a bay, of somewhat less breeding and bone, but still of great strength and price. Montreal finding the choice pressed upon him, gallantly selected the latter and less excellent.

Annibaldi was soon arrayed for the encounter, and Adrian gave the word to the trumpeters. The Roman was of a stature almost equal to that of Montreal, and though some years younger, seemed, in his armour, nearly of the same thews and girth, so that the present antagonists appeared at the first glance more evenly matched than the last. But this time Montreal, well horsed, inspired to the utmost by shame and pride, felt himself a match for an army; and he met the young Baron with such prowess, that while the very plume on his casque seemed scarcely stirred, the Italian was thrown several paces from his steed, and it was not till some moments after his visor was removed by his 'squires that he recovered his senses. This event restored Montreal to all his natural gaiety of humour, and effectually raised the spirits of his followers, who had felt much humbled by the previous encounter.

He himself assisted Annibaldi to rise with great courtesy, and a profusion of compliments, which the proud Roman took in stern silence, and then led the way to the pavilion, loudly ordering the banquet to be spread. Annibaldi, however, loitered behind, and Adrian, who penetrated his thoughts, and who saw that over their cups a quarrel between the Provençal and his friend was likely to ensue, drawing him aside, said:—" Methinks, dear Annibaldi, it would be better, if you, with the chief of our following, were to proceed onward to Fondi, where I will join you at sunset. My 'squires, and some eight lances, will suffice for my safeguard here; and, to say truth, I desire a few private words with our strange host, in the hope that he may be peaceably induced to withdraw from hence without the help of our Roman troops, who have enough elsewhere to feed their valour."

Annibaldi pressed his companion's hand: "I understand thee," he replied with a slight blush, "and, indeed, I could but ill brook the complacent triumph of the barbarian. I accept thy offer."

CHAPTER III

THE CONVERSATION BETWEEN THE ROMAN AND THE PROVENÇAL—ADELINE'S HISTORY—THE MOONLIT SEA—THE LUTE AND THE SONG

As soon as Annibaldi, with the greater part of the retinue, was gone, Adrian, divesting himself of his heavy greaves, entered alone the pavilion of the Knight of St. John. Montreal had already doffed all his armour, save the breastplate, and he now stepped forward to welcome his guest with the winning and easy grace which better suited his birth than his profession. He received Adrian's excuses for the absence of Annibaldi and the other knights of his train with a smile which seemed to prove how readily he divined the cause, and conducted him to the other and more private division of the pavilion in which the repast (rendered acceptable by the late exercise of guest and host) was prepared; and here Adrian for the first time discovered Adeline. Long inurement to the various and roving life of her lover, joined to a certain pride which she derived from conscious, though forfeited, rank, gave to the outward manner of that beautiful lady an ease and freedom which often concealed, even from Montreal, her sensitiveness to her unhappy situation. At times, indeed, when alone with Montreal, whom she loved with all the devotion of romance, she was sensible only to the charm of a presence which consoled her for all things; but in his frequent absence, or on the admission of any stranger, the illusion vanished—the reality returned. Poor lady! Nature had not formed, education had not reared, habit had not reconciled, her to the breath of shame!

The young Colonna was much struck by her beauty, and more by her gentle and high-born grace. Like her lord she appeared younger than she was; time seemed to spare a bloom which an experienced eye might have told was destined to an early grave; and there was something almost girlish in the lightness of her form—the braided luxuriance of her rich auburn hair, and the colour that went and came, not only with every movement, but almost with every word. The contrast between her and Montreal became them both—it was the contrast of devoted reliance and protecting strength: each looked fairer in the presence of the other; and as Adrian sate down to the well-laden board, he thought he had never seen a pair more formed for the poetic legends of their native Troubadours.

Montreal conversed gaily upon a thousand matters—pressed the wine flasks—and selected for his guest the most delicate portions of the delicious *spicola* of the neighbouring sea, and the rich flesh of the wild boar of the Pontine Marshes.

"Tell me," said Montreal, as their hunger was now appeased—"tell me, noble Adrian, how fares your kinsman, Signor Stephen? A brave old man for his years."

"He bears him as the youngest of us," answered Adrian.

"Late events must have shocked him a little," said Montreal, with an arch smile. "Ah, you look grave —yet commend my foresight;—I was the first who prophesied to thy kinsman the rise of Cola di Rienzi; he seems a great man—never more great than in conciliating the Colonna and the Orsini."

"The Tribune," returned Adrian, evasively, "is certainly a man of extraordinary genius. And now, seeing him command, my only wonder is how he ever brooked to obey—majesty seems a very part of him."

"Men who win power, easily put on its harness, dignity," answered Montreal; "and if I hear aright—(pledge me to your lady's health)—the Tribune, if not himself nobly born, will soon be nobly connected."

"He is already married to a Raselli, an old Roman house," replied Adrian.

"You evade my pursuit,—*Le doulx soupir! le doulx soupir!* as the old Cabestan has it"—said Montreal, laughing. "Well, you have pledged me one cup to your lady, pledge another to the fair Irene, the Tribune's sister—always provided they two are not one.—You smile and shake your head."

"I do not disguise from you, Sir Knight," answered Adrian, "that when my present embassy is over, I trust the alliance between the Tribune and a Colonna will go far towards the benefit of both."

"I have heard rightly, then," said Montreal, in a grave and thoughtful tone. "Rienzi's power must, indeed, be great."

"Of that my mission is a proof. Are you aware, Signor de Montreal, that Louis, King of Hungary——"

"How! what of him?"

"Has referred the decision of the feud between himself and Joanna of Naples, respecting the death of her royal spouse, his brother, to the fiat of the Tribune? This is the first time, methinks, since the death of Constantine, that so great a confidence and so high a charge were ever intrusted to a Roman!"

"By all the saints in the calendar," cried Montreal, crossing himself, "this news is indeed amazing! The fierce Louis of Hungary waive the right of the sword, and choose other umpire than the field of battle!"

"And this," continued Adrian, in a significant tone, "this it was which induced me to obey your courteous summons. I know, brave Montreal, that you hold intercourse with Louis. Louis has given to the Tribune the best pledge of his amity and alliance; will you do wisely if you——"

"Wage war with the Hungarian's ally," interrupted Montreal. "This you were about to add; the same thought crossed myself. My Lord, pardon me—Italians sometimes invent what they wish. On the honour of a Knight of the Empire, these tidings are the naked truth?"

"By my honour, and on the Cross," answered Adrian, drawing himself up; "and in proof thereof, I am now bound to Naples to settle with the Queen the preliminaries of the appointed trial."

"Two crowned heads before the tribunal of a plebeian, and one a defendant against the charge of murther!" muttered Montreal; "the news might well amaze me!"

He remained musing and silent a little while, till looking up, he caught Adeline's tender gaze fixed upon him with that deep solicitude with which she watched the outward effect of schemes and projects she was too soft to desire to know, and too innocent to share.

"Lady mine," said the Provençal, fondly, "how sayest thou? must we abandon our mountain castle, and these wild woodland scenes, for the dull walls of a city? I fear me so.—The Lady Adeline," he continued, turning to Adrian, "is of a singular bias; she hates the gay crowds of streets and thoroughfares, and esteems no palace like the solitary outlaw's hold. Yet, methinks, she might outshine all the faces of Italy,—thy mistress, Lord Adrian, of course, excepted."

"It is an exception which only a lover, and that too a betrothed lover, would dare to make," replied Adrian, gallantly.

"Nay," said Adeline, in a voice singularly sweet and clear, "nay, I know well at what price to value my lord's flattery, and Signor di Castello's courtesy. But you are bound, Sir Knight, to a court, that, if fame speak true, boasts in its Queen the very miracle and mould of beauty."

"It is some years since I saw the Queen of Naples," answered Adrian; "and I little dreamed then, when I gazed upon that angel face, that I should live to hear her accused of the foulest murther that ever stained even Italian royalty."

"And, as if resolved to prove her guilt," said Montreal, "ere long be sure she will marry the very man who did the deed. Of this I have certain proof."

Thus conversing, the Knights wore away the daylight, and beheld from the open tent the sun cast his setting glow over the purple sea. Adeline had long retired from the board, and they now saw her seated with her handmaids on a mound by the beach; while the sound of her lute faintly reached their ears. As Montreal caught the air, he turned from the converse, and sighing, half shaded his face with his hand. Somehow or other the two Knights had worn away all the little jealousy or pique which they had conceived against each other at Rome. Both imbued with the soldier-like spirit of the age, their contest in the morning had served to inspire them with that strange kind of respect, and even cordiality, which one brave man even still (how much more at that day!) feels for another, whose courage he has proved while vindicating his own. It is like the discovery of a congenial sentiment hitherto latent; and, in a life of camps, often establishes sudden and lasting friendship in the very lap of enmity. This feeling had been ripened by their subsequent familiar intercourse, and was increased on Adrian's side by the feeling, that in convincing Montreal of the policy of withdrawing from the Roman territories, he had obtained an advantage that well repaid whatever danger and delay he had undergone.

The sigh, and the altered manner of Montreal, did not escape Adrian, and he naturally connected it with something relating to her whose music had been its evident cause.

"Yon lovely dame," said he, gently, "touches the lute with an exquisite and fairy hand, and that plaintive air seems to my ear as of the minstrelsy of Provence."

"It is the air I taught her," said Montreal, sadly, "married as it is to indifferent words, with which I first wooed a heart that should never have given itself to me! Ay, young Colonna, many a night has my boat been moored beneath the starlit Sorgia that washes her proud father's halls, and my voice awaked the stillness of the waving sedges with a soldier's serenade. Sweet memories! bitter fruit!"

"Why bitter? ye love each other still."

"But I am vowed to celibacy, and Adeline de Courval is leman where she should be wedded dame. Methinks I fret at that thought even more than she,—dear Adeline!"

"Your lady, as all would guess, is then nobly born?"

"She is," answered Montreal, with a deep and evident feeling which, save in love, rarely, if ever, crossed his hardy breast. "She is! our tale is a brief one:—we loved each other as children: Her family was wealthier than mine: We were separated. I was given to understand that she abandoned me. I despaired, and in despair I took the cross of St. John. Chance threw us again together. I learned that her love was undecayed. Poor child!—she was even then, sir, but a child! I, wild—reckless—and not unskilled, perhaps, in the arts that woo and win. She could not resist my suit or her own affection!—We fled. In those words you see the thread of my after history. My sword and my Adeline were all my fortune. Society frowned on us. The Church threatened my soul. The Grand Master my life. I became a knight of fortune. Fate and my right hand favoured me. I have made those who scorned me tremble at my name. That name shall yet blaze, a star or a meteor, in the front of troubled nations, and I may yet win by force from the Pontiff the dispensation refused to my prayers. On the same day, I may offer Adeline the diadem and the ring.—Eno' of this;—you marked Adeline's cheek!—Seems it not delicate? I like not that changeful flush,—and she moves languidly,—*her* step that was so blithe!"

"Change of scene and the mild south will soon restore her health," said Adrian; "and in your peculiar life she is so little brought in contact with others, especially of her own sex, that I trust she is but seldom made aware of whatever is painful in her situation. And woman's love, Montreal, as we both have learned, is a robe that wraps her from many a storm!"

"You speak kindly," returned the Knight; "but you know not all our cause of grief. Adeline's father, a proud sieur, died,—they said of a broken heart,—but old men die of many another disease than that! The mother, a dame who boasted her descent from princes, bore the matter more sternly than the sire; clamoured for revenge,—which was odd, for she is as religious as a Dominican, and revenge is not Christian in a woman, though it is knightly in a man!—Well, my Lord, we had one boy, our only child; he was Adeline's solace in my absence,—his pretty ways were worth the world to her! She loved him so, that, but he had her eyes and looked like her when he slept, I should have been jealous! He grew up in our wild life, strong and comely; the young rogue, he would have been a brave knight! My evil stars led me to Milan, where I had business with the Visconti. One bright morning in June, our boy was stolen; verily that June was like a December to us!"

"Stolen!—how?—by whom?"

"The first question is answered easily,—the boy was with his nurse in the court-yard, the idle wench left him for but a minute or two—so she avers—to fetch him some childish toy; when she returned he was gone; not a trace left, save his pretty cap with the plume in it! Poor Adeline, many a time have I found her kissing that relic till it was wet with tears!"

"A strange fortune, in truth. But what interest could——"

"I will tell you," interrupted Montreal, "the only conjecture I could form;—Adeline's mother, on learning we had a son, sent to Adeline a letter, that well-nigh broke her heart, reproaching her for her love to me, and so forth, as if that had made her the vilest of the sex. She bade her take compassion on her child, and not bring him up to a robber's life,—so was she pleased to style the bold career of Walter de Montreal. She offered to rear the child in her own dull halls, and fit him, no doubt, for a shaven pate and a monk's cowl. She chafed much that a mother would not part with her treasure! She alone, partly in revenge, partly in silly compassion for Adeline's child, partly, it may be, from some pious fanaticism, could, it so seemed to me, have robbed us of our boy. On inquiry, I learned from the nurse—who, but that she was of the same sex as Adeline, should have tasted my dagger,—that in their walks, a woman of advanced years, but seemingly of humble rank, (that might be disguise!) had often stopped, and caressed and admired the child. I repaired at once to France, sought the old Castle of De Courval;—it had passed to the next heir, and the old widow was gone, none knew whither, but, it was conjectured, to take the veil in some remote convent."

"And you never saw her since?"

"Yes, at Rome," answered Montreal, turning pale; "when last there I chanced suddenly upon her; and then at length I learned my boy's fate, and the truth of my own surmise; she confessed to the theft—and my child was dead! I have not dared to tell Adeline of this; it seems to me as if it would be like plucking the shaft from the wounded side—and she would die at once, bereft of the uncertainty that rankles within her. She has still a hope—it comforts her; though my heart bleeds when I think on its vanity. Let this pass, my Colonna."

And Montreal started to his feet as if he strove, by a strong effort, to shake off the weakness that had crept over him in his narration.

"Think no more of it. Life is short—its thorns are many—let us not neglect any of its flowers. This is piety and wisdom too; Nature that meant me to struggle and to toil, gave me, happily, the sanguine heart and the elastic soul of France; and I have lived long enough to own that to die young is not an evil. Come, Lord Adrian, let us join my lady ere you part, if part you must; the moon will be up soon, and Fondi is but a short journey hence. You know that though I admire not your Petrarch, you with more courtesy laud our Provençal ballads, and you must hear Adeline sing one that you may prize them the more. The race of the Troubadours is dead, but the minstrelsy survives the minstrel!"

Adrian, who scarce knew what comfort to administer to the affliction of his companion, was somewhat relieved by the change in his mood, though his more grave and sensitive nature was a little startled at its suddenness. But, as we have before seen, Montreal's spirit (and this made perhaps its fascination) was as a varying and changeful sky; the gayest sunshine, and the fiercest storm swept over it in rapid alternation; and elements of singular might and grandeur, which, properly directed and concentrated, would have made him the blessing and glory of his time, were wielded with a boyish levity, roused into war and desolation, or lulled into repose and smoothness, with all the suddenness of chance, and all the fickleness of caprice.

Sauntering down to the beach, the music of Adeline's lute sounded more distinctly in their ears, and involuntarily they hushed their steps upon the rich and odorous turf, as in a voice, though not powerful, marvellously sweet and clear, and well adapted to the simple fashion of the words and melody, she sang the following stanzas:—

LAY OF THE LADY OF PROVENCE

1

Ah, why art thou sad, my heart? Why
  Darksome and lonely?
Frowns the face of the happy sky
  Over thee only?
          Ah me, ah me!
    Render to joy the earth!
    Grief shuns, not envies, Mirth;
    But leave one quiet spot,
    Where Mirth may enter not,
      To sigh, Ah me!—
          Ah me!

2

As a bird, though the sky be clear,
  Feels the storm lower;
My soul bodes the tempest near
  In the sunny hour;
          Ah me, ah me!
    Be glad while yet we may!
    I bid thee, my heart, be gay;
    And still I know not why,—
    Thou answerest with a sigh,
      (Fond heart!) Ah me!—
          Ah me!

3

As this twilight o'er the skies,
  Doubt brings the sorrow;
Who knows when the daylight dies,
  What waits the morrow?
      Ah me, ah me!
    Be blithe, be blithe, my lute,
    Thy strings will soon be mute;
    Be blithe—hark! while it dies,
    The note forewarning, sighs
      Its last—Ah me!—
        Ah me!

"My own Adeline—my sweetest night-bird," half-whispered Montreal, and softly approaching, he threw himself at his lady's feet—"thy song is too sad for this golden eve."

"No sound ever went to the heart," said Adrian, "whose arrow was not feathered by sadness. True sentiment, Montreal, is twin with melancholy, though not with gloom."

The lady looked softly and approvingly up at Adrian's face; she was pleased with its expression; she was pleased yet more with words of which women rather than men would acknowledge the truth. Adrian returned the look with one of deep and eloquent sympathy and respect; in fact, the short story he had heard from Montreal had interested him deeply in her; and never to the brilliant queen, to whose court he was bound, did his manner wear so chivalric and earnest a homage as it did to that lone and ill-fated lady on the twilight shores of Terracina.

Adeline blushed slightly and sighed; and then, to break the awkwardness of a pause which had stolen over them, as Montreal, unheeding the last remark of Adrian, was tuning the strings of the lute, she said—

"Of course, the Signor di Castello shares the universal enthusiasm for Petrarch?"

"Ay," cried Montreal; "my lady is Petrarch mad, like the rest of them: but all I know is, that never did belted knight and honest lover woo in such fantastic and tortured strains."

"In Italy," answered Adrian, "common language is exaggeration;—but even your own Troubadour poetry might tell you that love, ever seeking a new language of its own, cannot but often run into what to all but lovers seems distortion and conceit."

"Come, dear Signor," said Montreal, placing the lute in Adrian's hands, "let Adeline be the umpire between us, which music—yours or mine—can woo the more blandly."

"Ah," said Adrian, laughing; "I fear me, Sir Knight, you have already bribed the umpire."

Montreal's eyes and Adeline's met, and in that gaze Adeline forgot all her sorrows.

With a practised and skilful hand, Adrian touched the strings; and selecting a song which was less elaborate than those mostly in vogue amongst his countrymen, though still conceived in the Italian spirit, and in accordance with the sentiment he had previously expressed to Adeline, he sang as follows:—

LOVE'S EXCUSE FOR SADNESS

Chide not, beloved, if oft with thee
  I feel not rapture wholly;
For aye the heart that's fill'd with love,
  Runs o'er in melancholy.
To streams that glide in noon, the shade
  From summer skies is given;
So, if my breast reflects the cloud,
  'Tis but the cloud of heaven!

Thine image glass'd within my soul,
So well the mirror keepeth;
That, chide me not, if with the *light*
The *shadow* also sleepeth.

"And now," said Adrian, as he concluded, "the lute is to you: I but prelude your prize."

The Provençal laughed, and shook his head.—"With any other umpire, I had had my lute broken on my own head, for my conceit in provoking such a rival; but I must not shrink from a contest I have myself provoked, even though in one day *twice* defeated." And with that, in a deep and exquisitely melodious voice, which wanted only more scientific culture to have challenged any competition, the Knight of St. John poured forth

THE LAY OF THE TROUBADOUR

I

Gentle river, the moonbeam is hush'd on thy tide,
On thy pathway of light to my lady I glide.
My boat, where the stream laves the castle, I moor,—
All at rest save the maid and her young Troubadour!
As the stars to the waters that bore
My bark, to my spirit thou art;
Heaving yet, see it bound to the shore,
So moor'd to thy beauty my heart,—
Bel' amie, bel' amie, bel' amie!

2

Wilt thou fly from the world? It hath wealth for the vain
But Love breaks his bond when there's gold in the chain:
Wilt thou fly from the world? It hath courts for the proud;—
But Love, born in caves, pines to death in the crowd.
Were this bosom thy world, dearest one,
Thy world could not fail to be bright;
For thou shouldst thyself be its sun,
And what spot could be dim in thy light—
Bel' amie. bel' amie. bel' amie?

3

The rich and the great woo thee dearest; and poor,
Though his fathers were princes, thy young Troubadour!
But his heart never quail'd save to thee, his adored,—
There's no guile in his lute, and no stain on his sword.
Ah, I reck not what sorrows I know,
Could I still on thy solace confide;
And I care not, though earth be my foe,
If thy soft heart be found by my side,—
Bel' amie, bel' amie, bel' amie!

4

The maiden she blushed, and the maiden she sighed,
Not a cloud in the sky, not a gale on the tide;
But though tempest had raged on the wave and the wind,
That castle, methinks, had been still left behind!
Sweet lily, though bow'd by the blast,
(To this bosom transplanted) since then,
Wouldst thou change, could we call the past,
To the rock from thy garden again—
Bel' amie, bel' amie, bel' amie?

Thus they alternated the time with converse and song, as the wooded hills threw their sharp, long shadows over the sea; while from many a mound of waking flowers, and many a copse of citron and orange, relieved by the dark and solemn aloe, stole the summer breeze, laden with mingled odours; and, over the seas, coloured by the slow-fading hues of purple and rose, that the sun had long bequeathed to the twilight, flitted the gay fire-flies that sparkle along that enchanted coast. At length, the moon slowly rose above the dark forest-steeps, gleaming on the gay pavilion and glittering pennon of Montreal,—on the verdant sward,—the polished mail of the soldiers, stretched on the grass in various groups, half-shaded by oaks and cypress, and the war-steeds grazing peaceably together—a wild mixture of the Pastoral and the Iron time.

Adrian, reluctantly reminded of his journey, rose to depart.

"I fear," said he to Adeline, "that I have already detained you too late in the night air: but selfishness is little considerate."

"Nay, you see we are prudent," said Adeline, pointing to Montreal's mantle, which his provident hand had long since drawn around her form; "but if you must part, farewell, and success attend you!"

"We may meet again, I trust," said Adrian.

Adeline sighed gently; and the Colonna, gazing on her face by the moonlight, to which it was slightly raised, was painfully struck by its almost transparent delicacy. Moved by his compassion, ere he mounted his steed, he drew Montreal aside,—"Forgive me if I seem presumptuous," said he; "but to one so noble this wild life is scarce a fitting career. I know that, in our time, War consecrates all his children; but surely a settled rank in the court of the Emperor, or an honourable reconciliation with your knightly brethren, were better——"

"Than a Tartar camp, and a brigand's castle," interrupted Montreal, with some impatience. "This you were about to say—you are mistaken. Society thrust me from her bosom; let society take the fruit it hath sown. 'A fixed rank,' say you? some subaltern office, to fight at other men's command! You know me not: Walter de Montreal was not formed to obey. War when I will and rest when I list, is the motto of my escutcheon. Ambition proffers me rewards you wot not of; and I am of the mould as of the race of those whose swords have conquered thrones. For the rest, your news of the alliance of Louis of Hungary with your Tribune makes it necessary for the friend of Louis to withdraw from all feud with Rome. Ere the week expire, the owl and the bat may seek refuge in yon gray turrets."

"But your lady?"

"Is inured to change.—God help her, and temper the rough wind to the lamb!"

"Enough, Sir Knight: but should you desire a sure refuge at Rome for one so gentle and so highborn, by the right hand of a knight, I promise a safe roof and an honoured home to the Lady Adeline."

Montreal pressed the offered hand to his heart; then plucking his own hastily away, drew it across his eyes, and joined Adeline, in a silence that showed he dared not trust himself to speak. In a few moments Adrian and his train were on the march; but still the young Colonna turned back, to gaze once more on his wild host and that lovely lady, as they themselves lingered on the moonlit sward, while the sea rippled mournfully on their ears.

It was not many months after that date, that the name of Fra Moreale scattered terror and dismay throughout the fair Campania. The right hand of the Hungarian king, in his invasion of Naples, he was chosen afterwards vicar (or vicegerent) of Louis in Aversa; and fame and fate seemed to lead him triumphantly along that ambitious career which he had elected, whether bounded by the scaffold or the throne.

BOOK IV

THE TRIUMPH AND THE POMP

" Allora fama e paura di si buono reggimento, passa in ogni terra."—*Vita di Cola di Rienzi,* lib. i. cap. 21.

" Then the fame and the fear of that so good government passed into every land."—*Life of Cola di Rienzi.*

CHAPTER I

THE BOY ANGELO—THE DREAM OF NINA FULFILLED

The thread of my story transports us back to Rome. It was in a small chamber, in a ruinous mansion by the base of Mount Aventine, that a young boy sate, one evening, with a woman of a tall and stately form, but somewhat bowed both by infirmity and years. The boy was of a fair and comely presence; and there was that in his bold, frank, undaunted carriage, which made him appear older than he was.

The old woman, seated in the recess of the deep window, was apparently occupied with a Bible that lay open on her knees; but ever and anon she lifted her eyes, and gazed on her young companion with a sad and anxious expression.

" Dame," said the boy, who was busily employed in hewing out a sword of wood, " I would you had seen the show to-day. Why, every day is a show at Rome now! It is show enough to see the Tribune himself on his white steed—(oh, it is so beautiful!)—with his white robes all studded with jewels. But to-day, as I have just been telling you, the Lady Nina took notice of me, as I stood on the stairs of the Capitol: you know, dame, I had donned my best blue velvet doublet."

"And she called you a fair boy, and asked if you would be her little page; and this has turned thy brain, silly urchin that thou art——"

"But the words are the least: if you saw the Lady Nina, you would own that a smile from her might turn the wisest head in Italy. Oh, how I should like to serve the Tribune! All the lads of my age are mad for him. How they will stare, and envy me at school to-morrow! You know too, dame, that though I was not always brought up at Rome, I am Roman. Every Roman loves Rienzi."

"Ay, for the hour: the cry will soon change. This vanity of thine, Angelo, vexes my old heart. I would thou wert humbler."

"Bastards have their own name to win," said the boy, colouring deeply. "They twit me in the teeth, because I cannot say who my father and mother were."

"They need not," returned the dame, hastily. "Thou comest of noble blood and long descent, though, as I have told thee often, I know not the exact names of thy parents. But what art thou shaping that tough sapling of oak into?"

"A sword, dame, to assist the Tribune against the robbers."

"Alas! I fear me, like all those who seek power in Italy, he is more likely to enlist robbers than to assail them."

"Why, la you there, you live so shut up, that you know and hear nothing, or you would have learned that even that fiercest of all the robbers, Fra Moreale, has at length yielded to the Tribune, and fled from his castle, like a rat from a falling house."

"How, how!" cried the dame; "what say you? Has this plebeian, whom you call the Tribune—has he boldly thrown the gage to that dread warrior? and has Montreal left the Roman territory?"

"Ay, it is the talk of the town. But Fra Moreale seems as much a bugbear to you as to e'er a mother in Rome. Did he ever wrong you, dame?"

"Yes!" exclaimed the old woman, with so abrupt a fierceness, that even that hardy boy was startled.

"I wish I could meet him, then," said he, after a pause, as he flourished his mimic weapon.

"Now Heaven forbid! He is a man ever to be shunned by thee, whether for peace or war. Say again this good Tribune holds no terms with the Free Lances."

"Say it again—why all Rome knows it."

"He is pious, too, I have heard; and they do bruit it that he sees visions, and is comforted from above," said the woman, speaking to herself. Then turning to Angelo, she continued,—"Thou wouldst like greatly to accept the Lady Nina's proffer?"

"Ah, that I should, dame, if you could spare me."

"Child," replied the matron, solemnly, "my sand is nearly run, and my wish is to see thee placed with one who will nurture thy young years, and save thee from a life of licence. That done, I may fulfil my vow, and devote the desolate remnant of my years to God. I will think more of this, my child. Not under such a plebeian's roof shouldst thou have lodged, nor from a stranger's board been fed: but at Rome, my last relative worthy of the trust is dead;—and at the worst, obscure honesty is better than gaudy crime. Thy spirit troubles me already. Back, my child; I must to my closet, and watch and pray."

Thus saying, the old woman, repelling the advance, and silencing the muttered and confused words, of the boy—half affectionate as they were, yet half tetchy and wayward—glided from the chamber.

The boy looked abstractedly at the closing door, and then said to himself—"The dame is always talking riddles: I wonder if she know more of me than she tells, or if she is any way akin to me. I hope not, for I don't love her much; nor, for that matter, anything else. I wish she would place me with the Tribune's lady, and then we'll see who among the lads will call Angelo Villani bastard."

With that the boy fell to work again at his sword with redoubled vigour. In fact, the cold manner of this female, his sole nurse, companion, substitute for parent, had repelled his affections without subduing his temper; and though not originally of evil disposition, Angelo Villani was already insolent, cunning, and revengeful; but not, on the other hand, without a quick susceptibility to kindness as to affront, a natural acuteness of understanding, and a great indifference to fear. Brought up in quiet affluence rather than luxury, and living much with his protector, whom he knew but by the name of Ursula, his bearing was graceful, and his air that of the well-born. And it was his carriage, perhaps, rather than his countenance, which, though handsome, was more distinguished for intelligence than beauty, which had attracted the notice of the Tribune's bride. His education was that of one reared for some scholastic profession. He was not only taught to read and write, but had been even instructed in the rudiments of Latin. He did not, however, incline to these studies half so fondly as to the games of his companions, or the shows or riots in the street, into all of which he managed to thrust himself, and from which he had always the happy dexterity to return safe and unscathed.

The next morning Ursula entered the young Angelo's chamber. "Wear again thy blue doublet to-day," said she; "I would have thee look thy best. Thou shalt go with me to the palace."

"What, to-day?" cried the boy joyfully, half leaping from his bed. "Dear dame Ursula, shall I really then belong to the train of the great Tribune's lady?"

"Yes; and leave the old woman to die alone! Your joy becomes you,—but ingratitude is in your blood. Ingratitude! Oh, it has burned my heart into ashes—and yours, boy, can no longer find a fuel in the dry crumbling cinders."

"Dear dame, you are always so biting. You know you said you wished to retire into a convent, and I was too troublesome a charge for you. But you delight in rebuking me, justly or unjustly."

"My task is over," said Ursula, with a deep-drawn sigh.

The boy answered not; and the old woman retired with a heavy step, and, it may be, a heavier heart. When he joined her in their common apartment, he observed what his joy had previously blinded him to—that Ursula did not wear her usual plain and sober dress. The gold chain, rarely assumed then by women not of noble birth—though, in the other sex, affected also by public functionaries and wealthy merchants—glittered upon a robe of the rich flowered stuffs of Venice, and the clasps that confined the vest at the throat and waist were adorned with jewels of no common price.

Angelo's eye was struck by the change, but he felt a more manly pride in remarking that the old lady became it well. Her air and mien were indeed those of one to whom such garments were habitual; and they seemed that day more than usually austere and stately.

She smoothed the boy's ringlets, drew his short mantle more gracefully over his shoulder, and then placed in his belt a poniard whose handle was richly studded, and a purse well filled with florins.

"Learn to use both discreetly," said she; "and whether I live or die, you will never require to wield the poniard to procure the gold."

"This, then," cried Angelo, enchanted, "is a real poniard to fight the robbers with! Ah, with this I should not fear Fra Moreale, who wronged thee so. I trust I may yet avenge thee, though thou didst rate me so just now for ingratitude."

"I *am* avenged. Nourish not such thoughts, my son, they are sinful; at least I fear so. Draw to the board and eat; we will go betimes, as petitioners should do."

Angelo had soon finished his morning meal, and sallying with Ursula to the porch, he saw, to his surprise, four of those servitors who then usually attended persons of distinction, and who were to be hired in every city, for the convenience of strangers or the holyday ostentation of the gayer citizens.

"How grand we are to-day!" said he, clapping his hands with an eagerness which Ursula failed not to reprove.

"It is not for vain show," she added, "which true

nobility can well dispense with, but that we may the more readily gain admittance to the palace. These princes of yesterday are not easy of audience to the over humble."

"Oh! but you are wrong this time," said the boy. "The Tribune gives audience to all men, the poorest as the richest. Nay, there is not a ragged boor, or a barefooted friar, who does not win access to him sooner than the proudest baron. That's why the people love him so. And he devotes one day of the week to receiving the widows and the orphans;—and you know, dame, I am an orphan."

Ursula, already occupied with her own thoughts, did not answer, and scarcely heard, the boy; but leaning on his young arm, and preceded by the footmen to clear the way, passed slowly towards the palace of the Capitol.

A wonderful thing would it have been to a more observant eye, to note the change which two or three short months of the stern but salutary and wise rule of the Tribune had effected in the streets of Rome. You no longer beheld the gaunt and mail-clad forms of foreign mercenaries stalking through the vistas, or grouped in lazy insolence before the embattled porches of some gloomy palace. The shops, that in many quarters had been closed for years, were again open, glittering with wares and bustling with trade. The thoroughfares, formerly either silent as death, or crossed by some affrighted and solitary passenger with quick steps, and eyes that searched every corner,—or resounding with the roar of a pauper rabble, or the open feuds of savage nobles, now exhibited the regular, and wholesome, and mingled streams of civilised life, whether bound to pleasure or to commerce. Carts and waggons laden with goods which had passed in safety by the dismantled holds of the robbers of the Campagna, rattled cheerfully over the pathways. "Never, perhaps,"—to use the translation adapted from the Italian authorities, by a modern and by no means a partial historian*—"Never, perhaps, has the energy and effect of a single mind been more remarkably felt than in the sudden reformation of Rome by the Tribune Rienzi. A den of robbers was converted to the discipline of a camp or convent. 'In this time,' says the historian,† 'did the woods begin to rejoice that they were no longer infested with robbers; the oxen began to plough; the pilgrims visited the sanctuaries;‡ the roads and inns were replenished with travellers: trade, plenty, and good faith, were restored in the markets; and a purse of gold might be exposed without danger in the midst of the highways.'"

Amidst all these evidences of comfort and security to the people—some dark and discontented countenances might be seen mingled in the crowd, and whenever one who wore the livery of the Colonna or the Orsini felt himself jostled by the throng, a fierce hand moved involuntarily to the sword-belt, and a half-suppressed oath was ended with an indignant sigh. Here and there too,—contrasting the redecorated, refurnished, and smiling shops—heaps of rubbish before the gate of some haughty mansion testified the abasement of fortifications which the owner impotently resented as a sacrilege. Through such streets and such throngs did the party we accompany wend their way, till they found themselves amidst crowds assembled

* Gibbon.

† Vita di Cola di Rienzi, lib. i. c. 9.

‡ Gibbon: the words in the original are "*li pellegrini cominciaro a fere le cerca per la santuaria.*"

before the entrance of the Capitol. The officers there stationed kept, however, so discreet and dexterous an order, that they were not long detained; and now in the broad place or court of that memorable building, they saw the open doors of the great justice-hall, guarded but by a single sentinel, and in which, for six hours daily, did the Tribune hold his court, for "patient to hear, swift to redress, inexorable to punish, his tribunal was always accessible to the poor and stranger."*

Not, however, to that hall did the party bend its way, but to the entrance which admitted to the private apartments of the palace. And here the pomp, the gaud, the more than regal magnificence, of the residence of the Tribune, strongly contrasted the patriarchal simplicity which marked his justice court.

Even Ursula, not unaccustomed, of yore, to the luxurious state of Italian and French principalities, seemed roused into surprise at the hall crowded with retainers in costly liveries, the marble and gilded columns wreathed with flowers, and the gorgeous banners wrought with the blended arms of the Republican City and the Pontifical See, which blazed aloft and around.

Scarce knowing whom to address in such an assemblage, Ursula was relieved from her perplexity by an officer attired in a suit of crimson and gold, who, with a grave and formal decorum, which indeed reigned throughout the whole retinue, demanded, respectfully, whom she sought? "The Signora Nina!" replied Ursula, drawing up her stately person, with a natural, though somewhat antiquated, dignity. There was something foreign in the accent, which influenced the officer's answer.

* Gibbon.

"To-day, madam, I fear that the Signora receives only the Roman ladies. To-morrow is that appointed for all foreign dames of distinction."

Ursula, with a slight impatience of tone, replied—

"My business is of that nature which is welcome on any day, at palaces. I come, Signor, to lay certain presents at the Signora's feet, which I trust she will deign to accept."

"And say, Signor," added the boy, abruptly, "that Angelo Villani, whom the Lady Nina honoured yesterday with her notice, is no stranger but a Roman; and comes, as she bade him, to proffer to the Signora his homage and devotion."

The grave officer could not refrain a smile at the pert, yet not ungraceful, boldness of the boy.

"I remember me, Master Angelo Villani," he replied, "that the Lady Nina spoke to you by the great staircase. Madam, I will do your errand. Please to follow me to an apartment more fitting your sex and seeming."

With that the officer led the way across the hall to a broad staircase of white marble, along the centre of which were laid those rich Eastern carpets which at that day, when rushes strewed the chambers of an English monarch, were already common to the greater luxury of Italian palaces. Opening a door at the first flight, he ushered Ursula and her young charge into a lofty ante-chamber, hung with arras of wrought velvets; while over the opposite door, through which the officer now vanished, were blazoned the armorial bearings which the Tribune so constantly introduced in all his pomp, not more from the love of show, than from his politic desire to mingle with the keys of the Pontiff the heraldic insignia of the Republic.

"Philip of Valois is not housed like this man!" muttered Ursula. "If this last, I shall have done better for my charge than I recked of."

The officer soon returned, and led them across an apartment of vast extent, which was indeed the great reception chamber of the palace. Four-and-twenty columns of the Oriental alabaster which had attested the spoils of the later emperors, and had been disinterred from forgotten ruins, to grace the palace of the Reviver of the old Republic, supported the light roof, which, half Gothic, half classic, in its architecture, was inlaid with gilded and purple mosaics. The tesselated floor was covered in the centre with cloth of gold, the walls were clothed, at intervals, with the same gorgeous hangings, relieved by panels freshly painted in the most glowing colours, with mystic and symbolical designs. At the upper end of this royal chamber, two steps ascended to the place of the Tribune's throne, above which was the canopy wrought with the eternal armorial bearings of the Pontiff and the City.

Traversing this apartment, the officer opened the door at its extremity, which admitted to a small chamber, crowded with pages in rich dresses of silver and blue velvet. There were few amongst them elder than Angelo; and, from their general beauty, they seemed the very flower and blossom of the city.

Short time had Angelo to gaze on his comrades that were to be:—another minute, and he and his protectress were in the presence of the Tribune's bride.

The chamber was not large—but it was large enough to prove that the beautiful daughter of Raselli had realised her visions of vanity and splendour.

It was an apartment that mocked description—it seemed a cabinet for the gems of the world. The daylight, shaded by high and deep-set casements of stained glass, streamed in a purple and mellow hue over all that the art of that day boasted most precious, or regal luxury held most dear. The candelabras of the silver workmanship of Florence; the carpets and stuffs of the East; the draperies of Venice and Genoa; paintings like the illuminated missals, wrought in gold, and those lost colours of blue and crimson; antique marbles, which spoke of the bright days of Athens; tables of disinterred mosaics, their freshness preserved as by magic; censers of gold that steamed with the odours of Araby, yet so subdued as not to deaden the healthier scent of flowers, which blushed in every corner from their marble and alabaster vases; a small and spirit-like fountain, which seemed to gush from among wreaths of roses, diffusing in its diamond and fairy spray, a scarce felt coolness to the air;—all these, and such as these, which it were vain work to detail, congregated in the richest luxuriance, harmonised with the most exquisite taste, uniting the ancient arts with the modern, amazed and intoxicated the sense of the beholder. It was not so much the cost, nor the luxury, that made the character of the chamber; it was a certain gorgeous and almost sublime phantasy,—so that it seemed rather the fabled retreat of an enchantress, at whose word genii ransacked the earth, and fairies arranged the produce, than the grosser splendour of an earthly queen. Behind the piled cushions upon which Nina half reclined, stood four girls, beautiful as nymphs, with fans of the rarest feathers, and at her feet lay one older than the rest, whose lute, though now silent, attested her legitimate occupation.

But, had the room in itself seemed somewhat too fantastic and overcharged in its prodigal ornaments, the form and face of Nina would at once have rendered all appropriate: so completely did she seem the natural Spirit of the Place; so wonderfully did her beauty, elated as it now was with contented love, gratified vanity, exultant hope, body forth the brightest vision that ever floated before the eyes of Tasso, when he wrought into one immortal shape the glory of the Enchantress with the allurements of the Woman.

Nina half rose as she saw Ursula, whose sedate and mournful features involuntarily testified her surprise and admiration at a loveliness so rare and striking, but who, undazzled by the splendour around, soon recovered her wonted self-composure, and seated herself on the cushion to which Nina pointed, while the young visitor remained standing, and spell-bound by childish wonder, in the centre of the apartment. Nina recognised him with a smile.

"Ah, my pretty boy, whose quick eye and bold air caught my fancy yesterday! Have you come to accept my offer? Is it you, madam, who claim this fair child?"

"Lady," replied Ursula, "my business here is brief: by a train of events, needless to weary you with narrating, this boy from his infancy fell to my charge—a weighty and anxious trust to one whose thoughts are beyond the barrier of life. I have reared him as became a youth of gentle blood; for on both sides, lady, he is noble, though an orphan, motherless and sireless."

"Poor child!" said Nina, compassionately.

"Growing now," continued Ursula, "oppressed by years, and desirous only to make my peace with Heaven, I journeyed hither some months since, in the design to place the boy with a relation of mine; and, that trust fulfilled, to take the vows in the City of the Apostle. Alas! I found my kinsman dead, and a baron of wild and dissolute character was his heir. Here remaining, perplexed and anxious, it seemed to me the voice of Providence when, yester-evening, the child told me you had been pleased to honour him with your notice. Like the rest of Rome, he has already learned enthusiasm for the Tribune—devotion to the Tribune's bride. Will you, in truth, admit him of your household? He will not dishonour your protection by his blood, nor, I trust, by his bearing."

"I would take his face for his guarantee, madam, even without so distinguished a recommendation as your own. Is he Roman? His name then must be known to me."

"Pardon me, lady," replied Ursula: "he bears the name of Angelo Villani—not that of his sire or mother. The honour of a noble house for ever condemns his parentage to rest unknown. He is the offspring of a love unsanctioned by the church."

"He is the more to be loved, then, and to be pitied—victim of sin not his own!" answered Nina, with moistened eyes, as she saw the deep and burning blush that covered the boy's cheeks. "With the Tribune's reign commences a new era of nobility, when rank and knighthood shall be won by a man's own merit—not that of his ancestors. Fear not, madam: in my house he shall know no slight."

Ursula was moved from her pride by the kindness of Nina; she approached with involuntary reverence, and kissed the Signora's hand—

"May our Lady reward your noble heart!" said she: "and now my mission is ended, and my earthly goal is won. Add only, lady, to your inestimable favours one more. These jewels"—and Ursula drew from her robe a casket, touched the spring, and the lid flying back, discovered jewels of great size and the most brilliant water,—"these jewels," she continued, laying the casket at Nina's feet, "once belonging to the princely house of Thoulouse, are valueless to me and mine. Suffer me to think that they are transferred to one whose queenly brow will give them a lustre it cannot borrow."

"How!" said Nina, colouring very deeply; "think you, madam, my kindness can be bought? What woman's kindness ever was? Nay, nay—take back the gifts, or I shall pray you to take back your boy."

Ursula was astonished and confounded: to her experience such abstinence was a novelty, and she scarcely knew how to meet it. Nina perceived her embarrassment with a haughty and triumphant smile, and then, regaining her former courtesy of demeanour, said, with a grave sweetness—

"The Tribune's hands are clean,—the Tribune's wife must not be suspected. Rather, madam, should I press upon *you* some token of exchange for the fair charge you have committed to me. Your jewels hereafter may profit the boy in his career: reserve them for one who needs them."

"No, lady," said Ursula, rising and lifting her eyes to heaven;—"they shall buy masses for his mother's soul; for him I shall reserve a competence when his years require it. Lady, accept the thanks of a wretched and desolate heart. Fare you well!"

She turned to quit the room, but with so faltering and weak a step, that Nina, touched and affected, sprung up, and with her own hand guided the old woman across the room, whispering comfort and soothing to her; while, as they reached the door, the boy rushed forward, and, clasping Ursula's robe, sobbed out—"Dear dame, not one farewell for your little Angelo! Forgive him all he has cost you! Now, for the first time, I feel how wayward and thankless I have been."

The old woman caught him in her arms, and kissed him passionately; when the boy, as if a thought suddenly struck him, drew forth the purse she had given him, and said, in a choked and scarce articulate voice,—"And let this, dearest dame, go in masses for my poor *father's* soul; for *he* is dead, too, you know!"

These words seemed to freeze at once all the tenderer emotions of Ursula. She put back the boy with the same chilling and stern severity of aspect and manner which had so often before repressed him: and recovering her self-possession, at once quitted the apartment without saying another word. Nina, surprised, but still pitying her sorrow and respecting her age, followed her steps across the pages' ante-room and the reception-chamber, even to the foot of the stairs,—a condescension the haughtiest princes of Rome could not have won from her; and returning, saddened and thoughtful, she took the boy's hand, and affectionately kissed his forehead.

"Poor boy!" she said, "it seems as if Providence had made me select thee yesterday from the crowd, and thus conducted thee to thy proper refuge. For to whom should come the friendless and the orphans of Rome, but to the palace of Rome's first Magistrate?" Turning then to her attendants, she gave them instructions as to the personal comforts of her new charge, which evinced that if power had ministered to her vanity, it had not steeled her heart. Angelo Villani lived to repay her *well!*

She retained the boy in her presence, and conversing with him familiarly, she was more and more pleased with his bold spirit and frank manner. Their conversation was however interrupted, as the day advanced, by the arrival of several ladies of the Roman nobility. And then it was that Nina's virtues receded into shade, and her faults appeared. She could not resist the woman's triumph over those arrogant signoras who now cringed in homage where they had once slighted with disdain. She affected the manner of, she demanded the respect due, to a queen. And by many of those dexterous arts which the sex know so well, she contrived to render her very courtesy a humiliation to her haughty guests. Her commanding beauty and her graceful intellect saved her, indeed, from the vulgar insolence of the upstart; but yet more keenly stung the pride, by forbidding to those she mortified the retaliation of contempt. Hers were the covert taunt—the smiling affront—the sarcasm in the mask of compliment—the careless exaction of respect in trifles, which could not outwardly be resented, but which could not inly be forgiven.

"Fair day to the Signora Colonna," said she to the proud wife of the proud Stephen; "we passed your palace yesterday. How fair it now seems, relieved from those gloomy battlements which it must often have saddened you to gaze upon. Signora" (turning to one of the Orsini), "your lord has high favour with the Tribune, who destines him to great command. His fortunes are secured, and we rejoice at it; for no man more loyally serves the state. Have you seen, fair Lady of Frangipani, the last verses of Petrarch in honour of my lord?—they rest yonder. May we so far venture as to request you to point out their beauties to the Signora di Savelli? We rejoice, noble Lady of Malatesta, to observe that your eyesight is so well restored. The last time we met, though we stood next to you in the revels of the Lady Giulia, you seemed scarce to distinguish us from the pillar by which we stood!"

"Must this insolence be endured!" whispered the Signora Frangipani to the Signora Malatesta.

"Hush, hush; if ever it be *our* day again!"

CHAPTER II

THE BLESSING OF A COUNCILLOR WHOSE INTERESTS AND HEART ARE OUR OWN.—THE STRAWS THROWN UPWARD—DO THEY PORTEND A STORM

It was later that day than usual, when Rienzi returned from his tribunal to the apartments of the palace. As he traversed the reception hall, his countenance was much flushed; his teeth were set firmly, like a man who has taken a strong resolution from which he will not be moved; and his brow was dark with that settled and fearful frown which the describers of his personal appearance have not failed to notice as the characteristic of an anger the more deadly because invariably just. Close at his heels followed the Bishop of Orvietto and the aged Stephen Colonna. "I tell you, my Lords," said Rienzi, "that ye plead in vain. Rome knows no distinction between ranks. The law is blind to the agent—lynx-eyed to the deed."

"Yet," said Raimond, hesitatingly, "bethink thee,

Tribune; the nephew of two cardinals, and himself once a senator."

Rienzi halted abruptly, and faced his companions. "My Lord Bishop," said he, "does not this make the crime more inexcusable? Look you, thus it reads:—A vessel from Avignon to Naples, charged with the revenues of Provence to Queen Joanna, on whose cause, mark you, we now hold solemn council, is wrecked at the mouth of the Tiber; with that, Martino di Porto—a noble, as you say—the holder of that fortress whence he derives his title,—doubly bound by gentle blood and by immediate neighbourhood to succour the oppressed—falls upon the vessel with his troops (what hath the rebel with armed troops?)—and pillages the vessel like a common robber. He is apprehended—brought to my tribunal—receives fair trial—is condemned to die. Such is the law;—what more would ye have?"

"Mercy," said the Colonna.

Rienzi folded his arms, and laughed disdainfully. "I never heard my Lord Colonna plead for mercy when a peasant had stolen the bread that was to feed his famishing children."

"Between a peasant and a prince, Tribune, *I*, for one, recognise a distinction:—the bright blood of an Orsini is not to be shed like that of a base plebeian——"

"Which, I remember me," said Rienzi, in a low voice, "you deemed small matter enough when my boy-brother fell beneath the wanton spear of your proud son. Wake not that memory, I warn you; let it sleep.—For shame, old Colonna—for shame; so near the grave, where the worm levels all flesh, and preaching, with those gray hairs, the uncharitable distinction between man and man. Is there not distinction enough at the best? Does not one wear purple, and the other rags? Hath not one ease and the other toil? Doth not the one banquet while the other starves? Do I nourish any mad scheme to level the ranks which society renders a necessary evil? No. I war no more with Dives than with Lazarus. But before man's judgment-seat, as before God's, Lazarus and Dives are made equal. No more."

Colonna drew his robe round him with great haughtiness, and bit his lip in silence. Raimond interposed.

"All this is true, Tribune. But," and he drew Rienzi aside, "you know we must be politic as well as just. Nephew to two cardinals, what enmity will not this provoke at Avignon?"

"Vex not yourself, holy Raimond, I will answer it to the Pontiff." While they spoke the bell tolled heavily and loudly.

Colonna started.

"Great Tribune," said he, with a slight sneer, "deign to pause ere it be too late. I know not that I ever before bent to you a suppliant; and I ask you now to spare mine own foe. Stephen Colonna prays Cola di Rienzi to spare the life of an Orsini."

"I understand thy taunt, old Lord," said Rienzi, calmly, "but I resent it not. You are foe to the Orsini, yet you plead for him—it sounds generous; but hark you,—you are more a friend to your order than a foe to your rival. You cannot bear that one, great enough to have contended with you, should perish like a thief. I give full praise to such noble forgiveness; but I am no noble, and I do not sympathise with it. One word more:—if this were the sole act of fraud and violence that this bandit baron had committed, your prayers should plead for him; but is not his life notorious? Has he not been from boyhood the terror and disgrace of Rome! How many matrons violated, merchants pillaged, peaceful men stilettoed in the daylight, rise in dark witness against the prisoner? And for such a man do I live to hear an aged prince and a pope's vicar plead for mercy?—Fie, fie! But I will be even with ye. The next *poor* man whom the law sentences to death, for your sake will I pardon."

Raimond again drew aside the Tribune, while Colonna struggled to suppress his rage.

"My friend," said the Bishop, "the nobles will feel this as an insult to their whole order; the very pleading of Orsini's worst foe must convince thee of this. Martino's blood will seal their reconciliation with each other, and they will be as one man against thee."

"Be it so: with God and the People on my side, I will dare, though a Roman, to be just. The bell ceases—you are already too late." So saying, Rienzi threw open the casement; and by the Staircase of the Lion rose a gibbet from which swung with a creaking sound, arrayed in his patrician robes, the yet palpitating corpse of Martino di Porto.

"Behold!" said the Tribune, sternly, "thus die all robbers. For *traitors*, the same law has the axe and the scaffold!"

Raimond drew back and turned pale. Not so the veteran noble. Tears of wounded pride started from his eyes; he approached, leaning on his staff, to Rienzi, touched him on his shoulder, and said,—

"Tribune, a judge has lived to envy his victim!"

Rienzi turned with an equal pride to the Baron.

"We forgive idle words in the aged. My Lord, have you done with us?—we would be alone."

"Give me thy arm, Raimond," said Stephen. "Tribune—farewell. Forget that the Colonna sued thee,—an easy task, methinks; for, wise as you are, you forget what every one else can remember."

"Ah, my Lord, what?"

"Birth, Tribune, birth—that's all!"

"The Signor Colonna has taken up my old calling, and turned a wit," returned Rienzi, with an indifferent and easy tone.

Then following Raimond and Stephen with his eyes, till the door closed upon them, he muttered, "Insolent! were it not for Adrian, thy gray beard should not bear thee harmless. Birth! what Colonna would not boast himself, if he could, the grandson of an emperor?—Old man, there is danger in thee which must be watched." With that he turned musingly towards the casement, and again that grisly spectacle of death met his eye. The people below, assembled in large concourse, rejoiced at the execution of one whose whole life had been infamy and rapine—but who had seemed beyond justice—with all the fierce clamour that marks the exultation of the rabble over a crushed foe. And where Rienzi stood, he heard their shouts of "Long live the Tribune, the just judge, Rome's liberator!" But at that time other thoughts deafened his senses to the popular enthusiasm.

"My poor brother!" he said, with tears in his eyes, "it was owing to this man's crimes—and to a crime almost similar to that for which he has now suffered—that thou wert entrained to the slaughter; and they who had no pity for the lamb, clamour for compassion to the wolf! Ah, wert thou living now, how these proud heads would bend to thee; though dead, thou wert not worthy of a thought. God rest thy gentle soul, and keep my ambition pure as it was when we walked at twilight, side by side together!"

The Tribune shut the casement, and turning away, sought the chamber of Nina. On hearing his step without, she had already risen from the couch, her eyes sparkling, her bosom heaving; and as he entered, she threw herself on his neck, and murmured as she nestled to his breast,—"Ah, the hours since we parted!"

It was a singular thing to see that proud lady, proud of her beauty, her station, her new honours;—whose gorgeous vanity was already the talk of Rome, and the reproach to Rienzi,—how suddenly and miraculously she seemed changed in his presence! Blushing and timid, all pride in herself seemed merged in her proud love for him. No woman ever loved to the full extent of the passion, who did not venerate where she loved, and who did not feel humbled (delighted in that humility) by her exaggerated and overweening estimate of the superiority of the object of her worship.

And it might be the consciousness of this distinction between himself and all other created things, which continued to increase the love of the Tribune to his bride, to blind him to her failings towards others, and to indulge her in a magnificence of parade, which, though to a certain point politic to assume, was carried to an extent which, if it did not conspire to produce his downfall, has served the Romans with an excuse for their own cowardice and desertion, and historians with a plausible explanation of causes they had not the industry to fathom. Rienzi returned his wife's caresses with an equal affection, and bending down to her beautiful face, the sight was sufficient to chase from his brow the emotions, whether severe or sad, which had lately darkened its broad expanse.

"Thou has not been abroad this morning, Nina!"

"No, the heat was oppressive. But nevertheless, Cola, I have not lacked company—half the matronage of Rome has crowded the palace."

"Ah, I warrant it.—But yon boy, is he not a new face?"

"Hush, Cola, speak to him kindly, I entreat: of his story anon. Angelo, approach. You see your new master, the Tribune of Rome."

Angelo approached with a timidity not his wont, for an air of majesty was at all times natural to Rienzi, and since his power it had naturally taken a graver and austerer aspect, which impressed those who approached him, even the ambassadors of princes, with a certain involuntary awe. The Tribune smiled at the effect he saw he had produced, and being by temper fond of children, and affable to all but the great, he hastened to dispel it. He took the child affectionately in his arms, kissed him, and bade him welcome.

"May we have a son as fair!" he whispered to Nina, who blushed, and turned away.

"Thy name, my little friend?"

"Angelo Villani."

"A Tuscan name. There is a man of letters at Florence, doubtless writing our annals from hearsay at this moment, called Villani. Perhaps akin to thee?"

"I have no kin," said the boy, bluntly; "and therefore I shall the better love the Signora and honour you, if you will let me. I am Roman—all the Roman boys honour Rienzi."

"Do they, my brave lad?" said the Tribune, colouring with pleasure; "that is a good omen of my continued prosperity." He put down the boy, and threw himself on the cushions, while Nina placed herself on a kind of low stool beside him.

"Let us be alone," said he; and Nina motioned to the attendant maidens to withdraw.

"Take my new page with you," said she; "he is yet, perhaps, too fresh from home to enjoy the company of his giddy brethren."

When they were alone, Nina proceeded to narrate to Rienzi the adventure of the morning; but though he seemed outwardly to listen, his gaze was on vacancy, and he was evidently abstracted and self-absorbed. At length, as she concluded, he said, "Well, Nina, you have acted as ever, kindly and nobly. Let us to other themes. I am in danger."

"Danger!" echoed Nina, turning pale.

"Why, the word must not appal you—you have a spirit like mine, that scorns fear; and, for that reason, Nina, in all Rome you are my only confidante. It was not only to glad me with thy beauty, but to cheer me with thy counsel, to support me with thy valour, that Heaven gave me thee as a helpmate."

"Now, our Lady bless thee for those words!" said Nina, kissing the hand that hung over her shoulder; "and if I started at the word danger, it was but the woman's thought of thee,—an unworthy thought, my Cola, for glory and danger go together. And I am as ready to share the last as the first. If the hour of trial ever come, none of thy friends shall be so faithful to thy side as this weak form but undaunted heart."

"I know it, my own Nina; I know it," said Rienzi, rising, and pacing the chamber with large and rapid strides. "Now listen to me. Thou knowest that to govern in safety, it is my policy as my pride to govern justly. To govern justly is an awful thing, when mighty barons are the culprits. Nina, for an open and audacious robbery, our court has sentenced Martin of the Orsini, the Lord of Porto, to death. His corse swings now on the Staircase of the Lion."

"A dreadful doom!" said Nina, shuddering.

"True; but by his death thousands of poor and honest men may live in peace. It is not that which troubles me: the Barons resent the deed, as an insult to them that law should touch a noble. They will rise—they will rebel. I foresee the storm—not the spell to allay it."

Nina paused a moment,—"They have taken," she then said, "a solemn oath on the Eucharist not to bear arms against thee."

"Perjury is a light addition to theft and murder," answered Rienzi, with his sarcastic smile.

"But the people are faithful."

"Yes, but in a civil war (which the saints forefend!) those combatants are the stanchest who have no home but their armour, no calling but the sword. The trader will not leave his trade at the toll of a bell every day; but the Baron's soldiery are ready at all hours."

"To be strong," said Nina,—who summoned to the councils of her lord, shewed an intellect not unworthy of the honour,—"to be strong in dangerous times, authority must *seem* strong. By shewing no fear, you may prevent the cause of fear."

"My own thought!" returned Rienzi, quickly. "You know that half my power with these Barons is drawn from the homage rendered to me by foreign states. When from every city in Italy the ambassadors of crowned princes seek the alliance of the Tribune, they must veil their resentment at the rise of the Plebeian. On the other hand, to be strong abroad I must seem strong at home: the vast design I have planned, and, as by a miracle, begun to execute, will fail at once if it seem abroad to be intrusted to an unsteady and fluctuating power. That design" (continued Rienzi, pausing, and placing his hand on a marble bust of the young Augustus) "is greater than his, whose profound yet icy soul united Italy in subjection,—for it would unite Italy in freedom;—yes! could we but form one great federative league of all the States of Italy, each governed by its own laws, but united for mutual and common protection against the Attilas of the North, with Rome for their Metropolis and their Mother, this age and this brain would have wrought an enterprise which men should quote till the sound of the last trump!"

"I know thy divine scheme," said Nina, catching his enthusiasm; "and what if there be danger in attaining it? Have we not mastered the greatest danger in the first step?"

"Right, Nina, right! Heaven" (and the Tribune, who ever recognised, in his own fortunes, the agency of the hand above, crossed himself reverently) "will preserve him to whom it hath vouchsafed such lofty visions of the future redemption of the Land of the true Church, and the liberty and advancement of its children! This I trust: already many of the cities of Tuscany have entered into treaties for the formation of this league; nor from a single tyrant, save John di Vico, have I received aught but fair words and flattering promises. The time seems ripe for the grand stroke of all."

"And what is that?" demanded Nina, wonderingly.

"Defiance to all foreign interference. By what right does a synod of stranger princes give Rome a king in some Teuton Emperor? Rome's people alone should choose Rome's governor;—and shall we cross the Alps to render the title of our master to the descendants of the Goth?"

Nina was silent: the custom of choosing the sovereign by a diet beyond the Rhine, reserving only the ceremony of his subsequent coronation for the mock assent of the Romans, however degrading to that people, and however hostile to all notions of substantial independence, was so unquestioned at that time, that Rienzi's daring suggestion left her amazed and breathless, prepared as she was for any scheme, however extravagantly bold.

"How!" said she, after a long pause; "do I understand aright? Can you mean defiance to the Emperor?"

"Why, listen: at this moment there are two pretenders to the throne of Rome—to the imperial crown of Italy—a Bohemian and a Bavarian. To their election our assent—Rome's assent—is not requisite—not asked. Can we be called free—can we boast ourselves republican—when a stranger and a barbarian is thus thrust upon our necks? No, we will be free in reality as in name. Besides," (continued the Tribune, in a calmer tone,) "this seems to me politic as well as daring. The people incessantly demand wonders from me: how can I more nobly dazzle, more virtuously win them, than by asserting their inalienable right to choose their own rulers? The daring will awe the Barons, and foreigners themselves; it will give a startling example to all Italy; it will be the first brand of an universal blaze. It shall be done, and with a pomp that befits the deed!"

"Cola," said Nina, hesitatingly, "your eagle spirit often ascends where mine flags to follow; yet be not over bold."

"Nay, did you not, a moment since, preach a different doctrine? To be strong, was I not to seem strong?"

"May fate preserve you!" said Nina, with a foreboding sigh.

"Fate!" cried Rienzi; "there is *no* fate! Between the thought and the success, God is the only agent; and" (he added with a voice of deep solemnity) "I shall not be deserted. Visions by night, even while thine arms are around me; omens and impulses, stirring and divine, by day, even in the midst of the living crowd—encourage my path, and point my goal. Now, even now, a voice seems to whisper in my ear—'Pause not; tremble not; waver not;—for the eye of the All-Seeing is upon thee, and the hand of the All-Powerful shall protect!'"

As Rienzi thus spoke, his face grew pale, his hair seemed to bristle, his tall and proud form trembled visibly, and presently he sunk down on a seat, and covered his face with his hands.

An awe crept over Nina, though not unaccustomed to such strange and preternatural emotions, which appeared yet the more singular in one who in common life was so calm, stately, and self-possessed. But with every increase of prosperity and power, those emotions seemed to increase in their fervour, as if in such increase the devout and overwrought superstition of the Tribune recognised additional proof of a mysterious guardianship mightier than the valour or art of man.

She approached fearfully, and threw her arms around him, but without speaking.

Ere yet the Tribune had well recovered himself, a slight tap at the door was heard, and the sound seemed at once to recall his self-possession.

"Enter," he said, lifting his face, to which the wonted colour slowly returned.

An officer, half-opening the door, announced that the person he had sent for waited his leisure.

"I come!—Core of my heart," (he whispered to Nina,) "we will sup alone to-night, and will converse more on these matters:" so saying, with somewhat less than his usual loftiness of mien, he left the room, and sought his cabinet, which lay at the other side of the reception chamber. Here he found Cecco del Vecchio.

"How, my bold fellow," said the Tribune, assuming with wonderful ease that air of friendly equality which he always adopted with those of the lower class, and which made a striking contrast with the majesty, no less natural, which marked his manner to the great. "How now, my Cecco! Thou bearest thyself bravely, I see, during these sickly heats; we labourers—for both of us labour, Cecco—are too busy to fall ill as the idle do, in the summer, or the autumn, of Roman skies. I sent for thee, Cecco, because I would know how thy fellow-craftsmen are like to take the Orsini's execution."

"Oh! Tribune," replied the artificer, who, now familiarised with Rienzi, had lost much of his earlier awe of him, and who regarded the Tribune's power as partly his own creation; "they are already out of their honest wits, at your courage in punishing the great men as you would the small."

"So;—I am repaid! But hark you, Cecco, it will bring, perhaps, hot work upon us. Every Baron will dread lest it be his turn next, and dread will make them bold, like rats in despair. We may have to fight for the Good Estate."

"With all my heart, Tribune," answered Cecco, gruffly. "I, for one, am no craven."

"Then keep the same spirit in all your meetings with the artificers. I fight for the people. The people at a pinch must fight with me."

"They will," replied Cecco; "they will!"

"Cecco, this city is under the spiritual dominion of the Pontiff—so be it—it is an honour, not a burthen. But the *temporal* dominion, my friend, should be with Romans only. Is it not a disgrace to Republican Rome, that while we now speak, certain barbarians, whom we never heard of, should be deciding beyond the Alps on the merits of two sovereigns whom we never saw? Is not this a thing to be resisted? An Italian city,—what hath it to do with a Bohemian Emperor?"

"Little eno', St. Paul knows!" said Cecco.

"Should it not be a claim questioned?"

"I think so!" replied the smith.

"And if found an outrage on our ancient laws, should it not be a claim resisted?"

"Not a doubt of it."

"Well, go to! The archives assure me that never was Emperor lawfully crowned but by the free votes of the people. *We* never chose Bohemian or Bavarian."

"But, on the contrary, whenever these Northmen

come hither to be crowned, we try to drive them away with stones and curses,—for we are a people, Tribune, that love our liberties."

"Go back to your friends—see—address them, say that your Tribune will demand of these pretenders to Rome the right to her throne. Let them not be mazed or startled, but support me when the occasion comes."

"I am glad of this," quoth the huge smith; "for our friends have grown a little unruly of late, and say——"

"What do they say?"

"That it is true you have expelled the banditti, and curb the Barons, and administer justice fairly;—"

"Is not that miracle enough for the space of some two or three short months?"

"Why, they say it would have been more than enough in a noble; but you, being raised from the people, and having such gifts and so forth, might do yet more. It is now three weeks since they have had any new thing to talk about; but Orsini's execution to-day will cheer them a bit."

"Well, Cecco, well," said the Tribune, rising, "they shall have more anon to feed their mouths with. So you think they love me not quite so well as they did some three weeks back?"

"I say not so," answered Cecco. "But we Romans are an impatient people."

"Alas, yes!"

"However, they will no doubt stick close enough to you; provided, Tribune, you don't put any new tax upon them."

"Ha! But if, in order to be free, it be necessary to

fight—if to fight, it be necessary to have soldiers, why then the soldiers must be paid:—won't the people contribute something to their own liberties;—to just laws, and safe lives?"

"I don't know," returned the smith, scratching his head as if a little puzzled; "but I know that poor men won't be overtaxed. They say they are better off with you than with the Barons before, and therefore they love you. But men in business, Tribune, poor men with families, must look to their bellies. Only one man in ten goes to law—only one man in twenty is butchered by a Baron's brigand; but every man eats, and drinks, and feels a tax."

"This cannot be your reasoning, Cecco!" said Rienzi, gravely.

"Why, Tribune, I am an honest man, but I have a large family to rear."

"Enough; enough!" said the Tribune quickly; and then he added abstractedly as to himself, but aloud,—"Methinks we have been too lavish; these shows and spectacles should cease."

"What!" cried Cecco; "what, Tribune!—would you deny the poor fellows a holiday. They work hard enough, and their only pleasure is seeing your fine shows and processions; and then they go home and say,—'See, *our* man beats all the Barons! what state he keeps!'"

"Ah! they blame not my splendour, then!"

"Blame it; no! Without it they would be ashamed of you, and think the *Buono Stato* but a shabby concern."

"You speak bluntly, Cecco, but perhaps wisely. The saints keep you! Fail not to remember what I told you!"

"No, no. It is a shame to have an Emperor thrust upon us;—so it is. Good evening, Tribune."

Left alone, the Tribune remained for some time plunged in gloomy and foreboding thoughts.

"I am in the midst of a magician's spell," said he; "if I desist, the fiends tear me to pieces. What I have begun, that must I conclude. But this rude man shews me too well with what tools I work. For *me* failure is nothing. I have already climbed to a greatness which might render giddy many a born prince's brain. But with my fall—Rome, Italy, Peace, Justice, Civilisation—all fall back into the abyss of ages!"

He rose; and after once or twice pacing his apartment, in which from many a column gleamed upon him the marble effigies of the great of old, he opened the casement to inhale the air of the now declining day.

The Place of the Capitol was deserted save by the tread of the single sentinel. But still, dark and fearful, hung from the tall gibbet the clay of the robber noble; and the colossal shape of the Egyptian lion rose hard by, sharp and dark in the breathless atmosphere.

"Dread statue!" thought Rienzi, "how many unwhispered and solemn rites hast thou witnessed by thy native Nile, ere the Roman's hand transferred thee hither—the antique witness of Roman crimes! Strange! but when I look upon thee I feel as if thou hadst some mystic influence over my own fortunes. Beside thee was I hailed the republican Lord of Rome; beside thee are my palace, my tribunal, the place of my justice, my triumphs, and my pomp:—to thee my eyes turn from my bed of state: and if fated to die in power and peace, thou mayst be the last object my eyes will mark! Or if myself a victim——"—he paused—shrank from the thought presented to him—turned to a recess of the chamber—drew aside a curtain, that veiled a crucifix and a small table, on which lay a Bible and the monastic emblems of the skull and cross-bones—emblems, indeed, grave and irresistible, of the nothingness of power, and the uncertainty of life. Before these sacred monitors, whether to humble or to elevate, knelt that proud and aspiring man; and when he rose, it was with a lighter step and more cheerful mien than he had worn that day.

CHAPTER III

THE ACTOR UNMASKED

"In intoxication," says the proverb, "men betray their real characters." There is a no less honest and truth-revealing intoxication in prosperity, than in wine. The varnish of power brings forth at once the defects and the beauties of the human portrait.

The unprecedented and almost miraculous rise of Rienzi from the rank of the Pontiff's official to the Lord of Rome, would have been accompanied with a yet greater miracle, if it had not somewhat dazzled and seduced the object it elevated. When, as in well-ordered states and tranquil times, men rise slowly, step by step, they accustom themselves to their growing fortunes. But the leap of an hour from a citizen to a prince—from the victim of oppression to the dispenser of justice—is a transition so sudden as to render dizzy the most sober brain. And, perhaps, in proportion to the imagination, the enthusiasm, the genius of the man, will the suddenness be dangerous—excite too extravagant a hope—and lead to too chimerical an ambition. The qualities that made him rise, hurry him to his fall; and victory at the Marengo of his fortunes, urges him to destruction at its Moscow.

In his greatness Rienzi did not so much acquire new qualities, as develop in brighter light and deeper shadow those which he had always exhibited. On the one hand he was just—resolute—the friend of the oppressed—the terror of the oppressor. His wonderful intellect illumined everything it touched. By rooting out abuse, and by searching examination and wise arrangement, he had trebled the revenues of the city without imposing a single new tax. Faithful to his idol of liberty, he had not been betrayed by the wish of the people into despotic authority; but had, as we have seen, formally revived, and established with new powers, the Parliamentary Council of the city. However extensive his own authority, he referred its exercise to the people; in their name he alone declared himself to govern, and he never executed any signal action without submitting to them its reasons or its justification. No less faithful to his desire to restore prosperity as well as freedom to Rome, he had seized the first dazzling epoch of his power to propose that great federative league with the Italian States which would, as he rightly said, have raised Rome to the indisputable head of European nations. Under his rule trade was secure, literature was welcome, art began to rise.

On the other hand, the prosperity which made more apparent his justice, his integrity, his patriotism, his virtues, and his genius, brought out no less glaringly his arrogant consciousness of superiority, his love of display, and the wild and daring insolence of his ambition. Though too just to avenge himself by retaliating on the patricians their own violence, though, in his troubled and stormy tribuneship, not one unmerited or illegal execution of baron or citizen could be alleged against him, even by his enemies; yet sharing, less excusably, the weakness of Nina, he could not deny his proud heart the pleasure of humiliating those who had ridiculed him as a buffoon, despised him as a plebeian, and who, even now slaves to his face, were cynics behind his back. "They stood before him while he sate," says his biographer: "all these Barons, bareheaded; their hands crossed on their breasts; their looks downcast;—oh, how frightened they were!" a picture more disgraceful to the servile cowardice of the nobles than the haughty sternness of the Tribune. It might be that he deemed it policy to break the spirit of his foes, and to awe those whom it was a vain hope to conciliate.

For his pomp there was a greater excuse: it was the custom of the time; it was the insignia and witness of power; and when the modern historian taunts him with not imitating the simplicity of an ancient tribune, the sneer betrays an ignorance of the spirit of the age, and the vain people whom the chief magistrate was to govern. No doubt his gorgeous festivals, his solemn processions, set off and ennobled—if parade can so be ennobled—by a refined and magnificent richness of imagination, associated always with popular emblems, and designed to convey the idea of rejoicing for Liberty Restored, and to assert the state and majesty of Rome Revived—no doubt these spectacles, however otherwise judged in a more enlightened age and by closest sages, served greatly to augment the importance of the Tribune abroad, and to dazzle the pride of a fickle and ostentatious populace. And taste grew refined, luxury called labour into requisition, and foreigners from all states were attracted by the splendour of a court over which presided, under republican names, two sovereigns,* young and brilliant, the one renowned for his genius, the other eminent for her beauty. It was, indeed, a dazzling and royal dream in the long night of Rome, spoiled of her Pontiff and his voluptuous train—that holyday reign of Cola di Rienzi! And often afterwards it was recalled with a sigh, not only by the poor for its justice, the merchant for its security, but the gallant for its splendour, and the poet for its ideal and intellectual grace!

As if to show that it was not to gratify the more vulgar appetite and desire, in the midst of all his pomp, when the board groaned with the delicacies of every clime, when the wine most freely circled, the Tribune himself preserved a temperate and even rigid abstinence.† While the apartments of state and the chamber of his bride were adorned with a profuse luxury and cost, to his own private rooms he transported precisely the same furniture which had been familiar

* Rienzi, speaking in one of his letters of his great enterprise, refers it to the ardour of youth. The exact date of his birth is unknown; but he was certainly a young man at the time now referred to. His portrait in the Museo Barberino, from which his description has been already taken in the first book of this work, represents him as beardless, and, as far as one can judge, somewhere above thirty—old enough, to be sure, to have a beard; and seven years afterwards he wore a long one, which greatly displeased his *naïve* biographer, who seems to consider it a sort of crime. The head is very remarkable for its stern beauty, and little, if at all, inferior to that of Napoleon; to which, as I before remarked, it has some resemblance in expression, if not in feature.

† Vita di Cola di Rienzi.—The biographer praises the abstinence of the *Tribune*.

to him in his obscurer life. The books, the busts, the reliefs, the arms which had inspired him heretofore with the visions of the past, were endeared by associations which he did not care to forego.

But that which constituted the most singular feature of his character, and which still wraps all around him in a certain mystery, was his religious enthusiasm. The daring but wild doctrines of Arnold of Brescia, who, two centuries anterior, had preached reform, but inculcated mysticism, still lingered in Rome, and had in earlier youth deeply coloured the mind of Rienzi; and as I have before observed, his youthful propensity to dreamy thought, the melancholy death of his brother, his own various but successful fortunes, had all contributed to nurse the more zealous and solemn aspirations of this remarkable man. Like Arnold of Brescia, his faith bore a strong resemblance to the intense fanaticism of our own Puritans of the Civil War, as if similar political circumstances conduced to similar religious sentiments. He believed himself inspired by awful and mighty commune with beings of the better world. Saints and angels ministered to his dreams; and without this, the more profound and hallowed enthusiasm, he might never have been sufficiently emboldened by mere human patriotism, to his unprecedented enterprise: it was the secret of much of his greatness,—many of his errors. Like all men who are thus self-deluded by a vain but not inglorious superstition, united with, and coloured by, earthly ambition, it is impossible to say how far he was the visionary, and how far at times he dared to be the impostor. In the ceremonies of his pageants, in the ornaments of his person, were invariably introduced mystic and figurative emblems. In times of danger he publicly professed to have been cheered and directed by divine dreams; and on many occasions the prophetic warnings he announced having been singularly verified by the event, his influence with the people was strengthened by a belief in the favour and intercourse of Heaven. Thus, delusion of self might tempt and conduce to imposition on others, and he might not scruple to avail himself of the advantage of seeming what he believed himself to be. Yet, no doubt this intoxicating credulity pushed him into extravagance unworthy of, and strangely contrasted by, his soberer intellect, and made him disproportion his vast ends to his unsteady means, by the proud fallacy, that where man failed, God would interpose. Cola di Rienzi was no faultless hero of romance. In him lay, in conflicting prodigality, the richest and most opposite elements of character; strong sense, visionary superstition, an eloquence and energy that mastered all he approached, a blind enthusiasm that mastered himself; luxury and abstinence, sternness and susceptibility, pride to the great, humility to the low; the most devoted patriotism and the most avid desire of personal power. As few men undertake great and desperate designs without strong animal spirits, so it may be observed, that with most who have risen to eminence over the herd, there is an aptness, at times, to a wild mirth and an elasticity of humour which often astonish the more sober and regulated minds, that are "the commoners of life:" and the theatrical grandeur of Napoleon, the severe dignity of Cromwell, are strangely contrasted by a frequent, nor always seasonable buffoonery, which it is hard to reconcile with the ideal of their characters, or the gloomy and portentous interest of their careers. And this, equally a trait in the temperament of Rienzi, distinguished his hours of relaxation, and contributed to that marvellous versatility with which his harder nature accommodated itself to all humours and all men. Often from his austere judgment-seat he passed to the social board an altered man; and even the sullen Barons who reluctantly attended his feasts, forgot his public greatness in his familiar wit; albeit this reckless humour could not always refrain from seeking its subject in the mortification of his crest-fallen foes—a pleasure it would have been wiser and more generous to forego. And perhaps it was, in part, the prompting of this sarcastic and unbridled humour that made him often love to astonish as well as to awe. But even this gaiety, if so it may be called, taking an appearance of familiar frankness, served much to ingratiate him with the lower orders; and, if a fault in the prince, was a virtue in the demagogue.

To these various characteristics, now fully developed, the reader must add a genius of designs so bold, of conceptions so gigantic and august, conjoined with that more minute and ordinary ability which masters details; that with a brave, noble, intelligent, devoted people to back his projects, the accession of the Tribune would have been the close of the thraldom of Italy, and the abrupt limit of the dark age of Europe. With such a people, his faults would have been insensibly checked, his more unwholesome power have received a sufficient curb. Experience familiarising him with power, would have gradually weaned him from extravagance in its display: and the active and masculine energy of his intellect would have found field for the more restless spirits, as his justice gave shelter to the more tranquil. Faults he had, but whether those faults or the faults of the people, were to prepare his downfall, is yet to be seen.

Meanwhile, amidst a discontented nobility and a fickle populace, urged on by the danger of repose to the danger of enterprise; partly blinded by his outward power, partly impelled by the fear of internal weakness; at once made sanguine by his genius and his fanaticism, and uneasy by the expectations of the crowd,—he threw himself headlong into the gulf of the rushing Time, and surrendered his lofty spirit to no other guidance than a conviction of its natural buoyancy and its heaven-directed haven.

CHAPTER IV

THE ENEMY'S CAMP

While Rienzi was preparing, in concert, perhaps, with the ambassadors of the brave Tuscan States, whose pride of country and love of liberty were well fitted to comprehend, and even share them, his schemes for the emancipation from all foreign yoke of the Ancient Queen, and the Everlasting Garden of the World; the Barons, in restless secrecy, were revolving projects for the restoration of their own power.

One morning, the heads of the Savelli, the Orsini, and the Frangipani, met at the disfortified palace of Stephen Colonna. Their conference was warm and earnest—now resolute, now wavering, in its object—as indignation or fear prevailed.

" You have heard," said Luca di Savelli, in his usual soft and womanly voice, " that the Tribune has proclaimed, that, the day after to-morrow, he will take the order of knighthood, and watch the night before in the church of the Lateran! He has honoured me with a request to attend his vigil."

"Yes, yes, the knave. What means this new fantasy?" said the brutal Prince of the Orsini.

"Unless it be to have the cavalier's right to challenge a noble," said old Colonna, "I cannot conjecture. Will Rome never grow weary of this madman?"

"Rome is the more mad of the two," said Luca di Savelli; "but methinks, in his wildness, the Tribune hath committed one error of which we may well avail ourselves at Avignon."

"Ah," cried the old Colonna, "that must be our game; passive here, let us fight at Avignon."

"In a word then, he hath ordered that his bath shall be prepared in the holy porphyry vase in which once bathed the Emperor Constantine."

"Profanation! profanation!" cried Stephen. "This is enough to excuse a bull of excommunication. The Pope shall hear of it. I will despatch a courier forthwith."

"Better wait and see the ceremony," said the Savelli; "some greater folly will close the pomp, be assured."

"Hark ye, my masters," said the grim Lord of the Orsini; "ye are for delay and caution; I for promptness and daring; my kinsman's blood calls aloud, and brooks no parley."

"And what do?" said the soft-voiced Savelli; "fight without soldiers, against twenty thousand infuriated Romans? not I."

Orsini sunk his voice into a meaning whisper. "In Venice," said he, "this upstart might be mastered without an army. Think you in Rome no man wears a stiletto?"

"Hush," said Stephen, who was of far nobler and better nature than his compeers, and who, justifying to himself all other resistance to the Tribune, felt his conscience rise against assassination; "this must not be—your zeal transports you."

"Besides, whom can we employ? scarce a German left in the city; and to whisper this to a Roman were to exchange places with poor Martino—Heaven take him, for he's nearer heaven than ever he was before," said the Savelli.

"Jest me no jests," cried the Orsini, fiercely. "Jests on such a subject! By St. Francis I would, since thou lovest such wit, thou hadst it all to thyself; and, methinks, at the Tribune's board I have seen thee laugh at his rude humour as if thou didst not require a cord to choke thee."

"Better to laugh than to tremble," returned the Savelli.

"How! darest thou say I tremble?" cried the Baron.

"Hush, hush," said the veteran Colonna, with impatient dignity. "We are not now in such holiday times as to quarrel amongst ourselves. Forbear, my lords."

"Your greater prudence, Signor," said the sarcastic Savelli, "arises from your greater safety. Your house is about to shelter itself under the Tribune's; and, when the Lord Adrian returns from Naples, the innkeeper's son will be brother to your kinsman."

"You might spare me that taunt," said the old noble, with some emotion. "Heaven knows how bitterly I have chafed at the thought; yet I would Adrian were with us. His word goes far to moderate the Tribune, and to guide my own course, for my passion beguiles my reason; and since his departure methinks we have been the more sullen without being the more strong. Let this pass. If my own son had wed the Tribune's sister, I would yet strike a blow for the old constitution as becomes a noble, if I but saw that the blow would not cut off my own head."

Savelli, who had been whispering apart with Rinaldo Frangipani, now said—

"Noble Prince, listen to me. You are bound by your kinsman's approaching connection, your venerable age, and your intimacy with the Pontiff, to a greater caution than we are. Leave to us the management of the enterprise, and be assured of our discretion."

A young boy, Stefanello, who afterwards succeeded to the representation of the direct line of the Colonna, and whom the reader will once again encounter ere our tale be closed, was playing by his grandsire's knees. He looked sharply up at Savelli, and said, "My grandfather is too wise, and you are too timid. Frangipani is too yielding, and Orsini is too like a vexed bull. I wish I were a year or two older."

"And what would you do, my pretty censurer?" said the smooth Savelli, biting his smiling lip.

"Stab the Tribune with my own stiletto, and then hey for Palestrina!"

"The egg will hatch a brave serpent," quoth the Savelli. "Yet why so bitter against the Tribune, my cockatrice?"

"Because he allowed an insolent mercer to arrest my uncle Agapet for debt. The debt had been owed these ten years; and though it is said that no house in Rome has owed more money than the Colonna, this is the first time I ever heard of a rascally creditor being allowed to claim his debt unless with doffed cap and bended knee. And I say that I would not live to be a Baron, if such upstart insolence is to be put upon me."

"My child," said old Stephen, laughing heartily, "I see our noble order will be safe enough in your hands."

"And," continued the child, emboldened by the applause he received, "if I had time after pricking the Tribune, I would fain have a second stroke at——"

"Whom?" said the Savelli, observing the boy pause.

"My cousin Adrian. Shame on him, for dreaming to make one a wife whose birth would scarce fit her for a Colonna's leman!"

"Go play, my child—go play," said the old Colonna, as he pushed the boy from him.

"Enough of this babble," cried the Orsini, rudely. "Tell me, old lord; just as I entered, I saw an old friend (one of your former mercenaries) quit the palace—may I crave his errand?"

"Ah, yes; a messenger from Fra Moreale. I wrote to the Knight, reproving him for his desertion on our ill-starred return from Corneto, and intimating that five hundred lances would be highly paid for just now."

"Ah," said Savelli; "and what is his answer?"

"Oh, wily and evasive: He is profuse in compliments and good wishes; but says he is under fealty to the Hungarian king, whose cause is before Rienzi's tribunal; that he cannot desert his present standard; that he fears Rome is so evenly balanced between patricians and the people, that whatever party would permanently be uppermost must call in a Podesta; and this character alone the Provençal insinuates would suit him."

"Montreal our Podesta?" cried the Orsini.

"And why not?" said Savelli; "as good a well-born Podesta as a low-born Tribune! But I trust we may do without either. Colonna, has this messenger from Fra Moreale left the city?"

"I suppose so."

"No," said Orsini; "I met him at the gate, and knew him of old: it is Rodolf, the Saxon (once a hireling of the Colonna), who has made some widows among my clients in the good old day. He is a little disguised now; however, I recognised and accosted him, for I thought he was one who might yet become a friend, and I bade him await me at my palace."

"You did well," said the Savelli, musing, and his eyes met those of Orsini. Shortly afterwards a conference, in which much was said and nothing settled, was broken up; but Luca di Savelli, loitering at the porch, prayed the Frangipani, and the other Barons, to adjourn to the Orsini's palace.

"The old Colonna," said he, "is well-nigh in his dotage. We shall come to a quick determination without him, and we can secure his proxy in his son."

And this was a true prophecy, for half-an-hour's consultation with Rodolf of Saxony sufficed to ripen thought into enterprise.

CHAPTER V

THE NIGHT AND ITS INCIDENTS

With the following twilight, Rome was summoned to the commencement of the most magnificent spectacle the Imperial City had witnessed since the fall of the Cæsars. It had been a singular privilege, arrogated by the people of Rome, to confer upon their citizens the order of knighthood. Twenty years before, a Colonna and an Orsini had received this popular honour. Rienzi, who designed it as the prelude to a more important ceremony, claimed from the Romans a similar distinction. From the Capitol to the Lateran swept, in long procession, all that Rome boasted of noble, of fair, and brave. First went horsemen without number, and from all the neighbouring parts of Italy, in apparel that well befitted the occasion. Trumpeters, and musicians of all kinds, followed, and the trumpets were of silver; youths bearing the harness of the knightly war-steed, wrought with gold, preceded the march of the loftiest matronage of Rome, whose love for show, and it may be whose admiration for triumphant fame (which to women sanctions many offences,) made them forget the humbled greatness of their lords: amidst them Nina and Irene, outshining all the rest; then came the Tribune and the Pontiff's Vicar, surrounded by all the great Signors of the city, smothering alike resentment, revenge, and scorn, and struggling who should approach nearest to the monarch of the day. The high-hearted old Colonna alone remained aloof following at a little distance, and in a garb studiously plain.

But his age, his rank, his former renown in war and state, did not suffice to draw to his gray locks and high-born mien a single one of the shouts that attended the meanest lord on whom the great Tribune smiled. Savelli followed nearest to Rienzi, the most obsequious of the courtly band; immediately before the Tribune came two men; the one bore a drawn sword, the other the *pendone*, or standard usually assigned to royalty. The Tribune himself was clothed in a long robe of white satin, whose snowy dazzle (*miri candoris*) is peculiarly dwelt on by the historian, richly decorated with gold; while on his breast were many of those mystic symbols I have before alluded to, the exact meaning of which was perhaps known only to the wearer. In his dark eye, and on that large tranquil brow, in which thought seemed to sleep, as sleeps a storm, there might be detected a mind abstracted from the pomp around; but ever and anon he aroused himself, and conversed partially with Raimond or Savelli.

"This is a quaint game," said the Orsini, falling back to the old Colonna: "but it may end tragically."

"Methinks it may," said the old man, "if the Tribune overhear thee."

Orsini grew pale. "How—nay—nay, even if he did, he never resents words, but professes to laugh at our spoken rage. It was but the other day that some knave told him what one of the Annibaldi said of him—words for which a true cavalier would have drawn the speaker's life's blood; and he sent for the Annibaldi, and said, 'My friend, receive this purse of gold—court wits should be paid.'"

"Did Annibaldi take the gold?"

"Why, no; the Tribune was pleased with his spirit,

and made him sup with him; and Annibaldi says he never spent a merrier evening, and no longer wonders that his kinsman, Ricardo, loves the buffoon so."

Arrived now at the Lateran, Luca di Savelli fell also back, and whispered to Orsini; the Frangipani, and some other of the nobles, exchanged meaning looks; Rienzi, entering the sacred edifice in which, according to custom, he was to pass the night watching his armour, bade the crowd farewell, and summoned them the next morning "To hear things that might, he trusted, be acceptable to heaven and earth."

The immense multitude received this intimation with curiosity and gladness, while those who had been in some measure prepared by Cecco del Vecchio, hailed it as an omen of their Tribune's unflagging resolution. The concourse dispersed with singular order and quietness; it was recorded as a remarkable fact, that in so great a crowd, composed of men of all parties, none exhibited licence or indulged in quarrel. Some of the barons and cavaliers, among whom was Luca di Savelli, whose sleek urbanity and sarcastic humour found favour with the Tribune, and a few subordinate pages and attendants, alone remained; and, save a single sentinel at the porch, that broad space before the Palace, the Basilica and Fount of Constantine, soon presented a silent and desolate void to the melancholy moonlight. Within the church, according to the usage of the time and rite, the descendant of the Teuton kings received the order of the Santo Spirito. His pride or some superstition equally weak, though more excusable, led him to bathe in the porphyry vase which an absurd legend consecrated to Constantine; and this, as Savelli predicted, cost him dear. These appointed ceremonies concluded, his arms were placed in that part of the church, within the columns of St. John. And here his state bed was prepared.*

The attendant barons, pages and chamberlains, retired out of sight to a small side chapel in the edifice; and Rienzi was left alone. A single lamp, placed beside his bed, contended with the mournful rays of the moon, that cast through the long casements, over aisle and pillar, its "dim religious light." The sanctity of the place, the solemnity of the hour, and the solitary silence round, were well calculated to deepen the high-wrought and earnest mood of that son of fortune. Many and high fancies swept over his mind—now of worldly aspirations, now of more august but visionary belief, till at length, wearied with his own reflections, he cast himself on the bed. It was an omen which graver history has not neglected to record, that the moment he pressed the bed, new prepared for the occasion, part of it sank under him: he himself was affected by the accident, and sprung forth, turning pale and muttering; but, as if ashamed of his weakness, after a moment's pause, again composed himself to rest, and drew the drapery round him.

The moonbeams grew fainter and more faint as the time proceeded, and the sharp distinction between light and shade faded fast from the marble floor; when from behind a column at the furthest verge of the building, a strange shadow suddenly crossed the sickly light—it crept on—it moved, but without an echo,—from pillar to pillar it flitted—it rested at last behind the column nearest to the Tribune's bed—it remained stationary.

* In a more northern country, the eve of knighthood would have been spent without sleeping. In Italy, the ceremony of watching the armour does not appear to have been so rigidly observed.

The shades gathered darker and darker round; the stillness seemed to deepen; the moon was gone; and, save from the struggling ray of the lamp beside Rienzi, the blackness of night closed over the solemn and ghostly scene.

In one of the side chapels, as I have before said, which, in the many alterations the church has undergone, is probably long since destroyed, were Savelli and the few attendants retained by the Tribune. Savelli alone slept not; he remained sitting erect, breathless and listening, while the tall lights in the chapel rendered yet more impressive the rapid changes of his countenance.

"Now pray Heaven," said he, "the knave miscarry not! Such an occasion may never again occur! He has a strong arm and a dexterous hand, doubtless; but the other is a powerful man. The deed once done, I care not whether the doer escape or not; if not, why we must stab him! Dead men tell no tales. At the worst, who can avenge Rienzi? There is no other Rienzi! Ourselves and the Frangipani seize the Aventine, the Colonna and the Orsini the other quarters of the city; and without the master-spirit, we may laugh at the mad populace. But if discovered;——" and Savelli, who, fortunately for his foes, had not nerves equal to his will, covered his face and shuddered;—"I think I hear a noise!—no—is it the wind? —tush, it must be old Vico de Scotto, turning in his shell of mail!—silent—I like not that silence! No cry —no sound! Can the ruffian have played us false? or could he not scale the casement? It is but a child's effort;—or did the sentry spy him?"

Time passed on: the first ray of daylight slowly gleamed, when he thought he heard the door of the church close. Savelli's suspense became intolerable: he stole from the chapel, and came in sight of the Tribune's bed—all was silent.

"Perhaps the silence of death," said Savelli, as he crept back.

Meanwhile the Tribune, vainly endeavouring to close his eyes, was rendered yet more watchful by the uneasy position he was obliged to assume—for the part of the bed towards the pillow having given way, while the rest remained solid, he had inverted the legitimate order of lying, and drawn himself up as he might best accommodate his limbs, towards the foot of the bed. The light of the lamp, though shaded by the draperies, was thus opposite to him. Impatient of his wakefulness, he at last thought it was this dull and flickering light which scared away the slumber, and was about to rise, to remove it further from him, when he saw the curtain at the other end of the bed gently lifted: he remained quiet and alarmed;—ere he could draw a second breath, a dark figure interposed between the light and the bed; and he felt that a stroke was aimed against that part of the couch, which, but for the accident that had seemed to him ominous, would have given his breast to the knife. Rienzi waited not a second and better-directed blow; as the assassin yet stooped, groping in the uncertain light, he threw on him all the weight and power of his large and muscular frame, wrenched the stiletto from the bravo's hand, and dashing him on the bed, placed his knee on his breast.—The stiletto rose—gleamed—descended—the murtherer swerved aside, and it pierced only his right arm. The Tribune raised, for a deadlier blow, the revengeful blade.

The assassin thus foiled was a man used to all form

and shape of danger, and he did not now lose his presence of mind.

"Hold!" said he; "if you kill me, you will die yourself. Spare me, and I will save *you*."

"Miscreant!"

"Hush—not so loud, or you will disturb your attendants, and some of them may do what I have failed to execute. Spare me, I say, and I will reveal that which were worth more than my life; but call not—speak not aloud, I warn you!"

The Tribune felt his heart stand still: in that lonely place, afar from his idolising people—his devoted guards—with but loathing barons, or, it might be, faithless menials, within call, might not the baffled murtherer give a wholesome warning?—and those words and that doubt seemed suddenly to reverse their respective positions, and leave the conqueror still in the assassin's power.

"Thou thinkest to deceive me," said he, but in a voice whispered and uncertain, which shewed the ruffian the advantage he had gained: "thou wouldst that I might release thee without summoning my attendants, that thou mightst a second time attempt my life."

"Thou hast disabled my right arm, and disarmed me of my only weapon."

"How camest thou hither?"

"By connivance."

"Whence this attempt?"

"The dictation of others."

"If I pardon thee——"

"Thou shalt know all."

"Rise," said the Tribune, releasing his prisoner, but with great caution, and still grasping his shoulder with one hand, while the other pointed the dagger at his throat.

"Did my sentry admit thee? There is but one entrance to the church, methinks."

"He did not; follow me, and I will tell thee more."

"Dog! thou hast accomplices!"

"If I have, thou hast the knife at my throat."

"Wouldst thou escape?"

"I cannot, or I would."

Rienzi looked hard, by the dull light of the lamp, at the assassin. His rugged and coarse countenance, rude garb, and barbarian speech, seemed to him proof sufficient that he was but the hireling of others; and it might be wise to brave one danger present and certain, to prevent much danger future and unforeseen. Rienzi, too, was armed, strong, active, in the prime of life;—and at the worst, there was no part of the building whence his voice would not reach those within the chapel,—if they could be depended upon.

"Shew me then thy place and means of entrance," said he; "and if I but suspect thee as we move—thou diest. Take up the lamp."

The ruffian nodded; with his left hand took up the lamp as he was ordered; and with Rienzi's grasp on his shoulder, while the wound from his right arm dropped gore as he passed, he moved noiselessly along the church—gained the altar—to the left of which was a small room for the use or retirement of the priest. To this he made his way. Rienzi's heart misgave him a moment.

"Beware," he whispered, "the least sign of fraud, and thou art the first victim!"

The assassin nodded again, and proceeded. They entered the room; and then the Tribune's strange guide pointed to an open casement. "Behold my entrance," said he; "and if you permit me, my egress——"

"The frog gets not out of the well so easily as he came in, friend," returned Rienzi, smiling. "And now, if I am not to call my guards, what am I to do with thee!"

"Let me go, and I will seek thee to-morrow; and if thou payest me handsomely, and promisest not to harm limb or life, I will put thine enemies and my employers in thy power."

Rienzi could not refrain from a slight laugh at the proposition, but composing himself, replied—"And what if I call my attendants, and give thee to their charge?"

"Thou givest me to those very enemies and employers, and in despair lest I betray them, ere the day dawn they cut my throat—or thine."

"Methinks knave, I have seen thee before."

"Thou hast. I blush not for name or country. I am Rodolf of Saxony!"

"I remember me:—servitor of Walter de Montreal. He, then, is thy instigator!"

"Roman, no! That noble Knight scorns other weapon than the open sword, and his own hand slays his own foes. Your pitiful, miserable, dastard Italians, alone employ the courage, and hire the arm, of others."

Rienzi remained silent. He had released hold of his prisoner, and stood facing him; every now and then regarding his countenance, and again relapsing into thought. At length, casting his eyes round the small chamber thus singularly tenanted, he observed a kind of closet, in which the priests' robes, and some articles used in the sacred service, were contained. It suggested at once an escape from his dilemma: he pointed to it—

"There, Rodolf of Saxony, shalt thou pass some part of this night—a small penance for thy meditated crime; and to-morrow, as thou lookest for life, thou wilt reveal all."

"Hark ye, Tribune," returned the Saxon, doggedly; "my liberty is in your power, but neither my tongue nor my life. If I consent to be caged in that hole, you must swear on the crossed hilt of the dagger that you now hold, that, on confession of all I know, you pardon and set me free. My employers are enough to glut your rage an you were a tiger. If you do not swear this——"

"Ah, my modest friend!—the alternative?"

"I brain myself against the stone wall! Better such a death than the rack!"

"Fool, I want not revenge against such as thou. Be honest and I swear that, twelve hours after thy confession, thou shalt stand safe and unscathed without the walls of Rome. So help me our Lord and his saints."

"I am content!—*Donner und Hagel,* I have lived long enough to care only for my own life, and the great captain's next to it;—for the rest, I reck not if ye southerns cut each other's throats, and make all Italy one grave."

With this benevolent speech, Rodolf entered the closet; but ere Rienzi could close the door, he stepped forth again—

"Hold," said he: "this blood flows fast. Help me to bandage it, or I shall bleed to death ere my confession."

"*Per fede,*" said the Tribune, his strange humour

enjoying the man's cool audacity; "but, considering the service thou wouldst have rendered me, thou art the most pleasant, forbearing, unabashed, good fellow, I have seen this many a year. Give us thine own belt. I little thought my first eve of knighthood would have been so charitably spent!"

"Methinks these robes would make a better bandage," said Rodolf, pointing to the priests' gear suspended from the wall.

"Silence, knave," said the Tribune, frowning; "no sacrilege! Yet, as thou takest such dainty care of thyself, thou shalt have mine own scarf to accommodate thee."

With that the Tribune, placing his dagger on the ground, while he cautiously guarded it with his foot, bound up the wounded limb, for which condescension Rodolf gave him short thanks; resumed his weapon and lamp; closed the door; drew over it the long, heavy bolt without, and returned to his couch, deeply and indignantly musing over the treason he had so fortunately escaped.

At the first gray streak of dawn he went out of the great door of the church, called the sentry, who was one of his own guard, and bade him privately, and now ere the world was astir, convey the prisoner to one of the private dungeons of the Capitol. "Be silent," said he: "utter not a word of this to any one; be obedient, and thou shalt be promoted. This done, find out the councillor, Pandulfo di Guido, and bid him seek me here ere the crowd assemble."

He then, making the sentinel doff his heavy shoes of iron, led him across the church, resigned Rodolf to his care, saw them depart, and in a few minutes afterwards his voice was heard by the inmates of the neighbouring chapel; and he was soon surrounded by his train.

He was already standing on the floor, wrapped in a large gown lined with furs; and his piercing eye scanned carefully the face of each man that approached. Two of the Barons of the Frangipani family exhibited some tokens of confusion and embarrassment, from which they speedily recovered at the frank salutation of the Tribune.

But all the art of Savelli could not prevent his features from betraying to the most indifferent eye the terror of his soul;—and, when he felt the penetrating gaze of Rienzi upon him, he trembled in every joint. Rienzi alone did not, however, seem to notice his disorder; and when Vico di Scotto, an old knight, from whose hands he received his sword, asked him how he had passed the night, he replied, cheerfully—

"Well, well—my brave friend! Over a maiden knight some good angel always watches. Signor Luca di Savelli, I fear you have slept but ill: you seem pale. No matter!—our banquet to-day will soon brighten the current of your gay blood."

"Blood, Tribune!" said di Scotto, who was innocent of the plot: "thou sayest blood, and lo! on the floor are large gouts of it not yet dry."

"Now, out on thee, old hero, for betraying my awkwardness! I pricked myself with my own dagger in unrobing. Thank Heaven it hath no poison in its blade!"

The Frangipani exchanged looks,—Luca di Savelli clung to a column for support,—and the rest of the attendants seemed grave and surprised.

"Think not of it, my masters," said Rienzi: "it is a good omen, and a true prophecy. It implies that he who girds on his sword for the good of the state, must be ready to spill his blood for it: that am I. No more of this—a mere scratch: it gave more blood than I recked of from so slight a puncture, and saves the leech the trouble of the lancet. How brightly breaks the day! We must prepare to meet our fellow-citizens—they will be here anon. Ha, my Pandulfo—welcome!—thou, my old friend, shalt buckle on this mantle!"

And while Pandulfo was engaged in the task, the Tribune whispered a few words in his ear, which, by the smile on his countenance, seemed to the attendants one of the familiar jests with which Rienzi distinguished his intercourse with his more confidential intimates

CHAPTER VI

THE CELEBRATED CITATION

The bell of the great Lateran church sounded shrill and loud, as the mighty multitude, greater even than that of the preceding night, swept on. The appointed officers made way with difficulty for the barons and ambassadors, and scarcely were those noble visitors admitted ere the crowd closed in their ranks, poured headlong into the church, and took the way to the chapel of Boniface VIII. There, filling every cranny, and blocking up the entrance, the more fortunate of the press beheld the Tribune surrounded by the splendid court his genius had collected, and his fortune had subdued. At length, as the solemn and holy music began to swell through the edifice, preluding the celebration of the mass, the Tribune stepped forth, and the hush of the music was increased by the universal and dead silence of the audience. His height, his air, his countenance, were such as always command the attention of crowds; and at this time they received every adjunct from the interest of the occasion, and that peculiar look of intent yet suppressed fervour, which is, perhaps, the sole gift of the eloquent that Nature alone can give.

"Be it known," said he, slowly and deliberately, "in virtue of that authority, power, and jurisdiction, which the Roman people, in general parliament, have assigned to us, and which the Sovereign Pontiff hath confirmed, that we, not ungrateful of the gift and grace of the Holy Spirit—whose soldier we now are—nor of the favour of the Roman people, declare, that Rome, capital of the world, and base of the Christian church; and that every City, State, and People of Italy, are henceforth free. By that freedom, and in the same consecrated authority, we proclaim, that the election, jurisdiction, and monarchy of the Roman empire appertain to Rome and Rome's people, and the whole of Italy. We cite, then, and summon personally, the illustrious princes, Louis Duke of Bavaria, and Charles King of Bohemia, who would style themselves Emperors of Italy, to appear before us, or the other magistrates of Rome, to plead and to prove their claim between this day and the Day of Pentecost. We cite also, and within the same term, the Duke of Saxony, the Prince of Brandenburg, and whosoever else. potentate, prince, or prelate, asserts the right of Elector to the imperial throne—a right that, we find it chronicled from ancient and immemorial time, appertaineth only to the Roman people—and this in vindication of our civil liberties, without derogation of the spiritual power of the Church, the Pontiff, and the Sacred College.* Herald, proclaim the citation, at the greater and more formal length, as written and intrusted to your hands, without the Lateran."

As Rienzi concluded this bold proclamation of the liberties of Italy, the Tuscan ambassadors, and those of some other of the free states, murmured low appro-

* "Il tutto senza derogare all' autorità della Chiesa, del Tapa e del Sacro Collegio." So concludes this extraordinary citation, this bold and wonderful assertion of the classic independence of Italy, in the most feudal time of the fourteenth century. The anonymous biographer of Rienzi declares that the Tribune cited also the Pope and the Cardinals to reside in Rome. De Sade powerfully and incontrovertibly refutes this addition to the daring or the extravagance of Rienzi. Gibbon, however, who has rendered the rest of the citation in terms more abrupt and discourteous than he was warranted by any authority, copies the biographer's blunder, and sneers at De Sade, as using arguments "rather of decency than of weight." Without wearying the reader with all the arguments of the learned Abbé, it may be sufficient to give the first two.

1st. All the other contemporaneous historians that have treated of this event, G. Vallani, Hocsemius, the Vàtican MSS. and other chroniclers, relating the citation of the Emperor and Electors, say nothing of that of the Pope and Cardinals; and the Pope (Clement VI.), in his subsequent accusations of Rienzi, while very bitter against his citation of the Emperor, is wholly silent on what would have been to the Pontiff the much greater offence of citing himself and the Cardinals.

2d. The literal act of this citation, as published formally in the Lateran, is extant in Hocsemius, (whence is borrowed, though not at all its length, the speech in the text of our present tale;) and in this document the Pope and his Cardinals are *not* named in the summons.

Gibbon's whole account of Rienzi is superficial and unfair. To the cold and sneering scepticism, which so often deforms the gigantic work of that great writer, allowing nothing for that sincere and urgent enthusiasm which, whether of liberty or religion, is the most common parent of daring action, the great Roman seems but an ambitious and fantastic madman. In Gibbon's hands what would Cromwell have been? what Vane? what Hampden? The pedant, Julian, with his dirty person and pompous affectation, was Gibbon's ideal of a great man.

bation. The ambassadors of those States that affected the party of the Emperor looked at each other in silent amaze and consternation. The Roman Barons remained with mute lips and downcast eyes; only over the aged face of Stephen Colonna settled a smile, half of scorn, half of exultation. But the great mass of the citizens were caught by words that opened so grand a prospect as the emancipation of all Italy: and the reverence of the Tribune's power and fortune was almost that due to a supernatural being; so that they did not pause to calculate the means which were to correspond with the boast.

While his eye roved over the crowd, the gorgeous assemblage near him, the devoted throng beyond;—as on his ear boomed the murmur of thousands and ten thousands, in the space without, from before the Palace of Constantine (Palace now his own!) sworn to devote life and fortune to his cause; in the flush of prosperity that yet had known no check; in the zenith of power, as yet unconscious of reverse, the heart of the Tribune swelled proudly: visions of mighty fame and limitless dominion,—fame and dominion, once his beloved Rome's, and by him to be restored, rushed before his intoxicated gaze; and in the delirious and passionate aspirations of the moment, he turned his sword alternately to the three quarters of the then known globe, and said, in an abstracted voice, as a man in a dream, " In the right of the Roman people *this* too is mine!"*

Low though the voice, the wild boast was heard by all around as distinctly as if borne to them in thunder. And vain it were to describe the various sensations

* " Questo e mio."

it excited; the extravagance would have moved the derision of his foes, the grief of his friends, but for the manner of the speaker, which, solemn and commanding, hushed for the moment even reason and hatred themselves in awe; afterwards remembered and repeated, void of the spell they had borrowed from the utterer, the words met the cold condemnation of the well-judging; but at that moment all things seemed possible to the hero of the people. He spoke as one inspired—they trembled and believed; and, as rapt from the spectacle, he stood a moment silent, his arm still extended—his dark dilating eye fixed upon space —his lip parted—his proud head towering and erect above the herd,—his own enthusiasm kindled that of the more humble and distant spectators; and there was a deep murmur begun by one, echoed by the rest, "The Lord is with Italy and Rienzi!"

The Tribune turned, he saw the Pope's Vicar astonished, bewildered, rising to speak. His sense and foresight returned to him at once, and, resolved to drown the dangerous disavowal of the Papal authority for this hardihood, which was ready to burst from Raimond's lips, he motioned quickly to the musicians, and the solemn and ringing chant of the sacred ceremony prevented the Bishop of Orvietto all occasion of self-exoneration or reply.

The moment the ceremony was over, Rienzi touched the Bishop, and whispered, "We will explain this to your liking. You feast with us at the Lateran.—Your arm." Nor did he leave the good Bishop's arm, nor trust him to other companionship, until to the stormy sound of horn and trumpet, drum and cymbal, and amidst such a concourse as might have hailed, on the same spot, the legendary baptism of Constantine, the

Tribune and his nobles entered the great gates of the Lateran, then the Palace of the World.

Thus ended that remarkable ceremony and that proud challenge of the Northern Powers, in behalf of the Italian liberties, which, had it been afterwards successful, would have been deemed a sublime daring; which, unsuccessful, has been construed by the vulgar into a frantic insolence; but which, calmly considering all the circumstances that urged on the Tribune, and all the power that surrounded him, was not, perhaps, altogether so imprudent as it seemed. And, even accepting that imprudence in the extremest sense,—by the more penetrating judge of the higher order of character, it will probably be considered as the magnificent folly of a bold nature, excited at once by position and prosperity, by religious credulities, by patriotic aspirings, by scholastic visions too suddenly transferred from reverie to action, beyond that wise and earthward policy which sharpens the weapon ere it casts the gauntlet.

CHAPTER VII

THE FESTIVAL

The Festival of that day was far the most sumptuous hitherto known. The hint of Cecco del Vecchio, which so well depicted the character of his fellow-citizens, as yet it exists, though not to such excess, in their love of holyday pomp and gorgeous show, was not lost upon Rienzi. One instance of the universal banqueting (intended, indeed, rather for the people than the higher ranks) may illustrate the more than royal profusion that prevailed. From morn till eve, streams of wine flowed like a fountain from the nostrils of the Horse of the great Equestrian Statue of Constantine. The mighty halls of the Lateran palace, open to all ranks, were prodigally spread; and the games, sports, and buffooneries of the time, were in ample requisition. Apart, the Tribunessa, as Nina was rather unclassically entitled, entertained the dames of Rome; while the Tribune had so effectually silenced or conciliated Raimond, that the good Bishop shared his peculiar table—the only one admitted to that honour. As the eye ranged each saloon and hall, it beheld the space lined with all the nobility and knighthood—the wealth and strength—the learning and the beauty—of the Italian metropolis; mingled with ambassadors and noble strangers, even from beyond the Alps;*—envoys not only of the free states that had welcomed the rise of the Tribune, but of the high-born and haughty tyrants who had first derided his arrogance, and now cringed to his power. There, were not only the ambassadors of Florence, of Sienna, of Arezzo (which last subjected its government to the Tribune,) of Todi, of Spoleto, and of countless other lesser towns and states, but of the dark and terrible Visconti, prince of Milan; of Obizzo of Ferrara, and the tyrant rulers of Verona and Bologna; even the proud and sagacious Malatesta, lord of Rimini, whose arm afterwards broke for awhile the power of Montreal, at the head of his Great Company, had deputed his representative in his most honoured noble. John di Vico, the worst and most malignant despot of his

* The simple and credulous biographer of Rienzi declares his fame to have reached the ears of the Soldan of Babylon.

20

day, who had sternly defied the arms of the Tribune, now subdued and humbled, was there in person; and the ambassadors of Hungary and of Naples mingled with those of Bavaria and Bohemia, whose sovereigns that day had been cited to the Roman Judgment Court. The nodding of plumes, the glitter of jewels and cloth of gold, the rustling of silks and jingle of golden spurs, the waving of banners from the roof, the sounds of minstrelsy from the galleries above, all presented a picture of such power and state—a court and chivalry of such show—as the greatest of the feudal kings might have beheld with a sparkling eye and a swelling heart. But at that moment the cause and lord of all that splendour, recovered from his late exhilaration, sat moody and abstracted, remembering with a thoughtful brow the adventure of the past night, and sensible that amongst his gaudiest revellers lurked his intended murtherers. Amidst the swell of the minstrelsy and the pomp of the crowd, he felt that treason scowled beside him; and the image of the skeleton obtruding, as of old, its grim thought of death upon the feast, darkened the ruby of the wine, and chilled the glitter of the scene.

It was while the feast was loudest that Rienzi's page was seen gliding through the banquet, and whispering several of the nobles; each bowed low, but changed colour as he received the message.

"My Lord Savelli," said Orsini, himself trembling, "bear yourself more bravely. This must be meant in honour, not revenge. I suppose your summons corresponds with mine."

"He—he—asks—asks—me to supper at the Capitol; a fri—endly meeting—(pest on his friendship!)—after the noise of the day."

"The words addressed also to me!" said Orsini, turning to one of the Frangipani.

Those who received the summons soon broke from the feast, and collected in a group, eagerly conferring. Some were for flight, but flight was confession; their number, rank, long and consecrated impunity, reassured them, and they resolved to obey. The old Colonna, the sole innocent Baron of the invited guests, was also the only one who refused the invitation. "Tush!" said he, peevishly; "here is feasting enough for one day! Tell the Tribune that ere he sups I hope to be asleep. Gray hairs cannot encounter all this fever of festivity."

As Rienzi rose to depart, which he did early, for the banquet took place while yet morning, Raimond, eager to escape and confer with some of his spiritual friends, as to the report he should make to the Pontiff, was beginning his expressions of farewell, when the merciless Tribune said to him gravely—

"My Lord, we want you on urgent business at the Capitol. A prisoner—a trial—perhaps" (he added with his portentous and prophetic frown) "an *execution* waits us! Come."

"Verily, Tribune," stammered the good Bishop, "this is a strange time for execution!"

"Last night was a time yet more strange.—Come."

There was something in the way in which the final word was pronounced, that Raimond could not resist. He sighed, muttered, twitched his robes, and followed the Tribune. As he passed through the halls, the company rose on all sides. Rienzi repaid their salutations with smiles and whispers of frank courtesy and winning address. Young as he yet was, and of a handsome and noble presence, that took every advantage from splendid attire, and yet more from an appearance of intellectual command in his brow and eye, which the less cultivated signors of that dark age necessarily wanted—he glittered through the court as one worthy to form, and fitted to preside over, it; and his supposed descent from the Teuton Emperor, which, since his greatness, was universally bruited and believed abroad, seemed undeniably visible to the foreign lords in the majesty of his mien and the easy blandness of his address.

"My Lord Prefect," said he to a dark and sullen personage in black velvet, the powerful and arrogant John di Vico, prefect of Rome, "we are rejoiced to find so noble a guest at Rome: we must repay the courtesy by surprising you in your own palace ere long;—nor will you, Signor" (as he turned to the envoy from Tivoli,) "refuse us a shelter amidst your groves and waterfalls ere the vintage be gathered. Methinks Rome, united with sweet Tivoli, grows reconciled to the Muses. Your suit is carried, Master Venoni: the council recognises its justice; but I reserved the news for this holyday—you do not blame me, I trust." This was whispered, with a half-affectionate frankness, to a worthy citizen, who, finding himself amidst so many of the great, would have shrunk from the notice of the Tribune; but it was the policy of Rienzi to pay an especial and marked attention to those engaged in commercial pursuits. As, after tarrying a moment or two with the merchant, he passed on, the tall person of the old Colonna caught his eye—

"Signor," said he, with a profound inclination of his head, but with a slight emphasis of tone, "you will not fail us this evening."

"Tribune——" began the Colonna.

"We receive no excuse," interrupted the Tribune, hastily, and passed on.

He halted for a few moments before a small group of men plainly attired, who were watching him with intense interest; for they, too, were scholars, and in Rienzi's rise they saw another evidence of that wonderful and sudden power which intellect had begun to assume over brute force. With these, as if abruptly mingled with congenial spirits, the Tribune relaxed all the gravity of his brow. Happier, perhaps, his living career—more unequivocal his posthumous renown—had his objects as his tastes been theirs!

"Ah, *carissime!*" said he to one, whose arm he drew within his own,—"and how proceeds thy interpretation of the old marbles?—half unravelled? I rejoice to hear it! Confer with me as of old, I pray thee. To-morrow—no, nor the day after, but next week—we will have a tranquil evening. Dear poet, your ode transported me to the days of Horace; yet, methinks, we do wrong to reject the vernacular for the Latin. You shake your head? Well, Petrarch thinks with you: his great epic moves with the stride of a giant—so I hear from his friend and envoy,—and here he is. My Lælius, is that not your name with Petrarch? How shall I express my delight at his comforting, his inspiring letter? Alas! he overrates not my intentions, but my power. Of this hereafter."

A slight shade darkened the Tribune's brow at these words: but moving on, a long line of nobles and princes on either side, he regained his self-possession, and the dignity he had dropped with his former equals. Thus he passed through the crowd, and gradually disappeared.

" He bears him bravely," said one, as the revellers reseated themselves. " Noticed you the *we*—the style royal? "

" But it must be owned that he lords it well," said the ambassador of the Visconti: " less pride would be cringing to his haughty court."

" Why," said a professor of Bologna, " why is the Tribune called proud? I see no pride in him."

" Nor I," said a wealthy jeweller.

While these, and yet more contradictory, comments followed the exit of the Tribune, he passed into the saloon, where Nina presided; and here his fair person and silver tongue (" *Suavis coloratæque sententiæ*," according to the description of Petrarch) won him a more general favour with the matrons than he experienced with their lords, and not a little contrasted the formal and nervous compliments of the good Bishop, who served him on such occasions with an excellent foil.

But as soon as these ceremonies were done, and Rienzi mounted his horse, his manner changed at once into a stern and ominous severity.

" Vicar," said he, abruptly, to the Bishop, " we might well need your presence. Learn that at the Capitol now sits the Council in judgment upon an assassin. Last night, but for Heaven's mercy, I should have fallen a victim to a hireling's dagger. Knew you aught of this? "

And he turned so sharply on the Bishop, that the poor canonist nearly dropped from his horse in surprise and terror.

" I!—" said he.

Rienzi smiled—" No, good my Lord Bishop! I see you are of no murtherer's mould. But to continue:—

that I might not appear to act in mine own cause, I ordered the prisoner to be tried in my absence. In his trial (you marked the letter brought me at our banquet?)——"

"Ay, and you changed colour."

"Well I might: in his trial, I say, he has confessed that nine of the loftiest lords of Rome were his instigators. *They sup with me to-night!*—Vicar, forwards!"

BOOK V

THE CRISIS

"Questo ha acceso 'l fuoco e la fiamma laquale non la par spotegnere."—*Vit. di Col. di Rienzi*, lib. i. cap. 29.

"He has kindled fire and flames which he will not be able to extinguish."—*Life of Cola di Rienzi.*

CHAPTER I

THE JUDGMENT OF THE TRIBUNE

The brief words of the Tribune to Stephen Colonna, though they sharpened the rage of the proud old noble, were such as he did not on reflection deem it prudent to disobey. Accordingly, at the appointed hour, he found himself in one of the halls of the Capitol, with a gallant party of his peers. Rienzi received them with more than his usual graciousness.

They sate down to the splendid board in secret uneasiness and alarm, as they saw that, with the exception of Stephen Colonna, none, save the conspirators, had been invited to the banquet. Rienzi, regardless of their silence and abstraction, was more than usually gay—the old Colonna more than usually sullen.

"We fear we have but ill pleased you, my Lord Colonna, by our summons. Once, methinks, we might more easily provoke you to a smile."

"Situations are changed, Tribune, since you were my guest."

"Why, scarcely so. I have risen, but you have not fallen. Ye walk the streets day and night in security and peace; your lives are safe from the robber, and your palaces no longer need bars and battlements to shield you from your fellow-citizens. I have risen, but *we all* have risen—from barbarous disorder into civilised life! My Lord Gianni Colonna, whom we have made Captain over Campagna, you will not refuse a cup to the Buono Stato;—nor think we mistrust your valour, when we say, that we rejoice Rome hath no enemies to attest your generalship."

"Methinks," quoth the old Colonna, bluntly, "we shall have enemies enough from Bohemia and Bavaria, ere the next harvest be green."

"And, if so," replied the Tribune, calmly, "foreign foes are better than civil strife."

"Ay, if we have money in the treasury; which is but little likely, if we have many more such holydays."

"You are ungracious, my Lord," said the Tribune; "and, besides, you are more uncomplimentary to Rome than to ourselves. What citizen would not part with gold to buy fame and liberty?"

"I know very few in Rome that would," answered the Baron. "But tell me, Tribune, you who are a notable casuist, which is the best for a state—that its governor should be over-thrifty or over-lavish?"

"I refer the question to my friend, Luca di Savelli," replied Rienzi. "He is a grand philosopher, and I wot well could explain a much knottier riddle, which we will presently submit to his acumen."

The Barons, who had been much embarrassed by the bold speech of the old Colonna, all turned their eyes to Savelli, who answered with more composure than was anticipated.

"The question admits a double reply. He who is *born* a ruler, and maintains a foreign army, governing by fear, should be penurious. He who is *made* ruler, who courts the people, and would reign by love, must win their affection by generosity, and dazzle their fancies by pomp. Such, I believe, is the usual maxim in Italy, which is rife in all experience of state wisdom."

The Barons unanimously applauded the discreet reply of Savelli, excepting only the old Colonna.

"Yet pardon me, Tribune," said Stephen, "if I depart from the courtier-like decision of our friend, and opine, though with all due respect, that even a friar's coarse serge,* the parade of humility, would better become thee, than this gaudy pomp, the parade of pride!" So saying, he touched the large loose sleeve fringed with gold, of the Tribune's purple robe.

"Hush, father!" said Gianni, Colonna's son, colouring at the unprovoked rudeness and dangerous candour of the veteran.

"Nay, it matters not," said the Tribune, with affected indifference, though his lip quivered, and his eye shot fire; and then, after a pause, he resumed with an awful smile—"If the Colonna love the serge of the friar, he may see enough of it ere we part. And now, my Lord Savelli, for my question, which I pray you listen to; it demands all your wit. Is it best for a State's Ruler to be over-forgiving, or over-just? Take breath to answer: you look faint—you grow pale—you

* "Vestimenta da Bizoco," was the phrase used by Colonna; a phrase borrowed from certain heretics (*bizocchi*) who affected extreme austerity; afterwards the word passed into a proverb.—See the comments of Zefirino Re, in Vit. di Cola di Rienzi.

tremble—you cover your face! Traitor and assassin, your conscience betrays you! My Lords, relieve your accomplice, and take up the answer."

"Nay, if we are discovered," said the Orsini, rising in despair, "we will not fall unavenged—die, tyrant!"

He rushed to the place where Rienzi stood—for the Tribune also rose,—and made a thrust at his breast with his dagger; the steel pierced the purple robe, yet glanced harmlessly away—and the Tribune regarded the disappointed murtherer with a scornful smile.

"Till yesternight, I never dreamt that under the robe of state I should need the secret corselet," said he. "My Lords, you have taught me a dark lesson, and I thank ye."

So saying, he clapped his hands, and suddenly the folding doors at the end of the hall flew open, and discovered the saloon of the Council hung with silk of a blood-red, relieved by rays of white,—the emblem of crime and death. At a long table sate the councillors in their robes; at the bar stood a ruffian form, which the banqueters too well recognised.

"Bid Rodolf of Saxony approach!" said the Tribune.

And led by two guards, the robber entered the hall.

"Wretch, *you* then betrayed us!" said one of the Frangipani.

"Rodolf of Saxony goes ever to the highest bidder," returned the miscreant, with a horrid grin. "You gave me gold, and I would have slain your foe; your foe defeated me; he gives me life, and life is a greater boon than gold!"

"Ye confess your crime, my Lords! Silent! dumb! Where is your wit, Savelli? Where your pride, Rinaldo di Orsini? Gianni Colonna, is your chivalry come to this?"

"Oh!" continued Rienzi, with deep and passionate bitterness; "oh, my Lords, will nothing conciliate you —not to me, but to Rome? What hath been my sin against you and yours? Disbanded ruffians (such as your accuser)—dismantled fortresses—impartial law—what man, in all the wild revolutions of Italy, sprung from the people, ever yielded less to their licence? Not a coin of your coffers touched by wanton power, —not a hair of your heads harmed by private revenge. You, Gianni Colonna, loaded with honours, intrusted with command—you, Alphonso di Frangipani, endowed with new principalities,—did the Tribune remember one insult he received from you as the Plebeian? You accuse my pride;—was it my fault that ye cringed and fawned upon my power,—flattery on your lips, poison at your hearts? No, *I* have not offended you; let the world know, that in me you aimed at liberty, justice, law, order, the restored grandeur, the renovated rights of Rome! At these, the Abstract and the Immortal—not at this frail form, ye struck;—by the divinity of these ye are defeated;—for the outraged majesty of these,—criminals and victims,—ye must die!"

With these words, uttered with the tone and air that would have become the loftiest spirit of the ancient city, Rienzi, with a majestic step, swept from the chamber into the Hall of Council.*

All that night the conspirators remained within that

* The guilt of the Barons in their designed assassination of Rienzi, though hastily slurred over by Gibbon, and other modern writers, is clearly attested by Muratori, the Bolognese Chronicle, &c.—*They even confessed the crime.* (See Cron. Estens: Muratori, tom. xviii. p. 442.)

room, the doors locked and guarded; the banquet unremoved, and its splendour strangely contrasting the mood of the guests.

The utter prostration and despair of these dastard criminals—so unlike the knightly nobles of France and England—has been painted by the historian in odious and withering colours. The old Colonna alone sustained his impetuous and imperious character. He strode to and fro the room like a lion in his cage, uttering loud threats of resentment and defiance; and beating at the door with his clenched hands, demanding egress, and proclaiming the vengeance of the Pontiff.

The dawn came, slow and gray upon that agonised assembly: and just as the last star faded from the melancholy horizon, and by the wan and comfortless heaven, they regarded each other's faces, almost spectral with anxiety and fear, the great bell of the Capitol sounded the notes in which they well recognised the chime of death! It was then that the door opened, and a drear and gloomy procession of cordeliers, one to each Baron, entered the apartment! At that spectacle, we are told, the terror of the conspirators was so great, that it froze up the very power of speech.* The greater part at length, deeming all hope over, resigned themselves to their ghostly confessors. But when the friar appointed to Stephen approached that passionate old man, he waved his hand impatiently, and said—"Tease me not! tease me not!"

"Nay, son, prepare for the awful hour."

"Son, indeed!" quoth the Baron. "I am old enough to be thy grandsire; and for the rest, tell him

* "Diventarono sì gelati, che non poteano favellare."

who sent thee, that I neither am prepared for death, nor will prepare! I have made up my mind to live these twenty years, and longer too; if I catch not my death with the cold of this accursed night."

Just at that moment a cry that almost seemed to rend the Capitol asunder was heard, as, with one voice, the multitude below yelled forth—

"Death to the conspirators!—death! death!"

While this the scene in that hall, the Tribune issued from his chamber, in which he had been closeted with his wife and sister. The noble spirit of the one, the tears and grief of the other (who saw at one fell stroke perish the house of her betrothed,) had not worked without effect upon a temper, stern and just indeed, but naturally averse from blood; and a heart capable of the loftiest species of revenge.

He entered the Council, still sitting, with a calm brow, and even a cheerful eye.

"Pandulfo di Guido," he said, turning to that citizen, "you are right; you spoke as a wise man and a patriot, when you said that to cut off with one blow, however merited, the noblest heads of Rome, would endanger the State, sully our purple with an indelible stain, and unite the nobility of Italy against us."

"Such, Tribune, was my argument, though the Council have decided otherwise."

"Hearken to the shouts of the populace, you cannot appease their honest warmth," said the demagogue Baroncelli.

Many of the Council murmured applause.

"Friends," said the Tribune, with a solemn and earnest aspect, "let not Posterity say that Liberty loves blood; let us for once adopt the example and imitate the mercy of our great Redeemer! We have triumphed—let us forbear; we are saved—let us forgive!"

The speech of the Tribune was supported by Pandulfo, and others of the more mild and moderate policy; and after a short but animated discussion, the influence of Rienzi prevailed, and the sentence of death was revoked, but by a small majority.

"And now," said Rienzi, "let us be more than just; let us be generous. Speak—and boldly. Do any of ye think that I have been over-hard, over-haughty with these stubborn spirits?—I read your answer in your brows!—I have! Do any of ye think this error of mine may have stirred them to their dark revenge? Do any of you deem that they partake, as we do, of human nature,—that they are sensible to kindness, that they are softened by generosity,—that they can be tamed and disarmed by such vengeance as is dictated to noble foes by Christian laws?"

"I think," said Pandulfo, after a pause, "that it will not be in human nature, if the men you pardon, thus offending and thus convicted, again attempt your life!"

"Methinks," said Rienzi, "we must do even more than pardon. The first great Cæsar, when he did not crush a foe, strove to convert him to a friend——"

"And perished by the attempt," said Baroncelli, abruptly.

Rienzi started and changed colour.

"If you would save these wretched prisoners, better not wait till the fury of the mob become ungovernable," whispered Pandulfo.

The Tribune roused himself from his reverie.

"Pandulfo," said he, in the same tone, "my heart misgives me—the brood of serpents are in my hand—

I do not strangle them—they may sting me to death, in return for my mercy—it is their instinct! No matter: it shall not be said that the Roman Tribune bought with so many lives his own safety: nor shall it be written upon my grave-stone, 'Here lies the coward, who did not dare forgive.' What, ho! there, officers, unclose the doors! My masters, let us acquaint the prisoners with their sentence."

With that, Rienzi seated himself on the chair of state, at the head of the table, and the sun, now risen, cast its rays over the blood-red walls, in which the Barons, marshalled in order into the chamber, thought to read their fate.

"My Lords," said the Tribune, "ye have offended the laws of God and man; but God teaches man the quality of mercy. Learn at last, that I bear a charmed life. Nor is he whom, for high purposes, Heaven hath raised from the cottage to the popular throne, without invisible aid and spiritual protection. If hereditary monarchs are deemed sacred, how much more one in whose power the divine hand hath writ its witness! Yes, over him who lives but for his country, whose greatness is his country's gift, whose life is his country's liberty, watch the souls of the just, and the unsleeping eyes of the sworded seraphim! Taught by your late failure and your present peril, bid your anger against me cease; respect the laws, revere the freedom of your city, and think that no state presents a nobler spectacle than men born as ye are—a patrician and illustrious order—using your power to protect your city, your wealth to nurture its arts, your chivalry to protect its laws! Take back your swords—and the first man who strikes against the liberties of Rome, let *him* be your victim; even though that victim be the Tribune. Your cause has been tried—your sentence is pronounced. Renew your oath to forbear all hostility, private or public, against the government and the magistrates of Rome, and ye are pardoned—ye are free!"

Amazed, bewildered, the Barons mechanically bent the knee: the friars who had received their confessions, administered the appointed oath; and while, with white lips, they muttered the solemn words, they heard below the roar of the multitude for their blood.

This ceremony ended, the Tribune passed into the banquet-hall, which conducted to a balcony, whence he was accustomed to address the people; and never, perhaps, was his wonderful mastery over the passions of an audience (*ad persuadendum efficax dictator, quoque dulcis ac lepidus*)* more greatly needed or more eminently shown, than on that day; for the fury of the people was at its height, and it was long ere he succeeded in turning it aside. Before he concluded, however, every wave of the wild sea lay hushed.—The orator lived to stand on the same spot, to plead for a life nobler than those he now saved,—and to plead unheard and in vain!

As soon as the Tribune saw the favourable moment had arrived, the Barons were admitted into the balcony:—in the presence of the breathless thousands, they solemnly pledged themselves to protect the Good Estate. And thus the morning which seemed to dawn upon their execution witnessed their reconciliation with the people.

The crowd dispersed, the majority soothed and pleased;—the more sagacious, vexed and dissatisfied.

* Petrarch of Rienzi.

"He has but increased the smoke and the flame which he was not able to extinguish," growled Cecco del Vecchio; and the smith's appropriate saying passed into a proverb and a prophecy.

Meanwhile, the Tribune, conscious at least that he had taken the more generous course, broke up the Council, and retired to the chamber where Nina and his sister waited him. These beautiful young women had conceived for each other the tenderest affection. And their differing characters, both of mind and feature, seemed by contrast to heighten the charms of both; as in a skilful jewellery, the pearl and diamond borrow beauty from each other.

And as Irene now turned her pale countenance and streaming eyes from the bosom to which she had clung for support, the timid sister, anxious, doubtful, wistful;—the proud wife, sanguine and assured, as if never diffident of the intentions nor of the power of her Rienzi:—the contrast would have furnished to a painter no unworthy incarnation of the Love that hopeth, and the Love that feareth, all things.

"Be cheered, my sweet sister," said the Tribune, first caught by Irene's imploring look; "not a hair on the heads of those who boast the name of him thou lovest so well is injured.—Thank Heaven," as his sister, with a low cry, rushed into his arms, "that it was against my life they conspired! Had it been another Roman's, mercy might have been a crime! Dearest, may Adrian love thee half as well as I; and yet, my sister and my child, none can know thy soft soul like he who watched over it since its first blossom expanded to the sun. My poor brother! had he lived, your counsel had been his; and methinks his gentle spirit often whispers away the sternness which, otherwise, would harden over mine. Nina, my queen, my inspirer, my monitor—ever thus let thy heart, masculine in my distress, be woman's in my power; and be to me, with Irene, upon earth, what my brother is in heaven!"

The Tribune, exhausted by the trials of the night, retired for a few hours to rest; and as Nina, encircling him within her arms, watched over his noble countenance—care hushed, ambition laid at rest, its serenity had something almost of sublime. And tears of that delicious pride, which woman sheds for the hero of her dreams, stood heavy in the wife's eyes, as she rejoiced more, in the deep stillness of her heart, at the prerogative, alone hers, of sharing his solitary hours, than in all the rank to which his destiny had raised her, and which her nature fitted her at once to adorn and to enjoy. In that calm and lonely hour she beguiled her heart by waking dreams, vainer than the sleeper's; and pictured to herself the long career of glory, the august decline of peace, which were to await her lord.

And while she thus watched and thus dreamed, the cloud, as yet no bigger than a man's hand, darkened the horizon of a fate whose sunshine was well-nigh past!

CHAPTER II

THE FLIGHT

Fretting his proud heart, as a steed frets on the bit, old Colonna regained his palace. To him, innocent of the proposed crime of his kin and compeers, the whole scene of the night and morning presented but one feature of insult and degradation. Scarce was he in his palace, ere he ordered couriers, in whom he knew he could confide, to be in preparation for his summons. "This to Avignon," said he to himself, as he concluded an epistle to the Pontiff.—"We will see whether the friendship of the great house of the Colonna will outweigh the frantic support of the rabble's puppet.—This to Palestrina—the rock is inaccessible! —This to John di Vico, he may be relied upon, traitor though he be!—This to Naples; the Colonna will disown the Tribune's ambassador, if he throw not up the trust and hasten hither, not a lover but a soldier!—And may this find Walter de Montreal! Ah, a precious messenger he sent us, but I will forgive all—all, for a thousand lances." And as with trembling hands he twined the silk round his letters, he bade his pages invite to his board, next day, all the signors who had been implicated with him on the previous night.

The Barons came—far more enraged at the disgrace of pardon, than grateful for the boon of mercy. Their fears combined with their pride; and the shouts of the mob, the whine of the cordeliers, still ringing in their ears, they deemed united resistance the only course left to protect their lives, and avenge their affront.

To them the public pardon of the Tribune seemed only a disguise to private revenge. All they believed was, that Rienzi did not dare to destroy them in the face of day; forgetfulness and forgiveness appeared to them as the means designed to lull their vigilance, while abasing their pride: and the knowledge of crime detected forbade them all hope of safety. The hand of their own assassin might be armed against them, or they might be ruined singly, one by one, as was the common tyrant-craft of that day. Singularly enough, Luca di Savelli was the most urgent for immediate rebellion. The fear of death made the coward brave.

Unable even to conceive the romantic generosity of the Tribune, the Barons were yet more alarmed when, the next day, Rienzi, summoning them one by one to a private audience, presented them with gifts, and bade them forget the past: excused himself rather than them, and augmented their offices and honours.

In the Quixotism of a heart to which royalty was natural, he thought that there was no medium course; and that the enmity he would not silence by death, he could crush by confidence and favours. Such conduct from a born king to hereditary inferiors might have been successful; but the generosity of one who has abruptly risen over his lords, is but the ostentation of insult. Rienzi in this, and, perhaps, in forgiveness itself, committed a fatal error of *policy*, which the dark sagacity of a Visconti, or, in later times, of a Borgia, would never have perpetrated. But it was the error of a bright and a great mind.

Nina was seated in the grand saloon of the palace—it was the day of reception for the Roman ladies.

The attendance was so much less numerous than usual that it startled her, and she thought there was a coldness and restraint in the manner of the visitors present, which somewhat stung her vanity.

"I trust we have not offended the Signora Colonna," she said to the Lady of Gianni, Stephen's son. "She was wont to grace our halls, and we miss much her stately presence."

"Madam, my Lord's mother is unwell!"

"Is she so? We will send for her more welcome news. Methinks we are deserted to-day."

As she spoke, she carelessly dropped her handkerchief—the haughty dame of the Colonna bent not—not a hand stirred; and the Tribunessa looked for a moment surprised and disconcerted. Her eye roving over the throng, she perceived several, whom she knew as the wives of Rienzi's foes, whispering together with meaning glances, and more than one malicious sneer at her mortification was apparent. She recovered herself instantly, and said to the Signora Frangipani, with a smile, "May we be a partaker of your mirth? You seem to have chanced on some gay thought, which it were a sin not to share freely."

The lady she addressed coloured slightly, and replied, "We were thinking, madam, that had the Tribune been present, his vow of knighthood would have been called into requisition."

"And how, Signora?"

"It would have been his pleasing duty, madam, to succour the distressed." And the Signora glanced significantly on the kerchief still on the floor.

"You designed me, then, this slight, Signoras," said Nina, rising with great majesty. "I know not whether your Lords are equally bold to the Tribune; but this I know, that the Tribune's wife can in future forgive your absence. Four centuries ago, a Frangipani might well have stooped to a Raselli; to-day, the dame of a Roman Baron might acknowledge a superior in the wife of the first magistrate of Rome. I compel not your courtesy, nor seek it."

"We have gone too far," whispered one of the ladies to her neighbour. "Perhaps the enterprise may not succeed; and then——"

Further remark was cut short by the sudden entrance of the Tribune. He entered with great haste, and on his brow was that dark frown which none ever saw unquailing.

"How, fair matrons!" said he, looking round the room with a rapid glance, "ye have not deserted us yet? By the blessed cross, your Lords pay a compliment to our honour, to leave us such lovely hostages, or else, God's truth, they are ungrateful husbands. So, madam," turning sharp round to the wife of Gianni Colonna, "your husband is fled to Palestrina; yours, Signora Orsini, to Marino; yours with him, fair bride of Frangipani,—ye came hither to——. But *ye* are sacred even from a word!"

The Tribune paused a moment, evidently striving to suppress his emotion, as he observed the terror he had excited—his eye fell upon Nina, who, forgetting her previous vexation, regarded him with anxious amazement. "Yes," said he to her, "you alone, perhaps, of this fair assemblage, know not that the nobles whom I lately released from the headsman's gripe are a second time forsworn. They have left home in the dead of the night, and already the Heralds proclaim them traitors and rebels. *Rienzi forgives no more!*"

"Tribune," exclaimed the Signora Frangipani, who had more bold blood in her veins than her whole house, "were I of thine own sex, I would cast the words, Traitor and Rebel, given to my Lord, in thine own teeth!—Proud man, the Pontiff soon will fulfil that office!"

"Your Lord is blest with a dove, fair one," said the Tribune, scornfully. "Ladies, fear not, while Rienzi lives, the wife even of his worst foe is safe and honoured. The crowd will be here anon; our guards shall attend ye home in safety, or this palace may be your shelter—for, I warn ye, that your Lords have rushed into a great peril. And ere many days be past, the streets of Rome may be as rivers of blood."

"We accept your offer, Tribune," said the Signora Frangipani, who was touched, and, in spite of herself, awed by the Tribune's manner. And as she spoke, she dropped on one knee, picked up the kerchief, and, presenting it respectfully to Nina, said, "Madam, forgive me. I alone of these present respect you more in danger than in pride."

"And I," returned Nina, as she leaned in graceful confidence on Rienzi's arm, "I reply, that if there be danger, the more need of pride."

All that day and all that night rang the great bell of the Capitol. But on the following daybreak, the assemblage was thin and scattered; there was a great fear stricken into the hearts of the people, by the flight of the Barons, and they bitterly and loudly upbraided Rienzi for sparing them to this opportunity of mischief. That day the rumours continued; the murmurers for the most part remained within their houses, or assembled in listless and discontented troops. The next day dawned; the same lethargy prevailed. The Tribune summoned his Council, (which was a Representative assembly.)

"Shall we go forth as we are," said he, "with such few as will follow the Roman standard!"

"No," replied Pandulfo, who, by nature timid, was yet well acquainted with the disposition of the people, and therefore a sagacious counsellor. "Let us hold back; let us wait till the rebels commit themselves by some odious outrage, and then hatred will unite the waverers, and resentment lead them."

This counsel prevailed; the event proved its wisdom. To give excuse and dignity to the delay, messengers were sent to Marino, whither the chief part of the Barons had fled, and which was strongly fortified, demanding their immediate return.

On the day on which the haughty refusal of the insurgents was brought to Rienzi, came fugitives from all parts of the Campagna. Houses burned—convents and vineyards pillaged—cattle and horses seized—attested the warfare practised by the Barons, and animated the drooping Romans, by showing the mercies they might expect for themselves. That evening, of their own accord, the Romans rushed into the place of the Capitol:—Rinaldo Orsini had seized a fortress in the immediate neighbourhood of Rome, and had set fire to a tower, the flames of which were visible to the city. The tenant of the tower, a noble lady, old and widowed, was burnt alive. Then rose the wild clamour—the mighty wrath—the headlong fury. The hour for action had arrived.*

CHAPTER III

THE BATTLE

"I have dreamed a dream," cried Rienzi, leaping from his bed. "The lion-hearted Boniface, foe and victim of the Colonna, hath appeared to me, and promised victory.† Nina, prepare the laurel-wreath: this day victory shall be ours!"

* "Ardea terre, arse la Castelluzza e case, *e uomini*. Non si schifo di ardere una nobile donna Vedova, veterana, in una torre. Per tale crudeltade li Romani furo più irati," &c.—*Vita di C. di Rienzi*, lib. i. cap. 20.

† "In questa notte mi è apparito Santo Bonifacio Papa," &c.—*Vit. di Col. Rien.* cap. 32.

"Oh, Rienzi! to-day?"

"Yes! hearken to the bell—hearken to the trumpet. Nay, I hear even now the impatient hoofs of my white war-steed! One kiss, Nina, ere I arm for victory,—stay—comfort poor Irene; let me not see her—she weeps that my foes are akin to her betrothed; I cannot brook her tears; I watched her in her cradle. To-day, I must have no weakness on my soul! Knaves, twice perjured!—wolves, never to be tamed!—shall I meet ye at last sword to sword? Away, sweet Nina, to Irene, quick! Adrian is at Naples, and were he in Rome, her lover is sacred, though fifty times a Colonna."

With that, the Tribune passed into his wardrobe, where his pages and gentlemen attended with his armour. "I hear, by our spies," said he, "that they will be at our gates ere noon—four thousand foot, seven hundred horsemen. We will give them a hearty welcome, my masters. How, Angelo Villani, my pretty page, what do you out of your lady's service?"

"I would fain see a warrior arm for Rome," said the boy, with a boy's energy.

"Bless thee, my child; there spoke one of Rome's true sons!"

"And the Signora has promised me that I shall go with her guard to the gates, to hear the news——"

"And report the victory?—thou shalt. But they must not let thee come within shaft-shot. What! my Pandulfo, thou in mail?"

"Rome requires every man," said the citizen, whose weak nerves were strung by the contagion of the general enthusiasm.

"She doth—and once more I am proud to be a

Roman. Now, gentles, the Dalmaticum:* I would that every foe should know Rienzi; and, by the Lord of Hosts, fighting at the head of the imperial people, I have a right to the imperial robe. Are the friars prepared? Our march to the gates shall be preceded by a solemn hymn—so fought our sires."

"Tribune, John di Vico is arrived with a hundred horse to support the Good Estate."

"He hath!—The Lord has delivered us then of a foe, and given our dungeons a traitor!—Bring hither yon casket, Angelo.—So—Hark thee! Pandulfo, read this letter."

The citizen read, with surprise and consternation, the answer of the wily Prefect to the Colonna's epistle.

"He promises the Baron to desert to him in the battle, with the Prefect's banner," said Pandulfo. "What is to be done?"

"What!—take my signet—here—see him lodged forthwith in the prison of the Capitol. Bid his train leave Rome, and if found acting with the Barons, warn them that their Lord dies. Go—see to it without a moment's delay. Meanwhile, to the chapel—we will hear mass."

Within an hour the Roman army—vast, miscellaneous—old men and boys, mingled with the vigour of life, were on their march to the Gate of San Lorenzo; of their number, which amounted to twenty thousand foot, not one-sixth could be deemed men-at-arms; but the cavalry were well equipped, and consisted of the lesser Barons and the more opulent citi-

* A robe or mantle of white, borne by Rienzi; at one time belonging to the sacerdotal office, afterwards an emblem of empire.

zens. At the head of these rode the Tribune in complete armour, and wearing on his casque a wreath of oak and olive leaves, wrought in silver. Before him waved the great gonfalon of Rome, while in front of this multitudinous array marched a procession of monks, of the order of St. Francis, (for the ecclesiastical body of Rome went chiefly with the popular spirit, and its enthusiastic leader,)—slowly chanting the following hymn, which was made inexpressibly startling and imposing at the close of each stanza, by the clash of arms, the blast of trumpets, and the deep roll of the drum; which formed, as it were, a martial chorus to the song:—

ROMAN WAR-SONG

I

March, march for your hearths and your altars!
Cursed to all time be the dastard that falters,
Never on earth may his sins be forgiven
Death on his soul, shut the portals of heaven!
A curse on his heart, and a curse on his brain!—
Who strikes not for Rome, shall to Rome be her Cain!
  Breeze fill our banners, sun gild our spears,
  Spirito Santo, Cavaliers! *
    Blow, trumpets, blow,
    Blow, trumpets, blow,
      Gaily to glory we come;
    Like a king in his pomp,
    To the blast of the tromp,
      And the roar of the mighty drum!
  Breeze fill our banners, sun gild our spears,
  Spirito Santo, Cavaliers!

* Rienzi's word of battle was *Spirito Santo Cavaliere, i. e.* Cavalier in the singular number. The plural number has been employed in the text, as somewhat more animated, and therefore better adapted to the kind of poetry into the service of which the watchword has been pressed.

2

March, march for your Freedom and Laws!
Earth is your witness—all Earth is your cause!
Seraph and saint from their glory shall heed ye,
The angel that smote the Assyrian shall lead ye;
To the Christ of the Cross man is never so holy
As in braving the proud, in defence of the lowly!
  Breeze fill our banners, sun gild our spears,
  Spirito Santo, Cavaliers!
      Blow, trumpets, blow,
      Blow, trumpets, blow,
        Gaily to glory we come;
      Like a king in his pomp,
      To the blast of the tromp,
        And the roar of the mighty drum!
  Breeze fill our banners, sun gild our spears,
  Spirito Santo, Cavaliers!

3

March, march! ye are sons of the Roman,
The sound of whose step was as fate to the foeman!
Whose realm, save the air and the wave, had no wall,
As he strode through the world like a lord in his hall;
Though your fame hath sunk down to the night of the grave,
It shall rise from the field like the sun from the wave.
  Breeze fill our banners, sun gild our spears,
  Spirito Santo, Cavaliers!
      Blow, trumpets, blow,
      Blow, trumpets, blow,
        Gaily to glory we come;
      Like a king in his pomp,
      To the blast of the tromp,
        And the roar of the mighty drum!
  Breeze fill our banners, sun gild our spears,
  Spirito Santo, Cavaliers!

In this order they reached the wide waste that ruin and devastation left within the gates, and, marshalled in long lines on either side, extending far down the vistaed streets, and leaving a broad space in the centre, awaited the order of their leader.

"Throw open the gates, and admit the foe!" cried Rienzi, with a loud voice; as the trumpets of the Barons announced their approach.

Meanwhile the insurgent Patricians, who had marched that morning from a place called the Monument, four miles distant, came gallantly and boldly on.

With old Stephen, whose great height, gaunt frame, and lordly air, shewed well in his gorgeous mail, rode his sons,—the Frangipani and the Savelli, and Giordano Orsini, brother to Rinaldo.

"To-day the tyrant shall perish!" said the proud Baron; "and the flag of the Colonna shall wave from the Capitol."

"The flag of the Bear," said Giordano Orsini, angrily.—"The victory will not be *yours* alone, my Lord!"

"Our house ever took precedence in Rome," replied the Colonna, haughtily.

"Never, while one stone of the palaces of the Orsini stands upon another."

"Hush!" said Luca di Savelli; "are ye dividing the skin while the lion lives? We shall have fierce work to-day."

"Not so," said the old Colonna; "John di Vico will turn, with his Romans, at the first onset, and some of the malcontents within have promised to open the gates.—How, knave?" as a scout rode up breathless to the Baron. "What tidings?"

"The gates are opened—not a spear gleams from the walls!"

"Did I not tell ye, Lords?" said the Colonna, turning round triumphantly. "Methinks we shall win Rome without a single blow.—Grandson, where now are thy silly forebodings?" This was said to Pietro, one of his grandsons—the first-born of Gianni—a comely youth, not two weeks wedded, who made no reply. "My little Pietro here," continued the Baron, speaking to his comrades, "is so new a bridegroom, that last night he dreamed of his bride; and deems it, poor lad, a portent."

"She was in deep mourning, and glided from my arms, uttering 'Woe, woe, to the Colonna!'" said the young man, solemnly.

"I have lived nearly ninety years," replied the old man, "and I may have dreamed, therefore, some forty thousand dreams; of which, two came true, and the rest were false. Judge, then, what chances are in favour of the science!"

Thus conversing, they approached within bow-shot of the gates, which were still open. All was silent as death. The army, which was composed chiefly of foreign mercenaries, halted in deliberation—when, lo!—a torch was suddenly cast on high over the walls; it gleamed a moment—and then hissed in the miry pool below.

"It is the signal of our friends within, as agreed on," cried old Colonna. "Pietro, advance with your company!" The young nobleman closed his visor, put himself at the head of the band under his command; and, with his lance in his rest, rode in a half gallop to the gates. The morning had been clouded and overcast, and the sun, appearing only at intervals, now broke out in a bright stream of light—as it glittered on the waving plume and shining mail of the young horseman, disappearing under the gloomy arch, several paces in advance of his troop. On swept his followers—forward went the cavalry headed by Gianni Colonna, Pietro's father.—There was a minute's silence, broken only by the clatter of the arms, and tramp of hoofs,—when from within the walls rose the abrupt cry—"Rome, the Tribune, and the People! *Spirito Santo, Cavaliers!*" The main body halted aghast. Suddenly Gianni Colonna was seen flying backward from the gate at full speed.

"My son, my son!" he cried, "they have murdered him;"—he halted abrupt and irresolute, then adding, "But I will avenge!" wheeled round, and spurred again through the arch,—when a huge machine of iron, shaped as a portcullis, suddenly descended upon the unhappy father, and crushed man and horse to the ground—one blent, mangled, bloody mass.

The old Colonna saw, and scarce believed his eyes; and ere his troop recovered its stupor, the machine rose, and over the corpse dashed the Popular Armament. Thousands upon thousands, they came on; a wild, clamorous, roaring stream. They poured on all sides upon their enemies, who drawn up in steady discipline, and clad in complete mail, received and broke their charge.

"Revenge, and the Colonna!"—"The Bear and the Orsini!"—"Charity and the Frangipani!"* "Strike for the Snake† and the Savelli!" were then heard on high, mingled with the German and hoarse shout, "Full purses, and the Three Kings of Cologne." The

* Who had taken their motto from some fabled ancestor who had broken bread with a beggar in a time of famine.

† The Lion was, however, the animal usually arrogated by the heraldic vanity of the Savelli.

Romans, rather ferocious than disciplined, fell butchered in crowds round the ranks of the mercenaries: but as one fell, another succeeded; and still burst with undiminished fervour the counter cry of "Rome, the Tribune, and the People!—*Spirito Santo, Cavaliers!*" Exposed to every shaft and every sword by his emblematic diadem and his imperial robe, the fierce Rienzi led on each assault, wielding an enormous battle-axe, for the use of which the Italians were celebrated, and which he regarded as a national weapon. Inspired by every darker and sterner instinct of his nature, his blood heated, his passions aroused, fighting as a citizen for liberty, as a monarch for his crown, his daring seemed to the astonished foe as that of one frantic; his preservation that of one inspired: now here, now there; wherever flagged his own, or failed the opposing, force, glittered his white robe, and rose his bloody battle-axe; but his fury seemed rather directed against the chiefs than the herd; and still where his charger wheeled was heard his voice, "Where is a Colonna?"—"Defiance to the Orsini!"—"*Spirito Santo, Cavaliers!*" Three times was the sally led from the gate; three times were the Romans beaten back; and on the third, the gonfalon, borne before the Tribune, was cloven to the ground. Then, for the first time, he seemed amazed and alarmed, and, raising his eyes to heaven, he exclaimed, "O Lord, hast thou then forsaken me?" With that, taking heart, once more he waved his arm, and again led forward his wild array.

At eve the battle ceased. Of the Barons who had been the main object of the Tribune's assault, the pride and boast was broken. Of the princely line of the Colonna, three lay dead. Giordano Orsini was mortally wounded; the fierce Rinaldo had not shared the conflict. Of the Frangipani, the haughtiest signors were no more; and Luca, the dastard head of the Savelli, had long since saved himself by flight. On the other hand, the slaughter of the citizens had been prodigious;—the ground was swamped with blood—and over heaps of slain (steeds and riders) the twilight star beheld Rienzi and the Romans returning victors from the pursuit. Shouts of rejoicing followed the Tribune's panting steed through the arch; and just as he entered the space within, crowds of those whose infirmities, sex, or years, had not allowed them to share the conflict,—women, and children, and drivelling age, mingled with the bare feet and dark robes of monks and friars, apprised of the victory, were prepared to hail his triumph.

Rienzi reined his steed by the corpse of the boy Colonna, which lay half immersed in a pool of water, and close by it, removed from the arch where he had fallen, lay that of Gianni Colonna,—(that Gianni Colonna whose spear had dismissed his brother's gentle spirit.) He glanced over the slain, as the melancholy Hesperus played upon the bloody pool and the gory corselet, with a breast heaved with many emotions; and turning, he saw the young Angelo, who, with some of Nina's guard, had repaired to the spot, and had now approached the Tribune.

"Child," said Rienzi, pointing to the dead, "*blessed art thou who hast no blood of kindred to avenge!*—to him who hath, sooner or later comes the hour; and an awful hour it is!"

The words sank deep into Angelo's heart, and in after life became words of fate to the speaker and the listener.

Ere Rienzi had well recovered himself, and as were heard around him the shrieks of the widows and mothers of the slain—the groans of the dying—the exhortations of the friars—mingled with sounds of joy and triumph—a cry was raised by the women and stragglers on the battle-field without, of "The foe!—the foe!"

"To your swords," cried the Tribune; "fall back in order:—yet they cannot be so bold!"

The tramp of horses, the blast of a trumpet, were heard; and presently, at full speed, some thirty horsemen dashed through the gate.

"Your bows," exclaimed the Tribune, advancing; —"yet hold—the leader is unarmed—it is our own banner. By our Lady, it is our ambassador of Naples, the Lord Adrian di Castello!"

Panting—breathless—covered with dust—Adrian halted at the pool red with the blood of his kindred—and their pale faces, set in death, glared upon him.

"Too late—alas! alas!—dread fate!—unhappy Rome!"

"They fell into the pit they themselves had digged," said the Tribune, in a firm but hollow voice.—"Noble Adrian, would thy counsels had prevented this!"

"Away, proud man—away!" said Adrian, impatiently waving his hand,—"thou shouldst protect the lives of Romans, and——oh, Gianni!—Pietro!—could not birth, renown, and thy green years, poor boy—could not these save ye?"

"Pardon him, my friends," said the Tribune to the crowd,—"his grief is natural, and he knows not all their guilt.—Back, I pray ye—leave him to our ministering."

It might have fared ill for Adrian, but for the Tribune's brief speech. And as the young Lord, dismounting, now bent over his kinsmen—the Tribune also surrendering his charger to his 'squires, approached, and, despite Adrian's reluctance and aversion, drew him aside,—

"Young friend," said he, mournfully, "my heart bleeds for you; yet bethink thee, the wrath of the crowd is fresh upon them: be prudent."

"Prudent!"

"Hush—by my honour, these men were not worthy of your name. Twice perjured—once assassins—twice rebels—listen to me!"

"Tribune, I ask no other construing of what I see—they might have died justly, or been butchered foully. But there is no peace between the executioner of my race and me."

"Will *you*, too, be forsworn? Thine oath!—Come, come, I hear not these words. Be composed—retire—and if, three days hence, you impute any other blame to me than that of unwise lenity, I absolve you from your oath, and you are free to be my foe. The crowd gape and gaze upon us—a minute more, and I may not avail to save you."

The feelings of the young patrician were such as utterly baffle description. He had never been much amongst his house, nor ever received more than common courtesy at their hands. But lineage is lineage still! And there, in the fatal hazard of war, lay the tree and sapling, the prime and hope of his race. He felt there was no answer to the Tribune, the very place of their death proved they had fallen in an assault upon their countrymen. He sympathised not with their cause, but their fate. And rage, revenge alike forbidden—his heart was the more softened to the shock and paralysis of grief. He did not therefore speak, but continued to gaze upon the dead, while large and unheeded tears flowed down his cheeks, and his attitude of dejection and sorrow was so moving, that the crowd, at first indignant, now felt for his affliction. At length his mind seemed made up. He turned to Rienzi, and said, falteringly, "Tribune, I blame you not, nor accuse. If you have been rash in this, God will have blood for blood. I wage no war with you—you say right, my oath prevents me; and if you govern well, I can still remember that I am Roman. But—but—look to that bleeding clay—we meet no more!—your sister—God be with her!—between her and me flows a dark gulf!" The young noble paused some moments, choked by his emotions, and then continued, "These papers discharge me of my mission. Standard-bearers, lay down the banner of the Republic. Tribune, speak not—I would be calm—calm. And so farewell to Rome." With a hurried glance towards the dead, he sprung upon his steed, and, followed by his train, vanished through the arch.

The Tribune had not attempted to detain him—had not interrupted him. He felt that the young noble had thought—acted as became him best. He followed him with his eyes.

"And thus," said he gloomily, "Fate plucks from me my noblest friend and my justest counsellor—a better man Rome never lost!"

Such is the eternal doom of disordered states. The mediator between rank and rank,—the kindly noble—the dispassionate patriot—the first to act—the most hailed in action—darkly vanishes from the scene. Fiercer and more unscrupulous spirits alone stalk the field; and no neutral and harmonising link remains between hate and hate,—until exhaustion, sick with horrors, succeeds to frenzy, and despotism is welcomed as repose!

CHAPTER IV

THE HOLLOWNESS OF THE BASE

The rapid and busy march of state events has led us long away from the sister of the Tribune and the betrothed of Adrian. And the sweet thoughts and gentle day-dreams of that fair and enamoured girl, however full to *her* of an interest beyond all the storms and perils of ambition, are not so readily adapted to narration:—their soft monotony a few words can paint. They knew but one image, they tended to but one prospect. Shrinking from the glare of her brother's court, and eclipsed, when she forced herself to appear, by the more matured and dazzling beauty and all-commanding presence, of Nina,—to her the pomp and crowd seemed an unreal pageant, from which she retired to the *truth of life,*—the hopes and musings of her own heart. Poor girl! with all the soft and tender nature of her dead brother, and none of the stern genius and the prodigal ambition,—the eye-fatiguing ostentation and fervour of the living—she was but ill-fitted for the unquiet but splendid region to which she was thus suddenly transferred.

With all her affection for Rienzi, she could not conquer a certain fear which, conjoined with the difference of sex and age, forbade her to be communicative with him upon the subject most upon her heart.

As the absence of Adrian at the Neapolitan Court passed the anticipated date (for at no Court then, with a throne fiercely disputed, did the Tribune require a nobler or more intelligent representative,—and intrigues and counter-intrigues delayed his departure from week to week), she grew uneasy and alarmed. Like many, themselves unseen, inactive, the spectators of the scene, she saw involuntarily further into the time than the deeper intellect either of the Tribune or Nina; and the dangerous discontent of the nobles was visible and audible to her in looks and whispers, which reached not acuter or more suspected ears and eyes. Anxiously, restlessly, did she long for the return of Adrian, not from selfish motives alone, but from well-founded apprehensions for her brother. With Adrian di Castello, alike a noble and a patriot, each party had found a mediator, and his presence grew daily more needed, till at length the conspiracy of the Barons had broken out. From that hour she scarcely dared to hope; her calm sense, unblinded by the high-wrought genius which, as too often happens, made the Tribune see harsh realities through a false and brilliant light, perceived that the Rubicon was passed; and through all the events that followed she could behold but two images—danger to her brother, separation from her betrothed.

With Nina alone could her full heart confer; for Nina, with all the differences of character, was a woman who loved. And this united them. In the earlier power of Rienzi, many of their happiest hours had been passed together, remote from the gaudy crowd, alone and unrestrained, in the summer nights, on the moonlit balconies, in that interchange of thought, sympathy, and consolation, which to two impassioned and guileless women makes the most interesting occupation and the most effectual solace. But of late, this intercourse had been much marred. From the morning in which the Barons had received their pardon, to that on which they had marched on Rome, had been one succession of fierce excitements. Every face Irene saw was clouded and overcast—all gaiety was suspended—bustling and anxious councillors, or armed soldiers, had for days been the only visitors of the palace. Rienzi had been seen but for short moments: his brow wrapt in care. Nina had been more fond, more caressing than ever, but in those caresses there seemed a mournful and ominous compassion. The attempts at comfort and hope were succeeded by a sickly smile and broken words; and Irene was prepared, by the presentiments of her own heart, for the stroke that fell—victory was to her brother—his foe was crushed—Rome was free—but the lofty house of the Colonnas had lost its stateliest props, and Adrian was gone for ever!—She did not blame him; she could not blame her brother; each had acted as became his several station. She was the poor sacrifice of events and fate—the Iphigenia to the Winds which were to bear the bark of Rome to the haven, or, it might be, to whelm it in the abyss. She was stunned by the blow; she did not even weep or complain; she bowed to the storm that swept over her, and it passed. For two days she neither took food nor rest; she shut herself up; she asked only the boon of solitude: but on the third morning she recovered as by a miracle, for on the third morning the following letter was left at the palace:—

" Irene,—Ere this you have learned my deep cause of grief; you feel that to a Colonna, Rome can no longer be a home, nor Rome's Tribune be a brother.

While I write these words honour but feebly supports me: all the hopes I had formed, all the prospects I had pictured, all the love I bore and bear thee, rush upon my heart, and I can only feel that I am wretched. Irene, Irene, your sweet face rises before me, and in those beloved eyes I read that I am forgiven,—I am understood; and dearly as I know thou lovest me, thou wouldst rather I were lost to thee, rather I were in the grave with my kinsmen, than know I lived the reproach of my order, the recreant of my name. Ah! why was I a Colonna? why did Fortune make me noble, and nature and circumstance attach me to the people? I am barred alike from love and from revenge; all my revenge falls upon thee and me. Adored! we are perhaps separated for ever; but, by all the happiness I have known by thy side—by all the rapture of which I dreamed—by that delicious hour which first gave thee to my gaze, when I watched the soft soul returning to thine eyes and lip—by thy first blushing confession of love—by our first kiss—by our last farewell—I swear to be faithful to thee to the last. None other shall ever chase thine image from my heart. And now, when Hope seems over, Faith becomes doubly sacred; and thou, my beautiful, wilt thou not remember me? wilt thou not feel as if we were the betrothed of Heaven? In the legends of the North we are told of the knight who, returning from the Holy Land, found his mistress (believing his death) the bride of Heaven, and he built a hermitage by the convent where she dwelt; and, though they never saw each other more, their souls were faithful unto death. Even so, Irene, be we to each other—dead to all else—betrothed in memory—to be wedded above! And yet, yet ere I close, one hope dawns upon me. Thy brother's career, bright and lofty, may be but as a falling star; should darkness swallow it, should his power cease, should his throne be broken, and Rome know no more her Tribune; shouldst thou no longer have a brother in the judge and destroyer of my house; shouldst thou be stricken from pomp and state; shouldst thou be friendless, kindredless, alone—then, without a stain on mine honour, without the shame and odium of receiving power and happiness from hands yet red with the blood of my race, I may claim thee as my own. Honour ceases to command when thou ceasest to be great. I dare not too fondly indulge this dream, perchance it is a sin in both. But it must be whispered, that thou mayest know all thy Adrian, all his weakness and his strength. My own loved, my ever loved, loved more fondly now when loved despairingly, farewell! May angels heal thy sorrow, and guard *me* from sin, that *hereafter* at least we may meet again!"

"He loves me—he loves me still!" said the maiden, weeping at last; "and I am blest once more!"

With that letter pressed to her heart she recovered outwardly from the depth of her affliction; she met her brother with a smile, and Nina with embraces; and if still she pined and sorrowed, it was in that "concealment" which is the "worm i' the bud."

Meanwhile, after the first flush of victory, lamentation succeeded to joy in Rome; so great had been the slaughter that the private grief was large enough to swallow up all public triumph; and many of the mourners blamed even their defender for the swords of the assailant, "*Roma fu terribilmente vedovata.*"*

* "*Rome was terribly widowed.*"

The numerous funerals deeply affected the Tribune; and, in proportion to his sympathy with his people, grew his stern indignation against the Barons. Like all men whose religion is intense, passionate, and zealous, the Tribune had little toleration for those crimes which went to the root of religion. Perjury was to him the most base and inexpiable of offences, and the slain Barons had been twice perjured: in the bitterness of his wrath he forbade their families for some days to lament over their remains; and it was only in private and in secret that he permitted them to be interred in their ancestral vaults: an excess of vengeance which sullied his laurels, but which was scarcely inconsistent with the stern patriotism of his character. Impatient to finish what he had begun, anxious to march at once to Marino, where the insurgents collected their shattered force, he summoned his Council, and represented the certainty of victory, and its result in the complete restoration of peace. But pay was due to the soldiery; they already murmured; the treasury was emptied, it was necessary to fill it by raising a new tax.

Among the councillors were some whose families had suffered grievously in the battle—they lent a lukewarm attention to propositions of continued strife. Others, among whom was Pandulfo, timid but well-meaning, aware that grief and terror even of their own triumph had produced reaction amongst the people, declared that they would not venture to propose a new tax. A third party, headed by Baroncelli—a demagogue whose ambition was without principle—but who, by pandering to the worst passions of the populace, by a sturdy coarseness of nature with which they sympathised—and by that affectation of advancing what we now term the "movement," which often gives to the fiercest fool an advantage over the most prudent statesman, had quietly acquired a great influence with the lower ranks—offered a more bold opposition. They dared even to blame the proud Tribune for the gorgeous extravagance they had themselves been the first to recommend—and half insinuated sinister and treacherous motives in his acquittal of the Barons from the accusation of Rodolf. In the very Parliament which the Tribune had revived and remodelled for the support of freedom—freedom was abandoned. His fiery eloquence met with a gloomy silence, and finally, the votes were against his propositions for the new tax and the march to Marino. Rienzi broke up the Council in haste and disorder. As he left the hall, a letter was put into his hands; he read it, and remained for some moments as one thunderstruck. He then summoned the Captain of his Guards, and ordered a band of fifty horsemen to be prepared for his commands; he repaired to Nina's apartment, he found her alone, and stood for some moments gazing upon her so intently that she was awed and chilled from all attempt at speech. At length he said, abruptly—

"We must part."

"Part!"

"Yes, Nina—your guard is preparing; you have relations, I have friends, at Florence. Florence must be your home."

"Cola,——"

"Look not on me thus.—In power, in state, in safety—you were my ornament and counsellor. *Now* you but embarrass me. And——"

"Oh, Cola, speak not thus! What hath chanced? Be not so cold—frown not—turn not away! Am I not something more to thee, than the partner of joyous hours—the minion of love? Am I not thy wife, Cola—not thy leman?"

"Too dear—too dear to me," muttered the Tribune; "with thee by my side I shall be but half a Roman. Nina, the base slaves whom I myself made free desert me.—Now, in the very hour in which I might sweep away for ever all obstacles to the regeneration of Rome—now when one conquest points the path to complete success—now when the land is visible, my fortune suddenly leaves me in the midst of the seas! There is greater danger now than in the rage of the Barons—the Barons are fled; it is the People who are becoming traitors to Rome and to me."

"And wouldst thou have *me* traitor also! No, Cola; in death itself Nina shall be beside thee. Life and honour are reflected but from thee, and the stroke that slays the substance, shall destroy the humble shadow. I will not part from thee."

"Nina," said the Tribune, contending with strong and convulsive emotion,—"it may be literally of *death* that you speak.—Go! leave one who can no longer protect you or Rome!"

"Never—never."

"You are resolved?"

"I am."

"Be it so," said the Tribune, with deep sadness in his tone. "Arm thyself for the worst."

"There is no *worst* with thee, Cola!"

"Come to my arms, brave woman; thy words rebuke my weakness. But my sister!—if *I* fall, *you*, Nina, will not survive—your beauty a prey to the most lustful heart and the strongest hand. *We* will have the same tomb on the wrecks of Roman liberty. But

Irene is of weaker mould; poor child, I have robbed her of a lover, and now——"

"You are right; let Irene go. And in truth we may well disguise from her the real cause of her departure. Change of scene were best for her grief; and under all circumstances would seem decorum to the curious. I will see and prepare her."

"Do so, sweetheart. I would gladly be a moment alone with thought. But remember, she must part to-day—our sands run low."

As the door closed on Nina, the Tribune took out the letter and again read it deliberately. "So the Pope's Legate left Sienna:—prayed that Republic to withdraw its auxiliary troops from Rome—proclaimed me a rebel and a heretic;—thence repaired to Marino; —now in council with the Barons. Why, have my dreams belied me, then—false as the waking things that flatter and betray by day? In such peril will the people forsake me and themselves? Army of saints and martyrs, shades of heroes and patriots, have ye abandoned for ever your ancient home? No, no, I was not raised to perish thus; I will defeat them yet—and leave my name a legacy to Rome; a warning to the oppressor—an example to the free!"

CHAPTER V

THE ROTTENNESS OF THE EDIFICE

The kindly skill of Nina induced Irene to believe that it was but the tender consideration of her brother to change a scene embittered by her own thoughts, and in which the notoriety of her engagement with

Adrian exposed her to all that could mortify and embarrass, that led to the proposition of her visit to Florence. Its suddenness was ascribed to the occasion of an unexpected mission to Florence (for a loan of arms and money), which thus gave her a safe and honoured escort.—Passively she submitted to what she herself deemed a relief; and it was agreed that she should for a while be the guest of a relation of Nina's, who was the abbess of one of the wealthiest of the Florentine convents: the idea of monastic seclusion was welcome to the bruised heart and wearied spirit.

But though not apprised of the immediate peril of Rienzi, it was with deep sadness and gloomy forebodings that she returned his embrace and parting blessing; and when at length alone in her litter, and beyond the gates of Rome, she repented a departure to which the chance of danger gave the appearance of desertion.

Meanwhile, as the declining day closed around the litter and its troop, more turbulent actors in the drama demand our audience. The traders and artisans of Rome at that time, and especially during the popular government of Rienzi, held weekly meetings in each of the thirteen quarters of the city. And in the most democratic of these, Cecco del Vecchio was an oracle and leader. It was at that assembly, over which the smith presided, that the murmurs that preceded the earthquake were heard.

" So," cried one of the company—Luigi, the goodly butcher,—" they say he wanted to put a new tax on us; and that is the reason he broke up the Council today, because, good men, they were honest, and had bowels for the people: it is a shame and a sin that the treasury should be empty."

"I told him," said the smith, "to beware how he taxed the people. Poor men won't be taxed. But as he does not follow my advice, he must take the consequence—the horse runs from one hand, the halter remains in the other."

"Take *your* advice, Cecco! I warrant me his stomach is too high for that now. Why he is grown as proud as a pope."

"For all that, he is a great man," said one of the party. "He gave us laws—he rid the Campagna of robbers—filled the streets with merchants, and the shops with wares—defeated the boldest lords and fiercest soldiery of Italy——"

"And now wants to tax the people!—that's all the thanks we get for helping him," said the grumbling Cecco. "What would he have been without us?—we that make, can unmake."

"But," continued the advocate, seeing that he had his supporters—"but then he taxes us for our own liberties."

"Who strikes at them now?" asked the butcher.

"Why the Barons are daily mustering new strength at Marino."

"Marino is not Rome," said Luigi, the butcher. "Let's wait till they come to our gates again—we know how to receive them. Though, for the matter of that, I think we have had enough fighting—my two poor brothers had each a stab too much for them. Why won't the Tribune, if he *be* a great man, let us have peace? All we want now is quiet?"

"Ah!" said a seller of horse-harness. "Let him make it up with the Barons. They were good customers after all."

"For my part," said a merry-looking fellow, who

had been a grave-digger in bad times, and had now opened a stall of wares for the living, "I could forgive him all, but bathing in the holy vase of porphyry."

"Ah, that was a bad job," said several, shaking their heads.

"And the knighthood was but a silly show, an it were not for the wine from the horse's nostrils—*that* had some sense in it."

"My masters," said Cecco, "the folly was in not beheading the Barons when he had them all in the net; and so Messere Baroncelli says. (Ah, Baroncelli is an honest man, and follows no half measures!) It was a sort of treason to the people not to do so. Why, but for that, we should never have lost so many tall fellows by the gate of San Lorenzo."

"True, true, it was a shame; some say the Barons bought him."

"And then," said another, "those poor Lords Colonna—boy and man—they were the best of the family, save the Castello. I vow I pitied them."

"But to the point," said one of the crowd, *the richest* of the set; "*the tax is the thing*. The ingratitude to tax *us*.—Let him dare to do it!"

"Oh, he will not dare, for I hear that the Pope's bristles are up at last; so he will only have *us* to depend upon!"

The door was thrown open—a man rushed in open-mouthed—

"Masters, masters, the Pope's legate has arrived at Rome, and sent for the Tribune, who has just left his presence."

Ere his auditors had recovered their surprise, the sound of trumpets made them rush forth; they saw

Rienzi sweep by with his usual cavalcade, and in his proud array. The twilight was advancing, and torch-bearers preceded his way. Upon his countenance was deep calm, but it was not the calm of contentment. He passed on, and the street was again desolate. Meanwhile Rienzi reached the Capitol in silence, and mounted to the apartments of the palace, where Nina, pale and breathless, awaited his return.

"Well, well, thou smilest! No—it is that dread smile, worse than frowns. Speak, beloved, speak! What said the Cardinal?"

"Little thou wilt love to hear. He spoke at first high and solemnly, about the crime of declaring the Romans free; next about the treason of asserting that the election of the King of Rome was in the hands of the Romans."

"Well—thy answer."

"That which became Rome's Tribune: I re-asserted each right and proved it. The Cardinal passed to other charges."

"What?"

"The blood of the barons by San Lorenzo—blood only shed in our own defence against perjured assailants; this is in reality the main crime. The Colonna have the Pope's ear. Furthermore, the sacrilege—yes, the sacrilege (come laugh, Nina, laugh!) of bathing in a vase of porphyry used by Constantine while yet a heathen."

"Can it be! What saidst thou?"

"I laughed. 'Cardinal,' quoth I, 'what was not too good for a heathen is not too good for a Christian Catholic!' And verily the sour Frenchman looked as if I had smote him on the hip. When he had done, I asked him, in my turn, 'Is it alleged against me that

I have wronged one man in my judgment-court?'—Silence. 'Is it said that I have broken one law of the state?'—Silence. 'Is it even whispered that trade does not flourish—that life is not safe—that abroad or at home the Roman name is not honoured, to that point which no former rule can parallel?'—Silence. 'Then,' said I, 'Lord Cardinal, I demand thy thanks, not thy censure.' The Frenchman looked, and looked, and trembled, and shrunk, and then out he spoke. 'I have but one mission to fulfil, on the part of the Pontiff—resign at once thy Tribuneship, or the Church inflicts upon thee its solemn curse.'"

"How—how?" said Nina, turning very pale; "what is it that awaits thee?"

"Excommunication!"

This awful sentence, by which the spiritual arm had so often stricken down the fiercest foe, came to Nina's ears as a knell. She covered her face with her hands. Rienzi paced the room with rapid strides. "The curse!" he muttered; "the Church's curse—for me—for ME!"

"Oh, Cola! didst thou not seek to pacify this stern——"

"Pacify! Death and dishonour! Pacify! 'Cardinal,' I said, and I felt his soul shrivel at my gaze, 'my power I received from the people—to the people alone I render it. For my soul, man's words cannot scathe it. Thou, haughty priest, thou thyself art the accursed, if, puppet and tool of low cabals and exiled tyrants, thou breathest but a breath in the name of the Lord of Justice, for the cause of the oppressor, and against the rights of the oppressed.' With that I left him, and now——"

"Ay, now—now what will happen? Excommunication! In the metropolis of the Church, too—the superstition of the people! Oh, Cola!"

"If," muttered Rienzi, "my conscience condemned me of one crime—if I had stained my hands in one just man's blood—if I had broken one law I myself had framed—if I had taken bribes, or wronged the poor, or scorned the orphan, or shut my heart to the widow—then, then—but no! Lord, *thou* wilt not desert me!"

"But *man* may!" thought Nina mournfully, as she perceived that one of Rienzi's dark fits of fanatical and mystical reverie was growing over him—fits which he suffered no living eye, not even Nina's, to witness when they gathered to their height. And now, indeed, after a short interval of muttered soliloquy, in which his face worked so that the veins on his temples swelled like cords, he abruptly left the room, and sought the private oratory connected with his closet. Over the emotions there indulged let us draw the veil. Who shall describe those awful and mysterious moments, when man, with all his fiery passions, turbulent thoughts, wild hopes, and despondent fears, demands the solitary audience of his Maker?

It was long after this conference with Nina, and the midnight bell had long tolled, when Rienzi stood alone, upon one of the balconies of the palace, to cool, in the starry air, the fever that yet lingered on his exhausted frame. The night was exceedingly calm, the air clear, but chill, for it was now December. He gazed intently upon those solemn orbs to which our wild credulity has referred the prophecies of our doom.

"Vain science!" thought the Tribune, "and gloomy fantasy, that man's fate is pre-ordained—irrevocable—

unchangeable, from the moment of his birth! Yet, were the dream not baseless, fain would I know which of yon stately lights is my natal star,—which images—which reflects—my career in life, and the memory I shall leave in death." As this thought crossed him, and his gaze was still fixed above, he saw, as if made suddenly more distinct than the stars around it, that rapid and fiery comet which in the winter of 1347 dismayed the superstitions of those who recognised in the stranger of the heavens the omen of disaster and of woe. He recoiled as it met his eye, and muttered to himself, "Is such indeed my type! or, if the legendary lore speak true, and these strange fires portend nations ruined, and rulers overthrown, does it foretell my fate? I will think no more."* As his eyes fell they rested upon the colossal Lion of Basalt in the place below, the starlight investing its gray and towering form with a more ghostly whiteness; and then it was, that he perceived two figures in black robes lingering by the pedestal which supported the statue, and apparently engaged in some occupation which he could not guess. A fear shot through his veins, for he had never been able to divest himself of the vague idea that there was some solemn and appointed connection between his fate and that old Lion of Basalt. Somewhat relieved, he heard his sentry challenge the intruders; and as they came forward to the light, he perceived that they wore the garments of monks.

"Molest us not, son," said one of them to the sentry. "By order of the Legate of the Holy Father we affix

* Alas! if by the Romans associated with the fall of Rienzi, that comet was by the rest of Europe connected with the more dire calamity of the Great Plague that so soon afterwards ensued.

to this public monument of justice and of wrath, the bull of excommunication against a heretic and rebel. WOE TO THE ACCURSED OF THE CHURCH!"

CHAPTER VI

THE FALL OF THE TEMPLE

It was as a thunderbolt in a serene day—the reverse of the Tribune in the zenith of his power, in the abasement of his foe; when, with but a handful of brave Romans, determined to be free, he might have crushed for ever the antagonist power to the Roman liberties—have secured the rights of his country, and filled up the measure of his own renown. Such a reverse was the very mockery of Fate, who bore him through disaster, to abandon him in the sunniest noon of his prosperity.

The next morning not a soul was to be seen in the streets; the shops were shut—the churches closed; the city was as under an interdict. The awful curse of the papal excommunication upon the chief magistrate of the Pontifical city, seemed to freeze up all the arteries of life. The Legate himself, affecting fear of his life, had fled to Monte Fiascone, where he was joined by the Barons immediately after the publication of the edict. The curse worked best in the absence of the execrator.

Towards evening a few persons might be seen traversing the broad space of the Capitol, crossing themselves, as the bull, placarded on the Lion, met their eyes, and disappearing within the doors of the great palace. By and by, a few anxious groups collected in the streets, but they soon dispersed. It was a paralysis of all intercourse and commune. That spiritual and unarmed authority, which, like the invisible hand of God, desolated the market-place, and humbled the crowned head, no physical force could rally against or resist. Yet through the universal awe, one conviction touched the multitude—it was for them that their Tribune was thus blasted in the midst of his glories! The words of the Brand recorded against him on wall and column detailed his offences:—rebellion in asserting the liberties of Rome—heresy in purifying ecclesiastical abuses;—and to serve for a miserable covert to the rest, it was sacrilege for bathing in the porphyry vase of Constantine! They felt the conviction; they sighed—they shuddered—and, in his vast palace, save a few attached and devoted hearts, the Tribune was alone!

The staunchest of the Tuscan soldiery were gone with Irene. The rest of his force, save a few remaining guards, was the paid Roman militia, composed of citizens; who, long discontented by the delay of their stipends, now seized on the excuse of the excommunication to remain passive, but grumbling, in their homes.

On the third day, a new incident broke upon the death-like lethargy of the city; a hundred and fifty mercenaries, with Pepin of Minorbino, a Neapolitan, half noble, half bandit (a creature of Montreal's), at their head, entered the city, seized upon the fortresses of the Colonna, and sent a herald through the city, proclaiming, in the name of the Cardinal Legate, the reward of ten thousand florins for the head of Cola di Rienzi.

Then, swelled on high, shrill but not inspiring as of

old, the great bell of the Capitol—the people, listless, disheartened, awed by the spiritual fear of the papal authority (yet greater, in such events, since the removal of the see), came unarmed to the Capitol; and there, by the Place of the Lion, stood the Tribune. His 'squires, below the step, held his war-horse, his helm, and the same battle-axe which had blazed in the van of victorious war.

Beside him were a few of his guard, his attendants, and two or three of the principal citizens.

He stood bareheaded and erect, gazing upon the abashed and unarmed crowd with a look of bitter scorn, mingled with deep compassion; and, as the bell ceased its toll, and the throng remained hushed and listening, he thus spoke:—

"Ye come, then, once again! Come ye as slaves or freemen? A handful of armed men are in your walls: will ye who chased from your gates the haughtiest knights—the most practised battle-men of Rome, succumb now to one hundred and fifty hirelings and strangers? Will ye arm for your Tribune? You are silent!—be it so. Will you arm for *your own* liberties—*your own* Rome? Silent still! By the saints that reign on the thrones of the heathen gods! are ye thus fallen from your birthright? Have you no arms for your own defence? Romans, hear me! Have I wronged you?—if so, by *your* hands let me die: and then, with knives yet reeking with my blood, go forward against the robber who is but the herald of your slavery; and I die honoured, grateful, and avenged. You weep! Great God! you weep! Ay, and I could weep, too—that I should live to speak of liberty in vain to Romans—Weep! is this an hour for tears? Weep now, and your tears shall ripen harvests of crime, and licence, and despotism, to come! Romans, arm! follow me at once to the Place of the Colonna: expel this ruffian—expel your enemy (no matter what afterwards you do to me):" he paused; no ardour was kindled by his words—"or," he continued, "I abandon you to your fate."

There was a long, low, general murmur; at length it became shaped into speech, and many voices cried simultaneously: "The Pope's bull—thou art a man accursed!"

"What!" cried the Tribune; "and is it *ye* who forsake me, ye for whose cause alone man dares to hurl against me the thunders of his God? Is it not for *you* that I am declared heretic and rebel! What are my imputed crimes? That I have *made* Rome and *asserted* Italy to be free; that I have subdued the proud Magnates, who were the scourge both of Pope and People. And you—you upbraid me with what I have dared and done for you! Men, *with* you I would have fought, *for* you I would have perished. You forsake yourselves in forsaking me, and since I no longer rule over brave men, I resign my power to the tyrant you prefer. Seven months I have ruled over you, prosperous in commerce, stainless in justice—victorious in the field;—I have shown you what Rome could be; and since I abdicate the government ye gave me, when I am gone, strike for your own freedom! It matters nothing who is the chief of a brave and great people. Prove that Rome hath many a Rienzi, but of brighter fortunes."

"I would he had not sought to tax us," said Cecco del Vecchio, who was the very personification of the vulgar feeling: "and that he had beheaded the Barons!"

"Ay!" cried the ex-gravedigger; "but that blessed porphyry vase!"

"And why should we get our throats cut," said Luigi, the butcher, "like my two brothers?—Heaven rest them!"

On the face of the general multitude there was a common expression of irresolution and shame, many wept and groaned, none (save the aforesaid grumblers) *accused;* none upbraided, but none seemed disposed to arm. It was one of those listless panics, those strange fits of indifference and lethargy which often seize upon a people who make liberty a matter of impulse and caprice, to whom it has become a catchword, who have not long enjoyed all its rational, and sound, and practical, and blessed results; who have been affrayed by the storms that herald its dawn;—a people such as is common to the south: such as even the north has known; such as, had Cromwell lived a year longer, even England might have seen; and, indeed, in some measure, such a reaction from popular enthusiasm to popular indifference England *did* see, when her children madly surrendered the fruits of a bloody war, without reserve, without foresight, to the lewd pensioner of Louis, and the royal murderer of Sydney. To such prostration of soul, such blindness of intellect, even the noblest people will be subjected, when liberty, which should be the growth of ages, spreading its roots through the strata of a thousand customs, is raised, the exotic of an hour, and (like the Tree and Dryad of ancient fable) flourishes and withers with the single spirit that protects it.

"Oh, Heaven, that I were a man!" exclaimed Angelo, who stood behind Rienzi.

"Hear him, hear the boy," cried the Tribune; "ouc

of the mouths of babes speaketh wisdom! He wishes that he were a man, as ye are men, that he might do as ye should do. Mark me,—I ride with these faithful few through the quarter of the Colonna, before the fortress of your foe. Three times before that fortress shall my trumpet sound; if at the third blast ye come not, armed as befits ye—I say not all, but three, but two, but *one* hundred of ye—I break up my wand of office, and the world shall say one hundred and fifty robbers quelled the soul of Rome, and crushed her magistrate and her laws!"

With those words he descended the stairs, and mounted his charger; the populace gave way in silence, and their Tribune and his slender train passed slowly on, and gradually vanished from the view of the increasing crowd.

The Romans remained on the place, and after a pause, the demagogue Baroncelli, who saw an opening to his ambition, addressed them. Though not an eloquent nor gifted man, he had the art of uttering the most popular commonplaces. And he knew the weak side of his audience, in their vanity, indolence, and arrogant pride.

"Look you, my masters," said he, leaping up to the Place of the Lion; "the Tribune talks bravely—he always did—but the monkey used the cat for his chestnuts; he wants to thrust your paws into the fire; you will not be so silly as to let him. The saints bless us! But the Tribune, good man, gets a palace and has banquets, and bathes in a porphyry vase; the more shame on him!—in which San Sylvester christened the Emperor Constantine: all this is worth fighting for; but you, my masters, what do *you* get except hard blows, and a stare at a holyday spectacle? Why, if you beat these fellows, you will have another tax on the wine: *that* will be *your* reward!"

"Hark!" cried Cecco, "there sounds the trumpet, —a pity he wanted to tax us!"

"True," cried Baroncelli, "there sounds the trumpet; a *silver* trumpet, by the Lord! Next week, if you help him out of the scrape, he'll have a golden one. But go—why don't you move, my friends?—'tis but one hundred and fifty mercenaries. True, they are devils to fight, clad in armour from top to toe, but what then?—if they do cut some four or five hundred throats you'll beat them at last, and the Tribune will sup the merrier."

"There sounds the second blast," said the butcher. "If my old mother had not lost two of us already, 'tis odds, but I'd strike a blow for the bold tribune."

"You had better put more quicksilver in you," continued Baroncelli, "or you will be too late. And what a pity that will be!—if you believe the Tribune, he is the only man that can save Rome. What, you, the finest people in the world—you, not able to save yourselves!—you, bound up with one man—you, not able to dictate to the Colonna and Orsini! Why, who beat the Barons at San Lorenzo? Was it not you? Ah! you got the buffets, and the Tribune the *moneta!* Tush, my friends, let the man go; I warrant there are plenty as good as he to be bought a cheaper bargain. And, hark! there is the third blast; it is too late now!"

As the trumpet from the distance sent forth its long and melancholy note, it was as the last warning of the parting genius of the place; and when silence swallowed up the sound, a gloom fell over the whole assembly. They began to regret, to repent, when regret and repentance availed no more. The buffoonery of Baroncelli became suddenly displeasing; and the orator had the mortification of seeing his audience disperse in all directions, just as he was about to inform them what great things he himself could do in their behalf.

Meanwhile the Tribune, passing unscathed through the dangerous quarter of the enemy, who, dismayed at his approach, shrunk within their fortress, proceeded to the Castle of St. Angelo, whither Nina had already preceded him; and which he entered to find that proud lady with a smile for his safety,—without a tear for his reverse.

CHAPTER VII

THE SUCCESSORS OF AN UNSUCCESSFUL REVOLUTION—WHO IS TO BLAME—THE FORSAKEN ONE OR THE FORSAKERS?

Cheerfully broke the winter sun over the streets of Rome, as the army of the Barons swept along them. The Cardinal Legate at the head; the old Colonna (no longer haughty and erect, but bowed, and broken-hearted at the loss of his sons) at his right hand;—the sleek smile of Luca Savelli—the black frown of Rinaldo Orsini, were seen close behind. A long but barbarous array it was; made up chiefly of foreign hirelings; nor did the procession resemble the return of exiled citizens, but the march of invading foes.

"My Lord Colonna," said the Cardinal Legate, a small withered man, by birth a Frenchman, and full of the bitterest prejudices against the Romans, who had in a former mission very ill received him, as was their wont with foreign ecclesiastics; "this Pepin, whom Montreal has deputed at your orders, hath done us indeed good service."

The old Lord bowed, but made no answer. His strong intellect was already broken, and there was dotage in his glassy eye. The Cardinal muttered, "He hears me not; sorrow hath brought him to second childhood!" and looking back, motioned to Luca Savelli to approach.

"Luca," said the Legate, "it was fortunate that the Hungarian's black banner detained the Provençal at Aversa. Had he entered Rome, we might have found Rienzi's successor worse than the Tribune himself. Montreal," he added, with a slight emphasis and a curled lip, "is a gentleman, and a Frenchman. This Pepin, who is his delegate, we must bribe, or menace to our will."

"Assuredly," answered Savelli, "it is not a difficult task: for Montreal calculated on a more stubborn contest, which he himself would have found leisure to close——"

"As Podesta, or Prince of Rome! the modest man! We Frenchmen have a due sense of our own merits; but this sudden victory surprises him as it doth us, Luca; and we shall wrest the prey from Pepin, ere Montreal can come to his help! But Rienzi must die. He is still, I hear, shut up in St. Angelo. The Orsini shall storm him there ere the day be much older. To-day we possess the Capitol—annul all the rebel's laws—break up his ridiculous parliament, and put all the government of the city under three senators—Rinaldo Orsini, Colonna, and myself; you, my Lord, I trust, we shall fitly provide for."

"Oh! I am rewarded enough by returning to my palace; and a descent on the Jewellers' quarter will soon build up its fortifications. Luca Savelli is not an ambitious man. He wants but to live in peace."

The Cardinal smiled sourly, and took the turn towards the Capitol.

In the front space the usual gapers were assembled. "Make way! make way! knaves!" cried the guards, trampling on either side the crowd, who, accustomed to the sedate and courteous order of Rienzi's guard, fell back too slowly for many of them to escape severe injury from the pikes of the soldiers and the hoofs of the horses. Our friend, Luigi, the butcher, was one of these, and the surliness of the Roman blood was past boiling heat when he received in his ample stomach the blunt end of a German's pike. "There, Roman," said the rude mercenary, in his barbarous attempt at Italian, "make way for your betters; you have had enough crowds and shows of late, in all conscience."

"Betters!" gulped out the poor butcher; "a Roman has no betters; and if I had not lost two brothers by San Lorenzo, I would——"

"The dog is mutinous," said one of the followers of the Orsini, succeeding the German who had passed on, "and talks of San Lorenzo!"

"Oh!" said another Orsinist, who rode abreast, "I remember him of old. He was one of Rienzi's gang."

"Was he?" said the other, sternly; "then we cannot begin salutary examples too soon;" and, offended at something swaggering and insolent in the butcher's look, the Orsinist coolly thrust him through the heart with his pike, and rode on over his body.

"Shame! Shame!" "Murder! Murder!" cried the crowd: and they began to press, in the passion of the moment, round the fierce guards.

The Legate heard the cry, and saw the rush: he turned pale. "The rascals rebel again!" he faltered.

"No, your Eminence—no," said Luca; "but it may be as well to infuse a wholesome terror; they are all unarmed; let me bid the guards disperse them. A word will do it."

The Cardinal assented; the word was given; and, in a few minutes, the soldiery, who still smarted under the vindictive memory of defeat from an undisciplined multitude, scattered the crowd down the street without scruple or mercy—riding over some, spearing others—filling the air with shrieks and yells, and strewing the ground with almost as many men as a few days before would have sufficed to have guarded Rome, and preserved the constitution! Through this wild, tumultuous scene, and over the bodies of its victims, rode the Legate and his train, to receive in the Hall of the Capitol the allegiance of the citizens, and to proclaim the return of the oppressors.

As they dismounted at the stairs, a placard in large letters struck the eye of the Legate. It was placed upon the pedestal of the Lion of Basalt, covering the very place that had been occupied by the bull of excommunication. The words were few, and ran thus:

"TREMBLE! RIENZI SHALL RETURN!"

"How! what means this mummery!" cried the Legate, trembling already, and looking round to the nobles.

"Please your Eminence," said one of the councillors, who had come from the Capitol to meet the Legate, "we saw it at daybreak, the ink yet moist, as we entered the Hall. We deemed it best to leave it for your Eminence to deal with."

"*You* deemed! Who are *you*, then?"

"One of the members of the Council, your Eminence, and a stanch opponent of the Tribune, as is well known, when he wanted the new tax——"

"Council—trash! No more councils now! Order is restored at last. The Orsini and the Colonna will look to you in future. Resist a tax, did you? Well, that was right when proposed by a tyrant; but *I* warn you, friend, to take care how you resist the tax *we* shall impose. Happy if your city can buy its peace with the Church on any terms:—and his Holiness is short of the florins."

The discomfited councillor shrunk back.

"Tear off yon insolent placard. Nay, hold! fix over it our proclamation of ten thousand florins for the heretic's head! *Ten* thousand? methinks that is too much *now*—we will alter the cypher. Meanwhile Rinaldo Orsini, Lord Senator, march thy soldiers to St. Angelo; let us see if the heretic can stand a siege."

"It needs not, your Eminence," said the councillor, again officiously bustling up; "St. Angelo is surrendered. The Tribune, his wife, and one page, escaped last night, it is said, in disguise."

"Ha!" said the old Colonna, whose dulled sense had at length arrived at the conclusion that something extraordinary arrested the progress of his friends. "What is the matter? What is that placard? Will no one tell me the words? My old eyes are dim."

As he uttered the questions, in the shrill and piercing treble of age, a voice replied in a loud and deep tone—none knew whence it came; the crowd was reduced to a few stragglers, chiefly friars in cowl and serge, whose curiosity nought could daunt, and whose garb ensured them safety—the soldiers closed the rear: a voice, I say, came, startling the colour from many a cheek—in answer to the Colonna, saying:

"TREMBLE! RIENZI SHALL RETURN!"

BOOK VI

THE PLAGUE

"Erano gli anni dolla fruttifera Incarnazione del Figliuolo di Dio al numero pervenuti di millè trecento quarant'otto, quando nell' egregia città di Fiorenza oitre ad ogni altra Italica bellissima, pervenne la mortifera pestilenza."—Boccaccio, *Introduzione al Decamerone.*

"The years of the fructiferous incarnation of the Son of God had reached the number of one thousand three hundred and forty-eight, when into the illustrious city of Florence, beautiful beyond every other in Italy, entered the death-fraught pestilence."—*Introduction to the Decameron.*

CHAPTER I

THE RETREAT OF THE LOVER

By the borders of one of the fairest lakes of Northern Italy stood the favourite mansion of Adrian di Castello, to which in his softer and less patriotic moments his imagination had often and fondly turned; and thither the young nobleman, dismissing his more courtly and distinguished companions in the Neapolitan embassy, retired after his ill-starred return to Rome. Most of those thus dismissed joined the Barons; the young Annibaldi, whose daring and ambitious nature had attached him strongly to the Tribune, maintained a neutral ground; he betook himself to his castle in the Campagna, and did not return to Rome till the expulsion of Rienzi.

The retreat of Irene's lover was one well fitted to

feed his melancholy reveries. Without being absolutely a fortress, it was sufficiently strong to resist any assault of the mountain robbers or petty tyrants in the vicinity; while, built by some former lord from the materials of the half-ruined villas of the ancient Romans, its marbled columns and tessellated pavements relieved with a wild grace the gray stone walls and massive towers of feudal masonry. Rising from a green eminence gently sloping to the lake, the stately pile cast its shadow far and dark over the beautiful waters; by its side, from the high and wooded mountains on the background, broke a waterfall, in irregular and sinuous course—now hid by the foliage, now gleaming in the light, and collecting itself at last in a broad basin—beside which a little fountain, inscribed with half-obliterated letters, attested the departed elegance of the classic age—some memento of lord and poet whose very names were lost; thence descending through mosses and lichen, and odorous herbs, a brief, sheeted stream bore its surplus into the lake, And there, amidst the sturdier and bolder foliage of the North, grew, wild and picturesque, many a tree transplanted, in ages back, from the sunnier East; not blighted nor stunted in that golden clime, which fosters almost every produce of nature as with a mother's care. The place was remote and solitary. The roads that conducted to it from the distant towns were tangled, intricate, mountainous, and beset by robbers. A few cottages, and a small convent, a quarter of a league up the verdant margin, were the nearest habitations: and, save by some occasional pilgrim or some bewildered traveller, the loneliness of the mansion was rarely invaded. It was precisely the spot which proffered rest to a man weary of the world, and indulged the memories which grow in rank luxuriance over the wrecks of passion. And he whose mind, at once gentle and self-dependent, can endure solitude, might have ransacked all earth for a more fair and undisturbed retreat.

But not to such a solitude had the earlier dreams of Adrian dedicated the place. Here had he thought —should one bright being have presided—here should love have found its haven: and hither, when love at length admitted of intrusion, hither might wealth and congenial culture have invited all the gentler and better spirits which had begun to move over the troubled face of Italy, promising a second and younger empire of poesy, and lore, and art. To the graceful and romantic but somewhat pensive and inert, temperament of the young noble, more adapted to calm and civilised than stormy and barbarous times, ambition proffered no reward so grateful as lettered leisure and intellectual repose. His youth coloured by the influence of Petrarch, his manhood had dreamed of a happier Vaucluse not untenanted by a Laura. The visions which had connected the scene with the image of Irene made the place still haunted by her shade; and time and absence only ministering to his impassioned meditations, deepened his melancholy and increased his love.

In this lone retreat—which even in describing from memory, for these eyes have seen, these feet have trodden, this heart yet yearneth for, the spot—which even, I say, in thus describing, seems to me (and haply also to the gentle reader) a grateful and welcome transit from the storms of action and the vicissitudes of ambition, so long engrossing the narrative;—in this lone retreat Adrian passed the winter, which visits with so mild a change that intoxicating clime. The roar of the world without was borne but in faint and indistinct murmurings to his ear. He learned only imperfectly, and with many contradictions, the news which broke like a thunderbolt over Italy, that the singular and aspiring man—himself a revolution—who had excited the interest of all Europe, the brightest hopes of the enthusiastic, the profusest adulation of the great, the deepest terror of the despot, the wildest aspirations of all free spirits, had been suddenly stricken from his state, his name branded and his head proscribed. This event, which happened at the end of December, reached Adrian, through a wandering pilgrim, at the commencement of March, somewhat more than two months after the date; the March of that awful year 1348, which saw Europe, and Italy especially, desolated by the direst pestilence which history has recorded, accursed alike by the numbers and the celebrity of its victims, and yet strangely connected with some not unpleasing images by the grace of Boccaccio and the eloquence of Petrarch.

The pilgrim who informed Adrian of the revolution at Rome was unable to give him any clue to the present fate of Rienzi or his family. It was only known that the Tribune and his wife had escaped, none knew whither; many guessed that they were already dead, victims to the numerous robbers who immediately on the fall of the Tribune settled back to their former habits, sparing neither age nor sex, wealth nor poverty. As all relating to the ex-Tribune was matter of eager interest, the pilgrim had also learned that, previous to the fall of Rienzi, his sister had left Rome, but it was not known to what place she had been conveyed.

The news utterly roused Adrian from his dreaming life. Irene was then in the condition his letter dared to picture—severed from her brother, fallen from her rank, desolate and friendless. "Now," said the generous and high-hearted lover, "she may be mine without a disgrace to my name. Whatever Rienzi's faults, she is not implicated in them. *Her* hands are not red with my kinsman's blood; nor can men say that Adrian di Castello allies himself with a House whose power is built upon the ruins of the Colonnas. The Colonna are restored—again triumphant—Rienzi is nothing—distress and misfortune unite me at once to her on whom they fall!"

But how were these romantic resolutions to be executed—Irene's dwelling-place unknown? He resolved himself to repair to Rome and make the necessary inquiries: accordingly he summoned his retainers:—blithe tidings to them, those of travel! The mail left the armoury—the banner the hall—and after two days of animated bustle, the fountain by which Adrian had passed so many hours of reverie was haunted only by the birds of the returning spring; and the nightly lamp no longer cast its solitary ray from his turret chamber over the bosom of the deserted lake.

CHAPTER II

THE SEEKER

It was a bright, oppressive, sultry morning, when a solitary horseman was seen winding that unequalled road, from whose height, amidst fig-trees, vines, and olives, the traveller beholds gradually break upon his gaze the enchanting valley of the Arno, and the spires and domes of Florence. But not with the traveller's customary eye of admiration and delight passed that solitary horseman, and not upon the usual activity, and mirth, and animation of the Tuscan life, broke that noon-day sun. All was silent, void and hushed; and even in the light of heaven there seemed a sicklied and ghastly glare. The cottages by the road-side were some shut up and closed, some open, but seemingly inmateless. The plough stood still, the distaff plied not: horse and man had a dreary holiday. There was a darker curse upon the land than the curse of Cain! Now and then a single figure, usually clad in the gloomy robe of a friar, crossed the road, lifting towards the traveller a livid and amazed stare, and then hurried on, and vanished beneath some roof, whence issued a faint and dying moan, which but for the exceeding stillness around could scarcely have pierced the threshold. As the traveller neared the city, the scene became less solitary, yet more dread. There might be seen carts and litters, thick awnings wrapped closely round them, containing those who sought safety in flight, forgetful that the Plague was everywhere! And while these gloomy vehicles, conducted by horses, gaunt, shadowy skeletons, crawling heavily along, passed by, like hearses of the dead, sometimes a cry burst the silence in which they moved, and the traveller's steed started aside, as some wretch, on whom the disease had broke forth, was dropped from the vehicle by the selfish inhumanity of his comrades, and left to perish by the way. Hard by the gate a waggon paused, and a man with a mask threw out its contents in a green slimy ditch that bordered the road. These were garments and robes of all kind and value; the broidered mantle of the gallant, the hood and veil of my lady, and the rags of the peasant. While glancing at the labour of the masker, the cavalier beheld a herd of swine, gaunt and half famished, run to the spot in the hopes of food, and the traveller shuddered to think *what* food they might have anticipated! But ere he reached the gate, those of the animals that had been busiest rooting at the infectious heap, dropped down dead amongst their fellows.*

"Ho, ho," said the masker, and his hollow voice sounded yet more hollow through his vizard,—"comest thou here to die, stranger? See, thy brave mantle of triple-pile and golden broidery will not save thee from the gavocciolo.† Ride on, ride on;—to-day fit morsel for thy lady's kiss, to-morrow too foul for the rat and worm!"

Replying not to this hideous welcome, Adrian, for it was he, pursued his way. The gates stood wide open: this was the most appalling sign of all, for, at first, the most jealous precaution had been taken against the ingress of strangers. Now all care, all foresight, all vigilance, were vain. And thrice nine warders had died at that single post, and the officers to appoint their successors were dead too! Law and Police, and the Tribunals of Health, and the Boards of Safety, Death had stopped them all! And the Plague killed art itself, social union, the harmony and mechanism of civilisation, as if they had been bone and flesh!

So, mute and solitary, went on the lover, in his quest of love, resolved to find and to save his betrothed, and

* The same spectacle greeted, and is recorded by, Boccaccio.

† The tumour that made the fatal symptom.

guided (that faithful and loyal knight!) through the Wilderness of Horror by the blessed hope of that strange passion, noblest of all when noble, basest of all when base! He came into a broad and spacious square lined with palaces, the usual haunt of the best and most graceful nobility of Italy. The stranger was alone now, and the tramp of his gallant steed sounded ghastly and fearful in his own ears, when just as he turned the corner of one of the streets that led from it, he saw a woman steal forth with a child in her arms, while another, yet in infancy, clung to her robe. She held a large bunch of flowers to her nostrils (the fancied and favourite mode to prevent infection), and muttered to the children, who were moaning with hunger, —"Yes, yes, you shall have food! Plenty of food now for the stirring forth. But oh, *that stirring forth!*"—and she peered about and round, lest any of the diseased might be near.

"My friend," said he, "can you direct me to the convent of——"

"Away, man, away!" shrieked the woman.

"Alas!" said Adrian, with a mournful smile, "can you not see that I am not, as yet, one to *spread* contagion?"

But the woman, unheeding him, fled on; when, after a few paces, she was arrested by the child that clung to her.

"Mother, mother!" it cried, "I am sick—I cannot stir."

The woman halted, tore aside the child's robe, saw under the arm the fatal tumour, and, deserting her own flesh, fled with a shriek along the square. The shriek rung long in Adrian's ears, though not aware of the unnatural cause;—the *mother feared not for her infant, but herself.* The voice of Nature was no more heeded in that charnel city than it is in the tomb itself! Adrian rode on at a brisker pace, and came at length before a stately church; its doors were wide open, and he saw within a company of monks (the church had no other worshippers, and they were masked) gathered round the altar, and chanting the *Miserere Domine;*—the ministers of God, in a city hitherto boasting the devoutest population in Italy, without a flock!

The young Cavalier paused before the door, and waited till the service was done, and the monks descended the steps into the street.

"Holy fathers," said he then, "may I pray your goodness to tell me my nearest way to the convent Santa Maria de' Pazzi?"

"Son," said one of these featureless spectres, for so they seemed in their shroud-like robes, and uncouth vizards,—"son, pass on your way, and God be with you. Robbers or revellers may now fill the holy cloisters you speak of. The abbess is dead; and many a sister sleeps with her. And the nuns have fled from the contagion."

Adrian half fell from his horse, and, as he still remained rooted to the spot, the dark procession swept on, hymning in solemn dirge through the desolate street the monastic chaunt—

"By the Mother and the Son,
Death endured and mercy won;
Spare us, sinners though we be;
Miserere Domine!"

Recovering from his stupor, Adrian regained the brethren, and, as they closed the burthen of their song, again accosted them.

"Holy fathers, dismiss me not thus. Perchance the

one I seek may yet be heard of at the convent. Tell me which way to shape my course."

"Disturb us not, son," said the monk who spoke before. "It is an ill omen for thee to break thus upon the invocations of the ministers of Heaven."

"Pardon, pardon! I will do ample penance, pay many masses; but I seek a dear friend—the way—the way——"

"To the right, till you gain the first bridge. Beyond the third bridge, on the river side, you will find the convent," said another monk, moved by the earnestness of Adrian.

"Bless you, holy father," faltered forth the Cavalier, and spurred his steed in the direction given. The friars heeded him not, but again resumed their dirge. Mingled with the sound of his horse's hoofs on the clattering pavement, came to the rider's ear the imploring line—

"*Miserere Domine!*"

Impatient, sick at heart, desperate, Adrian flew through the street at the full speed of his horse. He passed the market-place—it was empty as the desert; —the gloomy and barricaded streets, in which the counter cries of Guelf and Ghibelline had so often cheered on the Chivalry and Rank of Florence. Now huddled together in vault and pit, lay Guelf and Ghibelline, knightly spurs and beggar's crutch. To that silence the roar even of civil strife would have been a blessing! The first bridge, the river side, the second, the third bridge, all were gained, and Adrian at last reined his steed before the walls of the convent. He fastened his steed to the porch, in which the door stood ajar, half torn from its hinges, traversed the court, gained the opposite door that admitted to the main building, came to the jealous grating, now no more a barrier from the profane world, and as he there paused a moment to recover breath and nerve, wild laughter and loud song, interrupted and mixed with oaths, startled his ear. He pushed aside the grated door, entered, and, led by the sounds, came to the refectory. In that meeting-place of the severe and mortified maids of heaven, he now beheld gathered round the upper table, used of yore by the abbess, a strange, disorderly, ruffian herd, who at first glance seemed indeed of all ranks, for some wore serge, or even rags, others were tricked out in all the bravery of satin and velvet, plume and mantle. But a second glance sufficed to indicate that the companions were much of the same degree, and that the finery of the more showy was but the spoil rent from unguarded palaces or tenantless bazaars; for under plumed hats, looped with jewels, were grim, unwashed, unshaven faces, over which hung the long locks which the professed brethren of the sharp knife and hireling arm had just begun to assume, serving them often instead of a mask. Amidst these savage revellers were many women, young and middle-aged, foul and fair, and Adrian piously shuddered to see amongst the loose robes and uncovered necks of the professional harlots the saintly habit and beaded rosary of nuns. Flasks of wine, ample viands, gold and silver vessels, mostly consecrated to holy rites, strewed the board. As the young Roman paused spell-bound at the threshold, the man who acted as president of the revel, a huge, swarthy ruffian, with a deep scar over his face, which, traversing the whole of the left cheek and upper lip, gave his large features an aspect preternaturally hideous, called out to him—

"Come in, man—come in! Why stand you there amazed and dumb? We are hospitable revellers, and give all men welcome. Here are wine and women. My Lord Bishop's wine and my Lady Abbess's women!

"Sing hey, sing ho, for the royal DEATH,
That scatters a host with a single breath;
That opens the prison to spoil the palace,
And rids honest necks from the hangman's malice.
Here's a health to the Plague! Let the mighty ones dread,
The poor never lived till the wealthy were dead.
A health to the Plague! may she ever as now
Loose the rogue from his chain and the nun from her vow;
To the gaoler a sword, to the captive a key,
Hurrah for Earth's Curse—'tis a blessing to me!"

Ere this fearful stave was concluded, Adrian, sensible that in such orgies there was no chance of prosecuting his inquiries, left the desecrated chamber and fled, scarcely drawing breath, so great was the terror that seized him, till he stood once more in the court amidst the hot, sickly, stagnant sunlight, that seemed a fit atmosphere for the scenes on which it fell. He resolved, however, not to desert the place without making another effort at inquiry; and while he stood without the court, musing and doubtful, he saw a small chapel hard by, through whose long casement gleamed faintly, and dimmed by the noon-day, the light of tapers. He turned towards its porch, entered, and saw beside the sanctuary a single nun kneeling in prayer. In the narrow aisle, upon a long table, (at either end of which burned the tall dismal tapers whose rays had attracted him,) the drapery of several shrouds showed him the half-distinct outline of human figures hushed in death. Adrian himself, impressed by the sadness and sanctity of the place, and the touching sight of that solitary and unselfish watcher of the dead, knelt down and intensely prayed.

As he rose, somewhat relieved from the burthen at his heart, the nun rose also, and started to perceive him.

"Unhappy man!" said she, in a voice which, low, faint, and solemn, sounded as a ghost's—"what fatality brings thee hither? Seest thou not thou art in the presence of clay which the Plague hath touched—thou breathest the air which destroys! Hence! and search throughout all the desolation for one spot where the Dark Visitor hath not come!"

"Holy maiden," answered Adrian, "the danger you hazard does not appal me;—I seek one whose life is dearer than my own."

"Thou needest say no more to tell me thou art newly come to Florence! Here son forsakes his father, and mother deserts her child. When life is most hopeless, these worms of a day cling to it as if it were the salvation of immortality! But for me alone, death has no horror. Long severed from the world, I have seen my sisterhood perish—the house of God desecrated—its altar overthrown, and I care not to survive,—the last whom the Pestilence leaves at once unperjured and alive."

The nun paused a few moments, and then, looking earnestly at the healthful countenance and unbroken frame of Adrian, sighed heavily—"Stranger, why fly you not?" she said. "Thou mightest as well search the crowded vaults and rotten corruption of the dead, as search the city for one living."

"Sister, and bride of the blessed Redeemer!" returned the Roman, clasping his hands—"one word I implore thee. Thou art, methinks, of the sisterhood of yon dismantled convent; tell me, knowest thou if Irene di Gabrini,*—guest of the late Abbess, sister of the fallen Tribune of Rome,—be yet amongst the living?"

"Art thou her brother, then?" said the nun. "Art thou that fallen Sun of the Morning?"

"I am her betrothed," replied Adrian, sadly. "Speak."

"Oh, flesh! flesh! how art thou victor to the last, even amidst the triumphs and in the lazar-house of corruption!" said the nun. "Vain man! think not of such carnal ties; make thy peace with heaven, for thy days are surely numbered!"

"Woman!" cried Adrian, impatiently—"talk not to me of myself, nor rail against ties whose holiness thou canst not know. I ask thee again, as thou thyself hopest for mercy and for pardon, is Irene living?"

The nun was awed by the energy of the young lover, and after a moment, which seemed to him an age of agonised suspense, she replied—

"The maiden thou speakest of died not with the general death. In the dispersion of the few remaining, she left the convent—I know not whither; but she had friends in Florence—their names I cannot tell thee."

"Now bless thee, holy sister! bless thee! How long since she left the convent?"

"Four days have passed since the robber and the harlot have seized the house of Santa Maria," replied the nun, groaning: "and they were quick successors to the sisterhood."

* The family name of Rienzi was Gabrini.

"Four days!—and thou canst give me no clue?"

"None—yet stay, young man!"—and the nun, approaching, lowered her voice to a hissing whisper—"Ask the *Becchini.*"*

Adrian started aside, crossed himself hastily, and quitted the convent without answer. He returned to his horse, and rode back into the silenced heart of the city. Tavern and hotel there were no more; but the palaces of dead princes were free to the living stranger. He entered one—a spacious and splendid mansion. In the stables he found forage still in the manger; but the horses, at that time in the Italian cities a proof of rank as well as wealth, were gone with the hands that fed them. The high-born Knight assumed the office of groom, took off the heavy harness, fastened his steed to the rack, and as the wearied animal, unconscious of the surrounding horrors, fell eagerly upon its meal, its young lord turned away, and muttered, "Faithful servant, and sole companion! may the pestilence that spareth neither beast nor man, spare thee! and may'st thou bear me hence with a lighter heart!"

A spacious hall, hung with arms and banners—a wide flight of marble stairs, whose walls were painted in the stiff outlines and gorgeous colours of the day, conducted to vast chambers, hung with velvets and cloth of gold, but silent as the tomb. He threw himself upon the cushions which were piled in the centre of the room, for he had ridden far that morning, and for many days before, and he was wearied and ex-

* According to the usual custom of Florence, the dead were borne to their resting-place on biers, supported by citizens of equal rank; but a new trade was created by the plague, and men of the lowest dregs of the populace, bribed by immense payment, discharged the office of transporting the remains of the victims. These were called Becchini.

hausted, body and limb; but he could not rest. Impatience, anxiety, hope, and fear, gnawed his heart and fevered his veins, and, after a brief and unsatisfactory attempt to sober his own thoughts, and devise some plan of search more certain than that which chance might afford him, he rose, and traversed the apartments, in the unacknowledged hope which chance alone could suggest.

It was easy to see that he had made his resting-place in the home of one of the princes of the land; and the splendour of all around him far outshone the barbarous and rude magnificence of the less civilised and wealthy Romans. Here, lay the lute as last touched—the gilded and illumined volume as last conned; there, were seats drawn familiarly together, as when lady and gallant had interchanged whispers last.

"And such," thought Adrian,—"such desolation may soon swallow up the vestige of the unwelcomed guest, as of the vanished lord!"

At length he entered a saloon, in which was a table still spread with wine-flasks, goblets of glass, and one of silver, withered flowers, half-mouldy fruits, and viands. At one side the arras, folding-doors opened to a broad flight of stairs, that descended to a little garden at the back of the house, in which a fountain still played sparkling and livingly—the only thing, save the stranger, living there! On the steps lay a crimson mantle, and by it a lady's glove. The relics seemed to speak to the lover's heart of a lover's last wooing and last farewell. He groaned aloud, and feeling he should have need of all his strength, filled one of the goblets from a half-emptied flask of Cyprus wine. He drained the draught—it revived him. "Now," he said, "once more to my task!—I will sally forth," when suddenly he heard heavy steps along the rooms he had quitted—they approached—they entered; and Adrian beheld two huge and ill-omened forms stalk into the chamber. They were wrapped in black homely draperies; their arms were bare, and they wore large shapeless masks, which descended to the breast, leaving only access to sight and breath in three small and circular apertures. The Colonna half drew his sword, for the forms and aspects of these visitors were not such as men think to look upon in safety.

"Oh!" said one, "the palace has a new guest to-day. Fear us not, stranger; there is room,—ay, and wealth enough for all men now in Florence! Per Bacco! but there is still one goblet of silver left—how comes that?" So saying, the man seized the cup which Adrian had just drained, and thrust it into his breast. He then turned to Adrian, whose hand was still upon his hilt, and said, with a laugh which came choked and muffled through his vizard—"Oh, we cut no throats, Signor; the Invisible spares us that trouble. We are honest men, state officers, and come but to see if the cart should halt here to-night."

"Ye are then——"

"Becchini!"

Adrian's blood ran cold. The Becchino continued —"And keep you this house while you rest at Florence, Signor?"

"Yes, if the rightful lord claim it not."

"Ha! ha! 'Rightful lord!' The Plague is Lord of all now! Why, I have known three gallant companies tenant this palace the last week, and have buried them all—all! It is a pleasant house enough, and gives good custom. Are you alone?"

"At present, yes."

"Shew us where you sleep, that we may know where to come for you. You won't want us these three days, I see."

"Ye are pleasant welcomers!" said Adrian;—"but listen to me. Can ye find the living as well as bury the dead? I seek one in this city who, if you discover her, shall be worth to you a year of burials."

"No, no! that is out of our line. As well look for a dropped sand on the beach, as for a living being amongst closed houses and yawning vaults; but if you will pay the poor grave-diggers beforehand, I promise you, you shall have the first of a new charnel-house:—it will be finished just about your time."

"There!" said Adrian, flinging the wretches a few pieces of gold—"there! and if you would do me a kinder service, leave me, at least while living; or I may save you that trouble." And he turned from the room.

The Becchino who had been spokesman followed him.

"You are generous, Signor, stay; you will want fresher food than these filthy fragments. I will supply thee of the best, while—while thou wantest it. And hark,—whom wishest thou that I should seek?"

This question arrested Adrian's departure. He detailed the name, and all the particulars he could suggest of Irene; and, with sickened heart, described the hair, features, and stature of that lovely and hallowed image, which might furnish a theme to the poet, and now gave a clue to the grave-digger.

The unhallowed apparition shook his head when Adrian had concluded. "Full five hundred such descriptions did I hear in the first days of the Plague, when there were still such things as mistress and lover;

but it is a dainty catalogue, Signor, and it will be a pride to the poor Becchino to discover or even to bury so many charms! I will do my best; meanwhile, I can recommend you, if in a hurry, to make the best of your time, to many a pretty face and comely shape——"

"Out, fiend!" muttered Adrian: "fool to waste time with such as thou!"

The laugh of the grave-digger followed his steps.

All that day did Adrian wander through the city, but search and questioning were alike unavailing; all whom he encountered and interrogated seemed to regard him as a madman, and these were indeed of no kind likely to advance his object. Wild troops of disordered, drunken revellers, processions of monks, or here and there, scattered individuals gliding rapidly along, and shunning all approach or speech, made the only haunters of the dismal streets, till the sun sunk, lurid and yellow, behind the hills, and Darkness closed around the noiseless pathway of the Pestilence.

CHAPTER III

THE FLOWERS AMIDST THE TOMBS

Adrian found that the Becchino had taken care that famine should not forestall the plague; the banquet of the dead was removed, and fresh viands and wines of all kinds,—for there was plenty then in Florence!—spread the table. He partook of the refreshment, though but sparingly, and shrinking from repose in beds beneath whose gorgeous hangings Death had been so lately busy, carefully closed door and window, wrapped himself in his mantle, and found his resting-place on the cushions of the chamber in which he had supped. Fatigue cast him into an unquiet slumber, from which he was suddenly awakened by the roll of a cart below, and the jingle of bells. He listened, as the cart proceeded slowly from door to door, and at length its sound died away in the distance.—He slept no more that night!

The sun had not long risen ere he renewed his labours; and it was yet early when, just as he passed a church, two ladies richly dressed came from the porch, and seemed through their vizards to regard the young Cavalier with earnest attention. The gaze arrested him also, when one of the ladies said, "Fair sir, you are over-bold: you wear no mask; neither do you smell to flowers."

"Lady, I wear no mask, for I would be seen: I search these miserable places for one in whose life I live."

"He is young, comely, evidently noble, and the plague hath not touched him: he will serve our purpose well," whispered one of the ladies to the other.

"You echo my own thoughts," returned her companion; and then turning to Adrian, she said, "You seek one you are not wedded to, if you seek so fondly?"

"It is true."

"Young and fair, with dark hair and neck of snow; I will conduct you to her."

"Signora!"

"Follow us!"

"Know you whom I am, and whom I seek?"

"Yes."

"Can you in truth tell me aught of Irene?"

"I can: follow me."

"To her?"

"Yes, yes: follow us!"

The ladies moved on as if impatient of further parley. Amazed, doubtful, and as if in a dream, Adrian followed them. Their dress, manner, and the pure Tuscan of the one who had addressed him, indicated them of birth and station; but all else was a riddle which he could not solve.

They arrived at one of the bridges, where a litter and a servant on horseback holding a palfrey by the bridle were in attendance. The ladies entered the litter, and she who had before spoken bade Adrian follow on the palfrey.

"But tell me——" he began.

"No questions, Cavalier," said she impatiently; "follow the living in silence, or remain with the dead, as you list."

With that the litter proceeded, and Adrian mounted the palfrey wonderingly, and followed his strange conductors, who moved on at a tolerably brisk pace. They crossed the bridge, left the river on one side, and, soon ascending a gentle acclivity, the trees and flowers of the country began to succeed dull walls and empty streets. After proceeding thus somewhat less than half and hour, they turned up a green lane remote from the road, and came suddenly upon the porticoes of a fair and stately palace. Here the ladies descended from their litter; and Adrian, who had vainly sought to extract speech from the attendant, also dismounted, and following them across a spacious court, filled on either side with vases of flowers and orange-trees, and then through a wide hall in the farther side of the quadrangle, found himself in one of the loveliest spots eye ever saw or poet ever sung. It was a garden plot of the most emerald verdure, bosquets of laurel and of myrtle opened on either side into vistas half overhung with clematis and rose, through whose arcades the prospect closed with statues and gushing fountains; in front, the lawn was bounded by rows of vases on marble pedestals filled with flowers! and broad and gradual flights of steps of the whitest marble led from terrace to terrace, each adorned with statues and fountains, half-way down a high but softly sloping and verdant hill. Beyond, spread in wide, various, and luxurious landscape, the vineyards and olive-groves, the villas and villages, of the Vale of Arno, intersected by the silver river, while the city, in all its calm, but without its horror, raised its roofs and spires to the sun. Birds of every hue and song, some free, some in network of golden wire, warbled round; and upon the centre of the sward reclined four ladies unmasked and richly dressed, the eldest of whom seemed scarcely more than twenty; and five cavaliers, young and handsome, whose jewelled vests and golden chains attested their degree. Wines and fruits were on a low table beside; and musical instruments, chess-boards, and gammon-tables, lay scattered all about. So fair a group, and so graceful a scene, Adrian never beheld but once, and that was in the midst of the ghastly pestilence of Italy!—such group and such scene our closet indolence may yet revive in the pages of the bright Boccaccio!

On seeing Adrian and his companions approach, the party rose instantly; and one of the ladies, who wore upon her head a wreath of laurel-leaves, stepping before the rest, exclaimed, "Well done, my Mariana!

welcome back, my fair subjects. And you, sir, welcome hither."

The two guides of the Colonna had by this time removed their masks; and the one who had accosted him, shaking her long and raven ringlets over a bright, laughing eye and a cheek to whose native olive now rose a slight blush, turned to him ere he could reply to the welcome he had received.

"Signor Cavalier," said she, "you now see to what I have decoyed you. Own that this is pleasanter than the sights and sounds of the city we have left. You gaze on me in surprise. See, my Queen, how speechless the marvel of your court has made our new gallant; I assure you he could talk quickly enough when he had only us to confer with: nay, I was forced to impose silence on him."

"Oh, then you have not yet informed him of the custom and origin of the court he enters?" quoth she of the laurel wreath.

"No, my Queen; I thought all description given in such a spot as our poor Florence now is would fail of its object. My task is done, I resign him to your Grace!"

So saying the lady tripped lightly away, and began coquettishly sleeking her locks in the smooth mirror of a marble basin, whose waters trickled over the margin upon the grass below, ever and anon glancing archly towards the stranger, and sufficiently at hand to overhear all that was said.

"In the first place, Signor, permit us to inquire," said the lady who bore the appellation of Queen, "thy name, rank, and birth-place."

"Madam," returned Adrian, "I came hither little dreaming to answer questions respecting myself; but what it pleases you to ask, it must please me to reply to. My name is Adrian di Castello, one of the Roman house of the Colonna."

"A noble column of a noble house!" answered the Queen. "For us, respecting whom your curiosity may perhaps be aroused, know that we six ladies of Florence, deserted by or deprived of our kin and protectors, formed the resolution to retire to this palace, where, if death comes, it comes stripped of half its horrors: and as the learned tell us that sadness engenders the awful malady, so you see us sworn foes to sadness. Six cavaliers of our acquaintance agreed to join us. We pass our days, whether many or few, in whatever diversions we can find or invent. Music and the dance, merry tales and lively songs, with such slight change of scene as from sward to shade, from alley to fountain, fill up our time, and prepare us for peaceful sleep and happy dreams. Each lady is by turns Queen of our fairy court, as is my lot this day. One law forms the code of our constitution—that nothing sad shall be admitted. We would live as if yonder city were not, and as if" (added the fair Queen, with a slight sigh) "youth, grace, and beauty, could endure for ever. One of our knights madly left us for a day, promising to return; we have seen him no more: we will not guess what hath chanced to him. It became necessary to fill up his place; we drew lots who should seek his substitute; it fell upon the ladies who have—not, I trust, to your displeasure—brought you hither. Fair sir, my explanation is made."

"Alas, lovely Queen," said Adrian, wrestling strongly, but vainly, with the bitter disappointment he felt—"I cannot be one of your happy circle; I am in myself a violation of your law. I am filled with but one sad and anxious thought, to which all mirth would seem impiety. I am a seeker amongst the living and the dead for one being of whose fate I am uncertain; and it was only by the words that fell from my fair conductor, that I have been decoyed hither from my mournful task. Suffer me, gracious lady, to return to Florence."

The Queen looked in mute vexation towards the dark-eyed Mariana, who returned the glance by one equally expressive, and then suddenly stepping up to Adrian she said,—

"But, Signor, if I should still keep my promise, if I should be able to satisfy thee of the health and safety of—of Irene."

"Irene!" echoed Adrian in surprise, forgetful at the moment that he had before revealed the name of her he sought—"Irene—Irene di Gabrini, sister of the once renowned Rienzi!"

"The same," replied Mariana, quickly; "I knew her, as I told you. Nay, Signor, I do not deceive thee. It is true that I cannot bring thee to her; but better as it is,—she went away many days ago to one of the towns of Lombardy, which, they say, the Pestilence has not yet pierced. Now, noble sir, is not your heart lightened? and will you so soon be a deserter from the Court of Loveliness; and perhaps," she added, with a soft look from her large dark eyes, "of Love?"

"Dare I, in truth, believe you, Lady?" said Adrian, all delighted, yet still half doubting.

"Would I deceive a true lover, as methinks you are? Be assured. Nay, Queen, receive your subject."

The Queen extended her hand to Adrian, and led him to the group that still stood on the grass at a little distance. They welcomed him as a brother, and soon forgave his abstracted courtesies, in compliment to his good mien and illustrious name.

The Queen clapped her hands, and the party again ranged themselves on the sward. Each lady beside each gallant. "You, Mariana, if not fatigued," said the Queen, "shall take the lute and silence these noisy grasshoppers, which chirp about us with as much pretension as if they were nightingales. Sing, sweet subjects, sing; and let it be the song our dear friend, Signor Visdomini,* made for a kind of inaugural anthem to such as we admitted to our court."

Mariana, who had reclined herself by the side of Adrian, took up the lute, and, after a short prelude, sung the words thus imperfectly translated:—

THE SONG OF THE FLORENTINE LADY

Enjoy the more the smiles of noon
  If doubtful be the morrow;
And know the Fort of Life is soon
  Betray'd to Death by Sorrow!

Death claims us all—then, Grief, away!
  We'll own no meaner master;
The clouds that darken round the day
  But bring the night the faster.

Love—feast—be merry while on earth,
  Such, Grave, should be thy moral!
Ev'n Death himself is friends with Mirth,
  And veils the tomb with laurel.†

* I know not if this be the same Visdomini who, three years afterwards, with one of the Medici, conducted so gallant a reinforcement to Scarperia, then besieged by Visconti d'Oleggio.

† At that time, in Italy, the laurel was frequently planted over the dead.

While gazing on the eyes I love,
  New life to mine is given—
If joy the lot of saints above,
  Joy fits us best for Heaven.

To this song, which was much applauded, succeeded those light and witty tales in which the Italian novelists furnished Voltaire and Marmontel with a model—each, in his or her turn, taking up the discourse, and with an equal dexterity avoiding every lugubrious image or mournful reflection that might remind those graceful idlers of the vicinity of Death. At any other time the temper and accomplishments of the young Lord di Castello would have fitted him to enjoy and to shine in that Arcadian court. But now he in vain sought to dispel the gloom from his brow, and the anxious thought from his heart. He revolved the intelligence he had received, wondered, guessed, hoped, and dreaded still; and if for a moment his mind returned to the scene about him, his nature too truly poetical for the false sentiment of the place, asked itself in what, save the polished exterior and the graceful circumstance, the mirth that he now so reluctantly witnessed differed from the brutal revels in the convent of Santa Maria—each alike in its motive, though so differing in the manner—equally callous and equally selfish, coining horror into enjoyment. The fair Mariana, whose partner had been reft from her, as the Queen had related, was in no mind to lose the new one she had gained. She pressed upon him from time to time the wine-flask and the fruits; and in those unmeaning courtesies her hand gently lingered upon his. At length, the hour arrived when the companions retired to the Palace, during the fiercer heats of noon—to come forth again in the declining sun, to sup by the side of the fountain, to dance, to sing, and to make merry by torchlight and the stars till the hour of rest. But Adrian, not willing to continue the entertainment, no sooner found himself in the apartment to which he was conducted, than he resolved to effect a silent escape, as under all circumstances the shortest, and not perhaps the least courteous, farewell left to him. Accordingly, when all seemed quiet and hushed in the repose common to the inhabitants of the South during that hour, he left his apartment, descended the stairs, passed the outer court, and was already at the gate, when he heard himself called by a voice that spoke vexation and alarm. He turned to behold Mariana.

"Why, how now, Signor di Castello, is our company so unpleasing, is our music so jarring, or are our brows so wrinkled, that you should fly as the traveller flies from the witches he surprises at Benevento? Nay, you cannot mean to leave us yet?"

"Fair dame," returned the cavalier, somewhat disconcerted, "it is in vain that I seek to rally my mournful spirits, or to fit myself for the court to which nothing sad should come. Your laws hang about me like a culprit—better timely flight than harsh expulsion."

As he spoke he moved on, and would have passed the gate, but Mariana caught his arm.

"Nay," said she, softly; "are there no eyes of dark light, and no neck of wintry snow, that can compensate to thee for the absent one? Tarry and forget, as doubtless in absence even *thou* art forgotten!"

"Lady," answered Adrian, with great gravity, not unmixed with an ill-suppressed disdain, "I have not sojourned long enough amidst the sights and sounds of woe, to blunt my heart and spirit into callousness to all around. Enjoy, if thou canst, and gather the rank roses of the sepulchre; but to me, haunted still by funeral images, Beauty fails to bring delight, and Love—even *holy* love—seems darkened by the Shadow of Death. Pardon me, and farewell."

"Go, then," said the Florentine, stung and enraged at his coldness; "go and find your mistress amidst the associations on which it pleases your philosophy to dwell. I did but deceive thee, blind fool! as I had hoped for thine own good, when I told thee Irene—(was that her name?)—was gone from Florence. Of her I know nought, and heard nought, save from thee. Go back and search the vault, and see whether thou lovest her still!"

CHAPTER IV

WE OBTAIN WHAT WE SEEK AND KNOW IT NOT

In the fiercest heat of the day, and on foot, Adrian returned to Florence. As he approached the city, all that festive and gallant scene he had quitted seemed to him like a dream; a vision of the gardens and bowers of an enchantress, from which he woke abruptly as a criminal may wake on the morning of his doom to see the scaffold and the deathsman;—so much did each silent and lonely step into the funeral city bring back his bewildered thoughts at once to life and to death. The parting words of Mariana sounded like a knell at his heart. And now as he passed on—the heat of the day, the lurid atmosphere, long fatigue, alternate exhaustion and excitement, combining with the sickness of disappointment, the fretting consciousness of precious moments irretrievably lost, and his utter despair of forming any systematic mode of search —fever began rapidly to burn through his veins. His temples felt oppressed as with the weight of a mountain; his lips parched with intolerable thirst; his strength seemed suddenly to desert him; and it was with pain and labour that he dragged one languid limb after the other.

"I feel it," thought he, with the loathing nausea and shivering dread with which nature struggles ever against death; "I feel it upon me—the Devouring and the Viewless—I shall perish, and without saving her; nor shall even one grave contain us!"

But these thoughts served rapidly to augment the disease which began to prey upon him; and ere he reached the interior of the city, even thought itself forsook him. The images of men and houses grew indistinct and shadowy before his eyes; the burning pavement became unsteady and reeling beneath his feet; delirium gathered over him, and he went on his way muttering broken and incoherent words; the few who met fled from him in dismay. Even the monks, still continuing their solemn and sad processions, passed with a murmured *bene vobis* to the other side from that on which his steps swerved and faltered. And from a booth at the corner of a street, four Becchini, drinking together, fixed upon him from their black masks the gaze that vultures fix upon some dying wanderer of the desert. Still he crept on, stretching out his arms like a man in the dark, and seeking with the vague sense that yet struggled against the gathering delirium, to find out the mansion in which he had fixed his home; though many as fair to live, and as meet to die in, stood with open portals before and beside his path.

"Irene, Irene!" he cried, sometimes in a muttered and low tone, sometimes in a wild and piercing shriek, "where art thou? Where? I come to snatch thee from them; they shall not have thee, the foul and ugly fiends! Pah! how the air smells of dead flesh! Irene, Irene! we will away to mine own palace and the heavenly lake—Irene!"

While thus benighted, and thus exclaiming, two females suddenly emerged from a neighbouring house, masked and mantled.

"Vain wisdom!" said the taller and slighter of the two, whose mantle, it is here necessary to observe, was of a deep blue, richly broidered with silver, of a shape and a colour not common in Florence, but usual in Rome, where the dress of ladies of the higher rank was singularly bright in hue and ample in fold—thus differing from the simpler and more slender draperies of the Tuscan fashion—"Vain wisdom, to fly a relentless and certain doom!"

"Why, thou wouldst not have us hold the same home with three of the dead in the next chamber—strangers too to us—when Florence has so many empty halls? Trust me, we shall not walk far ere we suit ourselves with a safer lodgment."

"Hitherto, indeed, we have been miraculously preserved," sighed the other, whose voice and shape were those of extreme youth; "yet would that we knew where to fly—what mount, what wood, what cavern, held my brother and his faithful Nina! I am sick with horrors!"

"Irene, Irene! Well then, if thou art at Milan or some Lombard town, why do I linger here? To horse, to horse! Oh, no! no!—not the horse with the bells! not the death cart."

With a cry, a shriek, louder than the loudest of the sick man's, broke that young female away from her companion. It seemed as if a single step took her to the side of Adrian. She caught his arm—she looked in his face—she met his unconscious eyes bright with a fearful fire. "It has seized him!" (she then said in a deep but calmer tone)—"the Plague!"

"Away, away! are you mad!" cried her companion; "hence, hence,—touch me not now thou hast touched him—go!—here we part!"

"Help me to bear him somewhere; see, he faints, he droops, he falls!—help me, dear Signora, for pity, for the love of God!"

But, wholly possessed by the selfish fear which overcame all humanity in that miserable time, the elder woman, though naturally kind, pitiful, and benevolent, fled rapidly away, and soon vanished. Thus left alone with Adrian, who had now, in the fierceness of the fever that preyed within him, fallen on the ground, the strength and nerve of that young girl did not forsake her. She tore off the heavy mantle which encumbered her arms, and cast it from her; and then, lifting up the face of her lover—for who but Irene was that weak woman, thus shrinking not from the contagion of death?—she supported him on her breast, and called aloud and again for help. At length the Becchini, in the booth before noticed, (hardened in their profession, and who, thus hardened, better than the most cautious, escaped the pestilence,) lazily approached—"Quicker, quicker, for Christ's love!" said Irene. "I have much gold: I will reward you well: help me to bear him under the nearest roof."

"Leave him to us, young lady: we have had our eye upon him," said one of the grave-diggers. "We'll do our duty by him, first and last."

"No, no! touch not his head—that is my care. There, I will help you; so,—now then,—but be gentle!"

Assisted by these portentous officers, Irene, who would not release her hold, but seemed to watch over the beloved eyes and lips (set and closed as they were), as if to look back the soul from parting, bore Adrian into a neighbouring house, and laid him on a bed; from which Irene (preserving as only women do, in such times, the presence of mind and vigilant providence which make so sublime a contrast with their keen susceptibilities) caused them first to cast off the draperies and clothing, which might retain additional infection. She then despatched them for new furniture, and for whatsoever leech money might yet bribe to a duty, now chiefly abandoned to those heroic Brotherhoods who, however vilified in modern judgment by the crimes of some unworthy members, were yet, in the dark times, the best, the bravest, and the holiest agents, to whom God ever delegated the power to resist the oppressor—to feed the hungry—to minister to woe; and who, alone, amidst that fiery Pestilence (loosed, as it were, a demon from the abyss, to shiver into atoms all that binds the world to Virtue and to Law), seemed to awaken, as by the sound of an angel's trumpet, to that noblest Chivalry of the Cross—whose faith is the scorn of self—whose hope is beyond the Lazar-house—whose feet, already winged for immortality, trample, with a conqueror's march, upon the graves of Death!

While this the ministry and the office of love—along

that street in which Adrian and Irene had met at last—came singing, reeling, roaring, the dissolute and abandoned crew who had fixed their quarters in the Convent of Santa Maria de' Pazzi, their bravo chief at their head, and a nun (no longer in nun's garments) upon either arm. "A health to the Plague!" shouted the ruffian: "A health to the Plague!" echoed his frantic Bacchanals.

"A health to the Plague, may she ever, as now,
Loose the rogue from his chain, and the nun from her vow;
To the gaoler a sword—to the captive a key,
Hurrah for Earth's Curse! 'tis a blessing to me."

"Holla!" cried the chief, stopping; "here, Margherita; here's a brave cloak for thee, my girl: silver enow on it to fill thy purse, if it ever grow empty; which it may, if ever the Plague grow slack."

"Nay," said the girl, who, amidst all the havoc of debauch, retained much of youth and beauty in her form and face, "nay, Guidotto; perhaps it has infection."

"Pooh, child, silver never infects. Clap it on, clap it on. Besides, fate is fate, and when it is thine hour there will be other means besides the *gavocciolo*."

So saying, he seized the mantle, threw it roughly over her shoulders, and dragged her on as before, half pleased with the finery, half frightened with the danger; while gradually died away, along the lurid air and the mournful streets, the chant of that most miserable mirth.

CHAPTER V

THE ERROR

For three days, the fatal three days, did Adrian remain bereft of strength and sense. But he was not smitten by the scourge which his devoted and generous nurse had anticipated. It was a fierce and dangerous fever, brought on by the great fatigue, restlessness, and terrible agitation he had undergone.

No professional mediciner could be found to attend him; but a good friar, better perhaps skilled in the healing art than many who claimed its monopoly, visited him daily. And in the long and frequent absences to which his other and numerous duties compelled the monk, there was one ever at hand to smooth the pillow, to wipe the brow, to listen to the moan, to watch the sleep. And even in that dismal office, when, in the frenzy of the sufferer, her name, coupled with terms of passionate endearment, broke from his lips, a thrill of strange pleasure crossed the heart of the betrothed, which she chid as if it were a crime. But even the most unearthly love is selfish in the rapture of being loved! Words cannot tell, heart cannot divine, the mingled emotions that broke over her when, in some of those incoherent ravings, she dimly understood that *for her* the city had been sought, the death dared, the danger incurred. And as then bending passionately to kiss that burning brow, her tears fell fast over the idol of her youth, the fountains from which they gushed were those, fathomless and countless, which a life could not weep away. Not an impulse of the human and the woman heart that was not stirred; the adoring gratitude, the meek wonder thus to *be* loved, while deeming it so simple a merit thus *to* love;—as if all sacrifice *in* her were a thing of course,—*to* her, a virtue nature could not paragon, worlds could not repay! And there he lay, the victim to his own fearless faith, helpless—dependent upon her—a thing between life and death, to thank, to serve—to be proud of, yet protect, to compassionate, yet revere—the saver, to be saved! Never seemed one object to demand at once from a single heart so many and so profound emotions; the romantic enthusiasm of the girl—the fond idolatry of the bride—the watchful providence of the mother over her child.

And strange to say, with all the excitement of that lonely watch, scarcely stirring from his side, taking food only that her strength might not fail her,—unable to close her eyes,—though, from the same cause, she would fain have taken rest, when slumber fell upon her charge—with all such wear and tear of frame and heart, she seemed wonderfully supported. And the holy man marvelled, in each visit, to see the cheek of the nurse still fresh, and her eye still bright. In her own superstition she thought and felt that Heaven gifted her with a preternatural power to be true to so sacred a charge; and in this fancy she did not wholly err:—for Heaven *did* gift her with that diviner power, when it planted in so soft a heart the enduring might and energy of Affection! The friar had visited the sick man late on the third night, and administered to him a strong sedative. "This night," said he to Irene, "will be the crisis: should he awaken as I trust he may, with a returning consciousness and a calm pulse, he will live; if not, young daughter, prepare for the worst. But should you note any turn in the disease, that may excite alarm, or require my attendance, this scroll will inform you where I am, if God spare me still, at each hour of the night and morning."

The monk retired, and Irene resumed her watch.

The sleep of Adrian was at first broken and interrupted—his features, his exclamations, his gestures, all evinced great agony, whether mental or bodily: it seemed, as perhaps it was, a fierce and doubtful struggle between life and death for the conquest of the sleeper. Patient, silent, breathing but by long-drawn gasps, Irene sate at the bed-head. The lamp was removed to the farther end of the chamber, and its ray, shaded by the draperies, did not suffice to give to her gaze more than the outline of the countenance she watched. In that awful suspense, all the thoughts that hitherto had stirred her mind lay hushed and mute. She was only sensible to that unutterable fear which few of us have been happy enough not to know. That crushing weight under which we can scarcely breathe or move, the avalanche over us, freezing and suspended, which we cannot escape from, beneath which, every moment, we may be buried and overwhelmed. The whole destiny of life was in the chances of that single night! It was just as Adrian at last seemed to glide into a deeper and serener slumber, that the bells of the death-cart broke with their boding knell the palpable silence of the streets. Now hushed, now revived, as the cart stopped for its gloomy passengers, and coming nearer and nearer after every pause. At length she heard the heavy wheels stop under the very casement, and a voice deep and muffled calling aloud, "Bring out the dead!" She rose, and with a noiseless step, passed to secure the door, when the dull lamp gleamed upon the dark and shrouded forms of the Becchini.

"You have not marked the door, nor set out the body," said one gruffly; "but this is the *third night!* He is ready for us."

"Hush, he sleeps—away, quick, it is not the Plague that seized him."

"Not the Plague?" growled the Becchino in a disappointed tone; "I thought no other illness dare encroach upon the rights of the gavocciolo!"

"Go—here's money; leave us."

And the grisly carrier sullenly withdrew. The cart moved on, the bell renewed its summons, till slowly and faintly the dreadful larum died in the distance.

Shading the lamp with her hand, Irene stole to the bed side, fearful that the sound and the intrusion had disturbed the slumberer. But his face was still locked, as in a vice, with that iron sleep. He stirred not—the breath scarcely passed his lips—she felt his pulse, as the wan hand lay on the coverlid—there was a slight beat—she was contented—removed the light, and, retiring to a corner of the room, placed the little cross suspended round her neck upon the table, and prayed, in her intense suffering, to Him who had known death, and who—Son of Heaven though he was, and Sovereign of the Seraphim—had also prayed, in his earthly travail, that the cup might pass away.

The Morning broke, not, as in the North, slowly and through shadow, but with the sudden glory with which in those climates Day leaps upon earth—like a giant from his sleep. A sudden smile—a burnished glow—and night had vanished. Adrian still slept; not a muscle seemed to have stirred: the sleep was even heavier than before: the silence became a burthen upon the air. Now, in that exceeding torpor so like unto death, the solitary watcher became alarmed and terrified. Time passed—morning glided to noon—still not a sound nor motion. The sun was midway in heaven—the Friar came not. And now again touching Adrian's pulse, she felt no flutter—she gazed on him, appalled and confounded; surely nought living could be so still and pale. "Was it indeed sleep, might it not be——" She turned away sick and frozen; her tongue clove to her lips. Why did the father tarry?—she would go to him—she would learn the worst—she could forbear no longer. She glanced over the scroll the Monk had left her: "From sunrise," it said, "I shall be at the Convent of the Dominicans. Death has stricken many of the brethren." The Convent was at some distance, but she knew the spot, and fear would wing her steps. She gave one wistful look at the sleeper and rushed from the house. "I shall see thee again presently," she murmured. Alas! what hope can calculate beyond the moment? And who shall claim the tenure of "*The Again?*"

It was not many minutes after Irene had left the room, ere, with a long sigh, Adrian opened his eyes—an altered and another man; the fever was gone, the reviving pulse beat low indeed, but calm. His mind was once more master of his body, and, though weak and feeble, the danger was past, and life and intellect regained.

"I have slept long," he muttered; "and oh, such dreams! And methought I saw Irene, but could not speak to her, and while I attempted to grasp her, her face changed, her form dilated, and I was in the clutch of the foul grave-digger. It is late—the sun is high—I must be up and stirring. Irene is in Lombardy.

No, no; that was a lie, a wicked lie; she is at Florence, I must renew my search."

As this duty came to his remembrance, he rose from the bed—he was amazed at his own debility: at first he could not stand without support from the wall; by degrees, however, he so far regained the mastery of his limbs as to walk, though with effort and pain. A ravening hunger preyed upon him, he found some scanty and light food in the chamber, which he devoured eagerly. And with scarce less eagerness laved his enfeebled form and haggard face with the water that stood at hand. He now felt refreshed and invigorated, and began to indue his garments, which he found thrown on a heap beside the bed. He gazed with surprise and a kind of self-compassion upon his emaciated hands and shrunken limbs, and began now to comprehend that he must have had some severe but unconscious illness. "Alone, too," thought he; "no one near to tend me! Nature my only nurse! But alas! alas! how long a time may thus have been wasted, and my adored Irene —— quick, quick, not a moment more will I lose."

He soon found himself in the open street; the air revived him; and that morning had sprung up the blessed breeze, the first known for weeks. He wandered on very slowly and feebly till he came to a broad square, from which, in the vista, might be seen one of the principal gates of Florence, and the fig-trees and olive-groves beyond. It was then that a Pilgrim of tall stature approached towards him as from the gate; his hood was thrown back, and gave to view a countenance of great but sad command; a face, in whose high features, massive brow, and proud, unshrinking gaze, shaded by an expression of melancholy more stern than soft, Nature seemed to have written majesty, and Fate disaster. As in that silent and dreary place, these two, the only tenants of the street, now encountered, Adrian stopped abruptly, and said in a startled and doubting voice: "Do I dream still, or do I behold Rienzi?"

The Pilgrim paused also, as he heard the name, and gazing long on the attenuated features of the young lord, said: "I am he that was Rienzi! and you, pale shadow, is it in this grave of Italy that I meet with the gay and high Colonna? Alas, young friend," he added, in a more relaxed and kindly voice, "hath the Plague not spared the flower of the Roman nobles? Come, I, the cruel and the harsh Tribune, *I* will be thy nurse: he who might have been my brother, shall yet claim from me a brother's care."

With these words, he wound his arm tenderly round Adrian; and the young noble, touched by his compassion, and agitated by the surprise, leaned upon Rienzi's breast in silence.

"Poor youth," resumed the Tribune, for so, since rather fallen than deposed, he may yet be called; "I ever loved the young, (my brother died young;) and you more than most. What fatality brought thee hither?"

"Irene!" replied Adrian, falteringly.

"Is it so, really? Art thou a Colonna, and yet prize the fallen? The same duty has brought me also to the city of Death. From the farthest south—over the mountains of the robber—through the fastnesses of my foes—through towns in which the herald proclaimed in my ear the price of my head—I have passed hither, on foot and alone, safe under the wings of the Almighty One. Young man, thou shouldst have left this task to one who bears a wizard's life, and whom Heaven and Earth yet reserve for an appointed end!"

The Tribune said this in a deep and inward voice; and in his raised eye and solemn brow might be seen how much his reverses had deepened his fanaticism, and added even to the sanguineness of his hopes.

"But," asked Adrian, withdrawing gently from Rienzi's arm, "thou knowest, then, where Irene is to be found; let us go together. Lose not a moment in this talk; time is of inestimable value, and a moment in this city is often but the border to eternity."

"Right," said Rienzi, awakening to his object. "But fear not, I *have dreamt* that I shall save her, the gem and darling of my house. Fear not, *I* have no fear."

"Know you where to seek?" said Adrian, impatiently; "the Convent holds far other guests."

"Ha! so said my dream!"

"Talk not now of dreams," said the lover; "but if you have no other guide, let us part at once in quest of her. I will take yonder street, you take the opposite, and at sunset let us meet in the same spot."

"Rash man!" said the Tribune, with great solemnity; "scoff not at the visions which Heaven makes a parable to its Chosen. Thou seekest counsel of thy human wisdom; I, less presumptuous, follow the hand of the mysterious Providence, moving even now before my gaze as a pillar of light through the wilderness of dread. Ay, meet me here at sunset, and prove whose guide is the most unerring. If my dream tell me true, I shall see my sister living, ere the sun reach yonder hill, and by a church dedicated to St. Mark."

The grave earnestness with which Rienzi spoke impressed Adrian with a hope which his reason would not acknowledge. He saw him depart with that proud and stately step to which his sweeping garments gave a yet more imposing dignity, and then passed up the street to the right hand. He had not got half-way when he felt himself pulled by the mantle. He turned, and saw the shapeless mask of a Becchino.

"I feared you were sped, and that another had cheated me of my office," said the grave-digger, "seeing that you returned not to the old Prince's palace. You don't know me from the rest of us I see, but I am the one you told to seek——"

"Irene!"

"Yes, Irene di Gabrini; you promised ample reward."

"You shall have it."

"Follow me."

The Becchino strode on, and soon arrived at a mansion. He knocked twice at the porter's entrance, an old woman cautiously opened the door. "Fear not, good aunt," said the grave-digger; "this is the young Lord I spoke to thee of. Thou sayest thou hadst two ladies in the palace, who alone survived of all the lodgers, and their names were Bianca de Medici, and —what was the other?"

"Irene di Gabrini, a Roman lady. But I told thee this was the fourth day they left the house, terrified by the deaths within it."

"Thou didst so: and was there anything remarkable in the dress of the Signora di Gabrini?"

"Yes, I have told thee: a blue mantle, such as I have rarely seen, wrought with silver."

"Was the broidery that of stars, silver stars," exclaimed Adrian. "with a sun in the centre?"

"It was."

"Alas! alas! the arms of the Tribune's family! I remember how I praised the mantle the first day she wore it—the day on which we were betrothed!" And the lover at once conjectured the secret sentiment which had induced Irene to retain thus carefully a robe so endeared by association.

"You know no more of your lodgers?"

"Nothing."

"And is this all you have learned, knave?" cried Adrian.

"Patience. I must bring you from proof to proof, and link to link, in order to win my reward. Follow, Signor."

The Becchino then passing through the several lanes and streets, arrived at another house of less magnificent size and architecture. Again he tapped thrice at the parlour door, and this time came forth a man withered, old, and palsied, whom death seemed to disdain to strike.

"Signor Astuccio," said the Becchino, "pardon me; but I told thee I might trouble thee again. This is the gentleman who wants to know, what is often best unknown—but that's not my affair. Did a lady—young and beautiful—with dark hair, and of a slender form, enter this house, stricken with the first symptom of the Plague, three days since?"

"Ay, thou knowest that well enough; and thou knowest still better, that she has departed these two days: it was quick work with her, quicker than with most!"

"Did she wear anything remarkable?"

"Yes, troublesome man: a blue cloak, with stars of silver."

"Couldst thou guess aught of her previous circum stances?"

"No, save that she raved much about the nunnery of Santa Maria de' Pazzi, and bravos, and sacrilege."

"Are you satisfied, Signor?" asked the grave-digger, with an air of triumph, turning to Adrian. "But no, I will satisfy thee better, if thou hast courage. Wilt thou follow?"

"I comprehend thee; lead on. Courage! What is there on earth now to fear?"

Muttering to himself, "Ay, leave me alone. I have a head worth something; I ask no gentleman to go by my word; I will make his own eyes the judge of what my trouble is worth," the grave-digger now led the way through one of the gates a little out of the city. And here, under a shed, sat six of his ghastly and ill-omened brethren, with spades and pickaxes at their feet.

His guide now turned round to Adrian, whose face was set, and resolute in despair.

"Fair Signor," said he, with some touch of lingering compassion, "wouldst thou really convince thine own eyes and heart?—the sight may appal, the contagion may destroy, thee,—if, indeed, as it seems to me, Death has not already written '*mine*' upon thee."

"Raven of bode and woe!" answered Adrian, "seest thou not that all I shrink from is thy voice and aspect? Show me her I seek, living or dead."

"I will show her to you, then," said the Becchino, sullenly, "such as two nights since she was committed to my charge. Line and lineament may already be swept away, for the Plague hath a rapid besom: but I have left that upon her by which you will know the Becchino is no liar. Bring hither the torches, comrades, and lift the door. Never stare; it's the gentleman's whim, and he'll pay it well."

Turning to the right, while Adrian mechanically followed his conductors, a spectacle whose dire philosophy crushes as with a wheel all the pride of mortal man—the spectacle of that vault in which earth hides all that on earth flourished, rejoiced, exulted—awaited his eye!

The Becchini lifted a ponderous grate, lowered their torches (scarcely needed, for through the aperture rushed, with a hideous glare, the light of the burning sun,) and motioned to Adrian to advance. He stood upon the summit of the abyss and gazed below.

* * * * *
* * * * *

It was a large deep and circular space, like the bottom of an exhausted well. In niches cut into the walls of earth around, lay, duly coffined, those who had been the earliest victims of the plague, when the Becchino's market was not yet glutted, and priest followed, and friend mourned the dead. But on the floor below, *there* was the loathsome horror! Huddled and matted together—some naked, some in shrouds already black and rotten—lay the later guests, the unshriven and unblest! The torches, the sun, streamed broad and red over Corruption in all its stages, from the pale blue tint and swollen shape, to the moistened undistinguishable mass, or the riddled bones, where yet clung, in strips and tatters, the black and mangled flesh. In many, the face remained almost perfect, while the rest of the body was but bone: the long hair, the human face, surmounting the grisly skeleton. There was the infant, still on the mother's breast; there was the lover, stretched across the dainty limbs of his adored! The rats, (for they clustered in numbers to that feast,) disturbed, not scared, sate up from their horrid meal as the light glimmered over them, and thousands of them lay round, stark, and dead, poisoned by what they fed on! There, too, the wild satire of the grave-diggers had cast, though stripped of their gold and jewels, the emblems that spoke of departed rank;—the broken wand of the Councillor; the General's baton; the Priestly Mitre! The foul and livid exhalations gathered like flesh itself, fungous and putrid, upon the walls, and the*——

* * * * *
* * * * *

But who shall detail the ineffable and unimaginable horrors that reigned over the Palace where the Great King received the prisoners whom the sword of the Pestilence had subdued?

But through all that crowded court—crowded with beauty and with birth, with the strength of the young and the honours of the old, and the valour of the brave, and the wisdom of the learned, and the wit of the scorner, and the piety of the faithful—one only figure attracted Adrian's eye. Apart from the rest, a late comer—the long locks streaming far and dark over arm and breast—lay a female, the face turned partially aside, the little seen not recognisable even by the mother of the dead,—but wrapped round in that fatal mantle, on which, though blackened and tarnished, was yet visible the starry heraldry assumed by those who claimed the name of the proud Tribune of Rome. Adrian saw no more—he fell back in the arms of the

* The description in the text is borrowed from the famous waxwork model [of the interior of the Charnel-house] at Florence.

grave-diggers: when he recovered, he was still without the gates of Florence—reclined upon a green mound—his guide stood beside him—holding his steed by the bridle as it grazed patiently on the neglected grass. The other brethren of the axe had resumed their seat under the shed.

"So, you have revived! Ah! I thought it was only the effluvia; few stand it as we do. And so, as your search is over, deeming you would now be quitting Florence if you have any sense left to you, I went for your good horse. I have fed him since your departure from the palace. Indeed I fancied he would be my perquisite, but there are plenty as good. Come, young sir, mount. I feel a pity for you, I know not why, except that you are the only one I have met for weeks who seems to care for another more than for yourself. I hope you are satisfied now that I showed some brains, eh! in your service: and as I have kept my promise, you'll keep yours."

"Friend," said Adrian, "here is gold enough to make thee rich; here, too, is a jewel that merchants will tell thee princes might vie to purchase. Thou seemest honest, despite thy calling, or thou mightest have robbed and murdered me long since. Do me one favour more."

"By my poor mother's soul, yes."

"Take yon—yon clay from that fearful place. Inter it in some quiet and remote spot—apart—alone! You promise me?—you swear it?—it is well! And now help me on my horse. Farewell Italy, and if I die not with this stroke, may I die as befits at once honour and despair—with trumpet and banner round me—in a well-fought field against a worthy foe!—Save a knightly death, nothing is left to live for!"

BOOK VII

THE PRISON

"Fu rinchiuso in una torre grossa e larga; avea libri assai, suo Tito Livio, sue storie di Roma, la Bibbia, &c.—*Vit. di Cola di Rienzi*, lib. ii. c. 13.

"He was immured in a high and spacious tower; he had books enough, his Titus Livius, his histories of Rome, the Bible," &c.

CHAPTER I

AVIGNON.—THE TWO PAGES.—THE STRANGER BEAUTY

There is this difference between the Drama of Shakspeare, and that of almost every other master of the same art; that in the first, the catastrophe is rarely produced by one single cause—one simple and continuous chain of events. Various and complicated agencies work out the final end. Unfettered by the rules of time and place, each time, each place depicted, presents us with its appropriate change of action, or of actors. Sometimes the interest seems to halt, to turn aside, to bring us unawares upon objects hitherto unnoticed, or upon qualities of the characters hitherto hinted at, not developed. But, in reality, the pause in the action is but to collect, to gather up, and to grasp, all the varieties of circumstance that conduce to the Great Result: and the art of fiction is only deserted for the fidelity of history. Whoever seeks to place before the world the true representation of a man's life and times, and enlarging the Dramatic into the Epic, extends his narrative over the vicissitudes of years, will find himself unconsciously, in this, the imitator of Shakspeare. New characters, each conducive to the end—new scenes, each leading to the last, rises before him as he proceeds, sometimes seeming to the reader to delay, even while they advance, the dread catastrophe. The sacrificial procession sweeps along, swelled by new comers, losing many that first joined it; before, at last, the same as a whole, but differing in its components, the crowd reach the fated bourn of the Altar and the Victim!

It is five years after the date of the events I have recorded, and my story conveys us to the Papal Court at Avignon—that tranquil seat of power, to which the successors of St. Peter had transplanted the luxury, the pomp, and the vices, of the Imperial City. Secure from the fraud or violence of a powerful and barbarous nobility, the courtiers of the See surrendered themselves to a holyday of delight—their repose was devoted to enjoyment, and Avignon presented, at that day, perhaps the gayest and most voluptuous society of Europe. The elegance of Clement VI. had diffused an air of literary refinement over the grosser pleasures of the place, and the spirit of Petrarch still continued to work its way through the councils of faction and the orgies of debauch.

Innocent VI. had lately succeeded Clement, and whatever his own claims to learning,* he, at least, appreciated knowledge and intellect in others; so that

* Matteo Villani (lib. iii. cap. 44) says that Innocent VI. had not much pretension to learning. He is reported, however, by other authorities, cited by Zefirino Re, to have been "eccellente canonista." He had been a professor in the University of Toulouse.

the graceful pedantry of the time continued to mix itself with the pursuit of pleasure. The corruption which reigned through the whole place was too confirmed to yield to the example of Innocent, himself a man of simple habits and exemplary life. Though, like his predecessor, obedient to the policy of France, Innocent possessed a hard and an extended ambition. Deeply concerned for the interests of the Church, he formed the project of confirming and re-establishing her shaken dominion in Italy; and he regarded the tyrants of the various states as the principal obstacles to his ecclesiastical ambition. Nor was this the policy of Innocent VI. alone. With such exceptions as peculiar circumstances necessarily occasioned, the Papal See was, upon the whole, friendly to the political liberties of Italy. The Republics of the Middle Ages grew up under the shadow of the Church; and there, as elsewhere, it was found, contrary to a vulgar opinion, that Religion, however prostituted and perverted, served for the general protection of civil freedom,—raised the lowly, and resisted the oppressor.

At this period there appeared at Avignon a lady of singular and matchless beauty. She had come with a slender but well-appointed retinue from Florence, but declared herself of Neapolitan birth; the widow of a noble of the brilliant court of the unfortunate Jane. Her name was Cesarini. Arrived at a place where, even in the citadel of Christianity, Venus retained her ancient empire, where Love made the prime business of life, and to be beautiful was to be of power; the Signora Cesarini had scarcely appeared in public before she saw at her feet half the rank and gallantry of Avignon. Her female attendants were beset with bribes and billets; and nightly, beneath her lattice, was heard the plaintive serenade. She entered largely into the gay dissipation of the town, and her charms shared the celebrity of the hour with the verse of Petrarch. But though she frowned on none, none could claim the monopoly of her smiles. Her fair fame was as yet unblemished; but if any might presume beyond the rest, she seemed to have selected rather from ambition than love, and Giles, the warlike Cardinal d'Albornoz, all powerful at the sacred court, already foreboded the hour of his triumph.

It was late noon, and in the ante-chamber of the fair Signora waited two of that fraternity of pages, fair and richly clad, who, at that day, furnished the favourite attendants to rank of either sex.

"By my troth," cried one of these young servitors, pushing from him the dice with which himself and his companion had sought to beguile their leisure, "this is but dull work! and the best part of the day is gone. Our lady is late."

"And I have donned my new velvet mantle," replied the other, compassionately eyeing his finery.

"Chut, Giacomo," said his comrade, yawning; "a truce with thy conceit.—What news abroad, I wonder? Has his Holiness come to his senses yet?"

"His senses; what, is he mad then?" quoth Giacomo, in a serious and astonished whisper.

"I think he is; if, being Pope, he does not discover that he may at length lay aside mask and hood. 'Continent Cardinal—lewd Pope,' is the old motto, you know; something must be the matter with the good man's brain if he continue to live like a hermit."

"Oh, I have you! but faith, his Holiness has proxies eno'. The bishops take care to prevent women,

Heaven bless them! going out of fashion; and Albornoz does not maintain your proverb, touching the Cardinals."

"True, but Giles is a warrior,—a cardinal in the church, but a soldier in the city."

"Will he carry the fort here, think you, Angelo?"

"Why, fort is female, but——"

"But what?"

"The Signora's brow is made for power, rather than love, fair as it is. She sees in Albornoz the prince, and not the lover. With what a step she sweeps the floor! it disdains even the cloth of gold!"

"Hark!" cried Giacomo, hastening to the lattice, "hear you the hoofs below? Ah, a gallant company!"

"Returned from hawking," answered Angelo, regarding wistfully the cavalcade, as it swept the narrow street. "Plumes waving, steeds curvetting—see how yon handsome cavalier presses close to that dame!"

"His mantle is the colour of mine," sighed Giacomo.

As the gay procession paced slowly on, till hidden by the winding street, and as the sound of laughter and the tramp of horses was yet faintly heard, there frowned right before the straining gaze of the pages, a dark massive tower of the mighty masonry of the eleventh century: the sun gleamed sadly on its vast and dismal surface, which was only here and there relieved by loopholes and narrow slits, rather than casements. It was a striking contrast to the gaiety around, the glittering shops, and the gaudy train that had just filled the space below. This contrast the young men seemed involuntarily to feel; they drew back, and looked at each other.

" I know your thoughts, Giacomo," said Angelo, the handsomer and elder of the two. " You think yon tower affords but a gloomy lodgment? "

" And I thank my stars that made me not high enough to require so grand a cage," rejoined Giacomo.

" Yet," observed Angelo, " it holds one, who in birth was not our superior."

" Do tell me something of that strange man," said Giacomo, regaining his seat; " you are Roman and should know."

" Yes! " answered Angelo, haughtily drawing himself up. " I *am* Roman! and I should be unworthy my birth, if I had not already learned what honour is due to the name of Cola di Rienzi."

" Yet your fellow-Romans nearly stoned him, I fancy," muttered Giacomo. " Honour seems to lie more in kicks than money. Can you tell me," continued the page in a louder key, " can you tell me if it be true, that Rienzi appeared at Prague before the Emperor, and prophesied that the late Pope and all the Cardinals should be murdered, and a new Italian Pope elected, who should endue the Emperor with a golden crown, as Sovereign of Sicilia, Calabria, and Apulia,* and himself with a crown of silver, as King of Rome, and all Italy? And——"

" Hush! " interrupted Angelo, impatiently. " Listen to me, and you shall know the exact story. On *last* leaving Rome (thou knowest that, after his fall, he was present at the Jubilee in disguise) the Tribune——" here Angelo, pausing, looked round, and then with a flushed cheek and raised voice resumed, " Yes, the

* An absurd fable, adopted by certain historians.

Tribune, that *was* and *shall* be—travelled in disguise, as a pilgrim, over mountain and forest, night and day, exposed to rain and storm, no shelter but the cave,—he who had been, they say, the very spoilt one of Luxury. Arrived at length in Bohemia, he disclosed himself to a Florentine in Prague, and through his aid obtained audience of the Emperor Charles."

"A prudent man, the Emperor!" said Giacomo, "close-fisted as a miser. He makes conquests by bargain, and goes to market for laurels,—as I have heard my brother say, who was under him."

"True; but I have also heard that he likes book-men and scholars—is wise and temperate, and much is yet hoped from him in Italy! Before the Emperor, I say, came Rienzi. 'Know, great Prince,' said he, 'that I am that Rienzi to whom God gave to govern Rome, in peace, with justice, and to freedom. I curbed the nobles, I purged corruption, I amended law. The powerful persecuted me—pride and envy have chased me from my dominions. Great as you are, fallen as I am, I too have wielded the sceptre and might have worn a crown. Know, too, that I am illegitimately of your lineage; my father the son of Henry VII.;* the blood of the Teuton rolls in my veins; mean as were my earlier fortunes and humble my earlier name! From you, O king, I seek protection, and I demand justice."†

"A bold speech, and one from equal to equal," said Giacomo; "surely you swell us out the words."

"Not a whit; they were written down by the Emperor's scribe, and every Roman who has once heard

* Uncle to the Emperor Charles.
† See, for this speech, "The Anonymous Biographer," lib. ii. cap. 12.

knows them by heart: once every Roman was the equal to a king, and Rienzi maintained our dignity in asserting his own."

Giacomo, who discreetly avoided quarrels, knew the weak side of his friend; and though in his heart he thought the Romans as good-for-nothing a set of turbulent dastards as all Italy might furnish, he merely picked a straw from his mantle, and said, in rather an impatient tone, "Humph! proceed! did the Emperor dismiss him?"

"Not so: Charles was struck with his bearing and his spirit, received him graciously, and entertained him hospitably. He remained some time at Prague, and astonished all the learned with his knowledge and eloquence."*

"But if so honoured at Prague, how comes he a prisoner at Avignon?"

"Giacomo," said Angelo, thoughtfully, "there are some men whom we, of another mind and mould, can rarely comprehend, and never fathom. And of such men I have observed that a supreme confidence in their own fortunes or their own souls, is the most common feature. Thus impressed, and thus buoyed, they rush into danger with a seeming madness, and from danger soar to greatness, or sink to death. So with Rienzi; dissatisfied with empty courtesies and weary of playing the pedant, since once he had played the prince;—some say of his own accord, (though others

* His Italian contemporary delights in representing this remarkable man as another Crichton. "Disputava," he says of him when at Prague, "disputava con Mastri di teologia; molto diceva, parlava cose meravigliose . . . . abbair fea ogni persona."—"He disputed with Masters of theology—he spoke much, he discoursed things wonderful—he astonished every one."

relate that he was surrendered to the Pope's legate by Charles,) he left the Emperor's court, and without arms, without money, betook himself at once to Avignon!"

"Madness indeed!"

"Yet, perhaps, his only course, under all circumstances," resumed the elder page. "Once before his fall, and once during his absence from Rome, he had been excommunicated by the Pope's legate. He was accused of heresy—the ban was still on him. It was necessary that he should clear himself. How was the poor exile to do so? No powerful friend stood up for the friend of the people. No courtier vindicated one who had trampled on the neck of the nobles. His own genius was his only friend; on that only could he rely. He sought Avignon, to free himself from the accusations against him; and, doubtless, he hoped that there was but one step from his acquittal to his restoration. Besides, it is certain that the Emperor had been applied to, formally to surrender Rienzi. He had the choice before him; for to that sooner or later it must come—to go free, or to go in bonds—as a criminal, or as a Roman. He chose the latter. Wherever he passed along, the people rose in every town, in every hamlet. The name of the great Tribune was honoured throughout all Italy. They besought him not to rush into the very den of peril—they implored him to save himself for that country which he had sought to raise. 'I go to vindicate myself, and to triumph,' was the Tribune's answer. Solemn honours were paid him in the cities through which he passed;* and I am told that never ambassador, prince, or baron, en-

* "Per tutto la via li furo fatti solenni onori," &c.—*Vit. di Col. di Rienzi*, lib. ii. cap. 13.

tered Avignon with so long a train as that which followed into these very walls the steps of Cola di Rienzi."

"And on his arrival?"

"He demanded an audience, that he might refute the charges against him. He flung down the gage to the proud cardinals who had excommunicated him. He besought a trial."

"And what said the Pope?"

"Nothing—by word. Yon tower was his answer!"

"A rough one!"

"But there have been longer roads than that from the prison to the palace, and God made not men like Rienzi for the dungeon and the chain."

As Angelo said this with a loud voice, and with all the enthusiasm with which the fame of the fallen Tribune had inspired the youth of Rome, he heard a sigh behind him. He turned in some confusion, and at the door which admitted to the chamber occupied by the Signora Cesarini, stood a female of noble presence. Attired in the richest garments, gold and gems were dull to the lustre of her dark eyes, and as she now stood, erect and commanding, never seemed brow more made for the regal crown—never did human beauty more fully consummate the ideal of a heroine and a queen.

"Pardon me, Signora," said Angelo, hesitatingly; "I spoke loud, I disturbed you; but I am Roman, and my theme was——"

"Rienzi!" said the lady, approaching; "a fit one to stir a Roman heart. Nay—no excuses: they would sound ill on thy generous lips. Ah, if—" the Signora paused suddenly, and sighed again; then in an altered and graver tone she resumed—"if fate restore Rienzi to his proper fortunes, he shall know what thou deemest of him."

"If you, lady, who are of Naples," said Angelo, with meaning emphasis, "speak thus of a fallen exile, what must I have felt who acknowledged a sovereign?"

"Rienzi is not of Rome alone—he is of Italy—of the world," returned the Signora. "And you, Angelo, who have had the boldness to speak thus of one fallen, have proved with what loyalty you can serve those who have the fortune to own you."

As she spoke, the Signora looked at the page's downcast and blushing face long and wistfully, with the gaze of one accustomed to read the soul in the countenance.

"Men are often deceived," said she, sadly, yet with a half smile; "but women rarely,—save in love. Would that Rome were filled with such as you! Enough! Hark! Is that the sound of hoofs in the court below?"

"Madam," said Giacomo, bringing his mantle gallantly over his shoulder, "I see the servitors of Monsignore the Cardinal d'Albornoz.—It is the Cardinal himself."

"It is well!" said the Signora, with a brightening eye; "I await him!" With these words she withdrew by the door through which she had surprised the Roman page.

CHAPTER II

THE CHARACTER OF A WARRIOR-PRIEST—AN INTERVIEW—THE INTRIGUE AND COUNTER-INTRIGUE OF COURTS

Giles, (or Egidio,*) Cardinal d'Albornoz, was one of the remarkable men of that remarkable time, so prodigal of genius. Boasting his descent from the royal houses of Aragon and Leon, he had early entered the church, and yet almost a youth, attained the archbishopric of Toledo. But no peaceful career, however brilliant, sufficed to his ambition. He could not content himself with the honours of the Church, unless they were the honours of a church militant. In the war against the Moors, no Spaniard had more highly distinguished himself; and Alphonso XI., king of Castile, had insisted on receiving from the hand of the martial priest the badge of knighthood. After the death of Alphonso, who was strongly attached to him, Albornoz repaired to Avignon, and obtained from Clement VI. the cardinal's hat. With Innocent he continued in high favour, and now, constantly in the councils of the Pope, rumours of warlike preparation, under the banners of Albornoz, for the recovery of the papal dominions from the various tyrants that usurped them, were already circulated through the court.†

* Egidio is the proper Italian equivalent to the French name Gilles,—but the Cardinal is generally called, by the writers of that day, Gilio d'Albornoz.

† It is a characteristic anecdote of this bold Churchman, that Urban V. one day demanded an account of the sums spent in his military expedition against the Italian tyrants. The Cardinal presented to the Pope a waggon, filled with the keys of the cities and fortresses he had taken. "This is

Bold, sagacious, enterprising, and cold-hearted,—with the valour of the knight, and the cunning of the priest, —such was the character of Giles, Cardinal d'Albornoz.

Leaving his attendant gentlemen in the ante-chamber, Albornoz was ushered into the apartment of the Signora Cesarini. In person, the Cardinal was about the middle height; the dark complexion of Spain had faded by thought, and the wear of ambitious schemes, into a sallow but hardy hue; his brow was deeply furrowed, and though not yet past the prime of life, Albornoz might seem to have entered age, but for the firmness of his step, the slender elasticity of his frame, and an eye which had acquired calmness and depth from thought, without losing any of the brilliancy of youth.

"Beautiful Signora," said the Cardinal, bending over the hand of the Cesarini with a grace which betokened more of the prince than of the priest; "the commands of his Holiness have detained me, I fear, beyond the hour in which you vouchsafed to appoint my homage, but my heart has been with you since we parted."

"The Cardinal d'Albornoz," replied the Signora, gently withdrawing her hand, and seating herself, "has so many demands on his time, from the duties of his rank and renown, that methinks to divert his attention for a few moments to less noble thoughts is a kind of treason to his fame."

"Ah, Lady," replied the Cardinal, "never was my ambition so nobly directed as it is now. And it were

my account," said he; "you perceive how I have invested your money." The Pope embraced him, and gave him no further trouble about his accounts.

a prouder lot to be at thy feet than on the throne of St. Peter."

A momentary blush passed over the cheek of the Signora, yet it seemed the blush of indignation as much as of vanity; it was succeeded by an extreme paleness. She paused before she replied; and then fixing her large and haughty eyes on the enamoured Spaniard, she said, in a low voice,

"My Lord Cardinal, I do not affect to misunderstand your words; neither do I place them to the account of a general gallantry. I am vain enough to believe you imagine you speak truly when you say you love me."

"Imagine!" echoed the Spaniard.

"Listen to me," continued the Signora. "She whom the Cardinal Albornoz honours with his love has a right to demand of him its proofs. In the papal court, whose power like his?—I require you to exercise it for me."

"Speak, dearest Lady; have your estates been seized by the barbarians of these lawless times? Hath any dared to injure you? Lands and titles, are these thy wish?—my power is thy slave."

"Cardinal, no! there is one thing dearer to an Italian and a woman than wealth or station—it is revenge!"

The Cardinal drew back from the flashing eye that was bent upon him, but the spirit of her speech touched a congenial chord.

"There," said he, after a little hesitation, "there spake high descent. Revenge is the luxury of the well-born. Let serfs and churls forgive an injury. Proceed, Lady."

"Hast thou heard the last news from Rome?" asked the Signora.

"Surely," replied the Cardinal, in some surprise, "we were poor statesmen to be ignorant of the condition of the capital of the papal dominions; and my heart mourns for that unfortunate city. But wherefore wouldst thou question me of Rome?—thou art—"

"Roman! Know, my Lord, that I have a purpose in calling myself of Naples. To your discretion I intrust my secret—I am of Rome! Tell me of her state."

"Fairest one," returned the Cardinal, "I should have known that that brow and presence were not of the light *Campania*. My reason should have told me that they bore the stamp of the Empress of the World. The state of Rome," continued Albornoz, in a graver tone, "is briefly told. Thou knowest that after the fall of the able but insolent Rienzi, Pepin, count of Minorbino, (a creature of Montreal's,) who had assisted in expelling him, would have betrayed Rome to Montreal,—but he was neither strong enough nor wise enough, and the Barons chased him as he had chased the Tribune. Some time afterwards a new demagogue, John Cerroni, was installed in the Capitol. He once more expelled the nobles; new revolutions ensued—the Barons were recalled. The weak successor of Rienzi summoned the people to arms—in vain: in terror and despair he abdicated his power, and left the city a prey to the interminable feuds of the Orsini, the Colonna, and the Savelli."

"Thus much I know, my Lord; but when his Holiness succeeded to the chair of Clement VI.——"

"Then," said Albornoz, and a slight frown darkened his sallow brow, "then came the blacker part of the history. Two senators were elected in concert by the Pope."

"Their names?"

"Bertoldo Orsini, and one of the Colonna. A few weeks afterwards, the high price of provisions stung the rascal stomachs of the mob—they rose, they clamoured, they armed, they besieged the Capitol——"

"Well, well," cried the Signora, clasping her hands, and betokening in every feature her interest in the narration.

"Colonna only escaped death by a vile disguise; Bertoldo Orsini was stoned."

"Stoned!—there fell one!"

"Yes, Lady, one of a great house; the least drop of whose blood were worth an ocean of plebeian puddle. At present, all is disorder, misrule, anarchy at Rome. The contests of the nobles shake the city to the centre; and prince and people, wearied of so many experiments to establish a government, have now no governor but the fear of the sword. Such, fair madam, is the state of Rome. Sigh not, it occupies now our care. It shall be remedied; and I, madam, may be the happy instrument of restoring peace to your native city."

"There is but one way of restoring peace to Rome," answered the Signora, abruptly, "and that is—The restoration of Rienzi!"

The Cardinal started. "Madam," said he, "do I hear aright?—are you not nobly born?—can you desire the rise of a plebeian? Did you not speak of revenge, and now you ask for mercy?"

"Lord Cardinal," said the beautiful Signora, earnestly, "I do not ask for mercy: such a word is not for the lips of one who demands justice. Nobly born

I am—ay, and from a stock to whose long descent from the patricians of ancient Rome the high line of Aragon itself would be of yesterday. Nay, I would not offend you, Monsignore; your greatness is not borrowed from pedigrees and tombstones—your greatness is your own achieving: would you speak honestly, my lord, you would own that you are proud only of *your own* laurels, and that, in your heart, you laugh at the stately fools who trick themselves out in the mouldering finery of the dead!"

"Muse! prophetess! you speak aright," said the high-spirited Cardinal, with unwonted energy; "and your voice is like that of the Fame I dreamed of in my youth. Speak on, speak ever!"

"Such," continued the Signora, "such as your pride, is the just pride of Rienzi. Proud that he is the workman of his own great renown. In such as the Tribune of Rome we acknowledge the founders of noble lineage. Ancestry makes not them—they make ancestry. Enough of this. I am of noble race, it is true; but my house, and those of many, have been crushed and broken beneath the yoke of the Orsini and Colonna—it is against them I desire revenge. But I am better than an Italian lady—I am a Roman woman—I weep tears of blood for the disorders of my unhappy country. I mourn that even you, my lord,—yes, that a barbarian, however eminent and however great, should mourn for Rome. I desire to restore her fortunes."

"But Rienzi would only restore his own."

"Not so, my Lord Cardinal; not so. Ambitious and proud he may be—great souls are so—but he has never had one wish divorced from the welfare of Rome. But put aside all thought of his interests—it is not of these I speak. You desire to re-establish the papal power in Rome. Your senators have failed to do it. Demagogues fail—Rienzi alone can succeed; he alone can command the turbulent passions of the Barons—he alone can sway the capricious and fickle mob. Release, restore Rienzi, and through Rienzi the Pope regains Rome!"

The Cardinal did not answer for some moments. Buried as in a reverie, he sate motionless, shading his face with his hand. Perhaps he secretly owned there was a wiser policy in the suggestions of the Signora than he cared openly to confess. Lifting his head, at length, from his bosom, he fixed his eyes upon the Signora's watchful countenance, and, with a forced smile, said,

"Pardon me, madam; but while we play the politicians, forget not that I am thy adorer. Sagacious may be thy counsels, yet wherefore are they urged? Why this anxious interest for Rienzi? If by releasing him the Church may gain an ally, am I sure that Giles d'Albornoz will not raise a rival?"

"My lord," said the Signora, half rising, "you are my suitor; but your rank does not tempt me—your gold cannot buy. If you love me, I have a right to command your services to whatsoever task I would require—it is the law of chivalry. If ever I yield to the addresses of mortal lover, it will be to the man who restores to my native land her hero and her saviour."

"Fair patriot," said the Cardinal, "your words encourage my hope, yet they half damp my ambition; for fain would I desire that love and not service should alone give me the treasure that I ask. But hear me, sweet lady; you overrate my power: I cannot deliver

Rienzi—he is accused of rebellion, he is excommunicated for heresy. His acquittal rests with himself."

"You can procure his trial?"

"Perhaps, Lady."

"That *is* his acquittal. And a private audience of his Holiness?"

"Doubtless."

"*That* is his restoration! Behold all I ask!"

"And then, sweet Roman, it will be *mine* to ask," said the Cardinal, passionately, dropping on his knee, and taking the Signora's hand. For one moment, that proud lady felt that she was woman—she blushed, she trembled: but it was not (could the Cardinal have read that heart) with passion or with weakness; it was with terror and with shame. Passively she surrendered her hand to the Cardinal, who covered it with kisses.

"Thus inspired," said Albornoz, rising, "I will not doubt of success. To-morrow I wait on thee again."

He pressed her hand to his heart—the lady felt it not. He sighed his farewell—she did not hear it. Lingeringly he gazed; and slowly he departed. But it was some moments before, recalled to herself, the Signora felt that she was alone.

"Alone!" she cried, half aloud, and with wild emphasis—"alone! Oh, what have I undergone—what have I said! Unfaithful even in thought to *him!* Oh, never! never! I that have felt the kiss of his hallowing lips—that have slept on his kingly heart—I!—holy Mother, befriend and strengthen me!" she continued, as, weeping bitterly, she sunk upon her knees; and for some moments she was lost in prayer. Then, rising composed, but deadly pale, and with the tears rolling heavily down her cheeks, the Signora passed slowly to the casement; she threw it open, and bent forward; the air of the declining day came softly on her temples; it cooled, it mitigated, the fever that preyed within. Dark and huge before her frowned, in its gloomy shadow, the tower in which Rienzi was confined; she gazed at it long and wistfully, and then, turning away, drew from the folds of her robe a small and sharp dagger. "Let me save him for glory!" she murmured; "and *this* shall save me from dishonour!"

CHAPTER III

HOLY MEN.—SAGACIOUS DELIBERATIONS.—JUST RESOLVES.—AND SORDID MOTIVES TO ALL

Enamoured of the beauty, and almost equally so of the lofty spirit, of the Signora Cesarini, as was the warlike Cardinal of Spain, love with him was not so master a passion as that ambition of complete success in all the active designs of life, which had hitherto animated his character and signalised his career. Musing, as he left the Signora, on her wish for the restoration of the Roman Tribune, his experienced and profound intellect ran swiftly through whatever advantages to his own political designs might result from that restoration. We have seen that it was the intention of the new Pontiff to attempt the recovery of the patrimonial territories, now torn from him by the gripe of able and disaffected tyrants. With this view, a military force was already in preparation, and the Cardinal was already secretly nominated the chief. But the force was very inadequate to the enterprise; and Albornoz depended much upon the moral strength of the cause in bringing recruits to his standard in his progress through the Italian states. The wonderful rise of Rienzi had excited an extraordinary enthusiasm in his favour through all the free populations of Italy. And this had been yet more kindled and inflamed by the influential eloquence of Petrarch, who, at that time, possessed of a power greater than ever, before or since, (not even excepting the Sage of Ferney,) wielded by a single literary man, had put forth his boldest genius in behalf of the Roman Tribune. Such a companion as Rienzi in the camp of the Cardinal might be a magnet of attraction to the youth and enterprise of Italy. On nearing Rome, he might himself judge how far it would be advisable to reinstate Rienzi as a delegate of the papal power. And, in the meanwhile, the Roman's influence might be serviceable, whether to awe the rebellious nobles or conciliate the stubborn people. On the other hand, the Cardinal was shrewd enough to perceive that no possible good could arise from Rienzi's present confinement. With every month it excited deeper and more universal sympathy. To his lonely dungeon turned half the hearts of republican Italy. Literature had leagued its new and sudden, and therefore mighty and even disproportioned, power with his cause; and the Pope, without daring to be his judge, incurred the odium of being his gaoler. "A popular prisoner," said the sagacious Cardinal to himself, "is the most dangerous of guests. Restore him as your servant, or destroy him as your foe! In this case I see no alternative but acquittal or the knife!" In these reflections that able plotter, deep in the Machiavelism of the age, divorced the lover from the statesman.

Recurring now to the former character, he felt some

disagreeable and uneasy forebodings at the earnest interest of his mistress. Fain would he have attributed, either to some fantasy of patriotism or some purpose of revenge, the anxiety of the Cesarini; and there was much in her stern and haughty character which favoured that belief. But he was forced to acknowledge to himself some jealous apprehension of a sinister and latent motive, which touched his vanity and alarmed his love. "Howbeit," he thought, as he turned from his unwilling fear, "I can play with her at her own weapons; I can obtain the release of Rienzi, and claim my reward. If denied, the hand that opened the dungeon can again rivet the chain. In her anxiety is my power!"

These thoughts the Cardinal was still revolving in his palace, when he was suddenly summoned to attend the Pontiff.

The pontifical palace no longer exhibited the gorgeous yet graceful luxury of Clement VI., and the sarcastic Cardinal smiled to himself at the quiet gloom of the ante-chambers. "He thinks to set an example—this poor native of Limoges!" thought Albornoz; "and has but the mortification of finding himself eclipsed by the poorest bishop. He humbles himself, and fancies that the humility will be contagious."

His Holiness was seated before a small and rude table bestrewed with papers, his face buried in his hands; the room was simply furnished, and in a small niche beside the casement was an ivory crucifix; below, the death's head and cross-bones, which most monks then introduced with a purpose similar to that of the ancients by the like ornaments,—mementos of the shortness of life. and therefore admonitions to make the best of it! On the ground lay a map of the Patrimonial Territory, with the fortresses in especial, distinctly and prominently marked. The Pope gently lifted up his head as the Cardinal was announced, and discovered a plain but sensible and somewhat interesting countenance. "My son!" said he, with a kindly courtesy to the lowly salutation of the proud Spaniard, "scarcely wouldst thou imagine, after our long conference this morning, that new cares would so soon demand the assistance of thy counsels. Verily, the wreath of thorns stings sharp under the triple crown; and I sometimes long for the quiet abode of my old professor's chair in Toulouse: my station is of pain and of toil."

"God tempers the wind to the shorn lamb," observed the Cardinal, with pious and compassionate gravity.

Innocent could scarcely refrain a smile as he replied, "The lamb that carries the cross must have the strength of the lion. Since we parted, my son, I have had painful intelligence; our couriers have arrived from the Campagna—the heathen rage furiously—the force of John di Vico has augmented fearfully, and the most redoubted adventurer of Europe has enlisted under his banner."

"Does his Holiness," cried the Cardinal, anxiously, "speak of Fra Moreale, the Knight of St. John?"

"Of no less a warrior," returned the Pontiff. "I dread the vast ambition of that wild adventurer."

"Your Holiness hath cause," said the Cardinal, drily.

"Some letters of his have fallen into the hands of the servants of the Church; they are here: read them, my son."

Albornoz received and deliberately scanned the letters; this done, he replaced them on the table, and remained for a few moments silent and absorbed.

"What think you, my son?" said the Pope, at length, with an impatient and even peevish tone.

"I think that, with Montreal's hot genius and John di Vico's frigid villany, your Holiness may live to envy, if not the quiet, at least the revenue, of the Professor's chair."

"How, Cardinal!" said the Pope, hastily, and with an angry flush on his pale brow.

The Cardinal quietly proceeded:

"By these letters it seems that Montreal has written to all the commanders of free lances throughout Italy, offering the highest pay of a soldier to every man who will join his standard, combined with the richest plunder of a brigand. He meditates great schemes then! —I know the man!"

"Well,—and our course?"

"Is plain," said the Cardinal, loftily, and with an eye that flashed with a soldier's fire. "Not a moment is to be lost! Thy son should at once take the field. Up with the Banner of the Church!"

"But are we strong enough? our numbers are few. Zeal slackens! the piety of the Baldwins is no more!"

"Your Holiness knows well," said the Cardinal, "that for the multitude of men there are two watchwords of war—Liberty and Religion. If Religion begins to fail, we must employ the profaner word. 'Up with the Banner of the Church—and down with the tyrants!' We will proclaim equal laws and free government;* and, God willing, our camp shall prosper

* In correcting the pages of this work, in the year 1847 . . . strange coincidences between the present policy of the Ro-

better with those promises than the tents of Montreal with the more vulgar shout of 'Pay and Rapine.'"

"Giles d'Albornoz," said the Pope, emphatically; and, warmed by the spirit of the Cardinal, he dropped the wonted etiquette of the phrase, "I trust implicitly to you. Now the right hand of the Church—hereafter, perhaps, its head. Too well I feel that the lot has fallen on a lowly place. My successor must requite my deficiencies."

No changing hue, no brightening glance, betrayed to the searching eye of the Pope whatever emotion these words had called up in the breast of the ambitious Cardinal. He bowed his proud head humbly as he answered, "Pray Heaven that Innocent VI. may long live to guide the Church to glory. For Giles d'Albornoz, less priest than soldier, the din of the camp, the breath of the war-steed, suggest the only aspirations which he ever dares indulge. But has your Holiness imparted to your servant all that——"

"Nay," interrupted Innocent, "I have yet intelligence equally ominous. This John di Vico,—pest go with him!—who still styles himself (the excommunicated ruffian!) Prefect of Rome, has so filled that unhappy city with his emissaries, that we have well-nigh lost the seat of the Apostle. Rome, long in anarchy, seems now in open rebellion. The nobles—sons of Belial!—it is true, are once more humbled; but how? —One Baroncelli a new demagogue, the fiercest—the most bloody that the fiend ever helped—has arisen—is invested by the mob with power, and uses it to butcher the people and insult the Pontiff. Wearied of

man Church and that by which in the 14th century it recovered both spiritual and temporal power cannot fail to suggest themselves.

the crimes of this man, (which are not even decorated by ability,) the shout of the people day and night along the streets is for 'Rienzi the Tribune.'"

"Ha!" said the Cardinal, "Rienzi's faults then are forgotten in Rome, and there is felt for him the same enthusiasm in that city as in the rest of Italy?"

"Alas! it is so."

"It is well, I have thought of this: Rienzi can accompany my progress——"

"My son! the rebel, the heretic——"

"By your Holiness's absolution will become a quiet subject and orthodox Catholic," said Albornoz. "Men are good or bad as they suit our purpose. What matters a virtue that is useless, or a crime that is useful, to us? The army of the Church proceeds against tyrants—it proclaims everywhere to the Papal towns the restoration of their popular constitutions. Sees not your Holiness that the acquittal of Rienzi, the popular darling, will be hailed an earnest of your sincerity?—sees not your Holiness that his name will fight for us?—sees not your Holiness that the great demagogue Rienzi must be used to extinguish the little demagogue Baroncelli? We must regain the Romans, whether of the city or whether in the seven towns of John di Vico. When they hear Rienzi is in our camp, trust me, we shall have a multitude of deserters from the tyrants—trust me, we shall hear no more of Baroncelli."

"Ever sagacious," said the Pope, musingly; "it is true we can use this man: but with caution. His genius is formidable——"

"And therefore must be conciliated; if we acquit, we must make him ours. My experience has taught me this, when you cannot slay a demagogue by law, crush him with honours. He must be no longer Tribune of the People. Give him the Patrician title of *Senator*, and he is then the Lieutenant of the Pope!"

"I will see to this, my son—your suggestions please, but alarm me: he shall at least be examined;—but if found a heretic——"

"Should, I humbly advise, be declared a saint."

The Pope bent his brow for a moment, but the effort was too much for him, and after a moment's struggle, he fairly laughed aloud.

"Go to, my son," said he, affectionately patting the Cardinal's sallow cheek. "Go to.—If the world heard thee, what would it say?"

"That Giles d'Albornoz had just enough religion to remember that the State is a Church, but not too much to forget that the Church is a State."

With these words the conference ended. That very evening the Pope decreed that Rienzi should be permitted the trial he had demanded.

CHAPTER IV

THE LADY AND THE PAGE

It wanted three hours of midnight, when Albornoz, resuming his character of gallant, despatched to the Signora Cesarini the following billet.

"Your commands are obeyed. Rienzi will receive an examination on his faith. It is well that he should be prepared. It may suit your purpose, as to which I am so faintly enlightened, to appear to the prisoner what you are—the obtainer of this grace. See how implicitly one noble heart can trust another! I send by the bearer an order that will admit one of your servitors to the prisoner's cell. Be it, if you will, your task to announce to him the new crisis of his fate. Ah! madam, may fortune be as favourable to me, and grant me the same intercessor—from thy lips my sentence is to come."

As Albornoz finished this epistle, he summoned his confidential attendant, a Spanish gentleman, who saw nothing in his noble birth that should prevent his fulfilling the various behests of the Cardinal.

"Alvarez," said he, "these to the Signora Cesarini by another hand; thou art unknown to her household. Repair to the state tower; this to the Governor admits thee. Mark who is admitted to the prisoner Cola di Rienzi. Know his name, examine whence he comes. Be keen, Alvarez. Learn by what motive the Cesarini interests herself in the prisoner's fate. All too of herself, birth, fortunes, lineage, would be welcome intelligence. Thou comprehendest me? It is well. One caution—thou hast no mission from, no connection with, me. Thou art an officer of the prison, or of the Pope,—what thou wilt. Give me the rosary; light the lamp before the crucifix; place yon hair-shirt beneath those arms. I would have it appear as if *meant* to be hidden! Tell Gomez that the Dominican preacher is to be admitted."

"Those friars have zeal," continued the Cardinal to himself, as, after executing his orders, Alvarez withdrew. "They would burn a man—but only on the Bible? They are worth conciliating, if the triple crown be really worth the winning; were it mine, I would add the eagle's plume to it."

And plunged into the aspiring future, this bold man forgot even the object of his passion. In real life, after a certain age, ambitious men love indeed; but it is only as an interlude. And indeed with most men, life has more absorbing though not more frequent concerns than those of love. Love is the business of the idle, but the idleness of the busy.

The Cesarini was alone when the Cardinal's messenger arrived, and he was scarcely dismissed with a few lines, expressive of a gratitude which seemed to bear down all those guards with which the coldness of the Signora usually fenced her pride, before the page Angelo was summoned to her presence.

The room was dark with the shades of the gathering night when the youth entered, and he discerned but dimly the outline of the Signora's stately form; but by the tone of her voice, he perceived that she was deeply agitated.

"Angelo," said she, as he approached, "Angelo—" and her voice failed her. She paused as for breath and again proceeded, "You alone have served us faithfully; you alone shared our escape, our wanderings, our exile—you alone know my secret—you of my train alone are Roman!—Roman! it was once a great name. Angelo, the name has fallen; but it is only because the nature of the Roman Race fell first. Haughty they are, but fickle; fierce, but dastard; vehement in promise, but rotten in their faith. You are a Roman, and though I have proved your truth, your very birth makes me afraid of falsehood."

"Madam," said the page, "I was but a child when you admitted me into your service, and I am yet only on the verge of manhood. But boy though I yet be, I would brave the stoutest lance of knight or freebooter, in defence of the faith of Angelo Villani, to his liege Lady and his native land."

" Alas! alas!" said the Signora, bitterly, " such have been the *words* of thousands of thy race. What have been their deeds? But I will trust thee, as I have trusted ever. I know that thou art covetous of honour, that thou hast youth's comely and bright ambition."

" I am an orphan and a bastard," said Angelo, bluntly! " And circumstance stings me sharply on to action; I would win my own name."

" Thou shalt," said the Signora. " We shall live yet to reward thee. And now be quick. Bring hither one of thy page's suits,—mantle and head-gear. Quick, I say, and whisper not to a soul what I have asked of thee."

CHAPTER V

THE INMATE OF THE TOWER

The night slowly advanced, and in the highest chamber of that dark and rugged tower which fronted the windows of the Cesarini's palace sate a solitary prisoner. A single lamp burned before him on a table of stone, and threw its rays over an open Bible; and those stern but fantastic legends of the prowess of ancient Rome, which the genius of Livy has dignified into history.* A chain hung pendant from the vault of the tower, and confined the captive; but so as to leave his limbs at sufficient liberty to measure at will the greater part of the cell. Green and damp were the mighty stones of the walls, and through a narrow aperture,

* " Avea libri assai, suo Tito Livio, sue storie di Roma, la Bibbia et altri libri assai, non finava di studiare."—*Vit. di Col. di Rienzi*, lib. ii. cap. 13. See translation to motto to Book VII., p. 419.

high out of reach, came the moonlight, and slept in long shadow over the rude floor. A bed at one corner completed the furniture of the room. Such for months had been the abode of the conqueror of the haughtiest Barons, and the luxurious dictator of the stateliest city of the world!

Care, and travel, and time, and adversity had wrought their change in the person of Rienzi. The proportions of his frame had enlarged from the compact strength of earlier manhood, the clear paleness of his cheek was bespread with a hectic and deceitful glow. Even in his present studies, intent as they seemed, and genial though the lecture to a mind enthusiastic even to fanaticism, his eyes could not rivet themselves as of yore steadily to the page. The charm was gone from the letters. Every now and then he moved restlessly, started, re-settled himself, and muttered broken exclamations like a man in an anxious dream. Anon, his gaze impatiently turned upward, about, around, and there was a strange and wandering fire in those large deep eyes, which might have thrilled the beholder with a vague and unaccountable awe.

Angelo had in the main correctly narrated the more recent adventures of Rienzi after his fall. He had first with Nina and Angelo betaken himself to Naples, and found a fallacious and brief favour with Louis, king of Hungary; that harsh but honourable monarch had refused to yield his illustrious guest to the demands of Clement, but had plainly declared his inability to shelter him in safety. Maintaining secret intercourse with his partisans at Rome, the fugitive then sought a refuge with the Eremites, sequestered in the lone recesses of the Monte Maiella, where in solitude and thought he had passed a whole year, save the time consumed in his visit to and return from Florence. Taking advantage of the Jubilee in Rome, he had then, disguised as a pilgrim, traversed the vales and mountains still rich in the melancholy ruins of ancient Rome, and entering the city, his restless and ambitious spirit indulged in new but vain conspiracies! * Excommunicated a second time by the Cardinal di Ceccano, and again a fugitive, he shook the dust from his feet as he left the city, and raising his hands towards those walls, in which are yet traced the witness of the Tarquins, cried aloud—"Honoured as thy prince—persecuted as thy victim—Rome, Rome, thou shalt yet receive me as thy conqueror!"

Still disguised as a pilgrim, he passed unmolested through Italy into the Court of the Emperor Charles of Bohemia, where the page, who had probably witnessed, had rightly narrated, his reception. It is doubtful, however, whether the conduct of the Emperor had been as chivalrous as appears by Angelo's relation, or whether he had not delivered Rienzi to the Pontiff's emissaries. At all events, it is certain, that from Prague to Avignon, the path of the fallen Tribune had been as one triumph. His strange adventures—his unbroken spirit—the new power that Intellect daily and wonderfully excited over the minds of the rising generation—the eloquence of Petrarch, and the common sympathy of the vulgar for fallen greatness,—all conspired to make Rienzi the hero of the age. Not a town through which he passed which would not have risked a siege for his protection—not a house that would not have sheltered him—not a hand that would not have struck in his defence. Refusing all offers of aid, disdaining all occasion of escape, inspired by

* Rainald, Ann. 1350, N. 4, E. 5.

his indomitable hope, and his unalloyed belief in the brightness of his own destinies, the Tribune sought Avignon—and found a dungeon!

These, his external adventures, are briefly and easily told; but who shall tell what passed within?—who narrate the fearful history of the heart?—who paint the rapid changes of emotion and of thought—the indignant grief—the stern dejection—the haughty disappointment that saddened while it never destroyed the resolve of that great soul? Who can say what must have been endured, what meditated, in the hermitage of Maiella;—on the lonely hills of the perished empire it had been his dream to restore;—in the Courts of Barbarian Kings;—and above all, on returning obscure and disguised, amidst the crowds of the Christian world, to the seat of his former power? What elements of memory, and in what a wild and fiery brain! What reflections to be conned in the dungeons of Avignon, by a man who had pushed into all the fervour of fanaticism—four passions, a single one of which has, in excess, sufficed to wreck the strongest reason—passions, which in themselves it is most difficult to combine,—the dreamer—the aspirant—the very nympholept of Freedom, yet of Power—of Knowledge, yet of Religion!

"Ay," muttered the prisoner, "ay, these texts are comforting—comforting. The righteous are not always oppressed." With a long sigh he deliberately put aside the Bible, kissed it with great reverence, remained silent, and musing for some minutes; and then as a slight noise was heard at one corner of the cell, said softly, "Ah, my friends, my comrades, the rats! it is their hour—I am glad I put aside the bread for them!" His eye brightened as it now detected those strange and unsocial animals venturing forth through a hole in the wall, and darkening the moonshine on the floor, steal fearlessly towards him. He flung some fragments of bread to them, and for some moments watched their gambols with a smile. "Manchino, the white-faced rascal! he beats all the rest—ha, ha! he is a superior wretch—he commands the tribe, and will venture the first into the trap. How will he bite against the steel, the fine fellow! while all the ignobler herd will gaze at him afar off, and quake and fear, and never help. Yet if united, they might gnaw the trap and release their leader! Ah, ye are base vermin, ye eat my bread, yet if death came upon me, ye would riot on my carcass. Away!" and clapping his hands, the chain round him clanked harshly, and the noisome co-mates of his dungeon vanished in an instant.

That singular and eccentric humour which marked Rienzi and which had seemed a buffoonery to the stolid sullenness of the Roman nobles, still retained its old expression in his countenance, and he laughed loud as he saw the vermin hurry back to their hiding-place.

"A little noise and the clank of a chain—fie, how ye imitate mankind!" Again he sank into silence, and then heavily and listlessly drawing towards him the animated tales of Livy, said, "An hour to mid-night!—waking dreams are better than sleep. Well, history tells us how men have risen—ay, and nations too—after sadder falls than that of Rienzi or of Rome!"

In a few minutes, he was apparently absorbed in the lecture; so intent indeed was he in the task, that he did not hear the steps which wound the spiral stairs that conducted to his cell. and it was not till the wards harshly grated beneath the huge key, and the door creaked on its hinges, that Rienzi, in amaze at intrusion at so unwonted an hour, lifted his eyes. The door had reclosed on the dungeon, and by the lonely and pale lamp he beheld a figure leaning, as for support, against the wall. The figure was wrapped from head to foot in the long cloak of the day, which, aided by a broad hat, shaded by plumes, concealed even the features of the visitor.

Rienzi gazed long and wistfully.

"Speak," he said at length, putting his hand to his brow. "Methinks either long solitude has bewildered me, or sweet sir, your apparition dazzles. I know you not—am I sure?—" and Rienzi's hair bristled while he slowly rose—"Am I sure that it is a living man who stands before me? Angels have entered the prison-house before now. Alas! an angel's comfort never was more needed."

The stranger answered not, but the captive saw that his heart heaved even beneath his cloak; loud sobs choked his voice; at length, as by a violent effort, he sprung forward, and sunk at the Tribune's feet. The disguising hat, the long mantle fell to the ground—it was the face of a woman that looked upward through passionate and glazing tears—the arms of a woman that clasped the prisoner's knees! Rienzi gazed mute and motionless as stone. "Powers and Saints of Heaven!" he murmured at last, "do ye tempt me further!—is it?—no, no—yet speak!"

"Beloved—adored!—do you not know me?"

"It is—it is!" shrieked Rienzi wildly, "it is my Nina—my wife—my——" His voice forsook him. Clasped in each other's arms, the unfortunates for some moments seemed to have lost even the sense of delight at their reunion. It was as an unconscious and deep trance, through which something *like* a dream only faintly and indistinctly stirs.

At length recovered—at length restored, the first broken exclamations, the first wild caresses of joy over—Nina lifted her head from her husband's bosom, and gazed sadly on his countenance—"Oh, what thou hast known since we parted!—what, since that hour when, borne on by thy bold heart and wild destiny, thou didst leave me in the Imperial Court, to seek again the diadem and find the chain! Ah! why did I heed thy commands?—why suffer thee to depart alone? How often in thy progress hitherward, in doubt, in danger, might this bosom have been thy resting-place, and this voice have whispered comfort to thy soul! Thou art well, my Lord—my Cola! Thy pulse beats quicker than of old—thy brow is furrowed. Ah! tell me thou art well!"

"Well," said Rienzi, mechanically. "Methinks so!—the mind diseased blunts all sense of bodily decay. Well—yes! And thou—thou, at least, art not changed, save to maturer beauty. The glory of the laurel-wreath has not faded from thy brow. Thou shalt yet—" then breaking off abruptly—"Rome—tell me of Rome! And thou—how camest thou hither? Ah! perhaps my doom is sealed, and in their mercy they have vouchsafed that I should see thee once more before the deathsman blinds me. I remember, it is the grace vouchsafed to malefactors. When *I* was a lord of life and death, I too permitted the meanest criminal to say farewell to those he loved."

"No—not so, Cola!" exclaimed Nina, putting her hand before his mouth. "I bring thee more auspicious tidings. To-morrow thou art to be heard. The favour of the Court is propitiated. Thou wilt be acquitted."

"Ha! speak again."

"Thou wilt be heard, my Cola—thou must be acquitted!"

"And Rome be free!—Great God, I thank Thee!"

The Tribune sank on his knees, and never had his heart, in his youngest and purest hour, poured forth thanksgiving more fervent, yet less selfish. When he rose again, the whole man seemed changed. His eye had resumed its earlier expressions of deep and serene command. Majesty sate upon his brow. The sorrows of the exile were forgotten. In his sanguine and rapid thoughts, he stood once more the guardian of his country,—and its sovereign!

Nina gazed upon him with that intense and devoted worship, which steeped her vainer and her harder qualities in all the fondness of the softest woman. "Such," thought she, "was his look eight years ago, when he left my maiden chamber, full of the mighty schemes which liberated Rome—such his look, when at the dawning sun he towered amidst the crouching Barons, and the kneeling population of the city he had made his throne!"

"Yes, Nina!" said Rienzi, as he turned and caught her eye. "My soul tells me that my hour is at hand. If they try me openly, they dare not convict—if they acquit me, they dare not but restore. To-morrow, saidst thou, to-morrow?"

"To-morrow, Rienzi; be prepared!"

"I am—for triumph! But tell me what happy chance brought thee to Avignon?"

"*Chance*, Cola!" said Nina, with reproachful tenderness. "Could I know that thou wert in the dungeons of the Pontiff, and linger in idle security at Prague? Even at the Emperor's Court thou hadst thy partisans and favourers. Gold was easily procured. I repaired to Florence—disguised my name—and came hither to plot, to scheme, to win thy liberty, or to die with thee. Ah! did not thy heart tell thee that morning and night the eyes of thy faithful Nina gazed upon this gloomy tower; and that one friend, humble though she be, never could forsake thee!"

"Sweet Nina! Yet—yet—at Avignon power yields not to beauty without reward. Remember, there is a worse death than the pause of life."

Nina turned pale. "Fear not," she said, with a low but determined voice; "fear not, that men's lips should say Rienzi's wife delivered him. None in this corrupted Court know that I am thy wife."

"Woman," said the Tribune, sternly; "thy lips elude the answer I would seek. In our degenerate time and land, thy sex and ours forget too basely what foulness writes a leprosy in the smallest stain upon a matron's honour. That thy heart would never wrong me, I believe; but if thy weakness, thy fear of my death should wrong me, thou art a bitterer foe to Rienzi than the swords of the Colonna. Nina, speak!"

"Oh, that my soul could speak," answered Nina. "Thy words are music to me, and not a thought of mine but echoes them. Could I touch this hand, could I meet that eye, and not know that death were dearer to thee than shame? Rienzi, when last we parted, in sadness, yet in hope, what were thy words to me?"

"I remember them well," returned the Tribune: "'I leave thee,' I said, 'to keep alive at the Emperor's Court, by thy genius, the Great Cause. Thou hast youth and beauty—and courts have lawless and ruffian suitors. I give thee no caution; it were beneath thee and me. But I leave thee the power of death.' And with that, Nina——"

"Thy hands tremblingly placed in mine this dagger. I live—need I say more?"

"My noble and beloved Nina, it is enough. Keep the dagger yet."

"Yes; till we meet in the Capitol of Rome!"

A slight tap was heard at the door; Nina regained, in an instant, her disguise.

"It is on the stroke of midnight," said the gaoler, appearing at the threshold.

"I come," said Nina.

"And thou hast to prepare thy thoughts," she whispered to Rienzi: "arm all thy glorious intellect. Alas! is it again we part? How my heart sinks!"

The presence of the gaoler at the threshold broke the bitterness of parting by abridging it. The false page pressed her lips on the prisoner's hand and left the cell.

The gaoler, lingering behind for a moment, placed a parchment on the table. It was the summons from the court appointed for the trial of the Tribune.

CHAPTER VI

THE SCENT DOES NOT LIE.—THE PRIEST AND THE SOLDIER

On descending the stairs, Nina was met by Alvarez.

"Fair page," said the Spaniard, gaily, "thy name, thou tellest me, is Villani?—Angelo Villani—why I know thy kinsman, methinks. Vouchsafe, young master, to enter this chamber, and drink a night-cup to thy lady's health; I would fain learn tidings of my old friends."

"At another time," answered the false Angelo, drawing the cloak closer round her face; "it is late—I am hurried."

"Nay," said the Spaniard, "you escape me not so easily;" and he caught firm hold of the page's shoulder.

"Unhand me, sir!" said Nina, haughtily, and almost weeping, for her strong nerves were yet unstrung. "Gaoler, at thy peril—unbar the gates."

"So hot," said Alvarez, surprised at so great a waste of dignity in a page; "nay, I meant not to offend thee. May I wait on thy pageship to-morrow?"

"Ay, to-morrow," said Nina, eager to escape.

"And meanwhile," said Alvarez, "I will accompany thee home—we can confer by the way."

So saying, without regarding the protestations of the supposed page, he passed with Nina into the open air. "Your lady," said he, carelessly, "is wondrous fair; her lightest will is law to the greatest noble of Avignon. Methinks she is of Naples—is it so? Art thou dumb, sweet youth?"

The page did not answer, but with a step so rapid that it almost put the slow Spaniard out of breath, hastened along the narrow space between the tower and the palace of the Signora Cesarini, nor could all the efforts of Alvarez draw forth a single syllable from his reluctant companion, till they reached the gates of the palace, and he found himself discourteously left without the walls.

"A plague on the boy!" said he, biting his lips;

"if the Cardinal thrive as well as his servant, by're Lady, Monsignor is a happy man!"

By no means pleased with the prospect of an interview with Albornoz, who, like most able men, valued the talents of those he employed exactly in proportion to their success, the Spaniard slowly returned home. With the licence accorded to him, he entered the Cardinal's chamber somewhat abruptly, and perceived him in earnest conversation with a Cavalier, whose long moustache, curled upward, and the bright cuirass worn underneath his mantle, seemed to betoken him of martial profession. Pleased with the respite, Alvarez hastily withdrew: and, in fact, the Cardinal's thoughts at that moment, and for that night, were bent upon other subjects than those of love.

The interruption served, however, to shorten the conversation between Albornoz and his guest. The latter rose.

"I think," said he, buckling on a short and broad rapier, which he laid aside during the interview,—"I think, my Lord Cardinal, you encourage me to consider that our negotiation stands a fair chance of a prosperous close. Ten thousand florins, and my brother quits Viterbo, and launches the thunderbolt of the Company on the lands of Rimini. On your part——"

"On my part it is agreed," said the Cardinal, "that the army of the Church interferes not with the course of your brother's arms—there is peace between us. One warrior understands another!"

"And the word of Giles d'Albornoz, son of the royal race of Aragon, is a guarantee for the faith of a Cardinal," replied the Cavalier, with a smile. "It is, my Lord, in your *former* quality that we treat."

"There is my right hand," answered Albornoz, too politic to heed the insinuation. The Cavalier raised it respectfully to his lips, and his armed tread was soon heard descending the stairs.

"Victory," cried Albornoz, tossing his arms aloof; "Victory, now thou art mine!"

With that he rose hastily, deposited his papers in an iron chest, and opening a concealed door behind the arras, entered a chamber that rather resembled a monk's cell than the apartment of a prince. Over a mean pallet hung a sword, a dagger, and a rude image of the Virgin. Without summoning Alvarez the Cardinal unrobed, and in a few moments was asleep.

CHAPTER VII

VAUCLUSE AND ITS GENIUS LOCI.—OLD ACQUAINTANCE RENEWED

The next day at early noon the Cavalier, whom our last chapter presented to the reader, was seen mounted on a strong Norman horse, winding his way slowly along a green and pleasant path some miles from Avignon. At length he found himself in a wild and romantic valley, through which wandered that delightful river whose name the verse of Petrarch has given to so beloved a fame. Sheltered by rocks, and in this part winding through the greenest banks, enamelled with a thousand wild flowers and water-reeds, went the crystal Sorgia. Advancing farther, the landscape assumed a more sombre and sterile aspect. The valley seemed enclosed or shut in by fantastic rocks of a thousand shapes, down which dashed and glittered a thousand rivulets. And, in the very wildest of the scene, the ground suddenly opened into a quaint and cultivated garden, through which, amidst a profusion of foliage was seen a small and lonely mansion,—the hermitage of the place. The horseman was in the valley of the Vaucluse and before his eye lay the garden and the house of PETRARCH! Carelessly, however, his eye scanned the consecrated spot; and unconsciously it rested for a moment, upon a solitary figure seated musingly by the margin of the river. A large dog at the side of the noonday idler barked at the horseman as he rode on. "A brave animal and a deep bay!" thought the traveller; to him the dog seemed an object much more interesting than its master. And so,—as the crowd of little men pass unheeding and unmoved those in whom Posterity shall acknowledge the landmarks of their age,—the horseman turned his glance from the Poet!

Thrice blessed name! Immortal Florentine!* not as the lover, nor even as the poet, do I bow before thy consecrated memory—venerating thee as one it were sacrilege to introduce in this unworthy page—save by name and as a shadow; but as the first who ever asserted to people and to prince the august majesty of Letters; who claimed to Genius the prerogative to influence states, to control opinion, to hold an empire over the hearts of men, and prepare events by animating passion, and guiding thought! What, (though but feebly felt and dimly seen)—what do we yet owe to Thee if Knowledge be now a Power; if MIND be a Prophet and a Fate, foretelling and foredooming the things to come! From the greatest to

*I need scarcely say that it is his origin, not his actual birth, which entitles us to term Petrarch a Florentine.

the least of us, to whom the pen is at once a sceptre and a sword, the low-born Florentine has been the arch-messenger to smooth the way and prepare the welcome. Yes! even the meanest of the aftercomers —even he who now vents his gratitude,—is thine everlasting debtor! Thine, how largely is the honour, if his labours, humble though they be, find an audience wherever literature is known; preaching in remotest lands the moral of forgotten revolutions, and scattering in the palace and the market-place the seeds that shall ripen into fruit when the hand of the sower shall be dust, and his very name, perhaps, be lost! For few, alas! are they whose *names* may outlive the grave; but the *thoughts* of every man who writes, are made undying;—others appropriate, advance, exalt them; and millions of minds unknown, undreamt of, are required to produce the immortality of one!

Indulging meditations very different from those which the idea of Petrarch awakens in a later time, the Cavalier pursued his path.

The valley was long left behind, and the way grew more and more faintly traced, until it terminated in a wood, through whose tangled boughs the sunlight broke playfully. At length, the wood opened into a wide glade, from which rose a precipitous ascent, crowned with the ruins of an old castle. The traveller dismounted, led his horse up the ascent, and, gaining the ruins, left his steed within one of the roofless chambers, overgrown with the longest grass and a profusion of wild shrubs; thence ascending, with some toil, a narrow and broken staircase, he found himself in a small room, less decayed than the rest, of which the roof and floor were yet whole.

Stretched on the ground in his cloak, and leaning

his head thoughtfully on his hand, was a man of tall stature and middle age. He lifted himself on his arm with great alacrity as the Cavalier entered.

"Well, Brettone, I have counted the hours—what tidings?"

"Albornoz consents."

"Glad news! Thou givest me new life. *Pardieu,* I shall breakfast all the better for this, my brother. Hast thou remembered that I am famishing?"

Brettone drew from beneath his cloak a sufficiently huge cask of wine, and a small panier, tolerably well filled; the inmate of the tower threw himself upon the provant with great devotion. And both the soldiers, for such they were, stretched at length on the ground, regaled themselves with considerable zest, talking hastily and familiarly between every mouthful.

"I say, Brettone, thou playest unfairly; thou hast already devoured more than half the pasty: push it hitherward. And so the Cardinal consents! What manner of man is he? Able as they say?"

"Quick, sharp, and earnest, with an eye of fire, few words, and comes to the point."

"Unlike a priest, then;—a good brigand spoilt. What hast thou heard of the force he heads? Ho, not so fast with the wine."

"Scanty at present.—He relies on recruits throughout Italy."

"What his designs for Rome? There, my brother, there tends my secret soul! As for these petty towns and petty tyrants, I care not how they fall, or by whom. But the Pope must not return to Rome. Rome must be mine. The city of a new empire, the conquest of a new Attila! There, every circumstance combines in my favour!—the absence of the Pope, the weakness of the middle class, the poverty of the populace, the imbecile though ferocious barbarism of the Barons, have long concurred to render Rome the most facile, while the most glorious conquest!"

"My brother, pray Heaven your ambition do not wreck you at last; you are ever losing sight of the land. Surely, with the immense wealth we are acquiring, we may——"

"Aspire to be something greater than Free Companions, generals to-day, and adventurers to-morrow. Rememberest thou, how the Norman sword won Sicily, and how the bastard William converted on the field of Hastings his baton into a sceptre. I tell thee, Brettone, that this loose Italy has crowns on the hedge that a dexterous hand may carry off at the point of the lance. My course is taken, I will form the fairest army in Italy, and with it I will win a throne in the Capitol. Fool that I was six years ago!—Instead of deputing that mad dolt Pepin of Minorbino, had I myself deserted the Hungarian, and repaired with my soldiery to Rome, the fall of Rienzi would have been followed by the rise of Montreal. Pepin was outwitted, and threw away the prey after he had hunted it down. The lion shall not again trust the chase to the jackal!"

"Walter, thou speakest of the fate of Rienzi, let it warn thee!"

"Rienzi!" replied Montreal; "I know the man! In peaceful times, or with an honest people, he would have founded a great dynasty. But he dreamt of laws and liberty for men who despise the first and will not protect the last. We, of a harder race, know that a new throne must be built by the feudal and not the civil system; and into the city we must transport the camp. It is by the multitude that the proud Tribune gained power,—by the multitude he lost it; it is by the sword that I will win it, and by the sword will I keep it!"

"Rienzi was too cruel, he should not have incensed the Barons," said Brettone, about to finish the flask, when the strong hand of his brother plucked it from him, and anticipated the design.

"Pooh," said Montreal, finishing the draught with a long sigh, "he was not cruel enough. He sought only to be just, and not to distinguish between noble and peasant. He should have distinguished! He should have exterminated the nobles root and branch. But this no Italian can do. This is reserved for me."

"Thou wouldst not butcher all the best blood of Rome?"

"Butcher! No, but I would seize their lands, and endow with them a new nobility, the hardy and fierce nobility of the North, who well know how to guard their prince, and *will* guard him, as the fountain of their own power. Enough of this now. And talking of Rienzi—rots he still in his dungeon?"

"Why, this morning, ere I left, I heard strange news. The town was astir, groups in every corner. They said that Rienzi's trial was to be to-day, and from the names of the judges chosen, it is suspected that acquittal is already determined on."

"Ha! thou shouldst have told me of this before."

"Should he be restored to Rome, would it militate against thy plans?"

"Humph! I know not—deep thought and dexterous management would be needed. I would fain not leave this spot till I hear what is decided on."

"Surely, Walter, it would have been wiser and safer

to have stayed with thy soldiery, and intrusted me with the absolute conduct of this affair."

"Not so," answered Montreal; "thou art a bold fellow enough, and a cunning ——, but my head in these matters is better than thine. Besides," continued the knight, lowering his voice, and shading his face, "I had vowed a pilgrimage to the beloved river, and the old trysting-place. Ah me!—— But all this, Brettone, thou understandest not—let it pass. As for my safety, since we have come to this amnesty with Albornoz, I fear but little danger even if discovered: besides, I want the florins. There are those in this country, Germans, who could eat an Italian army at a meal, whom I would fain engage, and their leaders want earnest-money—the griping knaves!—How are the Cardinal's florins to be paid?"

"Half now—half when thy troops are before Rimini!"

"Rimini! the thought whets my sword. Rememberest thou how that accursed Malatesta drove me from Aversa,* broke up my camp, and made me render to him all my booty? There fell the work of years! But for that, my banner now would be floating over St. Angelo. I will pay back the debt with fire and sword, ere the summer has shed its leaves."

The fair countenance of Montreal grew terrible as he uttered these words; his hands griped the handle of his sword, and his strong frame heaved visibly; tokens of the fierce and unsparing passions, by the

*This Malatesta, a signior of illustrious family, was one of the most skilful warriors in Italy. He and his brother Galeotto had been raised to the joint-tyranny of Rimini by the voice of its citizens. After being long the foes of the Church, they were ultimately named as its captains by the Cardinal Albornoz.

aid of which a life of rapine and revenge had corrupted a nature originally full no less of the mercy than the courage of Provençal chivalry.

Such was the fearful man who now (the wildness of his youth sobered, and his ambition hardened and concentered) was the rival with Rienzi for the mastery of Rome.

CHAPTER VIII

THE CROWD.—THE TRIAL.—THE VERDICT.—THE SOLDIER AND THE PAGE

It was on the following evening that a considerable crowd had gathered in the streets of Avignon. It was the second day of the examination of Rienzi, and with every moment was expected the announcement of the verdict. Amongst the foreigners of all countries assembled in that seat of the Papal splendour, the interest was intense. The Italians, even of the highest rank, were in favour of the Tribune, the French against him. As for the good townspeople of Avignon themselves, they felt but little excitement in anything that did not bring money into their pockets; and if it had been put to the secret vote, no doubt there would have been a vast majority for burning the prisoner, as a marketable speculation!

Amongst the crowd was a tall man in a plain and rusty suit of armour, but with an air of knightly bearing, which somewhat belied the coarseness of his mail; he wore no helmet, but a small morion of black leather, with a long projecting shade, much used by wayfarers in the hot climates of the south. A black patch covered nearly the whole of one cheek, and altogether he bore the appearance of a grim soldier, with whom war had dealt harshly, both in purse and person.

Many were the jests at the shabby swordsman's expense, with which that lively population amused their impatience; and though the shade of the morion concealed his eyes, an arch and merry smile about the corners of his mouth showed that he could take a jest at himself.

"Well," said one of the crowd (a rich Milanese), "I am of a state that *was* free, and I trust the People's man will have justice shown him."

"Amen," said a grave Florentine.

"They say," whispered a young student from Paris, to a learned doctor of laws, with whom he abode, "that his defence has been a masterpiece."

"He hath taken no degrees," replied the doctor, doubtingly. "Ho, friend, why dost thou push me so? thou hast rent my robe."

This was said to a minstrel, or jongleur, who, with a small lute slung round him, was making his way, with great earnestness, through the throng.

"I beg pardon, worthy sir," said the minstrel; "but this is a scene to be sung of! Centuries hence—ay, and in lands remote—legend and song will tell the fortunes of Cola di Rienzi, the friend of Petrarch and the Tribune of Rome!"

The young French student turned quickly round to the minstrel, with a glow on his pale face; not sharing the general sentiments of his countrymen against Rienzi, he felt that it was an era in the world when a minstrel spoke thus of the heroes of intellect—not of war.

At this time the tall soldier was tapped impatiently on the back.

"I pray thee, great sir," said a sharp and imperious voice, "to withdraw that tall bulk of thine a little on one side—I cannot see through thee; and I would fain my eyes were among the first to catch a glimpse of Rienzi as he passes from the court."

"Fair Sir page," replied the soldier, good-humouredly, as he made way for Angelo Villani, "thou wilt not always find that way in the world is won by commanding the strong. When thou art older thou wilt beard the weak, and the strong thou wilt wheedle."

"I must change my nature, then," answered Angelo (who was of somewhat small stature, and not yet come to his full growth), trying still to raise himself above the heads of the crowd.

The soldier looked at him approvingly; and as he looked he sighed, and his lips worked with some strange emotion.

"Thou speakest well," said he, after a pause. "Pardon me the rudeness of the question; but art thou of Italy?—thy tongue savours of the Roman dialect; yet I have seen lineaments like thine on this side the Alps."

"It may be, good fellow," said the page haughtily; "but I thank Heaven that I am of Rome."

At this moment a loud shout burst from that part of the crowd nearest the court. The sound of trumpets again hushed the throng into deep and breathless silence, while the Pope's guards, ranged along the space conducting from the court, drew themselves up more erect, and fell a step or two back upon the crowd.

As the trumpets ceased, the voice of a herald was heard, but it did not penetrate within several yards of the spot where Angelo and the soldier stood; and it was only by a mighty shout that in a moment circled through, and was echoed back by, the wide multitude—by the waving of kerchiefs from the windows—by broken ejaculations, which were caught up from lip to lip, that the page knew that Rienzi was acquitted.

"I would I could see his face!" sighed the page, querulously.

"And thou shalt," said the soldier; and he caught up the boy in his arms, and pressed on with the strength of a giant, parting the living stream from right to left, as he took his way to a place near the guards, and by which Rienzi was sure to pass.

The page, half-pleased, half-indignant, struggled a little, but finding it in vain, consented tacitly to what he felt an outrage on his dignity.

"Never mind," said the soldier, "thou art the first I ever willingly raised above myself; and I do it now for the sake of thy fair face, which reminds me of one I loved."

But these last words were spoken low, and the boy, in his anxiety to see the hero of Rome, did not hear or heed them. Presently Rienzi came by; two gentlemen, of the Pope's own following, walked by his side. He moved slowly, amidst the greetings and clamour of the crowd, looking neither to the right nor left. His bearing was firm and collected, and, save by the flush of his cheek, there was no external sign of joy or excitement. Flowers dropped from every balcony on his path: and just when he came to a broader space, where the ground was somewhat higher, and where he was in fuller view of the houses around, he paused—and, uncovering, acknowledged the homage he had received, with a look—a gesture—which each who beheld never forgot. It haunted even that gay and thoughtless court, when the last tale of Rienzi's life reached their ears. And Angelo, clinging then round that soldier's neck, recalled—but we must not anticipate.

It was not, however, to the dark tower that Rienzi returned. His home was prepared at the palace of the Cardinal d'Albornoz. The next day he was admitted to the Pope's presence, and on the evening of that day he was proclaimed Senator of Rome.

Meanwhile the soldier had placed Angelo on the ground; and as the page faltered out no courteous thanks, he interrupted him in a sad and kind voice, the tone of which struck the page forcibly, so little did it suit the rough and homely appearance of the man.

"We part," he said, "as strangers, fair boy; and since thou sayest thou art of Rome, there is no reason why my heart should have warmed to thee as it has done; yet if ever thou wantest a friend,—seek him" —and the soldier's voice sunk into a whisper—"in Walter de Montreal."

Ere the page recovered his surprise at that redoubted name, which his earliest childhood had been taught to dread, the Knight of St. John had vanished amongst the crowd.

CHAPTER IX

ALBORNOZ AND NINA

But the eyes which, above all others, thirsted for a glimpse of the released captive were forbidden that delight. Alone in her chamber, Nina awaited the result of the trial. She heard the shouts, the exclamations, the tramp of thousands along the street; she felt that the victory was won; and, her heart long overcharged, she burst into passionate tears. The return of Angelo soon acquainted her with all that had passed; but it somewhat chilled her joy to find Rienzi was the guest of the dreaded Cardinal. That shock, in which certainty, however happy, replaces suspense, had so powerful an effect on her frame, joined to her loathing fear of a visit from the Cardinal, that she became for three days alarmingly ill; and it was only on the fifth day from that which saw Rienzi endowed with the rank of Senator of Rome, that she was recovered sufficiently to admit Albornoz to her presence.

The Cardinal had sent daily to inquire after her health, and his inquiries, to her alarmed mind, had appeared to insinuate a pretension to the right to make them. Meanwhile Albornoz had had enough to divert and occupy his thoughts. Having bought off the formidable Montreal from the service of John de Vico, one of the ablest and fiercest enemies of the Church, he resolved to march to the territories of that tyrant as expeditiously as possible, and so not to allow him time to obtain the assistance of any other band of the mercenary adventurers, who found Italy the market for their valour. Occupied with raising troops, procuring money, corresponding with the various free states, and establishing alliances in aid of his ulterior and more ambitious projects at the court of Avignon, the Cardinal waited with tolerable resignation the time when he might claim from the Signora Cesarini the reward to which he deemed himself entitled. Meanwhile he had held his first conversations with Rienzi, and, under the semblance of courtesy to the acquitted

Tribune, Albornoz had received him as his guest, in order to make himself master of the character and disposition of one in whom he sought a minister and a tool. That miraculous and magic art, attested by the historians of the time, which Rienzi possessed over every one with whom he came into contact, however various in temper, station, or opinions, had not deserted him in his interview with the Pontiff. So faithfully had he described the true condition of Rome, so logically had he traced the causes and the remedies of the evils she endured, so sanguinely had he spoken of his own capacities for administering her affairs, and so brilliantly had he painted the prospects which that administration opened to the weal of the Church, and the interests of the Pope, that Innocent, though a keen and shrewd, and somewhat sceptical calculator of human chances, was entirely fascinated by the eloquence of the Roman.

" Is this the man," he is reported to have said, " whom for twelve months we have treated as a prisoner and a criminal? Would that it were on his shoulders only that the Christian empire reposed! "

At the close of the interview he had, with every mark of favour and distinction, conferred upon Rienzi the rank of Senator, which, in fact, was that of Viceroy of Rome, and had willingly acceded to all the projects which the enterprising Rienzi had once more formed —not only for recovering the territories of the Church, but for extending the dictatorial sway of the Seven-hilled City, over the old dependencies of Italy.

Albornoz, to whom the Pope retailed this conversation, was somewhat jealous of the favour the new Senator had so suddenly acquired, and immediately on his return home sought an interview with his guest. In his heart, the Lord Cardinal, emphatically a man of action and business, regarded Rienzi as one rather cunning than wise—rather fortunate than great—a mixture of the pedant and the demagogue. But after a long and scrutinising conversation with the new Senator, even he yielded to the spell of his enchanting and master intellect. Reluctantly Albornoz confessed to himself that Rienzi's rise was not the thing of chance; yet more reluctantly he perceived that the Senator was one whom he might treat with as an equal, but could not rule as a minion. And he entertained serious doubts whether it would be wise to reinstate him in a power which he evinced the capacity to wield and the genius to extend. Still, however, he did not repent the share he had taken in Rienzi's acquittal. His presence in a camp so thinly peopled was a matter greatly to be desired. And through his influence, the Cardinal more than ever trusted to enlist the Romans in favour of his enterprise for the recovery of the territory of St. Peter!

Rienzi, who panted once more to behold his Nina, endeared to him by trial and absence, as by fresh bridals, was not however able to discover the name she had assumed at Avignon; and his residence with the Cardinal closely but respectfully watched as he was, forbade Nina all opportunity of corresponding with him. Some half bantering hints which Albornoz had dropped upon the interest taken in his welfare by the most celebrated beauty of Avignon, had filled him with a vague alarm which he trembled to acknowledge even to himself. But the *volto sciolto** which, in common with all Italian politicians, concealed whatever

* *Volto sciolto, pensieri stretti*—the countenance open, the thoughts restrained.

were his *pensieri stretti*—enabled him to baffle completely the jealous and lynxlike observation of the Cardinal. Nor had Alvarez been better enabled to satisfy the curiosity of his master. He had indeed sought the page Villani, but the imperious manner of that wayward and haughty boy had cut short all attempts at cross-examination. And all he could ascertain was, that the real Angelo Villani was not the Angelo Villani who had visited Rienzi.

Trusting at last that he should learn all, and inflamed by such passion and such hope as he was capable of feeling, Albornoz, now took his way to the Cesarini's palace.

He was ushered with due state into the apartment of the Signora. He found her pale, and with the traces of illness upon her noble and statue-like features. She rose as he entered; and when he approached, she half bent her knee, and raised his hand to her lips. Surprised and delighted at a reception so new, the Cardinal hastened to prevent the condescension; retaining both her hands, he attempted gently to draw them to his heart.

"Fairest!" he whispered, "couldst thou know how I have mourned thy illness—and yet it has but left thee more lovely, as the rain only brightens the flower. Ah! happy if I have promoted thy lightest wish, and if in thine eyes I may henceforth seek at once an angel to guide me and a paradise to reward."

Nina, releasing her hand, waved it gently, and motioned the Cardinal to a seat. Seating herself at a little distance, she then spoke with great gravity and downcast eyes.

"My Lord, it is your intercession, joined to his own innocence, that has released from yonder tower the elected governor of the people of Rome. But freedom is the least of the generous gifts that you have conferred; there is a greater in a fair name vindicated, and rightful honours re-bestowed. For this, I rest ever your debtor; for this, if I bear children, they shall be taught to bless your name; for this the historian who recalls the deeds of this age, and the fortunes of Cola di Rienzi, shall add a new chaplet to the wreaths you have already won. Lord Cardinal, I may have erred. I may have offended you—you may accuse me of woman's artifice. Speak not, wonder not, hear me out. I have but one excuse, when I say that I held justified any means short of dishonour, to save the life and restore the fortunes of Cola di Rienzi. Know, my Lord, that she who now addresses you is his wife."

The Cardinal remained motionless and silent. But his sallow countenance grew flushed from the brow to the neck, and his thin lips quivered for a moment, and then broke into a withering and bitter smile. At length he rose from his seat, very slowly, and said, in a voice trembling with passion,

"It is well, madam. Giles d'Albornoz has been, then, a puppet in the hands, a stepping-stone in the rise, of the plebeian demagogue of Rome. You but played upon me for your own purposes; and nothing short of a Cardinal of Spain, and a Prince of the royal blood of Aragon, was meet to be the instrument of a mountebank's juggle! Madam, yourself and your husband might justly be accused of ambition——"

"Cease, my Lord," said Nina, with unspeakable dignity; "whatever offence has been committed against you was mine alone. Till after our last interview, Rienzi knew not even of my presence at Avignon."

"I have fulfilled my part—I claim yours."

"At our last interview, Lady, (you do well to recall it!) methinks there was a hinted and implied contract. I have fulfilled my part—I claim yours. Mark me! I do not forego that claim. As easily as I rend this glove can I rend the parchment which proclaims thy husband 'the Senator of Rome.' The dungeon is not death, and its door will open *twice*."

"My Lord—my Lord!" cried Nina, sick with terror, "wrong not so your noble nature, your great name, your sacred rank, your chivalric blood. You are of the knightly race of Spain, yours not the sullen, low, and inexorable vices that stain the petty tyrants of this unhappy land. You are no Visconti—no Castracani—you cannot stain your laurels with revenge upon a woman. Hear me," she continued, and she fell abruptly at his feet; "men dupe, deceive our sex—and for selfish purposes; they are pardoned—even by their victims. Did *I* deceive you with a false hope? Well—what my object?—what my excuse? My husband's liberty—my land's salvation! Woman,—my Lord, alas, your sex too rarely understand her weakness or her greatness! Erring—all human as she is to others—God gifts her with a thousand virtues to the one she loves! It is from that love that she alone drinks her nobler nature. For the hero of her worship she has the meekness of the dove—the devotion of the saint; for his safety in peril, for his rescue in misfortune, her vain sense imbibes the sagacity of the serpent—her weak heart, the courage of the lioness! It is this which, in absence, made me mask my face in smiles, that the friends of the houseless exile might not despair of his fate—it is this which brought me through forests beset with robbers, to watch the stars upon yon solitary tower—it was this which led my steps to the revels of your hated court—this which made me seek a deliverer in the noblest of its chiefs—it is this which has at last opened the dungeon door to the prisoner now within your halls; and this, Lord Cardinal," added Nina, rising, and folding her arms upon her heart—"this, if your anger seeks a victim, will inspire me to die without a groan,—but without dishonour!"

Albornoz remained rooted to the ground. Amazement—emotion—admiration—all busy at his heart. He gazed at Nina's flashing eyes and heaving bosom as a warrior of old upon a prophetess inspired. His eyes were riveted to hers as by a spell. He tried to speak, but his voice failed him. Nina continued:

"Yes, my Lord; these are no idle words! If you seek revenge, it is in your power. Undo what you have done. Give Rienzi back to the dungeon, or to disgrace, and you are avenged; but not on *him*. All the hearts of Italy shall become to him a second Nina! I am the guilty one, and I the sufferer. Hear me swear—in that instant which sees new wrong to Rienzi, this hand is my executioner.—My Lord, I supplicate you no longer!"

Albornoz continued deeply moved. Nina but rightly judged him, when she distinguished the aspiring Spaniard from the barbarous and unrelenting voluptuaries of Italy. Despite the profligacy that stained his sacred robe—despite all the acquired and increasing callousness of a hard, scheming, and sceptical man, cast amidst the worst natures of the worst of times—there lingered yet in his soul much of the knightly honour of his race and country. High thoughts and daring spirits touched a congenial string in his heart, and not the less, in that he had but rarely met them in his experience of camps and courts. For the first time in his life, he felt that he had seen the woman who could have contented him even with wedlock, and taught him the proud and faithful love of which the minstrels of Spain had sung. He sighed, and still gazing on Nina, approached her, almost reverentially; he knelt and kissed the hem of her robe. "Lady," he said, "I would I could believe that you have altogether read my nature aright, but I were indeed lost to all honour, and unworthy of gentle birth, if I still harboured a single thought against the peace and virtue of one like thee. Sweet heroine,"—he continued —"so lovely, yet so pure—so haughty, and yet so soft—thou hast opened to me the brightest page these eyes have ever scanned in the blotted volume of mankind. Mayest thou have such happiness as life can give; but souls such as thine make their nest like the eagle, upon rocks and amidst the storms. Fear me no more—think of me no more—unless hereafter, when thou hearest men speak of Giles d'Albornoz, thou mayest say in thine own heart,"—and here the Cardinal's lip curled with scorn—"he did not renounce every feeling worthy of a man, when Ambition and Fate endued him with the surplice of the priest."

The Spaniard was gone before Nina could reply.

BOOK VIII

THE GRAND COMPANY

" Montreal nourrissoit de plus vastes projets . . . . il donnoit à sa campagnie un gouvernement régulier. . . . . Par cette discipline il faisoit régner l'abondance dans son camp: les gens de guerre ne parloient, en Italie, que des richesses qu'on acquéroit à son service."—SISMONDI, *Hist. des Républiques Italiennes,* tom. vi. c. 42.

" Montreal cherished more vast designs . . . he subjected his company to a regular system of government. . . . . By means of this discipline he kept his camp abundantly supplied, and military adventurers in Italy talked of nothing but the wealth won in his service."—SISMONDI'S *Hist. of Ital. Republics.*

CHAPTER I

THE ENCAMPMENT

It was a most lovely day, in the very glow and meridian of an Italian summer, when a small band of horsemen were seen winding a hill which commanded one of the fairest landscapes of Tuscany. At their head was a Cavalier in a complete suit of chain armour, the links of which were so fine, that they resembled a delicate and curious network, but so strongly compacted, that they would have resisted spear or sword no less effectually than the heaviest corselet, while adapting themselves exactly and with ease to every movement of the light and graceful shape of the rider. He wore a hat of dark green velvet shaded by long plumes, while of two squires behind, the one bore his helmet and lance, the other led a strong war-horse, completely cased in plates of mail, which seemed, however, scarcely to encumber its proud and agile paces. The countenance of the Cavalier was comely, but strongly marked, and darkened, by long exposure to the suns of many climes, to a deep bronze hue: a few raven ringlets escaped from beneath his hat down a cheek closely shaven. The expression of his features was grave and composed even to sadness; nor could all the loveliness of the unrivalled scene before him dispel the quiet and settled melancholy of his eyes. Besides the squire, ten horsemen, armed cap-à-pié, attended the knight; and the low and murmured conversation they carried on at intervals, as well as their long fair hair, large stature, thick short beards, and the studied and accurate equipment of their arms and steeds, bespoke them of a hardier and more warlike race than the children of the south. The cavalcade was closed with a man almost of gigantic height, bearing a banner richly decorated, wherein was wrought a column, with the inscription, "ALONE AMIDST RUINS." Fair indeed was the prospect which with every step expanded yet more widely its various beauty. Right before stretched a long vale, now covered with green woodlands glittering in the yellow sunlight, now opening into narrow plains bordered by hillocks, from whose mosses of all hues grew fantastic and odorous shrubs; while, winding amidst them, a broad and silver stream broke into light at frequent intervals, snatched by wood and hillock from the eye, only to steal upon it again, in sudden and bright surprise. The opposite slope of gentle mountains, as well as that which the horsemen now descended, was covered with vineyards, trained in alleys and arcades: and the clustering grape laughed from every leafy and glossy covert, as gaily as when the Fauns held a holy-day in the shade. The eye of the Cavalier roved listlessly over this enchanting prospect, sleeping in the rosiest light of a Tuscan heaven, and then became fixed with a more earnest attention on the gray and frowning walls of a distant castle, which, high upon the steepest of the opposite mountains, overlooked the valley.

"Behold," he muttered to himself, "how every Eden in Italy hath its curse! Wherever the land smiles fairest, be sure to find the brigand's tent and the tyrant's castle!"

Scarce had these thoughts passed his mind, ere the shrill and sudden blast of a bugle that sounded close amongst the vineyards by the side of the path, startled the whole group. The cavalcade halted abruptly. The leader made a gesture to the squire who led his war-horse. The noble and practised animal remained perfectly still, save by champing its bit restlessly, and moving its quick ear to and fro, as aware of a coming danger,—while the squire, unencumbered by the heavy armour of the Germans, plunged into the thicket and disappeared. He returned in a few minutes, already heated and breathless.

"We must be on our guard," he whispered; "I see the glimmer of steel through the vine leaves."

"Our ground is unhappily chosen," said the Knight, hastily bracing on his helmet and leaping on his charger; and waving his hand towards a broader space in the road, which would permit the horsemen more room to act in union, with his small band he made hastily to the spot—the armour of the soldiers rattling heavily as two by two they proceeded on.

The space to which the Cavalier had pointed was a green semicircle of several yards in extent, backed by tangled copses of brushwood sloping down to the vale below. They reached it in safety; they drew up breast to breast in the form of a crescent: every visor closed save that of the Knight, who looked anxiously and keenly round the landscape.

"Hast thou heard, Giulio," he said, to his favourite squire, (the only Italian of the band,) "whether any brigands have been seen lately in these parts?"

"No, my Lord; on the contrary, I am told that every lance hath left the country to join the Grand Company of Fra Moreale. The love of his pay and plunder has drawn away the mercenaries of every Tuscan Signor."

As he ceased speaking, the bugle sounded again from nearly the same spot as before; it was answered by a brief and martial note from the very rear of the horsemen. At the same moment, from the thickets behind, broke the gleam of mail and spears. One after another, rank after rank, from the copse behind them, emerged men-at-arms, while suddenly, from the vines in front, still greater numbers poured forth with loud and fierce shouts.

"For God, for the Emperor, and for the Colonna!" cried the Knight, closing his visor; and the little band, closely serried, the lance in every rest, broke upon the rush of the enemy in front. A score or so, borne to the ground by the charge, cleared a path for the horsemen, and, without waiting the assault of the rest, the Knight wheeled his charger and led the way down the hill, almost at full gallop, despite the roughness of the descent: a flight of arrows despatched after them fell idly on their iron mail.

"If they have no horse," cried the Knight, "we are saved!"

And, indeed, the enemy seemed scarcely to think of pursuing them; but (gathered on the brow of a hill) appeared contented to watch their flight.

Suddenly a curve in the road brought them before a broad and white patch of waste land, which formed almost a level surface, interrupting the descent of the mountain. On the commencement of this waste, drawn up in still array, the sunlight broke on the breastplates of a long line of horsemen, whom the sinuosities of the road had hitherto concealed from the Knight and his party.

The little troop halted abruptly—retreat—advance alike cut off; gazing first at the foe before them, that remained still as a cloud, every eye was then turned towards the Knight.

"An thou wouldst, my Lord," said the leader of the Northmen, perceiving the irresolution of their chief, "we will fight to the last. You are the only Italian I ever knew whom I would willingly die for!"

This rude profession was received with a sympathetic murmur from the rest, and the soldiers drew closer around the Knight. "Nay, my brave fellows," said the Colonna, lifting his visor, "it is not in so inglorious a field, after such various fortunes, that we are doomed to perish. If these be brigands, as we must suppose, we can yet purchase our way. If the troops of some signor, we are strangers to the feud in which he is engaged. Give me yon banner—I will ride on to them."

"Nay, my Lord," said Giulio; "such marauders do not always spare a flag of truce. There is danger——"

"For that reason your leader braves it. Quick!"

The Knight took the banner, and rode deliberately up to the horsemen. On approaching, his warlike eye could not but admire the perfect caparison of their arms, the strength and beauty of their steeds, and the steady discipline of their long and glittering line.

As he rode up, and his gorgeous banner gleamed in the moonlight, the soldiers saluted him. It was a good omen, and he hailed it as such. "Fair sirs," said the Knight, "I come, at once herald and leader of the little band who have just escaped the unlooked-for assault of armed men on yonder hill—and, claiming aid, as knight from knight, and soldier from soldier, I place my troop under the protection of your leader. Suffer me to see him."

"Sir Knight," answered one, who seemed the captain of the band, "sorry am I to detain one of your gallant bearing, and still more so, on recognising the device of one of the most potent houses of Italy. But our orders are strict, and we must bring all armed men to the camp of our General."

"Long absent from my native land, I knew not," replied the Knight, "that there was war in Tuscany. Permit me to crave the name of the General whom you speak of, and that of the foe against whom ye march."

The Captain smiled slightly.

"Walter de Montreal is the General of the Grand Company, and Florence his present foe."

"We have fallen, then, into friendly, if fierce, hands," replied the Knight, after a moment's pause.

"To Sir Walter de Montreal I am known of old. Permit me to return to my companions, and acquaint them that if accident has made us prisoners, it is, at least, only to the most skilful warrior of his day that we are condemned to yield."

The Italian then turned his horse to join his comrades.

"A fair knight and a bold presence," said the Captain of the Companions to his neighbour, "though I scarce think it is the party we are ordered to intercept. Praised be the Virgin, however, his men seem from the North. Them, perhaps, we may hope to enlist."

The Knight now, with his comrades, rejoined the troop. And, on receiving their parole not to attempt escape, a detachment of thirty horsemen were despatched to conduct the prisoners to the encampment of the Grand Company.

Turning from the main road, the Knight found himself conducted into a narrow defile between the hills, which, succeeded by a gloomy track of wild forest-land, brought the party at length into a full and abrupt view of a wide plain, covered with the tents of what, for Italian warfare, was considered a mighty army. A stream, over which rude and hasty bridges had been formed from the neighbouring timber, alone separated the horsemen from the encampment.

"A noble sight!" said the captive Cavalier, with enthusiasm, as he reined in his steed, and gazed upon the wild and warlike streets of canvas, traversing each other in vistas broad and regular.

One of the captains of the Grand Company who rode beside him, smiled complacently.

"There are few masters of the martial art who equal

Fra Moreale," said he; "and savage, reckless, and gathered from all parts and all countries—from cavern and from market-place, from prison and from palace, as are his troops, he has reduced them already into a discipline which might shame even the soldiery of the Empire."

The Knight made no reply; but, spurring his horse over one of the rugged bridges, soon found himself amidst the encampment. But that part at which he entered, little merited the praises bestowed upon the discipline of the army. A more unruly and disorderly array, the Cavalier, accustomed to the stern regularity of English, French, and German discipline, thought he had never beheld: here and there, fierce, unshaven, half-naked brigands might be seen, driving before them the cattle which they had just collected by predatory excursions. Sometimes a knot of dissolute women stood—chattering, scolding, gesticulating—collected round groups of wild shagged Northmen, who, despite the bright purity of the summer-noon, were already engaged in deep potations. Oaths and laughter, and drunken merriment, and fierce brawl, rang from side to side; and ever and anon some hasty conflict with drawn knives was begun and finished by the fiery and savage bravoes of Calabria or the Apennines, before the very eyes and almost in the very path of the troop. Tumblers, and mountebanks, and jugglers, and Jew pedlers, were exhibiting their tricks or their wares at every interval, apparently well inured to the lawless and turbulent market in which they exercised their several callings. Despite the protection of the horsemen who accompanied them, the prisoners were not allowed to pass without molestation. Groups of urchins, squalid, fierce, and ragged, seemed to start from the ground, and surrounded their horses like swarms of bees, uttering the most discordant cries; and, with the gestures of savages, rather demanding than beseeching money, which, when granted, seemed only to render them more insatiable. While, sometimes mingled with the rest, were seen the bright eyes and olive cheek, and half-pleading, half-laughing smile of girls, whose extreme youth, scarce emerged from childhood, rendered doubly striking their utter and unredeemed abandonment.

"You did not exaggerate the decorum of the Grand Company!" cried the Knight, gravely, to his new acquaintance.

"Signor," replied the other, "you must not judge of the kernel by the shell. We are scarcely yet arrived at the camp. These are the outskirts, occupied rather by the rabble than the soldiers. Twenty thousand men from the sink, it must be owned, of every town in Italy, follow the camp, to fight if necessary, but rather for plunder, and for forage:—such you now behold. Presently, you will see those of another stamp."

The Knight's heart swelled high. "And to such men is Italy given up!" thought he. His reverie was broken by a loud burst of applause from some convivialists hard by. He turned, and under a long tent, and round a board covered with wine and viands, sate some thirty or forty bravoes. A ragged minstrel, or jongleur, with an immense beard and mustachios, was tuning, with no inconsiderable skill, a lute which had accompanied him in all his wanderings—and suddenly changing its notes into a wild and warlike melody, he commenced in a loud and deep voice the following song:—

THE PRAISE OF THE GRAND COMPANY

1

Ho, dark one from the golden South,—
  Ho, fair one from the North;
Ho, coat of mail and spear of sheen—
  Ho, wherefore ride ye forth?
"We come from mount, we come from cave,
  We come across the sea,
In long array, in bright array,
  To Montreal's Companiè."
    Oh, the merry, merry band,
    Light heart, and heavy hand—
      Oh, the Lances of the Free!

2

Ho, Princes of the castled height—
  Ho, burghers of the town;
Apulia's strength, Romagna's pride,
  And Tusca's old renown!
Why quail ye thus? why pale ye thus?
  What spectre do ye see?
"The blood-red flag, and trampling march
  Of Montreal's Companiè."
    Oh, the sunshine of your life—
    Oh, the thunders of your strife!
      Wild Lances of the Free!

3

Ho, scutcheons o'er the vaulted tomb
  Where Norman valour sleeps,
Why shake ye so? why quake ye so?
  What wind the trophy sweeps?
"We shake without a breath—below,
  The dead are stirred to see,
The Norman's fame revived again
  In Montreal's Companiè."
    Since Roger won his crown,
    Who hath equalled your renown,
      Brave Lances of the Free?

4

Ho, ye who seek to win a name,
  Where deeds are bravest done—
Ho, ye who wish to pile a heap,
  Where gold is lightest won;
Ho, ye who loathe the stagnant life,
  Or shun the law's decree,
Belt on the brand, and spur the steed,
  To Montreal's Companiè.
    And the maid shall share her rest,
    And the miser share his chest,
      With the Lances of the Free!
        The Free!
        The Free!
    Oh! the Lances of the Free!

Then suddenly, as if inspired to a wilder flight by his own minstrelsy, the jongleur, sweeping his hand over the chords, broke forth into an air admirably expressive of the picture which his words, running into a rude, but lively and stirring doggerel, attempted to paint.

THE MARCH OF THE GRAND COMPANY

Tirà, tiralà—trumpet and drum—
Rising bright o'er the height of the mountain they come!
German, and Hun, and the Islandrie,
Who routed the Frenchman at famed Cressiè,
When the rose changed its hue with the *fleur-de-lis;*
With the Roman, and Lombard, and Piedmontese,
And the dark-haired son of the southern seas.
Tirà, tiralà—more near and near
Down the steep—see them sweep;—rank by rank they appear!
With the Cloud of the Crowd hanging dark at their rear—
Serried, and steadied, and orderliè,
Like the course—like the force—of a marching sea!
Open your gates and out with your gold,
For the blood must be spilt, or the ransom be told!

Woe, Burghers, woe! Behold them led
By the stoutest arm and the wisest head,
With the snow-white cross on the cloth of red;—
With the eagle eye, and the lion port,
His barb for a throne, and his camp for a court:
Sovereign and scourge of the land is he—
The kingly Knight of the Companiè!
    Hurrah—hurrah—hurrah!
Hurrah for the army—hurrah for its lord—
Hurrah for the gold that is got by the sword—
    Hurrah—hurrah—hurrah!
        For the Lances of the Free!

Shouted by the full chorus of those desperate boon-companions, and caught up and re-echoed from side to side, near and far, as the familiar and well-known words of the burthen reached the ears of more distant groups or stragglers, the effect of this fierce and licentious minstrelsy was indescribable. It was impossible not to feel the zest which that daring life imparted to its daring followers, and even the gallant and stately Knight who listened to it, reproved himself for an involuntary thrill of sympathy and pleasure.

He turned with some impatience and irritation to his companion, who had taken a part in the chorus, and said, "Sir, to the ears of an Italian noble, conscious of the miseries of his country, this ditty is not welcome. I pray you, let us proceed."

"I humbly crave your pardon, Signor," said the Free Companion; "but really so attractive is the life led by Free Lances, under Fra Moreale, that sometimes we forget the——; but pardon me, we will on."

A few moments more, and bounding over a narrow circumvallation, the party found themselves in a quarter, animated indeed, but of a wholly different character of animation. Long lines of armed men were drawn up on either side of a path, conducting to a large marquee, placed upon a little hillock, surmounted by a blue flag, and up this path armed soldiers were passing to and fro with great order, but with a pleased and complacent expression upon their swarthy features. Some that repaired to the marquee were bearing packets and bales upon their shoulders—those that returned seemed to have got rid of their burthens, but every now and then, impatiently opening their hands, appeared counting and recounting to themselves the coins contained therein.

The Knight looked inquiringly at his companion.

" It is the marquee of the merchants," said the captain; " they have free admission to the camp, and their property and persons are rigidly respected. They purchase each soldier's share of the plunder at fair prices, and either party is contented with the bargain."

" It seems, then, that there is some kind of rude justice observed amongst you," said the Knight.

" Rude! *Diavolo!* Not a town in Italy but would be glad of such even justice, and such impartial laws. Yonder lie the tents of the judges, appointed to try all offences of soldier against soldier. To the right, the tent with the golden ball contains the treasurer of the army. Fra Moreale incurs no arrears with his soldiery."

It was, indeed, by these means that the Knight of St. John had collected the best equipped and the best contented force in Italy. Every day brought him recruits. Nothing was spoken of amongst the mercenaries of Italy but the wealth acquired in his service, and every warrior in the pay of Republic or of Tyrant sighed for the lawless standard of Fra Moreale. Already had exaggerated tales of the fortunes to be made in the ranks of the Great Company passed the Alps; and, even now, the Knight, penetrating farther into the camp, beheld from many a tent the proud banners and armorial blazon of German nobility and Gallic knighthood.

"You see," said the Free Companion, pointing to these insignia, "we are not without our different ranks in our wild city. And while we speak, many a golden spur is speeding hitherward from the North!"

All now in the quarter they had entered was still and solemn; only afar came the mingled hum, or the sudden shout of the pandemonium in the rear, mellowed by distance to a not unpleasing sound. An occasional soldier, crossing their path, stalked silently and stealthily to some neighbouring tent, and seemed scarcely to regard their approach.

"Behold! we are before the General's pavilion," said the Free Lance.

Blazoned with purple and gold, the tent of Montreal lay a little apart from the rest. A brooklet from the stream they had crossed murmured gratefully on the ear, and a tall and wide-spreading beech cast its shadow over the gorgeous canvas.

While his troop waited without, the Knight was conducted at once to the presence of the formidable adventurer.

CHAPTER II

ADRIAN ONCE MORE THE GUEST OF MONTREAL

Montreal was sitting at the head of a table, surrounded by men, some military, some civil, whom he called his councillors, and with whom he apparently debated all his projects. These men, drawn from various cities, were intimately acquainted with the internal affairs of the several states to which they belonged. They could tell to a fraction the force of a signor, the wealth of a merchant, the power of a mob. And thus, in his lawless camp, Montreal presided, not more as a general than a statesman. Such knowledge was invaluable to the chief of the Great Company. It enabled him to calculate exactly the time to attack a foe, and the sum to demand for a suppression of hostilities. He knew what parties to deal with—where to importune—where to forbear. And it usually happened that, by some secret intrigue, the appearance of Montreal's banner before the walls of a city was the signal for some sedition or some broil within. It may be that he thus also promoted an ulterior, as well as his present, policy.

The divan were in full consultation when an officer entered, and whispered a few words in Montreal's ear. His eyes brightened. "Admit him," he said hastily. "Messires," he added to his councillors, rubbing his hands, "I think our net has caught our bird. Let us see."

At this moment the drapery was lifted and the Knight admitted.

"How!" muttered Montreal, changing colour, and in evident disappointment. "Am I to be ever thus balked?"

"Sir Walter de Montreal," said the prisoner, "I am once more your guest. In these altered features you perhaps scarcely recognise Adrian di Castello."

"Pardon me, noble Signor," said Montreal, rising with great courtesy; "the mistake of my varlets disturbed my recollection for a moment.—I rejoice once more to press a hand that has won so many laurels since last we parted. Your renown has been grateful to my ears. Ho!" continued the chieftain, clapping his hands, "see to the refreshment and repose of this noble Cavalier and his attendants. Lord Adrian, I will join you presently."

Adrian withdrew. Montreal, forgetful of his councillors, traversed his tent with hasty strides; then summoning the officer who had admitted Adrian, he said, "Count Landau still keeps the pass?"

"Yes, General!"

"Hie thee fast back, then—the ambuscade must tarry till nightfall. We have trapped the wrong fox."

The officer departed, and shortly afterwards Montreal broke up the divan. He sought Adrian, who was lodged in a tent beside his own.

"My Lord," said Montreal, "it is true that my men had orders to stop every one on the roads towards Florence. I am at war with that city. Yet I expected a very different prisoner from you. Need I add, that you and your men are free?"

"I accept the courtesy, noble Montreal, as frankly as it is rendered. May I hope hereafter to repay it? Meanwhile permit me, without any disrespect, to say that had I learned the Grand Company was in this direction, I should have altered my course. I had heard that your arms were bent (somewhat to my mind more nobly) against Malatesta, the tyrant of Rimini!"

"They were so. He *was* my foe; he *is* my tributary. We conquered him. He paid us the price of his liberty. We marched by Asciano upon Sienna. For sixteen thousand florins we spared that city; and we now hang like a thunder-bolt over Florence, which dared to send her puny aid to the defence of Rimini.

Our marches are forced and rapid, and our camp in this plain but just pitched."

"I hear that the Grand Company is allied with Albornoz, and that its General is secretly the soldier of the Church. Is it so?"

"Ay—Albornoz and I understand one another," replied Montreal, carelessly; "and not the less so that we have a mutual foe, whom both are sworn to crush, in Visconti, the archbishop of Milan."

"Visconti! the most potent of the Italian princes. That he has justly incurred the wrath of the Church I know—and I can readily understand that Innocent has revoked the pardon which the intrigues of the Archbishop purchased from Clement VI. But I do not see clearly why Montreal should willingly provoke so dark and terrible a foe."

Montreal smiled sternly. "Know you not," he said, "the vast ambition of that Visconti? By the Holy Sepulchre, he is precisely the enemy my soul leaps to meet! He has a genius worthy to cope with Montreal's. I have made myself master of his secret plans—they are gigantic! In a word, the Archbishop designs the conquest of all Italy. His enormous wealth purchases the corrupt—his dark sagacity ensnares the credulous—his daring valour awes the weak. Every enemy he humbles—every ally he enslaves. This is precisely the Prince whose progress Walter de Montreal must arrest. For this" (he said in a whisper as to himself) "is precisely the Prince who, if suffered to extend his power, will frustrate the plans and break the force of Walter de Montreal."

Adrian was silent, and for the first time a suspicion of the real nature of the Provençal's designs crossed his breast.

"But, noble Montreal," resumed the Colonna, "give me, if your knowledge serves, as no doubt it does,—give me the latest tidings of my native city. I am Roman, and Rome is ever in my thoughts."

"And well she may," replied Montreal, quickly. "Thou knowest that Albornoz, as Legate of the Pontiff, led the army of the Church into the Papal Territories. He took with him Cola di Rienzi. Arrived at Monte Fiascone, crowds of Romans of all ranks hastened thither to render homage to the Tribune. The Legate was forgotten in the popularity of his companion. Whether or not Albornoz grew jealous—for he is proud as Lucifer—of the respect paid to the Tribune, or whether he feared the restoration of his power, I cannot tell. But he detained him in his camp, and refused to yield him to all the solicitations and all the deputations of the Romans. Artfully, however, he fulfilled one of the real objects of Rienzi's release. Through his means he formally regained the allegiance of Rome to the Church, and by the attraction of his presence swelled his camp with Roman recruits. Marching to Viterbo, Rienzi distinguished himself greatly in deeds of arms against the tyrant* John di Vico. Nay, he fought as one worthy of belonging to the Grand Company. This increased the zeal of the Romans; and the city disgorged half its inhabitants to attend the person of the bold Tribune. To the entreaties of these worthy citizens (perhaps the very men who had before shut up their darling in St. Angelo) the crafty Legate merely replied, 'Arm against John di Vico—conquer the tyrants of the Territory—re-establish the patrimony of St. Peter, and Rienzi shall then be proclaimed Senator, and return to Rome.'

* Vit. di Col. di Rienzi.

"These words inspired the Romans with so great a zeal, that they willingly lent their aid to the Legate. Aquapendente, Bolzena yielded, John di Vico was half reduced and half terrified into submission, and Gabrielli, the tyrant of Agobbio, has since succumbed. The glory is to the Cardinal, but the merit with Rienzi."

"And now?"

"Albornoz continued to entertain the Senator-Tribune with great splendour and fair words, but not a word about restoring him to Rome. Wearied with this suspense, I have learned by secret intelligence that Rienzi has left the camp, and betaken himself with a few attendants to Florence, where he has friends, who will provide him with arms and money to enter Rome."

"Ah then! now I guess," said Adrian, with a half smile, "for whom I was mistaken!"

Montreal blushed slightly. "Fairly conjectured!" said he.

"Meanwhile, at Rome," continued the Provençal—"at Rome, your worthy House, and that of the Orsini, being elected to the supreme power, quarrelled among themselves, and could not keep the authority they had won. Francesco Baroncelli,* a new demagogue, a

* This Baroncelli, who has been introduced to the reader in a former portion of this work, is called by Matteo Villani "a man of vile birth and little learning—he had been a Notary of the Capitol."

In the midst of the armed dissensions between the Barons, which followed the expulsion of Rienzi, Baroncelli contrived to make himself Master of the Capitol, and of what was considered an auxiliary of no common importance—viz. the *Great Bell*, by whose alarum Rienzi had so often summoned to arms the Roman people. Baroncelli was crowned Tribune, clothed in a robe of gold brocade, and invested with the crozier-sceptre of Rienzi. At first, his cruelty against the great took the appearance of protection to the humble; but the excesses of his sons (not exaggerated in the text), humble imitator of Rienzi, rose upon the ruins of the peace broken by the nobles, obtained the title of Tribune, and carried about the very insignia used by his predecessor. But less wise than Rienzi, he took the antipapal party. And the Legate was thus enabled to play the papal demagogue against the usurper. Baroncelli was a weak man, his sons committed every excess in mimicry of the high-born tyrants of Padua and Milan. Virgins violated and matrons dishonoured, somewhat contrasted the solemn and majestic decorum of Rienzi's rule;—in fine, Baroncelli fell, massacred by the people. And now, if you ask what rules Rome, I answer, 'It is the hope of Rienzi.'"

"A strange man, and various fortunes. What will be the end of both!"

"Swift murder to the first, and eternal fame to the last," answered Montreal, calmly. "Rienzi will be restored; that brave phœnix will wing its way through storm and cloud to its own funereal pyre: I foresee, I compassionate, I admire.—And then," added Montreal, "I look *beyond!*"

"But wherefore feel you so certain that, if restored, Rienzi must fall?"

"Is it not clear to every eye, save his, whom am-

and his own brutal but bold ferocity, soon made him execrated by the people, to whom he owed his elevation. He had the folly to declare against the Pope; and this it really was that mainly induced Innocent to restore, and oppose to their New Demagogue, the former and more illustrious Tribune. Baroncelli, like Rienzi, was excommunicated; and in his instance, also, the curse of the Church was the immediate cause of his downfall. In attempting flight he was massacred by the mob, December, 1353. Some, however, have maintained that he was slain in combat with Rienzi; and others, by a confusion of dates, have made him succeed to Rienzi on the *death* of the latter.—*Matteo Villani*, lib. iii. cap. 78. *Osservaz. Stor. di Zefirino Re. MS. Vat. Rip. dal Bzovio*, ann. 1353. N. 2.

bition blinds? How can mortal genius, however great, rule that most depraved people by popular means? The Barons—(you know their indomitable ferocity)—wedded to abuse, and loathing every semblance to law; the Barons, humbled for a moment, will watch their occasion, and rise. The people will again desert. Or else, grown wise in one respect by experience, the new Senator will see that popular favour has a loud voice, but a recreant arm. He will, like the Barons, surround himself by foreign swords. A detachment from the Grand Company will be his courtiers; they will be his masters! To pay them the people must be taxed. Then the idol is execrated. No Italian hand can govern these hardy demons of the north; they will mutiny and fall away. A new demagogue will lead on the people, and Rienzi will be the victim. Mark my prophecy!"

"And then the '*beyond*' to which you look?"

"Utter prostration of Rome, for new and long ages; God makes not two Rienzis; *or*," said Montreal, proudly, "the infusion of a new life into the worn-out and diseased frame,—the foundation of a new dynasty. Verily, when I look around me, I believe that the Ruler of nations designs the restoration of the South by the irruptions of the North; and that out of the old Franc and Germanic race will be built up the thrones of the future world!"

As Montreal thus spoke, leaning on his great war-sword, with his fair and heroic features—so different, in their frank, bold, fearless expression, from the dark and wily intellect that characterises the lineaments of the South—eloquent at once with enthusiasm and thought—he might have seemed no unfitting representative of the genius of that northern chivalry of which he spake. And Adrian half fancied that he saw before him one of the old Gothic scourges of the Western World.

Their conversation was here interrupted by the sound of a trumpet, and presently an officer entering, announced the arrival of ambassadors from Florence.

"Again you must pardon me, noble Adrian," said Montreal, "and let me claim you as my guest at least for to-night. Here you may rest secure, and on parting, my men shall attend you to the frontiers of whatsoever territory you design to visit."

Adrian, not sorry to see more of a man so celebrated, accepted the invitation.

Left alone, he leaned his head upon his hand, and soon became lost in his reflections.

CHAPTER III

FAITHFUL AND ILL-FATED LOVE.—THE ASPIRATIONS SURVIVE THE AFFECTIONS

Since that fearful hour in which Adrian Colonna had gazed upon the lifeless form of his adored Irene, the young Roman had undergone the usual vicissitudes of a wandering and adventurous life in those exciting times. His country seemed no longer dear to him. His very rank precluded him from the post he once aspired to take in restoring the liberties of Rome; and he felt that if ever such a revolution could be consummated, it was reserved for one in whose birth and habits the people could feel sympathy and kindred, and who could lift his hand in their behalf without becoming the apostate of his order and the judge of his own House. He had travelled through various courts, and served with renown in various fields. Beloved and honoured wheresoever he fixed a temporary home, no change of scene had removed his melancholy—no new ties had chased away the memory of the Lost. In that era of passionate and poetical romance, which Petrarch represented rather than created, Love had already begun to assume a more tender and sacred character than it had hitherto known, it had gradually imbibed the divine spirit which it derives from Christianity, and which associates its sorrows on earth with the visions and hopes of heaven. To him who relies upon immortality, fidelity to the dead is easy; because death cannot extinguish hope, and the soul of the mourner is already half in the world to come. It is an age that desponds of a future life—representing death as an eternal separation—in which, if men grieve awhile for the dead, they hasten to reconcile themselves to the living. For true is the old aphorism, that love exists not without hope. And all that romantic worship which the Hermit of Vaucluse felt, or feigned, for Laura, found its temple in the desolate heart of Adrian Colonna. He was emphatically the Lover of *his time!* Often as, in his pilgrimage from land to land, he passed the walls of some quiet and lonely convent, he seriously meditated the solemn vows, and internally resolved that the cloister should receive his maturer age. The absence of years had, however, in some degree restored the dimmed and shattered affection for his fatherland, and he desired once more to visit the city in which he had first beheld Irene. "Perhaps," he thought, "time may have wrought some unlooked-for change; and I may yet assist to restore my country."

But with this lingering patriotism no ambition was mingled. In that heated stage of action, in which the desire of power seemed to stir through every breast, and Italy had become the El Dorado of wealth, or the Utopia of empire, to thousands of valiant arms and plotting minds, there was at least one breast that felt the true philosophy of the Hermit. Adrian's nature, though gallant and masculine, was singularly imbued with that elegance of temperament which recoils from rude contact, and to which a lettered and cultivated indolence is the supremest luxury. His education, his experience, and his intellect, had placed him far in advance of his age, and he looked with a high contempt on the coarse villanies and base tricks by which Italian ambition sought its road to power. The rise and fall of Rienzi, who, whatever his failings, was at least the purest and most honourable of the self-raised princes of the age, had conspired to make him despond of the success of noble, as he recoiled from that of selfish aspirations. And the dreamy melancholy which resulted from his ill-starred love, yet more tended to wean him from the stale and hackneyed pursuits of the world. His character was full of beauty and of poetry—not the less so in that it found not a vent for its emotions in the actual occupation of the poet! Pent within, those emotions diffused themselves over all his thoughts and coloured his whole soul. Sometimes, in the blessed abstraction of his visions, he pictured to himself the lot he might have chosen had Irene lived, and fate united them—far from the turbulent and vulgar roar of Rome—but amidst some yet unpolluted solitude of the bright Italian soil. Before his eye there rose the lovely landscape—the palace by the borders of the waveless lake—the vineyards in the valley—the dark forests waving from the hill—and that home, the resort and refuge of all the minstrelsy and love of Italy, brightened by the "Lampeggiar dell' angelico riso," * that makes a paradise in the face we love. Often, seduced by such dreams to complete oblivion of his loss, the young wanderer started from the ideal bliss, to behold around him the solitary waste of way—or the moonlit tents of war—or, worse than all, the crowds and revels of a foreign court.

Whether or not such fancies now, for a moment, allured his meditations, conjured up, perhaps, by the name of Irene's brother, which never sounded in his ears but to awaken ten thousand associations, the Colonna remained thoughtful and absorbed, until he was disturbed by his own squire, who, accompanied by Montreal's servitors, ushered in his solitary but ample repast. Flasks of the richest Florentine wines—viands prepared with all the art which, alas, Italy has now lost!—goblets and salvers of gold and silver, prodigally wrought with barbaric gems—attested the princely luxury which reigned in the camp of the Grand Company. But Adrian saw in all only the spoliation of his degraded country, and felt the splendour almost as an insult. His lonely meal soon concluded, he became impatient of the monotony of his tent; and, tempted by the cool air of the descending eve, sauntered carelessly forth. He bent his steps by the side of the brooklet that curved, snakelike and sparkling, by Montreal's tent; and finding a spot somewhat solitary and apart from the warlike tenements around, flung himself by the margin of the stream.

The last rays of the sun quivered on the wave that

* "The splendour of the angel smile."—Petrarch.

danced musically over its stony bed; and amidst a little copse on the opposite bank broke the brief and momentary song of such of the bolder inhabitants of that purple air as the din of the camp had not scared from their green retreat. The clouds lay motionless to the west, in that sky so darkly and intensely blue, never seen but over the landscapes that a Claude or a Rosa loved to paint: and dim and delicious rose-hues gathered over the gray peaks of the distant Apennines. From afar floated the hum of the camp, broken by the neigh of returning steeds; the blast of an occasional bugle; and, at regular intervals, by the armed tramp of the neighbouring sentry. And opposite to the left of the copse—upon a rising ground, matted with reeds, moss, and waving shrubs—were the ruins of some old Etruscan building, whose name had perished, whose very uses were unknown.

The scene was so calm and lovely, as Adrian gazed upon it, that it was scarcely possible to imagine it at that very hour the haunt of fierce and banded robbers, among most of whom the very soul of man was embruted, and to all of whom murder or rapine made the habitual occupation of life.

Still buried in his reveries, and carelessly dropping stones into the noisy rivulet, Adrian was aroused by the sound of steps.

"A fair spot to listen to the lute and the ballads of Provence," said the voice of Montreal, as the Knight of St. John threw himself on the turf beside the young Colonna.

"You retain, then, your ancient love of your national melodies," said Adrian.

"Ay, I have not yet survived *all* my youth," answered Montreal, with a slight sigh. "But somehow or other, the strains that once pleased my fancy now go too directly to my heart. So, though I still welcome jongleur and minstrel, I bid them sing their *newest* conceits. I cannot wish ever again to hear the poetry I heard when *I was young!*"

"Pardon me," said Adrian, with great interest, "but fain would I have dared, though a secret apprehension prevented me hitherto,—fain would I have dared to question you of that lovely lady, with whom, seven years ago, we gazed at moonlight upon the odorous orange-groves and rosy waters of Terracina."

Montreal turned away his face; he laid his hand on Adrian's arm, and murmured, in a deep and hoarse tone, "I am alone now!"

Adrian pressed his hand in silence. He felt no light shock at thus learning the death of one so gentle, so lovely, and so ill-fated.

"The vows of my knighthood," continued Montreal, "which precluded Adeline the rights of wedlock—the shame of her house—the angry grief of her mother—the wild vicissitudes of my life, so exposed to peril—the loss of her son—all preyed silently on her frame. She did not die (die is too harsh a word!), but she drooped away, and glided into heaven. Even as on a summer's morn some soft dream fleets across us, growing less and less distinct, until it fades, as it were, into light, and we awaken—so faded Adeline's parting spirit, till the daylight of God broke upon it."

Montreal paused a moment, and then resumed: "These thoughts make the boldest of us weak sometimes, and we Provençals are foolish in these matters!—God wot, she was very dear to me!"

The Knight bent down and crossed himself devoutly, his lips muttered a prayer. Strange as it may seem to our more enlightened age, so martial a garb did morality then wear, that this man, at whose word towns had blazed and torrents of blood had flowed, neither adjudged himself, nor was adjudged by the majority of his contemporaries, a criminal. His order, half monastic, half warlike, was emblematic of himself. He trampled upon man, yet humbled himself to God; nor had all his acquaintance with the refining scepticism of Italy shaken the sturdy and simple faith of the bold Provençal. So far from recognising any want of harmony between his calling and his creed, he held that man no true chevalier who was not as devout to the Cross as relentless with the sword.

"And you have no child save the one you lost?" asked Adrian, when he observed the wonted composure of Montreal once more returning.

"None!" said Montreal, as his brow again darkened. "No love-begotten heir of mine will succeed to the fortunes I trust yet to build. Never on earth shall I see upon the face of her child the likeness of Adeline! Yet, at Avignon, I saw a boy I would have claimed; for methought she must have looked her soul into his eyes, they were so like hers! Well, well! the Provence tree hath other branches: and some unborn nephew must be—what? The stars have not yet decided! But ambition is now the only thing in the world left me to love."

"So differently operates the same misfortune upon different characters," thought the Colonna. "To me, crowns became valueless when I could no longer dream of placing them on Irene's brow!"

The similarity of their fates, however, attracted Adrian strongly towards his host; and the two Knights conversed together with more friendship and unreserve than they had hitherto done. At length Montreal said, "By the way, I have not inquired your destination."

"I am bound to Rome," said Adrian: "and the intelligence I have learned from you incites me thitherward yet more eagerly. If Rienzi return, I may mediate successfully, perchance, between the Tribune-Senator and the nobles; and if I find my cousin, young Stefanello, now the head of our house, more tractable than his sires, I shall not despair of conciliating the less powerful Barons. Rome wants repose; and whoever governs, if he govern but with justice, ought to be supported both by prince and plebeian!"

Montreal listened with great attention, and then muttered to himself, "No, it cannot be!" He mused a little while, shading his brow with his hand, before he said aloud, "To Rome you are bound. Well, we shall meet soon amidst its ruins. Know, by the way, that my object here is already won: these Florentine merchants have acceded to my terms; they have purchased a two years' peace; to-morrow the camp breaks up, and the Grand Company march to Lombardy. There, if my schemes prosper, and the Venetians pay my price, I league the rascals (under Landau, my Lieutenant) with the Sea-City, in defiance of the Visconti, and shall pass my autumn in peace amidst the pomps of Rome."

"Sir Walter de Montreal," said Adrian, "your frankness perhaps makes me presumptuous; but when I hear you talk, like a huxtering trader, of selling alike your friendship and your forbearance, I ask myself 'Is this the great Knight of St. John; and have men spoken of him fairly, when they assert the sole stain on his laurels to be his avarice?'"

Montreal bit his lips; nevertheless, he answered calmly, "My frankness has brought its own penance, Lord Adrian. However, I cannot wholly leave so honoured a guest under an impression which I feel to be plausible, but not just. No, brave Colonna; report wrongs me. I value Gold, for Gold is the Architect of Power! It fills the camp—it storms the city—it buys the market-place—it raises the palace—it founds the throne. I value Gold,—it is the means necessary to my end!"

"And that end——"

"Is—no matter what," said the Knight coldly. "Let us to our tents, the dews fall heavily, and the *malaria* floats over these houseless wastes."

The pair rose;—yet, fascinated by the beauty of the hour, they lingered for a moment by the brook. The earliest stars shone over its crisping wavelets, and a delicious breeze murmured gently amidst the glossy herbage.

"Thus gazing," said Montreal, softly, "we reverse the old Medusan fable the poets tell us of, and look and muse ourselves *out* of stone. A little while, and it was the *sunlight* that gilded the wave—it now shines as brightly and glides as gaily beneath the *stars;* even so rolls the stream of time: one luminary succeeds the other equally welcomed — equally illumining — equally evanescent!—You see, the poetry of Provence still lives beneath my mail!"

Adrian early sought his couch; but his own thoughts and the sounds of loud mirth that broke from Montreal's tent, where the chief feasted the captains of his band, a revel from which he had the delicacy to excuse the Roman noble, kept the Colonna long awake; and he had scarcely fallen into an unquiet slumber, when yet more discordant sounds again invaded his repose. At the earliest dawn the wide armament was astir—the creaking of cordage—the tramp of men—loud orders and louder oaths—the slow rolling of baggage-wains—and the clank of the armourers, announced the removal of the camp, and the approaching departure of the Grand Company.

Ere Adrian was yet attired, Montreal entered his tent.

"I have appointed," he said, "five score lances under a trusty leader, to accompany you, noble Adrian, to the borders of Romagna; they wait your leisure. In another hour I depart; the on-guard are already in motion."

Adrian would fain have declined the proffered escort; but he saw that it would only offend the pride of the chief, who soon retired. Hastily Adrian endued his arms—the air of the fresh morning, and the glad sun rising gorgeously from the hills, revived his wearied spirit. He repaired to Montreal's tent, and found him alone, with the implements of writing before him, and a triumphant smile upon his countenance.

"Fortune showers new favours on me!" he said gaily. "Yesterday the Florentines spared me the trouble of a siege: and to-day (even since I last saw you—a few minutes since) puts your new Senator of Rome into my power!"

"How! have your bands then arrested Rienzi?"

"Not so—better still! The Tribune changed his plan, and repaired to Perugia, where my brothers now abide—sought them—they have supplied him with money and soldiers enough to brave the perils of the way, and to defy the swords of the Barons. So writes my good brother Arimbaldo, a man of letters, whom the Tribune thinks rightly he has decoyed with old tales of Roman greatness, and mighty promises of grateful advancement. You find me hastily expressing my content at the arrangement. My brothers themselves will accompany the Senator-Tribune to the walls of the Capitol."

"Still, I see not how this places Rienzi in your power."

"No! His soldiers are my creatures—his comrades my brothers—his creditor myself! Let him rule Rome then—the time soon comes when the Vice-Regent must yield to——"

"The Chief of the Grand Company," interrupted Adrian, with a shudder, which the bold Montreal was too engrossed with the unconcealed excitement of his own thoughts to notice. "No, Knight of Provence, basely have we succumbed to domestic tyrants: but never, I trust, will Romans be so vile as to wear the yoke of a foreign usurper."

Montreal looked hard at Adrian, and smiled sternly.

"You mistake me," said he; "and it will be time enough for you to play the Brutus when I assume the Cæsar. Meanwhile we are but host and guest. Let us change the theme."

Nevertheless this, their latter conference, threw a chill over both during the short time the Knights remained together, and they parted with a formality which was ill-suited to their friendly intercourse of the night before. Montreal felt he had incautiously revealed himself, but caution was no part of his character, whenever he found himself at the head of an army, and at the full tide of fortune; and at that moment, so confident was he of the success of his wildest schemes, that he recked little whom he offended, or whom alarmed.

Slowly, with his strange and ferocious escort, Adrian renewed his way. Winding up a steep ascent that led from the plain,—when he reached the summit, the curve in the road showed him the whole army on its march;—the gonfalons waving—the armour flashing in the sun, line after line, like a river of steel, and the whole plain bristling with the array of that moving war;—while the solemn tread of the armed thousands fell subdued and stifled at times by martial and exulting music. As they swept on, Adrian descried at length the stately and towering form of Montreal upon a black charger, distinguished even at that distance from the rest, not more by his gorgeous armour than his lofty stature. So swept he on in the pride of his array—in the flush of his hopes—the head of a mighty armament—the terror of Italy—the hero that was—the monarch that might be!

BOOK IX

THE RETURN

"Allora la sua venuta fu a Roma sentita; Romani si apparecchiavano a riceverlo con letizia . . . furo fatti archi trionfali," &c., &c.—*Vita di Cola di Rienzi,* lib. ii. c. 17.

"Then the fame of his coming was felt at Rome; the Romans made ready to receive him with gladness . . . triumphal arches were erected," &c., &c.—*Life of Cola di Rienzi.*

CHAPTER I

THE TRIUMPHAL ENTRANCE

All Rome was astir!—from St. Angelo to the Capitol, windows, balconies, roofs, were crowded with animated thousands. Only here and there, in the sullen quarters of the Colonna, the Orsini, and the Savelli, reigned a death-like solitude and a dreary gloom. In those fortifications, rather than streets, not even the accustomed tread of the barbarian sentinel was heard. The gates closed—the casements barred—the grim silence around—attested the absence of the Barons. They had left the city so soon as they had learned the certain approach of Rienzi. In the villages and castles of the Campagna, surrounded by their mercenaries, they awaited the hour when the people, weary of their idol, should welcome back even those ferocious Iconoclasts.

With these exceptions, all Rome was astir! Triumphal arches of drapery, wrought with gold and silver, raised at every principal vista, were inscribed with mottoes of welcome and rejoicing. At frequent intervals stood youths and maidens, with baskets of flowers and laurels. High above the assembled multitudes —from the proud tower of Hadrian—from the turrets of the Capitol—from the spires of the sacred buildings dedicated to Apostle and to Saint—floated banners as for a victory. Rome once more opened her arms to receive her Tribune!

Mingled with the crowd—disguised by his large mantle—hidden by the pressure of the throng—his person, indeed, forgotten by most—and, in the confusion of the moment heeded by none—stood Adrian Colonna! He had not been able to conquer his interest for the brother of Irene. Solitary amidst his fellow-citizens, he stood—the only one of the proud race of Colonna who witnessed the triumph of the darling of the people.

"They say he has grown large in his prison," said one of the bystanders; "he was lean enough when he came by daybreak out of the Church of St. Angelo!"

"Ay," said another, a little man with a shrewd, restless eye, "they say truly; I saw him take leave of the Legate."

Every eye was turned to the last speaker; he became at once a personage of importance. "Yes," continued the little man with an elated and pompous air, "as soon, d'ye see, as he had prevailed on Messere Brettone, and Messere Arimbaldo, the brothers of Fra Moreale, to accompany him from Perugia to Monte Fiascone, he went at once to the Legate d'Albornoz, who was standing in the open air conversing with his captains. A crowd followed. I was one of them; and the Tribune nodded at me—ay, that did he!—and so, with his scarlet cloak, and his scarlet cap, he faced the proud Cardinal with a pride greater than his own. 'Monsignore,' said he, 'though you accord me neither money nor arms, to meet the dangers of the road and brave the ambush of the Barons, I am prepared to depart. Senator of Rome, his Holiness hath made me: according to custom, I pray you, Monsignore, forthwith to confirm the rank.' I would you could have seen how the proud Spaniard stared, and blushed, and frowned; but he bit his lip, and said little."

"And confirmed Rienzi Senator?"

"Yes; and blessed him, and bade him depart."

"Senator!" said a stalwart but gray-haired giant with folded arms; "I like not a title that has been borne by a patrician. I fear me, in the new title he will forget the old."

"Fie, Cecco del Vecchio, you were always a grumbler!" said a merchant of cloth, whose commodity the ceremonial had put in great request. "Fie! —for my part, I think Senator a less new-fangled title than Tribune. I hope there will be feasting enow, at last. Rome has been long dull. A bad time for trade, I warrant me!"

The artisan grinned scornfully. He was one of those who distinguished between the middle class and the working, and he loathed a merchant as much as he did a noble. "The day wears," said the little man; "he must be here anon. The Senator's lady, and all his train, have gone forth to meet him these two hours."

Scarce were these words uttered, when the crowd to the right swayed restlessly; and presently a horseman rode rapidly through the street. "Way there! Keep back! Way—make way for the Most Illustrious the Senator of Rome!"

The crowd became hushed—then murmuring—then hushed again. From balcony and casement stretched the neck of every gazer. The tramp of steeds was heard at a distance—the sound of clarion and trumpet;—then, gleaming through the distant curve of the streets, was seen the wave of the gonfalons—then, the glitter of spears—and then from the whole multitude, as from one voice, arose the shout,—"He comes! he comes!"

Adrian shrunk yet more backward amongst the throng; and, leaning against the wall of one of the houses, contemplated the approaching pageant.

First came six abreast, the procession of Roman horsemen who had gone forth to meet the Senator, bearing boughs of olive in their hands; each hundred preceded by banners, inscribed with the words, "Liberty and Peace restored." As these passed the group by Adrian, each more popular citizen of the cavalcade was recognised, and received with loud shouts. By the garb and equipment of the horsemen, Adrian saw that they belonged chiefly to the traders of Rome; a race who, he well knew, unless strangely altered, valued liberty, only as a commercial speculation. "A vain support these," thought the Colonna;—"what next?" On, then, came in glittering armour the German mercenaries, hired by the gold of the Brothers of Provence, in number two hundred and fifty, and previously in the pay of Malatesta of Rimini;—tall, stern, sedate, disciplined,—eyeing the crowd with a look, half of barbarian wonder, half of insolent disdain. No shout of gratulation welcomed these sturdy strangers; it was evident that their aspect cast a chill over the assembly.

"Shame!" growled Cecco del Vecchio, audibly. "Has the people's friend need of the swords which guard an Orsini or a Malatesta?—shame!"

No voice this time silenced the huge malcontent.

"His only real defence against the Barons," thought Adrian, "if he pay them well! But their number is not sufficient!"

Next came two hundred fantassins, or foot-soldiers, of Tuscany, with the corselets and arms of the heavy-armed soldiery—a gallant company, and whose cheerful looks and familiar bearing appeared to sympathise with the crowd. And in truth they did so,—for they were Tuscans, and therefore lovers of freedom. In them, too, the Romans seemed to recognise natural and legitimate allies,—and there was a general cry of "Vivano i bravi Toscani!"

"Poor defence!" thought the more sagacious Colonna; "the Barons can awe, and the mob corrupt them."

Next came a file of trumpeters and standard-bearers;—and now the sound of the music was drowned by shouts, which seemed to rise simultaneously as from every quarter of the city;—"Rienzi! Rienzi!—Welcome, welcome!—Liberty and Rienzi! Rienzi and the Good Estate!" Flowers dropped on his path, kerchiefs and banners waved from every house;—tears might be seen coursing, unheeded, down bearded cheeks;—youth and age were kneeling together, with uplifted hands, invoking blessings on the head of the Restored. On he came, the Senator-Tribune—"*the Phœnix to his pyre!*"

Robed in scarlet that literally blazed with gold. his

proud head bared in the sun, and bending to the saddle bow, Rienzi passed slowly through the throng. Not in the flush of that hour were visible on his glorious countenance, the signs of disease and care: the very enlargement of his proportions gave a greater majesty to his mien. Hope sparkled in his eye—triumph and empire sat upon his brow. The crowd could not contain themselves; they pressed forward, each upon each, anxious to catch the glance of his eye, to touch the hem of his robe. He himself was deeply affected by their joy. He halted; with faltering and broken words, he attempted to address them. "I am repaid," he said,—"repaid for all;—may I live to make you happy!"

The crowd parted again—the Senator moved on—again the crowd closed in. Behind the Tribune, to their excited imagination, seemed to move the very goddess of ancient Rome.

Upon a steed, caparisoned with cloth of gold;—in snow-white robes, studded with gems that flashed back the day,—came the beautiful and regal Nina. The memory of her pride, her ostentation, all forgotten in that moment, she was scarce less welcome, scarce less idolised, than her lord. And her smile all radiant with joy—her lip quivering with proud and elate emotion—never had she seemed at once so born alike for love and for command;—a Zenobia passing through the pomp of Rome,—not a captive, but a queen.

But not upon that stately form riveted the gaze of Adrian—pale, breathless, trembling, he clung to the walls against which he leaned. Was it a dream? Had the dead revived? Or was it his own—his living Irene—whose soft and melancholy loveliness shone sadly by the side of Nina—a star beside the moon?

The pageant faded from his eyes—all grew dim and dark. For a moment he was insensible. When he recovered, the crowd was hurrying along, confused and blent with the mighty stream that followed the procession. Through the moving multitude he caught the graceful form of Irene, again snatched by the closing standards of the procession from his view. His blood rushed back from his heart through every vein. He was as a man who for years had been in a fearful trance, and who is suddenly awakened to the light of heaven.

One of that mighty throng remained motionless with Adrian. It was Cecco del Vecchio.

"*He did not see me*," muttered the smith to himself; "*old friends are forgotten now!* Well, well, Cecco del Vecchio hates tyrants still—no matter what their name, nor how smoothly they are disguised. He did not see ME! Umph!"

CHAPTER II

THE MASQUERADE

The acuter reader has already learned, without the absolute intervention of the author as narrator, the incidents occurring to Rienzi in the interval between his acquittal at Avignon and his return to Rome. As the impression made by Nina upon the softer and better nature of Albornoz died away, he naturally began to consider his guest—as the profound politicians of that day ever considered men—a piece upon the great Chess-board, to be moved, advanced, or sacrificed, as best suited the scheme in view. His purpose accomplished, in the recovery of the patrimonial territory, the submission of John di Vico, and the fall and death of the Demagogue Baroncelli, the Cardinal deemed it far from advisable to restore to Rome, and with so high a dignity, the able and ambitious Rienzi. Before the daring Roman, even his own great spirit quailed; and he was wholly unable to conceive or to calculate the policy that might be adopted by the new Senator, when once more Lord of Rome. Without affecting to detain, he therefore declined to assist in restoring him. And Rienzi thus saw himself within an easy march of Rome, without one soldier to protect him against the Barons by the way. But Heaven had decreed that no *single* man, however gifted, or however powerful, should long counteract or master the destinies of Rienzi: and perhaps in no more glittering scene of his life did he ever evince so dexterous and subtle an intellect as he now did in extricating himself from the wiles of the Cardinal. Repairing to Perugia, he had, as we have seen, procured, through the brothers of Montreal, men and money for his return. But the Knight of St. John was greatly mistaken, if he imagined that Rienzi was not thoroughly aware of the perilous and treacherous tenure of the support he had received. His keen eye read at a glance the aims and the characters of the brothers of Montreal—he knew that while affecting to serve him, they designed to control—that, made the debtor of the grasping and aspiring Montreal, and surrounded by the troops conducted by Montreal's brethren, he was in the midst of a net which, if not broken, would soon involve fortune and life itself in its fatal and deadly meshes. But, confident in the resources and promptitude of his own genius, he yet sanguinely trusted to make those *his* puppets, who dreamed that he was their own; and, with empire for the stake, he cared not how crafty the antagonists he was compelled to engage.

Meanwhile, uniting to all his rasher and all his nobler qualities, a profound dissimulation, he appeared to trust implicitly to his Provençal companions; and his first act on entering the Capitol, after the triumphal procession, was to reward with the highest dignities in his gift, Messere Arimbaldo and Messere Brettone de Montreal!

High feasting was there that night in the halls of the Capitol; but dearer to Rienzi than all the pomp of the day, were the smiles of Nina. Her proud and admiring eyes, swimming with delicious tears, fixed upon his countenance, she but felt that they were re-united, and that the hours, however brilliantly illumined, were hastening to that moment, when, after so desolate and dark an absence, they might once more be alone.

Far other the thoughts of Adrian Colonna, as he sate alone in the dreary palace in the yet more dreary quarter of his haughty race. Irene then was alive,—he had been deceived by some strange error,—she had escaped the devouring pestilence; and something in the pale sadness of her gentle features, even in that day of triumph, told him he was still remembered. But as his mind by degrees calmed itself from its first wild and tumultuous rapture, he could not help asking himself the question whether they were not still to be divided! Stefanello Colonna, the grandson of the old Stephen, and (by the death of his sire and brother) the youthful head of that powerful House, had already raised his standard against the Senator. Fortifying himself in the almost impregnable fastness of Palestrina, he had assembled around him all the retainers of his family, and his lawless soldiery now ravaged the neighbouring plains far and wide.

Adrian foresaw that the lapse of a few days would suffice to bring the Colonna and the Senator to open war. Could he take part against those of his own blood? The very circumstance of his love for Irene would yet more rob such a proceeding of all appearance of disinterested patriotism, and yet more deeply and irremediably stain his knightly fame, wherever the sympathy of his equals was enlisted with the cause of the Colonna. On the other hand, not only his love for the Senator's sister, but his own secret inclinations and honest convictions, were on the side of one who alone seemed to him possessed of the desire and the genius to repress the disorders of his fallen city. Long meditating, he feared no alternative was left him but in the same cruel neutrality to which he had been before condemned; but he resolved at least to make the attempt—rendered favourable and dignified by his birth and reputation—to reconcile the contending parties. To effect this, he saw that he must begin with his haughty cousin. He was well aware that were it known that he had first obtained an interview with Rienzi—did it appear as if he were charged with overtures from the Senator—although Stefanello himself might be inclined to yield to his representations, the insolent and ferocious Barons who surrounded him would not deign to listen to the envoy of the People's chosen one; and instead of being honoured as an intercessor, he should be suspected as a traitor. He determined, then, to depart for Palestrina; but (and his heart beat audibly) would it not be possible first to obtain an interview with Irene? It was no easy enterprise, surrounded as she was, but he resolved to adventure it. He summoned Giulio.

"The Senator holds a festival this evening—think you that the assemblage will be numerous?"

"I hear," answered Giulio, "that the banquet given to the Ambassadors and Signors to-day is to be followed to-morrow by a mask, to which all ranks are admitted. By Bacchus,* if the Tribune only invited nobles, the smallest closet in the Capitol would suffice to receive his maskers. I suppose a mask has been resolved on in order to disguise the quality of the visitors."

Adrian mused a moment; and the result of his reverie was a determination to delay for another sun his departure to Palestrina—to take advantage of the nature of the revel, and to join the masquerade.

That species of entertainment, though unusual at that season of the year, had been preferred by Rienzi, partly and ostensibly because it was one in which all his numerous and motley supporters could be best received; but chiefly and secretly because it afforded himself and his confidential friends the occasion to mix unsuspected amongst the throng, and learn more of the real anticipations of the Romans with respect to his policy and his strength, than could well be gathered from the enthusiasm of a public spectacle.

The following night was beautifully serene and clear. The better to accommodate the numerous guests, and to take advantage of the warm and moonlit freshness of the air, the open court of the Capitol, with the Place of the Lion, (as well as the state apartments within,) was devoted to the festival.

As Adrian entered the festive court with the rush

* Still a common Roman expletive.

of the throng, it chanced that in the eager impatience of some maskers, more vehement than the rest, his vizard was deranged. He hastily replaced it; but not before one of the guests had recognised his countenance.

From courtesy, Rienzi and his family remained at first unmasked. They stood at the head of the stairs to which the old Egyptian Lion gave the name. The lights shone over that Colossal Monument—which, torn from its antique home, had witnessed, in its grim repose, the rise and lapse of countless generations, and the dark and stormy revolutions of avenging fate. It was an ill omen, often afterwards remarked, that the place of that state festival was the place also of the state executions. But at that moment, as group after group pressed forward to win smile and word from the celebrated man, whose fortunes had been the theme of Europe, or to bend in homage to the lustrous loveliness of Nina, no omen and no warning clouded the universal gladness.

Behind Nina, well contented to shrink from the gaze of the throng, and to feel her softer beauty eclipsed by the dazzling and gorgeous charms of her brother's wife, stood Irene. Amidst the crowd, on her alone Adrian fixed his eyes. The years which had flown over the fair brow of the girl of sixteen—then animated by, yet trembling beneath, the first wild breath of Love;—youth in every vein—passion and childish tenderness in every thought, had not marred, but they had changed, the character of Irene's beauty. Her cheek, no longer varying with every instant, was settled into a delicate and thoughtful paleness—her form, more rounded to the proportions of Roman beauty, had assumed an air of dignified and calm repose. No longer did the restless eye wander in search of some imagined object; no longer did the lip quiver into smiles at some untold hope or half-unconscious recollection. A grave and mournful expression gave to her face (still how sweet!) a gravity beyond her years. The bloom, the flush, the April of the heart, was gone; but yet neither time, nor sorrow, nor blighted love, had stolen from her countenance its rare and angelic softness—nor that inexpressible and virgin modesty of form and aspect, which, contrasting the bolder beauties of Italy, had more than aught else distinguished to Adrian, from all other women, the idol of his heart. And feeding his gaze upon those dark deep eyes, which spoke of thought far away and busy with the past, Adrian felt again and again that he was not forgotten! Hovering near her, but suffering the crowd to press one after another before him, he did not perceive that he had attracted the eagle eye of the Senator.

In fact, as one of the maskers passed Rienzi, he whispered, "Beware, a Colonna is among the masks! beneath the reveller's domino has often lurked the assassin's dagger. Yonder stands your foe—mark him!"

These words were the first sharp and thrilling intimation of the perils into which he had rushed, that the Tribune-Senator had received since his return. He changed colour slightly; and for some minutes the courtly smile and ready greeting with which he had hitherto delighted every guest, gave way to a moody abstraction.

"Why stands yon strange man so mute and motionless?" whispered he to Nina. "He speaks to none—he approaches us not—a churl, a churl!—he must be seen to."

"Doubtless some German or English barbarian," answered Nina. "Let not, my Lord, so slight a cloud dim your merriment."

"You are right, dearest; we have friends here; we are well girt. And, by my father's ashes, I feel that I must accustom myself to danger. Nina, let us move on; methinks we might now mix among the maskers—masked ourselves."

The music played loud and cheerily as the Senator and his party mingled with the throng. But still his eye turned ever towards the gray domino of Adrian, and he perceived that it followed his steps. Approaching the private entrance of the Capitol, he for a few moments lost sight of his unwelcome pursuer: but just as he entered, turning abruptly, Rienzi perceived him close at his side—the next moment the stranger had vanished amidst the throng. But that moment had sufficed to Adrian—he had reached Irene. "Adrian Colonna" (he whispered) "waits thee beside the Lion."

In the absorption of his own reflections, Rienzi fortunately did not notice the sudden paleness and agitation of his sister. Entered within his palace, he called for wine—the draught revived his spirits—he listened smilingly to the sparkling remarks of Nina; and enduing his mask and disguise, said, with his wonted cheerfulness, "Now for Truth—strange that in festivals it should only speak behind a vizard! My sweet sister, thou hast lost thine old smile, and I would rather see that than—Ha! has Irene vanished?"

"Only, I suppose, to change her dress, my Cola, and mingle with the revellers," answered Nina. "Let my smile atone for hers."

Rienzi kissed the bright brow of his wife as she

clung fondly to his bosom. "Thy smile is the sunlight," said he; "but this girl disturbs me. Methinks *now*, at least, she might wear a gladder aspect."

"Is there nothing of love beneath my fair sister's gloom?" answered Nina. "Do you not call to mind how she loved Adrian Colonna?"

"Does that fantasy hold still?" returned Rienzi, musingly. "Well, and she is fit bride for a monarch."

"Yet it were an alliance that would, better than one with monarchs, strengthen thy power at Rome!"

"Ay, were it possible; but that haughty race!—Perchance this very masker that so haunted our steps was but her lover. I will look to this. Let us forth, my Nina. Am I well cloaked?"

"Excellently well—and I?"

"The sun behind a cloud."

"Ah, let us not tarry long; what hour of revel like that when thy hand in mine, this head upon thy bosom, we forget the sorrows we have known, and even the triumphs we have shared?"

Meanwhile, Irene, confused and lost amidst a transport of emotion, already disguised and masked, was threading her way through the crowd back to the staircase of the Lion. With the absence of the Senator that spot had comparatively been deserted. Music and the dance attracted the maskers to another quarter of the wide space. And Irene now approaching, beheld the moonlight fall over the statue, and a solitary figure leaning against the pedestal. She paused, the figure approached, and again she heard the voice of her early love.

"Oh, Irene! recognised even in this disguise," said Adrian, seizing her trembling hand; "have I lived to gaze again upon that form—to touch this hand?

Did not these eyes behold thee lifeless in that fearful vault, which I shudder to recall? By what miracle wert thou raised again? By what means did Heaven spare to this earth one that it seemed already to have placed amongst its angels?"

"Was this, indeed, thy belief?" said Irene, falteringly, but with an accent eloquent of joy. "Thou didst not then willingly desert me? Unjust that I was, I wronged thy noble nature, and deemed that my brother's fall, my humble lineage, thy brilliant fate, had made thee renounce Irene."

"Unjust indeed!" answered the lover. "But surely I saw thee amongst the dead!—thy cloak, with the silver stars—who else wore the arms of the Roman Tribune?"

"Was it but the cloak then, which, dropped in the streets, was probably assumed by some more ill-fated victim; was it *that* sight alone, that made thee so soon despair? Ah! Adrian," continued Irene, tenderly, but with reproach; "not even when I saw *thee* seemingly lifeless on the couch by which I had watched three days and nights, not even then did *I* despair!"

"What, then, my vision did not deceive me! It was you who watched by my bed in that grim hour, whose love guarded, whose care preserved me! And I, wretch that I was!——"

"Nay," answered Irene, "your thought was natural. Heaven seemed to endow me with superhuman strength, whilst I was necessary to thee. But judge of my dismay. I left thee to seek the good friar who attended thee as thy leech; I returned, and found thee not. Heart-sick and terrified, I searched the desolate city in vain. Strong as I was while hope supported me, I sunk beneath fear.—And my brother found me senseless, and stretched on the ground, by the church of St. Mark."

"The church of St. Mark!—so foretold his dream!"

"He had told me he had met thee; we searched for thee in vain; at length we heard that thou hadst left the city, and—and—I rejoiced, Adrian, but I repined!"

For some minutes the young lovers surrendered themselves to the delight of reunion, while new explanations called forth new transports.

"And now," murmured Irene, "now that we have met——" she paused, and her mask concealed her blushes.

"Now that we have met," said Adrian, filling up the silence, "wouldst thou say further, 'that we should not part?' Trust me, dearest, that is the hope that animates my heart. It was but to enjoy these brief bright moments with thee, that I delayed my departure to Palestrina. Could I but hope to bring my young cousin into amity with thy brother, no barrier would prevent our union. Willingly I forget the past—the death of my unhappy kinsmen, (victims, it is true, to their own faults;) and, perhaps, amidst all the crowds that hailed his return, none more appreciated the great and lofty qualities of Cola di Rienzi, than did Adrian Colonna."

"If this be so," said Irene, "let me hope the best; meanwhile, it is enough of comfort and of happiness to know, that we love each other as of old. Ah, Adrian, I am sadly changed; and often have I thought it a thing beyond my dreams, that thou shouldst see me again and love me still."

"Fairer art thou and lovelier than ever," answered Adrian, passionately; "and time, which has ripened thy bloom, has but taught me more deeply to feel thy value. Farewell, Irene, I linger here no longer; thou wilt, I trust, hear soon of my success with my House, and ere the week be over I may return to claim thy hand in the face of day."

The lovers parted; Adrian lingered on the spot, and Irene hastened to bury her emotion and her raptures in her own chamber.

As her form vanished, and the young Colonna slowly turned away, a tall mask strode abruptly towards him.

"Thou art a Colonna," it said, "and in the power of the Senator. Dost thou tremble?"

"If I be a Colonna, rude masker," answered Adrian, coldly, "thou shouldst know the old proverb, 'He who stirs the column, shall rue the fall.'"

The stranger laughed aloud, and then lifting his mask, Adrian saw that it was the Senator who stood before him.

"My Lord Adrian di Castello," said Rienzi, resuming all his gravity, "is it as friend or foe that you have honoured our revels this night?"

"Senator of Rome," answered Adrian, with equal stateliness, "I partake of no man's hospitality but as a friend. A foe, at least to you, I trust never justly to be esteemed."

"I would," rejoined Rienzi, "that I could apply to myself unreservedly that most flattering speech. Are these friendly feelings entertained towards me as the Governor of the Roman people, or as the brother of the woman who has listened to your vows?"

Adrian, who when the Senator had unmasked had followed his example, felt at these words that his eye quailed beneath Rienzi's. However, he recovered himself with the wonted readiness of an Italian, and replied laconically,

"As both."

"Both!" echoed Rienzi. "Then, indeed, noble Adrian, you are welcome hither. And yet, methinks, if you conceived there was no cause for enmity between us, you would have wooed the sister of Cola di Rienzi in a guise more worthy of your birth; and, permit me to add, of that station which God, destiny, and my country, have accorded unto *me*. You dare not, young Colonna, meditate dishonour to the sister of the Senator of Rome. High-born as you are, she is your equal."

"Were I the Emperor, whose simple knight I but am, your sister were my equal," answered Adrian, warmly. "Rienzi, I grieve that I am discovered to you yet. I had trusted that, as a mediator between the Barons and yourself, I might first have won your confidence, and then claimed my reward. Know that with to-morrow's dawn I depart for Palestrina, seeking to reconcile my young cousin to the choice of the People and the Pontiff. Various reasons, which I need not now detail, would have made me wish to undertake this heraldry of peace without previous communication with you. But since we *have* met, intrust me with any terms of conciliation, and I pledge you the right hand, not of a Roman noble—alas! the *prisca fides* has departed from that pledge!—but of a Knight of the Imperial Court, that I will not betray your confidence."

Rienzi, accustomed to read the human countenance, had kept his eyes intently fixed upon Adrian while he spoke; when the Colonna concluded, he pressed the proffered hand, and said, with that familiar and winning sweetness which at times was so peculiar to his manner,

"I trust you, Adrian, from my soul. You were mine early friend in calmer, perchance happier years. And never did river reflect the stars more clearly, than your heart then mirrored back the truth. I trust you!"

While thus speaking, he had mechanically led back the Colonna to the statue of the Lion; there pausing, he resumed:

"Know that I have this morning despatched my delegate to your cousin Stefanello. With all due courtesy, I have apprised him of my return to Rome, and invited hither his honoured presence. Forgetting all ancient feuds, mine own past exile, I have assured him, here, the station and dignity due to the head of the Colonna. All that I ask in return is obedience to the law. Years and reverses have abated my younger pride, and though I may yet preserve the sternness of the Judge, none shall hereafter complain of the insolence of the Tribune."

"I would," answered Adrian, "that your mission to Stefanello had been delayed a day; I would fain have forestalled its purport. Howbeit, you increase my desire of departure, should I yet succeed in obtaining an honourable and peaceful reconciliation, it is not in disguise that I will woo your sister."

"And never did Colonna," replied Rienzi, loftily, "bring to his House a maiden whose alliance more gratified ambition. I still see, as I have seen ever, in mine own projects, and mine own destinies, the chart of the new Roman Empire!"

"Be not too sanguine yet, brave Rienzi," replied Adrian, laying his hand on the Lion of Basalt; "bethink thee on how many scheming brains this dumb image of stone hath looked down from its pedestal—schemes of sand, and schemers of dust. Thou hast enough, at present, for the employ of all thine energy—not to extend thy power, but to preserve thyself. For, trust me, never stood human greatness on so wild and dark a precipice!"

"Thou art honest," said the Senator; "and these are the first words of doubt, and yet of sympathy, I have heard in Rome. But the People love me, the Barons have fled from Rome, the Pontiff approves, and the swords of the Northmen guard the avenues of the Capitol. But these are nought; in mine own honesty are my spear and buckler. Oh, never," continued Rienzi, kindling with his enthusiasm, "never since the days of the old Republic, did Roman dream a purer and a brighter aspiration, than that which animates and supports me now. Peace restored—law established—art, letters, intellect, dawning upon the night of time; the Patricians, no longer bandits of rapine, but the guards of order; the People ennobled from a mob, brave to protect, enlightened to guide, themselves. Then, not by the violence of arms, but by the majesty of her moral power, shall the Mother of Nations claim the obedience of her children. Thus dreaming and thus hoping, shall I tremble or despond? No, Adrian Colonna, come weal or woe, I abide, unshrinking and unawed, by the chances of my doom!"

So much did the manner and the tone of the Senator exalt his language, that even the sober sense of Adrian was enchanted and subdued. He kissed the hand he held, and said earnestly,

"A doom that I will deem it my boast to share—a

career that it will be my glory to smooth. If I succeed in my present mission——"

"You are my brother!" said Rienzi.

"If I fail?"

"You may equally claim that alliance. You pause—you change colour."

"Can I desert my house?"

"Young Lord," said Rienzi, loftily, "say rather can you desert your country? If you doubt my honesty, if you fear my ambition, desist from your task, rob me not of a single foe. But if you believe that I have the will and the power to serve the state—if you recognise, even in the reverses and calamities I have known and mastered, the protecting hand of the Saviour of Nations—if those reverses were but the mercies of Him who chasteneth—necessary, it may be, to correct my earlier daring and sharpen yet more my intellect—if, in a word, thou believest me one whom, whatever be his faults, God hath preserved for the sake of Rome, forget that you are a Colonna—remember only that you are a Roman!"

"You have conquered me, strange and commanding spirit," said Adrian, in a low voice, completely carried away; "and whatever the conduct of my kindred, I am yours and Rome's. Farewell."

CHAPTER III

ADRIAN'S ADVENTURES AT PALESTRINA

It was yet noon when Adrian beheld before him the lofty mountains that shelter Palestrina, the *Præneste* of the ancient world. Back to a period before Romulus existed, in the earliest ages of that mysterious civilisation which in Italy preceded the birth of Rome, could be traced the existence and the power of that rocky city. Eight dependent towns owned its sway and its wealth; its position, and the strength of those mighty walls, in whose ruins may yet be traced the masonry of the remote Pelasgi, had long braved the ambition of the neighbouring Rome. From that very citadel, the Mural Crown* of the mountain, had waved the standard of Marius; and up the road which Adrian's scanty troop slowly wound, had echoed the march of the murtherous Sylla, on his return from the Mithridatic war. Below, where the city spreads towards the plain, were yet seen the shattered and roofless columns of the once celebrated Temple of Fortune; and still the immemorial olives clustered gray and mournfully around the ruins.

A more formidable hold the Barons of Rome could not have selected; and as Adrian's military eye scanned the steep ascent and the rugged walls, he felt that with ordinary skill it might defy for months all the power of the Roman Senator. Below, in the fertile valley, dismantled cottages and trampled harvests attested the violence and rapine of the insurgent Barons;

* Hence, apparently, its Greek name of Stephane. Palestrina is yet one of the many proofs which the vicinity of Rome affords of the old Greek civilisation of Italy.

and at that very moment were seen, in the old plain of the warlike Hernici, troops of armed men, driving before them herds of sheep and cattle, collected in their lawless incursions. In sight of that *Præneste*, which had been the favourite retreat of the luxurious Lords of Rome in its most polished day, the Age of Iron seemed renewed.

The banner of the Colonna, borne by Adrian's troop, obtained ready admittance at the Porta del Sole. As he passed up the irregular and narrow streets that ascended to the citadel, groups of foreign mercenaries,—half-ragged, half-tawdry knots of abandoned women,—mixed here and there with the liveries of the Colonna, stood loitering amidst the ruins of ancient fanes and palaces, or basked lazily in the sun, upon terraces, through which, from amidst weeds and grass, glowed the imperishable hues of the rich mosaics, which had made the pride of that lettered and graceful nobility, of whom savage freebooters were now the heirs.

The contrast been the Past and Present forcibly occurred to Adrian, as he passed along; and, despite his order, he felt as if Civilisation itself were enlisted against his House upon the side of Rienzi.

Leaving his train in the court of the citadel, Adrian demanded admission to the presence of his cousin. He had left Stefanello a child on his departure from Rome, and there could therefore be but a slight and unfamiliar acquaintance betwixt them, despite their kindred.

Peals of laughter came upon his ear, as he followed one of Stefanello's gentlemen through a winding passage that led to the principal chamber. The door was thrown open, and Adrian found himself in a rude hall, to which some appearance of hasty state and attempted comfort had been given. Costly arras imperfectly clothed the stone walls, and the rich seats and decorated tables, which the growing civilisation of the northern cities of Italy had already introduced into the palaces of Italian nobles, strangely contrasted the rough pavement, spread with heaps of armour negligently piled around. At the farther end of the apartment, Adrian shudderingly perceived, set in due and exact order, the implements of torture.

Stefanello Colonna, with two other Barons, indolently reclined on seats drawn around a table, in the recess of a deep casement, from which might be still seen the same glorious landscape, bounded by the dim spires of Rome, which Hannibal and Pyrrhus had ascended that very citadel to survey!

Stefanello himself, in the first bloom of youth, bore already on his beardless countenance those traces usually the work of the passions and vices of maturest manhood. His features were cast in the mould of the old Stephen's; in their clear, sharp, high-bred outline might be noticed that regular and graceful symmetry, which blood, in men as in animals, will sometimes entail through generations; but the features were wasted and meagre. His brows were knit in an eternal frown; his thin and bloodless lips wore that insolent contempt which seems so peculiarly cold and unlovely in early youth; and the deep and livid hollows round his eyes, spoke of habitual excess and premature exhaustion. By him sat (reconciled by hatred to one another) the hereditary foes of his race; the soft, but cunning and astute features of Luca di Savelli, contrasted with the broad frame and ferocious countenance of the Prince of the Orsini.

The young head of the Colonna rose with some cordiality to receive his cousin. "Welcome," he said, "dear Adrian; you are arrived in time to assist us with your well-known military skill. Think you not we shall stand a long siege, if the insolent plebeian dare adventure it? You know our friends, the Orsini and the Savelli? Thanks to St. Peter, or Peter's delegate, we have now happily meaner throats to cut than those of each other!"

Thus saying, Stefanello again threw himself listlessly on his seat, and the shrill, woman's voice of Savelli took part in the dialogue.

"I would, noble Signor, that you had come a few hours earlier: we are still making merry at the recollection—he, he, he!"

"Ah, excellent," cried Stefanello, joining in the laugh; "our cousin has had a loss. Know Adrian, that this base fellow, whom the Pope has had the impudence to create Senator, dared but yesterday to send us a varlet, whom he called—by our Lady!—his *ambassador!*"

"Would you could have seen his mantle, Signor Adrian!" chimed in the Savelli: "purple velvet, as I live, decorated in gold, with the arms of Rome: we soon spoiled his finery."

"What!" exclaimed Adrian, "you did not break the laws of all nobility and knighthood?—you offered no insult to a herald!"

"Herald, sayest thou?" cried Stefanello, frowning till his eyes were scarce visible. "It is for Princes and Barons alone to employ heralds. An I had had my will, I would have sent back the minion's head to the usurper."

"What did ye then?" asked Adrian, coldly.

"Bade our swineherds dip the fellow in the ditch, and gave him a night's lodging in a dungeon to dry himself withal."

"And this morning—he, he, he!" added the Savelli, "we had him before us, and drew his teeth, one by one;—I would you could have heard the fellow mumble out for mercy!"

Adrian rose hastily, and struck the table fiercely with his gauntlet.

"Stefanello Colonna," said he, colouring with noble rage, "answer me: did you dare to inflict this indelible disgrace upon the name we jointly bear? Tell me, at least, that you protested against this foul treason to all the laws of civilisation and of honour. You answer not. House of the Colonna, can such be thy representative!"

"To me these words!" said Stefanello, trembling with passion. "Beware! Methinks *thou* art the traitor, leagued perhaps with yon rascal mob. Well do I remember that thou, the betrothed of the Demagogue's sister, didst not join with my uncle and my father of old, but didst basely leave the city to her plebeian tyrant."

"That did he!" said the fierce Orsini, approaching Adrian menacingly, while the gentle cowardice of Savelli sought in vain to pluck him back by the mantle —"that did he! and but for thy presence, Stefanello——"

"Coward and blusterer!" interrupted Adrian, fairly beside himself with indignation and shame, and dashing his gauntlet in the very face of the advancing Orsini—"wouldst thou threaten one who has maintained, in every list of Europe, and against the stoutest Chivalry of the North, the honour of Rome, which thy deeds the while disgraced? By this gage, I spit upon and defy thee. With lance and with brand, on horse and on foot, I maintain against thee and all thy line, that thou art no knight to have thus maltreated, in thy strongholds, a peaceful and unarmed herald. Yes, even here, on the spot of thy disgrace, I challenge thee to arms!"

"To the court below! Follow me," said Orsini sullenly, and striding towards the threshold. "What, ho there! my helmet and breastplate!"

"Stay, noble Orsini," said Stefanello. "The insult offered to thee is my quarrel—mine was the deed—and against me speaks this degenerate scion of our line. Adrian di Castello—sometime called Colonna—surrender your sword: you are my prisoner!"

"Oh!" said Adrian, grinding his teeth, "that my ancestral blood did not flow through thy veins—else—but enough! Me! your equal, and the favoured Knight of the Emperor, whose advent now brightens the frontiers of Italy!—me—you dare not detain. For your friends, I shall meet them yet perhaps, ere many days are over, where none shall separate our swords. Till then, remember, Orsini, that it is against no unpractised arm that thou wilt have to redeem thine honour!"

Adrian, his drawn sword in his hand, strode towards the door, and passed the Orsini, who stood, lowering and irresolute, in the centre of the apartment.

"Savelli," whispered Stefanello. "He says, 'Ere many days be past!' Be sure, dear Signor, that he goes to join Rienzi. Remember, the alliance he once sought with the Tribune's sister may be renewed. Beware of him! Ought he to leave the castle? The name of a Colonna, associated with the mob, would distract and divide half our strength."

"Fear me not," returned Stefanello, with a malignant smile. "Ere you spoke, I had determined!"

The young Colonna lifted the arras from the wall, opened a door, and passed into a low hall, in which sate twenty mercenaries.

"Quick!" said he. "Seize and disarm yon stranger in the green mantle—but slay him not. Bid the guard below find dungeons for his train. Quick! ere he reach the gate."

Adrian had gained the open hall below—his train and his steed were in sight in the court—when suddenly the soldiery of the Colonna, rushing through another passage than that which he had passed, surrounded and intercepted his retreat.

"Yield thee, Adrian di Castello," cried Stefanello from the summit of the stairs; "or your blood be on your own head."

Three steps did Adrian make through the press, and three of his enemies fell beneath his sword. "To the rescue!" he shouted to his band, and already those bold and daring troopers had gained the hall. Presently the alarum bell tolled loud—the court swarmed with soldiers. Oppressed by numbers, beat down rather than subdued, Adrian's little train was soon secured, and the flower of the Colonna, wounded, breathless, disarmed, but still uttering loud defiance, was a prisoner in the fortress of his kinsman.

CHAPTER IV

THE POSITION OF THE SENATOR—THE WORK OF YEARS—THE REWARDS OF AMBITION

The indignation of Rienzi may readily be conceived, on the return of his herald mutilated and dishonoured. His temper, so naturally stern, was rendered yet more hard by the remembrance of his wrongs and trials; and the result which attended his overtures of conciliation to Stefanello Colonna stung him to the soul.

The bell of the Capitol tolled to arms within ten minutes after the return of the herald. The great gonfalon of Rome was unfurled on the highest tower; and the very evening after Adrian's arrest, the forces of the Senator, headed by Rienzi in person, were on the road to Palestrina. The troopers of the Barons had, however, made incursions as far as Tivoli with the supposed connivance of the inhabitants, and Rienzi halted at that beautiful spot to raise recruits, and receive the allegiance of the suspected, while his soldiers, with Arimbaldo and Brettone at their head, went in search of the marauders. The brothers of Montreal returned late at night with the intelligence, that the troopers of the Barons had secured themselves amidst the recesses of the wood of Pantano.

The red spot mounted to Rienzi's brow. He gazed hard at Brettone, who stated the news to him, and a natural suspicion shot across his mind.

"How!—escaped!" he said. "Is it possible? Enough of such idle skirmishes with these lordly robbers. Will the hour ever come when I shall meet them hand to hand? Brettone," and the brother of

Montreal felt the dark eye of Rienzi pierce to his very heart: "Brettone!" said he, with an abrupt change of voice, "are your men to be *trusted?* Is there no connivance with the Barons?"

"How!" said Brettone, sullenly, but somewhat confused.

"How me no hows!" quoth the Tribune-Senator, fiercely. "I know that thou art a valiant Captain of valiant men. Thou and thy brother Arimbaldo have served me well, and I have rewarded ye well! Have I not? Speak!"

"Senator," answered Arimbaldo, taking up the word, "you have kept your word to us. You have raised us to the highest rank your power could bestow, and this has amply atoned our humble services."

"I am glad ye allow thus much," said the Tribune.

Arimbaldo proceeded, somewhat more loftily, "I trust, my Lord, you do not doubt us?"

"Arimbaldo," replied Rienzi, in a voice of deep, but half-suppressed emotion; "you are a lettered man, and you have seemed to share my projects for the regeneration of our common kind. *You* ought not to betray me. There is something in unison between *us*. But, chide me not, I am surrounded by treason, and the very air I breathe seems to poison my lips."

There was a pathos mingled with Rienzi's words which touched the milder brother of Montreal. He bowed in silence. Rienzi surveyed him wistfully, and sighed. Then, changing the conversation, he spoke of their intended siege of Palestrina, and shortly afterwards retired to rest.

Left alone, the brothers regarded each other for some moments in silence. "Brettone," said Arimbaldo, at length, in a whispered voice, "my heart misgives me. I like not Walter's ambitious schemes. With our own countrymen we are frank and loyal, why play the traitor with this high-souled Roman?"*

"Tush!" said Brettone. "Our brother's hand of iron alone can sway this turbulent people; and if Rienzi be betrayed, so also his enemies, the Barons. No more of this! I have tidings from Montreal; he will be in Rome in a few days."

"And then!"

"Rienzi, weakened by the Barons (for he must not conquer)—the Barons, weakened by Rienzi—our Northmen seize the Capitol, and the soldiery, now scattered throughout Italy, will fly to the standard of the Grand Captain. Montreal must be first Podesta, then King, of Rome."

Arimbaldo moved restlessly in his seat, and the brethren conferred no more on their projects.

The situation of Rienzi was precisely that which tends the most to sour and to harden the fairest nature. With an intellect capable of the grandest designs, a heart that beats with the loftiest emotions, elevated to the sunny pinnacle of power and surrounded by loud-tongued adulators, he knew not among men a single breast in which he could confide. He was as one on a steep ascent, whose footing crumbles, while every bough at which he grasps seems to rot at his touch. He found the people more than ever eloquent in his favour, but while they shouted raptures as he passed, not a man was capable of *making a sacrifice for him!*

* The anonymous biographer of Rienzi makes the following just remark: "Sono li tedeschi, come discendon de la Alemagna, semplici, puri, senza fraude, come si allocano tra' taliani, diventano mastri coduti, viziosi, che sentono ogni malizia."—*Vit. di Col. di Rienzi*, lib. ii. cap. 16.

The liberty of a state is never achieved by a single individual; if not the people—if not the greater number—a zealous and fervent minority, at least, must go hand in hand with him. Rome demanded sacrifices in all who sought the Roman regeneration—sacrifices of time, ease, and money. The crowd followed the procession of the Senator, but not a single Roman devoted his life, *unpaid*, to his standard; not a single coin was subscribed in the defence of freedom. Against him were arrayed the most powerful and the most ferocious Barons of Italy; each of whom could maintain, at his own cost, a little army of practised warriors. With Rienzi were traders and artificers, who were willing to enjoy the fruits of liberty, but not to labour at the soil; who demanded, in return for empty shouts, peace and riches; and who expected that one man was to effect in a day what would be cheaply purchased by the struggle of a generation. All their dark and rude notion of a reformed state was to live unbutchered by the Barons and untaxed by their governors. Rome, I say, gave to her Senator not a free arm, nor a voluntary florin.* Well aware of the danger which surrounds the ruler who defends his state by foreign swords, the fondest wish, and the most visionary dream of Rienzi, was to revive amongst the Romans, in their first enthusiasm at his return, an organised and voluntary force, who, in protecting him, would protect themselves:—not, as before, in his first power, a *nominal* force of twenty thousand men, who at any hour might yield (as they did yield) to one hundred and fifty; but a regular, well disciplined and trusty body, numerous enough to resist aggression,

* This plain fact is thoroughly borne out by every authority.

not numerous enough to become themselves the aggressors.

Hitherto all his private endeavours, his public exhortations, had failed; the crowd listened—shouted—saw him quit the city to meet their tyrants, and returned to their shops saying to each other, "What a great man!"

The character of Rienzi has chiefly received for its judges men of the closet, who speculate upon human beings as if they were machines; who gauge the great, not by their merit, but by their success; and who have censured or sneered at the Tribune, where they should have condemned the People! Had but one-half the spirit been found in Rome which ran through a single vein of Cola di Rienzi, the august Republic, if not the majestic empire, of Rome, might be existing now! Turning from the people, the Senator saw his rude and savage troops, accustomed to the licence of a tyrant's camp, and under commanders in whom it was ruin really to confide—whom it was equal ruin openly to distrust. Hemmed in on every side by dangers, his character daily grew more restless, vigilant, and stern; and still, with all the aims of the patriot, he felt all the curses of the tyrant. Without the rough and hardening career which, through a life of warfare, had brought Cromwell to a similar power—with more of grace and intellectual softness in his composition, he resembled that yet greater man in some points of character—in his religious enthusiasm; his rigid justice, often forced by circumstance into severity, but never wantonly cruel or blood-thirsty; in his singular pride of country; and his mysterious command over the minds of others. But he resembled the giant Englishman far more in circumstance than original nature, and that circumstance assimilated their characters at the close of their several careers. Like Cromwell, beset by secret or open foes, the assassin's dagger ever gleamed before his eyes; and his stout heart, unawed by real, trembled at imagined, terrors. The countenance changing suddenly from red to white—the bloodshot, restless eye, belying the composed majesty of mien—the muttering lips—the broken slumber—the secret corselet;—these to both were the rewards of Power!

The elasticity of youth had left the Tribune! His frame, which had endured so many shocks, had contracted a painful disease in the dungeon at Avignon* —his high soul still supported him, but the nerves gave way. Tears came readily into his eyes, and often, like Cromwell, he was thought to weep from hypocrisy, when in truth it was the hysteric of overwrought and irritable emotion. In all his former life singularly temperate,† he now fled from his goading thoughts to the beguiling excitement of wine. He drank deep, though its effects were never visible upon him except in a freer and wilder mood, and the indulgence of that racy humour, half-mirthful, half-bitter, for which his younger days had been distinguished. Now the mirth had more loudness, but the bitterness more gall.

Such were the characteristics of Rienzi at his return to power—made more apparent with every day. Nina he still loved with the same tenderness, and, if pos-

* "Dicea che ne la prigione era stato ascarmato."—*Vit. di Col. di Rienzi*, lib. ii. cap. 18.

† "Solea prima esser sobrio, temperato, astinente, ora è diventato distemperatissimo bevitore," &c.—*Ibid.*

"At first he used to be sober, temperate, abstinent; now he is become a most intemperate drinker," &c.—*Life of Cola di Rienzi.*

sible, she adored him more than ever; but, the zest and freshness of triumphant ambition gone, somehow or other, their intercourse together had not its old charm. Formerly they talked constantly of the *future* —of the bright days in store for them. Now, with a sharp and uneasy pang, Rienzi turned from all thought of that "gay to-morrow." There was no "gay to-morrow" for him! Dark and thorny as was the present hour, all beyond seemed yet less cheering and more ominous. Still he had some moments, brief but brilliant, when, forgetting the iron race amongst whom he was thrown, he plunged into scholastic reveries of the worshipped Past, and half fancied that he was of a People worthy of his genius and his devotion. Like most men who have been preserved through great dangers, he continued with increasing fondness to nourish a credulous belief in the grandeur of his own destiny. He could not imagine that he had been so delivered, and for no end! He was the Elected, and therefore the Instrument, of Heaven. And thus, that Bible which in his loneliness, his wanderings, and his prison, had been his solace and support, was more than ever needed in his greatness.

It was another cause of sorrow and chagrin to one who, amidst such circumstances of public danger, required so peculiarly the support and sympathy of private friends,—that he found he had incurred amongst his old coadjutors the common penalty of absence. A few were dead; others, wearied with the storms of public life, and chilled in their ardour by the turbulent revolutions to which, in every effort for her amelioration, Rome had been subjected, had retired,—some altogether from the city, some from all participation in political affairs. In his halls, the Tribune-Senator was surrounded by unfamiliar faces, and a new generation. Of the heads of the popular party, most were animated by a stern dislike to the Pontifical domination, and looked with suspicion and repugnance upon one who, if he governed for the People, had been trusted and honoured by the Pope. Rienzi was not a man to forget former friends, however lowly, and had already found time to seek an interview with Cecco del Vecchio. But that stern Republican had received him with coldness. His foreign mercenaries, and his title of Senator were things that the artisan could not digest. With his usual bluntness, he had said so to Rienzi.

"As for the last," answered the Tribune, affably, "names do not alter natures. When I forget that to be delegate to the Pontiff is to be the guardian of his flock, forsake me. As for the first, let me but see five hundred Romans sworn to stand armed day and night for the defence of Rome, and I dismiss the Northmen."

Cecco del Vecchio was unsoftened; honest, but uneducated—impracticable, and by nature a malcontent, he felt as if he were no longer necessary to the Senator, and this offended his pride. Strange as it may seem, the sullen artisan bore, too, a secret grudge against Rienzi, for not having seen and selected him from a crowd of thousands on the day of his triumphal entry. Such are the small offences which produce deep danger to the great!

The artisans still held their meetings, and Cecco del Vecchio's voice was heard loud in grumbling forebodings. But what wounded Rienzi yet more than the alienation of the rest, was the confused and altered manner of his old friend and familiar. Pandulfo di Guido. Missing that popular citizen among those who daily offered their homage at the Capitol, he had sent for him, and sought in vain to revive their ancient intimacy. Pandulfo affected great respect, but not all the condescension of the Senator could conquer his distance and his restraint. In fact, Pandulfo had learned to form ambitious projects of his own; and but for the return of Rienzi, Pandulfo di Guido felt that he might now, with greater safety, and indeed with some connivance from the Barons, have been the Tribune of the People. The facility to rise into popular eminence which a disordered and corrupt state, unblest by a regular constitution, offers to ambition, breeds the jealousy and the rivalship which destroy union, and rot away the ties of party.

Such was the situation of Rienzi, and yet, wonderful to say, he seemed to be adored by the multitude; and law and liberty, life and death, were in his hands!

Of all those who attended his person, Angelo Villani was the most favoured; that youth who had accompanied Rienzi in his long exile, had also, at the wish of Nina, attended him from Avignon, through his sojourn in the camp of Albornoz. His zeal, intelligence, and frank and evident affection, blinded the Senator to the faults of his character, and established him more and more in the gratitude of Rienzi. He loved to feel that one faithful heart beat near him, and the page, raised to the rank of his chamberlain, always attended his person, and slept in his antechamber.

Retiring that night at Tivoli, to the apartment prepared for him, the Senator sat down by the open casement, through which were seen, waving in the starlight, the dark pines that crowned the hills, while the stillness of the hour gave to his ear the dash of the waterfalls heard above the regular and measured tread of the sentinels below. Leaning his cheek upon his hand, Rienzi long surrendered himself to gloomy thought, and, when he looked up, he saw the bright blue eye of Villani fixed in anxious sympathy on his countenance.

"Is my Lord unwell?" asked the young chamberlain, hesitating.

"Not so, my Angelo; but somewhat sick at heart. Methinks, for a September night, the air is chill!"

"Angelo," resumed Rienzi, who had already acquired that uneasy curiosity which belongs to an uncertain power,—"Angelo, bring me hither yon writing implements; hast thou heard aught what the men say of our probable success against Palestrina?"

"Would my Lord wish to learn all their gossip, whether it please or not?" answered Villani.

"If I studied only to hear what pleased me, Angelo, I should never have returned to Rome."

"Why, then, I heard a constable of the Northmen say, meaningly, that the place will not be carried."

"Humph! And what said the captains of my Roman Legion?"

"My Lord, I have heard it whispered that they fear defeat less than they do the revenge of the Barons, if they are successful."

"And with such tools the living race of Europe and misjudging posterity will deem that the workman is to shape out the Ideal and the Perfect! Bring me yon Bible."

As Angelo reverently brought to Rienzi the sacred book, he said,

"Just before I left my companions below, there was a rumour that the Lord Adrian Colonna had been imprisoned by his kinsman."

"I too heard, and I believe, as much," returned Rienzi: "these Barons would gibbet their own children in irons, if there were any chance of the shackles growing rusty for want of prey. But the wicked shall be brought low, and their strong places shall be made desolate."

"I would, my Lord," said Villani, "that our Northmen had other captains than these Provençals."

"Why?" asked Rienzi, abruptly.

"Have the creatures of the Captain of the Grand Company ever held faith with any man whom it suited the avarice or the ambition of Montreal to betray? Was he not, a few months ago, the right arm of John di Vico, and did he not sell his services to John di Vico's enemy, the Cardinal Albornoz? These warriors barter men as cattle."

"Thou describest Montreal rightly: a dangerous and an awful man. But methinks his brothers are of a duller and meaner kind; they dare not the crimes of the Robber Captain. Howbeit, Angelo, thou hast touched a string that will make discord with sleep to-night. Fair youth, thy young eyes have need of slumber; withdraw, and when thou hearest men envy Rienzi, think that——"

"God never made Genius to be envied!" interrupted Villani, with an energy that overcame his respect. "We envy not the sun, but rather the valleys that ripen beneath his beams."

"Verily, if I be the sun," said Rienzi, with a bitter and melancholy smile, "I long for night,—and come it will, to the human as to the celestial Pilgrim!—Thank Heaven at least, that our ambition cannot make us immortal!"

CHAPTER V

THE BITER BIT

The next morning, when Rienzi descended to the room where his captains awaited him, his quick eye perceived that a cloud still lowered upon the brow of Messere Brettone. Arimbaldo, sheltered by the recess of the rude casement, shunned his eye.

"A fair morning, gentles," said Rienzi; "the Sun laughs upon our enterprise. I have messengers from Rome betimes—fresh troops will join us ere noon."

"I am glad, Senator," answered Brettone, "that you have tidings which will counteract the ill of those I have to narrate to thee. The soldiers murmur loudly—their pay is due to them; and, I fear me, that without money they will not march to Palestrina."

"As they will," returned Rienzi, carelessly. "It is but a few days since they entered Rome; pay did they receive in advance—if they demand more, the Colonna and Orsini may outbid me. Draw off your soldiers, Sir Knight, and farewell."

Brettone's countenance fell—it was his object to get Rienzi more and more in his power, and he wished not to suffer him to gain that strength which would accrue to him from the fall of Palestrina: the indifference of the Senator foiled and entrapped him in his own net.

"That must not be," said the brother of Montreal, after a confused silence; "we cannot leave you thus to your enemies—the soldiers, it is true, demand pay——"

"And should have it," said Rienzi. "I know these mercenaries—it is ever with them, mutiny or money. I will throw myself on my Romans, and triumph—or fall, if so Heaven decrees, with them. Acquaint your constables with my resolve."

Scarce were these words spoken, ere, as previously concerted with Brettone, the chief constable of the mercenaries appeared at the door. "Senator," said he, with a rough semblance of aspect, "your orders to march have reached me, I have sought to marshal my men—but——"

"I know what thou wouldst say, friend," interrupted Rienzi, waving his hand: "Messere Brettone will give you my reply. Another time, Sir Captain, more ceremony with the Senator of Rome—you may withdraw."

The unforeseen dignity of Rienzi rebuked and abashed the constable; he looked at Brettone, who motioned him to depart. He closed the door and withdrew.

"What is to be done?" said Brettone.

"Sir Knight," replied Rienzi, gravely, "let us understand each other. Would you serve me or not? If the first, you are not my equal, but subordinate—and you must obey and not dictate; if the last, my debt to you shall be discharged, and the world is wide enough for both."

"We have declared allegiance to you," answered Brettone, "and it shall be given."

"One caution before I re-accept your fealty," replied Rienzi, very slowly. "For an open foe, I have my sword—for a traitor, mark me, Rome has the axe; of the first I have no fear; for the last, no mercy."

"These are not words that should pass between friends," said Brettone, turning pale with suppressed emotion.

"Friends!—ye are my friends, then!—your hands! Friends, so you are!—and shall prove it! Dear Arimbaldo, thou, like myself, art book-learned,—a clerkly soldier. Dost thou remember how in the Roman history it is told that the Treasury lacked money for the soldiers? The Consul convened the Nobles. 'Ye,' said he, 'that have the offices and dignity should be the first to pay for them.' Ye heed me, my friends; the nobles took the hint, they found the money—the army was paid. This example is not lost on you. I have made you the leaders of my force, Rome hath showered her honours on you. Your generosity shall commence the example which the Romans shall thus learn of strangers. Ye gaze at me, *my friends!* I read your noble souls—and thank ye beforehand. Ye have the dignity and the office; ye have also the wealth!—pay the hirelings, pay them!" *

Had a thunderbolt fallen at the feet of Brettone, he could not have been more astounded than at this simple suggestion of Rienzi's. He lifted his eyes to the Senator's face, and saw there that smile which he had already, bold as he was, learned to dread. He felt himself fairly sunk in the pit he had digged for another. There was that in the Senator-Tribune's brow that told him to refuse was to declare open war, and the moment was not ripe for that.

"Ye accede," said Rienzi; "ye have done well."

The Senator clapped his hands—his guard appeared.

"Summon the head constables of the soldiery."

The brothers still remained dumb.

* See the anonymous biographer, lib. ii. cap. 19.

The constables entered.

" My friends," said Rienzi, " Messere Brettone and Messere Arimbaldo have my directions to divide amongst your force a thousand florins. This evening we encamp beneath Palestrina."

The constables withdrew in visible surprise. Rienzi gazed a moment on the brothers, chuckling within himself—for his sarcastic humour enjoyed his triumph. " You lament not your devotion, *my friends!* "

" No," said Brettone, rousing himself; " the sum but trivially swells our debt."

" Frankly said—your hands once more!—the good people of Tivoli expect me in the Piazza—they require some admonitions. Adieu till noon."

When the door closed on Rienzi, Brettone struck the handle of his sword fiercely—" The Roman laughs at us," said he. " But let Walter de Montreal once appear in Rome, and the proud jester shall pay us dearly for this."

" Hush! " said Arimbaldo, " walls have ears, and that imp of Satan, young Villani, seems to me ever at our heels! "

" A thousand florins! I trust his heart hath as many drops," growled the chafed Brettone, unheeding his brother.

The soldiers were paid—the army marched—the eloquence of the Senator had augmented his force by volunteers from Tivoli, and wild and half-armed peasantry joined his standard from the Campagna and the neighbouring mountains.

Palestrina was besieged: Rienzi continued dexterously to watch the brothers of Montreal. Under pretext of imparting to the Italian volunteers the advantage of their military science, he separated them from their mercenaries, and assigned to them the command of the less disciplined Italians, with whom, he believed, they could not venture to tamper. He himself assumed the lead of the Northmen—and, despite themselves, they were fascinated by his artful, yet dignified affability, and the personal courage he displayed in some sallies of the besieged Barons. But as the huntsmen upon all the subtlest windings of their prey,—so pressed the relentless and speeding Fates upon Cola di Rienzi!

CHAPTER VI

THE EVENTS GATHER TO THE END

While this the state of the camp of the besiegers, Luca di Savelli and Stefanello Colonna were closeted with a stranger, who had privately entered Palestrina on the night before the Romans pitched their tents beneath its walls. This visitor, who might have somewhat passed his fortieth year, yet retained, scarcely diminished, the uncommon beauty of form and countenance for which his youth had been remarkable. But it was no longer that character of beauty which has been described in his first introduction to the reader. It was no longer the almost woman delicacy of feature and complexion, or the highborn polish, and graceful suavity of manner, which distinguished Walter de Montreal: a life of vicissitude and war had at length done its work. His bearing was now abrupt and imperious, as that of one accustomed to rule wild spirits, and he had exchanged the grace of persuasion for the sternness of command. His athletic form had grown more spare and sinewy, and instead of the brow half shaded by fair and clustering curls, his forehead, though yet but slightly wrinkled, was completely bald at the temples; and by its unwonted height, increased the dignity and manliness of his aspect. The bloom of his complexion was faded, less by outward exposure than inward thought, into a bronzed and settled paleness; and his features seemed more marked and prominent, as the flesh had somewhat sunk from the contour of the cheek. Yet the change suited the change of age and circumstance; and if the Provençal now less realized the idea of the brave and fair knight-errant, he but looked the more what the knight-errant had become—the sagacious counsellor and the mighty leader.

"You must be aware," said Montreal, continuing a discourse which appeared to have made great impression on his companions, "that in this contest between yourselves and the Senator, I alone hold the balance. Rienzi is utterly in my power—my brothers the leaders of his army; myself, his creditor. It rests with me to secure him on the throne, or to send him to the scaffold. I have but to give the order, and the Grand Company enter Rome; but without their agency methinks if you keep faith with me, our purpose can be effected."

"In the meanwhile, Palestrina is besieged by your brothers!" said Stefanello, sharply.

"But they have my orders to waste their time before its walls. Do you not see, that by this very siege, fruitless, as, if I will, it shall be, Rienzi loses fame abroad, and popularity in Rome."

"Sir Knight," said Luca di Savelli, "you speak as a man versed in the profound policy of the times; and under all the circumstances which menace us, your proposal seems but fitting and reasonable. On the one hand, you undertake to restore us and the other Barons to Rome; and to give Rienzi to the Staircase of the Lion——"

"Not so, not so," replied Montreal quickly. "I will consent either so to subdue and cripple his power, as to render him a puppet in our hands, a mere shadow of authority—or, if his proud spirit chafe at its cage, to give it once more liberty amongst the wilds of Germany. I would fetter or banish him, but not destroy; unless" (added Montreal, after a moment's pause) "fate absolutely drives us to it. Power should not demand victims; but to secure it, victims may be necessary."

"I understand your refinements," said Luca di Savelli, with his icy smile, "and am satisfied. The Barons once restored, our palaces once more manned, and I am willing to take the chance of the Senator's longevity. This service you promise to effect?"

"I do."

"And, in return, you demand our assent to your enjoying the rank of Podesta for five years?"

"You say right."

"I, for one, accede to the terms," said the Savelli: "there is my hand; I am wearied of these brawls, even amongst ourselves, and think that a Foreign Ruler may best enforce order; the more especially, if like you, Sir Knight, one whose birth and renown are such as to make him comprehend the difference between Barons and Plebeians."

"For my part," said Stefanello, "I feel that we have but a choice of evils—I like not a foreign Podesta; but I like a plebeian Senator still less;—there too is my hand, Sir Knight."

"Noble Signors," said Montreal, after a short pause, and turning his piercing gaze from one to the other with great deliberation, "our compact is sealed; one word by way of codicil. Walter de Montreal is no Count Pepin of Minorbino! Once before, little dreaming, I own, that the victory would be so facile, I intrusted your cause and mine to a deputy; your cause he promoted, mine he lost. He drove out the Tribune, and then suffered the Barons to banish himself. This time I see to my own affairs; and, mark you, I have learned in the Grand Company one lesson; viz. never to pardon spy or deserter, of whatever rank. Your forgiveness for the hint. Let us change the theme. So ye detain in your fortress my old friend the Baron di Castello?"

"Ay," said Luca di Savelli; for Stefanello, stung by Montreal's threat, which he dared not openly resent, preserved a sullen silence; "Ay, he is one noble the less to the Senator's council."

"You act wisely. I know his views and temper; at present dangerous to our interests. Yet use him well, I entreat you; he may hereafter serve us. And now, my Lords, my eyes are weary, suffer me to retire. Pleasant dreams of the New Revolution to us all?"

"By your leave, noble Montreal, we will attend you to your couch," said Luca di Savelli.

"By my troth, and ye shall not. I am no Tribune to have great Signors for my pages; but a plain gentleman, and a hardy soldier: your attendants will conduct me to whatever chamber your hospitality assigns to one who could sleep soundly beneath the rudest hedge under your open skies."

Savelli, however, insisted on conducting the Podesta that was to be. to his apartment. He then returned to Stefanello, whom he found pacing the saloon with long and disordered strides.

"What have we done, Savelli?" said he quickly; "sold our city to a barbarian!"

"Sold!" said Savelli; "to my mind it is the other part of the contract in which we have played our share. We have bought, Colonna, not sold—bought our lives from yon army; bought our power, our fortunes, our castles, from the Demagogue Senator; bought what is better than all, triumph and revenge. Tush, Colonna, see you not that if we had balked this great warrior, we had perished? Leagued with the Senator, the Grand Company would have marched to Rome; and, whether Montreal assisted or murdered Rienzi, (for methinks he is a Romulus, who would brook no Remus) *we* had equally been undone. *Now*, we have made our own terms, and our shares are equal. Nay, the first steps to be taken are in our favour. Rienzi is to be snared, and *we* are to enter Rome."

"And then the Provençal is to be Despot of the city."

"Podesta, if you please. Podestas who offend the people are often banished, and sometimes stoned—Podestas who insult the nobles are often stilettoed, and sometimes poisoned," said Savelli. "'Sufficient for the day is the evil thereof.' Meanwhile, say nothing to the bear, Orsini. Such men mar all wisdom. Come, cheer thee, Stefanello."

"Luca di Savelli, you have not such a stake in Rome as I have," said the young Lord, haughtily; "no Podesta can take from *you* the rank of the first Signor of the Italian metropolis!"

"An you had said so to the Orsini, there would have been drawing of swords," said Savelli. "But cheer thee, I say; is not our first care to destroy Rienzi, and then, between the death of one foe and the rise of another, are there not such preventives as Ezzelino da Romano has taught to wary men? Cheer thee, I say; and, next year, if we but hold together, Stefanello Colonna and Luca di Savelli will be joint Senators of Rome, and these great men food for worms!"

While thus conferred the Barons, Montreal, ere he retired to rest, stood gazing from the open lattice of his chamber over the landscape below, which slept in the autumnal moonlight, while at a distance gleamed, pale and steady, the lights round the encampment of the besiegers.

"Wide plains and broad valleys," thought the warrior, "soon shall ye repose in peace beneath a new sway, against which no petty tyrant shall dare rebel. And ye, white walls of canvas, even while I gaze—*ye* admonish me how realms are won. Even as, of old, from the Nomad tents was built up the stately Babylon,* that 'was not till the Assyrian founded it for them that dwell in the wilderness;' so by the new Ishmaelites of Europe shall a race, undreamt of now, be founded; and the camp of yesterday, be the city of to-morrow. Verily, when, for one soft offence, the Pontiff thrust me from the bosom of the Church, little guessed he what enemy he raised to Rome! How solemn is the night!—how still the heavens and earth!—the very stars are as hushed, as if intent on the events that are to pass below! So solemn and so still feels mine own spirit, and an awe unknown till now warns me that I approach the crisis of my daring fate!"

* Isaiah c. xxii.

BOOK X

THE LION OF BASALT

"Ora voglio contare la morte del Tribuno."—*Vit. di Cola di Rienzi*, lib. ii. cap. 24.

"Now will I narrate the death of the Tribune."—*Life of Cola di Rienzi.*

CHAPTER I

THE CONJUNCTION OF HOSTILE PLANETS IN THE HOUSE OF DEATH

On the fourth day of the siege, and after beating back to those almost impregnable walls the soldiery of the Barons, headed by the Prince of the Orsini, the Senator returned to his tent, where despatches from Rome awaited him. He ran his eye hastily over them, till he came to the last; yet each contained news that might have longer delayed the eye of a man less inured to danger. From one he learned that Albornoz, whose blessing had confirmed to him the rank of Senator, had received with special favour the messengers of the Orsini and Colonna. He knew that the Cardinal, whose views connected him with the Roman Patricians, desired his downfall; but he feared not Albornoz; perhaps in his secret heart he wished that any open aggression from the Pontiff's Legate might throw him wholly on the people.

He learned further, that, short as had been his absence, Pandulfo di Guido had twice addressed the populace, not in favour of the Senator, but in artful regrets of the loss to the trade of Rome in the absence of her wealthiest nobles.

"For this, then, he has deserted me," said Rienzi to himself. "Let him beware!"

The tidings contained in the next, touched him home: Walter de Montreal had openly arrived in Rome. The grasping and lawless bandit, whose rapine filled with a robber's booty every bank in Europe—whose Company was the army of a King—whose ambition, vast, unprincipled, and profound, he so well knew—whose brothers were in his camp—their treason already more than suspected;—Walter de Montreal was in Rome!

The Senator remained perfectly aghast at this new peril; and then said, setting his teeth as in a vice,

"Wild tiger, thou art in the Lion's den!" Then pausing, he broke out again, "One false step, Walter de Montreal, and all the mailed hands of the Grand Company shall not pluck thee from the abyss! But what can I do? Return to Rome—the plans of Montreal unpenetrated—no accusation against him! On what pretence can I with honour raise the siege? To leave Palestrina, is to give a triumph to the Barons—to abandon Adrian, to degrade my cause. Yet, while away from Rome, every hour breeds treason and danger. Pandulfo, Albornoz, Montreal—all are at work against me. A keen and trusty spy, now;—ha, well thought of—Villani!—What, ho—Angelo Villani!"

The young chamberlain appeared.

"I think," said Rienzi, "to have often heard, that thou art an orphan?"

"True, my Lord; the old Augustine nun who reared

my boyhood, has told me again and again that my parents are dead. Both noble, my Lord; but I am the child of shame. And I say it often, and think of it ever, in order to make Angelo Villani remember that he has a name to win."

"Young man, serve me as you have served, and if I live you shall have no need to call yourself an orphan. Mark me! I want a friend—the Senator of Rome wants a friend—only one friend—gentle Heaven! only one!"

Angelo sank on his knee, and kissed the mantle of his Lord.

"Say a follower. I am too mean to be Rienzi's friend."

"Too mean!—go to!—there is nothing mean before God, unless it be a base soul under high titles. With me, boy, there is but one nobility, and Nature signs its charter. Listen: thou hearest daily of Walter de Montreal, brother to these Provençals—great captain of great robbers?"

"Ay, and I have seen him, my Lord."

"Well, then, he is in Rome. Some daring thought—some well-supported and deep-schemed villany, could alone make that bandit venture openly into an Italian city, whose territories he ravaged by fire and sword a few months back. But his brothers have lent me money—assisted my return;—for their own ends, it is true: but the seeming obligation gives them real power. These Northern swordsmen would cut my throat if the Great Captain bade them. He counts on my supposed weakness. I know him of old. I suspect—nay I read, his projects; but I cannot prove them. Without proof, I cannot desert Palestrina in order to accuse and seize him. Thou art shrewd.

thoughtful, acute;—couldst thou go to Rome?—watch day and night his movements—see if he receive messengers from Albornoz or the Barons—if he confer with Pandulfo di Guido;—watch his lodgment, I say, night and day. He affects no concealment: your task will be less difficult than it seems. Apprise the Signora of all you learn. Give me your news daily. Will you undertake this mission?"

"I will, my Lord."

"To horse, then, quick!—and mind—save the wife of my bosom, I have no confidant in Rome."

CHAPTER II

MONTREAL AT ROME.—HIS RECEPTION OF ANGELO VILLANI

The danger that threatened Rienzi by the arrival of Montreal was indeed formidable. The Knight of St. John, having marched his army into Lombardy, had placed it at the disposal of the Venetian State in its war with the Archbishop of Milan. For this service he received an immense sum: while he provided winter quarters for his troop, for whom he proposed ample work in the ensuing spring. Leaving Palestrina secretly and in disguise, with but a slender train, which met him at Tivoli, Montreal repaired to Rome. His ostensible object was, partly to congratulate the Senator on his return, partly to receive the monies lent to Rienzi by his brother.

His secret object we have partly seen; but not contented with the support of the Barons, he trusted, by the corrupting means of his enormous wealth, to form a third party in support of his own ulterior designs. Wealth, indeed, in that age and in that land, was scarcely less the purchaser of diadems than it had been in the later days of the Roman Empire. And in many a city torn by hereditary feuds, the hatred of faction rose to that extent, that a foreign tyrant, willing and able to expel one party, might obtain at least the temporary submission of the other. His after-success was greatly in proportion to his power to maintain his state by a force which was independent of the citizens, and by a treasury which did not require the odious recruit of taxes. But more avaricious than ambitious, more cruel than firm, it was by griping exaction, or unnecessary bloodshed, that such usurpers usually fell.

Montreal, who had scanned the frequent revolutions of the time with a calm, and investigating eye, trusted that he should be enabled to avoid both these errors: and, as the reader has already seen, he had formed the profound and sagacious project of consolidating his usurpation by an utterly new race of nobles, who, serving him by the feudal tenure of the North, and ever ready to protect him, because in so doing they protected their own interests, should assist to erect, not the rotten and unsupported fabric of a single tyranny, but the strong fortress of a new, hardy, and compact Aristocratic State. Thus had the great dynasties of the North been founded; in which a King, though seemingly curbed by the Barons, was in reality supported by a common interest, whether against a subdued population or a foreign invasion.

Such were the vast schemes—extending into yet wider fields of glory and conquest, bounded only by the Alps—with which the Captain of the Grand Company beheld the columns and arches of the Seven-hilled City.

No fear disturbed the long current of his thoughts. His brothers were the leaders of Rienzi's hireling army —that army were his creatures. Over Rienzi himself he assumed the right of a creditor. Thus against one party he deemed himself secure. For the friends of the Pope, he had supported himself with private, though cautious letters from Albornoz, who desired only to make use of him for the return of the Roman Barons; and with the heads of the latter we have already witnessed his negotiations. Thus was he fitted, as he thought, to examine, to tamper with all parties, and to select from each the materials necessary for his own objects.

The open appearance of Montreal excited in Rome no inconsiderable sensation. The friends of the Barons gave out that Rienzi was in league with the Grand Company; and that he was to sell the imperial city to the plunder and pillage of Barbarian robbers. The effrontery with which Montreal (against whom, more than once, the Pontiff had thundered his bulls) appeared in the Metropolitan City of the Church, was made yet more insolent by the recollection of that stern justice which had led the Tribune to declare open war against all the robbers of Italy: and this audacity was linked with the obvious reflection, that the brothers of the bold Provençal were the instruments of Rienzi's return. So quickly spread suspicion through the city, that Montreal's presence alone would in a few weeks have sufficed to ruin the Senator. Meanwhile, the natural boldness of Montreal silenced every whisper of prudence; and, blinded by the dazzle of his hopes, the Knight of St. John, as if to give double importance to his coming, took up his residence in a sumptuous palace, and his retinue rivalled, in the splendour of garb and pomp, the display of Rienzi himself in his earlier and more brilliant power.

Amidst the growing excitement, Angelo Villani arrived at Rome. The character of this young man had been formed by his peculiar circumstances. He possessed qualities which often mark the Illegitimate as with a common stamp. He was insolent—like most of those who hold a doubtful rank; and while ashamed of his bastardy, was arrogant of the supposed nobility of his unknown parentage. The universal ferment and agitation of Italy at that day rendered ambition the most common of all the passions, and thus ambition, in all its many shades and varieties, forces itself into our delineations of character in this history. Though not for Angelo Villani were the dreams of the more lofty and generous order of that sublime infirmity, he was strongly incited by the desire and resolve to *rise*. He had warm affections and grateful impulses; and his fidelity to his patron had been carried to a virtue: but from his irregulated and desultory education, and the reckless profligacy of those with whom, in antechambers and guard-rooms, much of his youth had been passed, he had neither high principles nor an enlightened honour. Like most Italians, cunning and shrewd, he scrupled not at any deceit that served a purpose or a friend. His strong attachment to Rienzi had been unconsciously increased by the gratification of pride and vanity, flattered by the favour of so celebrated a man. Both self-interest and attachment urged him to every effort to promote the views and safety of one at once his benefactor and patron; and on undertaking his present mission, his only thought was to fulfil it with the most complete success. Far more brave and daring than was common with the Italians, something of the hardihood of an Ultra-Montane race gave nerve and vigour to his craft; and from what his art suggested his courage never shrunk.

When Rienzi had first detailed to him the objects of his present task, he instantly called to mind his adventure with the tall soldier in the crowd at Avignon. "If ever thou wantest a friend, seek him in Walter de Montreal," were words that had often rung in his ear, and they now recurred to him with prophetic distinctness. He had no doubt that it was Montreal himself whom he had seen. Why the Great Captain should have taken this interest in him, Angelo little cared to conjecture. Most probably it was but a crafty pretence—one of the common means by which the Chief of the Grand Company attracted to himself the youths of Italy, as well as the warriors of the North. He only thought now how he could turn the Knight's promise to account. What more easy than to present himself to Montreal—remind him of the words—enter his service—and thus effectually watch his conduct? The office of spy was not that which would have pleased every mind, but it shocked not the fastidiousness of Angelo Villani; and the fearful hatred with which his patron had often spoken of the avaricious and barbarian robber—the scourge of his native land, —had infected the young man, who had much of the arrogant and mock patriotism of the Romans, with a similar sentiment. More vindictive even than grateful, he bore, too, a secret grudge against Montreal's brother, whose rough address had often wounded his pride: and, above all, his early recollections of the fear and execration in which Ursula seemed ever to hold the terrible Fra Moreale, impressed him with a vague belief of some ancient wrong to himself or his race, perpetrated by the Provençal, which he was not ill-pleased to have the occasion to avenge. In truth, the words of Ursula, mystic and dark as they were in their denunciation, had left upon Villani's boyish impressions an unaccountable feeling of antipathy and hatred to the man it was now his object to betray. For the rest, every device seemed to him decorous and justifiable, so that it saved his master, served his country, and advanced himself.

Montreal was alone in his chamber when it was announced to him that a young Italian craved an audience. Professionally open to access, he forthwith gave admission to the applicant.

The Knight of St. John instantly recognised the page he had encountered at Avignon; and when Angelo Villani said, with easy boldness, "I have come to remind Sir Walter de Montreal of a promise——"

The Knight interrupted him with cordial frankness —"Thou needest not—I remember it. Dost thou now require my friendship?"

"I do, noble Signor!" answered Angelo; "I know not where else to seek a patron."

"Canst thou read and write? I fear me not."

"I have been taught those arts," replied Villani.

"It is well. Is thy birth gentle?"

"It is."

"Better still;—thy name?"

"Angelo Villani."

"I take thy blue eyes and low broad brow," said Montreal, with a slight sigh, "in pledge of thy truth. Henceforth, Angelo Villani, thou art in the list of my secretaries. Another time thou shalt tell me more of thyself. Thy service dates from this day. For the rest, no man ever wanted wealth who served Walter de Montreal; nor advancement, if he served him faithfully. My closet, through yonder door, is thy waiting room. Ask for, and send hither, Lusignan of Lyons; he is my chief scribe, and will see to thy comforts, and instruct thee in thy business."

Angelo withdrew—Montreal's eye followed him.

"A strange likeness!" said he, musingly and sadly; "my heart leaps to that boy!"

CHAPTER III

MONTREAL'S BANQUET

Some few days after the date of the last chapter, Rienzi received news from Rome, which seemed to produce in him a joyous and elated excitement. His troops still lay before Palestrina, and still the banners of the Barons waved over its unconquered walls. In truth, the Italians employed half their time in brawls amongst themselves; the Velletritrani had feuds with the people of Tivoli, and the Romans were still afraid of conquering the Barons;—"The hornet," said they, "stings worse after he is dead; and neither an Orsini, a Savelli, nor a Colonna, was ever known to forgive."

Again and again had the captains of his army assured the indignant Senator that the fortress was impregnable, and that time and money were idly wasted upon the siege. Rienzi knew better, but he concealed his thoughts.

He now summoned to his tent the brothers of Provence, and announced to them his intention of returning instantly to Rome. "The mercenaries shall continue the siege under our Lieutenant, and you, with my Roman Legion, shall accompany me. Your brother, Sir Walter, and I, both want your presence; we have affairs to arrange between us. After a few days I shall raise recruits in the city, and return."

This was what the brothers desired; they approved, with evident joy, the Senator's proposition.

Rienzi next sent for the lieutenant of his body-guard, the same Riccardo Annibaldi whom the reader will remember in the earlier part of this work, as the antagonist of Montreal's lance. This young man—one of the few nobles who espoused the cause of the Senator—had evinced great courage and military ability, and promised fair (should Fate spare his life *) to become one of the best Captains of his time.

"Dear Annibaldi," said Rienzi; "at length I can fulfil the project on which we have privately conferred. I take with me to Rome the two Provençal Captains—I leave you chief of the army. Palestrina will yield now—eh!—ha, ha, ha!—Palestrina will yield now!"

"By my right hand, I think so, Senator," replied Annibaldi. "These foreigners have hitherto only stirred up quarrels amongst ourselves, and if not cowards are certainly traitors!"

"Hush, hush, hush! Traitors! The learned Arimbaldo, the brave Brettone, traitors! Fie on it! No, no; they are very excellent, honourable men, but not lucky in the camp;—not lucky in the camp;—better speed to them in the city! And now to business."

* It appears that this was the same Annibaldi who was afterwards slain in an affray:—Petrarch lauds his valour and laments his fate.

The Senator then detailed to Annibaldi the plan he himself had formed for taking the town, and the military skill of Annibaldi at once recognised its feasibility.

With his Roman troop and Montreal's brothers, one at either hand, Rienzi then departed to Rome.

That night Montreal gave a banquet to Pandulfo di Guido, and to certain of the principal citizens, whom one by one he had already sounded, and found hollow at heart to the cause of the Senator.

Pandulfo sate at the right hand of the Knight of St. John, and Montreal lavished upon him the most courteous attentions.

"Pledge me in this—it is from the Vale of Chiana, near Monte Pulciano," said Montreal. "I think I have heard bookmen say (you know, Signor Pandulfo, we ought all to be bookmen now!) that the site was renowned of old. In truth, the wine hath a racy flavour."

"I hear," said Bruttini, one of the lesser Barons, (a stanch friend to the Colonna,) "that in this respect the innkeeper's son has put his book-learning to some use: he knows every place where the wine grows richest."

"What! the Senator is turned wine-bibber!" said Montreal, quaffing a vast goblet full; "that must unfit him for business—'tis a pity."

"Verily, yes," said Pandulfo; "a man at the head of a state should be temperate—*I* never drink wine unmixed."

"Ah," whispered Montreal, "if your calm good sense ruled Rome, then, indeed, the metropolis of Italy might taste of peace. Signor Vivaldi,"—and the host turned towards a wealthy draper,—"these disturbances are bad for trade."

"Very, very!" groaned the draper.

"The Barons are your best customers," quoth the minor noble.

"Much, much!" said the draper.

"'Tis a pity that they are thus roughly expelled," said Montreal, in a melancholy tone. "Would it not be possible, if the Senator (*I* drink his health) were less rash—less zealous, rather,—to unite free institutions with the return of the Barons?—*such* should be the task of a truly wise statesman."

"It surely might be possible," returned Vivaldi; "the Savelli alone spend more with me than all the rest of Rome."

"I know not if it be possible," said Bruttini; "but I do know that it is an outrage to all decorum that an innkeeper's son should be enabled to make a solitude of the palaces of Rome."

"It certainly seems to indicate too vulgar a desire of mob favour," said Montreal. "However, I trust we shall harmonize all these differences. Rienzi, perhaps,—nay, doubtless, *means* well!"

"I would," said Vivaldi, who had received his cue, "that we might form a mixed constitution—Plebeians and Patricians, each in their separate order."

"But," said Montreal, gravely, "so new an experiment would demand great physical force."

"Why, true; but we might call in an umpire—a foreigner who had no interest in either faction—who might protect the new Buono Stato; a Podesta, as we have done before—Brancaleone, for instance. How well and wisely he ruled! that was a golden age for Rome. A Podesta for ever!—that's my theory."

"You need not seek far for the president of your council," said Montreal, smiling at Pandulfo; "a citizen at once popular, well-born, and wealthy, may be found at my right hand."

Pandulfo hemmed, and coloured.

Montreal proceeded. "A committee of trades might furnish an honourable employment to Signor Vivaldi; and the treatment of all foreign affairs—the employment of armies, &c., might be left to the Barons, with a more open competition, Signor di Bruttini, to the Barons of the second order than has hitherto been conceded to their birth and importance. Sirs, will you taste the Malvoisie?"

"Still," said Vivaldi, after a pause—(Vivaldi anticipated at least the supplying with cloth the whole of the Grand Company)—"still, such a moderate and well-digested constitution would never be acceded to by Rienzi."

"Why should it? what need of Rienzi?" exclaimed Bruttini. "Rienzi may take another trip to Bohemia."

"Gently, gently," said Montreal; "I do not despair. All open violence against the Senator would strengthen his power. No, no, humble him—admit the Barons, and then insist on your own terms. Between the two factions you might then establish a fitting balance. And in order to keep your new constitution from the encroachment of either extreme, there *are* warriors and knights, too, who for a certain rank in the great city of Rome would maintain horse and foot at its service. We Ultra-Montanes are often harshly judged; we are wanderers and Ishmaelites, solely because we have no honourable place of rest. Now, if *I*——"

"Ay, if you, noble Montreal!" said Vivaldi.

The company remained hushed in breathless attention, when suddenly there was heard—deep, solemn, muffled,—the great bell of the Capitol!

"Hark!" said Vivaldi, "the bell: it tolls for execution: an unwonted hour!"

"Sure, the Senator has not returned!" exclaimed Pandulfo di Guido, turning pale.

"No, no," quoth Bruttini, "it is but a robber, caught two nights ago in Romagna. I heard that he was to die to-night."

At the word "robber," Montreal changed countenance slightly. The wine circulated—the bell continued to toll—its suddenness over, it ceased to alarm. Conversation flowed again.

"What were you saying, Sir Knight?" said Vivaldi.

"Why, let me think on't;—oh, speaking of the necessity of supporting a new state by force, I said that if *I*——"

"Ah, that was it!" quoth Bruttini, thumping the table.

"If *I* were summoned to your aid—*summoned*, mind ye, and absolved by the Pope's Legate of my former sins—(they weigh heavily on me, gentles)—I would myself guard your city from foreign foe and civil disturbance, with my gallant swordsmen. Not a Roman citizen should contribute a 'danaro' to the cost."

"*Viva Fra Moreale!*" cried Bruttini; and the shout was echoed by all the boon companions.

"Enough for me," continued Montreal, "to expiate my offences. Ye know, gentlemen, my order is vowed to God and the Church—a warrior monk am I! Enough for me to expiate my offences, I say, in the defence of the Holy City. Yet I, too, have my private and more earthly views,—who is above them? I——the bell changes its note!"

"It is but the change that preludes execution—the poor robber is about to die!"

Montreal crossed himself, and resumed:—"I am a knight and a noble," said he, proudly; "the profession I have followed is that of arms; but—I will not disguise it—mine equals have regarded me as one who has stained his scutcheon by too reckless a pursuit of glory and of gain. I wish to reconcile myself with my order—to purchase a new name—to vindicate myself to the Grand Master and the Pontiff. I have had hints, gentles,—hints, that I might best promote my interest by restoring order to the Papal metropolis. The Legate Albornoz (here is his letter) recommends me to keep watch upon the Senator."

"Surely," interrupted Pandulfo, "I hear steps below."

"The mob going to the robber's execution," said Bruttini; "proceed, Sir Knight!"

"And," continued Montreal, surveying his audience before he proceeded farther, "what think ye—(I do but ask your opinion, wiser than mine)—what think ye, as a fitting precaution against too arbitrary a power in the Senator—what think ye of the return of the Colonna, and the bold Barons of Palestrina?"

"Here's to their health!" cried Vivaldi, rising.

As by a sudden impulse, the company rose. "To the health of the besieged Barons!" was shouted aloud.

"Next, what if—(I do but humbly suggest)—what if you gave the Senator a colleague?—it is no affront to him. It was but as yesterday that one of the Colonna, who was Senator, received a colleague in Bertoldo Orsini."

"A most wise precaution," cried Vivaldi. "And where a colleague like Pandulfo di Guido?"

"*Viva Pandulfo di Guido!*" cried the guests, and again their goblets were drained to the bottom.

"And if in this I can assist ye by fair words with the Senator, (ye know he owes me monies—my brothers have served him), command Walter de Montreal."

"And if fair words fail?" said Vivaldi.

"The Grand Company—(heed me, *ye* are the councillors)—the Grand Company is accustomed to forced marches!"

"*Viva Fra Moreale!*" cried Bruttini and Vivaldi, simultaneously. "A health to all, my friends," continued Bruttini; "a health to the Barons, Rome's old friends; to Pandulfo di Guido, the Senator's new colleague; and to Fra Moreale, Rome's new Podesta."

"The bell has ceased," said Vivaldi, putting down his goblet.

"Heaven have mercy on the robber!" added Bruttini.

Scarce had he spoken, ere three taps were heard at the door—the guests looked at each other in dumb amaze.

"New guests!" said Montreal. "I asked some trusty friends to join us this evening. By my faith they are welcome! Enter!"

The door opened slowly; three by three entered, in complete armour, the guards of the Senator. On they marched, regular and speechless. They surrounded the festive board—they filled the spacious hall, and the lights of the banquet were reflected upon their corselets as on a wall of steel.

Not a syllable was uttered by the feasters, they were as if turned to stone. Presently the guards gave way, and Rienzi himself appeared. He approached the table, and folding his arms, turned his gaze deliberately from guest to guest, till at last, his eyes rested on Montreal, who had also risen, and who alone of the party had recovered the amaze of the moment.

And, there, as these two men, each so celebrated, so proud, able, and ambitious, stood front to front—it was literally as if the rival Spirits of Force and Intellect, Order and Strife, of the Falchion and the Fasces—the Antagonist Principles by which empires are ruled and empires overthrown, had met together, incarnate and opposed. They stood, both silent,—as if fascinated by each other's gaze,—loftier in stature, and nobler in presence than all around.

Montreal spoke first, and with a forced smile.

"Senator of Rome!—dare I believe that my poor banquet tempts thee, and may I trust that these armed men are a graceful compliment to one to whom arms have been a pastime?"

Rienzi answered not, but waved his hand to his guards. Montreal was seized on the instant. Again he surveyed the guests—as a bird from the rattlesnake,—shrunk Pandulfo di Guido, trembling, motionless, aghast, from the glittering eye of the Senator. Slowly Rienzi raised his fatal hand towards the unhappy citizen—Pandulfo saw—felt his doom,—shrieked,—and fell senseless in the arms of the soldiers.

One other and rapid glance cast the Senator round the board, and then, with a disdainful smile, as if anxious for no meaner prey, turned away. Not a breath had hitherto passed his lips—all had been dumb show—and his grim silence had imparted a more freezing terror to his unguessed-for apparition. Only, when he reached the door, he turned back, gazed upon the Knight of St. John's bold and undaunted face, and said, almost in a whisper, "Walter de Montreal!—you heard the death-knell!"

CHAPTER IV

THE SENTENCE OF WALTER DE MONTREAL

In silence the Captain of the Grand Company was borne to the prison of the Capitol. In the same building lodged the rivals for the government of Rome; the one occupied the prison, the other the palace. The guards forebore the ceremony of fetters, and leaving a lamp on the table, Montreal perceived he was not alone,—his brothers had preceded him.

"We are happily met," said the Knight of St. John; "we have passed together pleasanter nights than this is likely to be."

"Can you jest, Walter?" said Arimbaldo, half-weeping. "Know you not that our doom is fixed? Death scowls upon us."

"Death!" repeated Montreal, and for the first time his countenance changed; perhaps for the first time in his life he felt the thrill and agony of fear.

"Death!" he repeated again. "Impossible! He dare not, Brettone; the soldiers, the Northmen!—they will mutiny, they will pluck us back from the grasp of the headsman!"

"Cast from you so vain a hope," said Brettone sullenly; "the soldiers are encamped at Palestrina."

"How! Dolt—fool! Came you then to Rome *alone!* Are we *alone* with this dread man?"

"*You* are the dolt! Why came you hither?" answered the brother.

"Why, indeed! but that I knew thou wast the Captain of the army; and—but thou said'st right—the folly is mine, to have played against the crafty Tribune so unequal a brain as thine. Enough! Reproaches are idle. When were ye arrested?"

"At dusk—the instant we entered the gates of Rome. Rienzi entered privately."

"Humph! What can he know against me? Who can have betrayed me? My secretaries are tried—all trustworthy—except that youth, and he so seemingly zealous—that Angelo Villani!"

"Villani! Angelo Villani!" cried the brothers in a breath. "Hast thou confided aught to him?"

"Why, I fear he must have seen—at least in part—my correspondence with you, and with the Barons—he was among my scribes. Know you aught of him?"

"Walter, Heaven hath demented you!" returned Brettone. "Angelo Villani is the favourite menial of the Senator."

"Those eyes deceived me, then," muttered Montreal, solemnly and shuddering; "and, as if *her* ghost had returned to earth, God smites me from the grave!"

There was a long silence. At length Montreal, whose bold and sanguine temper was never long clouded, spoke again.

"Are the Senator's coffers full?—But that is impossible."

"Bare as a Dominican's."

"We are saved then. He shall name his price for

our heads. Money must be more useful to him than blood."

And as if with that thought all further meditation were rendered unnecessary, Montreal doffed his mantle, uttered a short prayer, and flung himself on a pallet in a corner of the cell.

"I have slept on worse beds," said the Knight, stretching himself; and in a few minutes he was fast asleep.

The brothers listened to his deep-drawn, but regular breathing, with envy and wonder, but they were in no mood to converse. Still and speechless, they sate like statues beside the sleeper. Time passed on, and the first cold air of the hour that succeeds to midnight crept through the bars of their cell. The bolts crashed, the door opened, six men-at-arms entered, passed the brothers, and one of them touched Montreal.

"Ha!" said he, still sleeping, but turning round. "Ha!" said he, in the soft Provençal tongue, "sweet Adeline, we will not rise yet—it is so long since we met!"

"What says he?" muttered the guard, shaking Montreal roughly. The Knight sprang up at once, and his hand grasped the head of his bed as for his sword. He stared round bewildered, rubbed his eyes, and then gazing on the guard, became alive to the present.

"Ye are early risers in the Capitol," said he. "What want ye of me?"

"*It* waits you!"

"*It!* What?" said Montreal.

"The rack!" replied the soldier, with a malignant scowl.

The Great Captain said not a word. He looked for one moment at the six swordsmen, as if measuring his single strength against theirs. His eye then wandered round the room. The rudest bar of iron would have been dearer to him than he had ever yet found the proofest steel of Milan. He completed his survey with a sigh, threw his mantle over his shoulders, nodded at his brethren, and followed the guard.

In a hall of the Capitol, hung with the ominous silk of white rays on a blood-red ground, sate Rienzi and his councillors. Across a recess was drawn a black curtain.

"Walter de Montreal," said a small man at the foot of the table, "Knight of the illustrious order of St. John of Jerusalem——"

"And Captain of the Grand Company!" added the prisoner, in a firm voice.

"You stand accused of divers counts: robbery and murder, in Tuscany, Romagna, and Apulia——"

"For robbery and murder, brave men, and belted knights," said Montreal, drawing himself up, "would use the words 'war and victory.' To those charges I plead guilty! Proceed."

"You are next accused of treasonable conspiracy against the liberties of Rome for the restoration of the proscribed Barons—and of traitorous correspondence with Stefanello Colonna at Palestrina."

"My accuser?"

"Step forth, Angelo Villani!"

"*You* are my betrayer, then?" said Montreal steadily. "I deserved this. I beseech you, Senator of Rome, let this young man retire. I confess my correspondence with the Colonna, and my desire to restore the Barons."

Rienzi motioned to Villani, who bowed and withdrew.

"There rests only then for you, Walter de Montreal, to relate, fully and faithfully, the details of your conspiracy."

"That is impossible," replied Montreal, carelessly.

"And why?"

"Because, doing as I please with my own life, I will not betray the lives of others."

"Bethink thee—thou wouldst have betrayed the life of thy judge!"

"Not betrayed—thou didst not trust me."

"The law, Walter de Montreal, hath sharp inquisitors—behold!"

The black curtain was drawn aside, and the eye of Montreal rested on the executioner and the rack! His proud breast heaved indignantly.

"Senator of Rome," said he, "these instruments are for serfs and villeins. I have been a warrior and a leader; life and death have been in my hands—I have used them as I listed; but to mine equal and my foe, I never proffered the insult of the rack."

"Sir Walter de Montreal," returned the Senator, gravely, but with some courteous respect, "your answer is that which rises naturally to the lips of brave men. But learn from me, whom fortune hath made thy judge, that no more for serf and villein, than for knight and noble, are such instruments the engincs of law, or the tests of truth. I yielded but to the desire of these reverend councillors, to test thy nerves. But, wert thou the meanest peasant of the Campagna, before my judgment-seat thou needst not apprehend the torture. Walter de Montreal, amongst the Princes of Italy thou hast known, amongst the Roman Barons thou wouldst have aided, is there one who could make that boast?"

"I desired only," said Montreal, with some hesitation, "to unite the Barons *with* thee; nor did I intrigue against thy *life!*"

Rienzi frowned—"Enough," he said, hastily. "Knight of St. John, I *know* thy secret projects, subterfuge and evasion neither befit nor avail thee. If thou didst not intrigue against my life, thou didst intrigue against the life of Rome. Thou hast but one favour left to demand on earth, it is the manner of thy death."

Montreal's lip worked convulsively.

"Senator," said he, in a low voice, "may I crave audience with thee *alone* for one minute?"

The councillors looked up.

"My Lord," whispered the eldest of them, "doubtless he hath concealed weapons—trust him not."

"Prisoner," returned Rienzi, after a moment's pause; "if thou seekest for mercy thy request is idle, and before my coadjutors I have no secret! speak out what thou hast to say!"

"Yet listen to me," said the prisoner, folding his arms, "it concerns not my life, but Rome's welfare."

"Then," said Rienzi, in an altered tone, "thy request is granted. Thou mayest add to thy guilt the design of the assassin, but for Rome I would dare greater danger."

So saying, he motioned to the councillors, who slowly withdrew by the door which had admitted Villani, while the guards retired to the farthest extremity of the hall.

"Now, Walter de Montreal, be brief, for thy time is short."

"Senator," said Montreal, "my life can but little profit you; men will say that you destroyed your creditor in order to cancel your debt. Fix a sum upon my life, estimate it at the price of a monarch's; every florin shall be paid to you, and your treasury will be filled for five years to come. If the '*Buono Stato*' depends on your government, what I have asked, your solicitude for Rome will not permit you to refuse."

"You mistake me, bold robber," said Rienzi sternly; "your *treason* I could guard against, and therefore forgive; your *ambition*, never! Mark me, I know you! Place your hand on your heart and say whether, could we change places, you, as Rienzi, would suffer all the gold of earth to purchase the life of Walter de Montreal? For men's reading of my conduct, that must I bear; for mine own reading, mine eyes must be purged from corruption. I am answerable to God for the trust of Rome. And Rome trembles while the head of the Grand Company lives in the plotting brain and the daring heart of Walter de Montreal. Man—wealthy, great, and subtle as you are, your hours are numbered; with the rise of the sun you die!"

Montreal's eyes, fixed upon the Senator's face, saw hope was over; his pride and his fortitude returned to him.

"We have wasted words," said he. "I played for a great stake, I have lost, and must pay the forfeit! I am prepared. On the threshold of the Unknown World, the dark spirit of prophecy rushes into us. Lord Senator, I go before thee to announce—that in Heaven or in Hell—ere many days be over, room must be given to one mightier than I am!"

As he spoke, his form dilated, his eye glared; and

Rienzi, cowering as never had he cowered before, shrunk back, and shaded his face with his hand.

"The manner of your death?" he asked, in a hollow voice.

"The axe: it is that which befits knight and warrior. For thee, Senator, Fate hath a less noble death."

"Robber, be dumb!" cried Rienzi, passionately; "Guards, bear back the prisoner. At sunrise, Montreal——"

"*Sets* the sun of the scourge of Italy," said the Knight, bitterly. "Be it so. One request more; the Knights of St. John claim affinity with the Augustine order; grant me an Augustine confessor."

"It is granted; and in return for thy denunciations, I, who can give thee no earthly mercy, will implore the Judge of all for pardon to thy soul!"

"Senator, I have done with man's mediation. My brethren? Their deaths are not necessary to thy safety or thy revenge!"

Rienzi mused a moment: "No," said he, "dangerous tools they were, but without the workman they may rust unharming. They served me once, too. Prisoner, their lives are spared."

CHAPTER V

THE DISCOVERY

The Council was broken up—Rienzi hastened to his own apartments. Meeting Villani by the way, he pressed the youth's hand affectionately. "You have saved Rome and me from great peril," said he; "the saints reward you!" Without tarrying for Villani's answer, he hurried on. Nina, anxious and perturbed, awaited him in their chamber.

"Not a-bed yet?" said he: "fie, Nina, even thy beauty will not stand these vigils."

"I could not rest till I had seen thee. I hear (all Rome has heard it ere this) that thou hast seized Walter de Montreal, and that he will perish by the headsman."

"The first robber that ever died so brave a death," returned Rienzi, slowly unrobing himself.

"Cola, I have never crossed your schemes,—your policy, even by a suggestion. Enough for me to triumph in their success, to mourn for their failure. Now, I ask thee one request—spare me the life of this man."

"Nina——"

"Hear me,—for thee I speak! Despite his crimes, his valour and his genius have gained him admirers, even amongst his foes. Many a prince, many a state that secretly rejoices at his fall, will affect horror against his judge. Hear me further; his brothers aided your return; the world will term you ungrateful. His brothers lent you monies, the world—(out on it!)—will term you——"

"Hold!" interrupted the Senator. "All that thou sayest, my mind forestalled. But thou knowest me—to thee I have no disguise. No compact can bind Montreal's faith—no mercy win his gratitude. Before his red right hand truth and justice are swept away. If I condemn Montreal I incur disgrace and risk danger—granted. If I release him, ere the first showers of April, the chargers of the Northmen will neigh in the halls of the Capitol. Which shall I hazard in this alternative, myself or Rome? Ask me no more—to bed, to bed!"

"Couldst thou read my forebodings, Cola, mystic—gloomy—unaccountable?"

"Forebodings!—I have mine," answered Rienzi, sadly, gazing on space, as if his thoughts peopled it with spectres. Then, raising his eyes to Heaven, he said with that fanatical energy which made much both of his strength and weakness—"Lord, mine at least not the sin of Saul! the Amalekite shall not be saved!"

While Rienzi enjoyed a short, troubled, and restless sleep, over which Nina watched—unslumbering, anxious, tearful, and oppressed with dark and terrible forewarnings—the accuser was more happy than the judge. The last thoughts that floated before the young mind of Angelo Villani, ere wrapped in sleep, were bright and sanguine. He felt no honourable remorse that he had entrapped the confidence of another—he felt only that his scheme had prospered, that his mission had been fulfilled. The grateful words of Rienzi rang in his ear, and hopes of fortune and power, beneath the sway of the Roman Senator, lulled him into slumber, and coloured all his dreams.

Scarce, however, had he been two hours asleep, ere he was wakened by one of the attendants of the palace, himself half awake. "Pardon me, Messere Villani," said he, "but there is a messenger below from the good Sister Ursula; he bids thee haste instantly to the convent—she is sick unto death, and has tidings that crave thy immediate presence."

Angelo, whose morbid susceptibility as to his parentage was ever excited by vague but ambitious hopes—started up, dressed hurriedly, and joining the messenger below, repaired to the Convent. In the Court of the Capitol, and by the Staircase of the Lion, was already heard the noise of the workmen, and looking back, Villani beheld the scaffold, hung with black—sleeping cloudlike in the gray light of dawn—at the same time the bell of the Capitol tolled heavily. A pang shot athwart him. He hurried on;—despite the immature earliness of the hour, he met groups of either sex, hastening along the streets to witness the execution of the redoubted Captain of the Grand Company. The Convent of the Augustines was at the farthest extremity of that city, even then so extensive, and the red light upon the hill tops already heralded the rising sun, ere the young man reached the venerable porch. His name obtained him instant admittance.

"Heaven grant," said an old Nun, who conducted him through a long and winding passage, "that thou mayst bring comfort to the sick sister: she has pined for thee grievously since matins."

In a cell set apart for the reception of visitors (from the outward world), to such of the Sisterhood as received the necessary dispensation, sate the aged Nun. Angelo had only seen her once since his return to Rome, and since then disease had made rapid havoc on her form and features. And now, in her shroudlike garments and attenuated frame, she seemed by the morning light as a spectre whom day had surprised above the earth. She approached the youth, however, with a motion more elastic and rapid than seemed possible to her worn and ghastly form. "Thou art come," she said. "Well, well! This morning after matins, my confessor, an Augustine, who alone knows the secrets of my life, took me aside, and told me that Walter de Montreal had been seized by the Senator—that he was adjudged to die, and that one of the Augustine brotherhood had been sent for to attend his last hours —is it so?"

"Thou wert told aright," said Angelo, wonderingly. "The man at whose name thou wert wont to shudder —against whom thou hast so often warned me—will die at sunrise."

"So soon!—so soon!—Oh, Mother of Mercy! fly! thou art about the person of the Senator, thou hast high favour with him; fly! down on thy knees—and as thou hopest for God's grace, rise not till thou hast won the Provençal's life."

"She raves," muttered Angelo, with white lips.

"I do *not* rave,—boy!" screeched the Sister, wildly, "know that my daughter was his leman. He disgraced our house,—a house haughtier than his own. Sinner that I was, I vowed revenge. His boy—they had only one!—was brought up in a robber's camp;—a life of bloodshed—a death of doom—a futurity of hell—were before him. I plucked the child from such a fate—I bore him away—I told the father he was dead—I placed him in the path to honourable fortunes. May my sin be forgiven me! Angelo Villani, thou art that child;—Walter de Montreal is thy father. But now, trembling on the verge of death, I shudder at the vindictive thoughts I once nourished. Perhaps——"

"Sinner and accursed!" interrupted Villani, with a loud shout:—"sinner and accursed thou art indeed! Know that it was *I* who betrayed thy daughter's lover! —by the son's treason dies the father!"

Not a moment more did he tarry: he waited not to witness the effect his words produced. As one frantic —as one whom a fiend possesses or pursues—he rushed from the Convent—he flew through the desolate streets. The death-bell came, first indistinct, then loud, upon his ear. Every sound seemed to him like the curse of God; on—on—he passed the more deserted quarter—crowds swept before him—he was mingled with the living stream, delayed, pushed back—thousands on thousands around, before him. Breathless, gasping, he still pressed on—he forced his way—he heard not—he saw not—all was like a dream. Up burst the sun over the distant hills;—the bell ceased! From right to left he pushed aside the crowd—his strength was as a giant's. He neared the fatal spot. A dead hush lay like a heavy air over the multitude. He heard a voice, as he pressed along, deep and clear—it was the voice of his father!—it ceased—the audience breathed heavily—they murmured—they swayed to and fro. On, on, went Angelo Villani. The guards of the Senator stopped his way;—he dashed aside their pikes—he eluded their grasp—he pierced the armed barrier—he stood on the Place of the Capitol. "Hold, hold!" he would have cried—but horror struck him dumb. He beheld the gleaming axe—he saw the bended neck. Ere another breath passed his lips, a ghastly and trunkless face was raised on high—Walter de Montreal was no more!

Villani saw—swooned not—shrunk not—breathed not!—but he turned his eyes from that lifted head, dropping gore, to the balcony, in which, according to custom, sate, in solemn pomp, the Senator of Rome——and the face of that young man was as the face of a demon!

"Ha!" said he, muttering to himself, and recalling the words of Rienzi seven years before—"*Blessed art thou who hast no blood of kindred to avenge!*"

CHAPTER VI

THE SUSPENSE

Walter de Montreal was buried in the Church of St. Maria dell' Araceli. But the "evil that he did lived after him!" Although the vulgar had, until his apprehension, murmured against Rienzi for allowing so notorious a freebooter to be at large, he was scarcely dead ere they compassionated the object of their terror. With that singular species of piety which Montreal had always cultivated, as if a decorous and natural part of the character of a warrior, no sooner was his sentence fixed, than he had surrendered himself to the devout preparation for death. With the Augustine Friar he consumed the brief remainder of the night in prayer and confession, comforted his brothers, and passed to the scaffold with the step of a hero and the self-acquittal of a martyr. In the wonderful delusions of the human heart, far from feeling remorse at a life of professional rapine and slaughter, almost the last words of the brave warrior were in proud commendation of his own deeds. "Be valiant like me," he said to his brothers, "and remember that ye are now the heirs to the Humbler of Apulia, Tuscany, and La Marca."*

This confidence in himself continued at the scaffold. "I die," he said, addressing the Romans—"I die contented, since my bones shall rest in the Holy City of

* "Pregovi che vi amiate e siate valorosi al mondo, come fui io, che mi feci fare obbedienza a la Puglia, Toscana, e a La Marca."—*Vit. di Cola di Rienzi*, lib. ii. cap. 22. "I pray you love one another, and be valorous as was I, who made Apulia, Tuscany and La Marca own obedience to me."—*Life of Cola di Rienzi.*

St. Peter and St. Paul, and the Soldier of Christ shall have the burial-place of the Apostles. But I die unjustly. My wealth is my crime—the poverty of your state my accuser. Senator of Rome, thou mayst envy my last hour—men like Walter de Montreal perish not unavenged." So saying, he turned to the East, murmured a brief prayer, knelt down deliberately, and said as to himself, "Rome guard my ashes!—Earth my memory—Fate my revenge;—and, now, Heaven receive my soul!—Strike!" At the first blow, the head was severed from the body.

His treason but imperfectly known, the fear of him forgotten, all that remained of the recollection of Walter de Montreal * in Rome, was admiration for his heroism, and compassion for his end. The fate of Pandulfo di Guido, which followed some days afterwards, excited a yet deeper, though more quiet, sentiment, against the Senator. "He was once Rienzi's friend!" said one man; "He was an honest, upright citizen!" muttered another; "He was an advocate of the people!" growled Cecco del Vecchio. But the Senator had wound himself up to a resolve to be inflexibly just, and to regard every peril to Rome as became a Roman. Rienzi remembered that he had never confided but he had been betrayed; he had never forgiven but to sharpen enmity. He was amidst a ferocious people, uncertain friends, wily enemies;

* The military renown and bold exploits of Montreal are acknowledged by all the Italian authorities. One of them declares that since the time of Cæsar, Italy had never known so great a Captain. The biographer of Rienzi, forgetting all the offences of the splendid and knightly robber, seems to feel only commiseration for his fate. He informs us, moreover, that at Tivoli one of his servants (perhaps our friend, Rodolf of Saxony), hearing his death, died of grief the following day.

and misplaced mercy would be but a premium to conspiracy. Yet the struggle he underwent was visible in the hysterical emotions he betrayed. He now wept bitterly, now laughed wildly. "Can I never again have the luxury to forgive?" said he. The coarse spectators of that passion deemed it,—some imbecility, some hypocrisy. But the execution produced the momentary effect intended. All sedition ceased, terror crept throughout the city, order and peace rose to the surface; but beneath, in the strong expression of a contemporaneous writer, "Lo mormorito quetamente suonava."*

On examining dispassionately the conduct of Rienzi at this awful period of his life, it is scarcely possible to condemn it of a single error in point of policy. Cured of his faults, he exhibited no unnecessary ostentation —he indulged in no exhibitions of intoxicated pride— that gorgeous imagination rather than vanity, which had led the Tribune into spectacle and pomp, was now lulled to rest, by the sober memory of grave vicissitudes, and the stern calmness of a maturer intellect. Frugal, provident, watchful, self-collected, "never was seen," observes no partial witness, "so extraordinary a man."† "In him was concentrated every thought for every want of Rome." Indefatigably occupied, he inspected, ordained, regulated all things; in the city, in the army, for peace, or for war. But he was feebly supported, and those he employed were lukewarm and lethargic. Still his arms prospered. Place after place, fortress after fortress, yielded to the Lieutenant of the Senator: and the cession of Palestrina itself was hourly expected. His art and address were always strik-

* "The murmur quietly sounded."

† Vit. di Cola di Rienzi, lib. ii. c. 23.

ingly exhibited in difficult situations, and the reader cannot fail to have noticed how conspicuously they were displayed in delivering himself from the iron tutelage of his foreign mercenaries. Montreal executed, his brothers imprisoned, (though their lives were spared,) a fear that induced respect was stricken into the breasts of those bandit soldiers. Removed from Rome, and, under Annibaldi, engaged against the Barons, constant action and constant success, withheld those necessary fiends from falling on their Master; while Rienzi, willing to yield to the natural antipathy of the Romans, thus kept the Northmen from all contact with the city; and, as he boasted, was the only chief in Italy who reigned in his palace guarded only by his citizens.

Despite his perilous situation—despite his suspicions, and his fears, no wanton cruelty stained his stern justice—Montreal and Pandulfo di Guido were the only state victims he demanded. If, according to the dark Machiavelism of Italian wisdom, the death of those enemies was impolitic, it was not in the act, but the mode of doing it. A prince of Bologna, or of Milan would have avoided the sympathy excited by the scaffold, and the drug or the dagger would have been the safer substitute for the axe. But with all his faults, real and imputed, no single act of that foul and murtherous policy, which made the science of the more fortunate princes of Italy, ever advanced the ambition or promoted the security of the Last of the Roman Tribunes. Whatever his errors, he lived and died as became a man, who dreamed the vain but glorious dream, that in a corrupt and dastard populace he could revive the genius of the old Republic.

Of all who attended on the Senator, the most assiduous and the most honoured was still Angelo Villani. Promoted to a high civil station, Rienzi felt it as a return of youth, to find one person entitled to his gratitude;—he loved and confided in the youth as a son. Villani was never absent from his side, except in intercourse with the various popular leaders in the various quarters of the city; and in this intercourse his zeal was indefatigable—it seemed even to prey upon his health; and Rienzi chid him fondly, whenever starting from his own reveries, he beheld the abstracted eye and the livid paleness which had succeeded the sparkle and bloom of youth.

Such chiding the young man answered only by the same unvarying words.

"Senator, I have a great trust to fulfil;"—and at these words he smiled.

One day Villani, while with the Senator, said rather abruptly, "Do you remember, my Lord, that before Viterbo, I acquitted myself so in arms, that even the Cardinal d'Albornoz was pleased to notice me?"

"I remember your valour well, Angelo; but why the question?"

"My Lord, Bellini, the Captain of the Guard of the Capitol, is dangerously ill."

"I know it."

"Whom can my Lord trust at the post?"

"Why, the Lieutenant."

"What!—a soldier that has served under the Orsini!"

"True. Well! there is Tommaso Filangieri."

"An excellent man; but is he not kin by blood to Pandulfo di Guido?"

"Ay—is he so? It must be thought of. Hast *thou*

any friend to name?" said the Senator, smiling, "Methinks thy cavils point that way."

"My Lord," replied Villani, colouring; "I am too young, perhaps; but the post is one that demands fidelity more than it does years. Shall I own it?—My tastes are rather to serve thee with my sword than with my pen."

"Wilt thou, indeed, accept the office? It is of less dignity and emolument than the one you hold; and you are full young to lead these stubborn spirits."

"Senator, I led taller men than they are to the assault at Viterbo. But, be it as seems best to your superior wisdom. Whatever you do, I pray you to be cautious. If you select a traitor to the command of the Capitol Guard!—I tremble at the thought!"

"By my faith, thou dost turn pale at it, dear boy; thy affection is a sweet drop in a bitter draught. Whom can I choose better than thee?—thou shalt have the post, at least during Bellini's illness. I will attend to it to-day. The business, too, will less fatigue thy young mind than that which now employs thee. Thou art over-laboured in our cause."

"Senator, I can but repeat my usual answer—I have a great trust to fulfil!"

CHAPTER VII

THE TAX

These formidable conspiracies quelled, the Barons nearly subdued, and three parts of the Papal territory reunited to Rome, Rienzi now deemed he might safely execute one of his favourite projects for the preservation of the liberties of his native city; and this was to raise and organise in each quarter of Rome a Roman Legion. Armed in the defence of their own institutions, he thus trusted to establish amongst her own citizens the only soldiery requisite for Rome.

But so base were the tools with which this great man was condemned to work out his noble schemes, that none could be found to serve their own country, without a pay equal to that demanded by foreign hirelings. With the insolence so peculiar to a race that has once been great, each Roman said, "Am I not better than a German?—Pay me, then, accordingly."

The Senator smothered his disgust—he had learned at last to know that the age of the Catos was no more. From a daring enthusiast, experience had converted him into a practical statesman. The Legions were necessary to Rome—they were formed—gallant their appearance and faultless their caparisons, How were they to be paid? There was but one means to maintain Rome—Rome must be taxed. A gabelle was put upon wine and salt.

The Proclamation ran thus:—

"Romans! raised to the rank of your Senator, my whole thought has been for your liberties and welfare; already Treason defeated in the City, our banners triumphant without, attest the favour with which the Deity regards men who seek to unite liberty with law. Let us set an example to Italy and the World! Let us prove that the Roman sword can guard the Roman Forum! In each Rione of the City is provided a Legion of the Citizens, collected from the traders and artisans of the town; they allege that they cannot leave their callings without remuneration. Your Senator calls upon you willingly to assist in your own defence. He has given you liberty; he has restored to you peace: your oppressors are scattered over the earth. He asks you now to preserve the treasures you have gained. To be free, you must sacrifice something; for freedom, what sacrifice too great? Confident of your support, I at length, for the first time, exert the right entrusted to me by office—and for Rome's salvation I tax the Romans!"

Then followed the announcement of the gabelle.

The proclamation was set up in the public thoroughfares. Round one of the placards a crowd assembled. Their gestures were vehement and unguarded—their eyes sparkled—they conversed low, but eagerly.

"He dares to tax us, then! Why, the Barons or the Pope could not do more than that!"

"Shame! shame!" cried a gaunt female; "we, who were his friends! How are our little ones to get bread?"

"He should have seized the Pope's money!" quoth an honest wine-vender.

"Ah! Pandulfo di Guido would have maintained an army at his own cost. He was a rich man. What insolence in the innkeeper's son to be a Senator!"

"We are not Romans if we suffer this!" said a deserter from Palestrina.

"Fellow-citizens!" exclaimed gruffly a tall man, who had hitherto been making a clerk read to him the particulars of the tax imposed, and whose heavy brain at length understood that wine was to be made dearer —"Fellow-citizens, we must have a new revolution! This is indeed gratitude! What have we benefited by restoring this man! Are we always to be ground to the dust? To pay—pay—pay! Is that all we are fit for?"

"Hark to Cecco del Vecchio!"

"No, no; not now," growled the smith. "To-night the artificers have a special meeting. We'll see—we'll see!"

A young man, muffled in a cloak, who had not been before observed, touched the smith.

"Whoever storms the Capitol the day after to-morrow at the dawn," he whispered, "shall find the guards absent!"

He was gone before the smith could look round.

The same night Rienzi, retiring to rest, said to Angelo Villani—"A bold but necessary measure this of mine! how do the people take it?"

"They murmur a little, but seem to recognise the necessity. Cecco del Vecchio *was* the loudest grumbler, but is now the loudest approver."

"The man is rough; he once deserted me;—but then that fatal excommunication! He and the Romans learned a bitter lesson in that desertion, and experience has, I trust, taught them to be honest. Well, if this tax be raised quietly, in two years Rome will be again the Queen of Italy;—her army manned—her Republic formed; and then—then——"

"Then what, Senator?"

"Why then, my Angelo, Cola di Rienzi may die in peace! There is a want which a profound experience of power and pomp brings at last to us—a want gnawing as that of hunger, wearing as that of sleep!—*my Angelo, it is the want to die!*"

"My Lord, I would give this right hand," cried Villani, earnestly, "to hear you say you were attached to life!"

"You are a good youth, Angelo!" said Rienzi, as

he passed to Nina's chamber; and in her smile and wistful tenderness, forgot for a while—that he was a great man!

CHAPTER VIII

THE THRESHOLD OF THE EVENT

The next morning the Senator of Rome held high Court in the Capitol. From Florence, from Padua, from Pisa, even from Milan, (the dominion of the Visconti,) from Genoa, from Naples,—came Ambassadors to welcome his return, or to thank him for having freed Italy from the freebooter De Montreal. Venice alone, who held in her pay the Grand Company, stood aloof. Never had Rienzi seemed more prosperous and more powerful, and never had he exhibited a more easy and cheerful majesty of demeanour.

Scarce was the audience over, when a messenger arrived from Palestrina. The town had surrendered, the Colonna had departed, and the standard of the Senator waved from the walls of the last hold of the rebellious Barons. Rome might now at length consider herself free, and not a foe seemed left to menace the repose of Rienzi.

The Court dissolved. The Senator, elated and joyous, repaired towards his private apartments, previous to the banquet given to the Ambassadors. Villani met him with his wonted sombre aspect.

"No sadness to-day, my Angelo," said the Senator, gaily; "Palestrina is ours!"

"I am glad to hear such news, and to see my Lord of so fair a mien," answered Angelo. "Does he not now desire life?"

"Till Roman virtue revives, perhaps—yes! But thus are we fools of Fortune;—to-day glad—to-morrow dejected!"

"To-morrow," repeated Villani, mechanically: "Ay —to-morrow perhaps dejected!"

"Thou playest with my words, boy," said Rienzi, half angrily, as he turned away.

But Villani heeded not the displeasure of his Lord.

The banquet was thronged and brilliant; and Rienzi that day, without an effort, played the courteous host.

Milanese, Paduan, Pisan, Neapolitan, vied with each other in attracting the smiles of the potent Senator. Prodigal were their compliments—lavish their promises of support. No monarch in Italy seemed more securely throned.

The banquet was over (as usual on state occasions) at an early hour; and Rienzi, somewhat heated with wine, strolled forth alone from the Capitol. Bending his solitary steps towards the Palatine, he saw the pale and veil-like mists that succeed the sunset, gather over the wild grass which waves above the Palace of the Cæsars. On a mound of ruins (column and arch overthrown) he stood, with folded arms, musing and intent. In the distance lay the melancholy tombs of the Campagna, and the circling hills, crested with the purple hues soon to melt beneath the starlight. Not a breeze stirred the dark cypress and unwaving pine. There was something awful in the stillness of the skies, hushing the desolate grandeur of the earth below. Many and mingled were the thoughts that swept over Rienzi's breast: memory was busy at his heart. How often, in his youth, had he trodden the same spot! —what visions had he nursed!—what hopes conceived! In the turbulence of his later life, Memory had long slept; but at that hour, she reasserted her shadowy reign with a despotism that seemed prophetic. He was wandering—a boy, with his young brother, hand in hand, by the river side at eve: anon he saw a pale face and gory side, and once more uttered his imprecations of revenge! His first successes, his virgin triumphs, his secret love, his fame, his power, his reverses, the hermitage of Maiella, the dungeon of Avignon, the triumphal return to Rome,—all swept across his breast with a distinctness as if he were living those scenes again!—and *now!*—he shrunk from the *present*, and descended the hill. The moon, already risen, shed her light over the Forum, as he passed through its mingled ruins. By the Temple of Jupiter, two figures suddenly emerged; the moonlight fell upon their faces, and Rienzi recognised Cecco del Vecchio and Angelo Villani. They saw him not; but, eagerly conversing, disappeared by the Arch of Trajan.

"Villani! ever active in my service!" thought the Senator; "methinks this morning I spoke to him harshly—it was churlish in me!"

He re-entered the place of the Capitol—he stood by the staircase of the Lion; there was a red stain upon the pavement, unobliterated since Montreal's execution, and the Senator drew himself aside with an inward shudder. Was it the ghastly and spectral light of the Moon, or did the face of that old Egyptian Monster wear an aspect that was as of life? The stony eyeballs seemed bent upon him with a malignant scowl; and as he passed on, and looked behind, they appeared almost preternaturally to follow his steps. A chill, he knew not why, sunk into his heart. He hastened to regain his palace. The sentinels made way for him.

"Senator," said one of them, doubtingly, "Messere Angelo Villani is our new captain—we are to obey his orders?"

"Assuredly," returned the Senator, passing on. The man lingered uneasily, as if he would have spoken, but Rienzi observed it not. Seeking his chamber, he found Nina and Irene waiting for him. His heart yearned to his wife. Care and toil had of late driven her from his thoughts, and he felt it remorsefully, as he gazed upon her noble face, softened by the solicitude of untiring and anxious love.

"Sweetest," said he, winding his arms around her tenderly; "thy lips never chide me, but thine eyes sometimes do! We have been apart too long. Brighter days dawn upon us, when I shall have leisure to thank thee for all thy care. And you, my fair sister, you smile on me!—ah, you have heard that your lover, ere this, is released by the cession of Palestrina, and to-morrow's sun will see him at your feet. Despite all the cares of the day, I remembered thee, my Irene, and sent a messenger to bring back the blush to that pale cheek. Come, come, we shall be happy again!" And with that domestic fondness common to him, when harsher thoughts permitted, he sate himself beside the two persons dearest to his hearth and heart.

"So happy—if we could have many hours like this!" murmured Nina, sinking on his breast. "Yet sometimes I wish——"

"And I too," interrupted Rienzi; "for I read thy woman's thought—*I* too sometimes wish that fate had placed us in the lowlier valleys of life! But it may come yet! Irene wedded to Adrian—Rome married to Liberty—and then, Nina, methinks you and I would find some quiet hermitage, and talk over old gauds and triumphs, as of a summer's dream. Beautiful, kiss me! Couldst thou resign these pomps?"

"For a desert with *thee*, Cola!"

"Let me reflect," resumed Rienzi; "is not to-day the seventh of October? Yes! on the seventh, be it noted, my foes yielded to my power! Seven! my fated number, whether ominous of good or evil! Seven months did I reign as Tribune—seven years was I absent as an exile; to-morrow, that sees me without an enemy, completes my seventh week of return!"

"And seven was the number of the crowns the Roman Convents and the Roman Council awarded thee, after the ceremony which gave thee the knighthood of the *Santo Spirito!*"† said Nina, adding, with woman's tender wit, "the brightest association of all!"

"Follies seem these thoughts to others, and to philosophy, in truth, they are so," said Rienzi; "but all my life long, omen and type and shadow have linked themselves to action and event: and the atmosphere of other men hath not been mine. Life itself a riddle, why should riddles amaze us? *The Future!*—what mystery in the very word! Had we lived all *through* the Past, since Time was, our profoundest experience of a thousand ages could not give us a guess of the events

*There was the lapse of one year between the release of Rienzi from Avignon, and his triumphal return to Rome: a year chiefly spent in the campaign of Albornoz.

† This superstition had an excuse in strange historical coincidences; and the number seven was indeed to Rienzi what the 3rd of September was to Cromwell. The ceremony of the seven crowns which he received after his knighthood, on the nature of which ridiculous ignorance has been shown by many recent writers, was, in fact, principally a religious and typical donation, (symbolical of the gifts of the Holy Spirit,) conferred by the heads of convents—and that part of the ceremony which was political, was republican, not regal.

that wait the very moment we are about to enter! Thus deserted by Reason, what wonder that we recur to the Imagination, on which, by dream and symbol, God sometimes paints the likeness of things to come? Who can endure to leave the Future all unguessed, and sit tamely down to groan under the fardel of the Present? No, no! that which the foolish-wise call Fanaticism, belongs to the same part of us as Hope. Each but carries us onward—from a barren strand to a glorious, if unbounded sea. Each is the yearning for the GREAT BEYOND, which attests our immortality. Each has its visions and chimeras—some false, but *some* true! Verily, a man who becomes great is often but made so by a kind of sorcery in his own soul—a Pythia which prophesies that he *shall* be great—and so renders the life one effort to fulfil the warning! Is this folly?—it were so, if all things stopped at the grave! But perhaps the very sharpening, and exercising, and elevating the faculties here—though but for a bootless end *on* earth—may be designed to fit the soul, thus quickened and ennobled, to some high destiny *beyond* the earth! Who can tell? not I!——Let us pray!"

While the Senator was thus employed, Rome in her various quarters presented less holy and quiet scenes.

In the fortress of the Orsini, lights flitted to and fro, through the gratings of the great court. Angelo Villani might be seen stealing from the postern-gate. Another hour, and the Moon was high in heaven; toward the ruins of the Colosseum, men, whose dress bespoke them of the lowest rank, were seen creeping from lanes and alleys, two by two; from these ruins glided again the form of the son of Montreal. Later yet—the Moon is sinking—a gray light breaking in the East—and the gates of Rome, by St. John of Lateran, are open! Villani is conversing with the sentries! The Moon has set—the mountains are dim with a mournful and chilling haze—Villani is before the palace of the Capitol—the *only* soldier there! Where are the Roman legions that were to guard alike the freedom and the deliverer of Rome?

CHAPTER THE LAST

THE CLOSE OF THE CHASE

It was the morning of the 8th of October, 1354. Rienzi, who rose betimes, stirred restlessly in his bed. "It is yet early," he said to Nina, whose soft arm was round his neck; "none of my people seem to be astir. Howbeit, *my* day begins before *theirs*."

"Rest yet, my Cola; you want sleep."

"No; I feel feverish, and this old pain in the side torments me. I have letters to write."

"Let me be your secretary, dearest," said Nina.

Rienzi smiled affectionately as he rose; he repaired to his closet adjoining his sleeping apartment, and used the bath, as was his wont. Then dressing himself, he returned to Nina, who, already loosely robed, sate by the writing-table, ready for her office of love.

"How still are all things!" said Rienzi. "What a cool and delicious prelude, in these early hours, to the toilsome day."

Leaning over his wife, he then dictated different letters, interrupting the task at times by such observations as crossed his mind.

"So, now to Annibaldi! By the way, young Adrian should join us to-day; how I rejoice for Irene's sake!"

"Dear sister—yes! she loves,—if any, Cola, can so love,—as we do."

"Well, but to your task, my fair scribe. Ha! what noise is that? I hear an armed step—the stairs creak—some one shouts my name."

Rienzi flew to his sword! the door was thrown rudely open, and a figure in complete armour appeared within the chamber.

"How! what means this?" said Rienzi, standing before Nina, with his drawn sword.

The intruder lifted his visor—it was Adrian Colonna.

"Fly, Rienzi!—hasten, Signora! Thank Heaven, I can save ye yet! Myself and train released by the capture of Palestrina, the pain of my wound detained me last night at Tivoli. The town was filled with armed men—not *thine*, Senator. I heard rumours that alarmed me. I resolved to proceed onward—I reached Rome, the gates of the city were wide open!"

"How!"

"Your guard gone. Presently I came upon a band of the retainers of the Savelli. My insignia, as a Colonna, misled them. I learned that this very hour some of your enemies are within the city, the rest are on their march—the people themselves arm against you. In the obscurer streets I passed through, the mob were already forming. They took me for thy foe, and shouted. I came hither—thy sentries have vanished. The private door below is unbarred and open. Not a soul seems left in thy palace. Haste—fly—save thyself!—Where is Irene?"

"The Capitol deserted!—impossible!" cried Rienzi. He strode across the chambers to the ante-room.

where his night-guard usually waited—it was empty! He passed hastily to Villani's room—it was untenanted! He would have passed farther, but the doors were secured without. It was evident that all egress had been cut off, save by the private door below, and *that* had been left open to admit his murtherers!

He returned to his room—Nina had already gone to rouse and prepare Irene, whose chamber was on the other side, within one of their own.

"Quick, Senator!" said Adrian. "Methinks there is yet time. We must make across to the Tiber. I have stationed my faithful squires and Northmen there. A boat waits us."

"Hark!" interrupted Rienzi, whose senses had of late been preternaturally quickened. "I hear a distant shout—a familiar shout, 'Viva l' Popolo!' Why, so say I! These must be friends."

"Deceive not thyself; thou hast scarce a friend at Rome."

"Hist!" said Rienzi, in a whisper; "save Nina—save Irene. I cannot accompany thee."

"Art thou mad?"

"No! but fearless. Besides, did I accompany, I might but destroy you all. Were I found with you, you would be massacred with me. Without me ye are safe. Yes, even the Senator's wife and sister have provoked no revenge. Save them, noble Colonna! Cola di Rienzi puts his trust in God alone!"

By this time Nina had returned; Irene with her. Afar was heard the tramp—steady—slow—gathering—of the fatal multitude.

"Now, Cola," said Nina, with a bold and cheerful air, and she took her husband's arm, while Adrian had already found his charge in Irene.

"Yes, *now,* Nina!" said Rienzi; "at length we part! If this is my last hour—*in* my last hour I pray God to bless and shield thee! for verily, thou hast been my exceeding solace—provident as a parent, tender as a child, the smile of my hearth, the—the——"

Rienzi was almost unmanned. Emotions, deep, conflicting, unspeakably fond and grateful, literally choked his speech.

"What!" cried Nina, clinging to his breast, and parting her hair from her eyes, as she sought his averted face. "Part!—never! This is my place—all Rome shall not tear me from it!"

Adrian, in despair, seized her hand, and attempted to drag her thence.

"Touch me not, sir!" said Nina, waving her arm with angry majesty, while her eyes sparkled as a lioness, whom the huntsmen would sever from her young. "I am the wife of Cola di Rienzi, the Great Senator of Rome, and by his side I will live and die!"

"Take her hence: quick!—quick! I hear the crowd advancing."

Irene tore herself from Adrian, and fell at the feet of Rienzi—she clasped his knees.

"Come, my brother, come! Why lose these precious moments? Rome forbids you to cast away a life in which her very self is bound up."

"Right, Irene; Rome is bound up with me, and we will rise or fall together!—no more!"

"You destroy us all!" said Adrian, with generous and impatient warmth. "A few minutes more and we are lost. Rash man! it is not to fall by an infuriate mob that you have been preserved from so many dangers."

"I believe it," said the Senator, as his tall form seemed to dilate as with the greatness of his own soul. "I shall triumph yet! Never shall mine enemies—never shall posterity say that a *second* time Rienzi abandoned Rome! Hark! 'Viva l' Popolo!' still the cry of 'THE PEOPLE.' That cry scares none but tyrants! I shall triumph and survive!"

"And I with thee!" said Nina, firmly. Rienzi paused a moment, gazed on his wife, passionately clasped her to his heart, kissed her again and again, and then said, "Nina, I command thee,—Go!"

"Never!"

He paused. Irene's face, drowned in tears, met his eyes.

"We will all perish with you," said his sister; "you only, Adrian, *you* leave us!"

"Be it so," said the Knight sadly; "we will *all* remain," and he desisted at once from further effort.

There was a dead but short pause, broken but by a convulsive sob from Irene. The tramp of the raging thousands sounded fearfully distinct. Rienzi seemed lost in thought—then lifting his head, he said, calmly, "Ye have triumphed—I join ye—I but collect these papers, and follow you. Quick, Adrian—save them!" and he pointed meaningly to Nina.

Waiting no other hint, the young Colonna seized Nina in his strong grasp—with his left hand he supported Irene, who with terror and excitement was almost insensible. Rienzi relieved him of the lighter load—he took his sister in his arms, and descended the winding stairs. Nina remained passive—she heard her husband's step behind, it was enough for her—she but turned once to thank him with her eyes. A tall Northman clad in armour stood at the open door. Rienzi placed Irene, now perfectly lifeless, in the soldier's arms, and kissed her pale cheek in silence.

"Quick, my Lord," said the Northman, "on all sides they come!" So saying, he bounded down the descent with his burthen. Adrian followed with Nina; the Senator paused one moment, turned back, and was in his room ere Adrian was aware that he had vanished.

Hastily he drew the coverlid from his bed, fastened it to the casement bars, and by its aid dropped (at a distance of several feet) into the balcony below. "I will not die like a rat," said he, "in the trap they have set for me! The whole crowd shall, at least, see and hear me."

This was the work of a moment.

Meanwhile, Nina had scarcely proceeded six paces, before she discovered that she was alone with Adrian.

"Ha! Cola!" she cried, "where is he? he has gone!"

"Take heart, Lady, he has returned but for some secret papers he has forgotten. He will follow us anon."

"Let us wait, then."

"Lady," said Adrian, grinding his teeth, "hear you not the crowd?—on, on!" and he flew with a swifter step. Nina struggled in his grasp—Love gave her the strength of despair. With a wild laugh she broke from him. She flew back—the door was closed—but unbarred—her trembling hands lingered a moment round the spring. She opened it, drew the heavy bolt across the panels, and frustrated all attempt from Adrian to regain her. She was on the stairs—she was in the room. Rienzi was gone! She fled, shrieking his name, through the State Chambers—all was desolate. She found the doors opening on the various passages that admitted to the rooms below barred without. Breathless and gasping, she returned to the chamber. She hurried to the casement—she perceived the method by which he had descended below—her brave heart told her of his brave design:—she saw they were separated,—"But the same roof holds us," she cried, joyously, "and our fate shall be the same!" With that thought she sank in mute patience on the floor.

Forming the generous resolve not to abandon the faithful and devoted pair without another effort, Adrian had followed Nina, but too late—the door was closed against his efforts. The crowd marched on—he heard their cry change on a sudden—it was no longer "LIVE THE PEOPLE!" but, "DEATH TO THE TRAITOR!" His attendant had already disappeared, and waking now only to the danger of Irene, the Colonna in bitter grief turned away, lightly sped down the descent, and hastened to the river side, where the boat and his band awaited him.

The balcony on which Rienzi had alighted was that from which he had been accustomed to address the people—it communicated with a vast hall used on solemn occasions for State festivals—and on either side were square projecting towers, whose grated casements looked into the balcony. One of these towers was devoted to the armoury, the other contained the prison of Brettone, the brother of Montreal. Beyond the latter tower was the general prison of the Capitol. For then the prison and the palace were in awful neighbourhood!

The windows of the Hall were yet open—and Rienzi

passed into it from the balcony—the witness of the yesterday's banquet was still there—the wine, yet undried, crimsoned the floor, and goblets of gold and silver shone from the recesses. He proceeded at once to the armoury, and selected from the various suits that which he himself had worn when, nearly eight years ago, he had chased the Barons from the gates of Rome. He arrayed himself in the mail, leaving only his head uncovered; and then taking, in his right hand, from the wall, the great Gonfalon of Rome, returned once more to the hall. Not a man encountered him. In that vast building, save the prisoners, and the faithful Nina, whose presence he knew not of—the Senator was alone.

On they came, no longer in measured order, as stream after stream—from lane, from alley, from palace and from hovel—the raging sea received new additions. On they came—their passions excited by their numbers—women and men, children and malignant age—in all the awful array of aroused, released, unresisted physical strength and brutal wrath; "Death to the traitor—death to the tyrant—death to him who has taxed the people!" "*Mora l'traditore che ha fatta la gabella!—Mora!*" Such was the cry of the people—such the crime of the Senator! They broke over the low palisades of the Capitol—they filled with one sudden rush the vast space;—a moment before so desolate,—now swarming with human beings athirst for blood!

Suddenly came a dead silence, and on the balcony above stood Rienzi—his head was bared and the morning sun shone over that lordly brow, and the hair grown gray before its time, in the service of that maddening multitude. Pale and erect he stood—neither fear nor anger, nor menace—but deep grief and high resolve—upon his features! A momentary shame—a momentary awe seized the crowd.

He pointed to the Gonfalon, wrought with the Republican motto and arms of Rome, and thus he began:—

"I too am a Roman and a Citizen! hear me!"

"Hear him not! hear him not! his false tongue can charm away our senses!" cried a voice louder than his own; and Rienzi recognised Cecco del Vecchio.

"Hear him not! down with the tyrant!" cried a more shrill and youthful tone: and by the side of the artisan stood Angelo Villani.

"Hear him not! death to the death-giver!" cried a voice close at hand, and from the grating of the neighbouring prison glared near upon him, as the eye of a tiger, the vengeful gaze of the brother of Montreal.

Then from Earth to Heaven rose the roar—"Down with the tyrant—down with him who taxed the people!"

A shower of stones rattled on the mail of the Senator,—still he stirred not. No changing muscle betokened fear. His persuasion of his own wonderful powers of eloquence, if he could but be heard, inspired him yet with hope; he stood collected in his own indignant, but determined thoughts!—but the knowledge of that very eloquence was now his deadliest foe. The leaders of the multitude trembled lest he *should* be heard; "*and doubtless,*" says the contemporaneous biographer, "*had he but spoken he would have changed them all, and the work been marred.*"

The soldiers of the Barons had already mixed themselves with the throng—more deadly weapons than stones aided tne wrath of the multitude—darts and arrows darkened the air; and now a voice was heard shrieking, "Way for the torches!" And red in the sunlight the torches tossed and waved, and danced to and fro, above the heads of the crowd, as if the fiends were let loose amongst the mob! And what place in hell *hath* fiends like those a mad mob can furnish? Straw, and wood and litter, were piled hastily round the great doors of the Capitol, and the smoke curled suddenly up, beating back the rush of the assailants.

Rienzi was no longer visible, an arrow had pierced his hand—the right hand that supported the flag of Rome—the right hand that had given a constitution to the Republic. He retired from the storm into the desolate hall.

He sat down;—and tears, springing from no weak and woman source, but tears from the loftiest fountain of emotion—tears that befit a warrior when his own troops desert him—a patriot when his countrymen rush to their own doom—a father when his children rebel against his love,—tears such as these forced themselves from his eyes and relieved, but *they changed*, his heart!

"Enough, enough!" he said, presently rising and dashing the drops scornfully away; "I have risked, dared, toiled enough for this dastard and degenerate race. I will yet baffle their malice—I renounce the thought of which they are so little worthy!—Let Rome perish!—I feel, at last, that I am nobler than my country!—she deserves not so high a sacrifice!"

With that feeling, Death lost all the nobleness of aspect it had before presented to him; and he resolved, in very scorn of his ungrateful foes, in very defeat of their inhuman wrath, to make one effort for his life!

He divested himself of his glittering arms; his address, his dexterity, his craft, returned to him. His active mind ran over the chances of disguise—of escape;—he left the hall—passed through the humbler rooms, devoted to the servitors and menials—found in one of them a coarse working garb—indued himself with it—placed upon his head some of the draperies and furniture of the palace, as if escaping with them; and said, with his old "*fantastico riso*"*—"When all other friends desert me, I may well forsake myself!" With that he awaited his occasion.

Meanwhile the flames burnt fierce and fast; the outer door below was already consumed; from the apartment he had deserted the fire burst out in volleys of smoke—the wood crackled—the lead melted—with a crash fell the severed gates—the dreadful entrance was opened to all the multitude—the proud Capitol of the Cæsars was already tottering to its fall!—Now was the time!—he passed the flaming door—the smouldering threshold;—he passed the outer gate unscathed—he was in the middle of the crowd. "Plenty of pillage within," he said to the bystanders, in the Roman *patois*, his face concealed by his load—"*Suso, suso a gliu traditore!*" † The mob rushed past him—he went on—he gained the last stair descending into the open streets—he was at the last gate—liberty and life were before him.

A soldier (one of his own) seized him. "Pass not—whither goest thou?"

"Beware, lest the Senator escape disguised!" cried a voice behind—it was Villani's. The concealing load was torn from his head—Rienzi stood revealed!

* "Fantastic smile or laugh."
† "Down, down with the traitor."

"I *am* the Senator!" he said in a loud voice. "Who dare touch the Representative of the People?"

The multitude were round him in an instant. Not led, but rather hurried and whirled along, the Senator was borne to the Place of the Lion. With the intense glare of the bursting flames, the gray image reflected a lurid light, and glowed—(that grim and solemn monument!)—as if itself of fire!

There arrived, the crowd gave way, terrified by the greatness of their victim. Silent he stood, and turned his face around; nor could the squalor of his garb, nor the terror of the hour, nor the proud grief of detection, abate the majesty of his mien, or reassure the courage of the thousands who gathered, gazing, round him. The whole Capitol wrapped in fire, lighted with ghastly pomp the immense multitude. Down the long vista of the streets extended the fiery light and the serried throng, till the crowd closed with the gleaming standards of the Colonna—the Orsini—the Savelli! Her true tyrants were marching into Rome! As the sound of their approaching horns and trumpets broke upon the burning air, the mob seemed to regain their courage. Rienzi prepared to speak; his first word was as the signal of his own death.

"Die, tyrant!" cried Cecco del Vecchio: and he plunged his dagger in the Senator's breast.

"Die, executioner of Montreal!" muttered Villani: "thus the trust is fulfilled!" and his was the second stroke. Then as he drew back, and saw the artisan in all the drunken fury of his brute passion, tossing up his cap, shouting aloud, and spurning the fallen lion,—the young man gazed upon him with a look of withering and bitter scorn, and said, while he sheathed his blade, and slowly turned to quit the crowd—

"Fool, miserable fool! *thou* and *these* at least had no *blood of kindred to avenge!*"

They heeded not his words—they saw him not depart; for as Rienzi, without a word, without a groan, fell to the earth,—as the roaring waves of the multitude closed over him,—a voice, shrill, sharp, and wild, was heard above all the clamour. At the casement of the Palace, (the casement of her bridal chamber,) Nina stood!—through the flames that burst below and around, her face and outstretched arms alone visible! Ere yet the sound of that thrilling cry passed from the air, down with a mighty crash thundered that whole wing of the Capitol,—a blackened and smouldering mass.

At that hour, a solitary boat was gliding swiftly along the Tiber. Rome was at a distance, but the lurid glow of the conflagration cast its reflection upon the placid and glassy stream: fair beyond description was the landscape! soft beyond all art of Painter and of Poet, the sunlight quivering over the autumnal herbage, and hushing into tender calm the waves of the golden River!

Adrian's eyes were strained towards the towers of the Capitol, distinguished by the flames from the spires and domes around;—senseless, and clasped to his guardian breast, Irene was happily unconscious of the horrors of the time.

"They dare not—they dare not," said the brave Colonna, "touch a hair of that sacred head!—if Rienzi fall, the liberties of Rome fall for ever! As those towers that surmount the flames, the pride and monument of Rome, he shall rise above the dangers of the hour. Behold, still unscathed amidst the raging element, the Capitol itself is his emblem!"

Scarce had he spoken, when a vast volume of smoke obscured the fires afar off, a dull crash, (deadened by the distance) travelled to his ear, and the next moment, the towers on which he gazed had vanished from the scene, and one intense and sullen glare seemed to settle over the atmosphere,—making all Rome itself the funeral pyre of THE LAST OF THE ROMAN TRIBUNES!

APPENDIX I

SOME REMARKS ON THE LIFE AND CHARACTER OF RIENZI

The principal authority from which historians have taken their account of the life and times of Rienzi is a very curious biography, by some unknown contemporary; and this, which is in the Roman *patois* of the time, has been rendered not quite unfamiliar to the French and English reader by the work of Père du Cerceau, called "Conjuration de Nicholas Gabini, dit de Rienzi,"* which has at once pillaged and deformed the Roman biographer. The biography I refer to was published (and the errors of the former editions revised) by Muratori in his great collection; and has lately been reprinted separately in an improved text, accompanied by notes of much discrimination and scholastic taste, and a comment upon that celebrated poem of Petrarch, "Spirto Gentil," which the majority of Italian critics have concurred in considering addressed to Rienzi, in spite of the ingenious arguments to the contrary by the Abbé de Sade.

This biography has been generally lauded for its rare impartiality. And the author does, indeed, praise and blame alike with a most singular appearance of stolid candour. The work, in truth, is one of those not uncommon proofs, of which Boswell's "Johnson" is the most striking, that a very valuable book may be written by a very silly man. The biographer of Rienzi appears more like the historian of Rienzi's clothes, so minute is he on all details of their colour and quality—so silent is he upon everything that could throw light upon the motives of their wearer. In fact, granting the writer every desire to be impartial, he is too foolish to be so. It requires some cleverness to judge accurately of a very clever man in very difficult circumstances; and the

* See for a specimen of the singular blunders of the Frenchman's work, Appendix II.

worthy biographer is utterly incapable of giving us any clue to the actions of Rienzi—utterly unable to explain the conduct of the man by the circumstances of the time. The weakness of his vision causes him, therefore, often to squint. We must add to his want of wisdom a want of truth, which the Herodotus-like simplicity of his style frequently conceals He describes things which had no witness as precisely and distinctly as those which he himself had seen. For instance, before the death of Rienzi, in those awful moments when the Senator was alone, unheard, unseen, he coolly informs us of cach motion, and each thought of Rienzi's, with as much detail as if Rienzi had returned from the grave to assist his narration. These obvious inventions have been adopted by Gibbon and others with more good faith than the laws of evidence would warrant. Still, however, to a patient and cautious reader the biography may furnish a much better notion of Rienzi's character, than we can glean from the historians who have borrowed from it piecemeal. Such a reader will discard all the writer's reasonings, will think little of his praise or blame, and regard only the facts he narrates, judging them true or doubtful, according as the writer had the opportunities of being himself the observer. Thus examining, the reader will find evidence sufficient of Rienzi's genius and Rienzi's failings. Carefully distinguishing between the period of his power as Tribune, and that of his power as Senator, he will find the Tribune vain, haughty, fond of display; but, despite the reasonings of the biographer, he will not recognise those faults in the Senator. On the other hand, he will notice the difference between youth and maturity—hope and experience; he will notice in the Tribune vast ambition, great schemes, enterprising activity—which sober into less gorgeous and more quiet colours in the portrait of the Senator. He will find that in neither instance did Rienzi fall from his own faults—he will find that the vulgar moral of ambition, blasted by its own excesses, is not the true moral of the Roman's life; he will find that, both in his abdication as Tribune, and his death as Senator, *Rienzi fell from the vices of the People.* The Tribune was a victim to ignorant cowardice—the Senator, a victim to ferocious avarice. It is this which modern historians have failed to represent. Gibbon records rightly, that the Count of Minorbino entered Rome with one hundred and fifty soldiers, and barricadoed the quarter of the Colonna—that the bell of the

Capitol sounded—that Rienzi addressed the People—that they were silent and inactive—and that Rienzi then abdicated the government. But for this he calls *Rienzi* "pusillanimous." Is not that epithet to be applied to *the People?* Rienzi invoked them to move against the Robber—the People refused to obey. Rienzi wished to fight—the People refused to stir. It was not the cause of Rienzi alone which demanded their exertions—it was the cause of the People—*theirs*, not his, the shame, if one hundred and fifty foreign soldiers mastered Rome, overthrew their liberties, and restored their tyrants! Whatever Rienzi's sins, whatever his unpopularity, *their* freedom, *their* laws, *their* republic, were at stake; and these they surrendered to one hundred and fifty hirelings! This is the fact that damns them! But Rienzi was not unpopular when he addressed and conjured them; they found no fault with him. "The sighs and the groans of the People," says Sismondi, justly, "replied to his,"—they could weep, but they would not fight. This strange apathy the modern historians have not accounted for. yet the principal cause was obvious—Rienzi was *excommunicated!** In stating the fact,

* And this curse I apprehend to have been the more effective in the instance of Rienzi, from a fact that it would be interesting and easy to establish: viz., that he owed his rise as much to religious as to civil causes. He aimed evidently to be a religious Reformer. All his devices, ceremonies, and watchwords, were of a religious character. The monks took part with his enterprise, and joined in the revolution. His letters are full of mystical fanaticism. His references to ancient heroes of Rome are always mingled with invocations to her Christian Saints. The Bible, at that time little read by the public civilians of Italy, is constantly in his hands, and his addresses studded with texts. His very garments were adorned with sacred and mysterious emblems. No doubt, the ceremony of his Knighthood, which Gibbon ridicules as an act of mere vanity, was but another of his religious extravagances; for he peculiarly dedicated his Knighthood to the service of the Santo Spirito; and his bathing in the vase of Constantine was quite of a piece, not with the vanity of the Tribune, but with the extravagance of the Fanatic. In fact, they tried hard to prove him a heretic; but he escaped a charge under the mild Innocent, which a century or two before, or a century or two afterwards, would have sufficed to have sent a dozen Rienzis to the stake. I have dwelt the more upon this point, because, if it be shown that religious causes operated with those of liberty, we throw a new light upon the whole of that most

these writers have seemed to think that excommunication in Rome, in the fourteenth century, produced no effect!—the effect it did produce I have endeavoured in these pages to convey.

The causes of the second fall and final murder of Rienzi are equally misstated by modern narrators. It was from no fault of his—no injustice, no cruelty, no extravagance—it was not from the execution of Montreal, nor that of Pandulfo di Guido—*it was from a gabelle on wine and salt that he fell.* To preserve Rome from the tyrants it was necessary to maintain an armed force; to pay the force a tax was necessary; the tax was imposed—and the multitude joined with the tyrants, and their cry was, " Perish the traitor *who has made the gabelle!* " This was their only charge—this the only crime that their passions and their fury could cite against him.

The faults of Rienzi are sufficiently visible, and I have not unsparingly shewn them; but we must judge men, not according as they approach perfection, but according as their good or bad qualities preponderate—their talents or their weaknesses—the benefits they effected, the evil they wrought. For a man who rose to so great a power, Rienzi's faults were singularly few—*crimes* he committed none. He is almost the only man who ever rose from the rank of a citizen to a power equal to that of monarchs without a single act of violence or treachery. When *in* power, he was vain, ostentatious, and imprudent,—always an enthusiast—often a fanatic; but his very faults had greatness of soul, and his very fanaticism at once supported his enthusiastic daring, and proved his earnest honesty. It is evident that no heinous charge could be brought against him even by his enemies, for all the accusations to which he was subjected, when excommunicated, exiled, fallen, were for two offences which Petrarch rightly deemed the proofs of his virtue and his glory: first, for declaring Rome to be free; secondly, for pretending

extraordinary revolution, and its suddenness is infinitely less striking. The deep impression Rienzi produced upon that populace was thus stamped with the spirit of the religious enthusiast more than that of the classical demagogue. And, as in the time of Cromwell, the desire for temporal liberty was warmed and coloured by the presence of a holier and more spiritual fervour:—" The Good Estate " (*Buono Stato*) of Rienzi reminds us a little of the Good Cause of General Cromwell.

that the Romans had a right of choice in the election of the Roman Emperor.* Stern, just, and inflexible, as he was when Tribune, his fault was never that of *wanton* cruelty. The accusation against him, made by the gentle Petrarch, indeed, was, that he was not determined enough—that he did not consummate the revolution by exterminating the patrician tyrants. When Senator, he was, without sufficient ground, accused of avarice in the otherwise just and necessary execution of Montreal.† It was natural enough that his enemies and the vulgar should suppose that he executed a creditor to get rid of a debt; but it was inexcusable in later, and wiser, and fairer writers to repeat so grave a calumny, without at least adding the obvious suggestion, that the avarice of Rienzi could have been much better gratified by sparing than by destroying the life of one of the richest subjects in Europe. Montreal, we may be quite sure, would have purchased his life at an immeasurably higher price than the paltry sum lent to Rienzi by his brothers. And this is not a probable hypothesis, but a certain fact, for we are expressly told that Montreal, "knowing the Tribune was in want of money, offered Rienzi, that if he would let him go, he, Montreal, would furnish him not only with twenty thousand florins, (four times the amount of Rienzi's debt to him,) but with as many soldiers and as much money as he pleased." This offer Rienzi did not attend to. Would he have rejected it had avarice been his motive? And what culpable injustice, to mention the vague calumny without citing the practical contradiction! When Gibbon tells us, also, that "the *most* virtuous citizen of Rome," meaning Pandulfo, or Pandulficcio di Guido,‡ was sacrificed to his jealousy, he a little exaggerates

* The charge of heresy was dropped.

† Gibbon, in mentioning the execution of Montreal, omits to state that Montreal was more than suspected of conspiracy and treason to restore the Colonna. Matthew Villani records it as a common belief that such truly was the offence of the Provençal. The biographer of Rienzi gives additional evidence of the fact. Gibbon's knowledge of this time was superficial. As one instance of this, he strangely enough represents Montreal as the head of the *first* Free Company that desolated Italy: he took that error from the Père du Cerceau.

‡ Matthew Villani speaks of him as a wise and good citizen, of great repute among the People—and this, it seems, he really was.

the expression bestowed upon Pandulfo, which is that of "virtuoso assai;" and that expression, too, used by a man who styles the robber Montreal "eccellente uomo—di quale fama suono per tutta la Italia di virtude" *—(so good a moral critic was the writer!) but he also altogether waves all mention of the probabilities that are sufficiently apparent, of the scheming of Pandulfo to supplant Rienzi, and to obtain the "Signoria del Popolo." Still, however, if the death of Pandulfo may be considered a blot on the memory of Rienzi, it does not appear that it was this which led to his own fate. The cry of the mob surrounding his palace was not, "Perish him who executed Pandulfo," it was—and this again and again must be carefully noted—it was nothing more nor less than "*Perish him who has made the gabelle!*"

Gibbon sneers at the military skill and courage of Rienzi. For this sneer there is no cause. His first attempts, his first rise, attested sufficiently his daring and brave spirit; in every danger he was present—never shrinking from a foe so long as he was supported by the People. He distinguished himself at Viterbo when in the camp of Albornoz, in several feats of arms,† and his end was that of a hero. So much for his courage; as to his military skill, it would be excusable enough if Rienzi—the eloquent and gifted student, called from the closet and the rostrum to assume the command of an army—should have been deficient in the art of war; yet, somehow or other, upon the whole, his arms prospered. He defeated the chivalry of Rome at her gates; and if he did not, after his victory, march to Marino, for which his biographer ‡ and Gibbon blame him, the reason is sufficiently clear—"Volea pecunia per soldati"—*he wanted money for the soldiers!* On his return as Senator, it must be remembered that he had to besiege Palestrina, which was considered even by the ancient Romans almost impregnable by position; but during the few weeks he was in power, Palestrina yielded—all his open enemies were defeated—the tyrants expelled—Rome free; and this without support from any party, Papal or Pop-

* "An excellent man whose fame for valour resounded throughout all Italy."

† Vit. di Col. di Rienzi, lib. ii. cap. 14.

‡ In this the anonymous writer compares him gravely to Hannibal, who knew how to conquer, but not how to use his conquest.

ular; or, as Gibbon well expresses it, "suspected by the People—abandoned by the Prince."

On regarding what Rienzi did, we must look to his means, to the difficulties that surrounded him, to the scantiness of his resources. We see a man without rank, wealth, or friends, raising himself to the head of a popular government in the metropolis of the Church—in the City of the Empire. We see him reject any title save that of a popular magistrate—establish at one stroke a free constitution—a new code of law. We see him first expel, then subdue, the fiercest aristocracy in Europe—conquer the most stubborn banditti, rule impartially the most turbulent people, embruted by the violence, and sunk in the corruption of centuries. We see him restore trade—establish order—create civilisation as by a miracle—receive from crowned heads homage and congratulation—outwit, conciliate, or awe, the wiliest priesthood of the Papal Diplomacy—and raise his native city at once to sudden yet acknowledged eminence over every other state, its superior in arts, wealth, and civilisation;—we ask what errors we are to weigh in the opposite balance, and we find an unnecessary ostentation, a fanatical extravagance, and a certain insolent sternness. But what are such offences—what the splendour of a banquet, or the ceremony of Knighthood, or a few arrogant words, compared with the vices of almost every prince who was his contemporary? This is the way to judge character; we must compare men with men, and not with ideals of what men should be. We look to the amazing benefits Rienzi conferred upon his country. We ask his means, and see but his own abilities. His treasury becomes impoverished—his enemies revolt—the Church takes advantage of his weakness—he is excommunicated—the soldiers refuse to fight—the People refuse to assist—the Barons ravage the country—the ways are closed, the provisions are cut off from Rome.* A handful of banditti enter the city—Rienzi proposes to resist them—the People desert—he abdicates. Rapine, Famine, Massacre, ensue—they who deserted, regret, repent—yet he is still unassisted, alone—now an exile, now a prisoner, his own genius saves him from every peril, and restores him to greatness. He

* "Allora le strade furo chiuse, li massari de la terre non portavano grano, ogni die nasceva nuovo rumores."—*Vit. di Col. Rienzi*, lib. i. cap. 37.

returns, the Pope's Legate refuses him arms—the People refuse him money. He re-establishes law and order, expels the tyrants, renounces his former faults *—is prudent, wary, provident—reigns a few weeks—taxes the People, in support of the People, and is torn to pieces! One day of the rule that followed is sufficient to vindicate his reign and avenge his memory—and for centuries afterwards, whenever that wretched and degenerate populace dreamed of glory or sighed for justice, they recalled the bright vision of their own victim, and deplored the fate of Cola di Rienzi. That he was not a tyrant is clear in this—when he was dead, he was bitterly regretted. The People never regret a tyrant! From the unpopularity that springs from other faults there is often a reaction; but there is no reaction in the populace towards their betrayer or oppressor. A thousand biographies cannot

* This, the second period of his power, has been represented by Gibbon and others as that of his principal faults, and he is evidently at this time no favourite with his contemporaneous biographer; but looking to what he *did,* we find amazing dexterity, prudence, and energy in the most difficult crisis, and *none of his earlier faults.* It is true, that he does not shew the same brilliant extravagance which, I suspect, dazzled his contemporaries, more than his sounder qualities; but we find that in a few weeks he had conquered all his powerful enemies—that his eloquence was as great as ever—his promptitude greater—his diligence indefatigable—his foresight unslumbering. "He alone," says the biographer, "carried on the affairs of Rome, but his officials were slothful and cold." This too, tortured by a painful disease—already—though yet young—broken and infirm. The only charges against him, as Senator, were the deaths of Montreal and Pandulfo di Guido, the imposition of the gabelle, and the renunciation of his former habits of rigid abstinence, for indulgence in wine and feasting. Of the first charges, the reader has already been enabled to form a judgment. To the last, alas! the reader must extend indulgence, and for it he may find excuse. We must compassionate even more than condemn the man to whom excitement has become nature, and who resorts to the physical stimulus or the momentary Lethe, when the mental exhilarations of hope, youth, and glory, begin to desert him. His alleged intemperance, however, which the Romans (a peculiarly sober people) might perhaps exaggerate, and for which he gave the excuse of a thirst produced by disease contracted in the dungeon of Avignon—evidently and confessedly did not in the least diminish his attention to business, which, according to his biographer, was at that time greater than ever.

decide upon the faults or merits of a ruler like the one fact, whether he is beloved or hated ten years after he is dead. But if the ruler has been murdered by the People, and is then regretted by them, their repentance is his acquittal.

I have said that the moral of the Tribune's life, and of this fiction, is not the stale and unprofitable moral that warns the ambition of an individual:—More vast, more solemn, and more useful, it addresses itself to nations. If I judge not erringly, it proclaims that, to be great and free, a People must trust not to individuals but themselves—that there is no sudden leap from servitude to liberty—that it is to institutions, not to men, that they must look for reforms that last beyond the hour—that their own passions are the real despots they should subdue, their own reason the true regenerator of abuses. With a calm and noble people, the individual ambition of a citizen can never effect evil:—to be impatient of chains is not to be worthy of freedom—to murder a magistrate is not to ameliorate the laws.* The People write their own condemnation whenever they use characters of blood; and theirs alone the madness and the crime, if they crown a tyrant or butcher a victim.

APPENDIX II

A WORD UPON THE WORK BY PÈRE DU CERCEAU AND PÈRE BRUMOY, ENTITLED "CONJURATION DE NICOLAS GABRINI, DIT DE RIENZI, TYRAN DE ROME"

Shortly after the romance of "Rienzi" first appeared, a translation of the biography compiled by Cerceau and Brumoy was published by Mr. Whittaker. The translator, in a short and courteous advertisement, observes, "That it has

* Rienzi was murdered because the Romans had been in the habit of murdering whenever they were displeased. They had, very shortly before, stoned one magistrate, and torn to pieces another. By the same causes and the same career a People may be made to resemble the bravo whose hand wanders to his knife at the smallest affront, and if to-day he poniards the enemy who assaults him, to-morrow he strikes the friend who would restrain.

always been considered as a work of authority; and even Gibbon appears to have relied on it without further research;" * . . . . . . that, "as a record of facts, therefore, the work will, it is presumed, be acceptable to the public." The translator has fulfilled his duty with accuracy, elegance, and spirit,—and he must forgive me, if, in justice to History and Rienzi, I point out a very few from amongst a great many reasons, why the joint labour of the two worthy Jesuits cannot be considered either a work of authority, or a record of facts. The translator observes in his preface, "that the general outline (of Du Cerceau's work) was *probably* furnished by an Italian life written by a contemporary of Rienzi." The fact, however, is, that Du Cerceau's book is little more than a wretched paraphrase of that very Italian life mentioned by the translator,—full of blunders, from ignorance of the peculiar and antiquated dialect in which the original is written, and of assumptions by the Jesuit himself, which rest upon no authority whatever. I will first shew, in support of this assertion, what the Italians themselves think of the work of Fathers Brumoy and Du Cerceau. The Signor Zefirino Re, who has proved himself singularly and minutely acquainted with the history of that time, and whose notes to the "Life of Rienzi" are characterised by acknowledged acuteness and research, thus describes the manner in which the two Jesuits compounded this valuable "record of facts."

"Father Du Cerceau for his work made use of a French translation of the life by the Italian contemporary printed in Bracciano, 1624, executed by Father Sanadon, another Jesuit, from whom he received the MS. This proves that Du Cerceau knew little of our 'volgar lingua' of the fourteenth century. But the errors into which he has run shew, that even that little was unknown to his guide, and still less to Father Brumoy, (however learned and reputed the latter might be in *French* literature) who, after the death of Du Cerceau, supplied the deficiencies in the first pages of the author's MS., which were, I know not how, lost; and in this part are found the more striking errors in the work, which shall be noticed in the proper place; in the meantime, one specimen will suffice. In the third chapter, book i., Cola, addressing the Romans, says, 'Che lo giubileo si approssima, che se la gente, la quale verrà al giubileo, li trova sproveduti

* Here, however, he does injustice to Gibbon.

di annona, le pietre (per metatesi sta scritto le preite) no porteranno da Roma per rabbia di fame, e le pietre non basteranno a tanta moltitudine. Il francese traduce. Le jubilé approche, et vous n'avez ni provisions, ni vivres; les étrangers . . . . trouveront votre ville denué de tout. Ne comptez point sur les secours des gens d'Eglise; ils sortiront de la ville, s'ils n'y trouvent de quoi subsister: et d'ailleurs pourroient-ils suffire à la multitude innombrable qui se trouvera dans vos murs?' "* "Buon Dio!" exclaims the learned Zefirino, "Buon Dio! le pietre prese per tanta gente di chiesa!"†

Another blunder little less extraordinary occurs in Chapter vi., in which the ordinances of Rienzi's Buono Stato are recited.

It is set forth as the third ordinance:—"Che nulla casa di Roma sia data per terra per alcuna cagione, ma vada in commune;" which simply means, that the houses of delinquents should in no instance be razed, but added to the community or confiscated. This law being intended partly to meet the barbarous violences with which the excesses and quarrels of the Barons had half dismantled Rome, and principally to repeal some old penal laws by which the houses of a certain class of offenders might be destroyed; but the French translator construes it, "*Que nulle maison de Rome ne saroit donnée en propre*, pour quelque raison que ce pût être; mais que les revenus en appartiendroient au public!"‡

But enough of the blunders arising from ignorance.—I must now be permitted to set before the reader a few of the graver offences of wilful assumption and preposterous invention.

When Rienzi condemned some of the Barons to death, the Père thus writes; I take the recent translation published by Mr. Whittaker:—

"The next day the Tribune, resolving more than ever to rid himself of his prisoners, ordered tapestries of two colours,

* The English translator could not fail to adopt the Frenchman's ludicrous mistake.

† See Preface to Zefirino Re's edition of the "Life of Rienzi," p. 9, note on Du Cerceau.

‡ The English translator makes this law unintelligible:—"That no family of Rome shall appropriate to their own use what they think fit, but that the revenues shall appertain to the public." ! ! !—The revenues of what?

red and white, to be laid over the place whereon he held his councils, and which he had made choice of to be the theatre of this bloody tragedy, as the extraordinary tapestry seemed to declare. He afterwards sent a cordelier to every one of the prisoners to administer the sacraments, and then ordered the Capitol bell to be tolled. At that fatal sound and the sight of the confessors, the Lords no longer doubted of sentence of death being passed upon them. They all confessed except the old Colonna, and many received the communion. In the meanwhile the people, *naturally prompt to attend, when their first impetuosity had time to calm, could not without pity behold the dismal preparations which were making. The sight of the bloody colour in the tapestry shocked them.* On this first impression they joined in opinion in relation to so many illustrious heads now going to be sacrificed, and lamented more their unhappy catastrophe, as no crime had been proved upon them to render them worthy of such barbarous treatment. *Above all, the unfortunate Stephen Colonna, whose birth, age, and affable behaviour, commanded respect, excited a particular compassion. An universal silence and sorrow reigned among them.* Those who were nearest Rienzi discovered an alteration. They took the opportunity of imploring his mercy towards the prisoners in terms the most affecting and moving."

Will it be believed, that in the original from which the Père Du Cerceau borrows or rather imagines this touching recital, *there is not a single syllable about the pity of the people, nor their shock at the bloody colours of the tapestry,* nor their particular compassion for the unfortunate Stephen Colonna! —in fine, the *People* are not even mentioned at all. All that is said is "Some Roman citizens, (alcuni cittadini Romani), considering the judgment Rienzi was about to make, interposed with soft and caressing words, and at last changed the opinion of the Tribune;" all the rest is the pure fiction of the ingenious Frenchman! Again, Du Cerceau, describing the appearance of the Barons at this fatal moment, says, "Notwithstanding the grief and despair visible in their countenances, *they showed a noble indignation, generally attendant on innocence in the hour of death.*" What says the authority from which alone, except his own, the good Father could take his account? Why, not a word about this noble indignation, or this parade of innocence! The original says simply, that "*the Barons were so frozen with terror that they* *were unable to speak,*" (diventaso si gelati che non poteano favellare;) "that the greater part humbled themselves," (e prese penitenza e comunione;) that when Rienzi addressed them, "*all* the Barons (come dannati) stood in sadness."* Du Cerceau then proceeds to state, that "although he (Rienzi) was grieved at heart to behold his victims snatched from him, he endeavoured to make a merit of it in the eyes of the People." *There is not a word of this in the original!*

So, when Rienzi, on a later occasion, placed the Prefect John di Vico in prison, this Jesuit says, "*To put a gloss upon this action* before the eyes of the people, Rienzi *gave out that* the Governor, John di Vico, keeping a correspondence with the conspirators, came with no other view than to betray the Romans." And if this scribbler, who pretends to have consulted the Vatican MSS., had looked at the most ordinary authorities, he would have seen that John di Vico *did* come with that view. (See for Di Vico's secret correspondence with the Barons, La Cron. Bologn. p. 406; and La Cron. Est. p. 444.)

Again, in the battle between the Barons and the Romans at the gates, Du Cerceau thus describes the conduct of the Tribune:—"The Tribune, amidst his troops, knew so little of what had passed, that seeing at a distance one of his standards fall, he looked upon all as lost, and, casting up his eyes to heaven full of despair, cried out, 'O God, will you then forsake me?' But no sooner was he informed of the entire defeat of his enemies, than his dread and cowardice even turned to boldness and arrogance."

Now in the original all that is said of this is, "That it is true that the standard of the Tribune fell—the Tribune astonished, (or if you please, dismayed, *sbigottio,*) stood with his eyes raised to heaven, and could find no other words than, 'O God hast thou betrayed me?'" This evinced, perhaps, alarm or consternation at the fall of his standard—a consternation natural, not to a coward, but a fanatic, at such an event. But not a word is said about Rienzi's cowardice in the action itself; it is not stated when the accident happened—nothing bears out the implication that the Tribune was remote from the contest, and knew little of what passed. And if this ignorant Frenchman had *consulted any other contemporaneous historian whatever*, he would have found it asserted

* See Vita di Col. di Rienzi, lib. i. cap. 29.

by them all, that the fight was conducted with great valour, both by the Roman populace and their leader on one side, and the Barons on the other.—G. Vill. lib. xii. cap. 105; Cron. Sen. tom. xv. Murat. p. 119; Cron. Est. p. 444. Yet Gibbon rests his own sarcasm on the Tribune's courage solely on the baseless exaggeration of this Père Du Cerceau.

So little, indeed, did this French pretender know of the history of the time and place he treats of, that he imagines the Stephen Colonna who was killed in the battle above mentioned was the *old* Stephen Colonna, and is very pathetic about his "venerable appearance," &c. This error, with regard to a man so eminent as Stephen Colonna the elder, is inexcusable; for, had the priest turned over the other pages of the very collection in which he found the biography he deforms, he would have learned that old Stephen Colonna was alive some time after that battle.—[Cron. Sen. Murat. tom. xv. p. 121.]

Again, just before Rienzi's expulsion from the office of Tribune, Du Cerceau, translating in his headlong way the old biographer's account of the causes of Rienzi's loss of popularity, says, "He shut himself up in his palace, and his presence was known only by the rigorous punishments which he caused his agents to inflict upon the innocent." Not a word of this in the original!

Again, after the expulsion, Du Cerceau says, that the Barons seized upon the "immense riches" he had amassed, —the words in the original are, "grandi ornamenti," which are very different things from immense riches. But the most remarkable sins of commission are in this person's account of the second rise and fall of Rienzi under the title of Senator. Of this I shall give but one instance:—

"The Senator, who perceived it, became only the more cruel. His jealousies produced only fresh murders. In the continual dread he was in, that the general discontent would terminate in some secret attempt upon his person, he determined to intimidate the most enterprising, by sacrificing sometimes one, sometimes another, and chiefly those whose riches rendered them the more guilty in his eyes. Numbers were sent every day to the Capitol prison. Happy were those who could get off with the confiscation of their estates."

Of these grave charges there is not a syllable in the original! And so much for the work of Père Cerceau and Père Brumoy, by virtue of which, historians have written of the life and times of Rienzi, and upon the figments of which, the most remarkable man in an age crowded with great characters is judged by the general reader!

I must be pardoned for this criticism, which might not have been necessary, had not the work to which it relates, in the English translation quoted from, (a translation that has no faults but those of the French original), been actually received as an historical and indisputable authority, and opposed with a triumphant air to some passages in my own narrative which were literally taken from the authentic records of the time.

THE END

www.ingramcontent.com/pod-product-compliance
Lightning Source LLC
LaVergne TN
LVHW030906080826
845145LV00010B/2789